Praise for Suhayl Saadi's novel *Psychoraag* and short story collection *The Burning Mirror*

'Suhayl Saadi's ambitious first novel, *Psychoraag,* an intimate 400-page sprawl covering six early-morning graveyard-shift hours in the life of an on-air Asian-Glaswegian DJ, came out earlier this year ... a book about race and invisibility, voice and silence, whose central theme is the question of whether anyone out there is actually listening.' **Ali Smith, The Guardian**

'*Psychoraag* is not just *Midnight's Children*-meets-*Trainspotting* because Saadi is more thoughtful than Welsh or Rushdie.' **Angus Calder, The Sunday Herald**

'You might expect the first-ever Asian Scottish novel to have a fair degree of ambition, but Suhayl Saadi's *Psychoraag* has it in towering abundance, plunging straight into an interior monologue that lasts for more than 400 pages and flashes with half a dozen different languages.' **David Robinson, The Scotsman**

'The title of the novel *Psychoraag* is inspired. The rest of the book is, too ... Saadi's trick ... is to combine the modern and the ancient, East and West. It's not a construct; not a clever idea designed to entrap a publisher and then a reader. It's how Suhayl lives and breathes. Five snatched minutes of conversation at a crossroads can spin easily from a discussion of the latest CD by Shakira to the social deprivation of Glasgow housing estates via a panegyric of anonymous 19th century flamenco lyricists. Suhayl's Scotland contains all of that, and it's one of the reasons why it's so important he's around.' **Chris Dolan, The Herald**

'It is a wonderfully audacious, linguistically elastic, verbally inventive, joyously irreverent work of literature.' **Alan Taylor, The Sunday Herald**

'*Psychoraag*—in its multi-vernacular, rambling, frenzied, helter-skelter fashion—sings.' **The Barcelona Review**

'While Suhayl is rushing away and I'm saying goodbye, I try to imagine what his next novel will be like: perhaps it will have the same lulling rhythm of songs played by Sufi minstrels, the same energy and anger of Indian rebel poet Kagi Nazrul Islam, the stream of consciousness of James Joyce and the visionary realism slightly tinted with historical and political themes of many Argentinean authors. After all, these elements can already be detected in *Psychoraag* and in other works by Saadi and are the reasons why his poems, prose, essays and articles are fresh, entertaining and will definitely help him to be included among the new exciting voices of contemporary literature. No, not of English, Scottish or British literature, but of international literature.'
Anna Battista, Erasing Clouds

'Suhayl Saadi's debut collection of short stories is a small treasure. His is such a unique voice in Scottish literature it is impossible not to get swept up in his many experiments with form and content ... Funny, clever and complex, his Scots Asian voice is very fresh, and reminiscent of masters like Salman Rushdie and Alan Warner and, on this evidence, Saadi may soon be at the point of having few contemporary rivals. Tricky and challenging but full of wit and repressed wisdom.' **The List**

'A second reading of this fine collection would undoubtedly reveal more structural and thematic connections. Its rich prose, which dares to be different with its unusual metaphors and striking turns of phrase, is the kind of language one often encounters with those not writing in their first language (Conrad, Nabokov, Kosinski), which is to say bold, fresh and wholly original. Of course, unlike them, Saadi's native language is English, but just as the ancestral religious strains rise up through the young boy in "Bandanna," so does an exotic linguistic strain work its way through Saadi's prose, giving it an innovative, distinctive literary flair. It is a striking debut collection – moving, passionate, and intellectually stimulating – which leaves you longing for more.' **The Barcelona Review**

Joseph's Box

SUHAYL SAADI

TWO RAVENS
PRESS

Published by Two Ravens Press Ltd.
Green Willow Croft
Rhiroy, Lochbroom
Ullapool
Ross-shire IV23 2SF

www.tworavenspress.com

ISBN: 978-1-906120-44-3

British Library Cataloguing in Publication Data: a CIP record for this book can be obtained from the British Library.

Designed and typeset in Sabon by Two Ravens Press. Cover design by David Knowles and Sharon Blackie.

Printed on Forest Stewardship Council-accredited paper by CPI Antony Rowe, Chippenham, Wiltshire

FSC
Mixed Sources
Product group from well-managed
forests and other controlled sources
Cert no. SGS-COC-2953
www.fsc.org
© 1996 Forest Stewardship Council

The publisher gratefully acknowledges subsidy from the Scottish Arts Council towards the publication of this volume.

Scottish
Arts Council

About the Author

Suhayl Saadi is a novelist and stage and radio dramatist based in Glasgow. His hallucinatory realist novel, *Psychoraag* (2004) won a PEN Oakland Josephine Miles Literary Award, was short-listed for the James Tait Black Memorial Prize and the Pakistan National Literary Award, was nominated for the Dublin-based IMPAC Prize and was acclaimed by *The List* magazine and the Scottish Book Trust as one of the Top 100 Scottish books of all time. Saadi's eclectic short story collection, *The Burning Mirror* (2001) was shortlisted for the Saltire First Book Prize. His work has been adapted for stage and screen, he has edited a number of anthologies and has penned song lyrics for modern classical compositions with the Dunedin Consort (The People's Mass), international choir (Project Paradisum) and with Scottish Opera (5:15). Driven often by music, his work has appeared from Cape Town to Kerala by way of Kiev and from San Diego to Singapore via New York City and Teheran. He has written extensively for the UK national press, the BBC and the British Council.

For more information about the author, and for additional reading material about the book, see

www.josephsbox.co.uk

Acknowledgements

Dedication:

For Nadia Afza Shirin Hawwa Mirza-Saadi, may you run with laughter always.

Acknowledgements:

The author wishes to acknowledge the support of the Scottish Arts Council for their kind provision of a writer's bursary, which facilitated time to write *Joseph's Box*.

Joseph's Box would not have been written had it not been for Tabassum Afza Sultana Ahmed, Salim Uddin Ahmed and Ellen Estella Mackrill, three souls who were there at the Beginning...

Grateful thanks to Sharon Blackie at Two Ravens Press for her creative courage and aesthetic genius, to Jenny Brown for her foresight, persistence, élan and encouragement and to Gavin Wallace, Head of Literature at the Scottish Arts Council for his intelligent sanguinity over the years.

Thanks also to:

Salman Ahmed
Miloud Aniba
Inam Baig
Aziz Balouch
Anna Battista
Sally Beamish
les Beaux Bébés
Kathryn Besio
Patrick Blaise
Boulus Ben Batal
Allan Cameron
Daniela Candiotta
Ruafza Zaliqa Chishti
Gaetano Cipolla
William Dalrymple

Adam Dawar
Claire Dawar
Melanie Desmoulins
Youhanna Dilber
Christopher M. Dolan
Mara Dompè
Caroline Mary Donaldson
elisatbd
Abu Nasr al-Farabi
Joseph Farrell
Asif Aslam Farrukhi
Venera Fazio
Paulo Fiorentino
Elisabetta Flamini
Phamie Gow
Shusha Guppy
The Habibiyya
Ruhi Hamid
Farideh Hasanzadeh
John Dobie Henderson
Jurj Ibn Sheikh
Nur ad-Din ar-Rahman Jami
Samina Khan
Jamila Khatoon
David Knowles
Oleksander Kyrylenko
Marc Lambert
Kenneth MacDonald
Rob MacKillop
Alistair McCall
Lynn McCall
Misha Maltsev
Marmot
Dawar Masaud
Leon Menezes
Samia Mikhail
Alan Milligan

Susan Milligan
Alina Mirza
Ricky Mirza
Sarmed Mirza
Necsus
Claudia Nocentini
Oliver3
Prince Paracletus of Pantiddirìa
Riccardo Pehlvani
Le Peru
Sophie Pilgrim
Eric Rahim
Raphillon
Jerome Richalot
Rashid Sami
Carla Sassi
Ronnie Scott
Salvatore Settis
Roman Turovsky-Savchuk
Adam Arnold Slotsky
Alan Smith
Hasan Zaidi
Maheen Zia
Various members of the 'Lute Web' and Oud, 'Ud and Lute
Societies from around the world

The Balti proverb on p 557 is acknowledged as being from: *Balti Proverbs, Hasni, G.H. (2004), Tam Lo (Balti Proverbs)*, Skardo: Shabbir Printing Press and Publishers.

This book also is dedicated to the memory of all those whom I have failed.

Life is weaker than death, and death is weaker than truth.

Khahlil Gibran, 1916

Never was there a beloved to compare with Yusuf, whose beauty exceeded that of all others ... among lovers, none was the equal of Zulaykha ... she loved from childhood to old age, both in omnipotence and destitution. She never ceased to devote herself to love: she was born, she lived and she died – in love.

Jami, from 'Yusuf and Zulaykha' (1414-1492)

BOX ONE: GLASGOW

One day, I saw,
Beneath the Clyde
A jewel that was an eye…

Melanie Desmoulins, 2002

Chapter One

She walks straight to the middle of the bridge, stops exactly midway between the two massive suspension props, removes her clothes, folds them carefully and places them in an ordered, pyramidal pile on the asphalt. Then, unzipping her holdall, she removes a set of exercise-weights, attaches the pig-iron to wrists and ankles using white twine of the unbreakable type, and mounts first the inner and then the outer railings. She clutches onto one of the coiled metal ropes that rise exponentially and which help maintain the perfect balance of the bridge. It is an engineering miracle, a big white bird.

Zuleikha has forgotten why she has walked from her car to the outer rail of the suspension bridge. A little further along there is some fresh, reinforced metal. She thinks that they would have to work on this bridge constantly, that no sooner would one deficit be remedied than another would appear. Yet there would come a time, surely, when even this degree of care would not suffice, when the bridge would be irreparable, when it would just be allowed to fall into the night.

Zuleikha laughs, and her voice is lost in the billowing seam. The wind is colder than night, yet she does not feel the cold well up from the emptiness, she does not feel it bite into her skin. In the sickly time after dawn, the dull gleam of human habitation resembles a carpet of fading stars flattened down against the hard earth. Everything begins to sway; beneath her naked feet she can sense the iron dance of the bridge, she feels it deform and crack, yet against her deadening skin the balustrade metal is perfectly smooth. In the whole universe, she is the only point of stillness. One deep breath. Eyes closed. Then, no breath. No body. Nothing. Jump. Jump. Jump.

Her naked body shoots down from the path at eighty kilometres per hour. The moment she hits the dark skin of the river, the cold shock shuts down every blood vessel and she is in complete darkness. Her movement slows as she sinks until, gently, the top of her head makes contact with the soft, reedy bed of the Clyde. Now in a foetal clasp, she rises perhaps a third of the way back up, until the density of the water reaches a level equal to that of her body plus the weights. There, in the pitch-black cold, the pull of the iron tethers her limbs, and her hair dances with the swaying heads of the reeds. Then, if her skull, neck and belly have not been split by the initial impact of the water, she begins to struggle as the oxygen starvation explodes inside her chest. A desperate regret as she attempts to free her legs and arms from the gravity that pulls her inexorably downwards.

Zuleikha has forgotten everything. Even the death of Daoudbehta has been lost. The minutiae of self-blame. All gone. In the depths of the river there is no logic, no compass. Even if she manages to free herself from the iron blocks, even if she senses the killing metal sink away, even if her limbs begin to thrash out a line which might just be a trajectory of heavy ascent, she is unable to tell, in the frozen gloom of her integument, in which direction she is slowly moving. She cannot hold the dioxide in the flowers of her lungs for a moment longer; the blooded carbon of her being is starving, screaming, exploding, and in one long contraction, silently, her whole body breathes out. She does not see the bubbles of her life. She can hold her contracted chest for only a couple of seconds before physics impels her to expand, to inhale deeply. Her neck swells as the cold river water fills her corpse. Everything freezes. One last desperate moment flecks before her eyes. Then the cold turns to warmth. A new energy. But the darkness remains.

The light breeze tinkered annoyingly with strands of her hair. She brushed them out of her eyes and thrust her hands into the pockets of her overcoat. She was walking along a narrow path which hugged the south bank. She wasn't sure why she had travelled to this part of the river, just upstream from the big suspension bridge that marked the de facto boundary between river and estuary. Between the sloping green banks, the clouds reached down and almost touched the surface of the water. The river was ashen, and was so still she could barely make out its flow. It was a misty morning, early. She had forgotten to scoop up her watch from the bedside table, but she reckoned that it was now around six o'clock. She hadn't been sleeping well recently; no matter what time she went to bed she would rise obsessively early, and the rapid ascent

4

from sleep left her weary, the ends of her consciousness ragged. The nights, the years. A diver coming up through deep water. Her brain had the bends. Too much inert gas building up behind her eyelids, too many loosened dreams.

The opposite bank was much steeper and the grass rolled right to the edge of the water. If someone were to try to perch on top of that bank they might easily lose their grip and, once the slide had begun, it would accelerate so that they would slip straight down into the glaucous waters of the Clyde River and be lost forever. There were no footholds, no lifebelts, no branches or rocky outcrops. There would be no escape. Since its construction in the early 1970s the bridge had been an extreme place, a favourite place for suicides.

Out here, the Clyde smelled quite different. It was hard to define. One moment, Zuleikha thought she caught a whiff of the sea which lay some twenty miles further west; the next, it was the oddly hypnotic stink of thick moss, rusty metal, lorry diesel and partial decomposition. A snakeskin, newly-shed. It was as though here, in this place beneath the bridge, all of the river's constituent parts had begun to merge and lose definition.

Several hundred feet above where she stood, the Erskine Bridge ran in a perfect spinal arc from south to north. No cars ran along the roads and no tiny figures dotted the slim eastern walkway. In any case, the land rose at too steep an angle for her to be able to make out anything much on the bridge, while mist shrouded the upper sections of the masts. It had rained the night before, and on the drive here the tarmac had gleamed almost painfully, yet the path on which she now stood was bone-dry. If she focused on one spot long enough and then rapidly shifted her eyes to the left, Zuleikha found that, just for a moment, she could arrest the flow of water, and then it was as though she had snapped a photograph of the river, so that for a moment she was able to see the long flow of the Clyde, Clwyd, Ctota in its entirety, every tiny ripple, every whirlpool, every hidden seepage which might indicate the presence of rocks, or reeds, or, far in the depths, the passage of cold, sleek fish. ·

Then it was gone and her eyes burned. She tried to blink away the monstrous angularity of the bridge. The coffee she had grabbed on the way had been far too strong and now it made her heart beat fast against the cage of her ribs. She'd wanted to wake, wholly, completely, and not be stuck in some kind of early morning limbo when secretions run on and the hair tautens, rank across the scalp. No. She'd wanted to awaken, to rise like the mist as the heat of the day moved in from the east. She'd wanted to become light, lighter even than air, and to float right out across the river and up along the sheer sides of the mountains which rose from the far bank. As the clouds began to clear, she began to make out the dark summits to the north. The heather was out of season and it clung to the rock like a rough skin. There was no-one else about. Still no cars up on the bridge. It was a public holiday, she remembered, the second one in May, and things today would be laid-back, easy.

She was standing beneath the south pillar. There was no wind and the mist rolled in heavy white curtains across the viscid water. She could feel the concrete through her dress, a yellow dress, thin, cotton, summery, incongruous. Yet she did not shiver. Life seethed just beneath the surface, transparent plankton, leaping salmon, estuary crabs which had crept upstream a little too far, and other murkier forms.

That was when, through the mist, she saw the head.

A small round shape, barely visible, shifting slowly on the edges of the current, somewhat upstream of her position. That was all it was at first. She made out a pair of eyes and a downward-curving mouth. The eyes were closed. The neck, if there was one, must still have lain beneath the waterline. She massaged her own eyes to try to recapture physiological normality.

But it was still there. It had moved away from the middle of the river and was growing larger as it drew closer to the bank. It was travelling diagonally, south-westwards. She'd seen enough of disembodied caputs as a medical student, back in the Old Century. Now she thought back on it, the whole thing seemed grossly bizarre. She'd walked into the anatomy dissection hall, where the temperature was kept around ten degrees below that in the rest of the building. Cold steel trolleys and Victorian columns had splintered the empty space. The bodies had been tightly swathed in sheets and laid face-up. Before her first day in the Hall, she had hardly thought death a credible thing. Although she had known that they would be dissecting real corpses, in some deep organ of her mind Zuleikha had imagined that when the day finally came for the teenage students, six to each trolley, to lean over and unwrap the white humps, they would discover life-sized facsimiles with synthetic flesh. It had taken her a few days of hard, messy cutting to realise that the thing beneath her scalpel was actually a human being, a woman, who only recently had been alive and had danced, sung, loved, made love. She was glad that throughout the long back-breaking months of dissection, the eyes of the corpse had remained closed. She was thankful the object floating in the river no longer resembled a head.

She ran down closer to the edge where the gradient was very gradual, yet still, at high tide, the ground on which she stood would be six feet under. The leather of her calf-length boots felt cold against her skin. Her sense of urgency had precluded any rummaging and anyway, at six am, no-one was going to be judging. She'd had to get out of her flat and into the fresh air. Then, once she'd got onto the street, she'd had to go somewhere else. Anywhere else. So in one movement she'd jumped into the driver's seat, rammed the keys into the ignition, and sped off. Sometimes, when she'd done this before, Zuleikha had felt the urge to swing the wheel violently either to the north or else due south and to keep going. There was something, she thought, about following the iron of the compass. In this part of the country, if you travelled along a west-to-east axis, all you ended up doing was moving between shopping-malls or industrial estates. If you really wanted to get away you had to head due north, up to where the old purple mountains hulked around bottomless lochs, or else south for a thousand miles until the temperature began at last to climb. She'd always had the urge to travel, to step unexpectedly onto the running-board of the magical evening plane. So why had she ended up as a functionary in a city whence there was little prospect of escape? She'd often asked herself that question as she'd peered at her own bleary face in the morning mirror, her gaze focusing always on the slightly bulbous tip of her long, typically Afghan nose. Her boots were strong, yet she had never left.

But she was glad of them now, because it meant that she could run painlessly over the rocks and rubbish of the riverbank and could go right up to the river's edge and stretch her body over the water, out as far as it would go. She would stretch spine, shoulders, elbows, fingers till she was almost horizontal, till she was like an arc, a bridge, and as the object floated past she would be able to grab hold of it. But suddenly it had turned over in the stream, so that now it looked like a bundle of rags. And what was wrapped in the rags? A dead cat? She shivered. A wrapped, amputated limb? A baby? She pushed the thought out of her mind and attempted to concentrate on the physicality of what she had to do. As it floated to within ten feet of her Zuleikha realised that, because of the curve of the river, the thing would touch neither the bank nor the tips of her fingers, but instead would float on past the pillar, beneath the bridge and out again into the main current, upon which it would be carried further and further westwards as the river swelled first into firth and then into the heaving, pellucid Irish Sea. From there, it might go north, through the Minch, and be washed up on some rocky Hebridean island where it would be picked up by some other woman who was wandering like a lunatic along the beach at six in the morning on a public holiday. She felt impelled to bring the object in. The trajectory of her whole life seemed at that moment to hinge upon whether or not she would be able to rescue what at first she had imagined, in her state of half-sleep, to be a large, dark brown head. Or perhaps its colour and apparent age were illusory; perhaps it had been fashioned thus over a period of time by nothing more than the turning lathe of the river water.

She glanced around. Panic was beginning to swell in her chest. Behind her, and about eight feet to her left, lay a long blackened branch, to which were still attached a few leafy twigs. She retreated onto the beach, bent down, fastened her right fist around the branch and yanked it up. It almost pulled her into the ground. She hadn't realised that it was tethered to something much larger, something which lay beneath the stones of the bank.

'Damn!'

Her voice made no echo, not even within her own skull, and the words immediately disappeared into the mist.

Bending down, Zuleikha fixed both hands around the branch and tugged, once, twice, three times, using more force with each succeeding effort so that at the third attempt she felt as though her

8

spine might crack. She glanced behind her. What she imagined had been a head was really a box, wrapped in old rags. Stupid bitch, she thought. She tried again. A ripping noise. A world, wheeling. Slowly, the box was slipping past her. She landed on her back, her legs suspended foolishly in the air like those of some up-ended crustacean. But she had the branch. From where she lay, she was just able to make out the top of a bag of old cement to which the branch had been attached. Leaping to her feet, she quickly pulled away most of the twigs. A phalanx of ants, suddenly disrupted in the middle of their labour, marched away into the scrubgrass.

The box had moved away and now was heading towards the bridge. Zuleikha knew that once it crossed an invisible line which ran between the pillars, it would be beyond capture. She ran down to the river's edge and, holding the stick almost at its end, again she stretched forwards her arms, her shoulders, her back, almost to the point of dislocation, so that now she felt like a cross between a fisherwoman and a madonna. But even with the stick, it was too far out for her to reach. The box bobbed up and down. She wondered why it had not sunk. Maybe it was air-tight. Or perhaps what she could see was only one-eighth of what was there. If that was the case, there was no way she would be able to hoist the box out of the water, let alone carry it home. She bent down and took off her boots.

When the water reached her waist, Zuleikha felt her feet begin to slip. Although, viewed from the bank, the river's surface had seemed unbroken, now that she was actually standing some way out, the river coursed upwards before her like the back of a great cow and threatened to knock her off her feet. She knew that balance, once lost, would not be regained. She sensed the pull of the current and of something beneath the current. She wondered whether the Atlantic undertow reached this far inland and decided that it wasn't worth finding out. The lower half of her body felt like a block of cold iron. Her only contact with the world was through the river-mud that swarmed around the soles of her feet.

Heads, floating in pots. More than twenty years earlier, back at Medical School (a term which already had become obsolete by then), Zuleikha had begun keenly to dissect the woman's body: first the arms, then the chest, abdomen, pelvis and legs. And thus, over a period of eighteen months, the bloodless bodies had been systematically deconstructed. Then one day many months later, when she had turned up as usual in the Anatomy Hall, she had found that all the corpses had vanished and the steel tables gleamed spotlessly in the morning light.

But on a shelf, set just above eye level and extending right the way around the hall, sat four hundred and one glass pots. An exact quantity of formaldehyde had been poured into each pot so that with the floating brain, the skin of the clear liquid reached to within five centimetres of the lid. Sometime during the night a team of hunch-backed, white-coated morticians had crept along the darkened corridors of the anatomy building, unlocked arcane cupboards and, using electrical saws, had performed multiple decapitations. Zuleikha could hardly bear to cut across the striations of the cortex, to disturb its sweeping symphonic patterns, its texture not unlike that of soft French cheese. There, she thought, my scalpel is slicing through the first smile, the tremulous steps, the last kiss. The simple desires and pleasures: food, sex, warmth, love, ambition, prayer. This brain, with its hundred billion neurons, had infused and enervated a body that had been worshipped by parents, friends, lovers and then, later, perhaps also by children and grandchildren who yet held within their heads the whispered last words. And perhaps there was some ineluctable node of transfiguration, some metaphysical point of contact with God through which right now she was dissecting. It was a violation, undertaken by the ignorant.

She swayed back on her heels and then, putting everything into the movement, she made one final stretch. She willed the branch onwards, so that at the last critical moment when she felt her legs buckle into the darkness, and as the first of the river-reeds arose and coiled their flared ends around her ankles, Zuleikha felt a tiny but satisfying judder as the branch leapt out and hooked its wavering tip around the far side of the box. The exhilaration fired through her body, enervating even those cells which she had thought deadened by the cold, and she moved deeper into the river. She felt as though now she was rising through the thick water, higher and higher until she was almost walking on its surface. She was in up to her chest and the river beat wildly against her heart so that it was all she could do to keep her balance. I could get used to this, she thought. Perhaps, every Sunday, she would come to the river's edge and peer across its surface; perhaps she would take to the water and swim among the dolphins, out to where the current was strongest, and then she would dive deep into the murk in search of something buried in the mud, clasped within a shell or hidden in a whisky bottle. It was like reverse dowsing. To seek out solidity in the endless flow of the river. But there weren't any dolphins hereabouts, she thought. Don't be silly.

'Yes, yes, you bastard, I've got you!' she hissed as she began gingerly to step backwards, pulling in the object as she went. Then she felt a little guilty at having sworn in the river, at the box. Until the moment she hauled it, dripping-wet and stinking, onto the hard rocks of the bank, Zuleikha did not take her eyes off the large bundle. Just when she thought she was safe, she overbalanced and half-fell into the river, and amidst the splashing and cursing some water found its way into her mouth.

In those days women surgeons had been few and far between, yet her decision really had been the result of her repulsion at the thought of the human form – and so Zuleikha Chashm Framareza had become Doctor MacBeth, General Practitioner, practitioner of generalities, scientific quack, Jill of all Trades and Mistress of Nothing. It had suited her personality. After all, when you really looked at things, nothing on earth could be mastered. The world was wild and infinitely inchoate. Even the most solid of objects ultimately would turn to liquid or smoke. And so, as time went on, that which she once had considered immutable began to shift – just as, once, she had imagined that her mother would live forever.

She sat, dripping and wet, on the stones of the small beach. She spat, tried to clear the foul taste of the Clyde out of her mouth. Then she began to shiver. She wrapped her hands tightly around her body, but the shivering just slipped inside and that was worse.

'I'll get fucking pneumonia,' she said through chattering teeth.

Zuleikha got up again and, arms still locked around her chest, began to jump up and down as though she was in an invisible straightjacket. That way, at least, she made herself out of breath, which somewhat distracted her body's attention from the cold. Her feet were streaked with mud, which warmed her skin a little as it dried. She stank of the river. Then she stopped moving, let her arms go loose, and bent down to inspect the object.

It was a bundle of old clothes, turned carp-grey in the river mud. Carefully, touching the thing with only the tips of her fingers, Zuleikha began to unwrap the bundle, layer by layer. Jacket, trousers, shirt – all had been tied in so many knots that she began to wish she'd brought along a pair of scissors – and finally (and at this point she found herself in that familiar fugue that lies beyond disgust, her index and middle fingers probing, laparotomy-style, at the seams) a pair of baggy Y-fronts. No socks? she thought, and then she smiled. The skin around her mouth was so tight and cold that she felt every crack. Without the garbage clothes, the object looked considerably smaller. It was a square box. Zuleikha knelt down, and with her bare hands began to scrape off the mud. She'd thought of using a stone, but had decided against it lest the sharp edges should damage the box. But beneath the wet outer layer the mud was scaled hard against the wooden walls, and she broke three nails just trying to uncover an area the size of a human palm.

The swishing sounds of cars traversing the bridge built up gradually into an urban hum. Zuleikha had lived all her life within its pulse, yet now she resisted the temptation to clap her palms over her ears. The bit of wood she could see was dark brown and had been carved in swirling shapes, some of which resembled waves and others which were more like chevrons. Then she realised that the watermarks were interlaced with the miniature designs of apple trees, rose bushes and other foliage. All this, in the space of four centimetres square! Someone was approaching. Oh shit! she thought, and she sat down on a rock and quickly pulled on her boots. She stood, and pretended to be gazing up at the bridge and toward the hills beyond the north bank of the river. The mist finally was clearing from around the tops of the masts and as it retreated, it left behind patches of cold, etiolated blue. When it came, the voice at her back was that of a man.

'You want a hand with that?'

She spun round. Felt the blood rush to her face.

'I saw you. That was very brave, but also rather stupid.'

A deep voice. White Russian bass. The shadow of a beard, hovering, disembodied, around the chin. Grigory Rasputin.

Unplaceable, class-wise. Broad face. Implacable. Clothes, hair – all black.

He was tall – six-three, or maybe six-four – and heavy. Not obese, really, just big. Broad shoulders, long fingers and shoes and lank black hair which he had grown to shoulder-length. Zuleikha thought that these days this look was confined mainly to bikers, computer hardware freaks and guys who worked in music shops. And yes – technically, medically, she thought, he probably is a little overweight; middling yellowish on those rising graphs of morbidity where red signifies imminent death, green, possible immortality, and yellow a sense of quotidian salvation. And beneath the belly of his coat and overspilling the waistband of his trousers, she thought, there must surely be a midriff of fat, yet she had an impetuous, flirtish sense that this stranger who had just appeared from nowhere – or rather, from the running shamble of modern houses which lay to the south-east of the bridge, was possessed of physical proportions that were almost perfectly suited to those of his being.

She nodded and then felt that she was staring at him, and she worried that he might think that she was insane or, at the very least, unbalanced or drug-crazed. The sun was breaking through the mist and her clothes were beginning to steam. She shifted her position so that she would be just a little higher than he on the slope of the bank, but no matter how far she moved, Zuleikha found that she was still gazing up into his face. There was no way she could be level with him: he was simply too tall. She would have needed to have risen an entire foot above the surface of the stones, and though the morning had been on the weird side of unusual, there were limits. Yes, there were. He was standing only a couple of metres away from her. Apart from the tiny scurrying bodies of metal and glass high up on the bridge road, they were alone. His hands were hidden in the pockets of his leather bomber jacket. She felt herself smile again. This time, though her face felt bright red, the skin did not crack. I must be warming up, she thought.

It occurred to her that it might not have been mere chance that he had seen her, that he actively might have been watching as she'd made a fool of herself in the water. The realisation that her arms had wrapped themselves around her breasts made her feel defensive and intensely self-conscious. I'm not some little Asian girl rushing in satins through the billowing thoroughfare – haven't been that for thirty years or more, she thought, and with a shudder she let her hands drop. He nodded.

'You'll catch your death of cold. Let's get that thing into your car. I assume you do want to take it with you, given the trouble you went to in getting it this far?'

He walked towards the box. He wasn't really Russian – it had been just a first impression, that certain gravitas. His jacket was too short for him and it bunched up stupidly around his hips. His buttocks were half-moons. They had not yet fallen.

The box was far heavier in the air than it had been in the water, and by the time they had carried it from the river bank to where her car was parked, she was out of breath. It didn't seem large enough, but she figured the water soaked into the wood must have imparted the extra weight. Nonetheless, she was surprised that it fitted into her boot. As they'd angled it in, its proportions had seemed implacably square.

'Don't suppose you'll want the rags,' he said, tossing them aside with the fluid yet hardly casual movement of someone perhaps not unaccustomed to manual labour. His eyes were small and airy blue like the patches of sky which were now beginning to join together through the mist.

'Thanks,' she said.

He shrugged.

As she slammed down the lid of the boot, he shoved his hands back into his pockets.

'I'd like to know what's inside,' he said.

'So would I,' she laughed, though her laughter did not seem to carry conviction.

He pulled out his right hand.

'Alex Wolfe.'

His hand seemed enormous and she expected hers to be crushed as it disappeared into the vault of his fingers. But no, his touch was gentle, the skin soft, a light pressure and then he was away. She couldn't resist looking down at her palm. She had expected to feel clamminess, a mess of sweat. She figured it must've rubbed off onto the material of his coat. Or onto the bottom of the box.

'Zulie MacBeth.'

'Zulie?'

'Yeah. It's short for Zuleikha, but no-one can pronounce that.'

'Why not?'

It was her turn to shrug.

'I'd better be going. Or I will catch pneumonia!' Her words were clumsy. She opened the car door. Clumsy.

He pointed beyond her.

'You're a doctor?'

She stopped in mid-movement. Her stethoscope lay looped like a sleeping, grey snake across the front passenger seat.

'Oh, yeah.'

'And what's a good doctor doing at this time of the morning, on a Late Spring Monday Holiday, leaping into the cold river?'

'Before I was a doctor, I was a person. Maybe one day I shall be a person again.'

He ran the middle finger of his right hand along the smooth line of the car bonnet. She knew she'd gone too far.

'Sorry,' she said. 'I didn't mean anything.'

He lifted his hand and slowly rubbed the dirt between the tips of his finger and thumb and then looked back at her.

She got into the car and swung the door to.

He tapped on the window. She pressed the button.

He poked his chin over the glass. He hadn't shaved. Must've rushed out to see what was happening, she thought.

'Seriously. I'd really like to find out what's in the box.'

Her hands slumped over the wheel. She felt the exhaustion rise like a wave over her shoulders. She just wanted to get back home. Thank God it was a public holiday. May 28th.

'Okay,' she said. 'Give me a phone number. Or an e-mail address.'

He unzipped his jacket and began to fish about, but he was having to bend almost double to reach the level of her window. He pulled the zip down further. The sides of his fingers were streaked with the same dun-coloured river mud that coated her feet. She could feel the skin tighten against the leather of her boots.

'Here.'

She leaned across, opened the glove-box and offered him a

white plastic biro. Her dress stuck to her breasts. Everything was uncomfortable. She was stinking of the river, and here, in the enclosed space of the car, the same scent which only half an hour earlier had seemed serpentine and mysterious now made her belly churn. By this time, Alex had managed to find something in the inside pocket of his jacket. He yanked it out. A bulging brown wallet sailed through the open window, flew across her lap, over the reclining stethoscope, and slithered down the space between the far side of the passenger seat and the door. Alex held a limp piece of paper between the thumb and index finger of his right hand as though he was holding aloft a winning ticket.

'Shit! Sorry.'

Instinctively, he moved round to the other side of the car.

'It's okay. I've got it,' she said, as she tossed the biro onto the dashboard and de-contorted herself from an almost impossible position.

She held the wallet and biro out of the window for him. He came back around and seemed nervous, clumsy, so that his apology and her acknowledgement of his apology almost overlapped. As he leaned on the car roof and scribbled down his contact details, Zuleikha noticed that he was wearing a white shirt, buttoned almost up to his Adam's apple, and a thin black woollen tie. She'd been right about his belly. Five months, she reckoned. He handed her the sheaf. Pregnant, that was.

'My pen...' she began.

'Oh yeah.'

The writing was neat, the letters small and black. Yet it was not the script of an obsessional neurotic – she'd read enough of those in her time – the cursive links between the letters were too elegant, too spontaneous, the arcs of the consonants too rounded and generous. But what did she know about people, other than that their brains were like the insides of deluxe cauliflowers? He hadn't been out of breath in the slightest as he had lifted the box. Through three feet of wood, she had sensed his strength. He could easily have carried it on his own. He probably hadn't wanted to embarrass her by posing as the macho man. She wouldn't have been embarrassed. Still, Zuleikha figured that, basically, she was unfit. In a purely physical sense, that was. Yeah, well. The smoking and no exercise. She ought to promote her own health for a change. But there never seemed to be time for that. You stupid cow, she thought, you spend your days and nights off wading chest-deep into freezing rivers, chasing after inanimate objects which change form as you touch them. What do you expect? She realised that the movement she'd thought had been produced by her heartbeat was actually her whole body shivering.

She placed the paper and the biro in the glove compartment, snapped it shut, then fished in her coat for her keys and thrust the largest one into the ignition. All in one smooth movement. Good, she thought, I'm on a roll again. Everything is physical. Her head felt light – not faint exactly, but heady, as though she'd had too much caffeine or not enough food. And when she thought about it, she hadn't had anything to eat since the night before. Hadn't felt hungry. But now she was ravenous. Her belly felt like a great empty sac. She had the sudden desire for a fry-up, a toxic plate of everything, and a cup of filter coffee with a jug of steaming-hot milk. Yeah, she would stop off somewhere, just for that. But she'd have to grab a shower first. She couldn't go into a café looking and smelling the way she did right now. Even as the last wisps of mist cleared from the sky, Zuleikha's car windows were steaming up from the dampness of her clothes. She raised herself up on one buttock and focused on the rear-view mirror. On the nose which she had inherited from her mother. Wiped the condensation off the glass. Her eyes looked tired, the whites seamed through with red, the hazel-brown muscles of her irises accommodating more sluggishly than usual as she tried to focus in on her face. Incipient crows' feet splayed out on either side of the orbits, pointing the way to the places dyed black where the roots were turning silver. She was forty-one, but thought she looked older. The lack of sleep, the exigencies of the job and this crazy march to, and beyond, the river's edge. She knew, but didn't dare admit to herself, that in more ways than one she was beginning to resemble her mother.

'Are you going to a funeral?' she asked, too loudly and without drawing her gaze away from the mirror. She attempted to poise herself by twisting her lips into an odd shape. Slowly, she drew the tip of her index finger down the surface of her right cheek. The skin felt rough. Too dry. Dead, almost.

There was a pause, a silence that was just long enough that Zuleikha realised she'd made a terrible mistake. She didn't dare look at him, but froze mid-movement, her fingertip still poised against the point of her cheekbone.

'My wife…' he said, then his voice choked off.

'Oh, I'm sorry,' she said, and then shut up as she became aware of the hyperbolic and fragmented tone of her voice.

'Yes, well. I'd better go.' He glanced at his watch. 'It begins in half an hour.'

Still shivering, she shook her head, slowly, sagely.

For a moment their eyes linked, and simultaneously they glanced away – he toward the gleaming red metal of the car's rear door, and she down at the sunlight bouncing off her key. An imprint of his facial structure hovered in front of her for a few seconds before slowly turning to a mess of silver and then vanishing altogether. There was nothing more to say. She switched on the engine.

He was too close to the side of the car. Might get his feet run over. Flesh crushed beneath the heavy rubber and metal. Half a ton of iron on bone. She'd seen that, too. She'd seen everything. No, she hadn't.

'Best move back a bit. I'm not that good at reversing!'

Why was she saying this stuff?

He stepped back and she thought she made out almost the flicker of a smile. No, it can't be, she thought. Not possible. There are limits.

As she drove away he seemed to say something – his lips didn't move, yet she thought she heard his voice. Low bass. Later, she wasn't certain whether it had been just a noise from the wheels as they'd dislodged from the mud. His figure receded in the rear-view mirror, fell back into chiaroscuro, and then as she turned onto the road that led towards the motorway, he vanished. He had made no attempt to begin walking away from the river bank. Zuleikha glanced at her watchless wrist.

'Eight-thirty a.m.,' she said aloud, as though to reassure herself, as she slipped back into the buzz and roar of the road.

She pondered on how two and a half hours could have passed so quickly. She had the desire to stop the car, right in the middle of the rush-hour traffic, and check whether the box was still there. Again, she caught her face in the mirror. She had assigned to her visage the talismanic self-deprecating nickname of 'The Nose'. A single deep furrow had etched itself across the skin of her forehead. She sat bolt upright and pressed the fingers of her right hand into the mould of the steering-wheel. Tightened her grip. Then she reached up with her left hand and massaged her forehead, attempted to smooth out the loose skin on both sides of the wrinkle. But it wouldn't budge. She put it down to insomnia and the drying effect of the Clyde. But then – she hadn't immersed her head, Dead Sea-style, in the river water. Had she? No, definitely not. The car moved more slowly than before; its acceleration up the gradient seemed inordinately sluggish, and she kept being overtaken on the inside. The sun had now broken through completely. She was heading due east. She cursed herself for forgetting to bring sunglasses and she pulled down the visor two-thirds of the way, so that it stuck out at an angle from the glass. The road gleamed silver from the heavy rain of the night before and the light bounced off the tarmac into her narrowed eyes. Wearing sunglasses in Scotland was more an act of faith than of style. The Catholics probably had a blinded patron saint of spectacles perched somewhere up on a bloody mountain.

As the car struggled up the light gradients of the motorway, Zuleikha had the irresistible urge to turn and look back. Like the hunger pangs in her belly, it was something physical – a fire, a rope, a whirlpool – and it was pulling her back toward the water and the mountains beyond. She told herself that to turn around at this time, in the middle lane of a busy motorway at eight thirty-five in the morning, would be suicidal. It was just plain stupid, a neurosis of a thing; it wasn't real. Yet she sensed the tendons of her right foot weaken and the accelerator pedal rise just a little, so that the car slowed even further in its ascent. At any moment it might stop and begin to roll backwards. The stretch of road ahead was dead straight for at least eight hundred metres, but in the blinding light of the morning it seemed as though it held no substance. The back of her head felt heavy and numb, as though it had been whacked with a cricket bat, or with the dead wood of an old tree. She bounced her occiput against the head-rest a couple of times, but that didn't help. She wound down the window, thinking that a little fresh air might blow away her madness. She rolled the glass right down so that the cold morning air punched into the cabin, blowing long strands across her face. Just like her son's face, on the morning of his death. Daoud.

Out on the water toward the middle of the river there was a large white sphere, a buoy of some sort, warning passing ships of rocks or embankments or other hidden dangers. Even a small rock could hole the hull of an ocean-going liner, and it would take just a hump of earth to ground a steamer, to stop its paddles from turning, its pistons from pumping. There was a spherical ball inflating in her abdomen, her pelvis. A leather ball. Pig-bladder. Air. Fucking emptiness. Her breathing grew shallow. The sunlight broke up into golden flecks. O fuck it, she said, and swung her head around so that she was gazing backwards from between the head-rests. As her car sped on at eighty-two kilometres an hour, Zuleikha saw the serpent at the heart of the Clyde writhe in the morning light, the river's surface turned by the sun to gleaming scales. And behind the silver body of the snake, on the north bank, a dark mound of earth and rock arose at the very edge of the water and, behind this, still greater mountains hulked and glowered silently. Rising through the back window of her hatchback, shimmering in the light, the whole picture was like an oil painting, one of those intensely accurate landscapes that had fallen out of favour as the fire and smoke of camera glass had hit the galleries. There was no sense of movement and it was as though the whole world was suffused in gold.

Into this idyllic vista an image inserted itself (at least that was how she explained it to herself): a picture of herself and the man – Alexander, Alex, yes, that's right, Alex – together by the pillar as the river flowed by, its surface calm as a brass shield. Beside them lay the box, dripping with water. They were naked, her back was up against the concrete and her thighs were broadly parted, her feet half-sunk into mud. Her hair was lank and mingled with his as he moved slowly against her, his hamstrings contracting rhythmically *like those of a frog just after its head has been severed*, she thought, and then she thought that she was a totally depraved and sick bastard: depraved, to have conjured up the first image, and sick, to have associated it with the second. Or maybe just desperate.

Then she was inside the image and he was inside her. He drove his feet into the mud and thrust more deeply into her, his substance enveloping, protecting her, and yet the vigour of his movement caused her skin to begin to rub off at the base of her spine. She closed her eyes and felt the blood pulse upwards from his calves until her clit was the centre of a web which extended all over her body, into every nerve-ending, each muscle, tendon, sulcus and into the essence of her being. As the warm waves of climax began to wash over her, Zuleikha opened her eyes and saw that beyond his still undulating white shoulder, the lid of the box had swung open and there was a light coming from inside, a brightness that was so intense it mingled with and synergised her orgasm.

A cacophony of car horns spun her round. Ahead of her, ballooning in size, was a tall green embankment. She spun the wheel maniacally and then later, as the beat of her heart at last began to steady, Zuleikha thanked her intuition for the fact that she'd turned in the correct direction and avoided hitting the rise at high speed. From time to time, though, she kept glancing in the mirror. There was a slight dampness between her legs. Fuck sake, she thought. But then she figured that she'd not quite dried herself properly of river water. Every time she looked up at the glass she expected the view to have changed, but no matter how far east the car moved the view remained the same: the snake river, the mound, the mountains, the sunlight on the water. The thing was, Zuleikha knew that it was the wrong view – that geographically, from where she was, there should've been nothing but fields filled with cattle and crops, not rivers and mountains and serpents. She knew that she should have lost sight of the Clyde long ago. And one other thing: the whole car now smelled of wood.

Chapter Two

He awoke covered in sweat which smelled of blood. He was lolling like a wooden ship in the ocean. Sails limp and salted white in the no-wind. Something was preventing him from exhaling. He could breathe in, but when he tried to push the air out of his chest, it wouldn't go beyond the point where the cartilages of his collar-bones met. It was a punishment. For betraying Margaret and never admitting his betrayal to her; for what he'd done to the whore all those years earlier. Perhaps, even, for the men he couldn't remember having shot out of the sky. His chest was expanding. He was a cartoon. It was a fucking joke, the ribs all pushed out like the bars of a parrot-cage. Pretty fuckin Polly. He'd heard that grey parrots could live for a hundred years. A century of talk. Blah blah blah. It didn't work. Focusing his mind on other things – on concrete images, as the head-therapist had told him to – just didn't work any more. Not in the daytime; not in the dark, when he was alone with the flapping of leaves against the windowpane. Summer nights. Margaret, naked in the light of three white candles, her body delicious like a fruit, like the body of an angel. Her hair grown long and silken over the skin of her shoulders, the way he'd told her to let it grow, so that it would be wild for him in the darkness. The distant sound of an orchestra playing some swing tune, hot jazz, American, from over-the-watter, brass cornets and sliding trombone elegies. Great black men. African breath. Fuck sake, it wasn't working. The block was still there. He forced his body to sit up. Maybe if he could vomit like in the dream, or retch even. He felt like a corpse on a table. Soon, Archie, soon.

He scratched his head, felt some hair come out in his hand, brought it down, gazed at it. Silver. Lank rotting wood, yeah – but once it had been close-cropped and a healthy mid-brown and when it had caught the sunlight it had been almost like wheat. Soon, in maybe a couple of months, or maybe six, you will feel the smoothness of morgue metal against your back. The fluorescence of permanent bliss. God's sake, now he was sounding like a Pape! The wallpaper was speckled with the wavering blue shapes of the leaves. The fecund orchard which they had planted in the garden of their post-war paradise. Some of the trees had borne fruit and they had eaten of the fruit, even though the pears had been bitter and they had discovered much later that those pears were used only for pig-feed. But they had eaten the white flesh of the fruit and had rejoiced in its pungency. It was a life. This was what life was about. The salt of the dark earth. He was meant to be a Proddy – not Orange or anything like that, he wasn't insane – but just solid Presbyterian, rock-faced in the face of adversity. Archibald Enoch McPherson. Aye. He had lost God during the War, or maybe God had lost him; yet there had been times over the years when he'd felt that it might have helped him to have believed in something. But you couldn't just conjure up faith like some giant white rabbit out of the hat of your ageing brain.

He felt the blood pound against the skin of his face. He knew he was turning blue. Like the wallpaper, like the night. He thrust his right arm out. Felt plastic. Pulled on the transparent skin of the mask. Then he reached out again and twisted the knob on the black metal cylinder, turned it clockwise as far as it would go. Almost broke it off in the process. A wave of oxygen gushed into his face, almost drowning him. The wave swept over his body, though he was now incapable of inhaling even one molecule of the stuff. Yet it was as though the very pores of his skin were absorbing the invisible gas, as though through necessity he was turning into some primeval, sensate creature. Perhaps that might be a way of avoiding pain, the pain which he had meted out in his time, the burning lumps of flesh that had fallen out of the sky, muscle and petrol and faeces admixed in the glorious war, the whore's blooded throat forever pulsating beneath him as her hunched, greatcoated spine retreats up the hill, Margaret's tired face, the hair, once a beauteous, luscious brown almost like the mane of a chestnut mare, gone wispy now in the grave, given an added lease of life, the Gorgon nails. Polished keratin. The shining faces of beatified popes. Perhaps, on the day of Resurrection, she would rise through the damp clay soil and would tear the eyes from his head that he might never again look upon the body of another woman. And perhaps the nameless whore and the ashen form into which she had risen – and which that day on the wind-blown street he and Margaret both had witnessed – had been only a spectre, a vision,

23

conjured by his own brain just to remind him that nothing is ever forgotten, that every word we utter is taken down and recorded somewhere in the blackness of space, every breath...

He was losing it, fuck sake, he was sinking or rising – it really made little difference in the midst of this blue darkness. Okay. Fuck. The doc – MacBeth or MacDuff or whatever her name was – Zulie, he'd been inside her head, yes, and now he would know something of what she was about even before she would know it herself. Maybe it was the chronic lack of oxygen, or the heroin, or the tumour which he hugged lovingly within the wall of his chest, but Archie had acquired the power to feel inside the thoughts of those with whom he came into physical contact. How was that, eh! Pretty bloody good. He was like that guy in the old film who had been able to see through skin and flesh and bone, the man who had been able to see right through people. Only in Archie's case, the visions didn't exactly come as visions – not like those of the Papist Saints: Kentigern, Columba and all that – no choirs of angels and hordes of rat-tailed devils for Archie-boy – no, what he knew could never be seen, but only sensed and felt like he could feel the smooth curves of Margaret's nails being buffed by the long bodies of white worms, or her hair bleached by the earth as it swept across her forehead. A swinging dance between the staves of the hangar, joyous orchestras overhead, the blood and oil of the skies. Archie, the whore, the doc and Margaret, all swinging together to the sound of Goodman's clarinet.

Archie had slipped through the eczematous fingers of young nurses and had groomed the firm backs of their beached boyfriends; he had dwelt for a time in the optimistic stretched cradle of the home help's thinned lips, and had found that beyond the grimace her husband was three-timing her with a pack of anal East End spine-dogs and that her darling son was hypodermicising his cerebral cortex with Pakhtun munnashiyaath, and that she knew all this yet still went on and on, hoping for salvation through mundanity, for redemption in mud. Yeah, inside other folk, Archie was multi-lingual, polyphonic, harmonious and dissonant at the same time. Inside the minds of other people he was all-feeling, ineffable. He was god. Joy of joy of joys! It almost made him believe again. Yet in that woman, Zulie MacBeth – and how the fuck did she ever get a name like that – there was a kernel which Archie could not penetrate, some inner vault that remained locked or sealed, as though by the mathematically approximating edges of closed pyramids. And what business of his was it anyway? The same driving force that had urged him forward across the concrete floor of the hangar and through which he had bled into the metal of every aircraft he had sent into the sky, the same leap of energy which had arced his fingers around the windpipe of the whore that sunny day in 1941, Vera Lynn serenading his acts of murder, the tightening bullskin muscles of his balls, the long perfect deception with Margaret's body which had meant that never once after death had her soul visited him. And he bathed deep in opiate senescence, in this pulse which kept him alive for just one more second, which pumped his heart muscle beyond the bounds of physiological possibility and which held together the long legs of his disunited axons.

And in the midst of his decline, Archibald Enoch McPherson prised open that which lay inside Zulie MacBeth. He did what he had done already to the others who had entered this last airspace of his life: he laid her bare before his blindness that he might feel the sweep of her soul. Maybe that way, lying against such a well-hidden piece of music, he might just begin to perceive his own truth. Fish philosophy, Archie thought, fucking haddock psychology, there in a glass on the rocks with oily swept-back coif, leaning tail-up against a bar in Purgatory. Fucking Andromeda, with whom rigid merman Perseus can only make love in the mirrored metal of his shield. Otherwise his love will turn to stone. I know what I am: a cunt. It's simple. A retching, hairy, vomiting, acidic whore's cunt. Sacrifice, foundation, truth, devotion ... lies, all. Worms. I've lain with every beast of the field there is, and some besides. The golden mean of the twitching leg and the arched back, of Junker bomb and shelter roof, of leaf on wall, of image blasted onto nitrate paper, of bulbous penis against bloated belly, nothing more. Only power meant anything at all. The angles formed by Margaret's bones as they shift about in the six-by-two, carried on the backs of millions of industrialised maggots or wingless ants. Parasites in her brain: his brain the parasite. Power.

And as, finally, his stomach heaved the bovine contents of his food supplements up over the coverlet of daisies which they had chosen together in some or other Christmas sale, Archie felt the green bolus that had been blocking his windpipe fly out from between his remaining teeth and plaster itself on the lightening blue flowers of the wall opposite, two – or possibly three – inches to the left of the golden frame of the photograph of his dead wife. Dawn on the stone as he rises from the bed of leaves upon which he has seeped his seed into the rearing yawn between her thighs. Archie the engineer goes off in a mess of guitar solos and acquires the geometer of words, letters, dancing figures. In the light of the morning, on the carbon of his brain, he rises and writes the next chapter of his life. Or perhaps it is the first.

Chapter Three

On the eve of her forty-second birthday, Zuleikha found that she could not decide whether or not to open the box.

Outside, veils of rain swept down onto the buildings, the tarmac, the trees, and even through her closed curtains Zuleikha could make out the amber droplets as they cascaded elegantly, High Glasgow-style, through the summer night. Well, it was June, right? The big box had been in her house for three days and two nights and still she'd done nothing with it. Yet every night she'd sat, smoking and sometimes drinking too, and had stared at the object and found herself completely subsumed into its existence.

She cursed as the stub of her cigar nipped the skin at the end of her finger and she tossed the stub onto the saucer which, for the past few weeks since she'd misplaced the original, had doubled as an ashtray. Or was it months? She rubbed her hands together to dispel the tingling and then inspected the skin of her index finger. Held it up close to the taut yellow lampshade. An ash mark matched the irregular pattern of her fingerprint. She stuck the phalange into her mouth and sucked on it a couple of times, but the action just made it nip all the more.

From the centre of the saucer, the cigar stub continued to smoulder and began to discolour the porcelain. The box sat between the smoking saucer and an almost empty mug of cold coffee. Along the sides of the mug, in a repetitive pattern, was stamped a red and yellow logo which consisted of a woman's head to which had been attached three legs, all bent at the knee, while its upper rim bore the imperfect red smudge of her lipstick. At the other end of the table, the weighty Saturday edition of the newspaper hulked ominously. It always contained the worst of the world. Quite why she had it delivered, she didn't know. You only stopped the papers if you were gone away or dead. And in some senses she had been away for several years – yet, paradoxically, she'd needed certain things to pin her down in this flat, this city, this world. And now she'd found another. Or maybe it had found her. At some point, she'd pulled out the glossy magazine insert and had laid it on top of the bundle of newspapers, so that now the front cover hawked a face whose muscles grinned almost beyond the point of anatomical possibility. Perfect teeth. Not like the photos ranged along her mantelpiece. Framed, sometimes awkward, monochrome images of her parents, taken before she'd been born. Zuleikha found that she was having increasing difficulty remembering anything specific about her distant past. Perhaps this is how it happens, she thought. A gradual disconnection.

Just after her mother had died, almost as the coffin – draped in black with the filigreed gold of the ninety-nine names of God – had vanished beneath the earth's surface, some tight-mouthed hijaabo had told her that one door to heaven had now been closed to her and that the other door would swing shut the moment she lost her remaining parent. Now every time she thought of her father, Zuleikha consciously had to resist imagining a closing door. A great carved wooden door like one of those she'd seen in picture books of the Paris catacombs. *Enter the House of the Dead.* Oak, elm or cedar. The letters of archaic languages, spelling out the names of the long-deceased: *Daniel John MacBeth, son of...* Now, in her mind, she protected her father as though he was one of the hollow porcelain figures she had arranged in a motionless dance on the mantelpiece. She hoped the woman was proud of herself and her religiosity.

And then there were the women with 1980s haircuts, people who talked far too much and who were fixated on the pusillanimous worship of next year's bottom line. These were the form-generators, the people who required everything to be printed out in quadruplicate; it was likely that they would doubt their own existence until they were certain that they were sitting on some lowest common denominator on a form somewhere. *I tick [boxes], therefore I am.* Nowadays the high streets of the towns were all exactly the same: the music, the phrases, the way people acted, unconsciously imitating characters from soap operas concocted by slick teams of script development editors. Mediated through Estuary English, enunciated so loudly it cracked elephants' eardrums, people mistook this dynamic for the working class taking over. In the face of all this crap, the miracle was not that people had turned into demand-feeders, but that there was any humanity left at all. And there was, loads of it. Deep down, the human spirit was stronger than all the shite. She hoped. Yes, she thought, it is – I see it every day. I see the reality that lies beneath the flickering screen, beneath the coprophagy of corporate jargon. And then there was the arrogance of never recognising the achievements of other societies. People had been brainwashed to believe that capitalism was the only way. Meanwhile, the earth was shaking and was readying itself for a cataclysm. But what if the truth – or at least a part of it – was contained not in some book, not in the word, not in a series of economic transactions or more-or-less syncretic myths, but in a box yet to be opened? A door behind a door. She pushed the thought from her mind.

Her father lived in a different part of the city, among dormer bungalows and well-pruned rowan trees and where all the properties were *south-facing sun-traps which harboured several rare breeds of cooking-apple.* Daniel John had never really been into that stuff before, and she suspected that now he did what he did partly in order to burn up useless energy, and partly in order not to stand out too much from the other residents. She'd advised him to get the whole place turfed or laid with stone or whatever would be needed to obviate the requirement to potter around in parodic gloved imitation of Hazrat Aadam in internal exile. He would decide on it eventually, she supposed, but meanwhile he went on doing what he thought ought to be done, his limbs growing thinner by the year, his face seamed with the musculature of weakness. Sometimes, by the evening, his eyes would be streaked red with the strain, though perhaps this last was as much due to the loss of his wife as to the necessity of endlessly performing the choreographed ritual dances of the petit-bourgeoisie. Had he always been like this, she wondered? She couldn't remember. The snapshot albums revealed nothing. Faces ageing, memories coiled, a slow shrinking, a darkening. No, she thought, that's wishful romantic thinking. His eyes were red because secretly he drank. No-one admitted to this, not even Zuleikha, but everyone knew it.

Like worms, such things came deep in the night. She had a pathological fear of things that crawled. She loved gardens, but hated gardening. Loved the countryside, but could never ever have been a farmer. Basically, she despised and feared the earth. Miserable pretentious bitch, she said aloud, and then laughed.

That's what comes from drinking too much, late at night. Bullshit words. There was no more truth in a book than there was in a stone.

Further along the mantelpiece was her graduation photo, bleached through a tremulous Scottish summer of twenty-odd years ago, an image of cold stone at her back. Even now, from the faded nitrate, her face shone without blemish in the light of the midsummer sun. She remembered that the long woollen gown in early July had been stifling, and the hall echoing and airless. Three hundred black-clad sweating individuals, standing in rows, listening to the distant speeches of the notables, while from far above, along the walls, the portraits of dead titans glowered into a static future. In the photo – not an official photograph, but merely a family snapshot – Zuleikha's parted lips displayed both rows of her teeth and her head was cocked slightly to one side, and this expression of feigned innocence, of High Summer and bourgeois picnics, somehow matched her black hair which was caught up above her ears in the long wavy disordered 'mop' style which had been all the rage back then. Long ago she had learned to moderate her smile, to cut her hair, to pull in her lips, to expose no more than the cracked edges of her teeth and, above all, not to swing her neck idiotically sideways. She had learned not to be cute. As a woman, if you wanted your mind to be taken seriously, you first had to reconstruct your body.

Standing beside and a little behind her on the stone steps outside the church hall, she made out the figures of her mother and father. At the time she had thought that they looked already past middle age, but now, over two decades on, her parents in the photo seemed merely worn. Daniel John's face glowed in the summer sunshine, and his cheeks still held a certain oval pink puffiness with slightly bucked teeth. He was gazing downwards, as though he had been forced to stand facing into the sun for just a little too long, so that his eyes were partially obscured by the angle of the shade cast from his brows. His hair was that kind of tawny grey which blond men tended to acquire ludicrously early. His slim form was stooped – partly, no doubt, in an attempt to squeeze the top of his head into the camera frame, but partly, she knew, because Daniel John had tended to tread through life searching for the foxhole. Even though his ancestors had been in this land for upwards of a century and a half, Zulie's father still held the mentality – and this was something to which he would never have admitted – that at any moment, the British – or Scottish – government might decide that it had had enough of the Irish, and kick them all back west. It was nonsensical, and she knew that he knew it. It was not something they had ever discussed at the dining table. It was not something that would ever come out, this insecurity that festered in the spirals of the genes, yet she had seen it, even by her mother's deathbed; she had heard it in his voice, in his cries; she had felt it in the timbre of his breath.

Her mother's last words to her had been spoken from a hospital bed where Nasrin Zeinab had been attached to numerous machines, each of them bleeping and flashing and pumping. As always, her mother's enunciation had been perfect: *Khuda Hafiz*. Her face had seemed serene, the light suffusing through the grime of the hospital window, turning the room into an illuminated chalice. Yet as the pentimento of the Pietà had faded, Zuleikha had begun to mistrust this memory. It had come to seem too much like the tale of a martyr – *God go with you!* – as though the primary colours of beatification which posthumously had accrued to her mother's absent persona had bled back into the past, as though this last, desperate illness had come to define her entire life. Zuleikha had been too upset to talk and too self-conscious to cry, there in the death room. She was a doctor, after all, and what would the nurses have thought?

Over by her shoulder, Zuleikha's father had shrunk visibly at the moment of his wife's death and had never regained his full size. Though her parents had been divorced for upwards of a decade, her father had never stopped loving her mother – whatever that meant. Zuleikha had never been able really to pin it down: a dampening of the glass at certain times of day, a slumping of his frame, or the way he startled whenever he heard either of his late wife's names being mentioned – *Nasrin, Zeinab* – even if the mention referred to another woman altogether. But she knew that all this was just fancifully romantic on her part. For most of Zuleikha's life, the obverse had not been true. Her mother had despised her ex-husband in an analytical manner; she had perceived him as weak, as a man who frankly was incapable of making decisions about even the simplest of things. Nasrin Zeinab had come to the conclusion that this was just evasion on his part, that Daniel John had always eschewed the responsibility he bore, as a man and as a human being, to confront situations and people. This was why they had rolled, not in money, but in angst – and later, in booze. His drinking had been subtle, but continuous – and above all, hermeneutic. Thimblefuls of single malt whisky, each one a tiny steel cop-out.

Eventually Nasrin Zeinab had cut loose of this man, of this Daniel John MacBeth – not because there was anyone else involved, nor because he was in any way overtly oppressive – but because, in her words, with him there was never any possibility of movement, of change. His polarity was as fixed as that of a sextant. In his paralysing fear of dispossession, he'd found his groove and had settled in it. His motto, engraved in brass or maybe even in gold, Roman Catholic-fashion, across his heart which was growing more sacred by the second: Habemus quae requirimus. We have what we need. Yessir! The drinking had always been merely part of it, neither properly cause nor effect but something in between. Spirit. Now Zuleikha laughed at the silly clichéd pun. But such idiotic conjunctions bore some truth. Daniel John had done what was required. He had fulfilled their material needs and had never lost a job in his life. Not that he had ever been a Marxist, not even in the days when it had been fashionable. He'd been a surveyor: one of those men in hard red hats who dance behind yellow tripods and take pictures of very interesting sections of the pavement. Sometimes he would get to daub, across the asphalt and in indelible yellow paint, cryptic symbols which would remain for years like mediaeval graffiti, long after their purpose had been forgotten. He was good with his spatial orientation, could see objects in multiple dimensions. In his time, Daniel John had staked out most of the city through the lenses of his sextant. Gles-ghu, in quantum. But the drink had sapped his initiative, it had made him less than he otherwise would have been. Might have been. And at times this knowledge had fuelled his irritability, an irritability which he had applied largely to his wife.

Nasrin Zeinab, on the other hand, had always dreamed of flying to America – by which she meant the United States of America (Paraguay was not on the agenda). Life across the water was faster, more fun; it leaped and danced and sang; it was Gene Kelly, Bette Davis, Malcolm X and Andy Warhol; it was great thoughts, fast dances and spacious barbecue-patios beneath unbroken blue skies. It was the land where even the dead rejoiced. Life out there was the future. Country & Western music sounded better as one rolled along the shining skin of tarmac laid straight amidst the wide open spaces and dreamed of Ernest Hemingway. A white bull, a yellow sun, plutonium spires, big tolling bells. The America of Nasrin Zeinab's imaginings was a science fiction state. Most of her friends had made the jump years earlier – from Britain, which they'd seen as a sinking ship badly moored somewhere off the crumbling edge of Europe – and in particular from Scotland, which was a holed dinghy bobbing in the ship's long wake. They'd gone to white-rock Boston, or august Washington State, or pink-granite Austin, or into the Absolute Zero air-conditioning of the dead-peyote New Mexican desert, or perhaps they had ended up caught somewhere in the commuter chains of Baltimore (where the Lady came from, after all) and such-like. They'd gone almost everywhere, in fact, except maybe Hawaii or Alaska. Because nobody went to those places unless they were stinking rich or stark raving mad. Or unless they were spies, studying the migration patterns of Arctic grey seals. And occasionally Zulie too had partaken of her mother's dreams. But now it was too late. She had reached that age when no prosperous foreign land would want either her or her skills. Over thirty-five, she thought, you were fucked. You had made your bed or you hadn't, but in either case you were destined to die where you lived – nails, fire and all. One day, she would have to lay down on her back and sink six feet, and she would sleep there forever, down in the wet clay soil of Kentigern's dream.

Whenever her parents had argued about it, her mother had accused Daniel John of attributing to her a shallow materialism, of popping her into one of those crassly decorated filigree plastic boxes bought at half price on the mohalla consciousness, the backstreet mind, which had used to be all the rage in South Asian households a while back, and labelling it *typical petit-bourgeois, court-shoe strutting, tap-tap-tap, Asian professional woman.*

It's the way they try to deal with us, she'd confided to Zuleikha. Their power having slipped away, all men could do was to strive for these ridiculous petulant victories. Or at least, *that's your father*. The below-the-belt man. The man who held in his most poisonous venom, and who operated on the premise that if the boat wasn't rocked then eventually, ultimately, it would tilt his way. *It doesn't work like that,* her mother had told her. *This life holds no favourable disposition towards inertia. You have to take the tiller and steer it through the tides, otherwise, sooner or later, like all the other losers, you will drown.* Zulie had wondered why Nasrin Zeinab had used so many naval metaphors in her pep-talks when, if her parents had gone anywhere, they surely would have flown. Perhaps it was some ancient folk memory, bleeding into her brain from the elongated time of gentlemanly ocean liners, the big blindingly white ships that'd brought Nasrin Zeinab's own parents over from the then newly roasted subcontinent. Flags fluttering in the breeze. Spats. Myths of the air, water dreams, blood on the balls of the croquet lawns.

There was a fundamental, yet unconscious, disconnection inherent in all their thinking. Both Zuleikha's parents had been born and brought up in Alba: specifically, between the undulations to the north and south that formed Glasgow's dear green Venusian delta, and where everyone dreamed of leaving – of flying off into a reddening ex-pat sunset to a place where the grass may not have been greener, but where the sun was certainly hotter, the sky bluer and life karmically more balanced. If only Mungo's hollow had been ten degrees warmer, in summer at least, and had had, say, half the rainfall ... the wilderness was only twelve miles away. It was a longing that was ubiquitous to the extent of being banal. Nasrin Zeinab and Daniel John were Glaswegian to their bones.

Because the area was perched at the top of a small incline, when they'd first moved in they'd had a good view of the hills, the mountains even – but as the years had gone on, more and more building work had meant that when the light was right and the clouds lifted towards the stratospheric, all you could see out of the well-tended back garden that faced due north from the dining-room window was the tiniest sliver of the dark shoulder of Ben Lomond. At least, that was what Daniel John told everyone who came to visit, during the full guided tour of his house which Zuleikha's father somehow managed to undertake every time. It was his kingdom and this was its highlight. A view of the mountain, hedged between several angled walls and cropped bushes. Resting against the petals of an off-white rose in summer, a row of reddish thorns in the snow season, there they were: the impossibly smooth shanks of the mountain that overlooked the north-eastern end of Loch Lomond, forty or so miles to the north. Everyone in Glasgow showed you the mountain, she thought. If it was visible from wherever you might be standing, they'd point it out to you. *There's Ben Lomond.* You felt, at that point, as though they were about to break into song – that really silly song with the single plaintive line that could still break your heart, that still, she thought, as she ran her fingers over the chair that once had been her mother's ... *But me and my true love will never meet again ...* that still broke Zuleikha's heart. Loch Laoiminn, the lake of the beacon, the blazing water. It was as though, unlike most towns, the centre of this city, the metaphysical heart of the metropolis, its defining point, lay not at its geographical centre but at the peak of that ancient hump-backed hill whose thousand metres rose, almost sheer, from the surface of the big loch and which formed the last outpost of the primeval country that lay to the north. She had never really known her maternal grandparents: they had died when she'd been a very young child. And so what she had – a vague, static image of their faces, enveloped in a kind of fuzz – in the cold light of scientific objectivity, she thought was likely to have been gleaned from photographs rather than from real-life memories.

He kept his old charts in a cupboard behind his bed. Zulie remembered that, as a child, she had been severely scolded for raking through and scrawling over his papers, and it was only much later that she had discovered that even at that time most of these maps had been obsolete. Daniel John could throw nothing away. He kept charts of roads which had never been constructed, or which had been churned up and built over, or which for obscure reasons had been re-named decades earlier. Over the years the roads and buildings would alternate, the landmarks would change one way and then the other in a kind of symphonic dance, so that eventually the maps which Daniel John kept secreted in the musty darkness of his bedroom cupboard, once again, would come to be accurate. At least, Zuleikha figured that maybe this was his reasoning. It was his one concession, save for his clipped consonants, to the intense Catholicism in which he had been raised. The rest of his home was normal; the usual pastel architectonics of retirement, walls and carpets the same colours as the clothes. Those who determined such things (themselves surely not mature citizens) seemed to imagine that, as a person crossed the threshold of sixty, all of a sudden they developed an allergy to bright colours and loud music. This seemed to Zuleikha an attitude that still held sway, even though those who had formed the original youth cults back in the boom years of the mid-twentieth century had long since reached pensionable age and certainly did not always fit this anaemic profile. Nonetheless, there was an element of circularity about such things. She remembered an uncle telling her that briefly he had been part of the Mod cult. And the Mods really went back to the nineteenth century, or maybe even the eighteenth, or maybe even to the humanism of Boccaccio and the luminous Middle Ages of Ziryab. She tried to picture her father as a Mod, but no, he would've been too old for that. A Beatnik, then. No. There hadn't been any Beatniks in Scotland.

Anyone who had been brought up by nuns, as Daniel John had been, was bound to carry intractable cerebral histories. The rumour went that his mother had been a one-time flapper-turned-opium-addict, his father some unknown punter – possibly a travelling magician or a song-and-dance waster – but it was something about which he almost never spoke. Yet there was a single faded photograph pressed between surveyors' charts, a dog-eared passport-sized black and white image of a gravestone leaned up against a brick wall with, beside it, a perfectly shaped mound of newly heaped earth. Zulie had come across this photo for the first time as a child of around ten or eleven, and she had stared at the slab for minutes, trying to make out the writing carved into its surface. But even when she'd gone back armed with a plastic magnifying-glass, she had been unable to make out anything much. In fact, it had seemed as though there was no writing at all. Years later, she had learned from her mother that this had been a picture of her paternal grandmother's grave and that it was surprising there was a stone at all. She'd wondered whether the inscription had been withheld by God, as a punishment for whatever sins the woman had committed. Or perhaps it was just that the stonemason hadn't yet got round to doing the job at the time when the snap had been taken. After all, it would've been a pauper's grave. When she had looked at it closely, Zuleikha had been able to tell that originally it had been a colour image and that over the years, even though it had been exposed to almost no light, the colours must have faded and the contrast become exaggerated. It must have been a very cheaply produced film, something quickly, and possibly furtively, developed along with a thousand others in one of those chemical factory machines by some insouciant cashier clad in a loose company tee-shirt. But no, she thought, it had been too early for those. The paper had obviously been crushed and bent and stained around its borders from being kept for long periods in leather wallets and between the pages of heavy books, so that even when she had found it, wedged between piles of maps and charts, it had seemed like something from the very deep past – like one of those pictures from the American Civil War where the level of contrast is paradoxically modernist and where the light seems to fall from the sky.

There was no sepia-tone softness to her father's past. In the blacks of his eyes the ghostly shades of opium hovered like the silver of the photograph, the spirits of a pain that burned still, somewhere beyond reach. The fact that he had gone to college and worked as a chartered surveyor would have been almost miraculous in itself, but the fact that he had met and married a scion of an exotic aristocracy might have been the stuff of romantic novels, or Technicolor films, except that the erstwhile noblewoman had been effectively broke, and relationships across class and race boundaries in Scotland – at least down to her parents' generation – had been modulated through discordant musical keys and shimmering veils of unawareness. Yet, for both parties, it'd had the effect of leap-frogging them up the social ladder, so that their only daughter had been able to become a member of the secular priest-class, a doctor, that final and most desirable destination of human evolution. And now her father, his skin turned to parchment yellow, his hair no longer billowing silver, the eyes in his face faded to veined autumn blue, dwelt in his voluminous yet cosy house of pastels that overlooked a pretty back garden and a distant, barely reachable peak. Whenever she visited she would be overwhelmed by despondency at the obscurity and pointlessness of human life. With the exception of a handful of prophets, kings and villains, she would think, most of us will quickly be forgotten, our tombstones rendered blank by the effects of time, light, shame. Most of us will have lived in a state of revolt against history.

Things girls do with their mothers: sewing, knitting, cooking, shopping, that kind of thing. Yeah, okay. But no, there had been none of that. Or at least, if there had, then it had been perfunctory; Nasrin Zeinab had condescended to do it because it was what her conscience told her mothers ought to do with their daughters. Girls need to be sent out into the world with skills, competencies, at least a degree of self-sufficiency, otherwise they would risk being no better than an old-style man. But Nasrin Zeinab hadn't been into all that stuff – no, she'd been a housewife who had hated housewifery. Tupper-blooming-ware. In the case of her mother, getting cancer had not turned her into a saint. In common with most health professionals, Zuleikha had long held strange ideas about patients, so that all of a sudden, people who had been thorough villains – drug-dealers, psychopaths and all – became miraculously transmogrified, the substance of their spirits cleansed as though with hydrochloric acid, formaldehyde or Dettol into those of incipient martyrs, and everyone began to treat them with hieratic kid gloves, as though their every emotion had assumed a cosmic significance. Getting cancer – it was the modern ascension. In the scheme of things, it was about as real as praying before the mazaar of a saint. Glossy pictures of light bulbs strung from the apex of a tomb dome, a structure resembling an extraterrestrial spacecraft and a strangely-worded communication born, it seemed, on the back of an old *Imperial 4* typewriter.

```
The Sacred Message of Love and Peace For Suffering
Humanity: Dear Postman Sahib: If undeliver please
deliver to any Indian/Pakistani/Bangladeshi/
Other Official worker of labourer who works in
your company and office.
```

38

Stamped in blue ink: BY SEA MAIL. Impossibly long – and quite possibly bogus – telephone numbers. Click, click, flutter. Tiny flags in the wind. Maybe you never learn by experience, Zuleikha thought, or maybe you just learn the wrong things. Those shrines, the white-washed walls, the domed vortices, the thousands of arms, millions of fingers, thrust desperately into the enclosure, worms grasping wildly at the rain. Some people swore by them.

She wished, now, that she had spoken to her mother at that last moment. She wished that she had leaned over and hugged her, removed the oxygen mask and kissed her on the lips – but she'd told herself that the machines would've got in the way, or that she'd have been too upset to do anything physical, that she had barely been able to hold the tears behind the skins of her eyes, that she'd had consciously to control her breathing, to bind the breath in her chest lest her body begin to heave uncontrollably and her throat emit ungainly sobbing noises. She'd told herself that she hadn't wanted to upset her mother by allowing her to see that she was upset. And Zuleikha had almost convinced herself that this concatenation of embarrassment, petrifaction and consideration had prevented her from touching her mother one last time before the heavy curtain of death had descended, separating them forever. People had intimated to her that because she was a doctor, a physician, a practitioner of generalities, she ought to have been inured to such things. But she had never got used to any of it. Not even after all that she had been through. The death, the hope, the futility, the comedy, the song. She had slipped into one box after another and had carried on her back many different skins, each of them heavier than the last.

She tore her gaze away from the photo. At the far end of the mantelpiece, the end nearest the window, were the faded colour prints of her son with his sandy hair, his blue eyes: Daoud, aged three months; Daoud, aged nine and a half months. The 'half' bore a leaden significance. Daoud, David; David, Daoud. His name, 'Daoud MacBeth', his birth and death dates inscribed on the rectangular silver plate that had been embedded two-thirds of the way up the small white coffin. His body held tight in its final swaddling, his face, his eyes, the lids, closed then, as the silken ropes eased him down into the earth. All the other dates were imaginary: Daoud, aged two years; Daoud, aged five; Daoud, aged ten. Perhaps his hair would have darkened as he grew older. Maybe now he would have been known as Davie, or even Dave. But she resented this ageing of her perfect child. She had re-formed her son as an icon, as though in so doing – in perfectly constructing these tiny stained-glass windows into the past – she might be rendering future life to him, as well as to herself, in some alternative universe, somewhere beyond the eleven dimensions of home that had killed him.

Somewhere, in a different box, a real one, a battered brown cardboard clip-file, she had pictures of Daoud which had been taken moments after his birth, and at which she could no longer bear to gaze. Over the ten-year chasm, the static images in her living space had become so familiar. She had learned to live with them in the room – indeed, she wasn't sure whether she would be able to live without them. She still occasionally dreamed of him. And in the dreams he would talk to her: he, Daoud, a nine-and-a-half month-old baby, like one of those miraculous Christ infants who had debated with the Sadducees. Tall hats, deep frowns and cherub cheeks. And all the while, as he raises his hands, palms pointing forwards, the incipience of iron. Like a nuclear shadow, his bones were burned into her flesh; beneath her right breast, a foot; over the ridge of her left shoulder, a chin. The scars in her womb, the place where he had lived and where, one screaming terrible joyous day, he had torn himself into life. She hadn't been able to breast-feed beyond three weeks – the fuckers had dried up, gone red, become sabres through her chest – but after he had died, suddenly her paps had begun to swell, to grow dark and to flow so that even at the funeral, and in spite of padding, her blouse had been soaked through. Her body was earth, becoming water; her mind, psychosis turning to stone. And now, every year at the time of the anniversary, the same thing happened: miraculously her mammaries would begin to deliver milk as though she was a premium cow.

First, he had pulsed through her vasculature like a rhythm or a melody, and then he had become the whole of her life. And he had taken the best of her down into the dark amnion of his perpetual babyhood. Every second of every day their bodies moved together;

her every unbreathing pause belonged to him. The place where he connected with her lay beyond reason. Part of it, she knew, was a set of conditioned responses, a combination of hormones and biochemical feedback loops; but she hadn't realised, before it had hit her in the gut, that even after all those years the tight whiff of Vaseline could rip the skin from her frame. Ten years of vomiting blood into the toilet pan, ten years of gazing at the smooth white enamel while her firstborn, her only child, erupted again from the lining of her stomach. Yet at some level Zuleikha relished the continuing physicality of his presence. The cries of cats in the night would draw the tips of her fingers to the cracks in the window-sill and the crack of her lips to the cold black glass. But most of the time her conjunction with her son could not be predicted or transmuted through metaphor; most of the time she could find no-one to blame and there was nothing in the universe she could hold down and rationalise. Instead she tasted the futility of burying herself in the flesh and juices of her body's remembrance. And then the grief was no longer tangible, no more a thing than life itself.

'Let us have music!' she declared.

She leapt to her feet, crossed the room, fished out a disc from the pile over in the far corner and slipped it into the bashed cherry-wood machine. Zuleikha enjoyed many different kinds of music – Western classical, roots and rock too – so long as it didn't rock too hard or hip-hop too stupidly – though the truth was, she felt passionate about none of these. Many years ago she had tried, somewhat half-heartedly, to learn a couple of instruments, but had discovered that she possessed neither the talent nor the inclination. For her, music was simply pleasant background noise. She lived in this big first-floor tenement flat in Bridgeton, a traditionally working-class area just north of the River Clyde and about a mile to the east of the city centre, which recently had been drawn somewhat upmarket – although the occupational use of the nearby Glasgow Green by hordes of prostitutes and the ferocious marches held fairly regularly by the local Orange Order tended to belie this aspiration. The King Billy Shop ran a thriving trade in sashes and bowler hats and, as though stuck metaphysically in the 1950s, up the closes half the young boys of the place seemed to be practising for one or other of the bands. The red stone buildings were well over a hundred years old now and remained in aspect beautiful – but, like all beautiful things, they had their obnoxious terrors.

I ought to buy a cat, she thought, to complete the sculpture of my various hoods: divorcee, spinster and widow. Okay, so I never had a husband who died – I just had an assortment of lovers who never lived. Yes, a sleek tabby would render to my world a certain concreteness leavened by a modicum of spirituality. All those trite poems about felines. There is one type of woman who substituted a horse for a lover and there is another type who stinks the abyss with prides of cats. I would become one of those Ancient Egyptian tarot cards, a kind of Southern Gothic Isis, long black hair and the sirocco of six thousand years billowing at my back. But then – I am not like those women. Like my mother, I am incomplete.

Six days earlier Zuleikha had carried the box from the boot of her car to the sitting-room of her flat and had set it down right in the middle of the coffee-table. And there it had stayed. Then, as light-classical music had filled the emptiness, she had bustled around in the kitchen, putting stuff out then clearing it up and finally making herself a large mug of coffee. When Zuleikha had returned from the kitchen, the sitting-room was flooded. A pool had formed around the base of the box and had flowed in a waterfall down over the edge of the table.

Now again, this evening, as once more she sipped at her insipid coffee, the box was exuding water. Cradling the mug in her palms she sat on a low chair some two metres away. The sides of the ceramic burned into her palms. She felt powerless. The music was still playing, though now it seemed crazy – like the orchestra on a sinking ship. She felt compelled to watch as the box denuded itself of the river. Eventually, it reached her bare feet – yet still she was unable to move. She simply sat there, waiting for the whole room to turn into a great pallid loch. What if it did? she thought. What if this box, which unwisely I carted into the city, should continue to exude water at this rate? In twelve hours' time the stone coffer of the tenement would be flooded. In one week the north side of Glasgow would unite with its parent river and flood over the embankments which guard the southern rise. In one month the Clyde, the Forth, the Don and the Tweed would have linked arms and Scotland would be the new Underwater Wonder World for visiting Yankees. Glass-bottomed boats, fish-tank souls, hooded sharks and giant kilted squids. Scylla and Charybdis. Within a year, the river which bubbled up from some mysterious unknown divot halfway up a yokel hillside would have conquered the world. And the football fans (who by then, would've sprouted gills from the sides of their branchial regions) would be lazily fish-mouthing:

Scoaaaaatlann!!!!!!!!

As gradually, at varying rates, the water had flowed out of it over the past three days, the upper part of the box had begun to dry out more quickly than she had expected. Yet this had been at the expense of her table and carpet, which she had swamped with towels, old newspapers and miscellaneous bits of rag in a frantic attempt to stem the tide. And at last the flow of water had begun to slow and, as the box became drier, she saw that the stain just beneath the padlocked clasp was still visible ... but that it had faded, its edge now traceable only when squinted at from a certain angle. The place was turning into a pig-sty. She would probably need to shampoo the carpet or something. Just what she needed right now. Still, it was her own fault. There was no-one else she could blame. Except maybe the man who had helped her haul it in. Alex what-was-his-name.

She reached forward and toyed with the padlock. If she rubbed it between finger and thumb and if she concentrated-without-concentrating, then perhaps the iron might just begin to melt, to liquefy, bend and crack. She tried this, but succeeded only in acquiring some painful metal splinters in her hands. She got up, brushed the rust from her skin and checked the box from all sides, in case there might be a label somewhere or other. Then she realised that she hadn't checked the bottom. It was awkward, tilting it over like that. It had an unbalancing effect, greater than she had expected. She had to release the box quickly to avoid her fingers being trapped and crushed to a pulp, the bones flattened white against the mid-brown MDF of her coffee-table. A doctor with no hands was pretty useless. You could become a psychiatrist or a faith-healer, perhaps. Or one of those ruddy-faced Presbyterian tanks who worked for the Benefits Agency, sifting the malingerers from the sick. Yes – but even as a gatekeeper you still occasionally needed to examine people. To frisk them down, to search for smoking guns, black market jobs like selling dirty movies down Paddy's Market or in the Gallowgate Barras. You could feel the grime come off their skin and could glimpse the pornography in their eyes. The foetid lager breath. Everything reduced to its lowest, theirs was a hindbrain world. She could see the attraction. Morbid thinking, she thought. Enough! Concentrate, Zulie, concentrate. She had mouthed these last words in a cod-Rumanian accent. Magician, necromancer, wizard, sorcerer, with a flourish too fast for the human eye, *I will now demonstrate the skinning of rabbits from a box!* No, that was from a hat, she thought. Oh, for God's sake, Zulie-gee, doctor sahb, get the fucking thing open!

She'd have to get hold of a tool.

She would have 'Guilty' stamped across her forehead, she was certain. She'd always been a terrible liar. Not like her mother, who had bent the truth with genetic elegance. With a flick of her coiffed hair, Zuleikha's mother had been capable of fashioning around herself innumerable delusions. The delusion that she'd been able to play the sarod; the façade of monogamy when, during the course of their marriage, she'd had at least five lovers other than Zuleikha's father; the fragmentary vision of love which had induced her to have Zuleikha; and, finally and most memorably of all, the old story which had been passed like a silver quaich from one generation to the next (mothers, it seemed, were skilled at such grotesque feats of remembrance) that she was descended from some or other scion of the last Mughal Court.

Zuleikha smiled, then took a sip of cooling coffee. The ultimate Mughal – Bahadur Shah Zafar, the poet-emperor of Old Delhi, who in 1857 rather reluctantly had backed a doomed attempt to cast out the red Angraise devils from the body of Mata Hindustan, only to find himself sans paper and pencils, sans muse, sans empire, incarcerated in a Rangoon jail (where, one dark night, he was almost certainly poisoned) and his wives, concubines and other fellow-travellers loosed upon the streets of Old Calicut, Delhi and Hyderabad Deccan. In the slums of India's great cities, not unlike the surviving Romanovs in Mother Russia (the ones who couldn't get to the Blue French Coast) some sixty years later, they had eked out a living, aggressively begging, selling tea on pavements or else whoring themselves to the lowest darkest bidder. And Zuleikha's mother had taken some pride in associating herself recombinantly with a certain Tohfah Bibi, junior-most, Afghan Durrani concubine-wife of the Shah-en-Shah, who apparently (according to family legend) had been summoned to meet only once with her Emperor – and then it had been merely to make use of her ear as a sounding-board for his latest epic love poem. The story continued that, when Bahadur Shah Zafar realised that the British had encircled the last bastion of Mughal power, the Tomb of the Emperor Humayun, he had taken up the scrolls of this epic (on which the ink had not yet dried) and gone to the boudoir of Tohfah Bibi, where he recited the entire tract to his almond-eyed young acolyte. She remained expressionless, impassive even, but as he read, the nastaliq metric running back on itself like the twisting ivory of white buffalo or black goat, her face (pale, yes) began to glow with a sense of inner illumination. She picked up her barbat and her mezrap, and across the shadows of imagined dasateen began to play a slow melancholic dastgah. The crescent moon of her lips parted, revealing a thin line of black, and in a sweet bulbul voice she began to sing the epic poem back to the King-Emperor. And Bahadur Shah Zafar let fall his wrinkled octogenarian eyelids and started (on the long, silken diwan) to sway, dervish-style, as the mesmerised coils of his cerebral cortex recorded the voice of this most recent addition to his haremic court.

It is said that, as the last notes of the barbat died away and the last breath of Tohfah's voice faded into the silken curtains around the diwan, her spirit lifted itself and flew from the shell of her body, and that she fell into a swoon from which she did not emerge for thirty years and five days. During this time she was returned to the Durrani court-in-exile in the great and ancient city of Ludhiana by one Captain Douglas Ainslie of Delgaty, Damascus and Mouaillart, godnephew of the rather better-known The Honourable Mountstuart Elphinstone of Dumbarton, Commissioner of the Deccan, Governor of Bombay, busy scribe of Amir Shah Shuja of Afghanistan and incipient delineator of the Afghan March. This progenitor and honourable imperial servant – the Tacitus, so to speak, of India – was a man who revelled in the fact that, in spite of catching a good-going case of Hindustani gonorrhoea, nevertheless he had managed to sustain erections of almost Herodotian dimensions. Presumably, while lifting his gaze to the pale-blue firmament of the morning mist over the bodies of the rivers Isis and Cam, this honourable deluxe Anglicised Scot had preferred his cunt dusky, oiled with snake-juice, and fringed with the scented foliage of coriander. Capt Ainslie, though, was of a rather different and somewhat holier bent, and his book – a florid epic-style poem on the subject of John of Damascus – was strung with a Trimurti of bookmarks: white for Christianity, yellow for Buddhism and green for 'Mohammedanism'.

The miraculous thing was that, when at last she awakened, Tohfah Bibi had aged not one second since the utterance of the last phrase of her song. It was as though the song had kept her alive somewhere beyond the reach of time and now her life had begun all over again. She took to wearing silver dresses and mounting horses and setting off on great hunts for gazelle and wild boar and to leaping behind rocks and strangling serpents by the skins of their necks. And before too long she married again, this time to a man of her choice: an ex-Kafir who had converted one night on the road that trails through the valley of Skardu, and who thus had turned from Kafir Kalash to Mussalmaan Qalash. Tohfah Bibi had seven children and lived to be a hundred and one, and in the last year of her life she learned to drive a glossy black Master Buick. In her will she expressed the wish to be buried, unmarked, in a place called The Goat's Horn, on the summit of a dark mountain overlooking the village of Bumburet.

While her body was being prepared for the journey, around her neck was discovered a silver locket on a chain, and when the clasp was undone and the locket opened, a paper scroll was found, rolled up and folded and crushed into a tiny white ball. It was assumed that this was a taawiz, and indeed one side of the paper was covered in a Quranic sura, penned in the nastaliq style. However, on the reverse of the scroll was what appeared to be a long poem, or perhaps a spell, but since it had been written in a language which no-one understood, the scroll was rolled up again and placed back in the locket, which was clasped shut and left around her neck, thus descending with her body into the unmarked grave. Some years later a terrible earthquake devastated the whole of the Hindu Kush – so much so that the geography of the entire area was quite altered, and the old Imperial maps – whether British, Mughal, Sikh or Durrani – became obsolete overnight. And so the content, and indeed the very existence of the poem, having already been forgotten, was now lost forever, along with the Emperor and his memory, somewhere on the road to Mandalay or Kathmandu or Jalalabad or Rumbur. Yet its shadow, its absence, the whiff of its spirit lived on down the generations, in the long tales of old women and in a tacit awareness that this branch of the family, this line of descent from Tohfah Bibi, in some mysterious manner, was different.

Her mother's eyes had manifested that flickering uncertain chorea which some actors attempt to cultivate but which really can only be pulled off by those absolutely certain of their interiority. Like rural Catholicism, it was natural and even attractive – but not true. As long as Zuleikha kept that before her, the knowledge that constantly to delude oneself is both the most facile and the greatest sin of all, she shouldn't go wrong. Yet things did not follow such simple aphorismic rules. Things just happened, regardless. Cancer. The worst. Each case she treated was tragic, and every time she genuinely felt for the family – yet those were vicarious sorrows, redemptive glimpses of a swelling darkness against which she was able firmly to close the gate. In some ways, the unremitting busy-ness of her job protected her. But when her mother had been diagnosed with a rare retroperitoneal cancer she'd known at once that the worst would come to pass, and over the nine months of its trajectory, in the moments of rising despair, she had longed for any kind of faith or even for the certainty of none.

And in those few terminal months she'd begun to understand the centrality of ritual in the lives of human beings, in her own life even, and the obsessional fresco into which, at any time, life could transmute. The pointless bargains, the tiny betrayals. Fool's silver. But she'd needed something to occupy her limbs, her brain, while she watched the woman who had brought her into the world inexorably recede from it. A little knowledge was worse, they said. Her partners at work had been sympathetic, but only up to a point, and she'd had to give up her full-time post and do locums instead. It had been more flexible and had allowed her to spend more time with her mother in those final months. Right now she was in the middle of a long-term maternity locum in a single-handed practice whose catchment area included every socio-economic group imaginable. That was good. She got to use every part of her mind, every nuance of voice and body posture.

The last thing to go had been the eyes. A few days before she died, after she'd conferred her last blessing on Zuleikha, a pall had passed over her mother's eyes. Zulie saw the change. It was a physical thing, as though a dark hand had been drawn across her face. From that moment on there was no real contact between them. When she gazed into her mother's eyes she saw only a reflection of her own worried face. Nasrin Zeinab sank by degrees into a bottomless coma, and for many weeks Zuleikha burned raw in the grief.

Zuleikha's tears dripped into the half-empty mug of cold coffee, where they pooled and slowly dissolved the light brown scum which had formed on its surface. The saline dried tartly into the skin of her cheeks. She put down the mug, wiped her face with the backs of both sleeves of her blouse, and gazed up through the big tenement window at the starless sky. Her eyes stung from the brightness of the street lights and for a while, as she blinked, the room remained slightly blurred.

She decided to leave the box just now and slip into the shower and then maybe head out into town. The 24/7 shops never closed. It was sad, she knew, yet she felt the need for multitudes: she wanted life to surround her, to blank out thought. She would be working all day tomorrow, so there would be no opportunity to buy metal-clippers until the day after that. She could wait. The box had waited for years.

She stripped off and headed for the shower, but stopped midway across her bedroom floor. How did she know that the box had remained sealed for years? After all, it might have been locked and cast into the river only a few days before she found it; iron rusted easily in the Clyde. Then there was the man she met on the riverbank. Alex. He'd even left her his number. He'd wanted to be there when she opened it. In her gratitude and through the strangeness of the morning she'd said yes then, but now she wasn't so sure about letting a strange man into her house. Who was he, and why was he at all interested? He'd just turned up at the right moment. She shivered, and wrapped her arms around her breasts. That in itself was slightly creepy. Why had he been watching? He'd just lost his wife. So he said. He did have a black tie and suit on. Perhaps he was another wanderer, someone who had lost the place somewhere along the line, and who felt the need to walk the land in hope of finding it again. From time to time during her own itinerant forays Zuleikha had seen them, these others. They were set apart. They were not so much wanderers as figures in the landscape. White towers, rising through a mist. They moved, and yet they went nowhere. But what did they hope to find, these lonely uncontrolled people, on their pointless criss-crossing journeys across rivers and mountains and city streets? Some of them would be married – with children, perhaps – yet still they sought solace or refuge or escape on the beat. Or perhaps it was deeper than that; perhaps it was a pagan need for rootedness, a craving for the arc of energy possessed by faith-healers or demons or very ancient trees. Maybe that was what this guy, Alex, was about. Yes, Zuleikha convinced herself, that's what it was: she'd seen it in his eyes. But eyes could lie, she reminded herself, and she drew her own gaze away from the full-length bathroom mirror as she stepped into the scalding wave of the shower.

Yeah, it was the physical things. It wasn't that Zulie hadn't been serious – no, quite the opposite. She'd thought about it, on and off, for years beforehand. But somehow the moment had grown ripe one rainy Glasgow night and she must've been positively bursting with fertility, with bags of eggs like some kind of pot-bellied slack-jawed amphibian scrambling across the beach, half here and half there, the ends of her legs slipping and sliding into the holy black waters of motherhood. In that part of Glasgow known as 'Dowager Dowanhill' her mother had been suitably shocked – but mothers, especially aristocratic mothers, will get used to almost anything; their capacity for syncretism, sublimation and transcendence is virtually infinite. And so she, too, had grown familiar with the idea, trans-substantiated into flesh, of baby Daoud. Daoud, Daoud, Daoud – who had begun as a shimmering white dot on a screen, who had expanded in her dreams into a chubby face with gleaming blue eyes and hair coiffed already with a fringe of slinky tan – had burst from her body on a stormy November's night, had emerged sleek, bloodied, perfect, straight out of a howling Polidori blackness, and then had lived and breathed and expanded into her life. Only to perish, seemingly without cause, one equally rainy but far warmer night nine months and fifteen-days later, a random archangelic travesty on the third floor of the abode of souls. Azrael's morning. Cold, blue, still. A cot-death. A few months later, she'd moved out of the flat. It would have been impossible for her to have remained. She knew that if she had stayed then, she would have stayed forever. But it had been too late. She had drowned long ago in the ocean of his gaze. His smile, breaking across her face.

Her mother had aged ten years that day, and she ... she had become ageless. Or rather, she had fallen into a state of ante-mortem. No-one had known what to say; she had not known what to say to herself. Or perhaps it was the night which had become eternal. Gloom leached into her life. She tried to run from it, tried to go on as before, yet it became like the gossamer that bound her brain. The entirety of her being was filtered through the ineffable fact of her son's existence. Azrael, the fourth Archangel, the Angel of Death. There was no possibility of escape, no chance of reversing time and streaming back along the line of the groove. It drove her to become a shaman.

At first, before Daoud, before even the Anatomy Hall, she'd dreamed of being a paediatrician, a healer of babies – but when she realised that it would've been too intense, too knife-edge, that she'd have to deal with dying children and their grieving parents, she plumped for general practice – where, generally, the children got better – or at least grew older, as her son had not.

A row of small plant-pots lay on the window-sill. No matter how much she watered them, the damn things insisted on dying on her. They'd had maximal light there in the window; they'd been fed that hyper plant-food stuff, given liberal though not excessive quantities of water – and yet, like every plant which Zuleikha had possessed after Daoud's death during that summer long ago, they thrived for only a few weeks before slowly they began to perish. She'd always thought she had purple fingers, mourning fingers, veins and bone and skin. But she had good times too – times which in retrospect she had denoted as wonderful or even great, and the fact that she did what she did meant that she would always have an income. As long as half the world was sick.

At the end of time I will plead insanity, or diminished responsibility, or nervous debility ... but the jury won't listen and will find me guilty and the judge will have a Presbyterian face, hard and silver like the bark of an old birch tree. Eyes cold, blue. Dead, like Daoud that last time. A summer's morning, golden sunlight through the window. She with glass arms, a fragmented body, a mind broken. Carrying his cold stiffened body around the house, whimpering, not believing, praying it was a nightmare. His lank hair, dead gold, scythed clean beneath the Glasgow sky. No, not like Daoud. Like the facsimile, then: the wise infant version of Daoud. The picture she'd never taken, but which like stained glass had been blown and burned in blood tints onto the base of her brain and through which now she felt the world. Zuleikha Chashm Framareza MacBeth, Zuleikha Bint Nasrin Zeinab, Zuleikha Om Daoud. I am like one of those mad Muscovites at the turn of the year: I dive, sky-clad, into cold rivers and rescue myself from myself. I find caskets that will not open.

The box filled the space on the table between the mug and the paper. She knew the proportions of its outer casing almost as well as she knew those of her own body. It was a perfect dark brown square. In the days since she'd found it Zuleikha had measured it many times, using both the imperial and the metric side of the tape. But the facts were immutable: no matter which way she looked at it, the box measured three feet in every direction. On one side, which she thought might have been hewn from cherry or oak, there was a blemish: the whorl patterns, depending on the angle of the light, tended to assume the likeness sometimes of a human head, at other times of the petals of an unfolding flower, and occasionally, in the very late evening, that of a strange Renaissance spaceship. She rubbed her finger up and down over the surface of the blemish. The wood was completely smooth; there was no sign of any damage to its surface. It looked as though perhaps the blemish – if that was what it was – had been acquired or inflicted some time prior to the application of the last coat of varnish. But then why hadn't they smoothed it out, planed it away? And who were 'they'? She imagined a lone Masonic craftsman hewing the wood from an aged fallen yew tree and then sculpting the box from this single piece, the dove-tails, the perfect angulation of its walls, the elegant carvings. Perhaps, like the fault woven into the underside of every Persian carpet, this imperfection was there to remind the artist of his own mortality, and that only God was infallible. Cherry, oak, yew ... the nature of the wood remained uncertain; its hue changed with the quality of the light. During the day, when sunlight – or more often, the blinding luminosity of the cloudy Scottish sky – streamed through the big tenement windows, the box seemed to gather within itself, a darkness which arose from somewhere beyond the electromagnetic. Paradoxically, at nightfall Zuleikha was confronted by the big box glowing with a pale green light. And as she watched, the whorls on its sides began to shift and quiver, the patterns which they formed seeming to swirl and twist like waves on the limpid surface of a river. She stood, open-mouthed like a chorister from an Eisenstein flick, and closed her eyes and let herself see images of gardens, dividing again and again in harmonic symmetries towards infinity. And in the gardens, in each of the chahar bagh, Zuleikha saw images of gazelles and peacocks, of bushes laden with fruit, of a hunter carrying a short-bow, of the sun, the moon and a couple of stars, and everywhere, of long, sinuous river-reeds.

What rubbish! she thought. It's probably some kid's toy-box, knocked up in a factory unit beneath a disused railway bridge, glued together for the global market by overall-ed, insouciant East European wood-women somewhere in the delta downstream of Bucharest. Cheap pouting hardwood girls, washing themselves and their whorls in the gleaming river and drowning, like lost princesses, in the sweep and pull of its current.

Looking at it from another perspective (as Zuleikha tended constantly to do) the box had filled up whatever space there had been in her life. It occupied her thoughts constantly. Even when she thought she'd forgotten about it, the dark claw of panic would rise from her stomach and would grab her by the throat until she managed to convince herself that, after all, it was most unlikely that the casket had been stolen while she'd been out. She found herself rushing home at odd times, even when she knew that she could ill-afford the time, even though it meant that she would drive maniacally, riskily down the side-roads, dodging potholes and parked cars in a desperate effort to continue to meet the inexorable demands of house-calls, surgeries, bank, post office and all the other things which, up until the day she had found the box, had set the tune to which Zuleikha MacBeth lifted up her feet and spun.

She dried her finger on the front of her jeans, ran it down over her right thigh, and got up off the sofa. Rolling up her sleeves, she went over to the window. She thrust aside the curtains and undid the catch at the top of the sash, then yanked the big plate of glass and wood upwards till it passed the brass at the side. The street smelled of damp toast and old petrol, but the air and rain felt cool on her skin. In another situation it might have been refreshing. There had been so many of these rainy nights, yet the skin of each drop held a different symbolism. Dochtarhood, doctorhood; love, motherhood; death, music. Time. She secured the window and then turned the trunk of her body around so that she was facing upwards, so she was facing the ceiling, and then she stuck her head and shoulders right out into the street. The billow of her jumper caught on a nail, tethering the wool at her back and causing it to tighten around the base of her neck. Without altering the tension on the threads, Zuleikha carefully reached down to the hem and freed the jumper. Then she swept back her hair and gazed up into the rain and the darkness.

Chapter Four

After the funeral, Alex dragged himself to the dowdy club where they'd laid on a buffet for relatives and friends, and there he forced himself to be courteous. It was something which they'd never discussed, but after she died he'd supposed that Susan would've preferred a short oration and no rituals. At that point, however, her mother had come in and insisted on the full Roman Catholic panoply. Incense and holy water, robed priests, bended knees, swinging censers, the lot. Midway through the service the madness had sucked him in too, so that Alex, who had not been inside the belly of a church for upwards of a decade – and who wasn't even Catholic, for God's sake – had almost begun to see the disembodied spirits of martyrs and saints and to feel the brush of angels' wings on his neck as they breezed their way down from the cracked stone roof. Now, as she lay invisible beneath the cloth and wood and earth, Alex wondered whether she might be annoyed at him for not following through, for giving in yet again to the demands of others. It had been the story of their lives. Nine years of surrender.

Drawn from the rationalist suburbs of Glasgow, his own family figured hardly at all in this hagiographical dynamic. He should've known that her family would take control, right from the first ink of the boxed obituary notice through the timing of the service, the green felt of the artificial turf that separated the soles of their very chaste shoes from the grubs and segmented monsters of the earth, and now this gracious reception where cold slim sandwiches were being consumed with piety, laced with conceit. And yet, after that day which had to have been the darkest in his life, Alex felt as though, like one of those Fifteenth Century Jews in Spain, he might easily become a Converso – just for the rabid power of the ritual and the feeling of not being utterly completely alone in the universe. But then he hadn't been a Jew or a Protestant or an atheist. He'd been what they referred to as the average postmodern British person, lacking in conviction about almost everything. Except his love for Susan. That had been real. Well, as solid as love can be. But it no longer mattered. Whatever he might tell himself would be delusion. Sweet or painful or comforting or amusing, maybe – but delusion nonetheless. The black magus had clapped his hands and everything had gone up in a puff of smoke. The sound of a car door closing, the scraping noise of the coffin lid as it covered her for the very last time. Alexander had been an only child in a lower-middle class Glasgow suburb on the edge of the green belt; his father was a printer, his mother a secretary. Both now were dead. There was absolutely nothing special about his upbringing. It had been the kind of childhood about which people in war-zones must dream, he thought. *Lower-middle class*. Prints, Fly-Mos and fake wood panelling. An only child, now again, he was alone. Just three weeks ago, life had been … In fact, to have spoken of his life would have been an inaccuracy; it had been *their* life. Some years earlier they had discovered that Alex was unable to father children. Words. Fuck. There were limits.

The cops. He had made out their shapes through the smoked glass of his front door, and had noticed the way that they switched off their radios, killed the metallic voices that spoke across the night in strange tangoing codes. Before he opened the door he had noticed them remove their hats, and he felt their staged but well-practised awkwardness as they asked if they could come in. The manner in which they offered him a seat in his own house. The way in which his heart pounded like a church bell. Blood, spirit and the night. All of a sudden the room, the house, the darkness had become alien. Every object had assumed independent being. In his chest, he was a pagan. But Alex had always been what those cod-psycho manuals called *empathetic*. In the dualistic world of those lavatorial books it was supposed to be a quality possessed primarily by women, but those writers didn't know the half of it. Bull-fucking-shit. They had men down, monolithically, as cave-burning brutes. Or Rangers supporters. Well, that night his fucking empathy had transported him into nightmare. They warned him that the face had been disfigured, they said that in such cases it was not necessary for a relative to perform an identification, that they could get that from documents around the person of the … deceased … from fingerprints and from DNA mined from the deep muscle of the thigh. For a while he had wondered obscenely at this, thinking of fish jaws and rough eel spines, until someone attempted gently to inform him that at that speed, from that height, a solid body of water hitting the glass of a windscreen had the force of a concrete wall. But he insisted. He had needed to see her just once more, one last time. They asked if they could borrow her toothbrush, and he stared uncomprehendingly at them until they informed him that it was for fingerprints and DNA and that after the body had been formally identified there would be a post-mortem to determine the exact cause of death.

The car ride to the mortuary. The false hope. Familiar landscapes, become suddenly scary in the pre-dawn light. The studied effortful silence of the mortuary attendant. Creaking metal. Antiseptic veins. The smooth movements of everything except his own body. He had confirmed to himself that it was her by the rings she was wearing and by a certain purplish birthmark which she bore on the left side of her neck, down where the collar-bone lay smashed. And anyway, he had known. There had been no doubt. But for Alex, Susan had been identified, not recognised. In the end, after all his insistence, when it came to the moment, he had not been able to look upon her face; beneath the clean white sheet it was a mass of dark red. He did not want to carry that memory of her to his... No. And then the whiteness of the cloth had grown enormous and the faceless mass before him had become terrible. Everything was drawn to a point of silence. Every movement, every sound, even his breathing, seemed intrusive, unreal. He became aware of the texture and solidity of each object in the morgue. One of the lights was fused and it flickered maddeningly so that he had the urge, there and then, to grab a step-ladder and rip it from its wires. He wished he could swoon, lose himself, become insane, but this state he was in was a moment of supreme awareness. This, he thought later, was the reason people had invented God. He had focused on her right foot, which protruded at an angle from beneath the sheet. The architecture of the bones, sinews and toenails was a perfect facsimile, and the skin seemed only a little paler than it had been in life. The crimson nail-polish that fell into cracks at the sides. Nothing was new. It was odd, but somehow he had expected there to be some drastic change, some signature of death upon the skin or on the nails with their flaked red paint. It was not that he was hoping now for some miracle, for the corpse not to have been hers – the certainty in his belly was granite – but he had thought that perhaps in death the idiosyncrasies, the deformities of the bones, might be dissipated somehow so that she – Susan – would float, sanitised, anonymised, dehumanised even, into oblivion. But no, the foot retained its agonising singularity; it was her foot and no-one else's. Whitened, motionless, dead. And yet it did seem inordinately pale and smooth like wax. He had the urge to stretch out the joints of his fingers and touch this simulacrum of his wife, and there, as in a dream, he half-imagined himself doing it, he drew the movement of the elbow ligaments as they stretched and pulled taut, he felt the release of the clenched fist at his side, the blood flowing from the palm where his nails had pierced the skin. It seemed he had been standing there, palsied, for minutes, the light falling from above and filling him with its atonal white noise.

And then everything had collapsed. The insulting presence of daylight, of cold air, of old music from some transistor. People's animated faces. There were no escape routes, no telescoping of the days. The nights. The whole world was pushed into the envelope of his body, his skull, yet the space within him seemed infinite, bottomless. One week. A pin-drop nightmare. He'd lost both parents some years earlier, one shortly after the other – but this, with its suddenness and lack of logical process, was far worse. It happened all the time, death on the roads. Of course it did. But this was different. As the police had said, there had been no other vehicle involved. Just her – their – third-hand Honda Civic, the one she'd paid for with the money from her call centre job. *Good afternoon, this is Mango Phones. You're through to Susan. How may I help you today? Hello, you're through to Strathclyde Gas, my name is Susan. How may I help you today? Welcome to Lizzie Ruddock's Kinky Knickers Chain Store (or had it been, Kinky Chain Knickers Store?). Susan speaking. What can I do for you today?* That had been ante-mortem. Post-mortem said this: A ruptured pulmonary vein, aorta, spleen and multiple vertebral and skull fractures; ribs all broken and head egg-shelled. There had never been a chance, and everyone hoped that death, or at least unconsciousness, had been immediate. The barriers on the bridge had been constructed so that it would have been very difficult to have crashed a vehicle over its edge. One would have had to have driven straight at the metal fence. It would have had to have been deliberate. A certain number of possible suicides were pronounced misadventure – or accidental, or whatever they called it in Scottish law – perhaps because often there was simply not enough evidence of a person's prior intention: if somebody falls under a train, they fall under a train – or perhaps (though Alexander thought that this was probably bullshit) to protect the family, where there had been any doubt; to allow them access to insurance monies, and probably also from some underlying unspoken religious repugnance. Now her body had been disembowelled, emptied of everything and then systematically reviscerated, zipped up like a handbag, readied for religion, made sweet-smelling for St Peter and the entire orchestra, choir and judges of the holy host. Yet suicide – he hated the word, he struggled even to enunciate it – damaged – destroyed so many people, the ones who were left forever with nothing but loss and guilt. So, as the Fiscal had decided on the basis of the police report, Susan's death had been an accident.

She'd not enjoyed the work; it wasn't something from which anyone with a sane brain could possibly have derived any enjoyment or fulfilment, but it had been a means to an end, the source of a steady flow of money with which to pay the bills while, as an out-of-work techie, he had scudded about doing a variety of casual jobs: working in bars or nightclubs, or else helping some catering company lug stuff around the map to various conferences and the like. The bar work could be interesting but was also very draining and, if you got too many aggressive drunks on one night, was potentially dangerous as well. Still, Alex had always been a big guy, even back when he was at school, so most trouble-makers would be deterred by that. Though you got the odd one – wee guy, usually, East-End-of-Glasgow, chips on their shoulders and flick-blades in their eyes... Yet Alex had managed to avoid real trouble and to continue with his life with Susan in their small modern house by the river.

He didn't know if he could bear to live in the place any more. Her presence was all over the house and he couldn't bring himself to alter it one iota. The frame of every jamb secreted an image. It was like some cinematic back-lot. The ghosts of dead cowgirls. Fractal whips. Her smell, the bottles of perfume she'd used, the girlish dresses, the workaday green dungarees she'd donned for washing the car that had made her look like a stereotypical lesbian – a private joke they'd shared, now turned to steel in his belly – the sticky shampoo stain running down the blue plastic bottle where she'd neglected to screw the cap back on tightly enough.

He had given up playing five-a-side football at least six years earlier. He had friends, but with guys, it was different. Talk was ... difficult. Spurious, maybe. Pointless, certainly. In the shower, Alex had gazed at that bottle for hours as the light coming through the window had flickered and faded and his skin had turned to red and begun to tear away from his flesh and still he had failed to bring himself to adjust the cap, to cry, or even to collapse. Then he had turned the water to cold, to freezing, so that he would be shocked out of his useless reverie and, standing there, his back against the glass, mechanically, forcefully, painfully, he had masturbated, had closed his eyes and had tried to re-imagine Susan's body around him, had tried to conjure up her breath in his ... but it hadn't worked and he had been left feeling dirty, unworthy of carrying even her memory. He had left untouched the stained half-empty coffee mug which she'd popped onto the flap of the kitchenette table. A sticky brown circle had formed around the base of the mug where she'd spilled some of the liquid as she'd rushed out of the house that night.

The cops had said no foul play was suspected. Nothing had proven to be amiss with the vehicle; its steering, brakes and gears had all been intact before the fall. So then it must have been driver error. Tiredness. Perhaps she'd fallen asleep at the wheel. Most accidents were caused that way. *Driver Inattention,* they called it. She'd had to go north across the Bridge to a place that lay somewhat beyond the untidy, drab and confusing town of Dumbarton, and she'd been late. She'd been working particularly hard in the past few months; she had mentioned saving for a holiday in the sun. Two weeks of escape for them both. He hadn't particularly liked the idea of lying on a beach, turning gradually to rare sirloin in bankrupt imitation of some cheap celebrity – but she'd insisted, saying that they never went away, it had been years and they'd gone no further than mid-Argyllshire. One long Glasgow Fair weekend. Well, it had been sunny that weekend, he'd riposted, and the water had been cool and clear … but then he'd given in and let her have her way. After all, it was her money, her silver. If she wanted a fortnight of Costa and sherry molasses, then as far as he was concerned she could have it. And he would go along with it, as she had gone along with his lute-playing. It was really quite pleasant, if irritating at times. Alex had known her feelings on the subject and he hadn't argued with her about it. Life was too short. Or it had been, till the night of the bridge.

But before that, the Costa. He'd even bought them a bottle of sherry to celebrate the booking. You could get into anything if you tried hard enough. It was like different pieces of music: some you might like, others you might find abstruse or pointless or repetitive or bland, yet once you'd made the effort you'd find that somehow they'd become part of the way you felt. It was a strange thing. He slung the dirty plate he'd used the night before into the sink. Turned on the hot water. Watched as the liquid began to lift off the grime. Fuck it. Psychology hadn't saved Susan. On that dark night up on the bridge no amount of longing for her day in the sun, no quality of love, had prevented her car from going off the edge. As the metal around her body pirouetted through the darkness, the sound of the air deafened her and as water and glass exploded into her face, the entire dark ocean of their love meant absolutely nothing. He wondered whether she'd been playing a CD when the accident had happened. If she had, it wouldn't have been his kind of music. No way. She'd been a straight-up, pyrotechnic soul woman. No quarter-tones. No quarter.

At the last minute Alex had made her a mug of milky coffee. He hadn't made one for himself, since the caffeine would've kept him up all night. He almost chuckled at the thought now, as he played his finger-tip around the top of the mug. The skin there was calloused; the porcelain could've been at boiling-point and he wouldn't have felt a thing. He'd gone to bed that evening and had fallen asleep quickly. Alex usually slept deeply and that night had been no exception. The police had almost had to break down the door to waken him. He'd drunk plenty of coffee since that night – God, his brain must be floating in the stuff! He felt suddenly claustrophobic in the small kitchenette, and stretched his arms out horizontally as if the movement itself might enlarge the volume of the room. He brought his palms together as though in prayer and then gazed at the ends of his fingers. There was a tiny smudge of red lipstick on the tip of his left index finger. He thrust it into his mouth, closed his eyes and let the end of his tongue play around the whorls. Then, using his tongue like an elephant's trunk, he brought the lipstick to the rear of his palate, right up where he could smell it. Normally, from outside, across the scraggy waste grounds and the darkening north-facing copses, Alex was able to make out even the most subtle of sounds. The rustling of feathers as birds nestled in for the night, the occasional hoot of a horn from the distant road, the slow waves of the breeze against the kitchenette window and beyond and beneath all of these, the pulse and sweep of the massive waters of the river as they flowed, ever westwards, into the fading light. Perhaps, if she'd finished her coffee ... nah, that was rubbish; up there it was cold and the darkness was absolute; the songs, silent.

He had never lived with silence. From an early age Alex had played a variety of instruments – guitar, piano, flute – until finally, some seven years earlier, he had acquired an etched, moulded, sixteen-course, double-headed, Tielke-style Baroque lute. Thirty-one wire-over-gut strings. Moveable frets tied around the neck. True intonation. There was something about the instrument. It had seemed odd at first: Alex was such a large man – six foot two, ninety-odd kilograms (ninety-eight in clothes and shoes) and his belly had expanded unstoppably, unnaturally almost, ever since he'd passed the age of thirty-four. This could have created difficulties in holding the lute upright, classical guitar-style, but Alex had figured out a pretty eccentric positioning which involved using the rather large rubber tyre around his waist as a cushion for the elliptical wooden body of the instrument. That way he could almost hug it to his chest, and at times he fancied that the lute too gained satisfaction from being so close to a human heart.

Or maybe not.

It hadn't been intentional. He hadn't just gone one day to a music shop and asked to see various different kinds of instrument. No – like most things that happened to Alex, it had been much more oblique than that. He'd been poring through second-hand bookshops in Glasgow on a Sunday in the middle of summer. A heatwave. Everybody had been going on about it endlessly. The radio, the TV, people in cafés and bars and in the street. Even the hooker sentinels of Hope Street had produced Factor 30 sun-tan lotion and had begun to plaster it all over their wiry viral bodies. The punters preferred their meat lean, pale and dying. Only the high-class call-girl types wore permanent fake tan, to give folk the impression that they had just flown back from some bikini-less Batista beach in Miami. But Alex had ignored the cream shadows which the hookers made against the big stones of the banking institutions, and had walked on eastwards along the north shoulder of the river until he had come to The Barrowlands ballroom. It had tanked it down the night before and, despite the morning heat, globules of water still hung from the glass bulbs that were strung across the brick frontage of the building. The *w* and the *s* had come unstuck and hung from the hoarding like the loosened fastenings of an old brassiere. This place went back a long way. It had been one of his teenage haunts. Twenty-five years – more. God! His very first visit to a gig had been here, his first wall-snog, to the pumping bass of The Clash. Spittle and hearts. Blacked eyes. Strummed lashes. Pale faces, sliding around a floor shining with sweat and saliva. Had it not been heaven? Alex shivered with a mixture of arousal and embarrassment. Christ! Vinegar memories. That was long before he'd got into other forms of music, but it had been his introduction – his rough baptism, if you like.

At weekends the whole area around the ballroom was taken over by an enormous chaotic covered market, and the entire east end of the city would descend to stroll among the stalls. The Barras sold everything from bits of car fender to skin hotdogs to old glitzy country-and-western records, but mostly it was a giant scam, a pretence of bargains when such things no longer existed. Alex had never bought anything at the Barras that hadn't turned out to be useless, ugly or a total rip-off. He went there for the bustling atmosphere and the inchoate sense of possibility. He went there for the ghosts. The stalls were surrounded by flickering fast-food joints and the permanent stink of fries, lager and crap music. The women were loud, the men surly. It was a hair-of-the-dog place, its cheap glamour calculated to blast hangovers to Purgatory – or at least to Shotts, that blistered village which lay somewhere to the north-east of the city, high up on a stone hill, a place where committing suicide would seem as easy as drawing breath from the north wind.

He'd explored the market hundreds of times; he knew all its illegal traders and its gastroenteritic hamburger joints and those dark corners where pornographers pushed their blank-cased medium-core across glass counters.

He grabbed a couple of bottles of cold cider. One long swallow each. He didn't usually drink cider: it tended to gas him up. Made him irritable. Dreamless. But today he had a sudden craving. It was this place, he thought: the Barras. It gave one an appetite for the base things of life. If you stayed long enough you'd end up looking as though you'd just stepped out of a sixteenth-century Breughel painting: one of those incipiently bubonic beggars with extreme features, big teeth. He began to spot them everywhere, slithering on scraggy slippers among the boob-tubed teen-idol look-alikes and the sickeningly pale obese kids whose blistering pock-marked skins resembled those of the very Scottish sausages which they'd used to flog back in the 1970s. The ones which, when cooked, turned out to be 99.9 per cent hog-fat and point-one per cent additives. Perhaps after a while, given the right circumstances, you would begin to resemble your forebears: your bone structure and the shadows around your face would shift subtly, the twist and curve of your spine would begin to move to a different and far older rhythm. Maybe it was just the intensity of humanity pressing in on you. Or perhaps it was the light – or the lack of it. A sense, a proximity, of the barely real. Funny the way that happened.

After downing his cider Alex wandered around aimlessly, the way he liked it. You could lose yourself here; amongst the complex labyrinth of stalls, dark corridors, unintelligible ejaculations, you could slip into a hypnotic trance as your soles pressed against the hot concrete and as you were burned and blinded by the sunlight which flashed through broken corrugations in the roof. Each time he visited he would tackle the market a different way. He would vary the point of entry and also would make certain that he never walked the same route twice. It gave him a thrill, wandering through the place; there was always the possibility that he might just stumble upon something he hadn't seen before, that he might actually buy something.

He'd almost given up and was on the point of turning around and heading for the bus station and home, when he realised that the lace of his left sneaker was undone. He moved to a corner where the density of the crowd seemed a little less intense. Perhaps he hadn't had enough water to drink that morning, or maybe he'd over-exerted himself in the belching, cidered heat – but as he bent down Alex began to feel light-headed. It shouldn't happen, he thought. You're supposed to faint when you stand up, not when you bend down. Quickly, he made a double knot. There was no air in the place; the old white-washed brick shut most things out, including ventilation. For God's sake! The crowd seethed around him, pushing rudely into the backs of his knees, his bum, almost toppling him over. Doing up the laces seemed to take forever. His fingers were lead. He knew he should have flexed his knee and crouched and not bent over like this, but there hadn't seemed to be room. He felt anger rise in his throat – but then maybe it was acid coming up from his belly, the cider billowing in dark waves through the flesh. His vision was beginning to fleck over with glittering silvery sequins like those which preceded the tromboned stage entry of a beauty queen.

O shit! He didn't want to keel over here. Everyone would just assume that he was drunk. Okay, so he'd had a couple of ciders. Surely not enough to do this. He had to get out. Just then, a little ahead of him and to his left, he noticed the entrance to a narrow corridor. Still bent almost double, he scrambled towards the stone arch. He sensed a couple of women staring at him from behind. He felt ridiculous – but then this was a ridiculous place. It wasn't as though he was on the last bus, or in a Presbyterian church, for Christ sake. Everybody here was slightly insane. He was panting like one of the dogs in the videos he hadn't watched. Alsatian orgasm. Fuck sake. Sounded like an early-Eighties rock band. He was laughing stupidly as he made it to the arch and leaned against the jamb, cooling his cheek on the dirty stone. He let his eyelids close. As his breathing eased, he wiped the sweat from his brow and ran his fingers through his long hair. The front of his skull thudded as though his brain was on the point of punching through the orbits. His tongue stuck to his palate. He blew the air out of his chest and then inhaled, very slowly, as though to clear his lungs of the cider, cigarette tar and diesel fumes which permeated the heat of the marketplace. But the smell here was different. It was so incongruous that at first Alex had difficulty identifying it. With his eyes still closed, he took a couple of steps forward. Then he stopped. Behind him, the sound of the Barras had sunk to a low growl. Black dogs across the water. As his breathing began to come more naturally, he realised that the smell was the scent of freshly cut wood. The silver flecks had eased off and he opened his eyes.

He was at the start of a long, narrow passageway, its walls newly whitewashed, with just enough room for a single person. There were no stalls here and no people, but at the end of the corridor Alex made out a flickering blue light. Its source was invisible and he figured it must be coming from a hollow somewhere to the right of the wall. But it took longer than he'd thought to get there; it was as though, barely perceptibly, the corridor was lengthening and growing more curvilinear with every step he took. He walked slowly and carefully, aware of every contact; he felt that only in this way might he hold things as they were, and prevent the floor and walls from slipping away.

The hubbub receded even further until, by the time he'd reached the far end of the corridor, it had faded altogether. The smell of wood here was much stronger. He trailed the fingers of both hands along the walls, tracing out the course of mortar between the bricks. The whitewash had been applied liberally, so that the surface was almost smooth. No daylight penetrated the dark brick roof. He wondered whether the passageway was brand new ... but then why was it there, and where did it lead? There were no enclaves for stalls, no green fire escape signs, no public conveniences. And no lights along the walls – just the flickering blue neon coming from what he thought must surely be an enclave, down at the far end. But for that single source of illumination everything here would have been completely dark, and because of the whitewash the light became magnified and was more than enough to see his way by. Then he realised that the gradient was slightly inclined. His instincts had been correct: he was going down into the earth. This place must be some kind of basement, right at the heart of the Barras. He'd never heard of one, but there you go. His head was clearing. He felt a sense of elation, the same almost mystical feeling he'd had occasionally when walking by the river or watching Susan's sleeping profile in the glow of a single bulb. His feet were lighter than before, so that it was as though he was tripping along the concrete. But the floor was no longer concrete: like the ceiling and the walls it was made of glazed whitened polished brick. He began to hear a sound – it seemed to issue from the far end of the corridor, from where the blue light was coming. He couldn't determine what it was at first, except that it was regular and soft, and had a swinging, almost syncopated cadence.

Eventually he reached the end. As if to make sure that it was the end, Alex placed both palms against the far wall and rubbed them up and down several times. Then he turned to his right to look into the alcove. It was a tiny space, little bigger than a priest-hole. To enter he would've had to have bowed his head and to have slid in sideways, to a sitting position. The light was coming from a gas fire tucked away in the far corner. The fire had no guard, not even the usual slim bars protecting the blue flames that shot up into the air, licking dangerously close to the glaze of the walls. He wondered why anyone could possibly have wanted to light a fire on a day like this, but then he remembered how cold it was down in this passageway, and he shivered and drew his arms around his ribs. The tiny black hairs on his forearms suddenly became punctuated by goose-pimples. He exhaled, and his breath drew a long chute of mist.

Virtually the entire space of the alcove from ceiling to floor was filled with slabs of wood of varying shapes, sizes and colours. In the middle of the space was a small dark man sitting on a low stool. The man seemed not to have noticed Alex's presence, and continued to chip away at a piece of wood. He was using a tool that resembled a roof-gutter, its blade gleaming blue as he cut and gouged. He was peeling slivers off the inner surface of a small log which he had balanced on his knee. Alex watched him for a while, figuring that either the man was too preoccupied to notice his presence, or else that he was blind. But then, he reasoned, blind men are supposed to have hyper-acute hearing, aren't they? So he would have heard me as I crept along the corridor, and even if he were both blind and deaf, the flames of his blue fire would surely have bent just a little as my bulk entered the corridor. Anyway, how could a blind man cut wood? He'd slice his finger off. And the man was deftly fashioning the log into something… Alex couldn't tell exactly what, yet it fascinated him that an artisan could hold one's gaze with even the humblest of tools: a pencil, a crayon, a chalk, a bone. His face was long and oval, with a mop of black hair tousled around the crown. It was as though he had shaved his head up to the top of his ears, and then combed the long hairs upward so that they gathered in a bunch on the pointed dome of his skull. His skin was swarthy, as though someone had rubbed walnut-juice into the pores and then left them to dry naturally. On the left side of his cheek, the side facing Alex, was a healed scar which ran right from his temple and down along the angle of his jaw. His eyelashes too were long and black – more like those of a woman, Alex thought. His sleeves were rolled up above his elbows, and the muscles of his forearms flexed and relaxed in a rhythmic cycle which made the whole appear more like a performance than a chore. In the changing inflections of the light his age seemed indeterminate, so that one moment he looked to be around forty, while the next he was a young boy, sitting cross-legged on a wooden stool, serving out his apprenticeship. Alex couldn't make out his eyes, since they were directed down at the log on which he was working. He was wearing a thick white woollen tunic, wide-legged trousers, skin shoes and a silver necklace inlaid with turquoise-coloured stones. The beaded necklace looped around the collarless tunic and ran down over his upper chest, making him resemble one of the loved ones in those sepia photographs people had used to put into Sterling lockets. Alex noticed that on the small table beside him was a monocle, attached to which was a silver chain, coiled like a snake. On the wall behind him, just above the level of the fire, was a round mirror the size of a face. The smell had become overwhelming – that scent of wood, of many types of wood. He became aware of a slight ache in his right calf, and shifted his position slightly. The man looked up.

Now Alex saw that his face was even longer than it had appeared in side profile. It was the longest face he had ever seen. It was obscenely, inhumanly long – and yet it reminded Alex of something…

'You found me,' the man said. 'I have been waiting for a while.'

His bass-baritone seemed too low for his diminutive stature, the inflection perfect, unaccented. Alex gestured.

'I just came down the corridor.'

He glanced back and was shocked to see that the corridor down which he had just shuffled was blind-ended to both left and right. There must be some mistake, he scrambled, it must be some optical thing. Maybe it curves round like one of those garden pergolas designed to fool. The man was smiling and his smile seemed to join up with the scar so that the whole of his face angled upwards, like the letter v.

'You might as well come in, now you're here. Have a seat.'

He motioned to a tiny space beyond where he sat, a compartment within a compartment close to the side of the fire. Alex took a step forward and then decided that the alcove's entrance was simply too low for him to be able to squeeze past.

'This way,' the man motioned again.

Drawing in his belly and standing almost on tiptoe, Alex inched his body past the man and his log and sat on a low stool. He watched as the man worked away at the piece of wood. It was of a light colour, sycamore maybe, but Alex didn't know much about wood. He was a city person, always had been, and the generations before him too – further back than he could go. Okay, he thought, okay; at some point we are all descended from peasants, and before that from cave- and forest-dwellers, but we lost all that long ago: our great-great-grandfathers sloughed it off when they turned the sand and seas into rock and glass. The wee man was still chipping away at the inner part of the log; sap trickled down over his hands as he cut. He was making several sorts of movement, and the concatenation of these movements, combined with the low hiss of the gas stove, was mesmeric.

Right through their brief exchange the man had not ceased working, and indeed now he was almost tearing at the log, so that chips flew out in all directions, some landing on Alex's jeans and tee-shirt. Meanwhile, the sap dribbled down onto the man's baggy brown trousers and onto the brick floor, where it gathered in a sticky opaque pool. The flames hissed and sputtered and gave off a stink which was a little like that of old-style lorry diesel.

Beneath the mirror was a narrow shelf filled with an array of tools. On the ground, beyond the far side of the fire, was a large dun-metal cylinder, a small saucepan containing a glass jar, and a pot of strong-smelling glue. Two cramps and a vice were clamped firmly to the table in front of the man, where an elaborate set of callipers and a hand-drill rested loose; while down beside his feet lay a round grey sharpening-stone. It was as though the alcove had been fashioned specifically for the task. Faster and faster the man worked, his brows knitted together, the skin pulled tight across his skull. As he laboured, the man's whole body began to sway back and forth over the wood. The blade reflected blue light from the fire into the man's face so that his eyes lit up with the flames, and it was as though his entire being was bent on the log and the form to which he was subjecting it.

Alex's body began to relax; the joints, muscles and ligaments slackened. Yet it was not sleep that hovered around his brain – rather it was the immanence of lucidity. His mind was a sword, his thoughts the sweep of a lark through a clear blue sky.

That which was emerging from the man's body, from the fire of his labour, was shaped like a bird with projecting tail-feathers, or an imaginary fifteenth-century spaceship, or a head with long flowing hair. He took a rough chunk of smooth-faced hardboard and, using sandpaper, coursed over both sides till they were completely smooth. Dust billowed out from the surface of the board and filled the small enclave so that for a while Alex could barely see the man as he worked. Oddly, he realised that the man with the long face and the knitted brows had been speaking to him all along, his lips barely moving, and yet so focused was he on his work that never once had the man actually looked directly at him. The joints of his fingers moved with almost impossible speed. And the man's voice now was high-pitched, like that of a jockey or a eunuch or someone who had just inhaled a pinch of helium. Yet all the while Alex was able to comprehend exactly what he was saying, as though his ears and his brain had become attuned somehow to the flow and assonance of his words. It was as though, as he constructed what was obviously some kind of musical instrument, the man's voice had begun to emote the essential nature of the sound the instrument would produce.

'The neckblock comes from cedar of Lebanon, the old crusader sentinels planted by those who sipped the wine of esoteric sects and who later scratched their names in hermeneutic codes on the pillars of ruined temples. The ribs are slab-sawn from ash, which dwells on the land yet lives in the sea, and once these ribs formed the hull of a trireme whose oars all were cut from the same tree. The rib spacers are of holly-oak, the tree of the scarlet hem. The endliner is made of battling pine, to hold firm belly and neck; the pegbox, of bass rider beech that it may sing the old songs, and the veneer is ebony that the musician might see his own face reflected in its surface. The grain of the soundboard is the most important of all, and must be cut dead straight with no run-off from Swiss pine. The year-rings of the bars must exactly parallel those of the soundboard, or the music produced will be weakened, dangerous.'

'Dangerous?' Alex interjected.

But the man ignored him, and went on. He was almost singing.

'The fingerboard will be ebony, since the language of music is unseen. Bridge and pegs are plumwood; an instrument is a machine after all, its musician an engineer, a pilot, a starless navigator through the dark waves of sound and silence.'

The man was swirling a paint-brush around in a ceramic pot filled with a glaucous steaming foul-smelling substance. The pot sat on the gas stove and the liquid within was beginning to bubble and smoke ominously. From a small tin in his other hand, occasionally he would spill some drops of a dark-brown substance into the pot.

'Hide-glue. The strongest known, it binds together beings.'

'Which animal is it from?' asked Alex, only just restraining himself from pinching his nose.

The man glanced up at him. He had not let go of the brush and was now holding it so that its end hovered some inches above Alex's jeans. The man held his gaze, however, so that Alex felt he could not look away without being terribly rude or breaking whatever spell had begun the moment he had walked into this place or perhaps earlier than that, though he was irritatingly conscious of the fact that at any moment the molten glue would drip off the end of the brush and land on his blue jeans. The inside of his thigh began to itch, and he had a vision of the gleaming globule of glue falling like lava through the air, monstrously consuming the

70

oxygen as it went. It would land on the cotton and within microseconds would burn right through. The hairs beneath would curl and crumble in a twisting hot chorea and the skin would melt into opalescent white, his Scots-Irish gene pool bubbling and rising into smoke. And then down through muscles, blood vessels, axonic threads, to crunching wet Woden bone. He could smell graphite and clay, the smell of a body trapped in a car, its substances mixed in with the oil and steel and zinc of the engine, the chassis, an extension of the personality, taken to extremes. His eyes began to water and he felt unable to stem, or even to wipe away, the tears that coursed down his cheeks. Must be the damned glue, he thought, the rising sawdust of pine, ash, beech, plum, holly, cedar. A ligneous alphabet beginning to play in his head, here, in this hollow at the end of an unknown corridor in the Barras where in the time before birth and death the Old Irish had used to come to ply folk with their wares. It's all you can do, Alex thought. There is nothing else. You must leap up and play your song, your coda, and then sink into dust, into light.

'Goat,' the man was intoning, 'from somewhere far away. The glue is melted from the hides of goats.'

He was concentrating on the pot once more, the brush safely back in the glue.

'Up on the sacred mountains, the goats roam free, their time is untrammelled. They do not die in the normal fashion, but slowly, turn to stone. The glue is immortal. Sometimes, it is necessary to add vinegar.'

Alex looked up. His neck was stiff, his whole body felt like cooling rock. Through the tears he saw that the mirror on the wall was made not of glass but of highly-polished bronze. Even though he was not level with the metal, he was able to see his own face reflected in its surface. He knew it was bronze. No glass mirror would have imparted such a tone to human integument, to the whites of the eyes even, so that as Alex stared at his image – which did not return his gaze – it seemed as though he was looking not at a scientific reflection of the light from polished metal, but at an ancient Byzantine fresco of pressed gold and dead skin.

'Who are you?' he asked the fresco.

'I am Rujari d'Alì.'

Alex shivered. Then he realised that it was not the image in the mirror who had spoken, but the instrument-maker.

Alex stuck out his hand. It was an automatic response, but he withdrew before it became too much of an embarrassment. He knew that there had been no intention to offend; it was simply that Rujari needed both hands to constantly create the instrument, that any break in this process would result in a less-than-perfect form. Or perhaps the craftsman had already made many thousands of such instruments, none of which were perfect. Just one tiny flaw would be enough. Not that anyone else would've noticed. Even a seasoned lutenist might not have perceived the infinitesimal slippage of tone, pitch or sonorousness, the lack of a certain depth because the glue had been applied a little too thickly, or the emergence of a tinny sound because it had been mixed with too much vinegar, or because, long ago, some crusading monk had been slaughtered against the trunk of the ancient Baalbek cedar from which the wood had been hewn, on account of him refusing to reveal the secret codes of Yeshva to the unwashed Farangi vigilantes who had trailed him all the way to the Levant. Rain on the ash, or tumoural fungus in the beech, flawed ebony, diseased holly-oak, djinn-infested Swiss pine, a stove temperature two degrees out either way, a gas-supply sputtering from the interceptive inhalations of junkies ... anything at all might throw the balance, and Rujari would have to start all over again, to fashion another lute, theorbo, pandor, 'ud, or even to convert an angelique. And in this manner, over the years, the maker had generated thousands of such melancholic instruments and by the constant exposure to goat-glue and sawdust his voice had risen far into the minor scales.

And that was how Alex had come to have a sixteen-course Baroque lute placed in the palms of his hands. By the time he had managed finally to stumble along the narrow corridor, the Barras were all closed up and dark and the doors sealed like those of the pyramids. Yet Alex had felt neither fear nor shame, and certainly not the over-riding and peculiar Glaswegian terror of appearing to stick out from the bulging beery crowd, for he had in his hands a warm being which he had watched being drawn up from the earth, and which now he would learn to play. For the only way to tell whether or not an instrument is perfect is to play it, and play it well, and by degrees; to become a maestro, a virtuoso, to turn the tired, stiffened fingers of one's soul into dancing tongues of fire. Or at least, of a candle-flame, the moment before it is extinguished by the dark hand. And so at last Alex fell asleep watching the orange light from the street-lamps drip into an angular niche formed by a fissure in the stone window-sill. The crack threw giant shapes onto the wall opposite a cartoon-stall.

And then, much later, years later, there was that woman down by the edge of the fat river. He wondered whether perhaps he had dreamed the whole encounter. When he thought about it afterwards, sitting at home, the photographs of his dead wife ranged in Vatican gold along the low modern mantelpiece, Alex almost convinced himself that it had been some kind of vivid dream in which all five senses had been operating not in a normal way, but at some highly-concentrated all-consuming level. The tips of his fingers remembered the touch of her collar, the swing of her dark hair, the particular manner in which her lips had moved.

He'd gone for a walk to clear his head after yet another sleepless night. First thing in the morning was good for that. Everything had tasted clean and fresh, but Alex had known that had been a delusion of the senses. He didn't know why, but he had found himself walking toward the foot of the bridge – the last place on earth he'd have wanted to walk toward. His original intention had been to stroll eastwards – in exactly the opposite direction. Yet some morbid sense had drawn him on. As he'd sat through the preceding night he'd watched the skin of the river go down, had watched as the lights reflected in its surface had sunk below the level of the banks, and he had thought that perhaps at the furthest low tide he might find some tracks, some remnant of the impact, some mark of the moment she had died. About halfway through his walk he had spotted the woman. He'd wondered then at what point upstream the Clyde River ceased being tidal. At the scythe of the Glasgow Green, perhaps, or was it beyond that? Upstream through the East End and then dipping south, down into the mossy gorges, the furze slopes, the ancient hump-backed hills and the desolate fields of South Lanarkshire. Maybe the sea exerted its force all the way to the springs of Gad Hill and the dark silent tributaries that garnered moisture from the forgotten segments of the earth. Perhaps that was really why he had turned and walked toward the bridge. Or perhaps, on that pristine morning of his wife's funeral, he had been gripped by the same curiosity which had driven him to the Barras seven years earlier, down the corridor which he had never again been able to find, and into the freezing-burning cave of Rujari d'Alì and his multifarious incipient lutes. But then, as he'd drawn closer to the muddy bank, he had stopped, and had wondered whether he might be hallucinating the entire scene, or whether perhaps the woman was an escaped lunatic or a shell-shocked WAAF ghost from the nearby Veterans' Hospital. Yet there had been something entirely unsymphonic about her bearing, about the way she had splayed out her arms and half-waded, half-swum towards the dark object as it slipped away from her grasping hands.

He had known that once it passed between the pillars of the bridge there would be no chance of the woman getting hold of whatever it was, and indeed, that there had been a fairly strong possibility that she would be sucked into the powerful current and pulled beneath the surface by rank malevolent weeds. Malevolent? Yeah, well, he'd begun to get those kinds of ideas recently. And for a moment Alex had imagined that maybe the bundle of rags was a piece of Susan. No-one had mentioned that her body hadn't been intact. Not that he'd seen all of her ... corpse. Hardly any of her at all. He'd dismissed the thought as irreverent idiocy, when he realised that since the object was flowing downriver and had not yet reached the bridge, it could hardly have arisen from the bridge. The mind plays tricks early in the morning, he thought; it is the most dangerous time. You think you're awake, and you're not. You're still dreaming, only the dreams are real, and the five senses discordant liars.

He'd made her promise to call him before she opened the box. He wasn't sure why. The woman was obviously not a lunatic – in fact, as he'd discovered rather clumsily, she was a doctor – and yet he'd sensed an instability as he'd held her in the water, the soft flesh of her waist rippling through the cotton of her dress like a lute-belly beneath his fingers, and then later too as he'd helped her drag the big box ashore and into the boot of her car. Well, she'd have to be pretty loopy to want to dive into the freezing Clyde River at six-thirty am, wouldn't she? Was it possible for a physician to be insane? Why did it seem so abhorrent, as though the very rubric of civilisation depended on such a thing not being imaginable? Yet he did not recall his clothes being sodden or mud-stained at the funeral. No, everything was in order: the censers had swung in perfect arcs, the priest's voice had lifted into the eaves, and towards the end he, Alexander Wolfe, had almost been singing. Perhaps he'd been exposed to too much incense, or maybe some holy water had spattered over his skin, and perhaps he'd imagined that he had circled his arms around her waist – yes, he was certain of it, he had constructed this fantasy as he had invented so many others in his life. A happy marriage was either a marriage which was about to begin, or one which had just ended. Every other relationship was conducted in varying states of denial and truce. Yet when he recounted the event in his mind, Alex found that it played like a complex harmony, a series of waves, of possibilities. And, after all, he had to be a little mad to have helped her. He hadn't run down and shouted to her because he'd wanted to save her life – though afterwards he'd told himself that had been part of it – no, the real reason Alex-the-autodidactic lutenist had joined Zuleikha MacBeth in the cool grey stream of the river was because, like her, he too had longed to discover what lay in the darkness beneath the waves, down among the killing reeds and the swirling mud, and now he figured a part of that must surely reside within such a casket or else it wouldn't have been cast by someone into the water. Yep, Alex thought, we're two of a kind, Zuleikha and I. Foundation stones. He wondered when the call would come.

Chapter Five

It was simple curiosity which impelled her to apply the jaws of the metal-clippers to the left arm of the padlock. Her arms felt heavy, as if she'd been out drinking the night before, or as though she'd just had sex – neither of which had been the case. She laughed at the thought. *No, I just imagine having sex while driving along motorways at ninety miles an hour.* The metal-cutters were not so weighty, the muscles of her forearms not so dainty. It must be guilt, she thought. Yet it had been she who had clutched its wood to her chest, and even amidst the cold swirling waters of the Clyde it had been she who felt her heart beat against its gnarled flank. So she was entitled to the first glance. *This ship, and all who sail in her.* It was a territorial thing:

This box and all it might
contain belongs to
Zuleikha MacBeth

She saw it, inscribed upon a brass plate, glinting in the sunlight on a sandstone wall. Or in matt black Victorian ink, scrawled across a watermarked wedge of embossed paper, the copperplate letters implying permanence, like spear-points on wood, marking out territory.

'Let it be mine!' she exclaimed.

Dearly beloved … no, no, that's wrong. Begin again. On this auspicious day, I launch this ship, as we, who have coursed across oceans and mountains, have come at last to understand (and as I, shahzadi-without-soil yet through whom all the rivers of the earth flow) that lunar cycles become synchronously confluent and over the centuries, thus do grand and secret energies gather as in a star ball. Bang! Whoosh! Trumpets, please! I launch this vessel upon the swirling, cinereous waters of the dearest, greenest metropolis in the universe, first drum-roll, I give you, ladies and gentlemen, second drum-roll:

ZULEIKHA'S BOX!

She inhaled sharply and snapped the jaws together. The padlock flew up into the air and whizzed past her left shoulder. The whoosh of the iron sailing through her sitting-room was accompanied by the sound of her breath as she ducked. Ah! Grand Guignol! she thought. Good job I've got quick reflexes! Clippers still clutched in her sweaty hands, she glanced behind her. The padlock had dented the far wall. She went over to it and burrowed her index finger into the crumbling plaster and the ivory-coloured paint that hung off the ends of the old horse-hairs. The flat was a recent thing, she remembered, a product of what was known as 'conversion' – in which builders took an old tenement town-house, inserted partitions, plumbing and so on, and turned each floor into a self-contained unit. An abode for souls – but scratch beneath and you got stallion hair and an odd powder the colour of desiccated blood.

She rubbed the dust off her skin. It smelled like iron. She'd heard of someone who'd caught tuberculosis from plaster, but later she'd wondered whether the story was apocryphal, like the tales of lions and tigers in the sub-basement of the old Art School or the kitchen-floor crucifixions effected by 1960s gangsters in the Gorbals. When she turned back towards the box, to her consternation Zuleikha found that the lid was stuck down to the upper rim, so that she had to fetch a chisel to use on the three unhinged sides in order to prise it open. She was out of breath the whole time. Not fit, she thought. All those cigars. Lung-rot and dementia. Spiders in the blood. I should know better.

She expected the stink of the river to blast into her face, and was fully prepared to jump back out of the way again. Once again she inhaled, more deeply this time, and then held her breath so that it swelled in her chest and she felt like an athlete performing a sprint beneath the gaze of fifty thousand spectators. She'd read somewhere that the women of Sparta had performed athletic feats with one breast hanging out, Amazonian-style. Cute. The root of her neck began to prickle and roast. The crazy things people did to one another. To themselves. The thing was fucking hard to prise open. She didn't dare let out her breath. The incipient suffocation coursed along her arms, her thighs, as she planted her feet wider apart to give her better leverage. It's all physics, she thought. All just numbers and letters and impossible concepts. The pungent stink of burning sulphur. Marie Anne Pierette Paulze Lavoisier. The decapitated neurologist. Vive Le Cerveau! Electric arcs, across the blackness of rigor. Police radios. Flowers, growing downwards into the earth. A stupid song, looping and reeling endlessly in her brain. For fuck's sake, it was just a box. A set of ribs.

She'd thought she might see a deep container, with perhaps a few dank reeds coiled in the bottom, or maybe a clutch of dead lugworms. But what she was presented with, after all the effort and involuntary cardiac responses, palpitations, sweaty hands, dry mouth, fight-or-flight-or-smoke, was just another lid with no visible sign of a lock of any kind. Yet she was unable to prise this lid open.

Deflated, she slumped back in her armchair and stared at the contraption. She should have called Alex. It was her mistake, and now it would go on and on. It had been her pride, the unreconstructed vodka joy of her secreted royalty. The feeling that she could be self-sufficient, that everything she did would always be directed by some unseen force with which her will was in total harmony. Perhaps it would have been better if she'd been born a foundling, like Hazrat Musa. Breast-fed from a basket. Miraculous fishes. But that's stupid, she thought. People aren't born foundlings, a foundling must be found. Enough! she said aloud, this is the sort of inane conversation lonely women have with themselves when they're singing themselves into oblivion. She kept seeing him in her dreams and sometimes the dreams would be filled with a kind of suppressed eroticism, whereas other nights he would appear through a mess of music. Enough bullshitting, she thought. It's time. She went over and pulled her overcoat off the peg by the door. Started ferreting about in the pockets.

The next day, at work, Zuleikha almost forgot about the box. If it was busy, which it usually was, she would find that most extraneous things would slip away somewhere between the end of her pen and the smooth clean surface of her prescription pad. From here, they might still pop back into her thoughts for a moment between patients – if there were no phone-calls, or if the light which filtered through the grilled rectangular ten-centimetre-diameter window set high up in the wall on her left grew strong and focused, so that a ray illuminated a particular section of carpet, holding her gaze for a few seconds. At times during her mother's illness she'd been able almost to forget the undertow of incipient loss. But the moment she'd realised that she'd forgotten, the whole thing would rush back. She'd rung the phone number Alex had given her, but had been met by a female voice on an answering machine – not the impersonal boffinesque speaking-clockish type of voice one usually got on answering services, but a real woman's voice, hesitant, fallible, inflected. And she too had hesitated for a few seconds before leaving her own name and number. As she'd tried not to mimic the dead woman's mechanised voice, she'd thought that perhaps her name was really the opposite of what she was, a kind of alter ego. Zuleikha, Zoolaykha, Zulaykha, Zulaikha, Zaliqa.

She'd felt somehow sacrilegious. The woman was dead, and he hadn't changed the message. You didn't fuck with a ghost.

Perhaps another reason she was able to push the box to the back of her mind was that today she had to pay a visit to Mr. McPherson. Archibald Enoch; or, as everyone increasingly referred to him, Archie. Calling a man of eighty-five by a diminutive of his first name was patronising, but they did it because the healers of the earth had opened up the door within themselves. Zuleikha had come to the conclusion that there was a definite transfer of energy that came of touch. At first, as a junior doctor, she had dispensed it like paracetamol, but it had been physically draining for her and as time had worn on and she realised the need to pace herself through life, she had grown more discriminating regarding upon whom and in what circumstances she might bestow her palms. It had to be directed and appropriate, if not always conscious, otherwise nothing would happen. It felt like a tingling, a warmth which flowed from the flexor surfaces of her hands. She'd been careful to avoid any kind of theatrics about all this; she didn't want either patients or colleagues to get the wrong idea – and besides, she didn't know herself, really, what on earth was going on during these episodes. For all she knew it might simply be a subjective reinforcement of her sublimated maternal instinct. Yet evidence was just a base, the foundations of a house – it mustn't be confused with the house itself. In any case, the transnational pharmaceutical industry directed most of the research that went on.

And all those guys 'n' gals with bow ties and stern specs followed the evidence produced by these billion-dollar conglomerates as though they actually relished the consequent paucity of thought. This was the current unquestioned dogma. And yet there remained no evidence for consciousness, for the pulse of thought and image and dream. *I think, therefore I don't know.* She'd never let this doubt show in her work, though: you simply couldn't do that sort of thing nowadays and get away with it. Patients would be the first to complain, report you, no-win-no-fee – and besides, she hadn't wanted to be seen as eccentric. And after Daoud had died, she'd seemed to lose both the will and the ability. Or maybe it was just that she'd let go of the delusion.

Archie's house was like a dark glove. It hadn't always been that way. Zuleikha remembered a time, some years ago, when she'd first worked as a locum in this practice; when the house – which after all was just a two-bedroom semi – had been simpler, its internal architecture solid, real, logical. Half of Scotland's houses were mid-twentieth-century pebble-dashed semis. Yet even then, she thought, as she turned into his street and into the face of the sun, even at the beginning there had been something. She'd forgotten her sunglasses.

Archie's wife had died quite suddenly, some years earlier, of a heart attack in the middle of the night. Zuleikha had heard the story which he kept wound in a coil of his brain, ready at any time for elastic recitation. It was as though perhaps he was afraid that if once he should fail to do this, his wife's memory, her image, her laughing eyes, her smell would cross over one final time, would exit from the well of his consciousness and go to dwell where those other dead friends and relatives now dwelt: in the dark untouchable places which rose to a semblance of life only in occasional dreams and through photographs pressed into bulky albums. He didn't have to dream about her; she had never really left. After she'd died, on that sudden winter's night hollowed and blackened by the empty light of snow, Archie had begun to reorganise the house which they'd shared for almost fifty years. But he hadn't had the heart for it, and after filling one small cardboard box with her personal things, he had found himself unable to continue. Margaret, the pearl of his life. A wondrous music. Never, never fade. Never, never die.

As night fell, the memories rose into swaying shadows on the wall. They'd met during the Second World War, when he'd been a technician with the RAF and she a WAAF volunteer. When Archie thought about it, it was an odd thing, to meet like this in the middle of a charnel world. But then, everything in that war had been strange. The very fact of the war itself now seemed unreal – as though it had been some distant dream of blood skies and dark receding aerodromes. All except the smells. Certain peculiar combinations of scents, the perfumes she had used with some thought – much as a factory-girl might tend to her smile – wafting through the opened door of a back-close, brought it all back. After Margaret had left that terrible night, 21st December, 3:15 a.m. – the official time as recorded on the Death Certificate was one hour and five minutes later, but he knew that this was wrong. He had been there at the actual moment, he had felt the darkness of the abyss move, just as so many times he had skinned the blue nightdress off her bony shoulders, so that it was the slippage, the friction, the movement, and not the state itself that had become real.

During World War Two, he'd been posted to the flatlands of Lincolnshire. Swaying fields of ripe wheat and barley had stretched to the horizon and the land had reeked of dark silos and of old blood. They'd met in an aircraft hangar during a regular lunchtime classical concert. Orchestras would dress up in tails and white ties and would bring along the instruments of a proper classical orchestra – all except the piano grand. Generally, it would be light classical, swing or popular shanties, jigs, reels and the like, or else themes from famous films – although occasionally the musicians would assume those postures of solemnity which denoted a proper classical performance. And it was during one of these that he had properly *met* Margaret, as opposed to merely spotting her from the other side of the runway or else as she leaned across the broad bonded expanse of northern Europe in the control-bunker where she took direct orders from the boffins and pushed cardboard squadrons around the diorama like a croupier in a gambling-hall. Up until then he'd been in the underground bunker only a couple of times, and then only when he'd been sent by one of the officers with some important message or other. But then, after he'd seen her up close at the concert and once she'd begun to smile every time she saw him, he had begun to volunteer to carry commands and messages between bunker and hangar.

The wardrobe lay always in darkness – and that, Archie thought, was as it should be. It was an alternative sepulchre, a tomb on the path. It, and not the grave in the cemetery up on the hill by the river, was the real eternal abode of the love of his life. Tentatively, conscious perhaps that he was performing some forbidden act, he would finger each one of her clothes; the soft waterproof sleek of the tropical-lime raincoat which had made her stand out a mile and about which on many rainy days they'd laughed till they were doubled up. In this city of rain, the coat had become almost another skin for Margaret. It had a silly floppy hood which was meant to roll up into the collar but which, once unwrapped, had simply refused to go back, so that as often as not Margaret had just worn it over her hair. And so, like some terrestrial whaler, her whole figure had been enclosed in the garment. Then there was the dark winter overcoat which he'd bought her on her fifty-fourth birthday. Pure lambswool. Her blue eyes had gleamed like those of a young child, or like those of the WAAF woman she had been when they had courted, back then in the war dream.

The aircraft hangar was huge, and even when full of people it retained a quality of emptiness connoted by the perpetual, albeit barely perceptible, echo. Each time a note was played it would be followed closely by itself – or rather, by an echo of itself. It wasn't obvious and you might not have picked it up if you hadn't been listening – really listening, that was, and not merely bathing in the emotive overlay of the piece. Archie had learned to listen; as a groundsman, he had learned that keeping your ears open might well save your life. The shadow notes pursued the real ones in a breakneck chase right through the trumpet solo and the strings, the woodwind, and especially along the ebony row of the upright piano. Archie was standing where the echo was strongest, several rows from the back. It was just the way it had turned out – he'd had to complete a particular task on a Hurricane wing. It was like that; you couldn't leave a job halfway through, break the flow. Every action was a bridge of sorts. And there were bridges aplenty that day in the hangar.

The first thing he'd noticed about her was the shadowing around her eyes. No, that wasn't true. Actually, the first thing he'd noticed was the fact that she was tapping her feet to some bizarre as-yet-uninvented rhythm, the syncopations of which were hidden even from him. He was a great admirer of Goodman's music, the dancing and all, and so it struck him as odd that he wasn't able to recognise the tune. At first he thought she was a typical woman, senseless of both ball-control and rhythmic cadence. But then as he watched her and as the shadow-notes came pouring down over them both, Archie realised that the WAAF volunteer had captured the elegant quintessence of this unknown piece of music in her being. He couldn't take his eyes off her. She seemed to be bathed in something akin to light. The echoes and the original notes appeared to come together in a fugue which he felt no-one else could hear.

Margaret – he found out her name later – was of average height and build and would not have been considered classically beautiful. Her hair was Lincolnshire earth-brown, and was not particularly sleek or silken: more grainy, tidy and functional. Her bosom in those days was really quite small, and her nose-bone ran straight down and outwards, without curve or break, so that it seemed as though she were perpetually seeking something. Her eyebrows were folded like a falcon's over the bone, and her eyes slanted slightly downwards at their outer ends – except when she smiled broadly or laughed and then, miraculously, her physiognomy would alter, her face would become highly animate, and in this plasticity he found himself viscerally aroused. But it wasn't just a physical arousal – he'd had that often enough with women – this was deeper. It was a sudden need to sweep her up, protect her. Through his obsession with her form, with the need to know her mind, Archie felt that he was beginning to mature. So this is what it feels like, he thought. Love.

The day was hot and the blue sleeves of her blouse had been rolled up to just above the elbows. Archie inched towards her through the tightly-packed crowd. As he drew closer he saw that, because she was sweating, the skin of her face, slightly overlaid with foundation, had begun to show through in irregular patches. He stopped, a distance of two bodies from her. She was plain; taken as individual qualities, everything about her was unremarkable. And yet, somehow, the whole possessed a subtle beauty which was as unrelated to prettiness as the beauty of rocks and pearls is distant from the attractiveness of village-church flower arrangements.

For Archie, the concert ended too soon. He had spotted her fleetingly before, and yet on those occasions she had seemed little different from the other WAAF women who worked on the base. They too wore regulation hair and shoes and Air Force-blue uniforms. No perfume. No lipstick. Not on duty, at any rate. Finally he plucked up the courage to ask her to dance, and then later, to take her out on a proper date. And one thing led to another, and because it was wartime, life was telescoped, and before they knew it, they had become engaged and married. All in the space of six weeks.

Margaret hailed from a hamlet some fifteen miles to the south-east of the aerodrome. A lot of the WAAF were home girls from the county, or even the Riding. Her family were tall north-Lincolnshire farmers with enormous bone-crushing hands and clothes full of holes. They lived under big skies and always seemed to carry iron buckets, filled with anything from eggs to straw to pig-manure. They were Lindsey people, and they thought it hilarious that the daughter of their house had been spliced with a *Scotchman*. But it went both ways. Archie chuckled as he remembered the look on his mother's face when he'd told her. She'd never even heard of Lincolnshire. At least, Archie felt relieved to remember, Margaret had had a kind of a Scottish name.

Anyway – they'd married swiftly, in one of the breaks between bombing-up aircraft, in her local village church, their signatures sandwiched between countless others, some of which already denoted the young deceased. His family had shifted awkwardly on the old oak pews. They'd kept glancing upwards, as though the praying hands of the Saxon eaves might suddenly begin to crumble and collapse on their heads. His pa would've been okay about it – if he'd been there. He'd fought in the Great War – so-called – and Archie felt certain that he would have understood the desperate need for permanence, for immortality, that can take hold of a man in the midst of total carnage. His pa would have known that in all wars, relationships are fluid. The soft touch of her large fingers along the lines of his palm, the slow movement of the joints as his fingers closed over her hand, the filtered milky light coming through the stained glass of the low kirk. Church. The imagined smile, so broad on his absent father's face, as though it might crack the bone of his jaw from end to end. His mother, diminutive and trying hard not to scowl beneath her simple pink hat. Everything had been basic, even the grizzled vicar, big-toothed and earthy like Margaret – yet perhaps it was this very solidity that, all these years on, made Archie able to recall the dead all the more clearly as they lifted off into dance. Aye.

He rolled over in bed and spat into the metal pan. He had some difficulty getting the stuff out of his mouth and it hung from one end of his upper lip like an auxiliary tongue until finally he flicked it off with the tip of his index finger. He inspected it, as always. As though he would ever discover anything new in the secretions which issued from his body. The gob lost its form in the large grey pool of sputum streaked through with green and red that wobbled at the bottom of the bowl. Exhausted by the effort of hewking up his lungs, he sank back onto his pillow and closed his eyes against the clean light of the morning. He knew that he ought to sip some water from the glass that sat on the bedside table, to clear his tubes, to break up the crap, but he was at the wrong angle and even the slight movement that would be required to perform such a function seemed now like some kind of marathon.

Days went by, slow within themselves, yet at a rate which he could no longer fathom. Time had pulled away from him like a flayed skin, and though he was aware of light and dark and sometimes of rain and hail against the glass of the window, Archie now slipped through a reality whose boundaries had receded. He supposed it must be the morphine which they'd given him in increasing doses as the cancer had progressed. Now that wee Doctor MacBeth had told him that he was taking a quantity of MST that would render an Indian elephant senseless, or more probably, dead. Two hundred and forty grams every twenty-four hours, in split doses. Slow-release. And he had top-up do-das for in between. And she should know, the wee doctor. Though she wasn't so short, that doctor; she would've been at least three inches taller than Margaret had been in those last years. He hated the way folk shrank as they grew older. He'd asked the doc and she'd said something about the spine crushing itself. Typical bloody human body. Crap on legs. Humans, that was, not the doc. No, she was good. The funny thing was, the top of her head reached the very same level against the jamb of the door as Margaret's had when they'd first moved into this house. That'd been around thirty years ago. No, it was more than three decades. Before he'd retired. Oh yeah. A while before. Sometime after he'd saved her life.

It had been no more than instinct. He'd just pushed her off the tarmac as a Messerschmitt Me 109 had come in really low and strafed the air with fire-shot and cannon. They'd ended up face-down on the ground, side-by-side and clutching hands. At least, that's how he'd rationalised it later when he'd played it down in front of his friends – though he was always glad that the friends had played it up to the level of the almost-miraculous. Well, if he'd been a Roman Catholic maybe he would've called it miraculous too, but since he had been brought up strictly red-brick Presbyterian, neither High nor Low but somewhere sensibly in between, Archie did not deem miracles realistically to be possible – though sometimes he did feel as though reality itself was a terrible miracle. At those times, like the time he had lain with Margaret afterwards, both of them smoking roll-ups with the orange light from the street-lamps dancing behind their eyes, Archie would find that the voice within him would fall silent – the cynical carping voice that for so long had poisoned his actions, his thoughts. The voice that always reminded him that he'd been with a baker's dozen of whores before he'd begun to save himself for Margaret, and that many years later he'd recognised one of them when he'd been visiting friends in that new town down by the river. A day when the rain had stopped dead.

She was just a figure, walking towards him along the wet road close to the site of the old hanging-tree. She was much older and darker than before, but there was something in her bearing that made him absolutely certain that she was the one. A small crushed face, albeit swarthier than he remembered. Black eyes. He felt Margaret at his side sense something, the way women did. Or maybe he was just imagining it; maybe it was just that fucking tree where at the end of the seventeenth century they had strung up the Great Erskine River Witch. When, against his will, Archie looked back over his shoulder, she had already vanished around a street-corner. As their paths had crossed, at the last moment he had averted his eyes. But he saw that she had looked full into his face and had known him. Miracles. Curses.

He'd had that last hooker in a top-floor tenement flat in Clydebank, one of the great loading-ports along the river, situated roughly midway between the upper and lower Clyde shipbuilders of Govan and Port Glasgow. It was the early spring of 1941. He'd been on a few days' leave that coincidentally followed a terrible air-raid in which he'd lost his best friend. The bomb had missed Archie by seconds. He'd just walked out of the room as the silence had come; his friend had not. Life: Death. It was that simple. Perhaps he'd gone to the whore as a means of assuagement or escape, or perhaps the touch of death had infected him. A man needs blood and seed, and a whore is as good as a kill.

It was a sunny afternoon, the sleepy time, but Archie was wide awake. His brain was electric; he felt as though he could direct events, swing aircraft across the sky, send subs down through the sea, and hoist the spines of women onto the end of his cock. She had long chestnut-brown hair, and skin the colour of marble. Although the rest of her looked and felt wan, sloppy, degenerate, the muscles of her buttocks, hips and lower back were sleek and lacked padding – she was akin to a machine, hard and almost wiry against his belly, his thighs, his groin. It was as though her whole existence, every brain-cell, every fibre of every sinew was directed simply at this one part of her anatomy. She made her living through her sphincters. On the wall, high up and almost at the line of junction with the ceiling, she had pinned a single cheap reproduction photograph of His Imperial Holiness Pope Pius XII in full ecclesiastical vestments, standing on a balcony and waving, smiling through thick spectacles at the invisible crowds gathered in Saint Peter's Square in Rome on what must have been another sunny day. Perhaps an afternoon just like this one, here in Clydebank – except that there would not have been an air-raid over St Peter's Basilica. The sirens went off and the whore tried to disengage, but Archie held her down against the bed and kept moving and with the overture of howling sirens and the full concerto of growling German aircraft punctuated arrhythmically by explosions from the docks, he became increasingly aroused. His cock felt like a holy sword, the sword of Saint Michael, with which he would disembowel this Luciferine whore, would take out her guts as if he were a shark and she some piss-shite mollusc lying at the bottom of the sea.

Well, as he was doing his thing, and as he was approaching some kind of difficult dark climax with this whisky-afternoon tart, Archie did something of which he was not in the least proud. And yet deep within the belly of his shame lay a rotting evil sense of triumph. The whore's skirt had been pushed up around her waist. Archie was naked, the way he liked it. His clothes were draped over a chair, right next to the bed: grey trousers, white shirt, vest and underpants (he'd been in civvies that day). Like the woman, the mattress was sagging; it was damp and older than its years and had been laid on a base of iron. Emptiness was fine for the Pope and all those priests shooting off their seed into the dark silence of hypocrisy, but a man needed a half-living receptacle.

The whore had her face turned to the net-curtained tenement window through which the sunlight cast the forms of their bodies into silhouette against the dirty cream-coloured wallpaper opposite. They were only a hundred yards or so from the water's edge. When he'd arrived in the bed-sit flat that reeked of stale spirit, over-ripe perfume and fossilised seminal fluid, and as they'd swigged some bitter black-market liquor straight from the bottle, he'd gazed out of the window and had looked through a large open space between the dock sheds, right across to the town of Renfrew and the rolling hills to the south. It was a great view for a screw, he'd thought; the elevation lent a certain airy feeling to the encounter, a sense of being not quite of this world. Or maybe that had been the booze. But now, on the dank creaking bed, it was the physical which anchored him: the acidic stench of the whore's cunt, the piquance of her arse-hole, which her fear was now transforming into a giddying efflorescence. She was trembling, he felt that; she was fucking terrified. The bombs were smashing up the docks, splintering ships, buildings and people, and with every explosion they were getting nearer. *We can do it in the shelter, she was saying, please, we can do it down there, sweetheart.* But he hardly heard.

Sweetheart, indeed! He was not her lover, he was a killer. It was as if he were a god, come down in the form of a beast to fuck a temple prostitute, to lay his silver seed into her perishing frame, that his spawn might erupt and cover the earth with their darkness.

Opposite the window, between the bed and the wall, there was a full-length swing mirror. Although it was broken, the glass was completely free of any impediment to vision – no dirt, no dust, no finger-marks – so that it appeared as though there was an identical but fractured room on the other side of the glass. The whore was gazing in one direction and he in the other. Two people fucking, one imagining fasces, sopranos and sacrificial slaughter, the other fearing an agonising death in a tower of fire – or else, perhaps, the distraction of a hot meal and some solitude. They were a pair of grunting corpses searching in common for a minute of peace amidst a lifetime spent staring into a grave, yet even in the midst of their act, each remained completely discrete from the other. They were opposites, enemies. Cain and Abel. Adam and Lilith. At another time, it might've been funny. Archie might have cracked up at the scene. Scots were meant to be good at laughing at themselves, but this was not another time, and time was critical. A few seconds this way or that. Time was absolute. The howling wolf of a bomb. Pulsing jugular dreams. Now he knew. The pilots probably came in their cockpits as they felt the bombs leave the seats of their pants, and so did the generals and air-marshals, stowed safely in their bunkers, the politicians doing deals in their counting-houses, the dark forces of the kings on their thrones, the popes leaning over the stone balcony, the gods in their stained glass palaces...

In the peeling glass Archie watched his slicked-back straw-brown hair, his body, broken and elongated by the crack; beneath his weight, the woman seemed to have disappeared into the mattress. She seemed like a ghost, or a corpse. A nothing. He reached over to the chair and removed the belt from its trouser-loops. In one movement, while continuing to thrust his pelvis against her sacral bone, he wound the leather around her neck, grabbed the ends with both hands, crossed them over and pulled tight. Her body convulsed, at first automatically and then deliberately, as she tried to throw him off her back. But he was strong on this day of broken light, with the deep metal beat of the bombs and the rising stench of sulphur, with the sun's shafts spearing their bodies with exploding hydrogen, with his bones hardening like those of a god, and up there, on heaven's ledge, the Pope, holy, holy, holy. It was a vignette, infallible both inside and out.

In her attempt to escape she had managed to twist her head halfway round, so that now both their faces were facing the same way, towards the wall. Her face was small, prematurely-lined and crushed into the material that stank of old tarpaulin, and his was long-boned and bare-toothed. Feral faces both, and he watched in the mirror as she turned first red and then blue, and then as her eyeballs bulged till they seemed on the verge of herniating, as her broken lips swelled and foam began to fleck the skin of her cheeks, to dissolve the cheap foundation of her make-up and as her thickened tongue began to protrude as though to accentuate her timeless ugliness. And then the transmutation was complete. The blacks of her eyes ruptured and spread over the whole. He felt her body tighten around his cock and her receding breath was like a song.

The whore was lucky that he hit orgasm a few seconds later. The pulse filled his whole body and extended out over the tenement stone, the city, the bombers, the river, and it seemed to go on forever. The sharp buckle of his belt had drawn blood from her neck: a thin red liquid which he scooped up on his index finger and brought to his tongue. As he left the room she looked like a piece of skin, all crumpled-up on the cheap messed bed. Just his waste.

Without washing, he'd wandered through the burning buildings as around his shoulders, in a single engagement, the town of Clydebank was almost completely destroyed. The next day he'd taken a train back down south and had returned to the aerodrome, to Margaret. He had looked straight into her cyanotic eyes and proposed to her.

Above the lapels of her dirty-brown overcoat that day in Erskine, he'd seen the scars. Just before he had climaxed, he had seen something in the mirror which he would never forget for as long as he lived. There was the whore, naked and standing with her hands on her hips, her teeth bared, and she was laughing at him. And as he shot out his seed, he saw her purse her lips and balloon

90

her cheeks as though they were bellows, and a golden spray flew from the surface of the glass, entered his widely opened mouth and coursed straight down his throat, filling his lungs with a substance that made his body feel like primordial stone the moment before it sets. The whore was inside him, a core of dock iron.

He shuddered as he buried the memory once more. For years he had feared that he might talk in his sleep. He had woken up covered in sweat that smelled of something else and had focused on the regular movement of the second hand on his bedside clock to help steady his breathing, to tame the beat of his heart against the wall of his chest. After Margaret had died there had been just a flicker from that same bastard cynical voice, and it had been pleased that he need no longer fear exposure. His relief had been short-lived, though, and recently Archie had become obsessed with the thought that in the middle of some opiate dwam he might come out with the whole tale. Sixty-odd years on, and riding down into the sunset. Yet now, at least, there was a chance that no-one would believe anything he said. He could tell them that a nuclear war was about to begin, or that the stock market had crashed, or that there was a lute-playing ghost sitting cross-legged on the nearest telegraph pole, and either they would have laughed silently and mixed some nutcase drug into the cocktail, or else would have comforted and humoured him – depending on how near the end they thought he might be. He'd even gone so far as to test out this theory on the home-help – or 'personal carer', or whatever it was they were called nowadays. She was a tubby red-faced woman who once – a long time ago, so she had told him – had been a mini-skirted toy hippie, a clockwork groover and possible groupie who had bedded a pop star or two and who had been completely obsessed with the acid music emanating at that time from, of all places, Austin, Texas … and it had worked! It was amazing how dishonest and downright nasty you could be when folk thought you were dying. They'd take almost anything, he thought. Well, you were dying, you are dying, but the thing's in the principle. Margaret's life saved, salved, or something. They had built no buildings, except in the sky.

Well, nowadays almost any woman under the age of fifty seemed to Archie to be pretty in some respect, though not necessarily beautiful: there was a difference. Doctor MacBeth. There was something about her: her eyes, the manner in which she held herself ... he couldn't put his finger on it, especially now that the poppy pills had made it difficult for him to focus properly. The way she moved. The way she never touched, unless it be to perform a clinical examination. He knew she had to maintain a certain professional distance. To be objective, for when the time came. She'd told him that she was divorced; he'd got that much out of her, and yet he wasn't even certain it was the truth. He hadn't dared ask her about kids. She was either scared or lying. But how could she possibly be frightened of him? Jesus! He could barely lift his dying frame from the winding-sheet onto the commode. Four feet, at most. At night, he wore a nappy. Christ, oh Christ. But he was probably wrong about her, as he had been about most things. His universe had contracted. These modern houses. They weren't like the old tenements he'd grown up in. Not like the old abodes of Govan. In those, you could stretch yourself till you were the length of a mediaeval rack-victim and still you wouldn't be able to touch the ceiling or to span the distance between the two walls. They'd been built around the turn of the century of white Giffnock sandstone, yet their templates had been raised from the forms of earlier slum tenements. So many generations living in the same cube of air. Screwing up the arse against the cold green walls, then sneaking off in the freezing darkness to the shame of the outside toilet at the end of the back-close. The heavy reek of old fries, the pudding-bowl wallow of mashed potatoes and cheap cabbage, the stinks pinned you to a place, swirled you down into the darkness of its time. From tallow to gaslight to amber, the flickering tenebrousness of existence had always been the same. Tenement whores, the touch of skin, lights going out, all over the ...

But that had been another world. A different universe. The people in it seemed now to have belonged almost to a preceding species. Hair grease and a bath once a week. Tea-rooms. Cold silver service. Over the years even he and Margaret had changed and had become unrecognisable, even – especially – to each other. He could feel the slippage in his bones. Theory of Evolution? Theory of Bullshit. Folk changed all the time, and not at all. Like in the photo of Margaret, the late-seventies garish colour slide, flared up into a six-by-six print and framed in gold. Well, obviously not real gold, but none of your cheap plastic lark either. And he was in the picture too, a younger version of him, his hand placed over her left shoulder, three of his fingers just visible amongst the rumples of her flowery summer frock. Both of them were smiling as they'd seldom smiled in life. It was like going up to a blank wall and grinning. If you did it to a wall, you'd be sent to the local loony bin; if you did it to a person, you'd be assaulted or else thrown behind the bars of the Bar L. Or maybe both. Archie knew that it had been taken using his old single-lens reflex camera; those were the days when Instamatiks were novelty machines, used most often as toys by children or by bored functionaries at drunken office parties. He couldn't recall whom he had asked to take the picture, nor even where they'd been, Margaret and he, when it had been snapped. It was obviously summer: you could see that from his own pale blue home-made Safari jacket, which Margaret obviously had modelled on a style beloved of witty Central African dictators bearing enigmatic azure Krishna smiles. Also, unusually for Scotland, the sun was shining.

He figured it must've been Millport, the only town on the tiny Isle of Cumbrae; for a while during the seventies they had gone there every summer for the two weeks of the Glasgow Fair. They had been a little too old for the Costa antics of those born after 1940. No, it had always been cold milk, tea and scones and the faint yet immanent possibility that sunlight might break its reclusive concubine smile through the netted windows of the clouds and begin to tease their surfaces. The skin just starting to sag then, the hair longer than now, whirling mercury over the tops of his ears and on his crown, the original barley-brown not yet flattened to tarnished silver. What folk didn't realise was that the appearance of your eyes was as much to do with the tautness of the skin around them as with the eyes themselves. When he pulled on his glasses Archie could just about make out the eyes of the people in the picture – of Margaret, with her face framed in a world of permed brown hair and of himself, as was. They stared from the photograph as though willing the future into being.

Compare that with the last time he had looked at Margaret's face, or rather, the time before the last, when he'd gazed into the face of a frightened woman, the blue of her eyes deadened. And then he had looked in the mirror and had realised that at some point, without him being aware of it, the same thing had happened to him. But in the photograph over the years the light had scumbled their features and illumined their skins as though from behind.

Recently, he had tended to avoid wearing his specs; the papers just had the same old shite as always and what would be the point of starting to read a novel? He might never finish it and anyway, no-one had ever learned anything from books, not really. He'd read too many books in his time. But, he told himself, those hadn't really been the reasons. The fact was, the photograph had been up on that wall for seven years, ever since she had died, and he no longer wished to gaze upon it. If there was something after the end of this crap, then he'd get to see her anyway – and if there wasn't, then fuck it. You couldn't trust a photo and you couldn't trust your eyes.

Anyway, he figured now that his entire consciousness was suspect. Soon there would be no handholds. Sometimes, in the depths of the night, in between bursts of rainfall on the glass, when the city at last fell into that state of silence which it had possessed in the beginning, Archie would awaken to the distant sound of gushing water. The unmistakeable sweep of a big ship, teetering, slipping like a giant steel ballerina down the launch shoot. See, he would tell himself at those times, you shut the fuck up, you welding bastard. Those ships are what gave you the asbestos, the cancer, blue, white and grey. Filaments, fine as those of heart's muscle. The sun is gleaming like a pearl set in a ring of sapphires. You're bare-backing the waves, riding along the stream that leads to the river that leads... Shut the fuck up! It's already starting.

Every hike in opiate dose made him throw up for a day and a half, and there was still pain, the discomfort of a disembodied jaw gnawing at his insides, and like those of an incubic foetus its teeth were growing larger every day, every hour, pulling him, inching him steadily closer to death. Well, then it would end, but first the long black mouth would have its gory fill. He had changed his will recently, though not to shut out the distant relatives – as a consequence of the miscarriage which had nearly killed her just before the end of the war, Margaret had been unable to bear children – but to ensure that after he had breathed his last, what remained of his emaciated body would be cremated and not buried. That way finally the tumour would be destroyed, but in the process he would've subjected it to the same hot vice of pain in which it had held him these six months, give or take. Bastard! Archie swore that in the burning tunnel of obliteration he would be laughing, gutting himself as the rat inside was ripped and flayed and seared by the white heat, while for the first time in ages he would feel no pain whatsoever. He got so excited by the prospect of posthumous revenge that he almost choked on another ball of shite heading up the way. He felt the crap linger tenaciously in his throat, teasing the mucosa like a whore's dildo, making it swell so that he couldn't get a breath, not one fucking molecule of oxygen for the entire flesh of his bones. He felt himself go blue, he heard his voice rasp, his cells screaming for air. *My soul, my soul, for a single fucking invisible atom!* Automatically he swung himself up on one elbow and tried to retch, but the muscles around his abdomen were not strong enough. The world was blurring over, the window, the Gainsborough print with its white plastic frame, the cart-horse whose ghost he had come to know so well, the lengthening shadows on the wall of morning. Ach, fuck. The world was turned upside-down and he, Archibald Enoch, Son-of-the-Son-of Pher, was hanging, unbreathing like a bat, from the roof of his darkened cave.

Somehow, perhaps by the use of some cell in his head which until that moment he hadn't known he had, Archie found the mask. And gradually, as the cool stream of the oxygen slipped into the trees of his lungs, the world – or at least that part of it which had come to exist within his bedroom – began to creep back, albeit reluctantly, into his thought-stream. A gloss-white stool and dressing-table. Synthetic, with a mirror that turned but only just – too much angulation and it would fall forwards into your face, tearing skin, smashing bone and spilling the perfumes all over the carpet. Alchemical bottles. Death sand. An entire city of sows' ears, turning. Miraculously, Margaret had managed to avoid such a fate. Archie had almost never used the thing. The bathroom mirror had always been enough for him. Fucking vanity.

Hubris, falling. Hadn't trusted fate, anyway. It was a cut-throat blade on a silken back; you could never take your eye off it, not even for one micro-nano-pico second, else it would have you. It would arrive and would fill the doorway.

The window was fire-proof and gloss paint had made it unopenable. Daylight coursed through the double layer of glass onto the side of his head. If ever a fire started inside the house, he'd have had it. He'd end as a crushed burning wasp, his guts smeared all over the white net and clear glass. Squeezing out stings. Underfoot – once during the day he had always worn slippers, but now his soles were bare, the skin hardened by the incipience of the earth and the shells of arthropods – the carpet was big-patterned and had been woven by huge looming machines high on lysergic acid. That was the thing: Archibald and Margaret had moved into this house nearly fifty years ago when it had been brand spanking new. They had needed to do it up only once in between flitting and dying, and that had been during the early 1970s – about the same time Archie had taken to growing Jewish-style sideburns and to wearing flared trousers and high-voltage nylon shirts. Shipyard innuendos, the hairy hookers of Govan Cross who like catamarans had sailed the world on the keels of their cunts. Static electricity. Artexed icing-sugar ceilings. Magnolia walls. Their bedroom now was neutral – clinical, even. A good place in which to lay out a body before it went stiff. The crescent of her cooling frame lying beside him. Through the white, the photographs, and turning in muslin sheets somewhere off to the side of his brain, the bark and scratch of a dead gramophone. Winding down. No air.

Then, sensing the cyanosis lift from his face, he became aware of rippling movements in his belly. It occurred to him that perhaps the demon had begun to evoke itself through the integument of his viscerae, or that perhaps he was going into some kind of bizarre opiate labour. Like in one of those science fiction films he sometimes watched late at night on his gleaming white plastic portable TV. But then he realised that for the first time in weeks he had begun to laugh.

He was still laughing when Zuleikha walked in, black bag and all. She smiled back at him. That made the dark circles around her eyes indent even more, and his awareness of this caused Archie's laughter to redouble.

'I'm glad you're feeling happy today, Archie.'

Her head was a silhouette against the gold-framed photo of Margaret. He yanked his thumb sideways.

'How did you get in?'

She swung her free arm backwards.

'You'd left the door open.'

He nodded.

'Aye. For the nurses.'

She sat down on the edge of his bed, inadvertently pushing herself up against his right thigh. He shifted a little to the left, in the direction of the window, to give her enough room. He didn't want her falling off Margaret's side of the bed.

'How are you? How's the pain?'

He shrugged. Pulled at the coverlet. Levered his shoulders up onto the double set of cushions.

'It's there, but it's the breathing, you know.'

She nodded. She obviously knew, so why did she ask?

He glanced down at her hands which were resting one on top of the other in the lap of her skirt. The fingers were long and bony and the skin was the colour of barley in June. Then he remembered that it was June. She was wearing a single silver band on the middle finger of her left hand. Very unusual, that. The ring had been carved in the shape of coiled serpents, or perhaps they were the entwined trunks of trees – he'd need his specs to figure it out. She'd not bothered to wear any make-up or lipstick, and that too was unusual for her. She snapped open her medical bag and removed her stethoscope. There was definitely something different about her today. Something had changed. Even her smell. Although she'd not worn anything on her face or lips, this morning it smelt as though Doctor MacBeth had bathed in perfume. Archie closed his eyes as he breathed slowly in and out. There wasn't much of a wave crest there, not much difference between in and out. Soon there would be none. A flat line. Sinking sand.

The cold steel rim of the stethoscope diaphragm lingered just a little too long in one place. She usually didn't listen so assiduously to his chest. After all, the diagnosis had already been made. There was nothing more to do. He'd had the gamma rays and the beta rays or whatever they called them nowadays, and everyone knew that the right side of his trunk was being eaten away by the creature gestating inside him. She listened for a moment too long, even though he had held his breath. Something he never did, something he had thought he would be incapable of ever doing again. Holding his breath. No effort. Normality. Light, hovering over the surface of a river. The moment before he opened his eyes, he had it. The new thing. The change in Zuleikha. Yes, he knew her first name. Hadn't dared call her by it yet. The invisible wall again. But today, during this long moment of unbreathing, the wall had been breached. The gate lay open, creaking as it swung back and forth on rusted hinges in the wind of no-breath. Just like in the aircraft hanger, sixty-odd years ago. Different time, same shadows. Archie held it in his mind for a second longer. When at last he exhaled, it was the longest breath he'd had for weeks. Months, even. And he had it. In the goat coil of his mid-brain, Archibald Enoch McPherson had it.

Zuleikha MacBeth smelled of death.

'You know you can use the mask whenever you want.'

He nodded.

'Are you eating?'

'A little. Mostly, I don't have the appetite.'

'The cartons?'

'Yeah.'

Archie had grown to hate the synthetic drinks, but often they were all he could keep down. And he needed fluid. When he got dehydrated he began to hallucinate pointlessly. And there was nothing worse than hallucinating without purpose.

The doc had twisted away from him, and now was gazing up at Margaret's picture. This was normal; ever since he'd met Doctor MacBeth she'd seemed fascinated by the photograph. She would glance at it as she walked in through the white doorway, and then again before she left. On one level, Archie felt that she was trespassing; the photograph was his property. No, it was more than that: it was part of him, it ran deep as his memory, and now this upstart scientist was walking in and freely violating his past. Raping him. He had not told her much beyond basic details about his wife, and she had never asked. It was as though their mutual ignorance was what kept them from confronting the issue. And yet Archie wished that he had confronted her at an earlier stage, the way people did in civilised situations, so that he could have explained to her what the picture meant to him, and then she would have understood that the silver of the image ran deeper than the paper, and perhaps she would have been more careful in future. But he wasn't sure about this woman; there was something about her which he couldn't pin down. Something that could not be held within the trammels of civility. Previously, he had feared visits from doctors. They had seemed like dark angels, carrying sugared bad news in their chemical black bags. But Doctor MacBeth was different. Her body, the tone of her voice, the look in her eyes.

Archie prided himself on his ability to judge character. When he'd been a foreman in the yards, he'd known the stamp of every man. It was a facility which had become sharpened as the years had gone on, so that eventually he had been able to gauge a man's timbre the moment he walked through the gates. Amidst the din and morass of a shipyard floor, the hammering, the welding, the cranking of the overhead cranes, it was something to do with bearing, the manner in which a body held itself, the tautness of its muscles, the template of its movements through space. It was really all engineering, geometry, music. And in the years since he'd retired this ability had become raised to an even higher pitch, perhaps partly because people no longer expected it of him. The second you retired, folk expected you to become a smiling retard, perpetually checking the date on your gold watch.

But Archie had become just the opposite. All his life, he had seen himself as an auto-didact. A bibliophile. Archie's father, William, had been a Red Clydesider and had marched with the Jarrow Men to Parliament in the thirties. One thing he'd always instilled into his seven children, of whom Archie was the youngest, was the need to get an education. Not just the education which the bosses dished out – enough to be able to function as a cog in their great steel wheel – but real learning that was broad and deep like the dock, like the Clyde, like the sea. To an extent Archie had idealised the man; he stood erect in Archie's brain, a socialist-realist stone. William McPherson had been the sort of man who would hang upside-down by his toes from the pan-rack in the kitchen and then curl his body upwards so that he could touch the rack with the ends of his fingers. These men with granite stomachs and golden hearts simply didn't exist any more. Yet Archie had always resented the fact that at one critical point his father had decided that freeing the masses in Spain had been more important than feeding his own family. And then, after the defeat of the Republican forces, he had escaped with some woman from the Andalusian Front to the south of Morocco. It was his father who had given Archie his middle name: Enoch.

Archie's mother had never been physically beaten by the docker, yet since the age of seventeen, when – in common with most women in those days – she had given up both her names, she had endured his politics, his dream speeches, the sweat of his knowledge, the blood anger of his oppression pushing down also on her. It had been his revenge. She had come from higher up the social scale than he; her father had been a clerk, her mother a seamstress. They'd had pretensions which the docker had despised, even though such ideas of wilful social progress might have been held intimately by ninety or more per cent of the membership of the various shipyard Orange Lodges. Wankers! A single smile from an aristocrat and they turned to water. Sawn-off silver flutes, big-bellied drums, faces stylised, fresco-white, the flapping of banners in the wind. The inertia of history. The Red Hand of the Grand Master, ferreting around inside the head.

After she'd married Archie's father, her own family swiftly had disowned her. If, after his act of betrayal, she'd gone to them, wooden begging-bowl teetering on the tips of trembling fingers and the admission of failure choking her voice, they might just have taken her back, unfrocked, to rot in porcelain spinsterhood – but she'd had her pride. The prospect of single-handedly bringing up seven children, born in symmetrical sequence, had been daunting enough; she had known that life would strip her of everything, that it would tear the flesh from her body and crumble her bones to dust. Yet she had folded the hate tightly inside of herself. She had come to hate the bosses, the workers, the council, the stones of her own tenement, the neighbours, the Germans, the English, the Fenians, the Orangemen, the radio, swing music, Gracie Fields, cemeteries, churches, ministers, prime ministers, young girls, ration-cards, black-market meat, postmen, factories, ships, cranes, planes, earth, air, water and fire. And her hatred had driven her to nurse her family as though she had been three women with six breasts. She wasn't alone, Archie remembered. Lots of women – widowed or abandoned – had done the same, though they at least had had their families behind them, helping out at every turn of the wash-house rollers that mangled the flesh and bone of Glasgow.

Another image was burned into Archie's brain: that of his aproned mother, leaning against the double sink in the evening kitchen, pressing her hands down onto the cracked white porcelain, the whole of her body shaking as she suppressed tears of rage. The bones of her fingers, reddened and swollen with the pressure, seemed as though they were about to crack and explode into a kitchen doubly darkened by the threat of rain. Big tenemental windows which opened onto the eye of an absentee God. Her teeth were clenched, the thin skin of her lips parted white across the bones of her jaw. Cold water gushed from the iron tap of the sink and splashed up into her face and onto her chest. A pool grew around her feet and, reflected in the pool, Archie saw the image of his father's face laughing in Arabic, ecstatic at his own sense of freedom.

There was no sin worse than envy – none, that was, except desire. Archie had been fourteen when his father had left home. And in spite of the hardship and the curses and fourth-floor spittle of his older sisters, Archie had moved through the sway and discord of adolescence and through the noisy inescapably claustrophobic love and hate of a large family, and all the while secretly he had worshipped the figure which his father had become. Yet the only physical contact he remembered having had with his father was a vision, box-Brownie'd in his mind, of the big docker wiping his cheek with a white handkerchief, the massiveness of the knuckled hand, unfisted for once, and a pressure gentle as the fall of the summer rain on the cropped grass of the Elder park.

And this was the image he took with him into the Air Force, which, much to the chagrin of his rapidly ageing mother, he had joined voluntarily right at the very start of the War. He finished his apprenticeship one day and joined up the next. And there it was! The second day of the Second World War, echoing in his ears.

The quivering elegance of Neville Chamberlain over the airwaves. In the sweep of his long strained vowels, you could smell the salt on his collar. The Prime Minister. He was a man already dead. The timing made it seem as though that failed artist Herr Hitler had invaded the flatlands of Silesia specifically so that Archie, like his father, could run off to war and to an unknown freedom. An Elysian field which lay fallow yet never forgotten, somewhere beyond the pulse of drink and muscle and spunk.

One by one, either through hasty park-bench marriages or the bellowing sirens of emigration, his brothers and sisters had moved out of the blackened tenement, had left the forecastles of Golspie Street and Neptune Street and Kellas Street, the Wine Alleys and the Teuchtar Hills and the dark, nameless places for good. One by one they had gone until only Archibald and his mother were left – she, though barely fifty, already broken and silver-haired, and he dreaming always of the spinning dancing women of the Aragonese jota. Her rage grew ever stronger as her children made their escape, her teeth splintered and crumbled as her jaw clenched on itself in a joyless syncopation with the night rain. Her love was beyond the human. She had brought up William McPherson's offspring as an act of revenge, as though, somewhere, perhaps from the souks of a Moroccan medina, her docker would be watching and sinking into icy madness at her implacable resilience in the face of his betrayal.

Archie's own need to escape the airless ruin of his mother's house had driven him to the great dark bellies of the hangars, to take shelter beneath the wings of Blenheim Bombers and De Havilland Dominies. He had wanted to fly, to soar through the emptiness and to engage in heroic sunset battles with the Hun. That had been his dream when he had signed the papers. He hadn't realised that his position in the anthill would remain static, that in spite of the massive shake-up which the exigencies of world war had injected into the system, there were some things which the kings of steel and fire simply would not allow. Archie and the other working-class lads would never be permitted to fly. And even if they did reach the interior of a Lancaster or a Wellington, it would be as mid-upper gunners, firing lead from rosy glass turrets whence, come the great fire, there would be no possibility of escape.

He was aware that she was looking at him. With a start

Archie focused on her face, her eyes. He began to panic again as he wondered how long she had been staring at him. The doc. MacBeth. What a strange name for a doctor to have. Well, you couldn't choose your name, he supposed. Neither the one under which you were christened, nor, as a woman, the one into which you marry. He had to get beneath the skin, as he had done after the War with all those work-mates, those potential killers, on the steel floors of battleships. And as he'd done beneath the big black wing of the Lancaster in the voluminous J-hangar where he'd used to make love to Margaret. The feeling, beneath his palms, of the curves of her body, the pull and stretch of the long muscles that lay beneath her skin, the silky whiteness of her form, floating like a beauteous wraith in the vast murk of the hangar. The pungent yet attractive smell of aircraft fuel. The sound of the lone trumpet blasting out a single perfect note.

'What's your name?'

The words had left his mouth before he'd had time to think.

She looked puzzled.

'My name? Macbeth. Doctor Macbeth.'

This could be fun. He knew her name – had overheard it being mentioned by the District Nurses – but it would be different coming from her own mouth. And asking people about themselves could be an underhand way of learning what they knew about you. Anyway, he would not be put off. He'd come this far.

'No, I mean your Christian name.'

Then he felt stupid. What if she wasn't Christian?

'I mean your first name.'

She inhaled. The noise and movement of her lips, the flare of her nostrils, the rise of her small breasts was just perceptible in the pallid morning light.

'Zuleikha.'

He attempted a pronunciation.

'I'm sorry,' he said.

She shrugged and looked away, down at the coverlet.

'It's okay. Most people have difficulty with the pronunciation. Most folk call me Zulie.'

'Zoolee?'

'Aye. Except it's more like Julie, but with a Z at the beginning.'

They looked at each other.

'OK. Zulee.'

She smiled.

'You're getting there.'

'I'm Archie.'

'I know.'

She knew everything about him. She knew his height, his weight, the level of oxygen in his blood, the daily volume of urine he passed, the bore of the hole in his penis, the operations he'd had, every single detail all the way back to 1948 when the National Health Service had been founded and when the soft cardboard Lloyd George pages, each measuring the span of a hand, had begun to be collated into a file. She knew of his two brothers, killed in bloody fighting on the Arakan Peninsula of the Burma Front, and of his four sisters who had died one by one, like falling queens of cards, in the darkness of their beds, from causes that were natural to their lives. She knew about the tumour and the treatment and she knew roughly how long he had left. But she wasn't saying. Was hedging her bets. He didn't blame her. After all, she was only a doctor; she was not God. You couldn't know when folk might just disappear. Fucking bastards, the lot of them. Best to stick to the straight and narrow lies which save you from useless hallucinations. He nodded towards the photograph.

'I was a flyer, you know.'

She wheeled around.

'Oh? You mean a pilot.'

He nodded, slowly. He bet that wasn't in the file. He had never talked about it. The rest, the stuff in his file, the births and deaths, had been just numbers, dates, noises. Now the music had begun.

'In the War. I flew over foreign lands.'

'Dropping bombs? TNT?'

'No! No, I never dropped bombs. I was a fighter pilot. Hurricanes, Spitfires. I shot down enemy aircraft.' He grinned. 'I was real good.'

She looked him straight in the eye. Maybe she knew. O fuck, what the hell. He was falling from a great height. Dying men should be allowed their fantasies. A last smouldering cigarette.

'Ever since I was a child, I always wanted to fly. To soar like

104

an eagle, high above the seas, the rivers, the land.'

That was it said. Embedding it in truth made the lie stronger, bolder, clearer. Maybe he was already hallucinating. Maybe the doc was mad, too.

She reached out. He saw her hand move, and he almost withdrew his beneath the covers. Her skin was soft and reminded him of the skins of the women he had had. Margaret, and the others. Yet there was more. Zulie's touch was electric. He felt his hand tingle, as though she had shut off the blood supply with a tourniquet. She curled the ends of her fingers around his hand, around the deadened palm and the withered joints. And her smile was a scimitar that swept across her face, drawing blood from the lines of her cheeks. She was not young. Her irises were deep, the colour of hazel, and he was pulled into her eyes, into the pupils, where there was sorrow, black as death, and into an echoing hangar so enormous he could not sense where the roof lay, and into the cold darkness of a room at the centre of which lay a wooden box.

This was not an hallucination he could remember ever having had. It was a sound he had never before heard, not in the swinging aerodrome concerts, not in the port and starboard steel of the shipyards, not in the cemetery where the remains of the woman he loved lay slowly rotting, the scimitar shape of her blasted forever into the cold concrete of the hangar.

From the centre of the box there came the sound of a lute. A single note, soundless, impossible to play.

Chapter Six

The sound of the doorbell was unexpected and seemed inordinately harsh and intrusive at that time of night. 11.30 p.m. Zuleikha had been on the point of tidying up, shutting things down and getting ready for bed. She had her system. It wasn't obsessionalism, though at times she had worried that she might be turning into some kind of young spinster. Well, at forty-two she would be considered young nowadays, when the average life-expectancy for females of her social class was pushing eighty-five. Not even halfway there yet! It irritated her that such thoughts popped into her mind as she went towards the bell, answering, snapping almost, at its second more insistent ring.

'OK! OK! I'm coming.'

She slipped the security chain on and angled open the glossed green door. Stepped back as she did so.

His form filled the passageway, blocking out the light from the electric ceiling disc. He had his hands in the pockets of his bomber jacket; a different jacket this time, but still the same colour: black. She couldn't see his face properly; it had acquired the qualities of a silhouette.

'You'd left a message on my machine.' When she didn't reply immediately, he went on. 'The other day. I was out – sorry – didn't get your message till the next morning. I tried phoning back, but I must've missed you.'

Still no reply.

'You remember? We met that morning. By the river's edge?'

Zuleikha recovered enough to blurt out some words.

'Oh yes, yes, of course. It's late, that's all. I didn't expect...'

'I'm sorry. I lost track of the time.' He glanced at his watch, then tapped its glass face, twice. Laughed. 'My watch is bust. Has been for weeks. I still wear it, though. Would feel naked without it.'

There was an awkward moment and then she clicked the door shut, flipped off the chain and then opened it again. For a moment he seemed uncertain, but she pulled back the door a little further and he shifted forwards. She was suddenly aware of the narrowness of the corridor, bookshelves and all, though she knew that really in architectural terms it was quite broad. He moved elegantly in spite of his bulk, and was careful to avoid brushing against her.

He looked different in casual clothes. Younger, perhaps, or just more relaxed. Yet there was no sense of ease about his face. The dark semi-circles beneath his eyes, the beginnings of crow's feet spanning out towards both temples. He's just lost his wife, for God's sake; what do you expect? Grief cut deep into people's faces. She'd seen it, too often. She'd seen it in the mirror. She glanced across at the tiny hollow in the wall which had been created by the flying padlock. Alexander Wolfe was too big for the flat. Anyone over six feet should move in different space, she thought. These Nordic types with their Viking bones bursting through the seams had never been made for civilisation. *Gorae loag*, her mother would've said. White people. Or, even more brutally, just *The Gora*: the White Man. Her mother had maintained that in spite of the fact that water in their countries had always been plentiful, until relatively recently they had never seemed to use it, and had remained in that primeval state of hairy filth whence all flesh had emerged. She sniffed.

'Have a seat.'

'Thanks.'

He took in the sitting room in one sweep, but avoided meeting her eyes, as though his doorstep confidence had suddenly gushed away. He must be wearing sci-fi wide-angle lenses, Zuleikha thought, and then she felt an odd sense of shame. It seemed as though the house was changing around them. Perhaps it had been happening for a while, maybe since the box had arrived, or even before that. Perhaps the horsehair and invisible cornicing of the old tenement flat had sensed the incipience of its arrival. Yet only now, when she really needed to appear … if not exactly happy, then at least controlled … she was behaving like a stereotypical career woman caught off-guard beneath the weight of his undirected gaze. She was regressing and was entering a state worse than childhood, a condition bordering on adolescence. Right there beneath her feet, for the first time in a hundred years, the long planks of dead wood were beginning to stretch. She could feel the dried sap moisten, the rings marking the seasons, and she could feel the whorls and knots tighten. She saw things she'd never before noticed, configurations of which she'd been conditioned to lose awareness, every creak and tug of leather and cotton and glass filling her ears as though it were her own pulse, and for the first time she realised that the air in the sitting-room had become permeated by the odour of old wood. She'd been breathing it for days – for almost two weeks, actually – and only now, with the entry of this other person, had she become aware of it. For God's sake. She was sliding again.

Control. Focus. Behave.

'Would you like a cup of tea?'

A momentary glance. Pallid blue, verging on grey – yes, typical Scottish eyes. Lochs, rain and a sky incipient with loss. The cousins of angels. Long black hair streaked with silver. Feathered wings. What nonsense. Too much cinema and majuscule.

'That'd be nice, thanks.' She had half-risen from the chair when he added: 'Zuleikha, isn't it?'

She nodded.

'That's right. Most people have difficulty with my name. So, to the world, I'm just Zulie.'

'Which do you prefer?'

She shrugged. God, white people were so hung up on names. For them, names were fixed, God-given. In the east, it was different. Not that she knew.

'Whichever's easier.'

'No, but I want to know what you like to be called.'

'Just call me Zulie, then. It's fine. Alex, yes?'

He nodded. Alexander, Sikander, Iskander. Emperor, folk-hero, sufi. He didn't know the half of it.

As she moved into the kitchen, she motioned casually back towards the box, which had remained on her centre table throughout, and at which they had both been trying to avoid looking.

'There it is.'

He nodded slowly. Folded his arms across his knees. Catholic, she thought. An ex-altar boy. Black cloth and white ruffs. Probably brought up by Jesuits. That would account for the nervousness around women. Once she'd thought that particular state of being was confined only to Asian guys, mama's boys, those brought up on a diet of virginal purity and commercial Indian cinema, a good recipe for efficient wanking, but not for life. No, no, she thought: that's applying the general to the particular. Or was it the particular to the general? – she couldn't remember which way round it went. Putting people into boxes. Or boxes into people.

When she returned with a tray of tea and biscuits he was still slumped awkwardly to the side as though the metal skeleton of the chair had been built to the wrong proportions for a man his size. He had one hand still hidden in his jacket pocket, which added to the impression of nervousness and which also reduced his bulk, compressed him into himself, so that oddly he seemed both larger and smaller at the same time. Is it Alex or Alice, she thought, and she felt a smile break across her jaws. She had no mushrooms, either magic or dumb, in the veg-basket.

She set the silver tray on the floor, before the mantelpiece. There was no room on the table. As she knelt and poured, she couldn't make Alex out as his words emerged from behind the box.

'You've already opened it.' There was a note of disappointment in his voice.

'I'm sorry, I…'

Why was she apologising, for God's sake? It didn't belong to him. Yet she had promised. They had discovered the box together. Without his intervention, she thought, it would be out to sea by now – as perhaps would she. The tide would have come in, and the box and she both would have been cast upon the heaving waves of Ireland, or Greenland, or Atlantis. No, that wasn't true. She was fantasising again.

Her hand was trembling as she set down his cup.

'D'you take sugar?' she asked, and she was reminded that her voice had an irritating tendency to rise in frequency at the ends of her sentences. This always happened when she was nervous, and she hated it. Men could have such rich velvety voices, and they didn't even have to try. That deep Ukrainian bass thing. After her mother had died, Zuleikha's voice had been pitched up a tone for weeks. Perhaps she needed elocution lessons. At times the frequency would get so high that her voice would be almost silent.

She slid a coaster across the table and set down the cup filled with steaming British tea, and then she noticed that above his upper lip, where he had neglected to shave properly, a few beads of sweat had already broken through and now glinted in the light in response to the movements of the muscles of his face. His pallid complexion made her think of footballs, the old-style pig's bladder spheres of the tenements that would grow heavy in the afternoon rain of the back courts. He had smiled apprehensively as she had come in. Typical Scot, she thought. In all the time I was clanking about in the kitchen, he did not move one millimetre from his seat, but remained frozen, immobilised on his bum as though he was afraid of causing a rent in the air, or of performing a sacrilegious ritual.

Maybe he's never been in an Asian woman's abode before. There were plenty of old photos on the mantelpiece, a couple of plant pots by the windows and bits and pieces of art pinned to the walls. She'd thought that, like most men, he might have succumbed to curiosity and paced around the room a little, exploring her external environment in feral fashion, gaining tiny sensory clues as to the appoggiaturas of her mind. But she had known, even as she had made her own temporary retreat into the kitchen, that he would not do this, that he would be terrified of being thought of as a snoop, an invader of her private space.

Sanity through barriers. It was the only way in this country, and yes, it had become her way too. Quite early on, Zuleikha had learned to relinquish that swirling and mixing of lives which had been the way of her mother and of those who had gone before. For those generations the unspoken rules had been altogether different, and yet, even in the midst of her relinquishment of this anthropological stream, it had always made her feel creepy – that taut Western envelope which would pullulate invisibly around individuals and subsequently around weathered couples who seemed, at least to the steadfastly single Zuleikha, to be floating like pairs of kidneys in hermetically-sealed containers.

He lifted the cup to his lips and sipped at the burning liquid. The coaster was covered in a fading photo of the summer promenade at Eastbourne. Flower-baskets, street lamps and no clouds. No wind. The sea, a slick azure skin, peeled from the sky.

'Just what I needed,' he said.

His teeth were set in a facial structure which belied her initial impressions of slack and weakness. His cheekbones were set high, so that the flesh of his lower face seemed to be hitched like the awnings of a tent to the bones of his skull. When he grows old he will seem cruel, she thought. God, she was always doing that, trying to imagine what people would look like at the moment of death. Paradoxically, when she visited the sheltered flats of the elderly, she would be drawn to the photographs with which they cluttered their rooms. Photos everywhere, on walls, mantelpiece, windowsills, on top of items of occasional furniture, on doily-draped centre tables, on fridges ... just about everywhere except the toilet-seat. What was that about? Didn't it just make them perpetually sad, to be prepossessed by those dearly beloved who were no longer with them, whose mortal frames were now ashes in a jar? Or by those who had been blown to bits in a V2 attack, or else drowned in the iron seas of the north. Sometimes while the person was speaking she would lose concentration, would lose track of their words and would find herself caught up among the cooling photographic plates of the past. And then she would be attempting to picture the person, the patient, as they had appeared, say, fifty or sixty years earlier during the Second World War, which in Britain, rather sadly, people still referred to as *The War*. She would imagine them making love to some gritty hero of Monte Casino or Biggin Hill, some terrified clerk turned intrepid paratrooper; she would see their bodies, lithe and simian, coursing upon each other in the faint light of some wood-wormed hotel, air-raid sirens howling cherubic symphonies into the darkness.

He nodded towards her television set, half-hidden behind a monkey plant.

'You've got an old-fashioned TV.'

She nodded.

'I hardly watch it, nowadays.' She shrugged. 'And anyway, mostly it just annoys me. The thing is, even as a kid, I always took the baddies' side. Still do, actually. You know, in those cheap American flicks, the ones "Made for TV": *Marvin's Fight Against Dyslexia in Association with a Crusading Biological Mother*; *The Father Who Was Not A Paedophile*; *Don't Worry, Missouri, The Drug-Dealing Villain Didn't Get Away (With It)*. The gloss-white, private aeroplane, accelerating across the hot tarmac, trying to escape from the square-headed cops in the Tin Lizzie. The sun, a clean disc in the Pacific sky. They must have people they pay big bucks to think up the worst possible titles.'

Alex made as if to draw a hoarding-sign in the air. He spoke in a wobbly fake version of an American accent.

'"From LA to Birnham Wood".'

Zuleikha laughed.

'You probably get that all the time,' he acknowledged.

'"Son of Beth". The lively one. Eventually, you know, he was beheaded and fell from the ramparts of his own castle.'

'In the play,' he ventured.

'Yes, of course,' she concurred.

The reality was always different.

Beneath the level of the table, his legs were crossed over each other. As she sat on a high-backed chair opposite him, it occurred to Zuleikha that the reason for his apparent immobility might lie not in Caledonian diffidence or subliminal Irish-Scots Catholic guilt or Presbyterian Scots-Irish reverence for boundaries, but partly in his stature and partly in their mutual hypnotic awkwardness around the box. It sat on the table between them, and because Alex was at a lower level than she, the upper edge of the box corresponded to the cut of their necks. Calvin would've been proud; neither of them had touched the chocolate-free biscuits.

She shuffled in her chair, her tail-bone roving for a plumper bit of cushion. It was her habit, which she sank into whenever she was nervous. The tea tasted good. She hid her gaze in the swirling steam of the cheap red porcelain and she felt her face begin to sweat. She looked up.

'I was very sorry to hear about your wife,' she began.

He turned away and gazed at the mantelpiece, suddenly interested in the old photos of her parents and other assorted family members. She wondered whether he was doing to her what she did to others, and the thought disconcerted her. She had expected an exchange of platitudes, though she was aware that such an expectation was presumptuous on her part. Nonetheless, the exposed nature of the situation prompted her to continue.

'Had she been ill for a while?'

She'd assumed that Alex's wife, whose name she still did not know, but whom she imagined must've been of a similar age to Alex, had died of natural causes. Cancer, perhaps, or some bizarre brain haemorrhage. It was unusual, though – a woman of that age, just dying. This wasn't the Age of Consumption, after all. He looked straight at her. She was going on instinct, and it had led her far, far out. She could walk on water for only so long. His expression was cool, the muscles of his face sat midway between the tensed and relaxed states, his eyes crystal. It was the opposite of what she'd expected. Too much mirror psychoanalysis. TV shows with immensely obese people screaming at one another. The ring-mistress clutching a mike. Estuary voices. Ranting populism. Fake soul music. Fake democracy. He shook his head.

'It wasn't illness.'

'Oh.' This was real. She wasn't sure whether he had shaken his head because he'd been annoyed at something she'd said, or because he was recalling the events surrounding his wife's death. Yet he didn't elaborate. 'I'm sorry. I didn't mean to pry.' Her finger curled more tightly around the thick lip of the cup's handle.

'You're not prying. There's no question of prying, because there's nothing to hide. No great secret, no mystery. Just death, pure and simple.'

'I didn't mean...'

Her skin was burning, the tiny muscles, the tendons that allowed the joints to move. Her hand, her face. Yet she was frozen. There was a pause.

'Listen, I came about the box.'

'Yes, I know.'

'I don't really know why. It seems so stupid, really. An old rotting piece of driftwood.'

She could see that at one time the box must have been covered in bright paint, though now the colours had become indeterminate, a dirtyish dark-brown, and all that remained were a few bits of hard flaking gloss. At last she removed her scalded index finger from the crescentic fire of the cup and ran it down over the cracked leaves of paint, cooling the skin-creases, the deeper flesh. Some of the pieces fell off as she did this, revealing beneath the outer shell other earlier layers, and because these had been protected from the elements, their colours had been better preserved. She hadn't noticed any of this before. In fact, she realised that, although she had obsessed over the box almost constantly, apart from when she had prised open the lid, she had hardly touched it since that morning when she – they – had plucked it from the river.

'I wonder whose it was,' she said.

'Is.'

'Pardon?' She swung round.

'It may still belong to someone.'

It hadn't occurred to her that the box might have an owner. Like a stray dog with an engraved studded collar. She wondered whether, perhaps, the box itself might contain some clue as to its age or provenance. It been thrown into the Clyde, right, but might it have been lost accidentally, or even stolen? Surely not the latter, she thought, since the padlock had been intact when she'd found it. And to whom had the clothes belonged? She gulped her tea, felt it sear the lining of her gullet. A burning bag in her belly.

'Nice place you've got here.' He was glancing around again. Searchlights.

'Thanks.'

She exhaled like a fire-eater, slowly, a measured ejection of used-up breath coursing invisibly across the room. It was a crazy way to drink tea, to burn out her insides, but she found the caffeine buzz happened faster and much more effectively that way. She liked the stuff really strong, two tea-bags per mug, swirled around, steeped in the hot liquid and then squeezed hard against the porcelain, leached of all the tannin they were worth. Sometimes she would leave the bags in, to fester right to the edge of bitterness. Tea-junky. Hyperactive vicar. Her one and only real vice. Typical Scot. Muslim, in the rain.

'What d'you do for a living, Zuleikha?'

She tensed on the edge of the chair, her hamstrings and the muscles of her buttocks and loins clenching tightly against the smooth wood. She'd pegged him wrong; he was not very Scottish at all. Too direct, too discomfiting. His deep voice a breath of fresh air. But maybe it was just the recent bereavement, she thought, it jarred people out of their usual orbits, and sometimes they never got back again. Just continued to float in perpetuity, in darkness.

'I work as a doctor. A GP.'

Even when she had been a fully paid-up partner in a group practice, she had never said, *I am a doctor.* There had seemed a definitive horror about stating it in totality, as though to have done so would have been to have admitted that her occupation had come to define her. Anyway, she knew that he'd already known what she did 'for a living', he'd seen the stethoscope in the car. Perhaps he'd just wanted her to be specific. Was she a brain surgeon, or a bladder specialist?

'What about you?'

He shrugged, and gazed down into his still-steaming half-empty cup. Swirled the tea around anti-clockwise, twice.

'I'm between jobs right now.' He looked up at her, put down the mug and spread out his palms. Six pink lines. Lots of creases. 'I've worked in offices, mainly, doing this and that, you know, white-collar stuff, pen-pushing. Short-term contracts. It's the way, nowadays. Bar work, too.' He lifted the mug to his lips and took a great gulp. In his eyes, in his face, suddenly, cynicism shifted into despair. 'Once I was a computer programmer. Listen, a drink would be great.' He glanced down again at the tea. 'I mean, a real drink.'

'You driving?'

Fucksake, what was she, the Health Promotion Unit? The Police?

'Nope. Came by bus. You got any spirits?'

'As opposed to spirit?'

He smiled. Caffeine buzz. High cheekbones. Very Nordic. Or Chinese. Or Yewpeean.

'Do the two not go together? Chinese and Nordic. And anyway, what's "Yoopian"?'

She startled, as she realised that she must have whispered the last couple of thoughts under her breath. She waved him away.

'Oh, never mind. It's not important.'

'Secrets...'

'No secrets. Je ne regrette rien.'

She wondered what else she'd said without realising. Sign of madness. There must be some kind of syndrome – named, probably, after a late-nineteenth-century French neurologist who had been a brothel buddy of Debussy, or Rodin, or one of those.

'Speaking of which, do you have absinthe?'

It was her turn to smile. Absinthe, indeed. Now we really are turning Frenchie.

'For God's sake, man, what d'you think this is, a trendy West-Endie bar?'

'Sorry.'

A smile played about the corners of his lips.

This is the normal state of his lips, she thought: they turn up a little at the ends. He can't help it. Like those Indian romantic leads, he often looks as though he's on the brink of happiness. Mothers' sons. She felt an odd jump in her chest. God, simple things.

'I have a bottle of Pernod ... was saving it up.'

'Saving it up? For what?'

She shrugged. That kind of lip architecture would mean that when he cried, he would tear apart the hearts of those around him.

'You want ice with it?'

He nodded.

She manoeuvred the mugs back onto the tray. Lifted it like an offering in her palms. Bastard.

She teetered back with a silver tray and two glasses.

'This okay?'

She held up the bottle so he could see the label. Alex fired a glance at her, nodded, and then watched as she poured the clear liquid from the bottle. She hesitated for a moment, then asked,

'Did your wife work? Outside the home, I mean.'

She dropped a lump of ice into each glass, watching as the liquid turned opaque. Her hands were liver-clamps, slow but steady. He took the glass which she offered, and for a brief moment their fingers touched. His were oddly cold, like bone. God. He does need a drink, she thought. So did she. He was already sipping. Holding her glass in her right hand, she sat down again and folded her legs diagonally like scissors, with her left hand and wrist placed horizontally across her lap. The nun position. If nuns had a position.

'She was a travelling saleswoman. Drove all over the country. She often stayed in motels, bed-and-breakfasts and so on. She used to phone me from the strangest places. Up in the farthest islands and beyond the reach of the mobile networks, it would be a red

116

iron box up on a hill by a one-track road overlooking a gleaming loch. She would describe the entire scene, you know, sands, smells and all. Big sky, clean air, sheep troddles – the lot. Made me really jealous, sitting there in the sick-building-syndrome office, buried in jargon and paper and cowered by psychopathic blue-suited bosses. Number One haircuts.'

'Yeah, I know the sort. Sharks. Wankers.'

'It was a bit of an escape for me, listening to her describing those vistas. Like I could almost smell the long waving grass, the white stones at the bottoms of lochs. Clean blue water. Sometimes, it was almost like poetry. Her voice…' He cleared his throat. 'Which is pretty good going, when you've been tramping around all day, knocking on people's doors, selling them life insurance.' He laughed, but his voice was bitter, cynical. He swirled the ice around in his glass, slowly at first, but then faster as though he were keen for it to melt, to seep into and strengthen the alcohol. 'Eventually, it was doubly ironic that she ended up working in call centres.'

There was a pause, during which Zuleikha almost began to wish she'd bought a fake antique grandfather clock. She reached across and extended the plate of biscuits towards him. Thank God for trivia.

It was nearly midnight. The amber shadows of leaves flickered across the walls. There was almost always a breeze of some sort in this city and now Zulie watched the fragmentary waltz of the shadows across her room, a whirling consort which made the old photographs on the mantelpiece seem somehow sinister. She drew her arms around her chest. She should really have gone and got a jumper and a cigar, but somehow she had felt unable to leave this table. Alex was sipping his fourth glass quickly, as though he was becoming frustrated at his inability, on this night, to become inebriated. He was eyeing the box. They had both been avoiding the large object that lay at the centre of the room, at the heart of her house. The mixture of liquids – tea and Pernod, what a combination, she thought – swirled around in her belly, causing her to bloat as though she were pregnant or dead. The box. It was like a giant blind-spot; it weighed heavily behind her eyelids and scumbled the substance of her brain. She was on her fourth glass too. In its silence, in the shared silence which they had spun around it, the box had grown huge, so that now it seemed to fill the whole room, the big city, the dark night, with its presence, and she knew that no matter how many glasses they both drank it would be impossible to slip around it and escape. She took a deep breath.

'I suppose we should open the lid,' she began, trying to catch his eye.

The bottle should have been emptied by now, given the amount they'd imbibed, but it was like a bottomless receptacle and it smelled of midnight.

'I just took off the padlock,' she said as they sat, a little later, allowing strong coffee to inflict first-degree burns on their palates. His sugar intake was worrying. Four spoons. Incipiently diabetic. Why was she bothering about this guy?

'And what did you find when you took off the padlock?' he asked.

She shrugged. Glanced up at the fake Constable print on the wall above his head. Late mad psychedelic Constable.

'Nothing,' she said.

'What, the box is empty?'

What was this, Jesuit interrogation? Mad eyes, broken twitching lips. Montgomery Clift. *Are you, or have you ever been, a homosexual?*

'No, not exactly.'

From somewhere, a clock began to tick. Fucking ridiculous, thought Zuleikha. How can a clock begin to tick? It's just that we become aware of its sound at a certain point in time and then, later, we lose awareness of it again. But the clock has never stopped. Its pendulum, or whatever digital circuit nowadays passes for a pendulum, has swung on beyond us. We cannot observe anything without altering that which we observe. In which case, nothing is real. Ah, the joyous light profundity of late-night caffeine. Every second person can be Einstein. Except Einstein, who is a pin-up poster. Then she remembered that she did not possess a mechanical clock.

She put down her cup and saucer, stood up and reached over the top of the box. As she did so, the hairs of her forearms brushed against its top. She felt a tingling along her skin. That had never happened to her with wood, and these days Zuleikha felt more like a sponge than an ecstatic. But this evening things were different. Impressions flooded into her like river-water into the sea. Alex smelled of animal hide, polished wood and music, while she smelled of the river, of a deep heaving death in the stone hollows which lay beneath the surface of the Clyde. First, Archie and the Luftwaffe and the swaying orchestras of the sky, and now this. It was all she could do to keep her bare feet planted firmly on the floor. They were in direct contact with boards which once had been measured out by the feet of the dead. *When much of Britain had been covered in forest, when kings had been gods and chapels had been carved in white stone in designs copied from secret, Byzantine formulae and when wise wandering bearded men had carried books in the deep whorls of their brains across the seas to this blank land of Alba...*

Alex had remained seated. She drew all ten digits towards the far edge of the box, the edge near Alex, and plunged her nails into the crack.

'Are you all right? Zulie...? Zuleikha?' he was mouthing, but his words seemed to come from some distant place, their meaning broken down into those of the separate letters. Her name... He was craning over her as she slumped back into her chair. In her cup, the surface of the coffee swayed and jigged with their movement. 'Are you okay?' he repeated, as though it was some kind of mantra. Hare hare.

'I'm fine. Just a bit dizzy. I must've got up too fast.'

Her feet suddenly felt very cold. She slid one over the other and rubbed, trying to warm the skin and muscle. Fuck sake, would it ever be summer in this country? The only land she had known was steeked down hard, like bone, like granite. The lid had fallen back from her, the box had closed again. The lid was not so heavy, she thought. At the last moment I lost my nerve. Huh! What's new? Her body was trembling all over as though an electric current had just shot through the axons.

'Have a sip of coffee. You should've put some sugar in it.'

He offered her the cup. He had removed his leather jacket at last, and as he leaned across her the logo on his tee-shirt, a large grinning eagle of some sort, filled most of her vision. His hands were large but elegant, the fingers long and tapered like the very fine fountain-pens with which, decades earlier, her mother had used to write letters home.

'Sugar's not good for you. I should know.'

Home sweet home.

'Heal thyself, doc.'

He was smiling. The sides of his head cracking apart with the smile. Death, so close to the skin. The box, falling into darkness.

She remembered her mother preparing to write, gazing out of the dining-room window and holding a maroon-coloured fountain-pen between her thumb and her forefinger, its tip hovering above blue airmail paper which had the thickness and transparency of human skin. Watermarks on the wood. Her mother's eyes, reflecting the clouds through the glass. Times past. Holy times. And Alex smelled of holiness, of cruet silver and blood wine, of trans-whatsit, of aftershave and horse spunk. Sikander, Alasdair, Alastair, Alistair, Alister. Alexis, Alexei, Iskander. Sasha, The Great Defender. The touch of his fingers as he handed her the porcelain cup. Rough sandy skin. Beryl blue irises. Silky, Persian, nastaliq. What's in a name?

At last her body began to warm up – everywhere, that is, except her feet. She knew she ought to go and put on some socks and slippers; she knew she should never have answered the door in the state she was in, bare feet and all, but his ringing had been so insistent and anyway, she was a post-modern woman. No hang-ups, her life and views a segue of half-truths, of observed – and therefore altered – phenomena, and her emotions deriving from these in a mixture of rational uncertainty, irrational analysis, necessary compromise, unremitting cynicism and an underlying hope of possible transfiguration. Yes, well; in this world of disappearing dots there was nothing wrong with strapping yourself to moveable anchors. Zuleikha could feel the iron points of the anchors scrape hidden calligraphies in the black sand of the ocean floor. Words which would never be read, save through the illiterate fibres and integuments of the body. She knew almost nothing about him, and what he had told her might well have been a pack of choir-boy lies. Jesuitical dialectics. Calvinistic elisions. Who, after all, was this Alex-man, this river-bank being? Maybe she was hallucinating him, perhaps his nervousness was merely a projection of her own insidious insecurities. And he had everything on her: her desperation that morning, her ridiculous Edwardian swooning now, her betrayal in forcing open the box when, if only she had waited for him to arrive, they might have been able to open it together, without force, and then perhaps the box would have yielded up more than fake static and the disordered visions and sky anchors of a dying flyer.

She reached over and pulled up the lid again.

She wondered whether perhaps the layers of boxes sealed by lids might form part of a single structure. It was not boxes-within-boxes – no, there was only one container, but it seemed to consist of countless levels, each cube just a little smaller than the last. What was this? Baboushka dolls? Scientific laws kept expanding while, like the universe, the box kept contracting. Perhaps it would go on forever. Like that book by some weird Ecuadorean, a story of mushrooms and Eros, which ended up being the story of just one letter that kept repeating, backwards and forwards across the text, from the first page to the last. Once you began to read the book, you would never be able to finish it. It was both infinite and infinitesimal. She couldn't recall now which letter of the alphabet it had been, not that it mattered much, since everything pointed towards it anyway. Wherever you began, you would always end up there. The heart of the labyrinth. *A*, perhaps: *Aleph*, maybe, or *Alba*, or *Alex*. His mellifluous voice. She looked straight at him, into his eyes, and this time he did not look away. Behind them was silence. There was no intrusive percussion of a timepiece, and no hum of the city. Even the breeze had been subsumed into the night. In the place where Zuleikha had made her house, a door opened silently.

'They're just numbers,' Zuleikha said, and as soon as she'd said it she felt stupid. Alex did not reply, but held up the piece of paper to the light as though he was trying to spot something in its substance. It was folio size, which was rather unusual. Zuleikha would've expected it to have been A1 or A3 or similar, but then, she thought, why am I expecting anything? This whole thing is so bizarre and yet somehow I find myself swept up in its crazy logic. She stepped back a couple of paces, as though there was a need physically to distance herself from both Alex and the box and all it contained. Or might contain. He had rolled the sleeves of his black cotton tee-shirt right up above the points of his shoulders as though he was intent on displaying the deltoids on either side, as though he was trying to impress her, as though he was a working man preparing for a long night-shift. It's crazy, she thought. Ever since the day by the river, I have been completely insane. If somebody – a patient, say – had come to her with this story, she would've been seriously worried about their mental state. Would've thought them, at the very least, some kind of incipient hysteric; at worst, a loculated psychotic. Someone who, to all intents and purposes, appeared and functioned quite normally but who carried an acorn of madness in them, well-hidden and pertaining to only one particular aspect of their lives.

Maybe that's what I am, she thought. Maybe I'm mad and don't know it. No trouble at all; the lid just comes open, as though it had never been in the water in the first place, as though the hinges are not rusted with years of oxidation, as though it recently had been oiled or greased. And in our drunkenness, what do we discover in the box? A sheet of paper. One sheet, folio size, cream paper. Clean as skin, no yellowing. Antique, this is not. Vintage, veteran? No-one held this piece of paper aloft in one hand while between the descending Zeppelin bombs, boom, boom, boom, they cranked up the front end of an automobile motor, round-and-round-and-round-and-round-and-round until their wrist snapped. No. And covering the top two-thirds of the paper, in what looks like size ten font, have been typed a series of numbers. Just meaningless random numbers. She blinked hard, twice, and then repeated the action to allow her contact lenses to slip over the surfaces of her corneas. Her vision was starting to blur; it was so bloody late – or early, she wasn't sure. At this time of year morning came quickly, but sometimes it was so dull, so overcast, that it might just as well have been midnight. She went over to the curtains and pulled aside the edge nearest the sash. Outside, the streetlights were still on, but their glow had turned anaemic and the rain was falling almost inaudibly from a steel-grey sky. Zuleikha sighed, whether from tiredness or depression she wasn't sure.

'They're numbers,' Alex repeated, as though her words of a few minutes earlier had only just reached him, as though between them there lay a thick layer of ether or else ice.

She turned back around. He was standing with his legs apart, holding the sheet in the palm of his right hand. He had rolled it up as though it were a scroll, and his clenched fingers were looped around it. His feet were planted firmly on the floor, as though he was preparing for battle. Or maybe he's just trying to stand up straight, she thought. Suddenly, every movement was leaden, cold. Glass.

'It's probably a joke,' she sneered. 'Some computer buff's idea of fun.'

'A joke ... or a code.'

'Oh, come on!'

He shook his head.

'There's something about the series of numbers. I don't know what it is, but I don't think they're just random.'

'How can you tell? Are you some kind of mathematician? I thought you said you worked in an office.'

'I did work in an office,' he corrected her, 'but now I don't work at all.'

'So how do you know?'

'I don't know.'

She took a deep breath. Her throat tasted of dry shit.

'I'm gonna get some water.'

'That would be good.'

I didn't offer you one, she thought as she tramped off towards the kitchen.

She re-emerged carrying a tray laden with two glasses of water, several slices of toast, a cafetière, mugs and a jug of steaming-hot milk. Alex hardly noticed, he was so busy poring over the paper. He had smoothed it out on the table before him so that its far edge brushed against the side of the box, and he was tracing along the lines of type as though searching for some hidden pattern, a picture perhaps, like those coloured dot-drawings they had back in the surgery, the ones they would use to tell whether or not someone was colour-blind. If you saw a number you were okay, but if it was a rabbit that popped out at you, if the dots joined together to make a snout and two ears, then you had the defective gene. But that generally applied only to men. Like so much shit in life, it was X-linked. They got it from their mothers.

Maybe that was why she hadn't inherited the essence of her mother's looks or aristocratic bearing. That precious sense of innate superiority which allows you to interact in a relaxed and normal manner with anyone and everyone, regardless of social station. It was important to be aware of the fact that, far from becoming a classless society (she wondered whether in the history of humankind such a thing had ever really existed) this country remained bound, fettered in tangles of words, in the way one spoke and in the manner of one's comportment. It was a kind of carnate ID card. The higher the score, the more access one gained. It applied to everything, to every walk of life. In the 1960s – long before Zuleikha's time – the barriers had become a little more permeable, but really the divisions had just become more subtle. Nasrin Zeinab had not been insane, but had possessed an immanent awareness of herself. More cod psychology. Okay, it's five-thirty in the morning. She set the tray down beside the paper, careful not to spill any of the hot milk.

'Thanks,' he said, without looking up. 'That's just what I need right now. Strong, I hope?'

'Two scoops per cup. Strength Number Five. Blows your bloody head off! You'll end up thinking you're Jesus Christ or the fifty-seventh Boddhisatva of Napoleon. And hot milk, too.' Not the pallid old British stuff, she was about to add, but thought better of it. You never knew who might be in the Territorial Army Reserve, or the SAS. She peered over his shoulder.

He had taken out a biro and was tracing thin lines between, or rather along, the rows of numbers. And as she watched, he drew lines downwards along the columns, light-blue looping lines that billowed off-course in the middle so that really they were more like arcs. It was as if he couldn't draw straight. Normally this kind of thing would've frustrated her and made her want to grab the biro from his hand and draw the lines herself (though she had no idea how he knew which columns and rows to link). But this time, the slow, barely certain movement of his pen, the manner in which he built the levels of ink, lightly going over each one again and again, began to have a hypnotic effect on her. But she was not sleepy. She was beginning to get a caffeine uplift and her mouth no longer tasted of excreta. As she leaned over him, her thin acrylic jumper was almost touching the angle of his left shoulder. He smelled of night sweat. Not night sweats, she thought: he's not got TB; but more like the smell of old burned leaves. He doesn't smoke. Yet he never said anything when I lit up. Usually, all you get is an opened mouth and: *Doctor, you should know better!* Even other smokers became self-righteous with guilt. You became like the old, dead Queen; you had to fart into a vacuum.

But Alex hadn't prejudged her. She hated herself for it, but that kind of thing always resulted in a sense of relief. For a long time she had fought against this relief, which seemed to her so much a sign of weakness or programming, the conditioning of a penta-millenium of patriarchy. But as she had grown older Zuleikha had come to rest more easily with her own emotions, she had stopped hectoring and told herself instead that it was simply her openness, her open heart, which made her respond in this way. And in spite of the tiredness which cramped behind her eyes and which laced her skin with a sweat cold and heavy as chain-mail; in spite of the oddness of the situation, Zuleikha felt more relaxed at that moment than she had felt for years. Somehow, in the concatenation of his smell, the quiet rhythm he made as he drew, the tousled swathe of his black hair in the lightening amber of the morning and the rough cotton of his dappled-black shirt (from which, she saw, two stitches close to the upturned horseshoe of the collar had come loose) Zuleikha felt the incipience of an unspoken, and perhaps wordless, knowledge about this man. And as she watched, though the numbers jumped around between the rows and columns, the ink of Alex's pen and the ink of the numbers seemed to merge into one blue-black sweep, *like his hair, like his eyes*, on the paper which was almost the colour of his skin, and through the curtains she felt the rain accelerate and disappear into the seeping dark of the tarmac and she felt it flood into streams and rivers which flowed like black blood towards the sea.

He must be a bit mad, she thought, but then we're in it together.

After around thirty minutes of this, Alex slumped back, tossed the biro down, closed his eyes and let out a long sigh. He folded his hands behind his head. He craned his neck backwards, then to the sides and upwards, and then he stretched. He flashed her

125

a look. The blue of his eyes had faded to gun-metal grey. He was exhausted.

'It's late,' he said.

She laughed.

'It's early.'

He glanced around the room, and then shook his head.

'I'm sorry. I should have left hours ago.'

'No, no, it's all right. I kept plying you with drink and caffeine.' She nodded at the tray. 'Have a toast,' she ventured, holding up a single, limp piece of browned bread. 'It's gone cold.' But he was still staring at her. She let her arm fall to her side. She looked at the box, and spoke slowly. 'We had to open it.'

'Perhaps we should never have lifted it from the river.'

'I lifted it.'

'Perhaps it wasn't meant to happen. Perhaps we were wrong.'

He was at it again. She felt a rising annoyance.

'If anyone was wrong, it was me.' She pointed forcefully at her chest, then felt idiotic as she realised that it was the hand with the toast.

He glanced down at the piece of paper.

'I think it's a code of some sort,' he began.

'Big deal.'

'What d'you mean?'

'I mean, we've been up all night, and I've really enjoyed it or whatever, but there's this piece of paper in the box and that's that.'

'But it's only the first lid, given that the one you opened by yourself wasn't really a lid, just an outer shell.'

'How d'you work that out?' she asked, shifting her bum against the springy synthetic stuffing of the chair.

'Well,' he said, and he brought his hands together as though preparing for a flamenco performance or a martial arts exhibition, 'you had to force open the lid, cut the padlock and all that.'

She nodded, slowly.

'So?'

'So the lid we opened tonight – last night – just opened. No force was required. It simply lifted on its hinges.' He sipped at the lukewarm coffee. Grimaced.

She leapt up.

'I'll make you a fresh cup. Strength Number Five.'

He shook his head.

'No, it's okay, really. I like...'

'... cold coffee?'

They burst into laughter. It was now properly morning. He got up.

'Look, Zuleikha...'

'Zulie.'

'Okay, Zulie. I'd really better be going.'

'Are you working? Oh no, I'm sorry, I forgot. You don't work.'

'No, I just play my lute.'

'Pardon?'

'The lute. A musical instrument.'

'Yes, Alex. I do know what a lute is. You never mentioned it before.'

'There was no reason to. I mean, it's not the first thing I come out with when I...'

She glanced down. He was holding the scroll – again he had rolled up the paper – in his right hand. She smiled.

'You must give me a performance.'

'No, no, it's not like that.'

'What, you're still learning?'

'With an instrument, one is always learning.'

'So you can play properly. I mean, you're not just a beginner.'

'Seven years ... maybe more.'

'So, next time we meet, you must play some. I've never heard the sound of a lute. Live, I mean.'

'Oh, the lute's dead. Dead wood.'

'Very funny.'

'I'll bring it with me next time. It's quite big, quite bulky.' He scanned the room. 'But it should fit here.'

Now he was smiling. He moved past her into the corridor.

She hesitated. He hadn't asked her round to his place. She found that slightly odd. It would have been the natural thing to have done. The normal, sane thing.

'It's an unusual instrument to want to play – nowadays, at least.'

'Not sexy, you mean.'

She flushed. Shook her head. Shrugged.

'No, but I mean that's a good thing – that someone should want to learn to play a quiet lute rather than a bawling electric guitar or a set of snare drums.'

'Yeah, I suppose it is a good thing.'

God, she thought, he's spent only a few hours in my house, in my life, and already he's managed to make me feel really stupid and gauche. This was why people went on those self-improvement courses. To improve themselves, so that they could riposte a line of words, flourish a silver foil to meet just such a statement. Her mother would've retorted with some intensely witty, possibly risqué comment, and the big man would have found himself (metaphorically-speaking; we're talking mind-games here) sprawled on the polished wooden floor. The image made her smile, and the embarrassing flush receded. Perhaps I need to learn some aristo manners. How to be elegantly rude. But first, there was the box.

As though he'd read her thoughts, he span back around and said:

'After all, we'll have to open the next lid.'

'We could do it now.'

He shook his head.

'I tried. While you were getting the coffee, I tried to prise open the next lid. But it wouldn't budge. I couldn't see how or where it might be fixed. No locks, no glue. And it wasn't as though it was wedged in awkwardly or anything. It was just immovable.'

Anger billowed in her throat. He had tried to open the box when she'd been out of the room. And now he was spiriting away the sheet, the dancing numbers. Whatever they might or might not mean, and however much she'd relaxed in his company, this was overstepping the mark. He had not pried into her belongings in a manner that might have been considered normal for a guy, yet now he was on the point of stealing that which lay at the centre of her home. The box, and all it might contain, belonged only to her. Not to the person who had cut the wood, not to the artisan who had built it, nor to the one who had typed out the numbers, nor to the one who had sealed the cask and set it adrift. No. Somehow, this box had sailed into her life, she had plucked it from the stream, and now it was hers. Perhaps it was like a transmigrating soul. It

128

could have only one owner at any one time. And right now, that owner was Zuleikha Chashm Framareza MacBeth. But it was difficult really to be angry at someone with whom you were in the first stages of infatuation.

'Immovable – like the rock?' she said quietly. He turned away again and headed for the door. She raised her voice. 'By the way, where are you going with that thing?' She was like a third-form teacher: *Bring that ruler back, now!*

'Umn?' He held up the scroll. 'Oh, this. I thought I'd continue working on it at home. You never know, when I'm fresh … I could feed it into a computer or something. See what comes out.'

She shook her head.

'The scroll stays here.'

He smiled.

'Scroll? What do you mean, scroll?'

She did not return the smile.

'Yeah. It stays in this house. If you want to come and work on it, you're more than welcome. But I cannot allow anyone to remove any part of the box from this place.'

'What? What are you talking about? We found it together.'

'No. I found the box. You helped me get it to the car. It could've been anyone.'

'Thanks.'

'Look, I know you probably saved me from slipping down into the deep current, and I'm really, really grateful for that…'

'Did I?' For a moment, he looked puzzled, and then he shrugged. 'Oh, any time.'

'But on this one point, I must insist.'

She was in doctor mode now. Thank God I'm not working today, she thought. If she had been, some poor unfortunate would've got purgatory.

He shrugged again.

'Okay. I could make a photocopy and work on that. It was what I did, when I had a job. You know, computers. I could try feeding this into a program – it's what I used to do, a long time ago. One of the things, anyway.'

'No. No copies. It stays here.'

She pointed down at the floor, and then felt ridiculous. A grown woman, she thought. Fuck sake. She blamed it on the insomnia. This. The intensity of it all.

Reluctantly, he held out the scroll. As she took it from him, their fingers became entangled so that the paper came loose and fell to the floor. They both bent down to retrieve it and their heads banged.

He didn't hold out his hand for her to shake. It was a Scottish thing, that. No physical contact. Just a kind of invisible tautness across the room. Yet perhaps it was more than cultural, perhaps it was a deliberate avoidance on his part. She felt a little guilty as she closed the door behind him, and a second later she had pulled it open again and was shouting down the stairwell. It happened so fast, she didn't have time to think about it.

'And next time, I'll make dinner!'

He turned, and smiled at her. Met her eyes for an instant, then looked back down at the worn stone of the staircase. A hundred and twenty years old, give or take. So many paces. She felt a sinking sensation in the vault of her chest as soon as she'd let out the words. Hardly a rapier, she thought. More like a soft, pliant cushion. A conditioned response which had been evinced from her because at some level she still expected it of herself. God! We set the bar so high, we end up spending our whole lives limbering up and never actually leaping. She remembered some Indian saying, one of those convenient aphorisms one found in glossy books for the uncomfortably-off, that went something like this:

A woman can be submissive because she has so much to give; she is ever-full.

Bull-fucking-shit, in any language. Empty or full, a woman is not a bloody vessel.

From the side of her large front-room window, Zuleikha watched Alex's form recede into the undefined grey of the morning. She gazed through the voile of the rain, but he disappeared before he reached the street corner.

Chapter Seven

Zuleikha felt a growing unease about going back to Archie's house. It was always the same with terminally ill patients; they reminded her of the basic fact that, in every case, ultimately she and her box of tricks would lose. In the stench of putrefaction which, she was convinced, began to arise long before the onset of multiple organ failure and clinical brain death, Zuleikha could smell her own mortality. And then, after she had lost her own mother to what people called 'The Big C', every time she had to confront it at work it brought the whole fucking thing back. And it always seemed to occur at the time when the day became set, at around eleven a.m. And she couldn't cope with it that early. Midnight was manageable: she was alone and that was better. This having to shore up a front, to be professionally adept, to be simultaneously dispassionate and empathetic, and all in the glare of a bulging July sun, this was becoming intolerable. Sometimes, she thought, it could be easier for a woman. It was probably the only thing in life that was easier; men had to maintain that awful macho thing and the expectation was mutual. Whereas Zulie once had hugged a tramp – well, he hadn't really been a tramp, but he had been technically homeless. An old guy in a hostel. So, technically she had hugged him. Well he'd been dying of cirrhosis, for Christ's sake. All these lonely people, they all came from somewhere, but their pasts were as inscrutable as … as the box whose secrets she felt she might never unlock.

Maybe there was something about that. Oldies. I prefer mature men, yes. Ahm … no, she thought, as she swung the car a little too recklessly into the long road which would take her to the post-war housing estate in which Archie lived. Actually, I don't. But the younger ones just aren't available any more.

And anyway, younger men didn't have pasts. A long swathe of darkness, a hidden period of silence could be attractive to a woman, no doubt about it: scars on the soul rendered a certain mystique. There should always be some a part of a person's life which would be forever unrevealed. Like Archie and his planes. Or 'aircraft', as he'd corrected her, more than once. RAF guys apparently never referred to flying machines as 'planes', but always as 'aircraft', or else as a specific model, like Junkers Ju 87 or Lancaster BI Special or Hawker Hurricane Mark IV. It was that kind of thing – she'd never have found out about Archie's Air Force days if he hadn't been dying on her.

All he had in the way of family were a couple of distant nephews, one in Australia and another in Dundee. When they'd come to visit, separately, the Australian one had seemed very pleasant and appreciative of what Zulie and her staff were doing, whereas the Dundonian had been all arched eyebrows and obsessional bourgeois innuendo. Like he'd had a medico-legal litigation lawyer stuffed somewhere up his very tight white, uhm, sleeve. Must be that biting easterly breeze, Zuleikha thought. It makes you purse your lips and pinch your words, and after a while it becomes your whole mindset. Searing wind across granite. Or was that Aberdeen? Anyway, Glasgow was different in that respect; an instant soaking made even the sternest lawyer look like Charlie Chaplin. Or perhaps it was the Hibernian seam. Argh, thank Gad for the Oirish! That glowing self-deprecation which was our salvation. Sometimes she'd wondered whether she might have some of those corpuscles in her blood, laughing genes scattered like seeds through her own DNA, a Cuchulain Aífe or two, offering tall heroes the friendship of the thighs and then leaping, armless, to lie between the sufi, Jahanara and the ray of light, Roshanak.

Even the big, heaving Proddy mobs of Ibrox and Bridgeton had it in them, they couldn't deny it. Under the Union hard-ons of their Jacks rippled a dark green sea, a swaying Beltane sun. One never knew from where one had really arisen. In spite of her mother's insistent genealogies, the long-toothed love-bite of Sunni Islam, the stencilled Afghan-Mughal-Persian axis and all, there might yet be a maverick in there somewhere. A traveller perhaps, or a merchant. Or even a friar, a Doctor Mirabilis who metaphysically had come to the Murcian lands of the Umma to learn science, anatomy and other secrets of the well. Maybe that was why she'd been impelled to become a doctor when really her temperament had always been much too soft for the job. She'd always been far too impressionable, too thin-skinned, they'd said. Not a good thing in Glasgow and not a good thing in this game.

You ended up trying to please everyone; you would do almost anything to avoid hurt, or at least confrontation. Though over the years you also learned how to pretend, to act like those small fishes who puffed themselves up to appear larger than they were. Still, she reminded herself tautly, I'm not the one dying of cancer.

It was something in his eyes, she decided, as yet again she examined his chest. The lank sparse hair growth was now confined to the upper areas of his shoulders and, together with a layer of cold sweat, this imparted an almost marine glow to his skin. And now she had it on her fingers: the smell of tumour. Mesothelioma. Technically it was not cancer, not carcinoma; it derived from other types of cells. But it behaved like a virulent form of cancer and was invariably fatal. Survival rate: zero per cent. Zuleikha had heard of a woman who had developed the disease simply because many years earlier, every evening on her father's return from the shipyards, she had used to leap up from the fireplace rug and run to embrace him and the fairy-dust he had carried on his clothes. There had been a number of years during which the bosses had known of the dangers, but had said and done nothing. So the bastard Gods of the Shipyards had rewarded love with death. Mesothelioma. It gestated in the middle of the lung, in the heart of the tissue, and it pushed out through the pores. She sat back down on the bed, played about with the coverlet, rolled the thick cotton beneath her fingers. It was an old-style coverlet, the type you hardly ever saw any more. It was light green and ribbed across its entire length, so that the effect was numbing like the sea. The light streamed in through the small rectangular bedroom window of the ground-floor maisonette. No, she thought, not the sea. Not yet. A loch, perhaps, into which he might dip and dream hippocanthic wordless dreams, a preparation for the ocean over which the darkness unfolds itself like God. She tapped the diaphragm of her stethoscope with the nail of her index finger. He was smiling at her.

'I slept better last night,' he said.

'Good,' she said.

And there was something fresh in his blue eyes. A glimpse, perhaps, of the man he once had been, the man who had wooed and loved Margaret, the man who had built planes – aircraft – the man who had jived furiously in empty hangars to the breath of hot swing trumpets.

'How's the pain?' Always the same questions. Regular ablutions. Keeps you on the straight and narrow. He shrugged. 'I could increase your morphine again.'

He shook his head.

'There'll be time enough for that.'

She flinched. It was the first time he had alluded to death. Did that mean he was beginning to accept it? Why should he? Why should anyone? Her mother had never accepted it. Not even at the end. She shook herself.

'Okay. Are you eating?'

'I don't need to eat, Zulie. I'd just be feeding the tumour. I can feel it growing inside.' He tapped his fingers against his protruding ribs. They made a hollow noise, like a tabla. He grinned at her. 'If I starve it, maybe it will suffer before it dies! Does a tumour die when a person dies?'

'Umn...'

He tilted his head to the side. He was smiling again. Must be the morphine, she thought. It's turned his mind.

'Or does it come alive in the grave and push its black roots up through the earth?'

'No. No, it doesn't.'

'How do you know, doc? Ever dug up a grave?'

'The cancer is just cells. They die like all cells. In fact, they often perish more quickly than normal cells. A disordered blood supply.'

'But like the worms, they feed on death. I once saw a foot-long worm, crawling through a wood. Forty segments or more.'

'Oh, that's horrible.' Zulie hated anything that had less than one leg or more than four.

'It was writhing and curling ... like this.' He was turning his bony fingers into a replica worm, coursing them along the ribbed coverlet which once had been the sea. Fucking monster. She couldn't move. The fingers inched closer, closer, until the tips of the pads brushed against the hairs of her forearm.

'No, it's all right,' she said, feeling suddenly nauseated. She couldn't move. It was almost a phobia.

'What's all right? Nothing's all right. Food for worms is what we are.'

She closed her eyes and inhaled deeply.

'Archie. Stop this.'

'Why? I'm a dying man. Indulge me.'

'You're not dying.'

'Eh? You mean I don't have lung cancer? I'm not wasting away by the hour?' She was silent. 'In a few months, if not weeks, I shall be inanimate as a cooling dog-turd.'

'Of course you have lung cancer. Well, mesothelioma.'

'Well then…'

'But I mean, you're not going to die right now.'

His fingers gripped her arm.

'No. And neither are you. And neither is Alexander.'

An electric shock. Zuleikha felt her mouth open and close like that of a fish. She felt her diaphragm rise, so that the words were more vomited than spoken.

'What?' His nails dug into the skin of her forearm. A shiver coursed through her body, so that it took all her strength to stop herself from falling to the side, into his lap. She had no air left in her lungs. Through her skin, she could feel his tumour, could feel its segments crawl. She took a deep breath. 'What did you say?' she repeated, intoning each word slowly and with considerable effort.

'Alexander and his dead wife. And his numbers.'

Her head was spinning. The room was coning like a diving Stuka. The old Air Force photos, the dead Margaret. A circular music. No ground.

'And you, Zulie. You and the river. Your mother in a box. The princess.'

He was staring straight into her eyes. Blue sea, just like Alex's. An old Alex, shrunken, dying. His dead wife, calling to him from beyond the grave. Her ashes, re-forming. Or had she been she buried, Catholic-style? Worms again. She was panting for air. His nails were drawing blood. She could feel it, hot on the coverlet. Red on green.

'Let go of my arm,' she said.

He laughed, a congested wheezy cackle, and his voice tasted of regurgitated shite.

'Let go!'

Saliva was drooling down his face. He was grinning. His head was skeletal. The light was pouring through the window.

'I'm a poet,' he said. 'I sing the songs of air and blood. Once, for inspiration, I almost killed a woman. No-one knows about it. Only me and the tart, and her tight wee neck. Gut strings, a broken lute. And now, you. Open your box, you fuckin' whore.' His voice was slow, turgid. Moscow bass. Hard ice. His grip tightened. Corpse nails. Sharpening. 'Open your box!'

She didn't dare use her other arm to remove his hand. There was too much electricity already.

'Get off me!' she yelled. With all her strength, Zulie yanked her arm away. She felt the skin tear but there was no pain, just white heat. With the momentum, she fell away from him and landed on the floor. Banged her head against the tap of the oxygen cylinder. A sudden hissing noise emanated from the discarded mask on the side-table.

'I jitterbug with the tumour,' he was saying. 'Ring-a-ring-a-roses! Benny Goodman, eh? Round and round and round we go ...'

He was still staring at her, but his eyes were somewhere else. Dead trombones. Deep psychotic blue. She shook her arm. Her legs felt like water. She propped herself up into a sitting position. What the fuck am I doing? she thought. She glanced at her skin. No blood. No marks. Nothing. He had turned away to face the wall. Beneath the coverlet his body was quivering slightly, yet he seemed to have fallen asleep. Tremulously, she forced her body to stand. The spinning had almost stopped, but she didn't dare move her neck in case it started up again. She half bent over him.

'Archie ...?'

It had obviously been an hallucination on his part. You couldn't blame him for it. He was like someone insane, or like a malevolent child. Not responsible for his words or actions. That was all. She was still breathless. She reached over and turned off the oxygen. Didn't want to be blown to smithereens, especially not with Archibald Enoch McPherson. Right now she needed white gleaming surfaces, she needed to be locked in a lab on the top floor of a sterile dry stainless-steel multi-storey with the kind of lighting that made sleep impossible. She wanted to be like someone on that anti-opiate drug, what was it called? The one that raised junkies from the dead. Naloxone. Yes, that was it. Archie's fit must've been just a side-effect of the heroin. A medical thing. Entirely understandable, given the circumstances. A clean, scientifically-provable phenomenon, evidence-based like an Edinburgh lawyer. Nothing more. The rest was bunkum, imaginary. The real world was space, invisible forces, coldness. And all of it was hurtling back towards Absolute Zero. In the Beginning there was light. There was nothing else.

But what about me? she thought. How did he know about Alex? And my mother? The river? What the fuck was going on? It was in his hands, it was on his skin. And, now she thought about it, she knew she'd felt it every time he'd touched her, a frisson. A something. He was like a leopard. Those nails needed trimming. She would leave a note for the district nurses. Actually, where were they, those angels of the morning? They surely should have been here by now. Where was their rattling, enematic cacophony of keys, needles and bonhomie? And meanwhile, she'd been left all alone with this flying maniac.

It was a good job he had been weakened by his illness. She thought of the woman he had mentioned during his rant, the woman he had called a whore. It was all in his imagination. Maybe he'd wanted to strangle someone. Irrationality was far from unusual in confused states, but never before had Zuleikha felt anything like the force that she now sensed from this man. It was odd, because up until this morning she had felt as though she'd known him for years. She also felt she'd known his wife, whom she had imagined to have been a small rather underweight woman who had been in no way out of the ordinary. Neither particularly submissive nor yet domineering, but like her husband, just plum middling normal. One or two pallid eccentricities, perhaps. Boat-modelling, or Tupperware parties. Or so it had always appeared, and Zuleikha had tended to think of herself as a reasonable judge of character. But perhaps that was just a cover for middle-class arrogance. You could never get blasé in this job; if ever you did, you would slip up.

Unlike those who viewed themselves as bourgeois intellectuals, working class people tended not to demand that the word *brain* be branded across their foreheads. But she'd got so she could tell a junkie from thirty metres. And, like many women, she could smell trouble a good decade before it hit, and had learned how best to head it off. She liked to think that most of the time she wandered around in a state of at least semi-awareness. She was not an aesthete, though. This was not some deep artistic sensitivity. That would have been positively dangerous in her line of work. It was more an internal alertness, like that of a sleeping cat. A readiness to jump – either into or out of a situation. Through silence, people survived. It wasn't always better to talk about things. Sometimes it was just asking for trouble. But she hadn't asked for trouble with Archie. She hadn't sought anything. It had all just come at her, like a tidal wave rolling towards the shore. Suddenly Zuleikha felt the need to tell Alex about what had happened. Yet he too was a stranger. She told herself to pull herself together. Which was kind of hard, if you were falling apart.

She made sure the oxygen cylinder was set at zero, then she went over and opened the window, inhaled several times. Not too deeply. She didn't want to faint. She looked at her watch. Almost no time had passed. Yet it had seemed like half an hour, or more. She glanced down at Archie. He was still curled up on his side. The movement had stopped. The effort had taken its toll. Through the coverlet she could just perceive the rise and fall of his chest, yet his breathing made no sound. He was sleeping, post-ictal. He seemed shrunken, foetal. His physical form was becoming an atomic shadow, as though, weeks or months before he was scheduled to die, already his reality lay elsewhere. She shivered as she remembered his crazy eyes staring right through her. He lived totally in the whirling propellers of his head. The blue baron. The flying ace. Steel and aluminium and fire. And now he was whirling in her head, too.

That night Zuleikha fell into a very deep sleep. She'd felt dog-tired. It was nothing unusual, just the normal weekday feeling, Wednesday onwards. On Mondays and Tuesdays it remained possible to believe in sunshine and redemption, even if it was chucking it down. But by Wednesday morning, all the energy which she had managed to recoup over the weekend had been sucked away by the constant grind of listening to the depressed, the obsessed, the needy, the angry, the hopeless, the dying.

The caring profession. It was infested with neurotics, Jesuit-types who needed constantly to prove to the world that their intelligence was superior to everyone else's. Or guilty Calvinists who drank only triple-strength tea. There were silent bigots, who had pals of only one confession. Then you got real crooks: people whose cheques would bounce on concrete and who, corporate-style, the moment you turned your back or went on holiday, would shaft you for a dime. There were doctors who would get you to do all the work and then take the dosh for themselves. Or some who set their managers – and, whether female or male, these would tend to prefer their haircuts cocained and scalped from the mullet corpses of 1980s pop stars – to spy on you, to take down fictitious figures based on nothing except their own little psy-op. It was a constant battle not to end up cynical, hard-bitten, shrewish and utterly morally exhausted. It seemed to burn out the guys internally, to destroy the fabric of their minds, so that the ones who in some way didn't get out ran the very real risk of ending up as alkies, druggies or incipient suicides. But the women wore it heavy on their skins; it greyed their hair and dulled their eyes, and day-by-day it flattened them down. Zuleikha had yet to meet a doctor over the age of forty-five who didn't look and smell ill.

Perhaps she should have gone to one of those Spiritualist Churches, where mediums spoke in tongues: *Is there a John in the house?* But they didn't have any answers. No-one did. Daoud. His cold skeleton never left her side; he had been drawn like Adam from her rib. He was the lost bone of her soul. His sea-blue eyes, one evening gleaming with life; the next morning slate-grey, sunken, dead. She hated mornings. For years she had lived in a vacuum, a continuous state of suffocating loss. During that time her realities had been tremulous and fragmented. Her anchors had been her work and her mother. But the healing had been reduced to a juggling act for people who had never had to save anyone in their entire lives, people who had never had to hold a child as it died. And everywhere around her she felt only despair, decay and death. Up on the swinging bridge she was crashing through the last barrier, crashing and falling into silence, the cold flaying her skin and the stars swaying like musical notes against the darkness.

The flying man was her last chance, yet even he was on the way out. The cancer was taking him down and she had let it get to her, she had let him inside her. That was why she kept going back, kept touching him, because every time she'd seen and felt something different, something that might lead her to find a reason for it all. But it could lead only to madness. Pox on the brain. Then had come the river… Clyde or Ravi, she was no longer certain onto which river bank she had strayed that other morning. Five of the clock, ante-meridiem, the time she always woke up with light clasped painfully, like solid silver coin, between her eyelids. The time, ten years earlier, when she had awoken knowing that her child was dead. Then the box, and the man. Alexander, and his dead wife. He hadn't mentioned her name or anything about her. What had she looked like, how had she laughed? It was all a secret. Yet, viscerally, Zuleikha had known. She had felt it that morning when she had found the box, when Alex had touched her cold skin. The woman had drowned. Had crashed her car over the edge of the bridge and drowned. Zuleikha had smelled the river water, she had taken it inside of herself, had let it flow through her veins and into the soft cream of her brain. Now it would never leave her. Perhaps it had been there all along, a dark stream flowing fast over hard stone. The Oxus, the Amu Darya. The smell of pine, sycamore and holm-oak. Lonely roads snaking across the high valleys. Women wearing tall head-dresses, dancing with loping steps in the House of Blood. Snow demons whistling through the boulders. Dead infants laid on beds of rushes, and sent out upon the waves of the river.

For years she'd had fantasies – not dreams; she'd been completely awake when she'd had them – of her son grown-up, a teenager, being difficult, being roughly loving. Daoud, King of the Jews, a slingshot life, and all the while his lips, a baby's lips, pressed up against the skin of her breast. Gradually the imaginings had become sepia shadows hulking in the recesses of her mind, drawing forth the ballooning muscle of her heart. Every word she had spoken since that morning had been a song to her dead child. Perhaps now the balm of death was all that remained for her. Zuleikha the con-woman, the juggler, the soldier, the malamati. Perhaps, like Aeroplane Archie, she was sinking joyously into the old stream, the darya of the heaving dark majority. So pondering, she fell into a deep sleep. A stone-bottomed Mariana Trench. Yet in spite of the depth Zuleikha found that her senses had become heightened, so that sleep rose into one of those very rare dreams where all five senses are used simultaneously. And, in the total darkness, she could see. It was as though she had been crushed flat into the rock and could now perceive with the consciousness of stone. A jangling musical perception.

And it was there, as she rolled on the cold featureless sea-floor, that Zuleikha dreamt of numbers. At first she was in her sitting-room and she was handling the scroll; she felt its high-quality cream finish impart to her skin a sense of completeness, of perfection – much as, many years earlier in primary school, she had run her fingers over the electric smooth surfaces of sheets of fresh white cartridge paper. And then the scroll began to elongate, so that as Zuleikha sifted it through her fingers it became more like a ream, the numbers shifting and proliferating over its surface. In dream-time she would be standing there, vaguely aware of the walls around her and of the hulking outline of the box close by. No, it was more than that: she could smell its constituent woods, and each of them carried into her brain a different and unique tone: sycamore, ebony, ash, oak, beech, pine, plum, aloe, hollyoak, cedar.

And as the music of the dream moved on, she was slipping into the worlds in which they had been formed, so that the rings and knots of the wood became the summers of a thousand years ago and she heard birdsong and smelled the scent of bright magenta flowers and felt in her own face the jaws of a goat, the muscles shifting upon bone, as it pulled the short tough grass from the mountainside. The air thin as a sheaf of paper. The sun a drop of gold in the sky. Just the undercurrent of a breeze. Silence. Solitude. A sense of existence which was simultaneously null and total, a feeling which she had had only twice before: once with the death of her son, and then again, years later, a reprise in the hospital room with its magnolia walls and its dead machines, a final coagulation. Death at both ends. A sense of time slowing, a fall through the thousand feet of a summer's morning. Grit beneath her nails as she climbs the sheer rock. The sun burning merciless on her back. Far below the sunlight catches on a fragment of breastplate, a scene, worked in aureate metal, of the River Choaspes, of forest and thorn bush and of Sikander Zulqarnain. A cool breeze siphoning from the back of a cave, the balm of sleep, the turning of nights and days and the splitting of bone. The dancing long-haired tsanrai steps of Qais of the Bani Israel, thirty-seventh son of Saul, from whose long loins issued the nations of the eastern satrapies. The Bani Afghan.

And as the spine of the maqam ran on, Zuleikha saw the numbers spill over the edge of the scroll. And the mountainside was no longer silent, but had become filled with the maqam sikah, the heptatonic scale of love, played on the tightly-wound gut strings of a Syrian oud. And accompanying – or possibly forming – the music was the tremolo of a lone male voice singing words in a language which she did not understand and yet which, like the numbers on the scroll, seemed constantly to transmute into streams and clouds and rocks. And, thin as a stick of incense, clad in wool and wearing a veil made from hair, Zuleikha wandered through the valleys and like the Zahra, the God-intoxicated Jerusalemite, the words and numbers were issuing from her throat, the song from her body. Zuleikha had become a poet, a one-toothed blue-eyed sha'iri who sings from the gut and whose night-dance causes carpets to rise and be suspended till morning.

Alex's eyes were shining as he stood there in her close. His eyes, that reminded her of her son's. He was carrying something in his left hand. Perhaps it was the angle of the late afternoon sunlight which streamed in through the long single-glazed tenement windows that imparted to his hair a tinge of russet, of high October. A sheen played over the surface of his face, over his elevated, almost Kirghizian cheekbones, his broad jaw, so that even the creases of his skin seemed luminous.

'Well, can I come in?'

He was smiling. Zuleikha knew that he had done a quick scan of her arms and of the sleeveless dress she was wearing, and that he had imprinted a static image of her body on the back of his brain. The hind of his mind. Men, and their fuck-shots.

Zulie realised that she too had been staring, and she swung the bulky blue door inwards. She saw now that it was a musical instrument case, shaped like a small black coffin. He was careful not to bang it as he slipped through the doorway. He held up the case as though it were a trophy.

'My lute,' he said.

She folded her arms, nodded.

'You gonna give us a tune, then?'

He turned around and went straight into the living-room. His back was huge.

'I hope so,' he replied, already out of sight.

He's already at home here, she thought, folding her arms. He moves with the alacrity and grace of a conqueror.

With immaculate care, he propped up the lute-case against her hi-fi and began to scan the scroll which she had left on the table by the box. From behind the sofa she stood and watched as he smoothed it out so that it became almost flat. It was no longer wrinkled and creased, and only at its ends did the paper still rise slightly; it was as though, beneath the hands of this lutenist, the scroll had accepted defeat and had become resigned to the fact that its form and meaning would be moulded to his will.

He swung round.

'Have a seat,' he motioned.

This time, Zuleikha sat next to him on the settee.

'Now, you see, I've figured out these numbers.'

'You've figured them out?'

'Exactly.' He paused, as though expecting her to comprehend. 'There's a pattern,' he explained. He was smiling triumphantly.

'Aren't we going to eat first?' She'd cooked a lamb pulaow of the Afghani type: no chillies, no fenugreek, no heavy-belly spices, but just big chunks of meat, sultanas and lots of skinned almonds, all mixed together in rice in which the water had been sealed. And just enough shorba to prevent it from tasting dry. It was virtually a trade secret. Perhaps old dervishes somewhere in the caves of Afghanistan might have known of it, but with the passage of years and the displacement of everything in that part of the world, it wouldn't have been the same. She'd made some aloo ghosht to go with it, since, as her mother had used to say, British people tended to find the pulaow on its own a little bland – not enough chillies or shorba – and both Alex and Zulie ate far too much and between them, emptied a bottle of vinho verde. Dessert was superfluous.

After dinner they made some green tea and sat across from each other, as before, with the box on the table in between. Alex took out a reporter's notepad and a blue biro and he began to draw all kinds of equations and other esoteric patterns, so that after a very short time Zuleikha lost track altogether and fell into a kind of semi-hypnotic state, lulled by the swirling motion of his pen nib across the smooth white paper. Eventually, he drew what looked like a stave, and then he began to fill in the spaces and lines of the stave with angular black notes that looked more like long ticks with retroflexed stems than the usual hollows and ovals which she'd tended to associate with musical scores.

'I can't read music,' she began, but he raised his left hand. He wanted silence.

She had been able to read music once on a day, but that had been some three decades earlier when she'd tried, unsuccessfully, to play the flute. It had been an exquisitely painful process; Zuleikha had found that she'd had neither the hand-eye coordination nor the lips nor the breath required to elicit meaningful sound from the instrument, and she'd felt immensely and suddenly free when the music teacher had relieved her of that peculiar burden. Now, as Alexander inscribed musical notes onto the paper, she began to feel the same irrational fear which she had experienced amidst the dry clarity, the brassy cymbals and matt-black metal stands, of the school music-room. Panic, light-headedness. But Alex was oblivious to her, and to everything except the flow of sound he was delineating on page-after-page of the notebook.

At last, after what seemed like half an hour, he sighed and flung his biro down with such gusto that it rolled and hit the side of the box, and he slumped against the back-rest of the settee.

'That's it?' she ventured.

He nodded.

'It's a piece of music. The numbers on the scroll form a complex pattern, a little like in those old school IQ tests. Once you've figured out the basic rubric, it becomes obvious that each number is separated from the next by a certain fraction, and that these fractions are actually musical intervals and combinations of notes, running vertically and horizontally, so that the whole can be turned into stave sheet music, or at the very least, into tablature.'

'Okay ... right.' She was trying to keep up. 'And have you tried

it? Tried playing it, I mean.'

He said nothing, but bent down, unclipped the steel fastenings on the lute case and carefully, almost reverentially, she thought, removed the instrument. It smelled of a mixture of musty leaves and very old wood. She closed her eyes and inhaled, but very slowly and not too audibly. Zuleikha liked smelling things: books, paper, furniture. She liked to think that it was one of her foibles. One of those precious little eccentricities that kept people sane. Then she exhaled, tasting the air as it flowed over her palate, the soft part and then the bone. It was like being in a forest, close to untouched places and the rattling, half-secreted skeletons of small animals. She thought of taking a second sniff, but decided against it. It could be dangerous, this breathing business, she decided. It could kill you, or drive you insane. And the lute was scuffed here and there and clearly was not just for show, though Alex treated it like a fragile-boned child. She wondered how old it really was. It's shaped like the musical notes he's drawn, she thought: fat body, tapered stem. Except that inside, it'll be hollow. But then, at the centres of musical notes, there is only silence. The body of the lute seemed to have been constructed from several types of wood: the fat belly of alternating light and dark strips, and the broad fretted neck which led to two independent peg boxes.

Alex balanced the belly of the instrument on his right thigh so that the peg-boxes were facing away from Zuleikha. Pulling out a large plectrum from a velvet side-pocket in the case he began to tune-up, making clipped rather dull sounds quite unlike those of an acoustic guitar, which was the only instrument apart from a descant school recorder and the gleaming mediaeval torture machine of the flute that Zulie had handled. He focused on the area where the neck and body overlapped and adjusted each of the metal strings until he thought he had attained perfect pitch, then made a series of resonant taps. He seemed to be trying to achieve maximal stretch of the top string. Instinctively, Zuleikha leaned away. If that string goes, she thought, I shall be blinded and like the defeated Emperors of Afghanistan; I will be forced to wander in darkness for the rest of my days. He broke in:

'It's an unusual tune, not like anything I've played before. This music is very, very old, I think. It's difficult and I've not even learned it. I'll probably make mistakes. In fact, I'm sure I will.'

'It's okay. It doesn't matter.'

'Actually, it does. If I make a mistake, then it means that the sequence of numbers won't have been followed.'

'Okay, well, you can correct it as you go along, then.'

'I suppose I could.'

'What alternative is there?'

He shrugged.

'None, really.'

'Then play it!'

God, he was so pernickety. Zuleikha wondered how his wife had dealt with all this. The lute, his painful attitude towards it. Such discord could permeate through the whole of a person's life.

'Wait!' she interjected at what seemed the last moment. She reached out towards him. Looked into his eyes. Ah, the blue… 'Can I hold it?' she asked.

She thought she saw just a flicker of alarm, but later she became unsure of this, since almost immediately afterwards his expression relaxed and, saying nothing, he simply offered her the lute across the sofa. But the distance across the top of the box was too far for her and so she got up, moved around the table and sat next to him. She accepted the instrument and laid it down, a little awkwardly, upon her thighs. Resting within the crescent of her body it felt warm, almost alive. But then, she thought, it's been in his lap for the past ten minutes. With her left hand she held onto the neck, while with her right she began to explore. Cautiously, not wanting to disturb the tuning, she plucked one of the middle strings with the nail of her right index finger. A single clean note sounded through the house. She looked up at him and smiled. If he was concerned, he was hiding it well. Most men get really uptight when you start fucking around with their things, like you're upsetting the cosmic balance. Then she remembered that Alex had had a wife, and that she must have handled his lute more than once. Had probably left her DNA on it.

The wood felt impossibly smooth against her skin. She caressed the neck, ran her fingertips over both peg-boxes. And then, last of all, she cupped the elliptical belly in her palm. She wondered whether Alex and his dead wife had made love to the sound of lute

146

music, whether he had played to her before coupling. She glanced up at him, afraid that he might have read her thoughts, or that inadvertently she might have begun to whisper them aloud. He seemed so big, there on her sofa. She had never had anyone so tall and bulky sitting next to her in her own house. Yet Zuleikha did not feel awe-inspired or fearful; she was merely aware of the disparity. Had he run his soft white hands over his wife's dead body? Over her skin, cold and puckered from the river-water? She wondered how she had known this and through how many hands this lute might have passed, over the centuries.

'It must be very old,' she ventured, gazing behind the strings into the darkness of the filigree'd rose.

'No. I got it in the Barras, just a few years ago. The shop must have been there for only a short time, because when I went back a week later it had gone. There was just an empty hollow in the wall. A dead-end passage. Bricked up, with not even the shape of a door. No-one I asked seemed to know anything about it. Maybe it was like those tanning salons and massage parlours. A fly-by-night musical instrument maker. Putting bad money after good. I don't know. But it is designed in Baroque style, which would have been fashionable around three hundred years ago.'

So, just two hands then, she thought.

'How do you know it's not old? I feel it's ancient.' She tapped the body. 'It looks worn.'

'Look. This guy made it in front of me. Cut the wood, boiled the glue, stuck it together. All in one, long day.'

'In the Barras? It must have cost a bomb! Thousands, I should imagine. I thought you said you didn't have any money.'

'You don't believe me.'

She looked up at him.

'No, no, I do. It just seems so odd.'

'Implausible, you mean.'

She shrugged.

'You think I've made it up, don't you. Look, if I'd bought it from a music shop, I would've said so. The man constructed this instrument before my very eyes and then he handed it to me. A gift, he said, a gift, given to you from Rujari d'Alì.'

'Who?'

Alex looked sheepish, as though he'd cranked the wire of credibility one turn too far.

'That's what happened, Zulie. He held it up to me – like this, at eye-level – and said: Un regalo per te da Rujari d'Alì.'

'He must be very skilled.'

'Then I had to learn how to play it.'

'A craftsman. An artist, even.'

'It took ages. Bloodied fingers, like the old rock guitarists.'

'Like the troubadours. Love and blood.'

'Animal glue, actually.'

'I wish I could play something,' she mused.

'Melted skin.'

'Perhaps it's ageing as we speak. Perhaps that's why it looks so old. Maybe the life-cycle of a lute is just different. What if it's dying, right now, in my arms?'

Zuleikha plucked a bum arpeggio and then jerked her head towards him.

'Did she like you playing?'

He looked away. Seemed momentarily to quiver, or tremble.

'Susan, you mean? She got a bit fed up with it. Men and their hobbies, you know.'

Susan. So there it was. Casually, just like that. A name, a life, a breath. Zuleikha inhaled, looked him straight in the eye and then whispered,

'How did she die, Alex?'

For a moment, she thought he would grab the lute from her, shove it back into the case, and leave. She felt his bulk tighten, the muscles of his face and his limbs turn to stone. For a moment, she was afraid. He held out his hands. She surrendered the lute.

Alex gazed in the direction of the window for a moment, as though fixing on the glass would help him to compose himself.

'She drowned in the river. Her car swerved off the bridge. Near where I met you. Near where you found the box. She was hurt but still alive when she hit the water. That's what they said. Because I asked.'

Zuleikha tried to focus on the wall, but nothing seemed to hold any solidity any more.

Then he began to play.

148

It was quite unlike any music Zuleikha had ever heard. In some senses Alex played lightly, his plectrum tripping over the gut strings as though he had hardly bothered to do any more than strike each one, but after a while she realised that this was the style, the sound of the instrument was like this, sweet and nasal like the flight of a small bird, a sparrow, say, or maybe a robin. The only birds left behind during the Scottish winter – or at least, the only ones you saw, the ravens and eagles being too high up in their cliff-edge eyries, and the crows and blackbirds ... well, you didn't really want to have anything to do with them, did you? You'd do anything not to have their malign flight-paths cross over your head in the shape of a Saint Andrew's Rood. No, definitely not. Bad luck, that would be. Cancer luck, or drowning. Or death before your time, right under the nose of your loving mother.

The more Alex played, the faster the plectrum moved, so that after a while it became just a blur of white. She wondered then why he didn't play using his fingernails; they were short, she was certain of that; she would've noticed, wouldn't she, if they'd been long and tapered like a guitarist's or a vampire's! Then she realised that in fact he was using his fingernails – those of the middle, ring and little fingers – while the plectrum remained clasped between thumb and index. His nails had grown since the funeral. He was using every part of himself to bring this instrument to life. He was creating new rules.

Zuleikha had no idea where on earth Alex was going with this; the very idea of a series of numbers leading to a musical piece seemed inherently ludicrous. Perhaps it was a practical joke played by some quack mathematician, a message in a bottle that meant nothing at all, but was simply a maze, a puzzle, existing for its own sake or else for the purpose of bamboozling fools like them who might have had the audacity and the madness to pluck it from the river. It had been meant to float right out into the Irish Sea, the Atlantic Ocean. Perhaps it would've billowed along in the Gulf Stream, all the way round the bony coast of Iceland and then back down south to the Gulf of Mexico. Or maybe it would've become caught up in the silver nets of Tangier and gone east into the Mediterranean, through the golden horns of old Byzantium and then into the Black Sea, or else down the Suez Canal into the

Red. Past Madinah, Makkah and the land of Bilqis and into the Arabian Sea, bumping along the southern Persian coast and into the Indian Ocean. A thousand and one nights, the box would sail, till at length it would reach the seven mouths of the Sindh Darya. There, reversing Alexander's course, it would leap upriver – or perhaps would be carried on the backs of large sacred goats and end in a mountain stream halfway up Tirich Mir where it would sink into a rock cavern under the branches of an ancient holm-oak and be dissolved in the spreading madness of a sleeping sufi-without-order.

Now Alex was playing a ricercas, two journeys in one, Zuleikha's and his own; or maybe those of the mystical Greek emperors, Sikander and Milinda, the tracings of their passage following elaborately opposite directions. Yet something had triggered this re-emergence, some concatenation of forces which even there, in the depths of the music, still eluded her. Or perhaps it was a folk-tale coiled within a nursery-rhyme, *King Fareweel*, perhaps, or *The Battle of the Harelaw*, its modes of the New Persian Tuning complete yet inaudible. And they would not open unless circumstances proved propitious. Some people got cancer and died early in great suffering, while others did not. Some perished in infancy while others lived on into dotage, for no reason whatsoever. Some fell in love, or committed suicide. Somewhere in all this mess there was an order, but it was beyond Zuleikha, it was beyond the reach of any human being, it could not be measured with the compass of words or philosophy – but perhaps, of music…

And as Alexander played, Zuleikha noticed that he had closed his eyes and that again a sweat had broken out across his brow. She worried that the sweat might drip onto the lute and cause rot or corrosion. The music was High Baroque; it was elegant to the point of madness. Yet beneath the formality, the mannerism, there were irregularities, odd dissonances, and in a state of aural lucidity which she had never before experienced, Zuleikha sensed that the lute and the music which emanated from it were older than history. The lute once had played Pythagorean music and had changed shape over the centuries, had progressed through various incarnations to the Baroque, the final and possibly the most perfect – but also the most effete – form, where structure and

150

sound had attained a complete match and whose every musical exploration, in the hands of a master – and whatever he said, whether he liked it or not, whether or not his dead wife had admitted it, Alexander was a master – might become a journey, a mapping out of possible coordinates. The fluttering pennants of rhythm. The bloody bursting forth of alphabets.

Then she saw it: the sweat on Alex's skin had coalesced into one large globule and the way he was perched, crook-backed over the instrument's belly, meant that sooner or later the shining droplet would detach itself from the edge of his brow and fall straight into the arabesque gul of the soundboard. And if that happened, he would never escape. Alexander would become a part of the lute, his substance would merge with the ancient wood and his fate would be played out through the yellowed scrolls of contrapuntal numbers, his life framed in the geometer of their music.

Yet this must have happened before, she thought; he must have sweated like this in the past, surely, when his wife had been sitting exactly where – in relation to him – I am sitting now, the fractal of her shape heavy upon mine, the blood cascading though the arteries of her thighs. Surely then Alexander must have bled into the wood of the lute. And the night she had died? Perhaps he had been playing at the very moment she'd lost control. The droplet began to thin at its base. How can he play so fast, she wondered, using only a plectrum? It's as though, like a juggler, he is dancing upon the tips of his fingers.

She realised that she was breathing fast and shallow, and that again she was becoming light-headed. You stupid cow, she thought, you're losing it. Consciousness, integrity, respect, everything. You're sinking into this man, this stranger, as he is sinking into the lute. Soon you will crave his substance, the oxbows of his mind; soon you too will be dancing beneath his fingers. The globule was turning into a teardrop. Zuleikha opened her mouth to warn him, to say: *Alex, stop!* She thought of closing her fingers over his, of holding firm the bone plectrum and staying its frenzied movement, its deadly course, light and sweet across the gut. She wanted to enclose his body in hers, to become a fecund moon around his darkness. It had become all-important. It had become everything. But she was too late.

It seemed to vanish. The droplet. Frantically, she searched for its course along the lute's body and then in amongst the petals of its rose. Yet she found nothing. Then she glanced down at the scroll.

The liquid was spreading like an amoeba, sucking in first one number and then the next. Zuleikha felt powerless to stop it. There were tissue-papers somewhere in the flat, but they would only have smudged things even more. Dabbing would have been useless. It was as though the sweat and ink had mingled and formed a substance whose only function was to gather to itself more and more of the music as it spread over the paper. The music itself was slowing through descending arpeggios and the ivory quill was visible once more. Yet Alex still had his eyes closed. His face was pale, the skin seeming to have forfeited its blood-supply – except around the eyes, where it had darkened and became sunken. He looked as though he was about to slump backwards. The music slowed even further, and then stopped in mid-note.

For a moment Alex swayed, and Zuleikha wasn't sure whether he would fall forwards or backwards. Then he sank to one side so that his head and upper body came to rest against hers, the soft bone of his temple, the dark sweep of his hair flowing towards the point of her shoulder. She flinched – partly because of his weight, partly because the sideways movement came unexpectedly; but mostly because, other than in a strictly clinical sense, she'd not been this close to a man for ages. He smelled of a certain kind of aftershave which she had encountered before on buses and on the subway, but she had never known its name: that slightly sweet scent that reminded her of cherry blossom. Though when she thought about it Zuleikha wasn't sure that cherry blossom had a scent at all. Well, okay, if it had an aroma, then Alex exuded it. How strange and hilarious, she thought, that such a huge man should smell of pink blossoms. But then Alex didn't strike her as a stereotypical west-of-Scotland male; that peculiar swaggering bull-reek machismo, honed over a thousand or more years, was singularly lacking. She craned her neck to look at the side of his face, at the strands of silver filigree'd through the black, and at the shifting delicate architecture of his nostrils as they flared. He was breathing more deeply now. Obviously, she reasoned, he was in some kind of profound sleep, or maybe even in an hypnotic state.

152

Perhaps he too could read her thoughts.

There was something familiar about the stain that was spreading across the paper. Perhaps it really was old, this scroll with its cryptic numbers that somehow had driven him to a frenzy of unconsciousness and her to ... what? Where were they going with all this stuff? Perhaps it was just a song to madness. A mathematical joke that would end up sucking the two of them — she said it to herself again – the two of them down into the endless dark well of clinical insanity. His body, resting against hers, seemed even bulkier than before. Yet through his clothes she felt that there would be little extraneous fat; he was all muscle and bone and sap. He was like a tree sawn through at the base with a single wire. In the hands of a master ...

But what if he were not quite good enough? For the lute. For Zuleikha.

'Alex...

'Alexander...?'

There was no response. Zuleikha shifted just a little to try and redistribute the weight of his body, but she was unable to control its movement and he slumped back, his limp fingers dragging the plectrum in a descending chromatic discord over the strings. The lute rolled a couple of times in his lap before coming to rest against his belly. For a moment she wondered whether he might die there, on her settee. She would never be able to drag his bulk onto the floor to try and resuscitate him. She didn't want him to die. Not again. Not another. Frantically she checked his radial pulse, but she was unable to feel anything because her own heart was thudding so violently against her ribs, almost as though she had run two miles non-stop uphill after inhaling forty cigars in ninety minutes. Fuck sake, she thought, then I'd be dead. I'd be grinning, up there in Havana Heaven. Stuyvesant Hell. Then she flattened the sensitive pulp of her right index and middle fingers lightly over his left carotid. She tried to turn him on his side, but only half managed it. His eyes remained closed, though once or twice she thought she saw the eyeballs begin to roll and flicker as though he was starting to dream.

As she pressed her fingers more deeply into the half-shaven skin of his neck, Zuleikha felt the rhythms of both their pulses slow and synchronise. She felt unable to remove her hand from his neck. Her whole body began to shiver, her frame, to tremble and she was thrown back by the force of it, yet still her hand did not move from his skin; it was as though something was leaving her and passing into him. She knew, even at that moment, that such a thing was medically impossible, yet she felt that his pulse was steadying against her pulse, his heartbeat against hers. She had gazed into Archie's soul and had seen the darkness at its centre, the tumour which had scattered like seeds from the high roof of the skies into his body right at the moment of first climax with his WAAF sweetheart, the hot jazz hangar tromboning in silver all around them. The whore's revenge, terrible, winged, rising, like the morning sky, like Iblis. Zuleikha had seen all this, and Archie had known that she had seen it. Well, fuck him! But there was more to Archie than worms and guilt. And now, in a sense, she was beholden to him. She would have to continue to visit him, not because of her Hippocratic duty, but because she needed to know the answers to questions which the rapier of allopathic Western Medicine, as it was presented in the early twenty-first century, simply was incapable of rendering. She needed to go further back, right back, and Archie was part of that journey.

The tears had stopped flowing across the surface of the paper and had begun to evaporate in places, so that parts of the script were turning sepia as they began to dry. Zuleikha knew that at the end the only real question was: Why? And she also knew that there could be no answer.

After a few minutes she realised that she still had her hand over his carotid. Gently, she removed her hand from his neck. The tendons were aching, the fingers felt cramped, and as she massaged her hand it seemed tiny, fragile, alien. She became conscious of the physiology of her own breathing, and when she looked down at the lute she saw that Alex was still holding the plectrum between his right thumb and index finger. Gently she reached across and pulled the plectrum away, laid it carefully on the table. It was then she noticed it.

The numbers which had covered the surface of the cream-coloured sheaf had vanished. In their place, rapidly drying, were the lines, furrows and rivers of a map.

Chapter Eight

The front door of Archie's house was bolted, so Zuleikha went around the back. Conversely, this door was open – not just unlocked as he sometimes left it, but wide open, and the late September wind was blowing straight through his kitchen into the hall. This was odd, as the district nurses would never have left it like that. But then Zuleikha remembered that she had arrived long before the nurses had even got out of bed. For a moment she wondered whether perhaps the house had been burgled during the night. Archie would've been powerless to stop them; he was bed-bound, for God's sake. There was hardly anything in his house worth stealing. Just an old colour TV, a radio and a few bits of brass, those trinkets purchased from tacky seafront shops that seemed ubiquitous among a certain class of the elderly. Nice mementos for the irretrievably lost. Brass was warm, brass was safe – so long as it wasn't musical.

He was lying face-down on the floor. He'd managed to crawl as far as the end of the wall, and his body was sprawled across the line which formed the doorway. His shoulder felt frozen, and at first Zuleikha thought that he might be dead. A merciful release, she thought, and then she wondered what it would be like to die, cold and alone, sprawled ignominiously on the floor. Like all clichés, it was common. Perhaps, one day, this was how she would end. But then, when she knelt on the soft carpet and leaned over him to try and feel for a pulse in his left wrist, he grunted and turned his head to face her. And he grinned. Once he'd had all his teeth. He'd always hated sweetness, had loved the sour, the bitter things of life. His mouth and his eyes were too close to her face, and she felt his breath on her cheek. Stale onions.

'Mornin, doc,' he said, as though this were quite a normal situation for him to be in.

Zuleikha shifted away. Removed her hand from his.

'Good morning, Archie. Are you hurt? What happened?'

The tunnels of his eyes were the heads of needles. Old-style, pig-iron ones. He was still attached to the infusion, she thought; the river of opium was flowing in. His voice came from far away.

'During the night, the door opened.'

Her brow furrowed with concern.

'Did the nurses not lock up?' she asked briskly.

'You're early.'

He seemed impossibly alert all of a sudden, but it was the viscid consciousness of morphine. The mechanism of a bedside battery-clock echoed through the hollow of the locker. Zuleikha sensed the faces in the photographs behind her. Above her. She stood up.

'Are you hurt?' she asked, in a measured clinical tone. She constantly needed to get things on an even keel with this guy.

'My ribs, at the front. Just a little. Mind you, I probably wouldn't feel it if I had snapped a bone, with all this poppy stuff going in. My whole body might fall apart and I wouldn't even know. Bliss, eh?'

After she'd helped him back into bed and had wrapped his body in as many blankets as she could find in his cupboard, she made him a mug of tea and fussed about by his bedside, checking the infusion pump, the boxes of vials, the scribbled lines of the nursing notes. The light was beginning to well out in the street. The sounds of the first cars came through the glass as though through thick water. It was going to be a nondescript early autumn day. Blustery, damp, overcast. On mornings like these Zuleikha would wonder how folk had lived here in the days before proper heating, running water, electricity, waterproofing. *This country is at the extreme edge of habitability*, her mother had used to say. *People only come here when they are forced to*. The tribes had always moved westwards, pushing one another further and further towards the sea-wall.

In her conversations with Zuleikha, her mother often had manifested a pervasive sense of dislocation. Even her words; the vowels had been Glaswegian, the consonants NWFP. Habits die hard, and accents, the songs of the ancestors, never die but go on sounding down through the generations. Perhaps, she thought, every one of us holds within ourselves the poetry of Ur. So what brought your parents here, Ummi, she thought, to this particular edge of the world? The Scots had arrived because even then they had been masochists; generations of Glaswegians had lived on *Dr Ratcliffe's Purging Elixir*, yet still, within their chests, behind the bone and muscle of their ribs, they held an overwhelming, an almost anatomical guilt.

No wonder Archie had difficulty breathing, she thought, as she poured boiling water over the tea-bag. She would make it strong for him. *Doctor MacBeth's Alchemical Tincture.* It might wake him up, rouse him from his poppy dreams. Fields of red that stretched far beyond the killing metal of the wing-tips. And the figure of Margaret, naked, curvaceous, painted in stylo beneath the glass side-window of the cockpit. Death, slumbering in its hull. Nine-hour runs each day over the Nordsee. Wheels rolled in blood. The Bloody Register. You could get used to anything.

After being back in bed for a while, Archie's body had warmed up – all except his fingers, which gripped the sides of the porcelain mug as though it was a Restoration tankard. He sipped.

'You make a good cup of tea.'

'Thanks. I made it strong.'

'Yeah. That's how I like it. Margaret could never seem to get the hang of that. Not in fifty-odd years.'

Zuleikha gazed at his quilt. Floral patterns, purple. Hydrangeas, maybe. Like the ones which grew, lean and rank, over the white marble tombstone of her mother's grave.

'Why have you come here so early in the morning?'

Zuleikha started at this. So he hadn't lost count of time, after all. Or maybe he dipped like a sick compass-needle, in and out of orientation. Bamboozled by the magnetism of rocks.

'I wanted to see how you were – before I started my surgery.'

'Don't get me wrong, but it's still only … what?' He glanced at the alarm clock.

'Seven in the morning.'

'Sometimes, if one begins early,' she began … and then she stopped. She looked into his eyes. The pupils had expanded just a little, as though the caffeine was partially reversing a little of the effect of the narcotic infusion. Or perhaps he's just waking up, she thought. She took a deep breath and leaped in. 'One might forget. Or remember.'

He sipped his tea silently. With the sweat of the night, his silver hair fell in clumps across his scalp, making him resemble a Brylcreemed forties lindyhopper. Cancer jived furiously through his system, changing the way things worked, altering the very nature of his mind. And yet, as she watched the rise and fall of his chest beneath the coverlet, it struck Zuleikha as odd that this morning Archie's breathing seemed a little easier than it had only a couple of days earlier. Sometimes with these things you got periods of partial remission. False dawns. The archangel Azrael, Farishta of Death, was back home, oiling and polishing his black wings, readying himself. Alone among the demons, Lucifer wielded wings of gleaming white. Down there in the deepest darkness of hell, the seraphim were invisible and there was only Whispering Iblis, the despairing diabolos.

Metaphysical theology by the bedside. Something which the medical schools had long forgotten, yet which had been there at the start and which even now, without anyone knowing it, underpinned everything. The four humours, and all that. Jalinoos, Ibn Sina, Ibn Nafis, Ibn Zuhr, Ibn Rabban, al-Razi, Ibn Rushd, al-Zahravi and many more. In the old days, when the mirrors and stones had been living beings, the makers of the world had been physicians. Now, Zuleikha thought, doctors were just refuse collectors.

'You've got insomnia, Zulie.'

The familiar form of address no longer seemed inappropriate.

'I haven't slept for years. Not properly.'

'Since you lost your baby.'

She inhaled sharply.

'I know about you, Zulie. The nurses gossip among themselves. They imagine that I am stupid, or riddled to the point of madness and light. And maybe I am all of these things, but I can still hear. Besides, when I touch your arm...'

She felt his free hand move beneath the sheets. She did not move away.

'We never had children, Margaret and I. It never seemed to happen. In those days, you didn't run to the doctor for that kind of thing. There was nothing that could be done. No glass baskets, filled with eggs. You just accepted it, as a judgement, perhaps. It was your life, dry and hard, and you got on with it. But it would've been worse if we'd had one and then lost it, I can see that.'

Excessive wakefulness can induce hallucinations. Which was

worse, the visions or the reality? Which was which? Would it have been better if Daoud had never been born, if the blastocyst had aborted itself at an imperceptibly early stage? If she had never gazed into those deep blue eyes whose flames had been lit by her sin? Her one-night stand. She had never told the father; in fact even the word stuck like a wormed apple in her craw. He had never known that he'd had a son who had lived and then died, who had been loved and then buried in the grass down by the dark river among the ageing mud-spattered plastic toys in the children's section of the Cathcart Cemetery. Not that there would've been any kind of terrible stigma attached; much of that rubbish had faded away as the oldies of the first – the immigrant – generation had died off during the previous decades. But in those days of her youth, she thought, there had been a sense of failure in such a thing, of letting down both the side and oneself. And the inelegant sordidness of fucking like cattle, just to conceive. We acquiesce in these idiocies, she thought, and yet we expect others to ignore them. And she had known that, sooner or later, bad blood would out. The whore, dying slowly in the dank alley, dreaming of fields of swaying red and white poppies.

'I still think of him, of Daoud.' Her voice trembled. She remembered having been surprised that below around three feet down, below the level of the clay, the earth had been dry.

Archie's hand now was touching hers. This was crazy. What if the district nurses turned up at this moment? What would they think? I'm the physician, she thought, not him: not this dying cancer patient, his shrunken asbestos body lying there, spinning like a wax cylinder in and out of flying scores.

'They are all with us.'

His voice had turned gruff, as though the mucous was beginning to well up again in his trachea. How stupid of her to imagine that he could've been granted any kind of respite. Fate versus free will? Nah. Fate won hands-down, every time. Apprentices. The asbestos snakes gripped them silently in their youth and never loosened their grip. Never.

'Who are with us?' she asked tremulously.

'The dead.'

Suddenly Zuleikha became intensely conscious of the picture

on the wall. Her neck began to burn; her cheeks to flush. Her chest was shaking. His breathing remained steady. Her hand gripped Archie's fingers as, through the rotting onions of his breath, she tasted the salt of her own tears.

Chapter Nine

It was the mildest autumn on record. Miraculously for Scotland; temperatures during the first half of October hit the low twenties. Although it was warm, the sun itself hardly appeared, and the days were stuffed with suffocating steel-grey clouds which, because of the absence of the usual westerly breezes, pooled in the dome of the sky. The leaves did not blow and swirl chaotically as they usually did, but simply spiralled on their axes like well-mannered Enlightenment balloonists. It was unbearably humid, and though people sweated salt on the subway and in the buses, cars and trains, like the leaves they did not dare dissent. The godfather of balloons would have been proud of the progress which this coastal nation had made across the span merely of one cosmic season.

It was on just such a morning, in the hours preceding dawn, that two figures, dark and insubstantial as silhouettes, climbed over the iron fence that surrounded the disused Botanic Gardens Railway Station. Eventually they made their way through the cold to what once had been the platform. Zuleikha gazed up at the rectangular section of a starless darkness which was modulated by the otherworldy efflorescence of the massed lights of the city reflected back from space. The opening seemed a lot smaller than it had when she'd peered at it from above. Then the stench hit her, and she covered her mouth with her gloved hand.

'God sake!'

Alex glanced over at her.

'It smells of shit,' he said, hardly breathing.

And God knows what else, she thought, but told herself not to think about that.

They stood there until their eyes grew accustomed to the murk. They had torches, but didn't want to rely completely on the narrow cones of light these would have cast. They figured that otherwise, once they were in the tunnels, where it was far darker than out here on the platform, their eyes would not become used to the lack of light and they'd be having to check their feet the whole time. The temperature down here was at least five degrees higher than it had been on the street, and beneath her thick clothes Zuleikha began to sweat. She removed two plastic torches from her back-pack, handed one to Alex, and then shone hers towards the right-hand platform. The clean white beam illuminated small sections of the wall, which looked as if it had been constructed of a mixture of cement and glazed brick. From time to time the torchlights would trace the outlines of scrawled graffiti. Zuleikha tried to read the words but they seemed nonsensical – not just ungrammatical, but totally without meaning. They might as well have been written in another language altogether, or else by somebody who had irreversible brain damage:

NOTAHOODA

What the hell did that mean?

The torch beams circled in the darkness as Zulie and Alex took one platform each. Occasionally, the streams of white light would cross paths in a swooping silent ballet, and at those times the lights would cancel out. Interference, Zuleikha thought, and she shivered a little in spite of the heat. We are interfering.

Then, as the daylight grew a little stronger and as their torches delineated more and more of the writing, Zuleikha realised that the reason the ancient graffiti seemed meaningless was simply because some of the spray-paint had worn away over the years, leaving only bits of words. As they walked from one end of the station to the other their feet crackled over all manner of bottles, cans, bollards and soft, indefinable and potentially repulsive objects. She tried to keep the thought of living creatures at bay. No, she thought, everything down here is dead. It's better that way. Less scary, somehow. Zuleikha decided to concentrate on not falling down any holes.

They'd done their research. The place had been opened in the late nineteenth century and had stopped functioning as a station just before the onset of the Second World War – though the Central Line, of which this station had been a part, had run until the mid-1960s. So that meant no trains had coursed along where Zuleikha was standing for the best part of half a century. Yet lots of people must have come here at one time or another. The graffiti seemed multi-layered, like frescos in an archaeological dig. Some of it must have dated back to the seventies at least: it referred to phrases, obsessions and rock groups which had been extant in those days. The authorities hadn't bothered to try and erase it. After all, no-one was really supposed to be gazing at these walls. Zuleikha felt a quiver of excitement as she shone her torch into the absolute darkness of the tunnel.

'Do you still want to do this?' Alex asked. Unlike Zuleikha he was carrying no bag, but had strapped an oblong case to his back.

She nodded.

He peered in her direction, then shone the torch-light straight into her eyes. She was blinded, and tried to shade her eyes with her hand.

'Was that a yes?' he insisted.

'Yes, yes. Stop shining that bloody light in my eyes, for God's sake.' The long beam slipped to the floor.

'Sorry, Zulie,' he said. 'I guess I'm just a little bit nervous. I've never done anything like this before.'

'But then you'd never waded, chest-deep, into a cold river before either.' It was the version they had come to accept.

'No. That's true.'

'And neither had I. So there it is. Let's just get on.'

Alex let out a deep breath.

'Which way?' he asked, swinging the torch along the parallel lengths of empty platform.

Zuleikha unzipped a small pocket over her right breast and took out an even smaller black plastic box. She knelt down. Then she unzipped the corresponding breast pocket on the left-hand side of her waterproofs, removed the map, knelt down and balanced it on her knee. In one movement she flipped open the box. The top was hinged and it swung back, revealing a compass. She placed the compass in the centre of her left palm and then, using her right hand, she shone the torch at the dial. She swung her body around, Cossack-style. She was facing away from Alex. She extended her compass-arm.

'This way. South-east. Towards the river.'

'The river, again,' Alex mouthed, then he wondered whether she might have read his lips. Maybe she can do that too, he thought, and he felt her breath almost upon his neck as they began to tread the course of the old sleepers. Cushioned in its case, the lute strapped across his back felt heavier than usual, so that every so often he had to re-adjust it slightly. But she had shown no sign of having heard, and now he really didn't want to glance backwards since the darkness ahead was like a wall and every sound was accentuated as though, as they moved forwards into the circular embrace of the tunnel, surreally, they were sliding down the mouths of one of those old brass gramophones.

At first the way was strewn with all kinds of detritus, from decaying milk-crates to half-empty plastic litre-bottles of cider to the obscenely large totally inflated tyres of an artic; deeper in, though, the rubbish turned foul and inchoate. This place must be a paradise for anaerobes, Zuleikha thought. No light, no fresh air, dark streams of brackish water trickling down the walls. A firdaus for the unseen crawling things of the world. She wondered about methane gas and explosions, and about all those Scottish laments about slaves who'd been trapped in the deepest levels of ancient metalliferous mines or who had drowned slowly behind a breached sea-wall. Then she forced herself to stop. They were following the lines on the scroll; the tremulous conjunction of Alex's musical notation and the ink stains of his sweat, or tears. There was a craziness about this whole thing that made Zuleikha feel as though she was leaping, almost flying along the tunnel over the rubbish, the mud, the decaying remnants of leaves that had blown in. It made her feel that through the dank air, through the very pores of her sweated-out skin, she was acquiring some kind of instinct, the nature of which she could not define any more than she had been able to define the instinct of motherhood that everyone went on about the whole time. With Archie, the incipience of death had sharpened her awareness of the shining and empty luminosity of every single moment – yes, even that moment when her mother had drawn, and then released, her very last autonomic breath. Or the moment Zuleikha had found the tiny, incandescent farishta of Daoud's spirit in the midst of his decorated bower. The dry riverbeds of hell were carved into her skin, one for each loss. The life-line, the heart-line, the marriage-line. They were the silences in her song. They had left her, broken and glowing, in the dark.

The place reeked of old pig-iron, and then Zuleikha realised that the milk-crates had turned from blue plastic to rusting metal and that the bottles over which her boots kept slipping were now all blown glass. The relics in the tunnel, and the tunnel itself, were going backwards in time. Maybe the vandals had been braver in those days, she thought; maybe, in their unreasonable flares, they had ventured deep into the spirit and knuckle dust of the old gangs. The Cheeky Forty, the Lollipops, the Kent Star Boys, the Baltic Fleet. The Billy Boys, the Shanley Boys, the Savoy Arcadians. The Black Book of Glasgow. What had happened to all those strange formations, those sweat and steel tribes? Perhaps, like the Botanic Gardens Station, they had been swept up into the greater cataclysm of world war and overnight had been turned into platoons of Tommy Scots.

She remembered the tales, told to her by her mother, of her great-grandfather's time on the road to Mandalay – or rather, through the jungles of Jahannam. The Burma Front. Only the more entertaining stories had come down through the generations, the vignettes of men burning sinuous invertebrates off the punctured backs of their comrades using lighted cigarettes, or worse, inducing them with pipe smoke to crawl slowly, segment by glistening segment, out of external auricular canals. Nothing about death, or about severed heads floating in pea-green swamps, the tranquil expression of their decomposition orchestrated by legions of dancing maggots. Nothing like that. Like so much of her family's real history, it had remained secreted in impregnable boxes of Sherwood oak. In the past, such tales would've been carved into the sides of men o' war or etched into the arcs of longbows.

After a while even the bits of glass and iron began to thin out and then they vanished altogether, and the walking became much easier, the ground drier, dustier. Alex's breathing was coming in short rasps. She touched him on the shoulder, and he nearly jumped out of his skin.

'What did you do that for?' he asked angrily.

'Calm down, Alex. I didn't mean to startle you. It's just I thought that maybe we ought to rest for a little.'

He looked around. Shook his head. There was only the hypnotic sound of water trickling down the walls. Zuleikha wondered whether this had grown louder the closer to the river they had drawn, but then she thought that probably it seemed that way because the crunching noise of their boots had ceased. The air in the tunnel was thick, black, unmoving.

From far away and long ago she seemed to be hearing the music of melting ice. The Ctota, frozen from its source to the span of the Jamaica Bridge. Booths and dram shops scattered across the white water. Wee women, shawled pawn-pieces, moving slowly over the river towards the creaking oil lamps of the Trongate.

As though to break the spell, Alex spread his arms out in a movement which reminded her somehow of a populist politician inviting the masses to come and be cradled in his bosom. But Alex wasn't inviting her to do anything.

'Rest?' she insisted. Her voice seemed a little too loud.

'Rest where? There's absolutely nowhere to sit, and I'm not sitting on that mud. God knows what's crawling through it.'

'We could just lean against the wall,' she suggested, trying to change the subject.

'With all that water coming down? No thanks.'

She shrugged.

'I just thought that maybe you ...'

'That was a mistake, then, wasn't it? This –' he swung his arm around in the darkness '– was a mistake!' He turned and walked away, more quickly than before.

The sound of his footsteps receded as it became subsumed into the echoes indigenous to the tunnel, and then the echoes multiplied, so that after only a few seconds it was as though Alex was being accompanied by a legion of shades. He'd told her that he too had been an only child. No siblings, no comparators. Just him, and death. Zuleikha took a step back. Inhaled. Something brushed softly against her neck, just below the hairline, and then swept over her cheek. She held her breath, tried to fan it off, tried not to panic. The torch-beam swung madly over her head, revealing a nest of bats high in the cupola. Their folded wings rippled like lips. Hairy snouts, inverted rats, Black Madonna cunts. O fuck. She let out her breath and almost dropped the torch. Her heart smashed against the backs of her ribs. In the distance she saw the light from Alex's torch swaying dimly against the tunnel walls. She was losing him. Gripping the hard plastic shell, she almost ran. This whole thing was slipping out of control. Yet she was part of it, they both were, they had brought with them their twin griefs, the multiple courses of their lives and of the lives that had gone before and they had begun to merge these with the cartogram of the city and its subterranean workings. They would have to follow the black streams of this tunnel, wherever they led. The bats were stirring.

She came to a burn, across which she half-leaped, half-waded. The freezing water splashed up over the rims of her boots, and Zuleikha shivered and massaged her arms. It was colder on the other bank; there seemed to be a breeze blowing from somewhere – she couldn't tell from which direction – and it was getting stronger, so that no matter where she positioned herself on the rock floor of the tunnel, still the wind kept coming.

'There must be a large opening hereabouts. This wind…' she began, and she was startled into silence by the echo of her own voice. She took out her compass and map and, crouching again, carefully traced her finger across the paper. She was glad that she had a good sense of direction. Not like her mother, who wouldn't have known east from west or north from south. Not that she'd needed to, really. Other people, her husband mainly, had always guided her over the rougher parts of her journeys. The trouble was, in everything except actual physical map-reading, his radar had been only slightly more efficient than that of his ex-aristocratic ex-wife, and so Zuleikha's parents had seemed to spend much of their time peering through a sextant, gazing for possible horizons.

She'd almost caught up with him now, their steps falling into virtually the same rhythm. She felt herself relax again. How long had they been down here, she wondered? She'd not kept as close an eye on her watch as she had on the map and compass. How long could it possibly have been?

'I think we're getting pretty close to the river-wall,' she began. She was aware of Alex moving back, just one step or maybe two, she wasn't too sure, it all happened so very quickly. One minute, he was there, huffing and puffing and sweating, and the next, there was the sound of crumbling, a single shout, a swaying and flailing of arms and hands, a clatter and a mess of light as he dropped his torch, a loud rumble as he fell and slid as though down a chute … and then everything was dark and silent, except for the flow

167

of the stream over black rock and the discrete, and maddening, sound of trickling water.

She dived to the floor and curled up. As though she had become instantly naked, Zuleikha was aware of her own body, of the smell of her sweat, of the timbre against her larynx of the breath she had just imbibed, of the panic that prickled along her skin, of the petrified vulnerability of her spine curved like that of the unknown woman in Roman Pompeii. Perhaps now the roof would fall in and turn her to fossil. It would take several centuries or more, but down here time was of little consequence. Or rather, it was all jumbled up together, a magic lantern of a thing. Then she sprang up. Adrenaline was pumping from her belly. God, how many of these could a body take? O fuck O fuck O fuck. Very carefully she unfurled herself, rose up and went over towards where Alex had been standing before he stepped back. She heard a muffled cough and then a scratching sound. The quantum movement of an impossibly long worm against the surface of her skin.

'Alex?'

No reply.

'Alex...?'

She was aware of the tremulousness of her second appeal and cleared her throat. But that sounded even worse. Fuck it. Louder this time. Scientific. Rational. Think. Am I. Therefore.

'Are you all right...? Alexander...?'

How ridiculous she sounded. Like his mother, or something. But the echo had altered. It seemed to be coming back at her from below. She peered forwards, not daring to take one more step. She shone her torch-beam at an angle to try to penetrate the darkness of the hole into which he had fallen. She even picked up his torch, switched it off, then on again, and then beamed its light at a different angle from that of her own torch. The cold breeze wafted into her face, freeing strands of her bound-back hair and scattering them across her cheeks. She tried to brush them away, but that sent the torch-beams crazy again so she desisted. She was breathless.

'Compose yourself!' she said aloud, but her voice sounded high-pitched, ludicrous and she was aware that she was panting.

After she'd taken maybe twenty or thirty steps she realised

that she'd left the map and compass on the ground by the hole. She swayed, trying to decide whether or not to go back for them. Her head pounded with the sound of the water all around. Drip-drip-drip. Water on the brain. Then, behind the stream, she heard something else. No, it couldn't be. Not here. It was crazy. She followed it, moving slowly and with some difficulty in the direction from which it seemed to be coming. It was odd, because it seemed to be issuing from two directions at once. She flashed the torches around, but the pointless vulgarity of their beams just distracted her. So she switched them off and waited for the darkness to leaven.

One stream of sound was coming from the place directly beneath where the floor had fallen in, and Zuleikha wasn't going there. No way. But the same hard noise – distant and distorted, as though its elements had been fractionated – was breaking from her left. From the east, she knew this without needing to consult the absent compass. Shining both torches before her as though she was some alkaline battery version of a Wild-West gunslinger, she trod gingerly on, testing the ground with each step, so that she felt that after today she would come to know this dangerous stretch of darkness better than anyone had ever known it. Even the illegal Irish navvies who, no doubt, had hewn this winding snake from the hard black rock had not known it as well as Zuleikha Chashm Framareza MacBeth. Even the mother of Friend Mungo, exiled for so long beyond memory's wake, had not borne the contours of her home city on her skin as did Zulie now, on the soles of her feet, along the lines of the bones of her toes-turned-to-fingers, on this day beneath the earth's impenetrable skin. The sound was getting louder, so she reckoned she must be on the right track. It led her down a short staircase to a place where the tunnel wall felt different, its stone softer and more friable, so that it flaked off and became trapped in the skin beneath her nails. She turned the ring handle and went through the door.

More steps, enhanced echoes, the sense of something spacious, breezy almost. And music. Yes, that was what the sound had been; all along she had known it, yet it had seemed so bizarre that she had been reluctant to admit it even to herself. Alex was playing the lute. She went down more steps. At first she tried to count them, but after the fiftieth she gave up because the attempt to reckon in the face of the melody was destabilising her feet. She needed all her concentration just to get down this dank staircase in one piece. And it was getting wetter, the further down she went. How far had he fallen? And if it was so far, how then had he managed to extract his undamaged instrument from its case – in pitch darkness, to boot – and then to play on it a tune which she had never heard him play before? And after their few months together, Zuleikha had heard quite a few. Madrigals, motets, arias and the rest – not that she was any kind of expert at distinguishing one from another. They all sounded basically baroque, elegant, clever, meditative, yet they lacked some basic element. Fire, perhaps. But then maybe that was too much to expect from a lute. A bit like trying to make the guitar perform like a clarinet. Or vice-versa. But she could tell that this piece was different. Something in the gaps.

At last, she came to the foot of the staircase.

She was in a large cavern. She wondered whether perhaps it had been some kind of storage place for the railway, or even for the mine which had preceded the railway. She moved with less caution now, towards the far corner from where the music was coming. She switched off the torch since its beam seemed the weaker. It must've been the one Alex had dropped, she thought. Several times she was on the point of calling out again, but even as she parted her lips and opened her mouth, some instinct stopped her. The smell here was also quite different. The air was fresher, though not as fresh as it would've been outdoors. Strange, though, that there was no light coming through. But then she stumbled – not dangerously, though nonetheless she was braced, her muscles tensed in readiness to grasp onto whatever was there, to swing the trunk of her body around, had even a whiff of any such danger presented itself – but just enough to cause the tiniest slip of her index finger over the switch of the torch. For a second she thought that the battery had failed, or that a wire had worked its way loose, and she began to fumble with the other, weaker torch. But then she stopped herself and stood quite still. Now she saw that there was light here after all, and that it was coming from above. As the music swirled around her in tetrachords Zuleikha stood quite still, and allowed the curtains of her eyes to widen.

She was relieved that Alex had not been badly injured; he must have slid down a kind of chute and he had come to rest here, in this cavern where light that resembled moonlight was streaming down from an opalescent roof that was more like alabaster than rock. As she gazed at the ceiling, Zuleikha made out the notes that streamed through the stone. Now he was playing a versi sdruccioli, an invocation. Rujari d'Alì, failed marriage broker, broken suitor. Lover of one woman too many. Prisoner of the convents, adulterer, murderer. He of the three lutes and the seven cities: Nepi, Bologna, Roma, Venezia, Torino, Genova and the last, the unknown place close to Agrigento where he had gazed into the waters of the White Sea and had dreamed of composing for this most beauteous face in the universe, a piece to be sung only in the most perfect castrati voice. Technically, his cantata would go further and higher than any before. And then, as he streamed into the river's flow, a shadow broke behind him, a swift blade. A sweep, a breach. Lying on the cobbles, the locks of his hair splayed out around his head, his warm blood flowing through each strand into the river and with it, the invocation of the spirits, his most beautiful act, the most supremely wondrous of all his compositions, the unwritten music dissolved itself into the pulse of the Great Sea.

Within the ornamental mannerism of the Baroque, as in her brain the shell of the music cracked and dissolved, there lay the splendiferous occultism of the Renaissance, and Zuleikha knew that the music had shifted back across the years. Just as always, she flew back to the absolute silence of her son's death. A skull, split on the still surface of the water, a flood of brain, a body, bloating in the river. Death comes slowly, as the stars pierce through the velvet curtain of the sky. A final lucid darkness. *Non havea il sole ancora.* Zuleikha fell to her knees. Her hair, finally, had all come loose and was falling in waves around her face and down onto her shoulders. And above her the entire weight of the Clyde, the Cluden, the unknown river, the Clwyd, the strong river, was seething through the infinitely thin diamond-hard stone of the impossible aria. And Alex was sitting cross-legged, blood streaming from his forehead, his lute cradled in his lap, its body scratched and torn but essentially, technically, mythically, undamaged. His eyes were closed, and with his fine ivory plectrum he was playing, faster and faster, the runs of notes which made up the bone and flesh patterns of the dead composer's features and the fractals of his thoughts. And the forms which emerged on the ceiling of the chamber were those of gate and well and cart and shallop and bones, the glacial marks of Thenew, Thaneu, Thaney, Thanetis, May Maa of Mungo, prodigal daughter of Northumbria and big mother of Glasgow. The violated, the unwilling, lover, denied by her own dear green place and hung, forever upside-down, to breathe among the fishes.

Where Alex's blood dripped onto the floor it did not congeal but streamed away in trails of notes and letters, cryptic symbols blown onto the bronze mirrors of the stone, and Zuleikha knew – could feel it in her fingers – that when eventually they managed to crawl through some neglected reed-stuffed crack in the bank of the Clyde or the Kelvin or whatever river it was, they would be able to open the second box without difficulty. At that moment she felt a terrible desire for him. A physical, animal desire. If he'd been there next to her she would have torn off his clothes and taken him and they would have copulated like dogs or rats down in the darkness of the disused railway. Away from the light, hidden by the ceaseless movement of the river and smothered by the thick mud of the past, in an act of communion, they would have steeked the smell of their bodies into the earth, stone and water. Like milt they would have spread themselves through the dank web that formed the city of Glasgow. She felt a moistness deep in her vagina and she realised that she was beginning to hyperventilate and she pressed her palms against the wall and forced her chest muscles to ease back into a steadier rhythm. Forced herself to think.

She took out a notebook and began to scribble down the markings. She had no idea what it might lead to; the deeper into this casket they sank, the wilder and more esoteric everything seemed to be getting. The darkness was warm, so she thought that perhaps it was the shuddering melancholic intensity of the music that was causing her to shiver violently.

Her heart was pounding, her legs felt weak, the muscles useless. In a sense they had both come from malleable pasts. No wonder the City Fathers had blocked off these tributaries. During the Second Great War, as the Messerschmidts and Hurricanes had howled across the skies, these tunnels had become places fit only for rats, djinns and crazy women. Not even adulterous couples had ventured down this far. Not even the castrati, the black and white eunuchs, the dancing uncle fairycakes had dared to slip this far into the caves lest the soles of their feet touch the burning metal of the earth's core.

She could feel the pulse and rhythm of his body, of every part of his physical being, as though it were her own. And even as he played, he swelled inside her and filled her with his bulk and with the light of his eyes, the colour of the Scottish sky in autumn. And again her chest heaved up and down and her heart pounded against her breasts and she knew that she was panicking down here in the deep darkness of the lute's endless belly, she knew that her sexual arousal was part of this, that she had come close to a man for the first time in years and that it was killing her, that the emotion would be all-consuming. The world which she had carefully constructed brick by brick over the years since Daoud's death was falling apart around her, falling into the flow of the green river of Queensberry Hill. A fear gripped her, and this time it was not claustrophobia but rather the terror of exposing herself again to the possibility of emotion and loss. And she tried to run from the cave – not the way she had come; that would have been impossible. You could never go back the way you came, not even Rujari d'Alì and all the collective lunatic lutenists of the world could have done that – but further out along the banks of the big burn, further out towards the sea. Something in her gut, some deep animal instinct, told Zuleikha that water and music both must flow towards light.

Chapter Ten

In the gentle folds of the west Lincolnshire countryside, Aircraft--man Archibald Enoch McPherson was tripping, one burning summer's afternoon in 1942. Tripping, that is, not in the post-1960s meaning of 'white bicycling' under the influence of numerous and diverse pharmacological compounds, but in the older sense of 'black bicycling' on a gearless hollow-iron contraption. These were his leave days, and this time around he had decided not to go into town. He had no map, since all the maps had been destroyed by order of the War Office. Although the threat of land invasion had receded somewhat compared to the fearful days of '39 and '40, you really couldn't be too careful.

Archie felt the air siphon deliciously around him. The road on both sides was guarded by deciduous trees quite unlike the perpendicular sentinels of Scotland. But the wilds of the far north and the border country remained as alien to him as these quiet, undulating fields of barley and wheat and the square Saxon church towers which connected each village to its Creator. They were not pretty; they were hardly the sorts of places that got lifted off onto biscuit tins. All the buildings except the churches were the colour of clotted blood, and some of the villages had had neither electricity nor running water till the RAF had arrived a couple of years earlier. This was the green and tan heart of the land of Angles and Danes; of wattle-and-daub, thane and brick; of common, monastic, feudal and enclosed lands. He had heard that at one time, from coast to coast, Britain had been covered with trees. The folk had lived in little clearings and one clearing had barely conceived of the existence of the next. Only the barons, the bishops, the thieves and the strange knights of stone and river had known of a world outside.

As he cycled on, the forest grew steadily more dense. The air had acquired a pungent stillness and the soothing pneumatism of his bicycle generated no echo. Up in the highest branches of the trees, clusters of rooks' nests broke up the deep blue of the sky into bucolic, yet vaguely ominous, asymmetries. There were neither birds nor vehicles. It was Sunday; people went to the early church service, where they caught a little stained glass sun. Even though he had no map he did have a compass, and he'd set off due east, vaguely in the direction of the sea. He'd known that he would never be able to reach the sea – it was around forty miles from the base to the North Sea coast – yet it had seemed like a normal thing to do. The forest air imparted a suppleness to his joints, and in the slipstream of this second wind he rose up and began to accelerate. The road ran die-straight for the next couple of hundred yards, and then it swung round to the left as it followed the dark green line of the forest – which itself clung to the banks of a stream which Archie could neither see nor hear but somehow knew to be there, flowing in the semi-darkness beneath the broad leaves of elm and ash and yew. I must be going upstream, he thought, and not towards the sea at all.

The land was flat and the march went on forever. Houses appeared and then vanished. No wonder people had imagined the carrs, fens and wolds to be haunted by the ghosts of those who had lost their way. Yet this part of the road was not entirely flat. In Scotland, the inclines would have been almost imperceptible like, say, the seven hills of Rome; but here on this eastern plain the gradients were singular, like the long cursive spines of unobtainable women. He had to keep that feeling under wraps, as he did the Type 440 Wellington B Mk Xs or the Avro Lancaster Mk IIIs before they took off on bombing runs. Sometimes he would watch as the aircraft became suddenly weightless, their noses tilting upwards, away from the shimmering runway, and he would long to be encased within their metal bodies and to gaze down upon the earth from a rose turret. It would be like seeing into the future. A tiny black speck. The attrition rate was almost as bad as during the Great War. Death and glory was all very well for officers and gentlemen. He pumped the pedals, harder now; he was breaking a sweat. The pungent, elemental reek of wheat soothed his senses as he caught a sharp bend just before the summit.

He rounded the bend and felt the pedals ease against his feet. He topped the crest, swung his tail back onto the hard leather of the saddle and took some slow, deep breaths as he allowed the frame to freewheel. The air was cooler here. He thought he might stop soon and have his sandwiches and the flask of cold tea he had brought with him. The bicycle was gathering speed. He closed his eyes and allowed his fingers to unclasp from the leather and chrome. Then he took his feet off the pedals and swung them forwards. Slowly, he turned his face from side to side. The air smoothed past his jowls, sculpting his shape into the blackness. He leaned back further and his body tautened. Before him, Margaret, lying open-mouthed and red with joy, her eyes a blue sky, emptied of battles, into which everything resolved. And through Margaret's supine whiteness, the Clyde River swelled and burst and carried all before it.

The pressure against Archie's thighs told him that the cycle was beginning to lean towards the right. He felt so confident that he could ride the curve by means of touch alone that at first he did not open his eyes or grab the handlebars, and even when the angle grew more acute so that his body was like the wing of a Spitfire as it wheeled in for the kill, still he did not reach for the cycle. It was as though he wanted to see how far it would go, possessed as he was by the knowledge that unlike in a Spitfire, control of the situation remained in his hands even if they were empty; that at any moment he would simply have to stretch back the skins of his lids and extend the tips of his fingers until they just touched and no more, and that he would be able to play the cycle as a maestro would, a piano grand. But then the rear tyre slipped sideways and he, his bicycle and his manifold visions flew into the air and tumbled chaotically, ignominiously, painfully to the ground. He was going fast downhill, and so his body tore along the rough surface of the road and he took a great thump in his ribs and then (or perhaps it was before; it all happened so quickly, the exact sequence of events was hard to know) another to the right side of his head, just above the temple.

The road and the trees and what remained of the sky circled before his eyes, and the right side of his body was shot through with a numbness which turned quickly to a searing pain and then, a little later, to a persistent throbbing ache. He swore aloud, and was alarmed at the shakiness of his voice and at the intensification of the silence. He took several deep breaths, tried to steady the world, and then again he tried to speak, but this time it was in a low, deliberately measured way.

'I am Archibald Enoch McPherson,' he said, 'and I am in the Royal Air Force. Today, I am in a forest in the north-western part of the English county of Lincolnshire, and I am lying in the middle of the road.'

Having spoken, he felt instantly ludicrous, lying crumpled by the broken bicycle, its black frame twisted, its front wheel buckled and its back wheel still spinning.

He spat hard, twice, and then gazed up at the sky which had been cut to pieces by the interlacing branches of the trees. Elms, he thought, or ash maybe, he wasn't sure. Now that the world had stopped spinning, the smells were growing stronger; the stink of himself and that of all the trees of the forest. Night would be here soon, but before that would come a silent summer twilight which would envelope the land like musk. Beneath the canopy of the leaves the road was warm, and Archie knew that he would have to get up at some point and begin to walk home. Then he laughed. Since when has the aerodrome been my home, he thought. Leaky Nissen huts, hastily grassed runways, echoing J-type hangars. The smell of black metal and roses. Glass turrets. And noise, always noise.

With some difficulty he levered himself up onto his side and then onto his feet. He noticed that the outer flap of his right boot had been badly scuffed. Bits of cheese were scattered over the road and there was something that had darkened the tarmac. For a moment he thought it was blood, but then he remembered that he had been carrying both food and liquid. His bag had been strapped to the flat metal plate that sat across the top of the rear mudguard. So much for that. He dragged the twisted bicycle-frame over to the side of the road and heaved it up onto the low embankment. He felt tiny glass splinters in his wrist. The hands of his watch were skewed at impossible angles, so that according to these it was now approaching midnight. He undid the leather strap and flung the watch into nearby bushes. He thought he heard a scuffling sound and wondered if the dead timepiece might have disturbed a rodent. Then he climbed down the other side of the embankment and entered the forest.

He had already gone so far in that he could no longer make out the road, when he discovered that he had also lost his compass.

The air around him was warmer than it had been out in the open, but the light was growing dim, and as though on the instruction of an invisible conductor, the night choir began to sing. He reasoned that eventually he would reach either the other side of the forest, or else a large clearing where he might spend the night. It was too late to walk back to the aerodrome, and no-one would be likely to open their doors to a strange man at this time. The farmers' big dogs would be out, guarding the barns. The thought occurred to him that he might be mistaken for a fox or even a spy, and shot. He was not a deserter, not yet. But that was fanciful. And fancy was something he could do without.

He wiped the blood out of his eyes. His skull was pounding, there was a painful swelling over his right temple, and he wished he had brought along some aspirin. Or maybe a hip-flask of whisky. I could sit in these woods and pour the gold into my mouth and get quietly, supremely drunk, he thought. But he had nothing, and darkness was falling fast. He thought he heard the sound of distant church bells, but when he drew to a halt in order to listen more carefully, he could make out nothing beyond the night sounds of the forest and the regular rise and fall of his own breathing.

As the light faded Archie slowed his pace, not wanting to trip over the branches, rocks and occasional hollows which punctuated the forest floor. He was convinced that the trees were drawing closer together. The grass was sparser here, and the ground was springy with dead leaves. It occurred to him that beneath some of this compost might lie bogs, reed-beds or snakes. Adders, with blue chevrons running down their backs. Old worms. The commons of England seethed with such things. In their own quiet way, they were as wild as the Highlands of Alba. In some of these places, he thought, nothing has changed since the last quill flourish of the Book of Domesday. Oh, what's the bloody difference, he thought. Die in a bombing-raid, or perish in the darkness of a forest. Or in bed at home, aged and pinioned under the glare of one's family. You'd be dead just the same. Finished. He shivered, though it was not cold. The air lay thick and still, and not even time moved across the surface of the forest. He paused, and leaned against a tree. Gazed up, tried to make out the stars, but the foliage was too dense.

Throughout the year, but especially during the autumn, sea haars would descend without warning upon the aerodrome for days, and then no flights would be possible. The RAF had brought in a fire-belching machine, but it wasn't always effective. There was something about the low level of the terrain around the aerodrome that was particularly conducive to the gathering of thick mist, and on those days visibility would drop to ten or twenty feet and the world would smell of salt and fishscales. And then, in spring, a glaucous green mist would rise slowly from the marshes. The land hereabouts had been drained by a series of energetic Dutchmen in the seventeenth century, enterprising Protestant men with names like Cornelius; yet beneath the vast silent fields, under the ordered rows of wheat and barley and the cubes of neatly harvested hay, its mudbanks shifted and its dark waters seethed and broiled and threatened to seep through the interstices of this most modern of wars.

He remembered that one night, in the depths of winter, he had been patrolling the perimeter fence. Snow and fog had reduced visibility to fifteen feet – and that, with a powerful military torch – and even though he was wearing his blue greatcoat over multiple layers of wool, every so often Archie had to stop and jump up and down five or six times just to get his circulation running again. Somewhere on the far side of the fence, a gurgling dyke; commonly in Lincolnshire, these would serve as both drain and enclosure, and on his rounds Archie was quite accustomed to hearing the sounds of splashing. He reasoned that otters would be emerging from their holes and were of no consequence – so long as they didn't burrow into the runways. But on this night it was something else. At first he thought that it was simply the reverberation from the tough leather of his boots hitting the tarmac, but then he remembered that the blanket of fog would have prevented any echo. He stopped moving, and tried to listen. From the sleek of the mist across his face, he realised that he had also stopped breathing.

There was nothing. Not even the rustle of the evergreens that grew beyond the perimeter fence and amongst which workmen had dumped piles of earth, rocks and muck. He clapped his gloved hands together and let his breath out. He began to walk away, a little more rapidly than before. Then he heard it again. He stopped in mid-stride. The sound fluctuated in volume, as though either it was coming from a long way off or else from somewhere far below the level of the airfield. He intoned a silent prayer: words which, in spite of the immanence of death wrought by war, he thought he had forgotten. *Forgive our debtors...* The Scottish version. Unlike the Anglican prayer it was not about land, privacy, transgression or violation, but poverty, coinage and guilt. It was a prayer of the poor.

> *Will our debtors forgive us? Those we have defiled.*
> *Those we have deceived,*
> *not in the heat of passion, but in the cold, clean*
> *air of the dawn gibbet.*

But then he seemed to forget the sequence. The skin and flesh of other tongues tore through the stone of this place, of Lindsey, Lincolnshire, Danelaw, the defiant laments of those who had lost everything, who had been nothing, and now all these voices inserted themselves into the meat of his throat and began to twist and churn and to evoke different songs, deeper dialects.

> *For behold, from henceforth: all generations shall call me blessed.*
> *For he that is mighty hath magnified me: and holy is his name.*
> *And his mercy is on them that fear him: throughout all generations.*
> *He hath shewed strength with his arm: he hath scattered the proud in the imagination of their hearts.*
> *He hath put down the mighty from their seat: and hath exalted the humble and meek.*
> *He hath filled the hungry with good things: and the rich he hath sent empty away.*

His father's song. His father, who had run away to foment revolution in other places. Archie felt a numbness spread over his body, but it was not the usual effect of the freezing weather, for it began not at his soles but at the crown of his head, and moved downwards as though the very substance of the fog was entering and filling him. He understood now how, over the years, so many strong men had died like blind horses in these Carrs, men who had thought they had known the land better than their own bodies. A loud clatter came from under his feet. The light swung crazily. He had dropped the torch. Ignoring orders, he ran and didn't stop until he was through the barracks door. Yet even then, with everyone else asleep, the noise did not cease but grew louder, so that still in full gear he lay down on his bed and clamped his gloves over the frozen cartilages of his ears and closed his eyes tightly. But that only caused the sound to reverberate as though he too were sitting at the bottom of a well, deep in the night forest, singing in falsetto the great Magnificat, over and over again for the undulating length of eternity. But there was more than that; there was something which, after that night, made Archie avoid being alone in that corner of the aerodrome for the remainder of the War. He had felt the tongues singing in his skull, intoning, whispering to him the moment of his own death. Words, sung in a woman's voice:

I wish my baby it was born
And smiling on his daddy's knee
And I poor girl was in my grave
With the long grass a-growing all over me

Dig me my grave long wide and deep
Put a marble stone at my head and feet
And at my breast place a white snow dove
For to let the world know that I died for love

The bark of the elder tree was becoming rough against the skin of his back. Even the insects seemed to have retreated; or perhaps, Archie thought, it is just that I have grown used to their sound. The paucity of light was beginning to play tricks on his eyes, and now as he gazed straight ahead between the trunks of two trees, the blackness seemed to assume the shape of a giant worm: a hideous prehistoric invertebrate with no eyes and a hidden mouth. He straightened up, brushed down his clothes. He wondered what he was doing here, a Scot uprooted and cast into this dark flat Angle land. Through the trees, he thought he saw a glimmer. He felt a ripple of relief; at last he must be approaching the far edge of the wood, and the lights would be coming from the farm-workers' cottages scattered around the outer borders of the fields.

As he followed the lights he had to stop at times, because the glimmer seemed to flicker and then vanish. Yet always it returned, and he reasoned that this must be simply an effect of the foliage. It was scientific, physical, lenticular like the trajectories of bombs, the billowing of thermals, the stacking of cumulus and cirrus and the flow of currents over the North Sea. Beneath the high tungsten of the hangars he would run his fingers along the warmed metal shanks of the bombers and fighters and reconnaissance aircraft, and he knew all about those, all about the death which they dispensed, the killing that lay at the centres of their existence, theirs and his, and he was an expert, he could tell which winds had buffeted their haunches, which steeples and streets they had seared and the smoke of which cities had risen to their bellies, bloated and blackened and screaming with song. The forest did not seem to be opening out as he had thought it would, though the scent of hyacinths was growing stronger the closer he got to the source of the light.

He stumbled out of the trees. He realised that he been almost running. He bent over and rested his hands on the shanks of his thighs, got his breath back. At first Archie thought that quite suddenly he had left the forest altogether, but then, when he looked up, he saw that he had simply entered a very large clearing. The stars shone brightly overhead, the way they did deep in the country where the night was at its blackest. There was no moon, or if there had been, then it had set awhile before. He must've been travelling through the forest for much longer than he had thought. He wished he had learned to read the sky. In the central part of the clearing was an area of complete darkness, and as he edged closer to this, he realised that it was a body of water. In the middle of the lake was a small island, connected to the rest of the clearing by a humpbacked stone bridge. Beyond the bridge, on the island, there was a two-storey house. He thought that the light must have been coming from one of the windows, but everything was dark now.

The shores of the lake seemed to run beyond the limits of his vision, back into the forest, and as he crossed the bridge he glanced over its side – it had neither wall nor railing – and then, when he had reached the highest point of the arch, he paused, picked up a stone, and dropped it into the darkness. It made a low-pitched sound as it struck the water, but the rippling died away within a few seconds. Although the water had remained invisible throughout, Archie had been counting, and listening. Twelve feet, he thought. Twelve feet from the bridge to the surface of the water. And then maybe another couple of fathoms down to the bottom. As he knelt, he noticed that cut into the stone flags was a mark which at first he had thought was just part of the natural architecture of the rock. As he traced his finger along its line, however, it seemed to form the shape of a cross whose long arm was pointing straight towards the house. From somewhere high in the trees, the sharp cry of a bird made him straighten up abruptly. The air was a little cooler here over the lake, and at least there was some movement, so that in spite of the fact that he was approaching this solitary building in the middle of the night, Archie felt less ill-at-ease than he had earlier, when he'd been hemmed in amongst the trees and the bracken. Here on the island, he could see where the land ended and the water began; he could feel the solidity of the earth beneath his boots – though if it had been any lower or flatter, he thought, the island surely would have sunk into the lake long before now. The place must be occupied: there had been the light, after all. But then, Archie thought, perhaps the light was just the glimmer of the heavens reflected back from the water. That would explain why it had shimmered and then vanished as he had approached. The fickleness of the stars. Yet, in a manner of speaking, they had led him out of the forest.

The house was almost cube-shaped and had been constructed of a gritstone which Archie had not seen anywhere else hereabouts: the buildings in North Lincolnshire mostly were made of fired red brick. It looked old – perhaps three hundred years old, he thought, though he was uncertain as to how he had come to that conclusion. It was something to do with the size of the windows: the small square sections of thick glass and the low level of the door lintel. Folk had been shorter in those days, or perhaps it was just that they had walked hunched-over, plague-ridden, witch-infested, laden with the weight of big black Breeches Bibles on their backs. All the curtains were drawn. He remembered that, apart from it being night-time, it was also the Blackout. He'd almost forgotten about the War. It was the first time since September '39 that he had been able to do that. When Clydeside had been bombed repeatedly he had sat by the aerodrome barracks' radio, listening to the broadcasts and wondering whether, at that moment, anyone he knew was being killed. The War had been a great morbid cloud that had descended upon the whole country, a highly technological Black Death. He could see that in places the stone had become lamp-black. He rubbed back and forth, feeling the tiny particles roll against his skin. He had half expected soot, but it wasn't that. The wall smelt musty like the stone on the inside of a vault, or like a tenement close at the end of a summer's day.

He went to the door. Knocked quietly, twice. No answer. So he knocked again, this time more firmly; but in his nervousness he overdid it, and the sound of his knocking pounded across the island. At this time of night, he thought, no-one was going to answer the door to a stranger. Quickly, he made up a story: He, a military man, had been patrolling the forest, searching for unexploded Jerry bombs. But then he wasn't in proper uniform. Anyone could've got hold of what he was wearing and anyway, with the accident, his clothes had been badly torn in places. People would wonder what he'd been through, how he'd ended up here. They might think he was a spy who had parachuted from an Axis aircraft and who spoke English with a slightly peculiar accent, or they might see him as a deserter. He might try to convince them that in fact he was a British spy, working undercover, and that he didn't want to draw attention to his work. But then why would he have to be incognito, here, in the heart of England – and in a deserted forest, in the middle of a summer's night? They would soon see through that one. In fact, lying might be extremely dangerous. The people around these parts weren't used to Scots voices. He knew of some Polish airmen who had been arrested on the spot by irate farmers wielding pitchforks and threshers. Red or black, Polish or Prussian, an eagle was an eagle.

No, it would be best simply to tell the truth. He had smashed up his bicycle and had wandered through the woods and got lost. And could they please direct him out of here? Him being an airman and it being a war, he would have to return to his base the day after next or he'd be in real trouble. Simple. Maybe they would even invite him in for a cup of tea, or else to stay the night. People in the countryside remained hospitable. A guest was treated with honour and given all manner of sugary cakes and flitches of bacon, of which the family members themselves partook only in small rationed quantities. Perhaps they would have some black market stuff. Such tiny cracks in the steel hull of war reminded one that people, after all, were human. Like Margaret and he, those nights in the hangar, the shelter, the woods, the wet cleft of a slow-flowing dyke. This conflict, even more than the first, had blown the breeches, clasps and staves apart so that now they fluttered like streams of burning aluminium in the sky. The fear of Hell, blitzed like Clydebank.

There was a brass handle at the left side of the door.

Still no reply. He couldn't just leave, not after he'd come this far. And anyway, he had no idea of compass direction. The trees formed a perfect ring all around the lake. If the house was empty, he would enter somehow and then would stay the night, and if it wasn't, he would try and explain himself to the occupants in as calm a manner as possible. He held his breath and turned the brass handle.

Inside the cottage was bare, save for one wooden chair and, in the far corner, a grandfather clock. The clock could not have been wound up, for its hands indicated the time as eleven o'clock and Archie was certain that it was long past that now. There was no fire in the grate, and though some old logs had been piled up, they had not been stripped and had turned green with moss. Next to the clock a narrow winding staircase led to the upper floor. It was one of those old cottages the ground floor of which consisted of just one room and a kitchen. And the kitchen was simply a narrow space on the left side of the house, quite bare save only for a log stove. It was clear that no-one had lived here for a good while. But he would check upstairs before making himself comfortable. Archie was surprised that it hadn't been despoiled by tramps and that it was pristine. No cobwebs, no dust. Someone had obviously taken care of it, though oddly they had neglected, on this night at least, to lock the door.

Upstairs, he found a single bed covered with a striped mattress and a coarse blanket. As far as he could make out there was no roof space, and in the starlight the shadows of the wooden beams criss-crossed the bed. The springs creaked loudly as Archie pressed down on the mattress. It was the sort of place that might have housed the family of a farm-worker. Yet they must have left some time before, he thought, since now there was none of the scent or detritus of human habitation. All that was left was the odour of gritstone and old rust. All the same, he went back down the stairs just to be sure, and searched behind the doors and in all the cupboards. It was as though the essence of the dwelling had been absorbed back into its four walls and roof.

And suddenly, Archie became aware of the deep architectonics of this far county: the low grass and wheel-ruts of the green roads, the church walls stained with the blood of murdered boy Bishops, the swaying notes of pig-iron and silver cornet and the silent miraculous darkness of saints' wells. The cold fingers of spirit children, long-dead of ague, typhus, cholera, plague. Belzybob, Bow Slasher and the Quack Doctor, Saint George and the Turkish Knight, and the slabs beneath which their bodies all turned quietly to earth.

Archie went upstairs again, removed his trousers, and lay down on the mattress. Since there was no pillow, he folded his coat and used that instead. The warmth of the summer night made him toss and turn on the creaking iron springs. He gazed up at the shadowy forms of the trees that keeled across the wattle and beams of the ceiling. It was as though he was lying at the bottom of the reed-bed of the lake and gazing up through the cold dark waters.

The world was fevered, fitful, attenuated, and likewise, the quality of the light in the room was etiolated, a smattering of dust from the stars, rising like mist from the surface of the lake. In this tenebrous state sleep would not come; his body sweated uncomfortably and his mind grew active, his perception painfully clear, like liquid glass.

He peeled off the remainder of his clothes and then went over and shoved open the rusted window. The full moon had risen. No bombing-runs then, he thought, as he went back to bed.

Something began to form on the floor in the darkness of the far corner of the room. At first he thought it might be just another shadow, or a pile of old rags, but as he watched it seemed to coil upon itself and acquire solidity. He propped himself up on his elbow and peered more closely. His curiosity unassuaged, he got up and went over. It was an earthenware carafe. It was heavier than he had thought, and he could hear the liquid sloshing about inside. He twisted off the cork and sniffed and then recoiled. It smelt of hagberry. He wondered how in God's name he had known that. Then he noticed something even more peculiar. On the floor, beside the place where the carafe had been, was a goblet. It was not of the common type, with slim stem and flat base; in fact, it was far larger than any glass Archie had ever seen, and had no stem at all. He put down the carafe and cradled the goblet in both palms. Around its rim was a band of highly-polished copper or brass. His head pounded. Sweat ran down his temples; his lips felt dry and puckered. The goblet itself seemed to have been made neither of metal, nor of glass. There were striations down its sides, a little akin to those on a very old parchment map, where the lines and squiggles represented rivers, paths and hills. Three jagged courses converged close to the base, while shallower indentations ran independently of one another. Quickly, Archie tipped a measure of the liquid into the cup, swirled it around, sniffed again and this time did not recoil. Then, briskly, he brought it to his lips and swallowed.

Nothing happened. It tasted of nothing. Not like water, exactly: more like air, had it been possible somehow to turn air into liquor. His lips felt even drier than before. So he poured more liberally this time, and drank again. And again. Soon the carafe was half-empty. He set both carafe and goblet down on the floor and went back to bed. As he pulled the rough blanket over his nakedness, again he thought he heard the sharp cry of the pyewipe; but by that point, he wasn't sure whether he might already have been dreaming.

The darkness in the room seemed to have faded slightly, and Archie wondered whether dawn at last might be arriving. But surely it must be a false dawn, he thought: of the sort that rises during a blitz or before a storm. He forced himself to think of tedious things like Air Force Regulations, or like his ration-card, or else concrete things like Margaret's welcoming nudity beneath the lights of the tungsten bunker. They had gone down, one dark summer's night, into the barely-used air-raid shelter out by the perimeter hedge. And in the darkness that had been so warm and intense it had seemed like the insides of their bodies, they had become naked and had made love for the first time. There, on the sandy earth floor, they had jived and sung breathlessly in each other's ears until their song had risen up and defied the searchlights and the growling Dornier 17s and the howling diving metal Stukas and the blood and hate of a thousand meaningless wars – and it was there, on that first night, in the time before they were married, that Archie had seen, through Margaret's body as though through a wall of alabaster, the bodies of all the lovers that had gone before and all that would come after. That knowledge had stayed with him all his life; it lived within him even now, within the filaments of tumour that perhaps had been born during the air-raid that night and upon which now his heart's blood began to play the notes of a lost, an unwritten symphony.

Slowly, as though he was a very old man, he got up and, hands on hips, began to pace around the walls of the room. He stopped as he passed by the half-opened window and rested his forehead against the glass. With both hands he gripped the casement. He closed his eyes and felt the night slip away behind his tired lids. He sighed. Then he felt something give, and he fell forwards. He felt the weight of his body heave out the window, and tried to alter his centre of gravity – but it all happened too fast, and Archie found himself falling through darkness.

Light streamed into his brain. A buzzing sound. The smell of honey. There was something close to his face. Something shaped like a guitar. But it was moving. In fact, it was singing. Archie opened his eyes properly. Then he coughed hard, twice. The bird almost smashed into his eyes as it flapped its wings and flew away. He was lying at the side of an unmetalled country road. The bicycle which he had been riding lay some twelve feet to his left, its twisted frame half-hidden in the straggly grass that grew on the fringes of the forest. The air smelled of tar and wheat. The sky was bright blue. He could tell from the position of the sun that it was mid-morning. His right temple ached and he was stiff all over. He moved his arm slowly to his scalp, to the site of a painful plum-sized swelling. Then he remembered. He had been cycling through the woods. He must have lain here all night. And in all that time, he thought, no-one had passed by. Archie saw a wasps' nest hanging from one of the low branches of the nearest of the trees, around eight feet above the ground. His body felt like wood as he hobbled the few paces it took to get to the tree. The nest's structure had been laid open to the elements so that he could see the rows, the passageways, the camerae, as though he were gazing at the innards of a modern building complex. The nest was clearly deserted. He rubbed his hands up and down over the fronts of his thighs and he noticed a laceration on the back of his left hand. It wasn't deep and must have stopped bleeding a while back, since a scab already had begun to form across its edges. The gash fascinated him for a few seconds and he attributed his fascination to exhaustion; yet it was this, he thought, the small, the inconsequential, the unavoidably physical, to which we return always.

He would have to get back to the aerodrome.

Still very stiff, he began to walk along the road, back in the direction whence he had come. As the dark mass of the forest receded, he had the feeling that there was a space where the night should have been – but Archie had learned not to pry into the dark closes of life, and so he forgot about it. There would be time enough for remembering, after this damned war was over. A whole lifetime, he hoped.

As he walked, he became aware that something was making his left side seem disproportionately heavy. Finally he paused, and thrust his left hand into his jacket pocket. His hand jumped out. His fingers had touched something – some object – that was intensely hot. He blew on the skin, then fished in his trousers for a handkerchief. Holding this gingerly, like a glove, Archie dipped back into his jacket pocket and removed and examined the object. It was a small book with a red leather cover across the front of which was inscribed a staff topped by a coiled serpent, and around this inscription was some faded gold lettering. Warily he spoke the words aloud, but his voice was swallowed by the breeze which had just got up, and which made the bulbous heads of the wheat and barley turn and sway upon their stalks. He spoke the words again, and though he knew that his pronunciation was clumsy, yet in his mind the words seemed quite clear.

'*Yussef va Zoleikha: The Memoirs of Lord Jack Ruthyn of Simnel Manor,*' he said. And though he had absolutely no idea what it meant, he repeated it again, just to be sure.

BOX TWO: ARGYLL

It is riches you love, and not people; when we were alive, it was people we loved.

From *The Lament of the Old Woman of Beare, c.900 AD*

Chapter Eleven

Mid-Argyll, mid-morning, mid-winter. Alex helped her over the last of the hillocks, and then they both stopped – partly to get their breath back, and partly because the view was so magnificent.

The body of the Black Loch was shaped like that of an enormous surahi, with a broad belly and a long stem that tapered as it fell away into the hazy sunlight. Over to their left, way beyond the far side of the loch, the shadowed mountains of Islay and Jura hulked like great stone whales. Zuleikha and Alexander were staring almost straight into the low sun, which at this time of day and in this season shone from due south. Running back from the shore closest to where they were standing, the sandy beach was dotted with white pebbles. This admixture threw up a luminescence over the surface of the water which made everything else look dark by comparison: the scrub-grass, which began close to the beach and which was patchy at first, but which grew thicker as it rose up the hill to where they were positioned; the winding fences of the enclosures that marked the outermost hilly boundaries of the farmland; the flattened fields devoid of livestock; the tight bushes of gorse and clematis that had caught at their ankles nearly the whole way as they had walked from the clearing where they had left their car. This morning was a world of extremes.

In this light, the usually dun brown skin exposed between the upper line of her gloves and the end of her anorak-sleeves glowed almost white, while Alex's face resembled a beacon. Zuleikha was glad she had brought her sun-glasses, even though at the time it had seemed a most unseasonal thing to do. Alex had not, and now wiped his face with the back of his glove. Her breath disappeared into the light and her head felt woozy. She hadn't eaten since she'd had some fruit around nine o'clock, and it was now eleven. She'd thought that a greasy meal would just slow her up, make her sleepy, but as they had clambered over the hills in this freezing weather her energy levels had soon run down and her limbs had begun to ache. It had not seemed so far on the Ordnance Survey map. Her calf and thigh muscles felt numb. She wobbled slightly, and then she noticed that he'd slipped his arm around her waist. Zuleikha began to tremble, but immediately stopped herself. She steadied her breathing. Deepened it, even though every inhalation was an icicle in her lungs.

'It's beautiful,' she exhaled.

He looked down at the side of her face.

'I'm glad we came,' he said quietly.

In the middle of the panorama, fifty yards or so from the water's edge, was a chapel with, at one end, a squat bell-tower. The air was hard and cold, yet there was only the hint of a breeze floating off the surface of the inland sea. The water most certainly did not appear to be black, but Zuleikha knew that such lochs – of which there were many in Scotland – got their name from the nature of the peat soil that formed their basins.

Zuleikha went right down to the water's edge and watched as a dark stain crept up the black leather of her boots. The clarity of the water acted as a magnifying-glass on the loch bed, so that she could make out the tiny tunnels which crabs had dug as the tide had gone out, and she could trace the ochre forms into which the rock had been torn ten thousand years earlier when the last of the icebergs had retreated, carrying bits of Scotland towards the North Pole. And then, as the floor of the beach angled gradually downwards, she sensed the enveloping darkness of the deep. She wondered what kinds of fish might circle in the cold still world of the Black Loch. Twelve-foot one-eyed singing fish, most probably. The kind that could live in water that was so far inland it was hardly salty any more: estuary fish, the beasts of the marches. Or maybe the kinds that could alter their form depending on where they found themselves. Like the lungfish they'd seen when they visited that place outside Edinburgh: the fish that had bucked over the tops of the waves like moustachio'd bandidos escaping from some dark-headed marshal of the deep. Everyone had been laughing, but how could such an unnatural thing be amusing? She'd thought they were monsters. She had half-expected them to open their oval mouths and speak, or sing of the death of God.

She removed a lighter and a packet of cigars from her coat pocket. Though she shaded the cigar in the cup of her hand, she really had no need to. She took a few gulps, swirled the smoke around in her mouth, let its flavour slink up the back of her nose and then exhaled, straight to heaven. I really ought to chuck this shit, she thought, and took another puff.

She saw that Alex was heading straight for the chapel door, and at this distance his figure was barely a speck against the backdrop. He seemed thinner than she remembered; his clothes hung off him as though he was on a diet, but it was probably just an effect of the light. He can't be on a diet: he eats me out of house and home. Yet still he hasn't invited me to his place. Perhaps he's afraid of Susan's ghost, or of the effect that her near-presence might have on me. Perhaps he's afraid that it might put me off. Or maybe he just likes eating curries. Says he cooks them himself. But they're probably not quite right. Perfection: you don't get that from cookery books. It's to do with fingers, touch, smell, taste – the things you were taught at your mother's elbow, stuff you could never learn. Like the way the rice grains in a pot of boiling water had to break easily into three pieces when massaged gently between thumb and forefinger. Muscle memory.

They had booked separate single rooms in the bed-and-breakfast, and they had brought the box with them in her car and had lodged it, along with her case and his lute, in her room. She had refused to allow the box out of her sight. You're crazy, he'd said. When you go to work, when you go visiting your patients, it is out of your reach. Your face takes on that Cecil B. de Mille, mother-of-God expression, and like an icon you suck their problems into your body. Meanwhile, your flat could be burgled; some invertebrate, copper-thieving, lag-eyed junkie could slip long fingers through the space between pane and frame and steal the box, carry it off to his den of pus, semen and hypoderm heaven – or, God forbid, there might be a fire and then the thing would go up in flames. When you got back home, a neat pile of white ashes would be waiting for you in the living-room.

She had wanted to say, *No, Alex; we Muslims do not cremate our dead. We bury them. That's why we ran out of space, first among the old gas-mask warriors in the Western Necropolis and then in the suburban mohallas of the Cathcart cemetery, so that now like bards and Druids we inter ourselves in fields and forests* – but she'd thought this would make her sound even more insane

195

than she already was, she, a woman in…

It had begun with a hiatus in sanity, that long May morning when the box had arrived. A veritable matchmaker, it had lit fires in their minds. But they'd not been lovers: not then and not for a while later – at least not in the carnal manner, though perhaps the postponement of consummation had deepened her feeling of dissolution. Maybe love was something through which you might annihilate yourself. Insanity, right enough.

She looked around. His body had disappeared into the chapel. He had fallen silent after their conversation about the box and the hypothetical fire. It must have been that phrase he quite casually had used: *Mother of God*. In view of the fact that her god had died aged nine and a half months, that King Herod the Great had been successful this time around and had ripped the salvation from her breasts, Alex probably had felt a little guilty about letting the phrase trip so carelessly from his lips. But she was guessing. You could never tell with men. They were like closed books. Or sealed boxes. Perhaps, like the brass rubbing of a dead Lady of the Loch, his Catholic wife had left her imprint on him. Mind you, she thought, they probably feel much the same about us. We are sparring, even when we do not intend it. It is a long pointless quadrille, yet still every time we leap joyously into it, or else into the fire.

At the far end of the long beach was a smashed-up breakwater, parts of which were swathed in white bedsheets and scuffs of polythene. A wave of sadness swept over her, and yet its aftertaste was pleasingly poetic: it held a quality of relinquishment, and its passage, like that of a tidal breath, left her mind clear. She felt suddenly intensely exposed there on the beach, almost as though she had stripped off and was preparing to make her way down the waters into blackness. She stubbed out the fag-end on a paper hankie and stuffed both into her pocket. She felt suddenly cold and, folding her arms, she left the water's edge and headed for the chapel.

They had opened the second box – or perhaps it had allowed itself to be opened – and there they had discovered another piece of paper. This one had been inscribed on one side with an unpetalled rose. A dead rose, you might say, or else a very young one, drawn in fine lines across the centre of the page. When Alex had flipped it over, there had been another set of cryptic numbers on which he had set to work almost immediately and which, after two days' work, he had converted into another map. This time it appeared to be the Clyde River and its tributaries, oxbows, digressions, the whole thing; a detailed water-map which, the longer she had gazed at it, had grown more and more to resemble the intricate vascular system of the human body, or more specifically of the human head. The absorptive area of a single gut spanned the rectangle of doubles tennis, she thought, while the transference of a lung was more or less on a par with the surface area of a squash court. So then, what equivalence did the human brain connote? The solar system, the galaxy, the universe? Each micro-tubule a thousand-and-one light years, rolled and secreted in obscure knots and whorls. Facts, facts, facts. Ah yes, these things had bothered her as she'd tuned to the classical music channel (the slow-paced one blissfully devoid of catchy melodies, hit parades or adverts) or as she'd steered her car around blind corners towards cooking-houses filled with snotty babes and blaring television sets, or as she had fallen into apartments where the temperature matched that of summer in central Africa and which rattled with bony oldies who smelt always of ninety-one-year-old underarm sweat.

Anyway, when she had compared the markings on the paper to the patterns and symbols which she had seen above her on the walls of the underground tunnel, they had matched perfectly. And one more thing: when held up to the light, the bald rose had shone through the paper onto the chart of the river system, and when the whole was superimposed upon an Ordnance Survey map of the area around the Clyde, the rose's centre lay not over any watercourse of the river itself, but rather somewhat to the north, right bang over this loch – or rather, over this pebbly beach and its ancient stone chapel. It had taken them a couple of months to figure all this out and for her to get time away from work in order to be able to come here. And now it was early winter, and the light came down bright, cold and almost perfect.

During those weeks Alex and she had gone out together on many occasions. The usual things: cinemas, restaurants, even a ten-pin bowling alley. Strange that neither of them previously had been into knocking over skittles – but then, she thought, neither had they made a pastime of reaching down deep into possibly empty boxes or deciphering cryptic codes. Perhaps these were the sorts of things you did when you were falling in love. That was what they all said, the liars, the singers, the storytellers. The poets and conjurors. Zulie had been there before: she'd engaged in a handful of glittering sojourns by the lake of romance. And yet, every time, it had been different. It was like a piece of folk music: it played always within a certain set of rules, it followed a particular sonic arc, but within those parameters there was almost infinite scope for variation. Like the best poetry, love arose always from a bed of misery.

Ah, now she was becoming a mistress of homilies, a sated repository of wisdom. Who was she fooling?

There was nothing logical or mathematical about it, and certainly nothing ecclesiastical. It was a craving to encompass, to possess, simultaneously to rule and be the subject. Human love was a Hindu thing: not the elevated stuff of the saadhus and gurus, but the mud and blood and spunk of the hairy backside statues, the stale sweated stones, the rivers filled with organic detritus and plastic and sick fishes into whose mouths you gazed and saw the cosmic whole.

Alexander. The quizzical look, the uncertainty of his brow, his irrepressible belly. The way he scratched his head. His mask had dissolved, as sooner or later it had to in a relationship. And behind it Alex was a comical figure really: plaster a moustache over his lip and he'd be something out of an Ealing comedy – well, a Scottish colour version of an Ealing comedy. A biscuit-tin man with a heart of jam. She'd seen a thousand Alexes come through the door of her consulting-room. His was a common-or-garden look. Middle, middle, middle, middle, middle class. Nothing out of the ordinary, nothing spectacular. Nothing to write to home about. Yet there was something singular about him, and it was not just his voice – which, she admitted, was so very hypnotic. And anyhow, there had been that day back in the late spring when she had found herself down by the riverbank, and now today – look at her – she was following this funny big man into a deserted freezing chapel by the shore of a loch in the middle of deepest

Argyll. Dál Riata, the first March of the Scots. God was not on the menu. Minor demons, maybe.

The chapel must have been a good deal older than the Reformation, since its sandstone walls bore the usual marks of rabid iconoclasm. Even in those days, she thought, Scotland had been full of headbangers. The evidence of vandalism continued all the way up to the slated roof, the fractured buttresses, the empty niches, the headless corpses. Saints, anonymised, eviscerated, flattened. Zuleikha craned her neck. Without the heads they were nothing. Alex had left the large wooden door open. But as soon as she crossed the granite lintel, it was as though she was entering a different world. Unlike on the outside, the statues and carvings here remained intact. It was puzzling that the interior had survived the ferocious axes of Knox and Co., but it had. Yes, okay: he was a reformer and the Vatican had created the motherfucking Inquisition, yet... Perhaps some important relative of his had had a quaint childhood fondness for the place, and given that this church had lain so far from anywhere, perhaps the interior of the chapel had been spared the breaker's axe.

It was surprising really, because Zuleikha had never seen such a richly decorated church in her life. Every centimetre of stone was used up, as though whoever had built it had been afraid of blank spaces or empty thoughts. While the bulk of the structure had been cut from white sandstone, the jambs, lintels and some of the pointing had been done in granite. A mixture, then, of soft and hard, of the west and east limbs of the body of Scotland. It wasn't the usual kind of church statuary either. The figures here were stumpy, and half-eroded so that they had all but lost any resemblance to the human body. Or perhaps they had never been human to begin with, but had been simulacra, Mediaeval jokes, patterns of lines and dots, fake structures formed by shadows and light.

They were not stupid, those masons, she thought. They had drawn their architectures of the mind from the hinterlands of Paradise, and this knowledge had been buried so deeply inside their heads that eventually they had forgotten its meaning. Like her father, cutting down the gladioli as the summer fell and binding back the heads of the witch hazel lest they should rise above their station. Summoning the cartoon magic of rowan and yew. These were the only ways to get by. Carve yourself in deep, so that five centuries later you come to be revealed in the stone whorls when the acid and the damp and the righteous mistakes of monochrome scientists have done their damage and eroded the rock right down to its core. And there in the letters, never before seen, the revealed, forbidden name of her Hibernian grandmother, and within the carving of a goat, there was a boy. Within the whale, there was a prophet. And inside the man ... who knows? An oak, perhaps. Alex was holding the piece of paper out from his body as though it was a dowsing-rod. The ink scrawled across it looked to her to spell the words:

VIDDRUS

A sense of the ridiculous overwhelmed her and she fully intended to be satirical, or worse; but she found that she had to shout, and this ameliorated the effect somewhat.

'Why are we here? This is really weird.'

He answered her in a quieter voice, and without looking at her.

'We're here because you found the box.'

She looked up at the sloping ceiling which was divided into thirds and which was decorated with golden stars and moons and symbols cut in a strange script. They looked Egyptian, or Jewish, or something like shorthand. She had tried to learn shorthand once, but had failed miserably. The problem had not been writing it – that had been relatively simple – but when she'd come to read over what she'd written, the act of translating what was a non-spoken language back into English had proved irritating and pointless.

'Zulie, we have to follow this to wherever it leads.'

Craning her neck made her dizzy, and she looked back down towards Alex.

'Wherever?' She was trying to be subtle, but her high-pitched voice was beginning to sound distinctly squeaky. Hysterical woman. Fuck sake.

'There's no other way. Once it's set in motion, we have to keep going.'

The church stopped spinning.

'No brakes, you mean. Like Susan.'

She wanted to bite back her lip, to bite deep into the flesh till she tasted heart's blood; she wanted to swallow her tongue, her mouth, her head, and to disappear or become one of those statues perched high up on the church walls, blasted by five hundred years of rain and wind and hate.

The paper trembled, but it was just the breeze coming in through the opened door. She took one step forward, her hand proffered in an uncertain gesture of apology, or support, or placation. He turned slowly. Looked at her. The man to whom she had made love, and who had made love to her, nineteen times. Or was it twenty? Or a hundred and one? It depended on whether you counted each session or each individual penetration. He had filled her with his whispering voice, with the tremulousness of its frequencies. At such volumes a low-pitched voice fragmented, became something which required her protection. All those church portals and mihrabs.

Or, to put it another way, it had been an autumn of cunt, cock and arse and, at times, the varied architectonics of fucking had become the only reality. Though perhaps, in reality, it had been merely an escape, an addiction, like watching, end-to-end, a series of feature films on dvd or munching on those cardiotoxic extra-large packets of crisps. His phallus was thicker than some; the smegma-and-gloss pornographers who were the core educational resource on sex never seemed to comprehend that it was not the length, but the diameter, that was of some importance to women. The performance value of a penis lay solely in its ability to stimulate the clitoris, not in its qualities as a battering-ram.

Nonetheless, sex was good for a Scottish autumn; it belied the darkening. Endorphins. Thor-finn. When the Vikings had been raiding along the west coast, there must surely have been a last fuck on Iona. Zuleikha and Alexander had tried all the positions in all the books, even some of most esoteric gymnastic ones – the ones that had been drawn only because the guys who had inscribed those texts (or at least, the bods who had translated them) – *The Perfumed Garden*, the *Kama Sutra* and those Indian weavings that had issued from the fingers of Shiva – all had had an abiding sense of humour. For God's sake! She probably had a half-litre of his stuff inside her. A loch of silver sperm, tiny archangels dancing over her waters. She felt as though the wind was blowing through all her orifices. And it was bloody cold. It was easier for frogs, she thought, but much less fun.

He shook his head very slowly, so that later, she was no longer certain that the movement had occurred at all. Spoke quietly, yet in that stone place his whispered words seemed to resonate far more than her screeching ever had.

'No. Not like Susan.'

And he went on with his search.

She hated herself, for feeling pity. This insane journey into which they had been sucked was as much his as it was Zuleikha's, and she needed to stop being envious of his abilities – musical, mathematical or otherwise. Or else whatever they had would be poisoned slowly like the stone in this church. No, that was wrong. Their spirits would be eroded from the inside out, the modern way. She thought the sound of the loch had grown louder. Perhaps it was tidal after all.

Alex had stopped next to a tall pillar. She came up beside him. The pillar was about ten feet in height and was lavishly decorated, even more so than the rest of the chapel. Sleek dragons curled around its base, their talons and bodies interlocking so that it was difficult to tell where one beast ended and the next began. They seemed almost Chinese, though she supposed that they couldn't possibly be – not here. Norse, maybe. Garlands of barley, wheat and peas were wrapped around the legs of the dragons, while from their bodies there grew a giant lavish vine, a vine so thick it resembled a tree that twisted around itself in a complex spiral right up to the crown of the pillar, where it melded into a series of friezes and statues that ran horizontally around the stone. Her voice was back to normal.

'It's funny that I've never been here before, after forty-odd years of living only a hundred miles to the south. Less, as the crow flies.'

'The crow?' Alex seemed distracted.

'Yes. Glasgow – I was brought up in Glasgow, and yet I'd never even heard of this place till a few weeks ago.'

He shrugged.

'Neither had I. Neither have most people in this country of ours. Perhaps that's just as well.'

She slipped off her black woollen glove and reached out a hand. In this light her skin seemed inordinately pale, the hairs on the dorsae of her fingers barely visible.

He trembled as she touched his waist. She leaned her head against his shoulder. His bulky anorak was bone cold against her cheek. She glanced up at him. Shit.

'I'm sorry, love,' she said.

He inclined his neck so that his temple came into contact with the top of her head, his lank black hair mingling with hers. He was putting Zuleikha's stupidity, like Satan, behind him. She felt relief but also shame, and wished she had brought along some salt.

They stayed that way for around thirty seconds, until it had begun to feel a little ridiculous, this melodramatic resolution of a monosyllabic lover's tiff. She pulled away first, mainly because she couldn't bear him to. She exhaled loudly, and her breath made steam at the lion and the goat.

'That's Isaac,' he said. 'See, he's kneeling, waiting to be sacrificed.'

'Or Ismail, depending on your point of view.'

He glanced around, focused critically.

'This is too busy,' he began. He swept his arm around the vista, dismissively.

'That's a typical Anglo-Saxon attitude.'

It was overplayed, she knew, this difference between East and West. Meaningless terms, erected by those with deep-seated and cruel agendas. In reality, there were no divisions. Yet you found yourself bound by such nonsense; every day you lied to your own face. Anyway, Alexander – her Alexander, not the Great Conqueror of the World – was a Celt, wasn't he? And the Celts had tied themselves up in knots, hadn't they? Yet the people of the Scottish Lowlands had been formed from very mixed stock – Angles, Scots, Normans, Picts, and other things thrown in for good measure. Her father's family had been from Ireland, though the 'Mac' form of the prefix 'son of' was very uncommon over there. It was a Highland Scottish thing. But originally the two had been interchangeable: MacBethad, MacBeth, McBeth. Anyway, all the haplo-this and haplo-that, all that fixation with genes, it was such a load of crap.

'No, no. It's not that,' he answered. 'I mean, I can't sit on a pew and play my lute here. There's too much going on. And what if somebody walks in?'

'No-one's going to walk in. It's Monday morning, and it's mid-winter.'

'You never know. A woman doing the hoovering, or a priest, or something.'

Zuleikha glanced at the long dirty rug that covered the central aisle.

'I'm not even sure whether it's still used. I mean, the door was open.' She drew her arms around herself. 'And there's no heating. Nowadays, churches still in use are locked and bolted against thieves and false prophets. Anyway, even if there is a minister covering, say, three or four different churches, he – or she – is likely to be out and about among their flock.' She wondered whether she and Alex were really thieves. Goats in sheep's clothing.

'How the hell do you know?' he asked.

'Don't blaspheme.'

She'd meant it as a joke, but it hadn't come out like that and a serious expression crossed Alex's face. He wasn't a son of the manse, was he…?

He pointed to a stairwell.

'Let's go down there.'

She shoved her hands into her coat pockets. A red rope slung between two brass poles bared their way.

'I'm not sure whether we're supposed to go down here,' Zuleikha began, but he had scissored over the rope and was already halfway down the stone stairs.

It was much darker in the crypt, since the only light there was came through a number of small square-shaped stained-glass windows set at either side.

'It's a crypt, or a cellar,' he said. His voice echoed.

'Or a vault.'

The place was longer than it was broad, and close to the far wall was what looked like the beginnings of another staircase, one which had obviously been blocked up, or perhaps never properly built. There were just the remains of the first two stairs and then half of a third, and then a wall. There were no chairs in the crypt, but beneath each window was a horizontal ledge.

'It's not so cold down here,' she said. 'More sheltered.' Her boots echoed on the stone as she paced around the walls. She peered out of the window, but the mixture of grime and coloured stain prevented her from being able to make out anything except sunlight. It made her eyes smart. The light always seemed brighter when she wore lenses. Ah, the price of vanity! But she'd never liked specs. They'd always seemed to imprison her face, somehow; their metal frames, even the lightest ones, compressed her and made her temples and the tops of her ears itch and sweat unbearably. She was really quite badly short-sighted, and was also slightly astigmatic, which complicated things somewhat. Now, though, she'd managed to lose even her emergency pair of spectacles. If I lose my lenses too, I will be blind, she thought. I will see the world as though through this shining window here, and there will be only light. The bliss of high myopia. She reached up and touched the surface of the glass. It was cold, but not as cold as she'd expected. In the background, the distant wash of the loch, the swoop of wings. Gulls, with their shifty yellow eyes and tight white skins: the great watchers who followed the lines and staves made by the fish as they coursed through the almost frozen water. The sunlight grew stronger as the day mounted towards noon.

A thumping sound made her turn.

Alex was jumping up and down on the stone flags. He had put his lute-case beside him and was leaping from one stone to another in a movement which resembled that of a Hollywood Apache and which quite belied his bulk.

'You're nuts!' she laughed. 'You're mad! What on earth are you doing?' She was thinking that maybe he was just trying to get warm.

'This floor is false. There is a room beneath it.' His boots were making a hollow sound on the old stone floor.

'Okay, I get the idea. You can stop bouncing now!'

He stopped. His face was flushed. He spoke breathlessly, as much from excitement as from the physical effort.

'I was trying to outline the walls below.' He shook open the paper. 'I think this is a plan of the crypt.'

'How in God's name do you know that?'

The blood was beginning to prick at the skin of her face. The first stage of hypothermia, she thought. Or was it the second? He didn't answer, but bent down and removed his lute from its case. Then he sat on the window-ledge, crossed one leg over the other, and balanced the belly of the instrument over the thigh of the crossed leg. Zuleikha levered her bum up onto the opposite ledge. Through the denim of her jeans the stone felt pleasantly cold, and as she swung her heels against the wall she began to feel as though she was only three years old. The light streaming in through the window behind him reduced Alex to a silhouette. She thought he was smiling at her, and she smiled back. But then she wasn't sure; he seemed to be gazing through her, or at a level just above her head. This feeling got so strong that she was tempted to glance upwards, but she resisted doing so and instead, tried to concentrate on the lute.

She was sure it was her imagination, but Zuleikha thought that the lute looked smaller than before. Otherwise how could he possibly have balanced its big belly on his thigh like that – what with his big belly and all! Mind you, she thought, I was right: he has lost weight. He's becoming leaner, fitter. All that love-making must be good for him. And maybe for his lute, too. The neck seemed less complex, and the peg-box had fewer pegs, which were shaped like Coptic Crucifixes and were ornate and adorned with foliage. It bore only fifteen strings and not the twenty-five which it had had before. And now it was a dark red colour. Maroon, almost. Maybe he had a selection of lutes at home. Not that she had been there. Not really. Well, perhaps once, briefly, when he'd realised he'd forgotten something they'd needed. But she hadn't seen them there. The other lutes. He'd kept her waiting by the jamb of the porch door. People were funny, she thought; people were damned funny. With their jealously guarded eccentricities, they made you pregnant with laughter, they made you want to belly-laugh, to scream, to weep. It was as if their humanity somehow was defined more by these neurotic foibles than by the commonalities. But she had crept in while he was in the bathroom.

The walls had been covered with icons of Susan. Susan, the Dead One, resurrected in silver nitrate upon the cardboard and plaster walls of a small white house in satellite Glasgow, a pebble-dashed asylum of howling grief. And Zulie was aware that it remained their sanctum, the place of Susan and Alexander's marital communion, and that even if, in due course, she did graduate to his double-bed – and this was something about which she had fantastised on more than one occasion – she knew that she would never be permitted to enter that place. Not really: not in spirit. Her cunt, maybe; her heart, never. For all she knew, Alexander Wolfe kept a whole stack of lutes, theorbos, pandoras, kobzas, in a cupboard in his bedroom. Perhaps he slept with them, when he wasn't with her. Perhaps every night he spat his seed into their rose windows as he prayed sorrowfully to the Late Renaissance clitoris of *My Lade Bekluch*. God, that was sick. And now the lute had changed. No, that was silly. It was just that she couldn't see properly. Those contact lenses of hers needed changing, all right. She'd had them in for too many weeks. It was always like this. She neglected to clean them properly, and as a consequence, every few months, ended up half-blind. It was especially bad in this duality of light and darkness. Her eyes began to throb against the backs of their sockets, and she let the lids close.

When she opened them again, Alex was already playing. There was something wrong, though. At first, she was unable to pin it down, this inconsistency in a morning full of inconsistencies. The last few months had been a pantechnicon of strangeness, and Zuleikha had felt as though, like a refugee, she was clinging desperately to its undercarriage, the river of the road flowing beneath her. She was swimming ever deeper into the nucleic acid of Archie McPherson's consciousness, into the vestiges of his life. Saint Michael, over the water. She trembled. It was not her place to hand over his Domesday book, it was not up to her to decide into which hand – the left or the right – the record of his deeds, his thoughts, his desires would fall.

But perhaps it was the wrong way round. After all, right now it was not Archie who was six feet under. Like those ladies of the mansions who long ago had perished in childbirth and who now, in a smoky eternity, watched over succeeding generations of young children, yes – Zuleikha and her lover were the ones trawling through the frozen earth. It had become all there was. They were just two naked creatures, trying to turn the geometries of sex into the calculus of love. The box had been a pretext. Perhaps they were hallucinating the whole damn thing. Perhaps even this cold stone church was not as they saw it. What if the maqam to which they had pinned their lives' melody was a false music? Rujari d'Alì, the Sicilian lutenist who had slaughtered his own wife and her lover with his bare hands in their consummatory bed. The Minstrel's Pillar. The symphony of a liar, a paranoiac, a philanderer, a man whose last sight had been a blood vision of his own face staring back at him from a night pool. Lutenist, murderer, genius, wife-killer, prince of dissonance. Yes, it was a well-secreted psychosis, a gospel of madness which had always been there, in Zuleikha and probably in her mother too, but which, like the fires on the summits of mountains, could only have ignited thus between herself and Alex. It was a confluence of insanity. Maybe Daoud and Susan too had lived and died in allegory. Who knows what happens between spirits?

Yet when she had held her naked dead baby in her arms, and had wept, and from the depths of her heart had cursed God, Allah, Allaha, Elohim, Khuda, Rubb, Deo – all of them – it had been more truly real than any other single moment in her life. More real, even, than the moment of his birth. His face, his closed lids, the pressure of his still-flaccid limbs over her forearms, his shock of ripening chestnut hair, electric on her skin – all of it was inscribed in the meat of her heart. She had traced the line of his spine all the way to the base of his skull – the skull whose fissures yet remained open, vulnerable; the fissures which, in spite of her love, had left his spirit unguarded; and then she had run her whitened bloodless fingers over the bowl of his scalp, in a slow imitation of her own movements during the minutes which had followed his birth. She had thought of the no-thought which his body contained.

It was crazy; the whole thing fucking crazy. An indecipherable carpet page of madness. She was supposed to be a woman of science, for God's sake. She was meant to be an anchor, a pillar of society and of the rationale upon which the world had been built these last few hundred years. Instead of which, she and her lover had leapt into a river that was carrying them back into a mediaevalist, nativist, night-counting frame of thought. A brain, filled with coruscating dots of red lead; a mind that fashioned swans draped in green silk and lips that sipped from jaams filled with spicy hippocras wine. Trembling with cold, Laux, Mahler and Hans Frei, deep in the night forests of High Germany, knives in hand, waiting for the round moon to ascend to its mid-point so that they might cut wood from the ancient yew and spruce trees from which they would fashion ribs and bodies. Drunken friars with dirty hands, playing gitterns into which had been carved women's faces. Emerald Khizr, singing wisdom from a well. Oblong lute-books. *The Romance of Alexander*. Thebus the Arab. Mystical, rhyming Thomas of Ercyldoune. Goat musicians, rising in fourths from dark lochs, playing tear-drop lutes, tuned to strange internal patterns.

She ought really to be cycling with the far galaxies, flying into the blades of black holes. Evidence-based medicine. No. Evidence was for crimes. Good and evil. Reality was more complex. Yet even long-haired Newton had seen visions of unearthly lights dancing above the hills of the marches. *O Freshest Flower, O Rosa Bella, Mine Heart's Lust, Of Such Complain, Toujours*. Fantasies. There was something wrong. Although he had no plectrum, his movements were so rapid that it seemed at times as though his nails were as long as quills.

The music was changing, too.

It was no longer polite, baroque, playfully melancholic. This was an earlier, more brutal music, where the gut sounded like iron and where every note was a weapon. And yet amidst the brash loudness were periods of exquisite silence, and a stillness that reminded her of the surface of the great loch that lay only a few yards away. It was a complex, almost unplayable music, the sort of thing you might find in a codex, covered in blood and hidden in a casket, deep in the wall of the vault of a Morisco-haunted Castilian monastery. A symbolic houlate symphony, constructed long before the form had even been invented. The sound resonated off the stone flags, making the floor seem to waver before her eyes, each flag another rhythmic progression of letters and numbers and fleeting diagonal accents. It was a murderous music, and it left the fingers of lutenists stained with their own heart's blood.

Then she saw, in the stained glass window behind Alexander, the figure of a lutenist with a turban on his head – but otherwise clad in the habit of a wandering friar. He was seated in exactly the same manner as Alex; it was a strangely modern posture, and their instruments too were identical. She blinked, twice. She thought that it might be her lenses: that finally they had given out and were displaying images to her in diplopia. And now it seemed as though it was the friar, and not Alex, whom she was seeing. Not her man of flesh-and-blood-and-semen whom, in the Quranic sense, she had known for some little time in this life. O fuck. What was going on?

She tried to talk, but her mouth was parched and her tongue stuck like a slick of old rubber to her palate. All that came out was a croak. She coughed, cleared her throat, breathed in, then out, and then managed to say:

'What do you want from me, Alex? What is all this about? What are we doing?' But it was too late. Either he couldn't hear her, or else he didn't want to. She should've known from the set of his mouth, and from the look in his eyes. If she'd gone up close to his face, she'd have seen her own reflection and nothing else. She felt like getting up and shaking him by the shoulders, the same shoulders onto which she had clutched as she had risen beneath him like some raving Persephone and which had turned to paper after his climax. But then maybe he knew only as much as she did. Maybe they were both ignorant together. *Ignorance is bliss.* Who wrote that? Idiot!

Sweat was breaking out over Alex's forehead.

Fuck fuck fuck.

Temporal lobe seizures. She'd figured it out. Alex was epileptic, and was having one of those most bizarre and unpredictable of fits – in his case brought on not by flashing lights or emotional shock, but by music of a certain kind. If music could be used as therapy, then surely it also could become a disease. Okay, that was the rational explanation. It was the explanation she'd have given to one of her patients. But here, in this ice chapel, with the huge body of the Black Loch heaving just a stone's throw from her skull – here, amidst the heavy scent of flowers, it was not so easy to be rational.

Something in the light had died. If she'd switched on a photometer she was sure it would've shown no difference, and yet still there was a subtle darkening. The afternoons up here, at this time of year, were shorter even than those in Glasgow, and there were no street-lights, no false pink dusks wheeling across the horizon. In the countryside, the darkness was complete. Even on cloudless days, in the depths of winter it would be pitch dark by four o'clock. The loch would lie invisibly in the pelvis of the mountains like a great black eye. She wondered where that elegant slightly sweet smell was coming from. At this time of year, surely nothing living could exude even the slightest aroma. Zuleikha felt that she would never be able to get up again, that her backside had become sculpted to the granite of the window-ledge. The cold had crept into her body; it had been an attack on two fronts, from wall and ledge, and now, after a period of trying to suppress it, her whole body began to shake violently.

Alex was still playing his melancholy music in a completely manic mode. He'd been playing for what seemed like hours. She would have to throw herself down onto her feet and shake him awake, or else, she thought, he will play until he kills himself. His heart will give out. This was like running a marathon with no training. He was not twenty-one. And neither was she. Zuleikha hadn't been to the gym for ages. Not since she'd met Alex. Not since that day down by the river. She'd begun to neglect herself in ways which in themselves were minimal, but which had a cumulative effect. At work she had become barely functional, she was so knackered all the time with this crazy chasing around. Not to mention the mental exhaustion inherent in the slow and slippery act of falling in love in such a manner, the nights spent ferociously and unpredictably screwing, and now she felt that she was close to the very limit of the humanly possible. And that mad old bastard, the airman, Archibald Enoch McPherson, with his tales of forests and poets and great metal war-birds. His WAAF wife and his holy whore. Fuck. It was just the touch of a hand. Her hand, the skin blistered, scarred, where she had held Archie's body. She knew it all. And if she knew, then he knew. Jesus, the other night she'd had a hypnagogic dream, set on 13th March 1941, in which she was the whore and Archie … enough! She felt like vomiting. Her stomach heaved. She scrunched up over the angle of her knees.

The waves of the loch were leaden with the weight of the sky and the music was unstoppable. She heaved again. This time, she felt her body rise onto its feet and, though she could no longer feel the soles, she made to go over to where Alex was slumped across the lute. But her knees buckled halfway, and she knew that if she got him up she wouldn't be able to climb the stairs. The light was now so dim that she could hardly make out the steps. She went on all fours up the staircase and crawled under the rope. She stumbled up the aisle towards the door, clutching onto the ends of pews and badly banging her left knee against something made of stone. Darkness had fallen upon the old church more completely than she had imagined possible. The door to the outside was closed. Panic swept over her. What if someone locked the door at night? They wouldn't have thought to check down in the vault. But wouldn't they have heard the music? Another recurring dream she'd had: She was floating on the surface of the shallow loch, lying on her back and staring at the sky as it turned from azure to orange to purple to black. Something brushed by beneath her, and she wheeled around. The skin of the water broke apart and she sank through cold blackness. She was out of her depth, and it was night.

She tried to recall whether or not she had closed the big door behind her when she'd come in after Alex, but her thoughts were all mixed up, and though she could not feel anything below her knees, she knew that the music was rising from the stone. And it was a strange, swaying, loping music. The sort of music that ghosts might play, their long insubstantial fingers trailing over the surfaces of old Crusader parchments, of Pre-Reformatory vellum-encased manuscripts from Rowallan or Panmure or Balcarres. Perhaps it was no longer Alex who was playing, but the elegant and beautiful Lady Margaret, tracing out the ninety lost scores of the dashing poet, William Mure of Carmel Water, who had been blooded at Marston Moor and who, in his old age, for some long-forgotten reason had tried to obliterate some of his own compositions. Currents, sarabands, ballets and braills … an atlas of scores, a diorama of streams – in musical form it seemed to encompass everything, Alexander and Zuleikha and Archibald and Susan and Daoud and Margaret and Daniel John and Nasrin Zeinab and the un-nameable whore who would never die but who would trail through history growing older and more haggard and becoming riddled with ever more deadly and esoteric diseases, poxes of the soul, firebombs, atom ordnance, neutron missiles, venereal explosives. War, sex, music. Death modal, death pentatonic and death hexatonic. Scotch snaps. Gray steil Afghan dastgahs, Yunani mousike, Hebrew zimrah. *I love my love in secret.*

She slammed herself against the door. It was locked. Tried again; almost broke her shoulder. The music was growing larger – not louder exactly, but broader, so that it spanned centuries from the howling hillsides of a wintry Scotland before electricity, roads, telephones and steam to the far southern latitudes of the Middle White Sea and the Time of Rebirth. It seemed to fill the church, and to resonate with the statues and carvings and the strange filigree'd plants that curled up the pillars and the glacial figures who endlessly performed the dance of death as they slipped down the slope of the ceiling. The chapel was in complete darkness, yet through the music Zuleikha could see it all; she knew every grain of dust, each cut stone; she knew every finger of every hand that had gripped the mallet, chisel and trowel; she knew the name, words, lips and tongue of every priest, minister, pastor who down through the centuries had preached in this place, and she had sat inside the vault of every skull of every member of the flock, from the edge of the loch onwards. Unlike people, music never died, but remained out there, caught in stone and air and river. Unseen, it animated a mathematical rubric of reality that in essence stood quite outside of time. It was the coat of many colours, the fabric of the spirit.

A crystalline fear turned her body to ice so that she could no longer breathe. Her legs gave way and she slumped down, her back to the door. She could feel nothing below the level of her hips. Yet somehow the scent had grown stronger and it seemed almost visible, now as it swirled around her. What if we die here? she thought. What if this is the end? A drumming in her ears. What would they make of it? A woman, lying beneath the frieze of the Dance of Death, and a man in the vault, propped up against the window-sill, his fingers rigor-mortised to the body of an old red lute. The last note, hanging suspended in the air.

Alex was down in the vault. He had watched her leave, and her body had seemed to be turning blue. It had seemed unreal, her going on all fours up the stairs. How strange, he had thought, even as his fingers had moved ruinously over the strings of the eight-course lute. My blue lady-love is leaving – ascending, you

213

might say, in the manner of a dog saint, and only I remain here in this place of wondrous darkness. All the women in my life have left in this manner. Slipped away, sanctified, in the night, to a place cold with the slab of steel and neon and the stench of preservative aldehydes. He assumed that she had gone back to the car. He was not ready yet to follow. The soles of his feet began to itch. He glanced down and saw the starlight burn like an exploding nucleus through the dust, through his arms, his legs. He glanced up at the window behind him. One of those naked roses again; just the centre of the flower and no petals. The silvery light was streaming through the stained glass and as it hit the floor; some physical effect on the stone conjured up the shape of another star. He scuffed his foot around, yet the shape did not disappear but slipped over the lace, leather and metal eyes of his boot, altering the rose's shape while leaving its structure intact. The itch got worse, and spread up his ankles.

He had stopped playing, yet in his head the music ran on and downwards. Alex undid his laces, kicked off his boots and slipped off his socks. Surprisingly, his feet did not feel at all cold. Perhaps he had been sitting in an awkward position, and this itch was just the lifeblood pumping back in. Carefully, he placed the lute beside the boots, its peg-box lying angled against the rough stone of the wall. He paced about slowly, to try and tease the air into movement around his feet. The floor felt warm. He remembered that the flags had sounded as though the space beneath was hollow. Perhaps, down there in the airless pitch darkness, someone is lighting a fire, he thought. Perhaps there is a secret tunnel, accessible only to poets, tramps and other idiot wanderers, through which they were able to enter the vault-beneath-the-vault. Perhaps it had been built back in the Days of Persecution. Alex imagined that it might lead to an opening far below, somewhere close to the foot of the landward side of the hill on which the chapel had been built, somewhere in the dense woods which Zuleikha and he earlier had avoided and which clustered around the small river that fed the loch. Or maybe it was just the heat generated by legions of dead bodies.

He remembered that once, many years earlier, on a visit to Paris, Susan and he had ventured via an obscure side-street into the famous catacombs. This place smelt the same. This church. Perhaps it was just its age, or the type of stone. In the past, whenever he'd thought about their experience in the tunnels beneath Paris, Alex had shivered and felt the pantomime urge to look behind him. But now, in this vault beneath the chapel by the loch's edge, the memory was no longer terrifying. It was as though something was coming together. Something which had always been there, around the next corner or just beneath the skin or coiled in dreams, but which he'd never been able to quite place or define. On the floor at the opposite end of the room, a different pattern was emerging. The light was so faint, Alex knew that it could not have been moonlight; he tried to remember when last he had seen the full moon, but it wasn't really the sort of thing of which he tended to make a note. He wasn't a lunatic. He went over, removed the piece of paper from his trouser pocket, uncrumpled it, and smoothed it down on the stone so that it lay directly over the pattern.

In the back of his head, the sound of each note had become prolonged as though the lute was being played in a decelerating motion. It was as though emerging from within each note were multiple other notes which had been there all along, but which, like an old god, Alexander was now revealing from the ends of his fingers. His nails had grown to corpse-length. They were long enough to slit the throat of a goat, to disembowel a naked wrestler, or to decapitate a man and, using them, he now shifted the paper to and fro, leaning back every so often to try and discern a pattern. There had been a certain melody which he had played on the night Susan had died and which, like spirit voices, he had never been able to recapture; it was as though he had been reproducing, by ear, a melody first heard from a dream. But that whole night had become a dream. As had these past few months with Zuleikha, Our Lady of the River-Mud, his very own Brown Madonna. Break open the skin and see what lies inside. Lie inside her and crack open your life. Susan, the lute, the box, the river, Zulie … the whole thing made him feel giddy, yet he couldn't stop. The lute slowed and then fell silent and the last note faded into the polished ashlar. Then Alex felt it all around him. The ceiling beams, the rough walls, the floor, the staircase up which Zuleikha had crawled, the empty space in between – the whole church was swaying. Until now it had been barely perceptible, but he realised that it had been happening all along. It was the reason his lute music had gone on, even though he had no longer been hitting the strings. The chapel was a giant repository of sound. It turned everything that had ever happened into an impossibly slow music. He glanced down again. The patterns matched. The numbers whose forms had seemed incomplete had been that way because they were actually parts of letters. Not simple Latin letters, but something else.

He had no idea what this meant. It looked like Arabic, or Hebrew, but it might just as well have been ancient Aramaic or Assyrian for all Alex knew. The shapes of the letters, while recognisably Latinate, yet had that angular, Middle Eastern look about them, a certain ambience of ziggurats and almond eyes. Strange slashes and dots. Each tiny mark would totally change the sound, the meaning. It was like old lute notation. He scuffed his feet against the floor. The itch had disappeared. But by this time the church was spinning like a planet, and Alex slumped to the ground with his back against the wall and his head in his hands. He tried to pull his thoughts around, tried to anchor his buttocks to the cold stone, but the heat was rising from the crypts, from the ageless bones and the darkened reliquaries, and with the warmth there came the stench of cedar oil and dried reeds. Alex was floating downstream, his mind was turning in blue water, its substance drowning in the heave and pull of the sub-currents, the undertows.

Anchor.

Last night, they had made love.

Anchor.

The first time they had slept together, he and Zulie, it had been in her house. He hadn't been ready to have another woman within his walls: it had seemed too soon somehow, what with Susan's manifold presence staring, smiling, illuminated by the light of past summers, each one twisted like twine, like silk around some chemical remembrance of reality. If so much of a house could be weighed in skin dust, then most of his home was filled with Susan. He might take a deep Hoover to it some day, but he hadn't had the heart – not yet. Sweep up his past and throw it away? Erase Susan's flesh from his mind, tear her presence from his lungs? No, it wasn't possible. He could have sex with this woman, this Zuleikha, and he could enjoy her company, he liked her smile, her intensity, the way she shrugged, the way her voice curled around the consonants and turned them almost into the phonemes of another language. But she could never be Susan, who went back decades into the dark warmth of his bones, into the vortex of his heart. Yet there was something…

Anchor.

How had it begun that first time, a couple of months back? How does it ever begin? he wondered. With a shudder, perhaps; a feeling of shared mortality, of suffering in common – not merely with each other, but with thousands of ancestors: a sense of communion with a family tree that reached to the moon and the stars, going right back to the point at which human consciousness emerged. A premonition of someone walking over their graves, cuboid sections of soil and clay and sand which, for all they knew, might end up lying thousands of miles apart. *You've made your grave, now lie in it!* Would he be buried next to Susan, on that blustery green hill overlooking the sweeping plain of the Clyde? Or would he end in some dusty place where the call to prayer was a world away from the sheeting rain and eddying currents of Dalriada? Stop. His head was spinning again. Anchor. Right. Months ago. But that first time it had not been a bed: it had been wood and wine and the civilised domesticity of a living room. It had seemed sacrilegious, making love on the sofa in front of the dead screen of the TV so that they had been able to watch their distorted silhouettes in the glass, and it had seemed at times as though it were they who were being watched and this, together with the immanence of the box, its scent all around them, its presence inside the whorls and rhythms of the very act, the very sap, of their copulation, had lent a certain devilish frisson to their coupling. A poor man's hard-core.

That first time. Two months ago – two months and six days. A shared smile, a congruent glance, that first deep gaze into a stranger's eyes – they had wished they could have held it intact forever, a moment of both acknowledgment and absolution. The touch of a hand, a play of breath on the skin. This was how it had begun. Their mutual affection lay in their flaws, their shared angles of inelegance. When you've bathed your body in sleek river-mud and felt the ends of the reeds curl sinuously around your ankles, when you've seen the desperation in the other person's face, when you've touched the howling burning envelope of their skin, when you've felt the broken rigor of their climax, when you've spanned the invertebrate arch of love's counterpoint and heard the sound of their throat's whispered pleas within your own cracked weeping voice, there can be no idols left in the charnel house.

Later, as he'd lain next to her, feeling the heat off her body and the curled dark waxiness of her skin, and gazing up at the barely defined shadows that flitted along the cracks in the cream-coloured ceiling, Alex had wondered how many others in that very room had done what they had just done, going back a hundred years or more, and in the shacks that had been there before the tenements and in the fields, forests and ditches wheeling back through the years, maybe five hundred, maybe a long-thousand. And thus, for a short time, he had felt at one with all of those unknown, dead lovers, the record of whose existence at most would be a name in a parish register. And then he had heard a noise from outside the window, from down in the back close where the lights recently had fused, and he had thought that it sounded awfully like the singing of a cat. As they had made love, he had moved at times clumsily – partly because her body had been unfamiliar, but also because, automatically, his body had reverted to the remembered hippocampal template of Susan, so that in every limbic kiss, every flitch of groping desperation, he had had first to break apart the bonds of her shade from around his flesh. That is why he had wept: he had felt like a murderer.

Alex straightened his neck. His head had stopped whirling. The vault was cold, not freezing yet, but there was a definite chill in the air. The moon must've come up after all, he thought, because it was far lighter than it had been before, and the light that shone through the windows did not create any particular patterns, but simply flooded like fresh water over the stone flags of the church floor. Wearily, Alex rose, pulled on his socks and laced up his boots. He clambered into his overcoat, then he collected his lute, placed it back in its case and began to climb the stairs.

He had expected the chapel above to be empty. So when he saw the figure crumpled up by the door, he stopped walking and almost dropped the lute case. He ran over. She was unconscious. Her skin was blue and very, very cold. Her eyes opened. She glanced at the lute-case, then up at him.

'It's you,' she whispered.

'Let's get you into the car.' He slipped off his coat and wrapped it as best he could around her body, which seemed smaller and thinner than before, as though the cold had caused her frame to contract within itself.

'I couldn't open the door,' she began, but Alex had already pulled on the iron loop and the night air that whooshed in smelled of the furthest ends of the loch. He felt his legs begin to buckle under her weight but also beneath the knowledge that the music had brought him, not just into this cold church and its luminous past, but also into the mind of Zuleikha, into the well of her desires and the pain of her loss. And now, as he carried her through the moonlight, with the waves meeting the rocky shore with a gentleness that could be evinced only by a killer, Alexander kissed her on the frozen lips that were cut in the shape of twin moons and, with death whirling all around them, he felt their emptiness become one.

Chapter Twelve

'So, you're leaving,' he said, looking up at her accusingly. 'You're leaving when I'm dying.' Even over the weekend, his face seemed to have shrunk a little further into the pillow and the bones to have punched through the skin, which more and more was coming to resemble waxed parchment.

'It's only for a little while,' she pleaded. 'Just a week or two. I'll be back as soon as I can.' She laughed, trying to lighten things and affecting casualness, but simply seeming pathetic. 'Anyway, I'll have to come back – I need the money!'

He did not smile, but looked away into the floral wallpaper. It was a Monday morning, it was raining, and she could ill-afford the time to placate the dying. Too much bloody paperwork, too many demands from the needy. She was like a religious icon, and by nightfall she, the physician, would end up completely drained, her brain unable to compute even the simplest logic.

'Look, Archie, I'd better check your chest.'

'Go to Hell!'

'Okay.' She straightened up, placed her left hand in the small of her back, and pushed her belly forwards. She had on a tartan skirt whose hem, now she realised, was probably a little too short. God, she thought, how prissy we've become! Whatever happened to the Sixties? Right now there was a dull ache in the lower part of her back. It was something which bothered Zulie from time to time and which she attributed to too much half-bending, too much empathising. Whether they were seated in a chair or lying in bed, patients always seemed to require that you bend toward them like some nineteenth-century French neurologist intent on defining an obscure perturbation of the synapses. She lifted up the back of his pyjama-top. His skin was cooler than she remembered. He didn't take the deep breaths through his mouth which she had requested, and so the examination was next to useless. In fact, she thought, it would have been useless in any case. The guy was on the way out and there was nothing anyone could do. Now, there was just the laying-on of hands, the application of balms, the imbibing of sleeping-draughts, the inculcation of dreams. Theirs was a Mediaeval relationship. She should have been wearing one of those bird-headed plague masks into whose beaks one secreted aromatic compounds. It had been illusory; they had provided no protection whatsoever. But they would have ameliorated the stench of the dead and would have scared away children and malingerers.

The light was barely beyond dawn. At this time of year, she thought, Scotland really does feel very northern. I should be used to the dampness and the cold: after all, I was born into it. Half my genes were grown on stalks of rowan and thistle. But then, at this time of year Lincolnshire will be even colder, with that piercing east wind that blows straight off the Siberian steppe.

She straightened up again.

'Ow!' Her back cracked and pain seared down her left leg. Archie spun around. For a dying man, he could move bloody fast.

'What's up?' His eyes were suddenly alive. Fucking devil, she thought, he can sense weakness a mile off. Fucking big cat bastard.

'Nothing,' she groaned. 'Just did my back in at the weekend.'

Mistake, mistake, mistake.

'Oh, really?' A smile broke across his face. He had six teeth left, all at the front. Enough to bite. Suck blood. 'And what were you doing to have acquired a broken back, Zulie?'

'Nothing,' she lied, and she shrugged just a little – then felt idiotic for having done so, as though Archie was a teacher and she a pupil.

She checked his syringe-driver, made sure the heroin was flowing in at exactly the correct rate, made certain it had been labelled properly and – most importantly – reassured herself that it wouldn't run out in the middle of the night, or worse still at five to six in the evening. Everything was in order. Except that it wasn't. She stood still, narrowed her eyes. She felt she might have done better with half-moon specs, but she wasn't quite old enough yet for those, not quite blind enough. She could still accommodate to light and dark, big words, small talk.

'Archie, have you been boosting the pump?' He shrugged. 'It's okay to do that, you know, if you're in pain.'

'It's not the pain.' There was a pause. He seemed to be breathing more rapidly all of a sudden. Bugger wouldn't breathe when I asked him to, she thought. He stared her down. 'I'm a flyer, you know, Zulie. Always was, always will be.' He pointed up at the ceiling as though he was a sufi, and automatically she found herself following his right index finger. 'I'm up there, thirty thousand feet in the clear blue, halfway to heaven's gate.'

'I didn't know Spitfires went that high.'

'Fuck Spitfires.'

She pottered about, knowing that really she had to, ought to, needed to leave, yet reluctant to do so.

'Why don't you sit down, Zulie? Rest your back for a while. Have a cup of tea. You'll have to make it yourself. Plenty of tea-bags, milk.'

'I don't have time. I'm … I'm sorry, Archie.'

'Aye you do. Sit.' He motioned her to sit on the edge of his bed. He was insistent, his voice suddenly gentle and seductive. 'Listen, my dear, the nurses will be here soon. Where are you going?'

'Back to the surgery.'

He shook his head.

'No, I mean where are you going that you'll not be here when I die.'

She looked away. Her thighs seemed oddly pallid beneath the fabric of her stockings. She rubbed her hands over them, felt the static rise. Gazed at her palms as though expecting the electricity to leap off the skin. The style of her outfit was modelled on those fashionable in the year 1965, and wearing it made her feel a little like a beat-girl, or else a flapper from the 1920s. Archibald McPherson's parents' generation, that would've been, right? But they wouldn't have been flappers. No way. Not middle-class enough. Not middle-class at all. She chuckled to herself.

'What's so funny?'

She looked at him. O fuck, she thought: the strange situations we get ourselves into. But she made sure she wasn't touching him as she thought this.

'Lincolnshire. We're going to Lincolnshire.' She'd expected him to ask, *Where's that?* People were so ignorant of geography, even within their own country. There were people who lived in, say, Govan, who'd never visited the centre of Glasgow, to whom the main streets were as alien as the ones in New York City or Paris. But he didn't ask.

'We...?'

Another mistake.

'My ... friend and I.'

'Boyfriend, girlfriend?'

What? Did he think she was lesbian or something? Or did he mean, 'girlfriend' in the contemporary, colloquial sense of 'a woman's female pal'? But no, he was too old for that, wasn't he? Too old by far. Wasn't he?

'He's a man.'

'Ah! That's good.' He patted her hand. 'You should get a man. A man's what you need.'

She smiled.

'You think so?'

'I know Lincolnshire well. Or at least, I did, sixty-odd years ago. Air Force.'

Yes, she thought, that was it.

'That was where I met Margaret. Kesteven, Lindsay, Holland – there are three parts, I remember that. It's very flat, you know, except for a bit in the middle, around where the capital is. But compared to Scotland, it's flat. In those days it was primitive, really. The sea haar and the cold east wind. No running water or electricity. Just wild forests, history. It was where we met, it was where I first had her, and it was like Heaven. After that, it was never the same. Nothing can ever be returned to what it was. Every moment of our lives, the position of the sun in every one of our skies, is unique. That's our tragedy. We're dancing slowly to the sound of flaring trumpets. Fire jazz. Can you hear it, Zulie? It's coming from the great hangars where the aircraft sleep, from where the men depart, from where they leave, to die...' He stared at her. 'Dance with me, Zulie, please. Before the bombs come down.'

Suddenly his eyes seemed intense, the blue fibres kindled with a wild light as though without her noticing he'd slipped over into another state of consciousness. Instinctively she glanced down at the syringe-driver to check she hadn't inadvertently knocked a button or something. She felt her cheek begin to burn and she looked away. Draped untidily over the back of an upright chair were Archie's daytime clothes, the clothes he never wore any more.

An unironed white shirt, big cotton underpants and grey-brown trousers. They seemed familiar to her. But then, she thought, they would. Half the men in the country over a certain age wore these things.

'Is ... is there a lake?' she began. She felt a weight pulling her down and she realised that he had grabbed her by the elbows. He had burned down to bone and spirit and now his fingers felt like metal. She tried to hoist him up so that they would both be sitting, but the inertia of his body and the force of his longing were too great, her back too painful, and she found herself sinking onto the bed beside him.

'You're a fool, Zulie,' he began, 'you're swimming against a tide. You're a salmon, an eel.' His breath was hot and heavy and tasted of earthenware, like some ancient Celtic perfume: Head of Horse. She tried to stop inhaling and closed her eyes, but then she felt her chest begin to explode very slowly from a point somewhere beneath where her heart would be – some plexus or other. Stuff they didn't teach at Medical School, stuff she would've denied had anybody asked. Energy meridians, whatever. They used it now, acupuncture, even though in the entire compass of the Western system there was no explanation for how it might work. And no-one seemed to think this the least bit incongruous. So why should she be at all surprised that this was happening to her now, here, as she lay down with a dying man. It suddenly seemed completely natural; she felt that in some way she knew everything about him and about the women he'd had. Margaret, his wife of five decades, the Lincolnshire lass, luminous now in her posthumous purity, the axis of her history fixed through a particular set of points which originally had seemed entirely casually determined, the logically disordered musical score of an ordinary life – but, as happened with the remembered dead, each element of which now took on an altogether more semiotic connotation.

And then there were those other, shadow women. The women who had been caught like flies in glass, the imagined woman of smoky pornographic image – there she was, posing nude on a chaise longue in some backstreet Glasgow studio, fleshy perfectly white thighs counterpointed by the black cigarette-holder tripping insouciantly from her fingers, the smoke curling upwards through the photographic plate, stinging Zuleikha's eyes and making them run. The real, imperfect women whom he had purchased and with whom on ancient sprung beds he had had sex during the desperate times of the air raids when it had seemed as though such an act was part of the War Effort. My God, he should've received a medal and so should she, the whore whose neck he had burned and bruised with his hardened body, his mortal soul. And he seemed to know everything about Zuleikha's life, her loves, the loss of her child, this odd journey upon which she had embarked. As he turned down the tops of her stockings and flipped up her skirt, he seemed to be drawing her body in precise patterns as though he knew its singular frequencies of arousal.

She flipped open the buttons of her blouse and loosened her bra. She felt she was fumbling, ungainly, clumsy, human, while he was already more than half-spirit. And yet she felt that every cell in her body could sense his carnality. Everything was extreme: his pallor, the attenuation of his frame, the virtual hairlessness of his skin, the way that she was able to feel beneath her the angular form of every single bone of his skeleton. He would soon be part of the earth, his flesh would curl and bloat, his innards would spill out into raw soil and beneath six feet of darkness his body would begin to dance. Zuleikha felt that she was fucking the land, his land, her land, the Land of Scota, the old Egyptian bride, and that the soil, rock and rivers were rising and heaving like the surface of an ocean. She felt that she was regressing through the species so that ultimately she would be simply a single pullulating cell, possessed of no consciousness of which to speak and yet clasping within it a sense of infinite possibility.

She felt his hands all over her, on her breasts, her belly, along the insides of her thighs and they were soothing hands, warm, soft, loving. They circled the areolae of her nipples, the fingertips drawing the dark flesh to points of stone. They massaged the small of her back, they healed her broken muscles so that she felt able to move freely over him. She pulled off his urosheath and gently, gently, with her long fingers she peeled back the foreskin and stiffened him and then mounted her pelvis over his, lowering herself carefully but allowing him to enter faster than she would have felt comfortable with. He was an airman and this was his final flight. And she was the machine with whom he had always dreamed of melding himself, so that its course and his would become the same, a trajectory into infinity. And all the time, he was calling her Margaret, Margaret my love, Margaret my sweet duck, Margaret my beauty, my soldier, my whore, my cat, my lioness. But then the pain from his body shot through her spine and made her cry out, made her howl like a banshee and she sank down and forgot about pain, loss, everything.

The light seemed to darken all around and the sound of the rain intensified and she wasn't sure whether the water actually was falling faster upon the city than before or whether it was just her own mental state, as beneath the frozen stare of his late wife she straddled the old airman and rocked the frail line of his body back and forth; as, like some brown earth mother, she encompassed his languid flesh in hers. Zuleikha was aware of the movement of the bed against the wall and the floor and she was aware of her own breathing and of his rasping as she slipped the oxygen mask over his thin face, reached behind her and swivelled the tap on the cylinder to its maximum setting. Given to the wrong kind of person, that much oxygen was poison. But then, she thought, I am the wrong kind of person. Otherwise I wouldn't be here, doing this, would I? It was funny, death could come from either too little air or too much. It was belly-busting, cunt-weeping, prick-teasing hilarious! And they were laughing together as they rocked, laughing like hyenas, laughing like wild wolves.

She had to inhale, she needed to breathe. And when it came, the great inward aromatic breath, it was as though she was breathing him in, the entirety of him, his past, his rotting present, his shortened future, and she knew that whether he would seep into the earth of a damp grave or be consumed in the fire of the crematorium, he was bequeathing himself to her. It was as though Archibald Enoch McPherson, with all of his ancestors going back to God-knows-where, with his father who had run off to Morocco, his mother, whose shade still cranked sheets through the rollers of the tenement wash-house, his dead howling sisters, his airman's hands that never till this moment had encircled the joystick and flown, everything he had ever been or imagined, or imagined himself to be, was slipping into the cells of her body, into the substance of her brain, into the cold empty darkness of her womb. She would carry him now and forever as she had carried her son, Daoud, king of the Jews, Hazrat David, Holy Prophet of Islam, Dave the Rave, the slingshot man who through a single act had risen from the lowest to the highest of the social classes. Daoud the musician, the chironomer, the leader of orchestras, the codifier of musical principles, the man who had made the Bible sing and who had had so many wives, concubines and miscellaneous women that surely by now he must be the father of everyone. Daoud, the archetypal Messiah who in his turn had fathered Suleiman, the King of the Djinns.

As she inhaled she was met by his lips, which she had expected to be limp, whitened, withered, coated in some horrible fungal growth, but which instead she found strangely vital, the tiny muscles coursing with power and yes, with passion. It was as though, on a hot spit somewhere inside of this eighty-five year old shell, there turned a young man: Aircraftman Archibald Idris McPherson, a man of air and light, a being of history. And yes, she knew that what she was doing was horrendous, illegal, unethical, wrong, repulsive; that she was taking advantage of a dying man who was in a state of altered consciousness; that he was confused, that he was not himself, that his brain was beyond repair, and that this was a clear violation of him and also of that modern version of the Hippocratic Oath which she had sworn all those years ago on that very sunny graduation day, to all those dead brains in aspic and formalin, the Rule by which she had pledged thenceforth to live her life. She knew that what she was doing was criminal and in some sense evil, yet that morning it really didn't seem that way. There seemed instead to be a morality which superseded all that previously she had learned and accepted. Hers was a historical, or even a mythical morality. She knew that deep down, where it mattered, Archie was intact, that he was purifying himself through the vessel of her body, that he was giving life to her as surely as if he had been re-starting her heart with electricity and light. She knew that if it had been she and not Margaret who had lived in his time, if she had been the WAAF maiden who had granted him succour in the darkness of the air-raid shelter and who had rendered unto him her virginity and her life and who even now, seven years dead, still gave him life and love, sweet Mother Margaret, Holy Mother Margaret, Saint Margaret of the Lincolnshire flats, then the bond between them would have been unbreakable, even by death, even by a thousand deaths. And as she ran her palm over the dry skin of his skull she could feel every line and indentation, as she incorporated every inch of his withered resurrected body into hers she knew him: whoring Archie of the Govan docks who never once had been permitted to lift off from the tarmac black of the aerodrome, yet who had cradled and sipped from the head of Lord Jack of the Lake, Lord Jack of the Roof of the World; and in his turn, Lord Jack had held in his palm and had drunk from the brain-pan of a still older head, though she was not yet able to make out to whom this ancient skull had belonged.

As she arched forwards over him Archie tore the mask off his face, reached up and planted it over her mouth, her lips. His face turned blue and his breathing became fast and shallow. His eyes rolled. The whites were streaked with distended blood vessels which writhed before her eyes like tiny parasites that were wriggling outwards from the substance of his brain, and as she let her own lids slip down like screens over her vision, she felt these same worms become fast to the hindmost mountains of her mind where they expanded and burst into a million streams. His chest heaved and then faltered. She could feel the beat of his heart flicker through her skin as it raced towards oblivion, she felt it grow irregular and then, as inside and behind her his cock and balls went into rigor and she felt it deep inside her belly, his tears of joy opening like glistening mistletoe leaves upon an acorn, her whole body went into waves of climax and a long, loud animal scream forced its way through the tight curtains of her throat, a scream that was louder than it had ever been, a quejío that would resound across the entire sleeping city – and then she felt both their heartbeats stop.

BOX THREE: LINCOLNSHIRE

Now Creeping Jane is dead and gone
And her body lies on the cold ground o
I'll go down to my master and tell the boy today
To keep her little body from the ground
Lal dee day dee o the diddle lie de day o
I'll go down to her master and tell the boy today
Just to keep her little body from the ground

Trad., sung by Joseph Taylor, from 'Unto Brigg Fair'
(arr. Percy Grainger)

Chapter Thirteen

Alexander had remained sober as, respectfully, he lifted up the lid of the box. It opened easily, as though acknowledging that they had paid their dues. Whatever was she thinking? This was nuts! She was attributing motive, consciousness and reflex to an inanimate object, something that quite literally was dead wood. Yet the box was changing. *Just as I am changing,* she thought. Its colour was no longer the dry dun-brown it had acquired during the few days following its rescue from the river. Over the past few weeks the box had gained, if not viridescence, then at least a hint of green. When Zuleikha looked straight at it this impression vanished completely, but it would re-emerge the moment she glanced away. Rods and cones, she thought, the flashing cells of the retina, halfway to the mind if not the soul. Their distribution allowed one to see colours most vividly at the centre rather than the periphery of the visual field. But that was the opposite of what was happening, she thought. What was happening had no basis in anatomical or physiological truth. To accept it would be to cast *I think, therefore I am* down a very deep drain.

And when Alex had pulled out a skull, or rather half a skull, Zuleikha had not jumped, or screamed, or exclaimed; neither had she swooned nor uttered a prayer or curse. She simply had accepted the object graciously from his proffered hands as though such a thing were natural – mundane, even. The cranium had been smoothed down and polished so that the bone shone, brilliant white.

'It's a glass,' he said, and she nodded.

'I don't fancy drinking anything from it, though.'

'The river water didn't damage it at all. It's as though it's been sealed all this time.'

The skull had a gold-coloured metal rim. This was melted down from a crucifix, she thought.

'All what time?' she asked.

'The music – these maps of the music – they're getting steadily older. I'm having real difficulty reading it. Notation's the same, but the way it's written changes.'

'But how can it change when it's you who's writing it down? I mean, you play and then you write, yeah?'

'It doesn't matter. When I write it down, it's as though it's not me.'

'Eh?'

'It's as though someone's directing the movements of the pen.'

'Oh, right. Spirits, you mean! Like on an Ouija board.' She laughed. 'You're completely screwed, Alex.'

'No – I mean, you...'

'What if I'd never met you, Alex? What then? What if I hadn't driven, that morning, down to the riverbank? None of this would be happening. We would both still be normal people, going about our everyday lives, working, sleeping, earning dosh, being ordinary. Ordi-fucking-nary. Instead of which, I'm now jacking in a good job – and for what? So I can follow you on some whacked-out voyage to the boring commuter wilds of Lincolnshire, and God-knows-where after that.'

He seemed perplexed. He hadn't expected this.

'I'm following you, Zulie. You started all this. It was you who saw the box and wanted to fish it out of the river. If it hadn't been for me...'

'You were bereaved. You needed someone to need you.'

'What's so wrong about that? Isn't that what love's about?' A pause. He took a step forward, tentative, uncertain. She knew what was coming. 'Don't you love me?' He took both her hands, lifted them to his lips. She felt that they would smell of bone, or worse still, of flesh. Archie's flesh. But Alex had already pulled away and turned to face the wall. There was a thin crack running down the plaster. She tried to follow the crack up as far as it went, but she lost it long before it reached the ceiling. 'We don't have to go,' he said, quietly. 'Why don't we junk the box? Forget about it altogether. We can still see each other. It's just a box, for Christ's sake!' He turned back slowly towards her. She shook her head.

'No, Alex. We can't do that.'

'Why not?' He picked up the skull goblet. 'What is this, after all? *Alas, poor Yorick?*' He laughed, and swung it from one hand to the other as though it were half a baseball.

'Don't!' She reached out, but he dodged away and began to

pace about the room.

'So, Yorick me old pal, whose skull are you, eh?' Alex cupped the skull over his left ear and inclined his head like a child listening for the sea. 'Well, well, you're very quiet tonight. What's the matter? Forgot your lines? Some whisky, perhaps?' He went over to her drinks cabinet, and before she'd had time to stop him, he had poured a liberal quantity of the single malt into the crown of the skull. He swirled it around, much as he might've done with a large clear glass, and then up-ended it and drank. All in one go. 'Ah!!!'

'You're a sick fuck, Alex. What do you think you're trying to prove?'

He re-filled the receptacle.

'No, Zuleikha Chashm Framareza MacBeth. You are the one who is a sick fuck.'

He began to move toward her. His eyes already carried that spirit glaze. 'You, my dear, are quite insane. Insane as the fucking wind in the trees. Like the great owls of the world, you are howling at the moon. Well, Macbeth,' he said, bringing his face right up to hers so that the fumes almost overwhelmed her senses, 'you know something? Banquo is back! And he isn't going anywhere.'

They kissed. She closed her eyes. His mouth tasted of whisky, but of something else as well. Something intensely dry, an aroma of extreme age. It wasn't unpleasant, though, and she wondered whether perhaps it wasn't merely the aftertaste of the aftertaste of the whisky. But then she took the skull from him, and she too drank from its edge, sipping at first, and then, as the golden warmth spread like a silk carpet over her body, she tipped back her head and emptied the goblet to the dregs. She knew now what the aroma had been.

Chapter Fourteen

There seemed to be no dichotomy between her making love that night with Alex, the skull glass sitting benignly on her bedside locker, peering at them through its eyeless sockets, and the fact that a couple of days earlier she'd had sex with Archie, her patient and a man twice Alex's age and half his size. That the old airman hadn't expired that morning had been a miracle, she thought. And then she found herself questioning whether it had really happened. Human beings were sewers, great humping pigs with enormous dribbling snouts. Especially when it came to fucking. Anything was possible. You never knew what your body or your mind would do next.

But now, this morning just before Christmas, they climbed a steep hill overlooking the capital city of the county. Alexander and Zuleikha sat on the cold grass and stone and marvelled at the elegant towers and spires of Lincoln Cathedral – the tallest in Europe, they said. And all around this sand-coloured Gothic structure, beyond the old Roman and Mediaeval centre, the city spilled out across the land in a quintessentially twentieth-century urban manner. Zuleikha knew that the streets would be comprised of the same rows of chain-stores and prettily pedestrianised areas with black iron bollards shaped like the lowest-ranked chess piece, and that the cuteness of this nauseatingly uniform 'heritage' planning had come to define the nerve-centres of our civilisation. Suburbs, she thought, for all their cars and lack of spirit at least did not pretend to be anything other than what they were. She remembered her father, endlessly pruning his roses. But at least he was doing something, he wasn't harming anyone, and she supposed that he must be happy. Well, through the filter of whisky, he must be happy. She had hardly seen him for the past few months. Just the odd stilted phone conversation. She felt the guilt rise in her throat. Well, she thought, I can't be everybody's bloody mother!

They were on the old Carrs of Lindsey, which once had been treacherous black wastelands where sterile earth had been punctuated only by bright green bogs in which countless travellers, drawn off-route by the glowing phosphorescent lights known as will-o'-the-wisps, had met their end. The air tasted of woodsmoke and ice and the cloudy sky was suffused with light as, some forty miles to the east, the sun rose over the invisible North Sea.

Alex removed the map from his rucksack and smoothed it out over his knees. Zulie sniffed and then huddled up close to him. Even on the highest ground there was no snow, though it felt as though there might be some later. He pointed out that the area towards which they needed to head was somewhat to the east and north of the last of the suburbs of the city. There was a dark green patch on the landscape which seemed strangely separate from the rigorously cultivated land, the meticulously planned towns. Separate, even, from the prettified commuter villages. She shuddered and burrowed closer into his side. She was convinced now that she had hallucinated the episode with Archie, or else dreamt it. The brain did funny things, didn't it? It was ludicrous, even the thought that she would have done such a thing. It was unthinkable. Well, not quite, since after all, she had thought it. But people thought things all the time – there wasn't a law against thinking, was there? Not yet, anyway. No, the reality was that she had finished her examination of his tumour-addled body, and then had said goodbye, and she had been aware that he had turned his face to the wall – literally, that was, not metaphorically – and that she had left and undertaken the rest of her day as though nothing had happened. Because nothing had happened. She couldn't remember that nothing had happened, but she was convinced that it had not.

Alexander had the skull there, too, in his rucksack, and now he removed it and pointed out to her the lines and fissures which ran across its surface. *Where blood once had flowed*, he said, but then she knew all about that: once on a day she'd had to memorise every last bump, so like those mounds which people in this county called hills, but which if you were from Scotland you hardly noticed.

She had been educated to be a physician in the old days when rote learning had been the mainstay and when students had had to stay up half the night, every night, trying to cram that stuff about the skull and about every single bone, every last redundant bit of the human body, into their own crania. Zuleikha did not enjoy remembering. She did not enjoy remembering the neat black coffee she'd had to drink every day, many times a day, in order simply to stay awake. Especially as it had come out of one of those awful machines. Chemical crap, it gradually did in the brain. And now, so many years later, what had popped out of the box but – guess what – a skull! And this skull should have been just as familiar to her as any other – except that, mercifully, she'd forgotten all that, and now one fissure, one hump was no different to her from any other. That was the comedy, she thought: things went into your brain and things fell out and you had little say over what did what!

They'd booked into a cheap hotel in Lincoln – a double room, this time – whose clientèle tended to be business travellers or else assorted bands of relatives come to bury one of the aged who seemed to comprise a disproportionately large segment of the population hereabouts. They'd positioned the box in a cupboard next to the small room-safe and had shut the door, convinced that nobody would want to steal such a thing. Anyway, it was too big, and they had received odd stares as they'd carried it in – as though, Alex later had joked, they'd been carrying in a corpse. Burke and Hare, grave-robbers in battered top hats, come to dismember the past, or the future, or whatever it is, was, or will be. Que fucking sera.

The ground was freezing and she hauled Alex up off the rocks. 'Let's go, then.'

He smiled, and followed her to the car. Alex had plotted the coordinates by drawing on his memory of the music, but the loops of notes were so long he wasn't certain whether or not he'd got all the correct figures. He worried that if he was out even by a small margin, they would be on a wild goose chase up and down a chimney. Like his lute, the music too was changing form. Every time he had played it in that state of which afterwards he had only metaphysical memory, the sound had seemed to be coming at him from further away, in both time and space. When he had been given the instrument by the man in the Barras, the man whom subsequently he had been unable to find, it had been a full sixteen-course Late Baroque lute, each course consisting of two strings except for the chantarelle, the highest, which remained single. So, at first, there had been thirty-one strings. And it had stayed that way until he had met Zuleikha, until the box had

236

floated down the river and landed in their hands. Everything had been normal – well, at least rational, logical, material. Two and two made four, right? Time was linear and moved, like the Light Brigade, onward, always onward. Right. Then all this weirdness had begun and every time he'd opened another box, every time he'd played this way, the music had generated the means of opening the next lid … but as this had happened, in a strange parallel, the lute had seemed to diminish in size and complexity. Not that it had become less difficult to play – with all these changes and this trekking around, Alex had become paranoid about keeping up his expertise – and he didn't know whether or not he might have some sort of epilepsy – that's what Zulie had said, though she'd also said that it didn't fit any syndrome she had ever seen. So, after the underground station in Glasgow the lute had had thirteen courses, twenty-five strings, and the strings had reverted from metal to gut, and following their visit to the church in Argyllshire it had shrunk yet again – to eight courses, fifteen strings – at least, that's what it had been the last time he'd checked, just that afternoon.

Furthermore, at some stage between the station and the church, Alex had begun to find it impossible to play with his fingers – whichever way he'd tuned it, the strings had seemed too dull and flat – and so he'd bought a variety of metal and plastic plectra, though none had seemed quite right. The nature of the music which he was able to produce on such an instrument also had altered – the tunings were all different and it was simply impossible to play polyphony on this simpler form of the lute – and so the structure had dictated that the melodic line become dominant and he had found himself embroidering loose texts around that line. Watching the text was not so important now that he was drawing on deep memory. Yet the playing – his playing – was not loose; in fact he had never played so well in his life. It gave him a real high every time he picked up the piece of wood, which as its form shifted also was becoming steadily lighter in weight. His fingers were now so supple that it was almost as though they were jointless. It was as though the glue from which the lute had been constructed was turning to fluid, so that in the same manner in which, over time, other lutes had been remoulded, necks extended or shortened and strings and peg-boxes added, it seemed that Alex's lute was reverting to its original form – whatever that might be.

The notation was becoming increasingly archaic, yes, and anarchic as well, yet it was perfectly suited to the music. Not all the music was set in the codes he had discovered from the box; it was as though he'd become attuned to picking up from the air something which had been lost in the substance of time. He found that only by actually playing the lute could he discover what this music might have been, and that even then, it was fast becoming impossible to write it down. How could you write down a note that curled across several frequencies simultaneously, or one that buried itself within another note, only to emerge at some later stage of the piece, having never really gone away in between? We weren't talking overtones, trills, sustains or harmonics here, but actual first-degree sounds, impossible sounds, pitches which he'd never heard before, not even played by those consorts who attempted to reconstruct what Early Mediaeval music might have sounded like. This wasn't simply sound. He'd tried recording it and then feeding it in a number of modes through his computer. He'd applied the panoply of the not quite out-of-date expertise he'd gained in his various high-tech jobs, yet still had drawn a blank. This was something which computers could not solve. Animals and plants shifted shape, yes, they grew and shrank and got fat or thin and their hair went grey. Okay, but stones and dead wood? In the sea, maybe – or in a river, over hundreds, thousands of years. Then there was evolution, but that didn't pertain to a single thing. Even the tiniest atom was unique and discrete. Perhaps their perceptions were warped, like those idiots who thought they could make out statues of the Virgin Mary weeping tears of blood.

Alexander sensed that it had something to do with that airman she'd talked so much about before, and about whom quite suddenly she had ceased talking shortly before their departure for Lincoln. The man was dying of meso-whatsit, some tumour to do with asbestos exposure in the shipyards, and he was Zulie's patient – yet Alex knew that there was much more to it than that. At a stretch, Archie had only a month or two left, but Zulie, who initially had seemed upset about this, now seemed nonchalant – elated, almost. It was probably just that, as a caring doctor, she felt guilty about leaving a vulnerable person to die on her watch in that horrible, strangulatory way. Alex couldn't imagine facing such a terrible death. But then, was it better to go as Susan had, in a sudden death-spin through the night? 'Archie' was over eighty; he had lived his life and had left behind tangible things of steel and iron, whereas Susan had been in her prime and what had she left behind, except him? Death was shit, no matter how or when it arrived. And anyway, why was he thinking about her like that, as though she were some impersonal historical figure? How could he think of her in that manner?

Alex felt the guilt sit like a stone, like a square box in the pit of his stomach. Every time he thought of her, the pain made him physically sick. He couldn't talk about her with anyone, least of all with Zuleikha. Susan, Susan, Susan. What happened that night, my love? He'd been dreaming that he'd been playing his lute when the police had arrived at the door. Playing fast, faster than ever before, he'd lost himself in its song. He'd never done that before. Not really. He'd dreamed of it like that. He'd told himself that he'd been fast asleep. He wasn't a sleep-walker, far less a sleep-player. Wasn't even sure such a thing existed. Yet his memory was playing tricks on him, just as it had with himself and Zuleikha down by the water. Had he helped her lift the box out of the swirling river, or had she already done that when he'd arrived on the scene? The more he thought about it all, the worse it got. He thought that maybe he was suffering from some kind of pre-senile dementia, that his brain was rotting from the inside out.

When he died, she would be waiting for him. Susan, that was. But then what about Zuleikha? Where did she fit in? What could be wrong about loving someone, even if – as he knew everyone would say – it was just on the rebound? He sensed that their relationship would outlast this journey. He had no idea how, but there was something all-encompassing and ferocious in the world which he and Zulie had created around themselves. The three things in his life that he had felt to be genuinely his, the three trajectories over which he felt he'd had at least some control, were Susan, Zuleikha and the music. Perhaps after death, if there was anything, it would exist in some kind of quantum state, so that on the one hand he and Susan would be together again, awaiting the Resurrection, and on the other Zuleikha and he would be here, exploring the freezing wastes of Lincolnshire, building their love on a series of squiggles and plucked catgut and drinking liquor from the half-world of a skull.

As they sped past the rank hedgerows and lightning-struck trees, Alex began to drift into a fitful sleep. It was just as well she was driving, he thought. Perhaps she would have grown wings – Susan, that was. But he knew that whichever weird multi-dimensional state he would find himself in after his physical demise, it would be filled with, and defined by, music.

White. White, everywhere. Alex blinked and keeled over, tried to grab a hold. She was shoving his shoulder, waking him up from a dreamless sleep.

'Is this it?' she asked. 'Are we here?'

Alex rubbed his eyes, then wiped a circle in the glass and peered through the steamed-up side-window.

'What is this...?' He opened the door. Stepped out, inhaled.

They were at the centre of a vast, empty space. Everything was lightly coated in the powdery snow which was still falling all around them.

'Right,' she said, quietly. 'It's an old runaway.'

Over to their left were some low red-brick buildings, overgrown almost to their roofs with earth and weeds, while what had been the runway had been fractured in places by dark-green clumps of bushes. They left the car and began to circle what might have been the perimeter. Around the aerodrome were the rusty remains of a fence, but long ago this had been subsumed into the vegetation, so that even in midwinter it was impossible to define the aerodrome's limit. There was an absence of echo which Zuleikha found disturbing. The snow didn't seem thick enough here to be swallowing up sound. Alex worried about his lute, sitting in its thin case in the car boot. Lutes did not react well to extremes of temperature or humidity, specifically coldness and dampness. They lost tone far more readily than, say, guitars. Like Zulie, they'd originated in hot dry countries. Or at least, like half of her, he thought with some amusement. Mind you, the lute too had been put together mechanically as though it was a piece of architecture, a kind of portable cathedral. An incarnation of High Art, cut and fired from the city's rough-and-tumble spiritual heart, the Barras, just a stone's throw away from the Glasgow Green, where glas cau – Glasgu, the dear people of the green hollow, or the dear place of the green people, or the … whatever! And the Barras was only a Brythonic headband's throw from the big old necropolis of the sacred oaks and the hill-fort that had overlooked both the holy grove and the Clyde. Strange, he thought, that a graveyard had been built where once human beings may have been sacrificed, where their spirits had been given up to the sky like Isaac's tears to Yahweh. Trees had a lot to answer for.

You really felt it, he thought, in these elemental places; the iron and song of the centuries seemed that much closer. Resurrected birds, burning branches, tolling bells. The unfaithful Langeoreth of Strathclyde, the Queen of ring and salmon. Alex still wore his wedding ring; indeed, chafed by the metal, his finger had grown thicker immediately distal to the plain band of 18-carat gold, so that it would have been very difficult for him to have removed it even if he'd wanted to. And he hadn't … wanted to. And was Zuleikha his Langeoreth? He chuckled, and then smiled at her and she smiled back. It's so easy, he thought, to grant a smile, a laugh, a song. To lie with someone was not so very hard. During that time between the sheets, which in spite of all the exploitation nevertheless remained the most intimate thing in which two adult human beings consensually could engage, you could pretend to forget. But the long term was more difficult. The long term was metal; it did not swell and flow and change like flesh and wood and water. It bound in one's history, fixed it to the ground, carved it into sandstone, granite and Corinthian bronze. But she seemed to be okay here in this place, he thought. Bundled up as she was, to look at her you'd think it was the Arctic and not rural Lindsey that she was visiting. Captain bloody Scott! He pulled out the chart from the inside pocket of his jacket.

'I don't know why we're here, in this place,' she said. Her voice seemed to come from far away. 'I thought it was a lake we were looking for, but this was where you'd marked on the map.'

'Yes, it was,' he said slowly. 'I don't know.' He paused. 'Perhaps I got it wrong.'

She turned on him.

'You can't get it wrong. I can't do what you do with that lute.'

She gestured back towards her car, which was now some two hundred metres behind them and which was fast being covered with snow.

He splayed his arms.

'Look, I'm not perfect. It's possible that I've got it wrong.'

'Why are we at a World War Two aerodrome?'

'How do you know that's what it is?'

'What else could it be, Alex? Besides, I've seen it before.' What was she saying?

'Pardon?'

'I've seen it before.'

'How?'

'With Archie, you know, the guy I told you about. He's dying.' So she was talking about him again. 'Yes. Archie,' she went on. 'He's dying. He might not last till the New Year.'

'What's he got to do with it?'

Suddenly, she seemed distant.

'He was posted here.'

But Alex seemed not to have heard properly, or maybe she had spoken too quietly.

'What did you say?'

She shrugged and gazed into the distance. She could just about make out what might have been the remains of the control tower, though now it seemed to resemble something more like a sheep-pen. Perhaps it was simply a sheep-pen. Or perhaps, slowly and in multifarious ways, the land was reclaiming everything man-made – the way it always did, sooner or later. For a few years, she thought, you are what you eat and then you sink down to your knees and are eaten. But things got preserved in the cold, didn't they? Things lasted for millions of years. As the world hotted up and the big ice-sheets retreated, people were finding perfectly preserved woolly mammoths all over Siberia, for God's sake. Perhaps, like some old monster, the box too had been released from an iceberg up by the North Pole and somehow had ended up coming doon the watter! *You're a salmon, Zulie. You're an eel.* His words, the airman's. *You're leaving me because once again you can't face seeing someone die before your eyes.* He didn't say that, did he? Did he? She couldn't remember what people had said and what

242

they hadn't said. His last words. *To me, it is nothing. During the War, I watched men – good friends – go up into the sky and never come back down. During the war, I went up into the sky…* But you did come back, Archibald; you did come back and you lived with Margaret, Bibi Margaret, in your semi in the Glasgow suburbs. So stop lying to me, Archie; stop spinning my thoughts into lies. Please.

You did not make love to me, you fucking, lying, dying bastard. You fucking human tumour.

She pulled her scarf more tightly around her neck and walked on towards the sheep-pen. The snow was coming down thicker, faster, so that somewhere behind her Alex's figure had become a series of Pointillist dots in a sea of white. When they reached the circle of rubble which they had supposed had been the control tower, they realised that actually it was just a pile of rubbish left over from the go-kart racing that took place on the aerodrome every Sunday. But behind and to the left of this area, Zuleikha noticed a tall hedge which seemed somehow out of place.

'So, it's a hedge,' said Alex, despondently.

But Zuleikha was wandering again, thinking of Archie and of her mother and of her dead son. It was the snow, she reasoned: it was this snow that was taking her back – years, decades – to the sirens and the fast death that came down like fog – yes, that was it: the anti-fog machine that had never seemed to work properly. Yes, she could see it now: she could see, looped like a magic circle around everything, around the old perimeter fence, around the bodies of the WAAF personnel, women's bodies, the flesh of those who had had to lie across the tails of aircraft as the camouflaged machines had wheeled and taxied, the rationed weight of the women counterbalancing that of the nose-cone. But sometimes the pilots would forget that there was a woman on the back of their craft, and wouldn't slow down before the final take-off run. Archie had known all this, and now Zuleikha also knew as she marched towards the dark green hedge. He was calling after her, he, Alexander, King of the Lute, Widower Alexander who seemed unable to grasp that Susan, his Susan, was rotting now, right now, in the steeked earth. And that she, Zuleikha, was all around, that she was the air he breathed, and that Susan's memory could only ever be a pale substitute, a shadow, a ghost in his life. Love was a bitch. Love was a killer.

The hedge was of that tough evergreen vegetation that in Britain had seemed never to have dropped its leaves since the time of William the Conqueror. You hardly noticed it during summer, but now, in the depths of winter, it came into its own. The myth was that the verdure kept the countryside from looking completely desolate, but in fact, Zuleikha thought, these resilient types of plants, bushes and hedges simply served to accentuate the feeling of wasteland. During the last Ice Age this whole area had been glacier, she thought, and before that it had been under a sea that had billowed with the exudates from cavernous underwater volcanoes, a sea that had been set at the temperature of human saliva. That, she thought as she kicked up the earth, was why the soil around these parts was virtually pure sand. You scratched a few centimetres down and you came up with gold under your nails. The water here was so hard; it came straight from limestone bedrock and was good for your health. But it ruined the kettles. During the raids, it had coated the insides of both the kettles and the teapots just as it had formed and grown inside Archibald, just as in this monochrome memory his eyes had joined with hers across the diorama board in the busy bunker. She had slipped inside him, pure and white and cut fresh off a cliff, and that had been long before the asbestos, the ships, the cancer. He had drunk deep of this land, he had sipped the marrow from its bones and now she, Zuleikha, had returned, she had followed the bone trail, she had gazed through the orbit sockets of a skull and had seen ... this place, this aerodrome, its horizontal perfection, its aroma, dissipating through sixty years or more of abandonment and useless pursuits. Yet she knew that even now, through the thickening snow, it still held the land in thrall with that stench, that scent, of death.

Alex had caught up with her and was attempting to hold her back as she pushed her body through the dense growth of the hedge.

'What are you doing?' he shouted. 'Are you mad? Don't you see the thorns? Zuleikha! Are you listening to me?'

And perhaps she was insane and had been so for a while, but she didn't see or feel the thorns as they tore at her flesh and as they drew the blood to the surface of her skin, her almond-brown, hazelnut-brown, Lincolnshire earth-brown skin, and she felt the blood seep from between Margaret's legs as he entered her that first time – her first time – in the shelter; as, far away and high above, the orchestra had played a jolly tune, the upright piano lingering a little too long on a particular syncopation. It was the virtuoso's special treat for the masses: light classical music for everyman, music which brought noise but no light. And Zuleikha knew every inch of him, his body, his mind, and as she emerged into a clearing she knew that this was where he had been patrolling that night he had dropped his torch and run back to the barracks. This was where, sixty-eight years earlier, Archie first had heard the music. Lord Jack's music, the music of the mountains. Lord Jack Ruthyn's skull, which had been bequeathed to a strange craftsman, to fashion in the manner of the goblet of the old monk. Corinthian brass. And in that, there was no syncopation.

'Bring the lute,' she commanded Alexander, who was so dumbfounded as he looked at her face, which had turned marsh-like and archaic, that he spun on his heel. But by the time he had returned to the spot, having negotiated his way, carrying lute case and all, through the snow thicket, the tangle, the wild gorse – this last of which, with its dense sprawling bushiness, had grown taller even than he – she had gone. She had disappeared into the snow, leaving only footprints which, as the snowfall intensified, rapidly were becoming erased. He hurried on. He gave up calling her name only when he realised that his voice was being completely absorbed into the thick white blanket which the world had become.

Chapter Fifteen

Before she'd left for Lincolnshire, Zuleikha had gone to visit her father. She wasn't sure exactly why; after all, it wasn't as though she was going to the far ends of the earth or emigrating to America. Not that it would have required an event as momentous as that to have spurred her into paying a visit to Daniel John. Not quite. Every time she went to see him, it was as though she had to hold her breath, to try and forget the passage of time – even though, in the fading photographs which filled the walls of his house, time seemed to be the major, the comforting obsession. Comforting for him, maybe. It was as though his home had been turned into a kind of Orthodox necropolis. Everywhere you looked, there was an icon. And then there was the big secret of his drinking – a secret with which, even in her medical mode, Zuleikha had never quite managed to confront him. It had never been admitted to by either of them, and her complicity in his self-deceit filled her with guilt. To have admitted it would have been to have acknowledged that icons fail, that saints were no longer beatific, that the last remaining bulwark between herself and the grave was riddled with woodworm. It was easy to give advice to others, she thought. But those weren't the only reasons for Zuleikha's tentativeness. He still lived in the house which for so many years they had all occupied as a family, she and her parents. He'd kept all her childhood things: the toys, the books, even the steel-blue school jotters which were emblazoned on their back covers with a red-stone version of the Ten Commandments:

DO NOT TALK IN THE CLASS
DO NOT CHEW GUM
DO NOT SLOUCH
DO NOT TRY TO APPEAR CLEVER
DO NOT SHAKE HANDS
DO NOT REVEAL YOURSELF TO YOURSELF
DO NOT REACH ABOVE YOUR SHOULDER
DO NOT DREAM

DO NOT STEP OUT OF LINE
OR RAISE YOUR HEAD ABOVE THE PARAPET

Mostly they were stored in vertiginous Dickensian piles up in the loft, but they were also scattered around the fabric of the house, and inexplicably she would find them here and there, as though the long-abandoned ferocious jotters now had acquired independent vitality. *Dreaming is for fools.* But the main reason she had to hold taut a maximal inhalation and, with it, her tongue, was his tendency always to assume control. This hadn't been his way in the days when the persona of Nasrin Zeinab had filled the foreground of their lives. She had always been the assertive one. Yes, that was how middle management-speakers would have had it: assertive, loud, dominant. In fact, people had often commented on how Daniel John had been such a quiet man in comparison, so respectful and all – when really, Zuleikha now understood, his quietude had been his means simultaneously of escape and control. Now he no longer needed the former, and he had Nasrin Zeinab held there permanently, her image pinned like a representation of the life-cycle of a butterfly to the walls of every room – even to the insides of the kitchen cupboards, for God's sake. Well, that was love for you, she thought. Very romantic. But for anyone outside of that axis, it was profoundly disconcerting. And Zuleikha was most definitely outside. Always had been.

There was a particular set of traffic-lights through which she had to drive in order to enter his part of town. Well, she didn't have to go that way, but the other routes were so much longer – and anyway, whichever of the routes she took, there was always a specific set of lights, the broken end of a wall, a vanished gable-end. Whenever she crossed any of these lines it was as though she was flipping back twenty or thirty years. It all felt so much like second nature, and yet every time she ventured across that frontier, structurally – geologically, almost – more would have changed. A new development here, a brightly polished refurbishment there. Old buildings gone overnight. Roads turned one-way. Hills turned to valleys, and valleys turned to hills. There hadn't been so much construction work going on in Glasgow since the early 1970s. She supposed it must be for the good of the economy. And some of that soulless post-War stuff did need pulling down. But, as with all of Britain, the roads were about three times as busy as they had been forty years ago. No, that was wrong. Five times as busy. With less and less space, smaller rooms, narrower corridors, tighter driveways, lower ceilings, the suburbs seemed perpetually to exist in a sub-acute state of road-rage. Visiting her father involved transporting herself through a series of dislocations. But then, she thought, it won't be forever. And then she hated herself.

How to bring up the subject? By the time they had eaten dinner and had had a post-prandial cup of weak English tea, she still hadn't decided. And so, as usual, she just blurted it out at what she knew would turn out to be the wrong moment. His face remained expressionless as she told him. She had hoped for some inroad, some half-sign of beckoning. He was a good cook for a man of his age, but the food was generally a little too laden with oil, or perhaps with onions, and now the meal sat in her upper abdomen, heavy and dead, forcing her to hyperventilate slightly. She ought really to have got up and gone for a walk, but then she would have lost the moment. She shifted to the right, then to the left. He seemed calm; expectant, even. Then she told him again.

'Where are you going?' he asked. Daniel John often pretended to be deaf – at least, when it suited him. So she had to repeat it, as she knew she would, and in the repetition she found herself stumbling over her words, becoming inchoate, imbecilic, dyslexic, dyspraxic, autistic, child-like again before him.

'Lincolnshire. It's in the east of England.'

'Why are you going there? Nice, is it?'

She nodded.

'Yes, and I'm taking a friend.'

'Oh?'

'His name's Alexander.'

'Andrew?'

'No, Dad. Alexander.' She virtually spelled out the letters, then realised that she was talking too loudly. Just like her mother. His face was long, Scots-Irish. Yes, he was Roman Catholic, but his ancestors must've been bears, she thought. That's where she had got her elongated, almost rectangular features from: some howling Orangeman who in the seventeenth century had been assigned land by the Crown for services rendered. Some acolyte of John Knox, the great Scottish reformer. At some point, someone must have married heretically, and most probably had been disowned as a consequence. Such cataclysmic implications of inter-marriage between Catholics and Protestants had continued well into the 1970s and probably beyond. Back in the early days, she thought, Orangeism had meant liberation, enlightenment, rationalism and the beginnings of democracy and industrial capitalism. No-one nowadays seemed to want to hear of that history, nor of the principle of vigorous debate that underpinned much Protestant ideology. But then later, as so often was the way, it had become a symbol of oppression, discrimination and mindless bigotry, and a peculiarly bitter form of royalist imperialism. So often, unionists or loyalists – so-called from their stance over the status of Northern Ireland – had made themselves into a laughing-stock. Rip Van Winkles who hadn't woken up to the fact that they were no longer under threat from the forces of the Whore of Babylon, or at least that the Whore now was living in … Babylon. And not Dublin. It was, she thought, the unconscious mal-directed anger of the white working-classes, trans-substantiated into a vortex of cloth. How things change! How adroitly and with what perfection we turn into our enemies.

He looked away.

'Your life is your own,' he said. As he did, always. A tiny movement of his lip, a slight angulation of his left eyebrow, and that was it. Once upon a time perhaps his face would have held more expression, and perhaps even there would have been a surfeit of change, like the Irish Sea on those days when it gleamed blue beneath the windy sky. You could never smell the drink off him. It was bloody miraculous! He was like one of those saints whose bodies, in the moments immediately post-mortem, had exuded the scent of roses. It was his mantra. *Your life is your own.* Her life was her own, meaning that whatever she did with her existence, wherever she went and with whomever she slept, the fault lay only with her. He was washing his hands in Pontius Pilate's golden bowl. Or, to be more accurate, in the black box of the confessional. As though anyone's life was really their own. Even Eve and Adam had had God, the apple tree and the Devil. And they'd been in the

Garden of Heavenly Delights. She knew – she felt – that she was being inordinately harsh, but like certain types of expression or a specific shape of face, it brought out the worst in her. Perhaps, she thought, this was his way of dealing with loss. But no – that was bullshit; he'd always been like this. The older you got, the sharper your obsessions became. By the time you died, she thought, you would be like the edge of a bone. You would be like Archie.

No, she thought, no-one could be like Archie.

'It's just for a little while, Dad; a week, or maybe two. We're searching for something.'

'Searching? Searching for what?'

Just when she'd thought she could ramble on, that really he wouldn't be hearing or comprehending what she said, he was suddenly alert. Never underestimate the not-so-deaf, or the very old. They've seen it all. They may not have done it all, but they've certainly imagined doing it.

'I don't know yet. A place, a person, a piece of music. I really don't know.'

Daniel John shrugged, then looked her in the eye and took her hand. His hands were still massive, and though it was true that the rest of him had shrivelled, even when he'd been drinking they bore no tremulousness. He could crush a heart in those hands, she thought. Maybe he crushed my mother's. Suffocated the life out of her. Not rapidly, like the cancer, but insidiously over the years. By the things he'd never done, the words he'd never said. Nasrin Zeinab had fuelled his drinking, though, that was for sure. She'd bought him bottles that he could stow away. Oh yes, she thought, his drinking had long preceded his wife's illness and death. How strange people are, Zuleikha thought. You create your own demons and then you feed them as though they are malevolent household pets. You become like a woman who can't let go of a high-rise electrified cable. It kills you, but you'd rather cling to it than fall. Once, those same hands had cradled Zuleikha's entire being and yet still, every time, in spite of herself, she resented coming here. She felt like a heel, like a stinking turd desiccating slowly on a pavement in the summer sun. But it wasn't summer; hadn't been for a while.

The heating was full-on and she was suffocating with the weight of memory. Her own and that of her mother – which, now that her mother was no more, she could see much more clearly, as though she was able to shift behind the pigment and light of the photographic prints, as though she was able to seek out the spirit that lay in the smiles, the tiredness, the mundanities that gleamed with the fire of stained glass. The Old Ones were dead right, she thought. The power of hands lay not in the physical weight of muscle and bone, but in the shape they made as they joined together, the light barely glinting through the undulations of the palms – Mons Javis, Via Solis, Mons Veneris – as they prayed in the unashamedly Catholic position, finger-ends apposed in a dead perfect symmetry, the conjuration of spine, shoulders, skull and phalanges together forming the shape of a symphony – or rather of a sanctus, set at the seraphic feet of the Throne of God. Every night Daniel John prayed with those hands; they were his conduit to his immortal soul. Perhaps, she thought, he had prayed before he had laid the seed of his loins into Nasrin Zeinab, that night – she supposed it must've been night – when Zuleikha had had her own personal Genesis. Let there be light! The electric evening darkness seemed to accentuate his still-full head of hair, and then she thought that perhaps at the last minute he would end up being buried in a Catholic cemetery, far away from her mother's resting-place. No, she thought, they'd bought the plot together when she'd been diagnosed with cancer. So Daniel John MacBeth would be the sole baptised Roman Catholic in a Muslim graveyard. But his hair will not die, she thought: it will continue to grow, long and silver; it will sift its way through the coffin walls and will sleek through the cold earth and will wrap around the caskets of others, of the skeletal and the still-fleshed, alike as one row of stones succeeds the next. Beneath the roots of the ancient yew tree, his hair will circle the dead wood and slip into the sap channels, will climb through trunk, branches, twigs, and then, one spring, three or perhaps four years later, Daniel John MacBeth will emerge, glorious and triumphant, in the form of a cherubic burst of leaves. Hosannah in Excelsis!

But that life could begin only after this one was over, and when all was said and not said, or thought and unthought, he was her dad. This was the man who had dreamed her into being, for God's sake – who had taken her by the hand that first time, so that she wouldn't fall and hurt herself. Who had sat with her for hours on end as she'd attempted to learn how to read a sequence of simple words, and who had taken her to sail tiny boats on the undulating waves of laughter and sunshine that would always be her vision of the pond in the local park. His body once had held within it cells of endless possibility, and his silhouette, framed against the dun white sky, still tended at times towards the heroic. Yet now destiny, or random chance, or nothing at all, had left him beached here, in this suburban land of jannats, of moderately spacious tightly-hedged plots where people walked the dog and were polite to the point of insouciance – except, of course, on the roads, where it was all Freud – and where, even on the brightest days, an unrelenting gloom leached through the stones and earth and through the white plastic of the sweet pea trellises.

Chapter Sixteen

And now there was light, but it was of a quite different sort. There was nothing remotely heavenly about the blinding white sheets of snow which cascaded down from the sky and covered the flat land of Lindo with a layer of solid water, several feet deep. It was unusual in these days when the world was rapidly over-heating, but every so often a storm of Victorian proportions would descend like a whirling ghost upon the east of England. And when that happened, a nation which prided itself on no longer being used to extremes of climate, temperament or disposition suddenly acquired a frenetic nervous energy that lasted two or perhaps three days. The news bulletins would be filled with reports of the existential state of the snow and ice, and intrepid reporters clad in full Antarctic expeditionary gear would scour the furthest reaches of Danelaw in search of heartwarming stories of grace and fortitude, tales of Blitz spirit plucked from among the Plebeian Estate. During those days it was England against the World, a contest with predetermined narrative, coordinates, end-point.

But on that day Zuleikha was not concerned with any of this persiflage: she was following a trail that meandered like a pre-industrial river, leaving stagnation and bogs in its wake. Her father had understood that her journey had begun many years earlier, the day she had left home to work in her first hospital post, some two hundred miles to the north of Glasgow. He had known that she was prone to unexpected twists and turns, that he would have to accept that any rational comprehension of her trajectory would have to wait months, years or even decades.

And Zuleikha found herself preoccupied with thoughts of her father and of the unfairness of the way in which she had learned to treat him, not making sufficient allowance for his own emotional state, nor for the fact that he was a being sufficient unto himself who had been born without relation to her. She was angry at herself for inheriting her mother's inherent disdain of men, and specifically of Daniel John. Why then, Zuleikha thought, if Nasrin Zeinab had held her husband in such contempt, why on earth had she married him in the first place and then stayed with him for so many years, almost till the end? Why had she not only tolerated his long-standing drinking habit, but also fuelled it? Why, eventually, had she been the one who had moved out, relocated herself and her life to some anonymous newly-built one-bedroom apartment on the Southside?

Secretly, Zuleikha had always blamed the shock of this move on the cancer that had seemed to erupt out of nowhere. She'd seen it before. Major life-change leading to physical pathology. Something to do with the energy meridians and their effect on the immune system. Inflammatory markers. Moving out, breaking free had killed her mother, and even though it had been the right thing to do, Zuleikha was angry at her – firstly for not having done it many years earlier, and then for having done it when it was too late. Guilt, guilt, guilt. Yeah, maybe that was it. O fuck, she thought, how could you understand someone else's mind when you couldn't even figure out your own? If language was a trap, its meanings infinitely malleable, then that which remained unspoken and out of sight was surely much more so. Relationships between women and men nowadays seemed tenuous and conditional, dependent as they were on some hierophantic conjunction of romantic fantasy, physical lust and a sense of history's terrible weight.

She no longer knew whether or not Alexander was following her. She supposed he must be, but the snow blanked out sound and she dared not glance backwards for fear of losing the silver thread which seemed to draw her not out of, but deeper into the labyrinth. After a while she realised that the snow had thinned to nothing underfoot and that she was walking on a damp springy bed of leaves. She had lost count of time and distance, but reasoned that she must surely have gone far beyond the outermost boundary of the aerodrome – though she didn't recall noticing any hedges laid out in a deliberate manner. Or perhaps, she thought, such an amorphous border would be invisible from close-up: that, like the political divisions on maps, it would hold no reality when you were actually standing on it.

She was surrounded by tall elms, the bareness of whose branches accentuated the natural architecture of the wood. Then she corrected herself. They couldn't be elms. Most of that species had been wiped out by Dutch Elm Disease during the 1960s just as, fifty years before that, a substantial proportion of the population had been despatched to an early grave by Spanish Influenza. In Britain, mass destroyers always had foreign names. It wasn't like in Hinduism, she thought, in the view of which, destruction arises from inside, from the very spirit of reality. Ironic, then, that while India had been invaded countless times, usually from the north and west, the sea-wall of this small rickettsian figure of an island had not been breached for almost a thousand years. Here, she thought, it had always been England versus the Ocean. The state of siege had never been more real, though, than when the aerodrome had been hastily constructed from cheap concrete and corrugated sheet metal. And while at first its runways had been formed merely by flattening down the earth, later massive slabs of concrete had been laid and then sometimes covered in liquid tarmacadam and emblazoned with thick white arrows which pointed always in one direction. She knew that the attrition rate had been horrendous; scarcely conceivable in these days of risk aversion, when one is encouraged to proceed through life minding all the gaps and when claxon announcers seem to find it absolutely necessary to remind travellers very seriously and in a decidedly obsessional manner that, as the sun sinks in the sky, it tends to get dark. Beware the dark! Beware the dog! Beware the stars, the moon, love, hate, sex, and remember that life itself holds little but a legion of fears, large, small and unquantifiable, each with unknown yet indefinably horrific consequences.

But in those days, in Archie's days ... and then she lost the thread as she shuddered. Though hardly any snow now was managing to penetrate the deep cover of the trees, and Zuleikha was unsure whether or not the stray flakes which did tickle at her face constituted fresh fall from the clouds, or secondary cascade from the gnarled branches of the dark green aspen tree which towered above her.

The vegetation had drawn in closer now, so that from time to time as she proceeded through the forest a particularly long twig would brush against her coat, her thick woollen hat, and against even the suede of her boots. The light seemed to have contracted, and Zuleikha found herself trying to remember what time of day it was. She stopped momentarily and glanced at her left wrist, but found only the imprint of a loop, and she realised that she had left her watch behind in the hotel. She listened for footsteps. Surely, she thought, now that there was no longer any snow to shut out sound, she would be able to hear Alex as he approached over the still loosely packed leaves. But though she waited and listened for what she fancied was two minutes or more, the only sound was that of her own breathing against the stillness. The lack of even the slightest breeze imparted a sense of eeriness which began as a vague sensation across the epidermis in the small of her back and rapidly spread over her whole body, penetrating deep into her flesh, becoming in the process visceral, primal, terrifying. She realised that she was hyperventilating again, and so like an opera singer in warm-up, she placed her right palm over the upper part of her abdomen, tried to slow down its movement, breath-by-breath, tried to steady herself. She found that it was easier to do this when she was walking, and so she decided to continue forward, deeper into the forest.

The branches now had drawn so closely together that they almost formed a pergola around and above her, and presumably because of the protection afforded by the matted wood, the trees here had not shed their leaves. Indeed, the further in she went, the more leaves there seemed to be – leaves that were brown at first and later a dark winter green, until after a while Zuleikha could barely make out any sky at all, and the light grew so dim that she found herself groping along, her hands held out before her as though she was dowsing, her face lined with the strain of trying to see. The foliage which pressed into her body now was thick and green and its scent was heavy, aromatic, fecund.

The temperature seemed to be rising, though she couldn't tell whether or not this perception was simply a result of her exertions and her panic. There seemed to be a noise coming from somewhere to her left, but now her progress occasioned such a volume of dissonant sound that she was unsure as to whether the new noise was simply part of the cacophony produced by her own movement. She dared not stop, but now her concern lay not in a worry that she might lose the path – though 'path' seemed an inordinately civilised word to describe this narrow tunnel through which she was passing, a bit like referring to a jungle as a forest and to a forest as a wood – but rather from an inchoate fear that if she were to stop, whatever was producing the sound might catch up with her. She tried to reassure herself. Perhaps it's just Alex, she thought, crashing like an elephant through the undergrowth, carrying his lute-case.

Alex had thought that Zulie would have waited for him to return with the lute, but when he got back to what he thought was the place where they'd been standing, he found that the freshly fallen snow had obscured both sets of footprints. He stood and wheeled around on the spot, his breath turning ghosts through the cold air, and this made him dizzy and slightly anxious and it seemed to take longer than usual for him to regain his equanimity. He felt a slight ache in the sides of his jawbone, and then the discomfort spread to his forehead. He knew it would get worse the longer he was out in the cold. Looking at the distribution of trees, bushes and rubble, there seemed only one way she could have gone – but then the snowflakes whipped into his face, stinging his eyes and momentarily blinding him, and he felt a terrible sense of despondency.

He began to move forward, but there was something resistant in the ground near the boot of his right foot. He looked down and kicked the object. It felt more like metal than stone. He knelt, brushed off the snow and hardened sand and, using both hands and the toe of his boot, managed to exhume the object. It was a long metal torch. He pressed on the buttons, but they were jammed. It looked old: its design was archaic; but then, he thought, anything made of metal which had been in the ground for any length of time would look older than it was. Yet there wasn't a single speck of rust on the torch's outer casing. He took out a hankie and wiped the lens, then peered into the mouth of the torch. The glass was so clear it wouldn't reflect. It was probably just something the go-kart enthusiasts had left behind. People had no respect for anything: they just dumped their rubbish wherever was convenient to them. They had no respect for the countryside or for its history. Where he was standing, somewhere beneath the snow and ice and sandy soil, there would still be the indentations made by high-velocity bullets spouted from the ends of Messerschmitt Bf 110 machine-gun barrels. Bullets that had carried flesh and bone into the concrete of the runway. In this air, the air that was biting into the face of his skull, in this cold white emptiness, people had danced together and made love. People had been destroyed.

Carefully, Alex placed the torch back where he had found it and covered it with powdery snow. He stood up and, cupping his hands, he called out her name loudly, several times. But his voice went no further than the boundaries of the clearing. It was as though he was sitting in the cockpit of a Hurricane, screaming at the top of his lungs. No-one would ever hear.

She leaped across becks which were almost hidden by ferns and whose water bubbled, fast and cold, over worn stones, and she was weaving so fast that at times she barely avoided ramming her skull into one of the trunks of the thousand-year old crack willows that grew out of the darkness. She ran up small inclines – the ground was becoming slightly less flat, the further away from the aerodrome she got – and each breath seemed to tumble over the next so that eventually there seemed to be no difference between inhalation and its opposite. Her heart seemed ready to burst out from between her collar-bones, and a cold ache was developing deep within the muscles of the insides of her thighs. She thought she'd spotted a large fish in one of the streams, and the fish had been silver and had seemed to gaze up at her as she'd prepared to jump across, and beneath the rippling semi-frozen water it had seemed to be swimming – but in fact it was lying, quite still on the surface of the stones that formed the bed of the stream. It had been here for centuries, she'd thought; it was here when Archie had brought Margaret, or else one of those other women, into the forest. And perhaps the fish had watched as the couple had stripped off their clothes, the uniforms of battle and market, and slowly had coupled amongst the ferns and the moss and the dancing butterflies. It must have been summer, surely, or else they'd have been frozen to the spot. The summers in the 1940s had been sunny and warm – they'd been real childhood summers (never mind the War). But perhaps it had been midwinter, and perhaps it had been just like today, right in the middle of a snowstorm. Yes, the winters too in those days had been more extreme, verging on the Victorian, and perhaps Archie and his woman had remained more or less clothed and had stayed standing, up against one of the ancient elms that had towered over the water, and perhaps it had been this very same elongated fish that had witnessed and felt everything that she had witnessed and had felt when she had touched his skin – skin that had been already yellowing from the incipience of the grave.

As she had stared into the eye of the silver fish, snow had fallen against Margaret's cheek and she had felt him moving deep inside her belly, moving painfully inside, ramming the small of her back up against the rough bark of the tree till she'd felt that even beneath the thick protective layers of her standard WAAF-issue clothes, the skin over her spine must surely be torn and bleeding. Just as, when he had taken her for the first time, she had bled from inside in the way in which the other girls had told her she would – but differently, somehow, from the way she had imagined. This time, it was as if she was being turned inside-out, as though her very being was inverting, as though she was being changed into a different person. And she gazed over Archie's shoulder into the stream, into the overwhelming brightness of the sky that was reflected in its surface, and she saw there an ugly silver-coloured fish lying on a stone, and in the eye of the fish she saw the dark spirits of the Hurricanes and Spitfires, Messerschmitts and Stukas dancing through the smoke and blood of the war which had conjured them into being.

And then she saw a woman with a dusky face who was dressed rather strangely She was preparing to jump across the water, but at the last minute the woman turned and stared at Margaret and Archie as, fully-clothed, they made love against the elm tree. And Margaret felt no embarrassment; there was no sense that what they were doing was in any way wrong. After all, she thought as she watched the stream, up there in the sky men were dying in their scores, and indeed Archie and she might be next if the bombers followed on. And Margaret was used now to giving Archie what he needed, allowing him to grobble at every inch of her flesh as though he were some lungeous hobnail risen just now from the carr. Yes, she let him have his way with her, even though she knew that he went to whores, because she loved him more than she

259

loved the sky and the earth and the fast-flowing water and indeed life itself, and her love went far beyond this dirty furtive act. But today, on this freezing mid-winter's afternoon, in the middle of this quite unexpected snowstorm, Margaret felt a great warmth begin to rise from the rock and soil, and she felt her arm stretch up the tree-trunk as though it were a serpent; she felt the silver bracelet which carried her name on its inner surface catch on a snag of bark.

And she felt Archie reach up and grab her hands, felt his fingers entwine feverishly with hers, and as the sweeping rhythm of his body accelerated it was as though he was crucifying her there against the tree. Iron, silver, steel. Out there in the tight metallic world of the aerodrome it was winter, yet down here in the forest there remained the possibility of something else: of summers that would never end, of youth that would never fade, of a love that would never die, of music whose final chord would play on into infinity to a place where pain, loss and furtiveness did not exist. She no longer felt any pain, but only heat, and the heat rose up her legs, her abdomen, her chest, in waves that were so powerful they forced her eyes shut. This was better than High Church holy communion. And she thought that perhaps she had conjured up this lady of the silver stream as a symbol of her virginity. She was unable to draw away her gaze from the face, and even through closed lids Margaret could still see the woman's odd figure, her black hair and her burned, almost Gypsy complexion, and the shape of her head which was seared onto the back of Margaret's brain, the part of her brain that was almost touching the skin of the tree, the part which knew that in this forest filled with the foetid breath of todlowries there was no such thing as sin ... until eventually, as she let her eyes close with the heavy perfume of ecstasy, she saw the judy turn away and jump across the stream. When at length she opened them again, the figure had vanished.

After a while Zuleikha leapt across the water, but because she had not backed up first she found herself wheeling through the air in an attempt to reach the other side. Her left foot landed in the mud of the far bank, but because the bank was steep – she saw now that the watercourse was a dyke rather than a beck – she fell backwards, and in order to prevent herself falling right into the water she had to sacrifice her right foot and let it land straight in the dyke. The water threatened to splash over the top of her boot, but with a great effort she managed to pull herself forward and grab onto a branch, and then she used that to haul herself out of the mud. She almost lost first the right and then the left boot in the process, but still she did not give up. It was as though she was gripped by the same madness that had held her in its thrall ever since she'd crossed paths with the box. No, she thought, it hadn't begun then. It had begun much earlier, perhaps when her child had died. Deep down, she thought, ever since that morning, I have been insane. This has been the only truth and everything else has been myth. Anyway, when she'd gazed back into the dyke from the far bank the fish had no longer been there. She'd thought that it must have been disturbed by her infraction and swum quickly away. She decided then that actually pain, loss and furtiveness were what made her tick.

Zuleikha felt her eyes begin to lose clarity and at one point she felt her heart almost stop. She knew that she couldn't go on, and so she stood with her legs wide apart and her hands pressed against the fronts of her thighs, the fingers facing inwards, and her back bent almost double so that the crown of her head was down at waist level. She dared not breathe, it had become so painful. She promised herself that she would chuck cigars the week after. No, she wouldn't wait till New Year: by then she might be dead. So she made a Christmas resolution, even though she was not Christian. So then Christ was good for something after all, she thought through her pain, almost enjoying the heresy.

'You okay?'

The woman's voice came at her from ahead. She straightened up. Flecks completely obscured her vision and she spoke without seeing.

'I'm fine,' she lied. 'Who are you?' Zuleikha was aware that the person was moving toward her, and it took all of her resolution not to step back. She stuck her hand out and instantly felt stupid. Her vision began to return, and as the woman came toward her she looked as if she was walking through a glittering silver shower. She took Zuleikha's hand and shook it a little too firmly, making Zuleikha imagine that perhaps she was one of those management types out on a power-walk through the country. Either that, or a born-again whatsit. But she didn't fit into either of those boxes. She was slightly shorter and plumper than Zuleikha and the undulations in her face seemed buffed, so that although Zuleikha could see that the woman was somewhere over fifty-five, she had the appearance of someone much younger.

'Laila Sciaccia.' She nodded, as though acknowledging Zulie's quick mental assessment of her. 'You looked like you'd overdone it!'

Zulie smiled.

'Zuleikha MacBeth. I'm not as fit as I ought to be.' Or as young, she thought, but she wasn't going to say that. Laila had on the full winter country-walking outfit: purple waterproofs for the upper body and orange trousers to … well, not exactly to match, Zuleikha thought, her eyes beginning to smart in a quite different way from before. She glanced at the other woman's impregnable dark brown boots, then back up at the rucksack on her back. She wasn't shorter in height than Zulie; it had been merely the impression imparted by a combination of the latter's near-blindness and the effect on the former's posture of the sack on her back. In fact, she was somewhat taller than Zuleikha, though perhaps the shape of her spine had altered with age and had given her that slightly hunched-over appearance. 'What are you doing here?' she asked Laila.

Laila threw out her arms.

'Walking, what else?'

'It's a strange time to go for a walk.'

'Well, it wasn't snowing when I started.'

'No,' Zuleikha acknowledged.

Laila's skin was as white as paper and tufts of silvery hair bunched out from beneath her multicoloured woollen cap. Her lips were thin, though Zulie wasn't sure whether this was genuine or whether it was an effect of the low temperature. But she wasn't cyanosed. She stopped herself there. It was automatic, this attempting to diagnose a person, to assign them a pathology in advance, as though their very humanity was a kind of illness. Madame Blavatsky, medium and theosophist extraordinaire. *I can know the exact time, date, cause and whereabouts of your death. Call down the spirits!* Or rather, don't. The old Ruskie had been a con-artist. Perhaps Laila too was a crook. Blue eyes again. Fuck that. Where was Alex? she wondered.

'My ... friend. Back there.' She jerked her thumb over her shoulder in the vague direction of where she had come.

Laila seemed puzzled.

'But that's just sinking sand and the Common. I wouldn't be walking over there. At this time of year the adders are very sleepy. In fact, they're asleep.'

'Adders?' Zulie shuddered.

'Yeah, bush eels. This place is swarming with them. Well, okay, that's a slight exaggeration. But in the summer and early autumn they come out to bask in the sun, down by the river. They're said to be immortal during daylight hours. Rubbish, of course – but I wouldn't want to test it. They like sand, you see, and this county is very sandy.'

Zuleikha kicked at the ground a couple of times.

'I had noticed.'

'And also, sometimes, by the lake.'

'Lake? What lake?'

'Tut Lake. It's frozen over right now. A couple of miles east of here. There used to be a house there, but that's long gone. Now it's just the lake and the snakes.' Laila peered around Zulie. 'No sign of your friend, then?'

Zuleikha shrugged and shook her head.

'I hope he's all right. It's pretty wild out there.'

'That's why I came in here when it began to snow. It's always so protected: cool and shady in summer and not so extreme in winter. I could see there was going to be a storm. Actually I knew all along, even before I set out this morning.'

'How did you know?'

'Red sky. You know what they say.'

Zuleikha thought for a moment.

'Red sky at night, shepherd's delight...'

Laila nodded.

'Or sailor's. My father was a ship's captain in the Merchant Navy. He always used to say "sailor's delight". *An evening rainbow means good weather in the morning, but a rainbow in the morning fills wells and fountains.* He used to say things like that. He was

263

full of maxims, aphorisms, nuggets of wisdom. At least, according to my mother. I never met him, or if I did I don't remember it. It was a bit odd – he took his mother's maiden name of Asunsi. I think now that perhaps he wanted to divorce himself from the long generations of peasanthood, of patriarchy.' There was an awkward silence. The snowstorm was barely present here. Just the occasional drop of cold water from some high branch. Otherwise it had been almost as though she had entered some kind of outdoor botanical garden. 'Was your friend following you?' Laila asked.

'Yes – how did you know?'

'I just assumed.'

A thought occurred to Zuleikha.

'Were you back there, I mean in the tunnel thing?'

Laila shook her head.

'What tunnel thing? I came from the other direction.'

'I mean, the aerodrome…'

'Aerodrome?'

'Yes, you know … are you from here?'

'Do I sound like I'm from here?' Laila smiled. Zuleikha wasn't familiar with the variety of northern English accents. 'Liverpool. A long time ago, granted – when it was a proper port. I mean, I lived in London for ages. Too long, perhaps. Then I sold up and moved here. I'm older than I look.'

Yes, Zuleikha thought. You are. Still, better than being younger than you look. Was it? Wasn't it?

'What part of London?' she asked. She felt suddenly stupid again. Here they were, two women dressed like cosmonauts having this bus-stoppish conversation, and her partner was missing – or at least was lost in a snowstorm, and the leaves around them were in full flower. Could leaves be in flower? Is that possible? she wondered, and then realised that the scents which she had noticed earlier had grown even stronger now, overwhelmingly so, and that even though those awful flecks had long gone from her vision, she was beginning to feel light-headed again. This time, it was as though she was drunk.

'Crouch End,' the woman was saying, but it barely registered with Zuleikha. 'Where the clock tower is. Very pretty nowadays.'

She felt herself stumble, and she reached out to try and grab a branch which she thought was there but which obviously can't have been, as she then tumbled sideways and fell into a tree-stump. At least, that was what she reasoned must have happened as, later, she sat on the same tree-stump nursing the laceration on the outside of her left calf. The blood had almost dried, but it had stained the inside of her trouser-leg and sock. Laila was crouching down in front of her, asking her again whether she was all right, but Zuleikha wasn't really and she knew this when she realised that she was repeating, *Where's the aerodrome? Where's Archie?*

She shut herself up.

'Is Archie your friend's name?'

'What...? Who...?' Zuleikha shook her head, as much to clear her thoughts as to answer the question. 'He's just someone I know. Not a friend. Alexander is who was with me, Alex. He just went to the car. I should've waited for him.' She glanced over her shoulder with a worried expression.

'You don't have a phone?' Laila asked.

Zuleikha shook her head.

'It's as good as dead.' She took her mobile from her coat pocket and shook it about. 'It seems to have to said "No Network Available" ever since we came to Lincolnshire – it's very annoying actually – and he doesn't have one. Stupid, I suppose.'

'It's easy to underestimate the wildness of this country.'

Zuleikha spun back round. What a peculiar thing to say, she thought. *The wildness of this country.* What did she mean? And anyway, Laila was an unusual name for a white woman.

'Yes, I know. We're not really experienced hillwalkers or anything like that.'

'There are basic precautions, though. Countryside codes.'

Oh fuck off, Zulie felt like saying. What was this, health promotion, rustic-style? They were in Lincolnshire, not the Himalayas for God's sake, and it was the twenty-first century.

'Alex has the map.' She almost added, *and he's carrying a lute and that's better than a sextant,* but thought better of it.

'Well, we can't just wait here,' said Laila.

'No.'

'Further on there's the lake. It'd be easier to wait there, actually, because he'd be able to see us more easily. There's more open space.'

265

'I think that's where I was heading.'

'Oh?'

'Just a feeling.' She wondered why Laila was out here in this same blizzard, and why this area seemed protected from not only the extreme weather conditions pertaining today, but from winter itself. It was as though this part of the forest had its own micro-climate, like the ones which hovered over those outdoor gardens up in the north-west of Scotland and in which you could find all manner of exotic, almost subtropical plants. The Gulf Stream. But this was the wrong side of the country, she thought. It was, wasn't it? Clocktowers, control towers … how was she supposed to know where these places were? It was a wild Lincolnshire goose chase. She laughed out loud and Laila turned to her and smiled, the type of warm full smile with which strangers in the most unexpected places sometimes surprised her, and which she then realised she craved most of the time. Zuleikha found herself smiling back.

He was sure they must've taken different routes. There was no way she could've moved that fast across such uneven country. He wasn't exactly fit, he acknowledged, and he was carrying this case, with its delicate instrument inside. It really should never have been brought out in weather conditions like these: the wood might warp irreparably; the lute's tone might become damaged beyond recognition. I might never be able to play it again, he thought. How could he have been so stupid? Following this mad woman across the Wild East. He knew that he was part of it, that without him she would not have been able to have come even this far, and that it was as much his obsession as it was hers – but you had to hang on to a modicum of rationality; you had to believe that what you were doing was at the very least purposeful.

He seemed to be moving down a grass path surrounded by bushes and low trees. Although nearly all the vegetation was deciduous and therefore without leaves, Alex found it almost impossible to see through to the open land beyond. He supposed that it must consist of vast fields of agribusiness: wheat, barley, all manner of vegetables, and that they would lie bare at this time of year as they were readied for the spring onslaught of tractors and other machinery. He negotiated a broken stile and landed heavily

266

on the other side. Further on there was a small hunting gate of the type one found in the countryside, designed to allow passage to humans, whether mounted or on foot, but to prevent animals from escaping. The winter seemed to be intensifying, and now it was as though he had moved from the semi-deserted scrublands of the aerodrome into a total wilderness. The air was freezing, and its very stillness bit through his clothes, impelling him to quicken his pace in an attempt to generate some body heat. The ground seemed to be rising steadily, and the effort of climbing the slight but prolonged incline brought a sharp pain to the right side of his chest which got worse every time he breathed in. It's okay – it's the right side. It's not my heart, he thought, and he pushed on – but there was no sign of the gradient easing off, and eventually the pain became like daggers, forcing him to stop and get his breath back.

He set down his lute-case against a nearby tree trunk, wiped the dry snow off a broken bit of fence, and tested that the wood would take his weight. As the pain in his chest subsided and his breathing became more measured, Alex thought he made out a sound which did not seem to be coming from the falling snow. There was no wind, so it couldn't be that. However, because he was unable to see out of the tunnel created by the trees and bushes, Alexander was unsure from which direction the sound was coming. It was steady, neither rising nor falling but simply continuing, unbroken like the sound of a long exhalation. He wondered whether it might be a snow-plough, or some massive farm contraption, but it didn't sound mechanical or electrical – and anyway, who would be out doing anything in the fields in this weather? He took out the map and smoothed it down over his thigh. He had marked everything clearly, yet nothing made sense any more. The aerodrome was there, right at the centre of the map, and over to the left was the control tower … but then, as he gazed at the white paper, the coordinates seemed to shift and he was no longer certain whether what he was inspecting was a map of the land, or an anatomical drawing of the inside of a particular skull – a skull which, while bearing aspects common to all human crania, would nevertheless remain without mimic in the whole of history.

'Bloody bizarre!' he said aloud, and then he looked around to check no-one had heard. Stupid bastard, he thought: there's no-one here! There's not been anyone here since ... Yet, in the white purity of winter, his voice seemed almost sacrilegious there on the old bridle-path down which so many dead souls still passed. Alex felt that the branches, the twigs, the broken pieces of fence were all closing in on him, that the grassy path was narrowing down to nothing, and he felt like an intruder. 'Bloody bizarre!' he shouted, as though in challenge to the cold spirits of the place, to the lovers on the shepherd race, to Archie, the mad airman who, it seemed, had possessed Zuleikha's soul. Just as he was coming closer to her, he was losing her. Today he had lost her. *If Susan's ghost had walked along these paths green and silent...*

The noise was louder, closer. He sprang off the fence.

'Shut it! Fuck off!' He quickly folded the map, put it back into the inside pocket of his jacket, picked up the lute case, and walked on toward the narrowing of the path.

It got so narrow that he could barely squeeze his way through, and his shoulders and hair became covered with a cloak of fine snow. The snow here was different from that in Scotland – though nowadays in Glasgow it hardly ever snowed. Up there it was nearly always damp and would quickly melt and soak through your clothes, causing you to freeze, but here in Lincolnshire the snow was dry and could sit on you for ages – and even then might not melt, but just gently evanesce. It was so fine you could blow it off like dust, like the caster sugar you sprinkled over strawberries. But right here there was no room to turn and blow anything off; there was barely enough room for him to carry the lute case through the tunnel of vegetation.

He was hoping that somehow he and Zulie would find their way through the dense forest and would emerge roughly on the same side, though he admitted to himself that he'd had absolutely no idea of how big, nor of how old, the forest was. Perhaps he was approaching the Lincolnshire Cliff, the great limestone escarpment that divided the county north-to-south, and beyond which lay the Wolds. Or perhaps he was already in the Wolds. Perhaps he was walking along some ancient Roman road, a tributary of Ermine Street which had run dead straight from London through Lincoln to York. The noise was getting louder, and Alex began to imagine that it was the sound of a small plane coming in to land on one of the disused runways, or else to bomb some control tower. Perhaps, as in Argyllshire, the MOD still used these areas for target practice. Perhaps the scent which he could not yet identify was that of human skin rising off the concrete of deserted J-hangars, or maybe it was the smell of brass from the French horns of the lunchtime orchestras. The grip of old rubber on rough Tarmacadam, the sound of a bicycle wheeling around a corner, the swish of long-haired hog-bristle on vellum, the calm visage of a lord of the manor as he posed before the painter who had come all the way from London to steady the moment in oil, the feel of bone beneath his fingertips, the same mind thrice over: Alexander Wolfe, Lord Jack Ruthyn and Archibald Idris McPherson, Man of the Sky.

He found himself slipping into a very old habit which he had thought long-dead, and he began to whistle. Usually, when men whistled – and after all, he thought, it was always men who whistled – it was some nondescript tune, some jolly, early-to-mid-twentieth-century ditty from the time when jazz had not yet reinvented itself. Yes, that was it: the daft songs which working-class guys of a certain age put out through pursed lips were drawn from the vaults of New Orleans jazz. They whistled nowadays not just for the joy of it; no longer was there any sense of cloth-capped, socialist-realist stamp-head orgasm marching to and from the factory, whistling:

We make things with our hands
And we enjoy the land, mud, earth 'n' sand!
And weren't 'er buttocks fat, hey-ho!
But in the dark you don't notice that, no, no!
With a hey-ho diddly-dee, a hey-ho diddly-dum,
From head to prick, comrade, the truth, here, see
Gleaming through the old, old tree, is that
One night we'll all be free!

They whistled now rather to demonstrate to the reconstructed, terrified women of the newly ascendant ruling classes that they, working-class males, were no longer a threat, on either a personal (virginity) or a class (redistribution) basis. Whistling had become the proletarian bugle-call of surrender. Perhaps some sociologist had undertaken a study of this phenomenon, thought Alex, as he whistled his way through another thicket. But really he knew that now he was whistling to fend off the madness of the concept that through music he was able to slip in and out of other people's ruminations, and that perhaps they were able to do the same with his – and also because he had an irrational fear of looking up, lest in the moment before explosive death he should see only the black-painted undercarriage of an old German bomber. But mostly he whistled in order to blank out the sound of water coming from somewhere ahead. A flutter of wings close by almost sent him flying into a gorse bush.

'Okay, here we are,' said Laila as though she was a tourist guide, though no tourists ever came here. They were back in mid-winter again and had emerged into a large clearing, at the centre of which lay a pond. The storm had snowed itself out, and both the land and forest had acquired a postcard beauty. It was apparent that they were still deep in the forest; trees ringed the clearing on all sides and Zuleikha could see no light through them, but at least now there was some air, some proper – albeit fading – daylight, and some room in which to move. The water had frozen solid, and the ice was covered with a blanket of snow. In the middle of the pond was a hump of land on which grew a number of tousled bushes and deformed blackened trees which looked as though they had been struck by lightning some decades earlier. As in a child's drawing, new twigs had sprouted like mutants from the most improbable of places. Laila smiled broadly, as though she had just guided Zuleikha to some auspicious monument.

And now, as this woman gazed and smiled at her, Zuleikha began to wonder whether she and Alex might be the victims of a vast practical joke. Maybe they were being monitored, filmed through a certain type of tree-trunk, or else via a spy satellite that from two hundred miles up could look through stone and soul and identify the internal structure of a grasshopper, or perhaps even that of a wooden box. Laila was a funny name for an Englishwoman, unless perhaps her father had been a romantic colonialist who'd been posted to some dusty territory east of Suez. Yes, thought Zuleikha, she would be about the right age for that.

270

Asunsi, though. That wasn't very English, either. Her paternal grandmother's maiden name, she'd said. Peasanthood, patriarchy. Zulie spread her hands, palms-up, before her.

'What's here?' she asked.

'Well, from here, it's a fairly straight course to the far side of the forest. The side from which I entered – that's where I live, right on the forest edge.'

'But our car is back there, in the opposite direction. And Alex won't know where to come. I mean, where is he?' Zuleikha felt herself beginning to become upset and she didn't want that, so she began to walk towards the pond. 'D'you think it's safe to walk on?' she asked. 'The ice?'

'I think so,' Laila replied, though she didn't sound at all certain. Zuleikha went right to the pond's edge and turned around. Laila's figure seemed to have shrunk inordinately and suddenly she was far away. 'Don't worry, Zulie, he'll probably come here,' she shouted. 'And if not, the forest's not that big. He'll get out, one way or another. I mean, it's not the Amazonian jungle! This is Lincolnshire, duck!' She laughed.

Laila's voice seemed to have reverted from light Generic Northern to a deep Lindsey drawl: an accent that was broadly akin to that of the East Riding of Yorkshire or, to be more accurate, to that of Hull, but in which the vowels were prolonged rather than flattened. Not that I'm becoming an expert, Zuleikha thought as she stepped onto the ice, with just the slightest niggle at the back of her mind that Laila had not followed her onto the pond. She'd called her 'Zulie' without being prompted. How the hell did she, a woman of her age living out here in the middle of England, know that 'Zulie' was a diminutive of 'Zuleikha'?

'Is it deep?' she called out, but Laila didn't reply. Perhaps she really doesn't know, Zuleikha thought, after all, she's lived in London for the past ... how long did she say it was? What did she say she did? Did she say what she did? The temperature was lower out here on the open ice and Zuleikha felt the cold bite like a wolf into her cheeks. She brushed away the snow with the tip of her boot and, sitting on her haunches, swung back and forth. She needed some wine, mulled properly with all the correct spices and herbs and then ladled with a big wooden spoon into sycamore tankards. Why sycamore? she thought, as she gazed down through the clear window which she had made in the ice.

'Alex, with your wondrous lute and your beautiful ice-white body, where the fuck are you?' she said quietly into the glass.

Chapter Seventeen

He stood before the waterfall, watching it cascade into the pool below, fascinated by its crazy, swirling movement and by the way it seemed to create its own depth. The river upstream must be partly frozen, he thought, and this waterfall was pouring forth like a deluge from the edge of the last ice sheets. Had this been the line where they had ended, all those years ago, or had that been further South? So many maps, shifting over one another like – well, like the sand that served as earth in these parts. What once had been seabed became permafrost that was buried beneath six miles of ice, and this in turn rose up again and became forest, aerodrome, the inside of a skull, the dark space enclosed by a box, the sweep of a musical score. The spray from the waterfall did not quite reach him and Alex dared not venture any closer lest water get into the lute-case, but then he noticed a narrow winding path up by the side of the falls. The path was shielded from the cascading water by a row of enormous grey boulders.

He had to bend almost double in order to enter the cave. He lifted the lute-case in first; held it out in front of him as though it was a rifle or a spear. It occurred to him that it was fortunate that the lute had grown lighter in weight (though its case had not). The cave did not smell musty as he had expected, yet there had been a definite change in the atmosphere the moment he had crossed the threshold. It wasn't completely dark, but simply murky, so that right from the moment he entered and despite his eyes having to accommodate from the brightness of a snowy winter's sky, Alex was able to make out vague shapes, protuberances, and towards the rear, a door.

The floor of the cave was quite smooth and was strewn mainly with old dry leaves, but with remarkably little detritus. He had expected to find used syringes, condoms, fag-ends, beer cans, dead cats, snakeskins and the stink of piss, shit and semen, but instead there was this scent … what was it? It was almost like incense, but not quite as pungent. Carefully he went towards the door, bent down and gripped the iron handle. The first couple of times he attempted to turn it, it did not budge, so he put down the lute-case and, using both hands, he formed a kind of double-fist around it, pulled his entire body weight to one side, and jerked hard. With a great wrenching sound the thing came off, and the momentum threw him diagonally backwards so that he landed in a corner of the cave, clutching the metal handle and feeling rather stupid. Fortunately, because leaves had drifted into the cave, he was unhurt. He threw down the handle and got up. Went over to the door. He bent down to pick up his lute and as he did so, his right shoulder brushed against the door. He turned to leave the cave, but stopped when he noticed that the pile of vegetation which had cushioned his fall was beginning to disperse, the dry leaves fluttering like wizened butterflies around his boots. His back felt colder here than it had outside. Slowly, Alexander turned around. The door lay open, and behind it was a dark passageway down which he could see for only a few metres. The scent was much stronger now, and he felt tempted to close his eyes and let the breeze blow over his face. Instead, he walked through the doorway and entered the passage.

He half-expected the door to creak shut like in a corny horror-flick, but it didn't, and as he progressed downwards – there was a definite incline – the patch of daylight behind him became steadily smaller but more focused, until eventually it was merely a point of light like that of a distant nova. The passageway was dry and was about six feet wide and perhaps seven high; it had been cut straight through the limestone common to this area, so that the walls were a perfect white. Alex wondered if this had been the source of the scent, but no: limestone had a particular smell and taste and this wasn't it. The light reflected from one wall to another, creating a dull luminescence within the passage. Not enough to read by. Anyway, he thought, there's no point consulting the chart. I've lost Zulie somewhere and I have no idea where I am. The whole thing has got beyond the map. Or perhaps we're just rambling idiots. Again he had a fleeting terror of the door closing, of the light vanishing, and of him being trapped underground forever. But then, he thought, I can simply re-trace my steps. The walls are smooth and clean: I can do it by touch if I need to. The moment of terror was succeeded by a giddying recklessness. Or perhaps it was the scent. The temperature rose slowly as he descended. *Beware the*

House of the Dead! came into his mind, the catacombs of Paris and Susan's face, her smile, the taste of the cave of her mouth in the night. He felt a smile break out across his face. What with the station in Glasgow, the church vault in Argyllshire, and now this passageway cut into the Lincolnshire Cliff, it seemed that the subterranean was becoming his natural habitat. *We are the moles.* Well, he thought, we shall all spend eternity beneath the earth, so I might as well get used to it. No-one knew when death would come to turn the rusted handle of our lives and take us down. Such platitudes kept us safe, he thought, yet like all totems, they are far from harmless.

After perhaps ten minutes (but since he couldn't make out the hands of his watch, he couldn't be certain that it had not been longer) the ground began to flatten out and the walls to sink away into darkness on either side. His footsteps began to echo on the limestone, and Alex realised that he was in a chamber of some sort. He had half-expected to find water at the bottom, but like the cave and the passageway, this place too was completely dry. However, it seemed lit from above, and when he craned his neck he could just about make out, between the dry dead limestone stalactites, shafts which had been cut into the roof. He remembered that at the aerodrome it had been early afternoon, and he wondered whether perhaps the daylight ought to have faded by now, but time seemed to have acquired a somewhat elastic quality and anyway, Alex had found that it was not profitable to dwell on such things.

The scent down here was so strong that he began to feel positively yet lightly stoned, as though he'd just had a first joint. He put down his lute-case and sat cross-legged on the floor, his back against the wall. He noticed now that the floor had been cut virtually flat, though the markings of the stalagmite bases were clearly visible. Once, this place must have been dripping with the heavy liquid of mineral deposits. So what had changed? he wondered. It was obviously a natural cave which at some point in history had been enlarged by men to suit some purpose, but what purpose might that have been? The smell really was unbearable: toxic, almost. It made him want to swoon, to focus on the far distance. Time and space were rubber bands and his mind was clear, cool water running over flat stones. Millions of years, drip-by-drip, water-into-rock, here, in this place at the bottom of the world. He let his eyes close, then forced them to open. He had to get somewhere, he had a very important meeting, or at least there was something of great importance which he had to do. He chuckled to himself, *I'm the white rabbit,* but it couldn't have been just to himself because then he heard the echo of his voice, falling off into the darkness.

The light was fading, evening was coming on fast, and shifting across the clean white walls of the chamber, Alexander began to make out the shapes of dancers holding tambourines: figures that were half-women, half-foxes, and then other figures with human bodies but the heads of horses. He heard the cracking sound of seven foot-long gad-whips on ox skin, the fluttering of the wings of a flock of white sparrows as they rose from an old barn, and from the centre of the troupe there emerged a figure shaped like a bull. He could see that while its head was horned, the lower body was that of a woman with blue skin. The bull-woman came off the wall and strode to the middle of the chamber, and sat on a chair made from old gibbet-wood.

'I am Old Mother Nightshade,' she said, without opening her mouth. '*On the night of the fourteenth moon, I take the form of a wolf. On the night of the new moon, I enter the corpse of Holy Hannah and I dance the round dance to the beat of a red tambourine. In the Year of Our lord, 999, on the Eve of the Feast of Saint Thomas, in this white cave, did I lie with a tinker and conceived a son and he was called Jesus Wiseman.*'

And Alex found that he had taken out his lute and that, in spite of the extreme weather conditions through which it had passed on that day, the twenty-first of December, which somehow he knew was the Feast Day of St Thomas the Twin, it was perfectly tuned. Okay, he thought, eight courses. The bass strings which he had known so well were disappearing off the end, a future vanishing into silence. He began to play using a quill plectrum, and as he played, still without opening her bull-mouth, the woman began to sing. Alexander's fingers stretched across the body of the lute as though they were extending over the corpus of a woman, of Zuleikha, perhaps, or else over this wondrous body before him, the glistening, beauteous, bull-headed Hannah.

As the song progressed, it seemed to switch back over a river of sound to something far older, something which Alexander recognised as the vieil ton, the old tuning, and his lute seemed to follow suit, becoming set to the mean. Or perhaps it was he who had tuned it, his fingers, palms, wrists, seeming to have a mind and rhythm all of their own.

'I wish my baby was born
And smiling on his daddy's knee
And I poor girl was in my grave
With the long green grass a-growing all over me'

Her song echoed off the chalk, creating a resonance that filled his head, and he knew that he had been here before, that inside his skull was the skull of Lord Jack, of Mister William Michael Jacobus de Ruthyn the imperial adventurer, and that inside Lord Jack's skull was the skull of the great monk, the master of Monks, whose face once had been captured in an image that had been painted on the black shank skin of a bull. And her song was the song of the Dead Cart, the dark carriage drawn by blind creeping horses that trundled the old salt roads of Lindsey every night of the full moon, carrying the naked bodies of those destined to die in the coming month. She had lain with King John the night before he had perished, and he and his treasure had been in her song, the gold of England, turned to lead and brass that had been carried on the hundred-foot washes into the nets of dreaming fishermen and brought by a Fen Gang here, to this cave, where the alchemists of the ages had striven to turn it back into gold and where the great Doctor Mirabilis had succeeded only in forging a large brass head which had foretold the future and changed the past.

And on his return from the land of high peaks, Lord Jack had discovered the means by which a dead body could be revived and made to tell of the secrets it had witnessed. He had exhumed the body of the Lincolnshire Forger and had made his throat open and sing of his last hidden book, which in his turn he had copied directly from the dead mouth of the Master of the Monastery of Black Monks. The monastery had been built directly over this spot, on the island in the lake, and had contained the notation for eight-course lute composed by Rujari d'Alì on the very night he had murdered his wife and her lover. He had thrown them through the plaintive, almost polytonal strains of il liuto, into the rigor of a fixed and macabre embrace before the castle walls on the marital bed. And Alexander was disgusted by this man who, slowly, thrust by thrust, had stabbed his wife to death and slit open her belly as though she were a fish or a hog, and then left the raw flesh of her sex clearly visible out in the open air to be consumed by the public and by whatever verminous creatures happened by. When Susan had hit the water, her body had exploded. Yet he could not stop playing; his fingers moved irrespective of his thoughts and emotions. He was a mechanical toy, strumming into eternity.

'It was I,' went on the bull-headed woman, 'who lay with Rujari d'Alì on that night of stars and white Marsala wine, the night of God on which Rujari murdered his lady, and in our great conjoining, there came to him a musical piece such as had never been heard before, a piece that would turn back time and revert all things to their source. And after our love-making had ended he went for a stroll, parchment, ink-pot and quill in hand. And the ink-pot was filled with his lady's blood. Yahya of Dimashq, Mikhail of the Tweed, Roger of Alì, I was with them all. They said that I was mad. That I was their slave, their minstrel, their 'aref. And I too played the wood, yet in reality it was I who was their Master. I prayed and swooned by the banks of an-nil, Ganga, Sindh, Oxus. In the dust mohallas of Pataliputra I was stoned by children because I claimed to have seen God standing by a certain pillar in the Tavern of the Black House. In the secret deserts of Abyssinia I painted my eyelids with the henna of Divine love before setting off on a journey through the Lands of Wodewose, Rus and Varangian in search of Maud of the White Cloak, and at the summit of the high mountains I was born of a goat who was born of a prophet who was born of a tree. I am less, and more, than reality. And now you are my slave and I am your Master. My name is Tohfah, I am the Gift. Be grateful for me.'

'And what is the aim of all this?' Alexander asked the bull-headed woman. 'Why am I journeying with Zuleikha, why am I playing music this way, what is in the box, what is the box? Why do you have the head of a bull?'

'*Truth resides in eighteen worlds,*' she replied. '*In this mehrab you may catch a glimpse of the Real, but only for a fleeting moment, for if you were to behold its full magnificence, you would not live to tell the tale. Like Bibiak of Marv, you would leave your body and never return. And so does one night become a thousand years. Live in the night, not as a journey but as truth, for in this life truth is the only journey possible.*'

Then Alexander saw that the woman wore a blue robe made of hair, and that beneath the robe she was so thin that her body quivered like a reed even though there was no breeze. In her right hand was a pitcher of white honey. She lifted her left hand, palm inclined upwards, and said – or rather, half-sang, for now it seemed as though her voice was emanating from the substance of a metalliferous cylinder –

'*Snowfall is the fluttering of the pages of the Book.*
At the fall of the night, letters come down from heaven.
I fasted for forty years and became a skeleton.'

He saw that on the fourth finger of her left hand was a golden ring. And then he saw that it was his wedding-ring, the band of gold which he'd thought would never leave his finger. He glanced down at his hand and saw only an indentation in the skin. The ring opened and Alexander continued to play without even having to look at the strings of his lute. Its structure indeed had changed, so that while the pegbox remained at an angle to the neck, its body now was vaulted, its soundboard entirely flat, and the strings themselves were no longer twisted catlines but simple tautened sections of gut. He knew that he ought to have been playing this kind of music on this type of lute using a plectrum and not with his bare fingers, because the strings now were slacker than before and needed to be hit rather than simply plucked. But he had dropped the plectrum, and his fingers coaxed from the lute stanzas most beauteous, qasa'ed, muwash'shahat, nubat, kharjat and sonnets and in the pitch of many voices, the bull-headed woman sang the verses of her song simultaneously in twelve languages and Alex found that there, in the white cave, he was able to understand every one of them as though each was his mother tongue. And suddenly he saw strands of light stretching down from the shafts in the roof and each strand was connected to the woman. And her eyes turned back in their sockets and wept blood.

'I cried for forty years, until blindness overcame me.
Then I began to dance.'

And she embarked on a rotunda and her measured steps at first paced out the journey of Christ into the Underworld, but later her movements grew faster and more frenzied as she swayed in caricature parodies of the clergy, and she began to thrust her hips outwards in Alexander's direction, and then to tear off her robe. He saw that underneath the hair-robe, she was completely naked. Her skin held a faint blueish tinge, and as she spun he saw that her breasts were large and muscular. She was shaking her head wildly as though afflicted by some delirium, yet her features suggested that she was closer to ecstasy than confusion. The bull-mouth was fixed in a grin so severe, it seemed as though it might rip apart her face, and the huge black eyes burned and stared as though they would sear through rock. Through the feet of countless peasants her dance had spanned mountains, steppes and sacred rivers, while in the spring tide of the ocean, always it incarnated itself in the same round formation, with always the same monstrous climax and always, in every movement, there hovered the shadow of death. The chorea now had become asymmetric, and she raised herself up over Alexander.

A blue light began to emanate from the figure. At first it was soothing, but then it grew bright and painful and Alexander had to struggle to keep his eyes open. He was playing faster than he had ever played, yet he felt nothing: there was no discomfort in his fingers which by now should have been bleeding.

She knelt down, opened his trousers and took hold of his penis, which already had swollen to the half-erect position. Straddling him, she peeled back his foreskin, placed his cock in the centre of her wet vulva, and began to move up and down on him, her upper body and head continuing to sway in the dance. She reeked of the earth, of that stench which earlier had intoxicated him and which now in its very repulsiveness stimulated his desire. Her fingernails were like claws and, lifting up his coat, jumper, shirt, she drew them along the delicate skin of his flanks, causing him almost to convulse with pleasure. She was mechanical, instinctual; there was hint of neither emotion nor thought in her being. Her eyes were thick and glassy and held no depth, but simply reflected his face. She was working him for seed, that was all. He was a surahi, a receptacle full of fig juice, and she was a magician, an elemental, and was drawing out the liquid from the jar of his mortal body. As though energised by the woman, his fingers were unstoppable; they moved across the lute's belly, delivering sounds for her pleasure. A voice, old as the hills, a beldering woman's voice.

'As I went out one morning on the fourteenth of July
I met a maid and I asked her age and she gave me this reply:
"I have a little meadow I've kept for you in store
And it's only due I should tell you true, it never was mowed
    before."

'She said: "Me handsome young man, if a mower that you be
I give you good employment, so come along with me."
Well it was me good employment to wander up and down
With me tearing scythe all to contrive to mow her meadow
down.

'Now me courage being undaunted, I stepped out on the ground
And with me tearing scythe I then did strive to mow her meadow
    down
I mowed from nine till dinnertime, it was far beyond my skill
I was obliged to yield and to quit the field and the grass was
    growing still.

'Now the mower she kissed and did pretest, this fair maid bein'
    so young
Her little eyes they glittered like to the rising sun
She said: "I'll strive to sharpen your scythe, so set it in me hand
And then perhaps you will return again to mow me meadow
    land."'

At the moment of climax he closed his eyes, and the bull-woman let out a bellow so loud he felt his eardrums would burst. Behind his closed lids, Alexander saw the woman remove the bull's head from her body. It was as though she was inside the sound – both of the song that was coming from her own throat, and the music which he was playing on the lute. It was as though through all the years he had been working the instrument, through all the intense difficulties of studying its mechanics, of learning to read tablature and musical notation, through the terrible grief and unrequitedness of life and now through his love for Zuleikha – yes, it was love, it felt like love and not simply infatuation or displacement – the music carried with it the awful feeling of incipient tragedy which lay at the centre of all the closest human relationships. It was as though all that time there had been some force that lay in the music and in the very act of making music, a force which fundamentally was erotic in nature. It was as though whenever he played a particular piece, all those who had gone before and who had acted in some way intentionally – the composers, the luthiers, the lutenists, and those who had inspired all of these, the animals from whose intestines the strings had been made, the lovers of the composers, those who had murdered them, or been murdered by them, the very spirits of the dead buried deep within the wood – all of these were moving in the bones of his fingers, in his ears, in the substance of his brain. It was only at those moments that Alexander felt that he would be able to comprehend anything at all. It was as though more of the universe was held taut in a single string of his lute than in all the rest of his life put together. Just before the light blinded him, in the black space where the woman's head had been, he thought he made out Susan's face.

Chapter Eighteen

Zuleikha climbed to the top of the mound that lay at the centre of the pond. This was not as easy as at first it had appeared, since toward the upper sections of the hillock the ground was slippery with ice and was covered in thorn bushes, the branches of which she had to part carefully as she climbed. From time to time her foot would catch on a piece of angular brownish-black stone that told her that at some point in the past there had been a house on this site. She was aware of Laila, not moving from her position on the bank, watching. She must think I'm mad! Zuleikha thought.

Eventually, she got to the top. From where she stood, from the distribution of the pattern of the vegetation, she could see quite clearly what had been the plan of a fairly large house. There was also the hint of what might have been a bridge, or at least a causeway that may have linked the island with the main body of the forest. She closed her eyes and sighed. This was how she'd seen it in Archie's house, when she'd … touched his skin. That was all that had happened. The rest was ridiculous imagination, some kind of weird Freudian thing to do with grandfathers, or maybe a Jungian thing to do with wizards. Anyway, it had been a lie. Archie had been here in this house, he had slept as the bombs had torn down heaven. How had Laila known where to bring her? It seemed too much of a coincidence.

She opened her eyes. Laila was still there, smiling at her. She'd half-expected the woman to have vanished into the darkening air. And it was getting dark. They would have to leave the forest soon, and what about Alex? What if he'd twisted his ankle, hurt himself? What if he were stranded somewhere, with no phone, no means of calling for help? Perhaps they should re-trace their steps, go right back to the aerodrome. But darkness would descend long before they got there and then they too would be stuck. Perhaps they should call the police, or the fire brigade, or whatever one did in situations like these. The woman had a funny name, so what? People had all kinds of names. Like Zuleikha Chashm Framareza MacBeth. Perhaps Laila had Muslim or Jewish blood. Perhaps things were not quite as they seemed, perhaps Laila had been drawn somehow to her, perhaps she needed something from Zuleikha even if she didn't realise it. She was startled out of her reverie by Laila shouting at her.

'You'd better come back now! Your friend…!'

'Okay, I'm coming down!' she shouted back. Yes, Zuleikha thought, I have been remiss and irresponsible in the extreme, haven't I? I have not minded the gap. But her own passivity now began to irritate her. She had always been the life-saver – or, at least, the life-placator. But maybe this was her true self. Looking at it objectively, this whole journey seemed like a collective psychosis. We should all go onto psychotropic medication, she thought. Hearing voices, music, telepathic messages from the dead and the dying … this was the stuff of madness. Or else hilarity.

She began to descend the hillock. She skated the last few feet to the bank. It made her feel like a girl again; that one flourish held so many memories – regular visits with her mother and father to the local park in midwinter – though even in those days, in the west of Britain, ponds had very rarely frozen over. She remembered always being disappointed that winter had never lived up to its reputation, that it had never been like on the biscuit tins or in the films and story books. With all that fluffy snow and those enormous log fires, winter in Victorian times had seemed so much more fun! Apart, that was, from the kids dying of consumption, phthisis, rheumatic fever, scarlet fever, measles and malnutrition, and their mothers perishing en masse from all these diseases and from the added joys of puerperal fever, malposition or blood loss during childbirth. Those things never appeared in films or on chocolate boxes. No, it was always men who resembled Prince Albert, an entire regiment of Saxe-Coburg and Gotha clones with ladies done up in furs and mufflers who climbed like icicles oh-so-delicately into sleighs. And everyone clearly must have had baths daily since they all looked so clean and shiny, and there could not possibly have been outside toilets or loony bins for women who had fallen pregnant out of wedlock. Tragically, by the time Zuleikha had met such women, they had become indistinguishable from the legions of the genuinely mentally ill with whom they had been forced to co-habit for the preceding sixty years. The baby would have been have been removed at birth and sent out for adoption.

Purgatorial treatments would have been administered on the precise instructions of zealous whitecoats who really truly believed that they were advancing the cause of science, that through such entirely reasonable actions, indubitably and indomitably, they were pulling humanity by its stays, bootstraps and girdles up to the next evolutionary stage. Those women too had lost their children.

Laila was staring at her, more with concern than curiosity.

'Where were you? I was talking to you and you seemed miles away.' Zuleikha was about four feet away from the other woman, and they had left the bank and now were standing almost at the edge of the clearing. And Zuleikha had remembered none of it.

'I was thinking. Sorry.'

'You're worried about your friend.'

'I guess.'

'I'm sure he'll be all right. Probably gone back to your car by now. Actually, it's more likely that he'll be worried about you.'

This had never occurred to Zuleikha, but now she thought yes, for certain: Alex will be fretting. He loves me, doesn't he, and so he will be terrified that he might lose another woman to the vagaries of … what? Fate? Evolution? God? Did she and Susan both have weaknesses in their characters which had led one (she supposed) to commit suicide and the other to embark on some mad escapist journey? You couldn't trust God with a woman. He was a right jealous bastard, and after even a glimpse of his golden shower, likely as not the woman would end up wrapped in a black shroud or else turned into a pillar of salt. Who was that woman who had opened the box, unleashing all the demons of the cosmos? Pandora. Right. All-gifted. According to the legend, only Hope had been trapped inside. Poor old Dora. Was that what Zuleikha had been looking for? Hope? Pandora, Alexander, it all went back to the Greeks, the Yunanis, the Yona, may God fuck 'em well and truly right down the centuries. Well, the men, anyway.

'Can we get to a phone?' she asked Laila.

'You can use mine. It's only about a mile from here. My house, I mean.'

Thanks, that's very kind of you.' Why on earth hadn't Laila said that before? Why hadn't she taken Zuleikha there, instead of to this ruined hill in the middle of a lake?

As though Laila had read her thoughts, she said,

'It was on the way, Lord Jack's Summer House. Or at least, what remains of it. I thought that your friend might well stumble upon it.'

Zuleikha stopped in her tracks.

'Lord Jack?'

'Yes... What? You've heard of him?'

'Must've read it somewhere,' Zuleikha mumbled as they trudged through the forest.

'He belonged to a famous family who once owned most of the land around here. They used to hunt wild boar in the forest. That was a very long time ago. Jack's ancestors had built the summer-house, partly as a hunting-lodge and partly as a retreat, but like the mansion it fell into disuse, though I think it may have been inhabited until sometime in the 1960s.' She smiled. 'I've been here a long time.'

'I thought you said you lived in London.'

'I did, but I bought the place up here well before I retired. I used to escape sometimes at weekends and during breaks.'

'What happened to him?'

'Who? Lord Jack?' Laila shrugged. 'Don't know. He died, obviously. I think he was the last of the line. I live in one of the cottages on the old estate. It became the vicarage. The manor house itself was torn down – before it fell down – years ago, way before the War. He was an explorer, a traveller, an adventurer. A Romantic! Went east, as did they all.'

'Where is he buried?'

'In St Cuthman's churchyard, in a large stone tomb.'

'And ... his skull?'

Laila half-turned to look at her.

'With the rest of him, I suppose. What a strange question! Why on earth do you ask that?'

Zuleikha did not answer. They had left the forest and now were walking over rough fields which quite evidently had been left fallow for at least a couple of seasons. Every so often they would have to leap across a dyke. These were the conduits which, many years ago, had been dug by those intrepid and much-loathed Dutchies as a means of draining this bog-ridden county. Zuleikha saw no more fish, and it was approaching twilight, though the moon – a little beyond full – was bright enough that she could even make out colours. Several centuries of urbanisation have alienated us from our own countryside, she thought. And yet, not so very long ago, we all were either peasants or else lords of the land. Mother Earth. Pandora, formed from mud, reluctantly opens her celestial box. Fuck Freud, she thought. Or on second thoughts, don't.

The cottage had looked deceptively small from the outside. Or maybe that's just the way with these conversions. Laila told her that it was three hundred and twenty-six years old and that part of it originally had been the stables. Zuleikha thought that it would be easy to lose one's way in the narrow corridors and half-hidden doors that were placed across three floors. She had to step down to enter, and the beamed ceilings were low – though not as low as in a modern semi. Zuleikha phoned the police and told them about Alexander: gave a description. But she felt guilty that she did not feel more panicky. She should have been panicking: the situation, after all, was potentially extremely serious. To be lost in the open countryside in the middle of winter, even in Lincolnshire in the twenty-first century, was not a laughing matter. He's bound to come across some farmhouse or other, she thought; it's not Caithness, for goodness sake. But then, would anyone open the door to a stranger in the middle of the night? Britain had become a rather paranoid place. And all those nice country cottages were guarded by ferocious dogs and pathologically angry farmers wielding four-wheel drives and shotguns. It was no place to be wandering around with no fixed abode. In that sense, it was probably a lot more dangerous than Caithness would've been. There, at least, if you were lost, you were lost. No robber would venture up that far. SIS assassins, maybe.

'In this big friendly county, which is not as flat as folk make out,' Laila said as they cradled scalding mugs of tea, 'in some of the craft shops they sell golliwogs – they're back in fashion, you know. They're sold quite casually, as though there were nothing in the least offensive about them. I won't buy from those shops. Deepest England. There is much that I love about it. But there is also much that is extremely disturbing.'

287

Yes, Zuleikha thought; here it was the humans and their best friends from whom you had the most to fear. You would be assumed to be criminal until proved otherwise.

'I'll get a taxi back to Lincoln,' Zuleikha suggested. 'I can pick up the car in the morning.'

There was a slight pause as Laila plumped up cushions on the enormous, wooden settee.

'You're welcome to stay the night. There's a spare room – several, actually – it's no trouble.' She looked up.

Zuleikha wondered why she was being so helpful, but then she reprimanded herself for her cynicism. In spite of the big business paranoia, among ordinary people there was still a certain level of trust – of collectivity, even, though perhaps that was going a little far.

'Are you sure?'

Laila nodded.

'Definitely. Anyway, the snow's pretty thick out there. I don't fancy your chances of a taxi even agreeing to come here at this time of night. It would be suicidal. You'd need a four-wheel drive, at least.' Hands on hips, Laila sighed. 'You must be famished.'

'No – it's okay. Please don't…'

'No, no.' Laila leapt up with the alacrity and vigour of a woman half her age. 'There's food; it just needs warming up!'

The house was filled with books, scrolls, charts, all kinds of bric-a-brac, and the apparent chaos of it all convinced Zuleikha that Laila was either single or else was engaged only in some kind of long-distance relationship with someone – the man, perhaps, whom she'd spotted in several faded colour photographs tastefully positioned on the walls and mantelpiece. Or maybe that was a brother. And there was a younger Laila, a Laila with long fox-coloured hair and impossibly white skin. She was about to ask, then thought better of it. English people generally didn't like you prying into their affairs so early on. Laila's shoulder-length hair now was silvery and her face, warmed up, was ruddy rather than pale – and yet there was the same cool luminescence from her eyes, the way some blue-eyed people were: when you looked at them it felt as though you were gazing through tiny portholes into a vast sea. It could be quite distracting, so that you found yourself constantly losing the thread of what they were saying, and you had to keep pulling your gaze away in order to concentrate. She was broad-hipped and big-breasted, but not really obese ... again Zuleikha stopped herself even as she made this quick mental assessment, and burrowed deeper into the comfortable armchair, let her head fall back, and closed her eyes. The room was warm, though not uncomfortably so. She was surprised the woman didn't have a big stupid (male) dog and a log fire. But why should she?

Zuleikha was relieved in some ways to be out of it, at least for a while. Medicine, that was. Why had she become a sawbones? Who knows? There were a thousand rationalisations, but really, when all was said and done, it hadn't been 'to help people'. It had been much more complex than that, and the complexity itself was depressing for her to contemplate. Whether or not you liked it, in so many ways it came to shape the way you thought. You are what you do. Doctor sahiba. So what did that make her, chasing around after an old box? So thinking, she fell asleep.

She was in a wood – not unlike the one she had just left, except that here it was properly spring and the sun was shining. She was standing in a large clearing formed by towering trees of a species she'd never seen before, and over to her left was the pond, much larger than it had been in reality. In her dream it was more like a small lake, and through the dense foliage she was unable to make out the far corners. Behind her stood the house, now unbroken – though possibly deserted, since the green wooden shutters were all closed and the door bolted. There was music coming from somewhere – lute music – yet the sound seemed slightly distorted, as though it was issuing from under water or from the end of a long tunnel. Nonetheless, the music seemed harder and cleaner than before.

As she pulled away some light branches, down by the lake's edge, just beyond the end of the clearing, Zuleikha saw a man sitting bolt-upright on a log, one leg crossed over the other. He was dressed in black trousers and shirt and was playing a lute, and though he stared in her direction he did not seem to notice her presence. She had the feeling that she had seen him somewhere before, but she was unable to place the memory. His fingers moved quickly across the strings of the lute, which was similar in appearance to the one Alexander had had at the start of his relationship with her. A baroque sixteen-course lute with double pegboard, but played without a plectrum.

She was able to feel every string as though the sinews were her own, as though they had been cut from her own gut. How strange! she thought. Perhaps, I am a goat or a sheep. She glanced down at herself, but she was still a woman. Even though it was spring, she was still wearing the clothes she'd had on at the aerodrome, yet there seemed no incongruity. And even though her formal knowledge of musical notation and tablature was at best nominal, Zuleikha found that in the dream, as far as music was concerned, she was almost omniscient. And when the man began to sing it was in the alto range, the register a little too high, and yet this too seemed entirely in keeping with the internal logic of the situation. In fact, in the dream she was able to identify the limitless number of chordal coincidences, the manifest reality that the same chord, played over and over, cannot be replicated by any other chord, but that one can still add or subtract notes from above and below and retain the same sound while forfeiting the singularity. This meant that, down through time, the sounds produced by a single lute would reverberate into those of all other lutes, identical yet slightly altered in some manner, either by the conglomerate of possible notes or by mechanical and anatomical factors such as the quality of the instrumentalist's fingers, how many men she had had over the course of her life, the degree of melodrama suffered – or else inflicted – by the composer, the corn on which the sheep had been fed whose guts had been used to make the strings, the tree from which wood had been hewn in order to construct the body of the instrument … and so on. In other words, every time, everything in the universe goes into a single musical performance.

And as she watched, or to be more precise – and music is nothing if not absolutely precise – as she listened, the man's face began to shift, like a police photofit. His features began to alter, subtly at first but then more grossly, so that while at the start it had been a younger, perhaps idealised or romanticised version of Alexander Wolfe who had been playing the lute, now (s)he seemed more like Lady Margaret Wemyss. And then the features became almost Italianate, the complexion a deep shade of cream rather than paper-white, and they now seemed to encapsulate a certain chastity – belonging, as they did, to Alessia Aldobrandini: handmaiden, if not bridesmaid, of Christ and keeper of the figs of the convent garden. From this virtual nun to the rake, adulterer, murderer and typical male genius Rujari d'Alì, and then back further still to the great king of the magical isle, Manfred the German, the Sultan of Lucera, who bathed in Arab waters and who carried the good seed of civilisation into the barren belly of Europe. But the truly freaky, the entheogenic, the dreamadelic thing was that behind and within all of these visages brought on by the Lincolnshire winter were the faces of herself and her ancestors. On one side there was the poet-emperor of Delhi who wrote only sad songs, and there were the Sadozai Kings of Afghanistan, and then – who knows – perhaps she went back to Milinda of the Greeks, Menander of the Yavanas, King of Patna, Lord of the Biharis, Duke of Mathura and Magadha, Disciple of the Greater Vehicle who, breaking from the Horned One's army and passing through seven deserted valleys, had climbed the lonely stretches of Kaspapuros and entered the cave of light and who had lived on as general and sage, far beyond mortal span.

And on her other side, there were the translucent bards of Hiber who had sung to and sailed with Gaythelos and Scota, all the way, they said, from the singing mouth of Africa. And the lute too became like fluid, so that it was as though Zuleikha, the musician and indeed the entire forest were simply reflections in the surface of the lake, and that the reality must lie on the other side of the water, somewhere deep in the limestone of eastern England, beyond the screaming cacophony of Messerschmitts and V2 rockets, beyond the chalky taste of the whisky from Lord Jack's skull-cup, beyond even the smile, cut into bone, of the holy man who had learned fifty-three languages and imparted them all, one hot June night, to his mentor and friend, Frederici, the King of Sicily. And the music which Zuleikha the Lover heard was identical to that played deep in the cave by Alexander the Lutenist of the New Town of Erskine, and in the dream she knew this, and she knew also that he had come to no harm in the midwinter's night, for the cave had been warmed by the spirits of history, the spirits of the earth going back ten thousand years, to the very edge of the Great Ice.

Laila woke her gently, so that the first thing Zuleikha smelled was the perfume which the other woman had donned. During dinner, and then later, over wine, Laila explained that she had been a hippy in London during the late Sixties and that she had crossed paths – that was how she put it – with a number of well-known musicians and activists of the time. And that later, for a time, she had been a Radical Feminist, and that over the course of this development she had lived in a variety of squats in London, but that ultimately she had grown disillusioned with all that – and it had got seriously violent with the Pigs and the NF and the grandstanding that had been going on … and so by degrees she had drifted back into respectable society.

Many years later, she had come here to live on the fringes of the deep past, in this place where she had felt she would be able to grow her own future. But with the encroachment of commuterland it had palled a little as, bereft of fig-tree vicars and hand-cut harvest festival fasces, like so much of rural England, Lincolnshire had become an estate agent's paradise. And she had discovered that the developers, speculators and corporate shit-kickers who were messing up the countryside now were the same ones who had destroyed the social and architectural fabric of London during the 1970s and 80s. Laila was no longer vegetarian, having subscribed instead to the Jewish doctrine that one should partake of God's creation without prejudice. Not that she was Jewish – well, Zuleikha hadn't noticed any obvious symbols around the house, but that didn't necessarily mean … after all, she herself didn't have any obvious Islamic symbols around her flat. Though what with the vicissitudes of history and the name-, not to mention shape-, changing that had gone on down the centuries, one never really knew.

'There was a time,' Laila said, her voice seeming to drop half an octave, 'when Lincolnshire was out there. You know, right out there, along with the great rolling mists and the ghosts of wrecked wooden ships. Did you know that half the county used to be under water?'

'Why are you called Laila?' Zuleikha asked, and she knew instantly that she'd had too much wine. The lamb was delicious, though: roast lamb – okay, re-heated, but lots of gravy, home-made – my God, thought Zuleikha, this woman is Mother Earth!

At first Laila made no reply, and Zuleikha wondered whether she'd gone too far, or whether perhaps she had phrased the question rudely.

'My full name is Laila Sciaccia Asunsi. My father was probably Jewish, though he was also Sicilian. My mother was most definitely C of E.' She stroked her cheek. 'I take after her in looks.'

Zuleikha chuckled.

'What do you mean, "probably Jewish"?'

'In those days in England – remember, we're talking about the 1930s and 40s – it wasn't exactly fashionable to admit that you were a Jew. Now, of course, it's the opposite. His family came from a very poor part of Sicily – well, I mean Sicily in general was very poor, but they were from one of the worst areas. It was way back, the Jewishness; they didn't do any of the rituals, it was really just a folk memory. They had run away during the twenties and had come to Liverpool, where they worked as sailors and dockers. My father was the blue-eyed boy. Well, actually he had brown eyes! Being Jewish and Sicilian – it was too complicated; there were too many things you had to uphold, while you were just trying to get by. It can't have been easy in those days. And with the passing of the generations some people just let it go; they became Gentiles, or at any rate they allowed their children to become Gentiles – especially if their wives were local. It became a legend, nothing more.'

'But he gave you his name. I mean your name is totally ...'

Laila smiled.

'He gave me his mother's maiden name. Perhaps it was his way of fighting back. I don't know. He died before I was born.'

'Oh. I'm sorry.'

'We lived in the East End of London. I was supposed to have been born during an air-raid in the War, you know; so many children were born during air-raids. He'd worked his way up to being a Merchant Navy captain; he went through U-boats, torpedoes, the lot. And then, at the age of forty-four, while on leave, he was killed in an air-raid. My mother survived, but during the same air-raid that killed my father she went into labour.'

'My God!'

'After the war, we moved to Liverpool. I don't miss him, or anything. I mean, I never knew him. And now it's history.' She smiled. 'Though sometimes when I was growing up I used to fantasise. As young girls do.'

'The man in the photos – I hope you don't mind me asking?'

'Not at all. That's Joe.'

'Joe,' Zuleikha repeated.

Laila looked her in the eye. Zulie flinched and looked at a watercolour on the wall. Rustic art.

'My lover.'

'Oh.'

Zulie looked back.

'He's dead, too.'

'Oh, I'm sorry…'

Laila waved her off.

'When you get to my age, so many of the people you know are dead people.'

Suddenly, Zulie remembered Daoud. His hyacinth eyes, his hair, the colour of the sun.

'He died fairly young. A haemorrhage of some sort; internal bleeding. They never really found out what had happened. It came totally out of the blue. It wrecked me, for a good while.'

'Do you have children?' Zuleikha asked. Stupid cow. Why did she have to ask that?

'No.'

'I see.' She paused. 'Sorry, I'm being very rude.'

'No, you're not.' A pause. 'And you…?'

Zuleikha answered a little too quickly.

'No. None.'

Peter denied Christ thrice. So they said. But then, according to Islam, Christ was never crucified: he simply Ascended. And according to Judaism, he was nothing. And now Zuleikha was denying Daoud. Not because she was in any way ashamed of having had him, of having brought his body out of hers as God had brought forth Man (and presumably, Woman, too, though perhaps like Pandora she had been fashioned from mud, a golem-for-fucking, a kind of blow-up doll for Holy Joes) but because she had never been able to talk about him – it, the subject, the object,

294

the loss, the great black hole inside her which, as she had grown older, had expanded and filled her eyes with nothing but darkness. She wished for a moment that she had acquired the equanimity of the older woman, wished that she had developed the ability to talk calmly about the dead people who surrounded her with their absence, but she didn't know how. To Zuleikha, every loss had seemed final, definitive. Archie, even. Well, he wasn't dead yet. She wondered how she knew that. After all, it had been a week since she'd last seen him, since ... but in her gut, in the empty box that was her womb, she knew. She feared what might happen when he finally went. She feared what might happen to Alex and her. Because if she could dream about the music he was playing and the changes it wrought, then why shouldn't Alex know everything that had passed between her and Archie? And exactly what had passed between them? she wondered. Nothing, she decided. A few bankrupt memories of a drug-addled, cancer-riddled pensioner – that was all. And the future imaginings of a very sick doc. A matri addulurata.

After Turkish coffee, served properly in demitasse cups, Zuleikha retired to bed. She knew, though, that she wouldn't be able to sleep. Her room was on the first floor at the end of a long narrow corridor bracketed on one side by a row of small windows and on the other by a series of framed psychedelic prints – a corridor which Laila told her had been constructed across the roof around a hundred and fifty years earlier, in order to link the main body of the house with what had been the servants' quarters. Laila said she presumed that this was for ease of access – both ways. And then she'd given Zuleikha a sort of woman-to-woman look, the meaning of which was obvious.

After Laila had left her alone, Zuleikha went back out into the corridor. The posters ran from Op Art, with its circling, hypnotic, monochrome dot-and-line effects, to the full joyous psychosis of psychedelia. Art Nouveau for the Baby Boomers. There, she couldn't get it out of her mind. Babies. For fuck sake. Yet gazing at the paintings soothed her. Some were pure works of art, while others advertised gigs and happenings. Bands with fantastic pot-names like *The Giant Sun Trolley*, bands that seemed to have erupted from another world. Or, to be more accurate, acid names.

Yes, LSD had been the thing then ... overnight, the phrase, 'dropping cups of tea' had assumed another meaning. When Zuleikha ran her hand across the clear glass of the framed posters, the swirls of paint brought to her attention the fact that these were not prints at all: they were signed, original paintings from 1960s London. Signed with the name, 'Laila S'. So that's what Laila had been doing back then, she thought. She wasn't a groupie at all: she was an artist. Perhaps for a short time they had almost grasped something, those bands, those artists. And perhaps Laila too had seen it, but then it had fallen away, maybe forever. An eccentric and fearless inventiveness, an ability to hear correspondences and, running through it all, the essence of something called hope. Ah, she thought, as she wheeled around in the guest room, I'm just a Romantic! Or else I've had too much wine tonight. She eased open the casement window just a fraction, swept up a tin ashtray from the sill, went back to the bed, arranged herself in cross-legged fashion, and lit a cheroot.

At around two a.m. (though since there was no clock in the room and since Zuleikha had forgotten to bring her watch that day, she couldn't be sure) there came the knock on the door which she'd been half-expecting. The branches of the ash tree outside her window waved crazy shadows; its trunk sprouted some fifty or so feet from the house, but its outermost twigs almost brushed against the walls, doors, windows.

'I thought it was a ghost,' she joked with Laila as, sitting cross-legged on the bed, they shared a strong joint. There was a CD player on the window-sill, and Laila slipped in a silver disc which gave out music that sounded to Zuleikha like some kind of acid rumba.

'This house is full of them. It was the vicarage once, and before that it was a guest cottage on the estate. And before that, there was another house on this site – same foundations, I think, though I'm not sure – there seem to be a number of different stories. It belonged to a priest, or monks, or nuns, or something. In the old days, this forest was full of repressed romance. Besides, any respectable ancient building must contain least one white lady, one green lady, one blue lady ...'

'It's crowded, then.'

Laila nodded.

'Crowded, but organic. I grow my own.' She swirled her joint through the air, then brought it to Zuleikha's lips.

'What, ghosts?'

They dissolved into girlish giggles.

Outside the room, in the darkened corridor, the prints began to dance a lithe tropicalia to an Arabesque of contrapuntal minor keys and Phrygian modal raga-rock runs, with the dead from the bands of those days emerging from their urns and sarcophagi and playing power chords to the swaying trees of the ancient forest and to the two strangers who felt now that they had known each other always. And later, Zuleikha wasn't certain whether what she had imagined during that night had really happened, or whether it had been an effect of the drug or else of loose wishful thinking. They began to touch hands like adolescents on a first date, and then, on the pretext of a relaxing mutual massage, tentatively to touch other parts of each other's bodies – but still only through their clothes. Behind the other woman, Zuleikha made out the billowing shadow of the ash tree as its branches too began to quiver and then to sway madly. Then, at a certain ineffable point which neither of them could have predetermined, their lips met. She found that even the taste was quite different. Because they both had long noses, there was a little farce in their movements – and, more than once, they erupted in laughter. But, she thought, while with a man there would have been irritation at this, with a woman it tended to heighten the sense of relaxation necessary for effective love-making. And Laila whispered something, though Zuleikha didn't see her lips part as she spoke:

'Cosi amari, ténili cari; cosi duci, ténili 'nchiusi.'

And she found that in the midst of the night and beneath the swaying, glittering blanket of the stars, she understood. And she whispered back, though she was not at all certain whether or not her own mouth opened as she spoke, save to receive the essence of the other woman.

Bitter things, hold them dear; sweet things, keep them enclosed.

At first, Laila was the dominant one. It was she who peeled off Zuleikha's garments, and it was she who began to touch Zuleikha's body with the skill born of countless relationships, of assorted lysergic encounters in forest and city, conjoined with the deep cornucopia of pagan, hippy, tantric knowledge. Laila Sciacca Asunsi was a witch, a follower of moon and mother goddess, a believer in the sanctity of earth, water and sky and in the sacredness of sex. When the witches pranced naked in a circle, it was she who held aloft the black-handled athame and chose her partner for the consecration of the rite, and now she drew the nude Zuleikha in circles around the room. Or at least that was how it felt to Zuleikha: her head was spinning, but in a not unpleasant manner, and she was seeing visions – or perhaps they were part of the visions that Leila was seeing and through which she was acting.

All edges had become immaterial; the borders between herself and Laila had evaporated in the heat of the entheogen, and now Zuleikha felt as if she was lying naked on a sandy shore, tucked beneath the awning of a tufa cliff that sloped steeply into a turquoise sea. Beneath her back, the fine grains of sand mingled with slightly larger rounded pebbles, and as she basted her skin in the hot sunlight, as she became aware of an itching sensation that meant she was beginning to burn in its rays, there was a frisson, an undulating flexibility about this mixture of sensation that aroused her intensely. Behind her was a rough stone staircase, cut into the side of the cliff. As she let her eye drift across the waves, she saw the water turn from a light shade of turquoise to azure, then to a deeper blue, and finally to a terrifying greenish-grey. And there, only some fifty feet from the shoreline, from the hollows formed in the soft silver sand by her heels, Zuleikha watched the sea move like a single muscle – not so much individual waves as a uniform mindless entity that at any moment might simply sweep up onto the beach and pull her out into the emptiness. From behind, from inland, from the weave and sway of sleek eucalyptus trees, the pleasantly hypnotic music of cicadas filled her head with a buzzing high-pitched tone. And there was Laila Sciacca Asunsi, rising from the ocean, swimming from the belly of the sea, from those same glaucous depths where Zuleikha knew the water would be cold as death. And yet, in spite of her age, Laila's movement seemed assured, sinuous, and behind and around her, her hair gathered up the sea in silver nets. As Laila reached the shallows and stood up, Zuleikha saw that she too was stark-naked, and as the undertow

298

pulled at her calves and as the water cascaded like a shower of liquid gold from her skin, she seemed almost like a statue – not some man-made idealisation of womanhood, but a real living, breathing incarnation of spirit drawn from earth and ocean. Her body, sculpted by decades of vegetarianism, was long, thin and a little bony – though perhaps, because more recently she had resumed meat-eating, her sinews were bulkier and more powerful than one might have expected, and though she was fair-skinned, the water and light cast over her a fluctuating sheen, thin as voile. Her pubic hair too was silvery and plentiful, and her breasts, far from being limp, seemed to coruscate with a taut muscularity. Her fingers were long, thin and bony, and the nails had been cut elegantly to medium length. And though Laila did not seem to be opening her mouth, yet the muscles of her neck and throat pulled and swelled as she sang.

> *I wish my baby it was born*
> *And smiling on his daddy's knee*
> *And I poor girl was in my grave*
> *With the long grass a-growing all over me*
>
> *Dig me my grave long wide and deep*
> *Put a marble stone at my head and feet*
> *And at my breast place a white snow dove*
> *For to let the world know that I died for love*

Zuleikha rose onto her elbows as Laila sank down beside her. They kissed, long and deep, and Zuleikha felt the scent of the sea rub off from the other woman onto her skin. She turned fully to face Laila, whose face was beautiful, stained and browned with salt, and the bright blue glint in her eyes electrified Zuleikha's being. Then they were back in the room in Lincolnshire in the depths of a winter's night and they were naked on the bed beneath the ash tree whose twigs teased their backs, buttocks, breasts, the insides of their knees, the soles of their feet and they were turning and twisting upon each other, turning and twisting and grinding like two rough tufa stones, now soft, now hard, so that Zuleikha felt the tiny pebbles cut into her back in a thousand different places and she felt herself release her lifeblood into the glistening silvery earth.

Laila turned down and away from her and, opening her own thighs, she wheeled her body over that of her lover and sank her lips into Zuleikha's vulva, simultaneously offering hers to Zuleikha's straining mouth. Laila's vagina tasted of moon-lemons, of a bitterness which mingled with the scent of sea-pine that wafted over the cliff's edge, a bitterness that burned – yet as Zuleikha flicked her tongue in and out, as she massaged the soft velvet walls of Laila's box, Zuleikha began to feel more and more like a snake. Her organ seemed to elongate until she was able to tickle the twin clasps of Laila's womb, to rime off the thick bung as though she were dissolving the plug of a surahi of Suleiman, and to take onto the spine of her muscle the flooding egg-sac, to slip it into her mouth, to feel its delicateness and vulnerability beneath the hard stones of her teeth and, finally, to puncture its transparent membrane as though she was entering the very core of the other woman. At the same moment, Zuleikha felt her own belly release its wondrous golden entrails, and a burning wave swept over her.

Their interlocking bodies formed a serpent, joined at the font of joy that was the clitoris. Perhaps in truth it had been this tiny snake that had been the saamnp of original sin, when Lilith had taken Hawwa to the burning well. So this, Zuleikha thought, was what they'd meant by the phrase 'radical squat'! Two women, one lying supine, the other squatting over her, the only parts of their bodies in contact being the four millimetres, the eight thousand nerves, the dendritic, explosive tapers of their shared womanhood, hidden, secreted behind layers of labia, major and minor, like a magical note that had been there always at the centres of their beings, yet which reached a perfect fruition only in the luscious grinding of one bone upon another. Those fools who declared that a woman should cover herself from head to toe failed to understand that while they tried to destroy – or rather, control – every aspect of a woman's sexuality, in fact, ironically, they were sculpting a life-size statue, a walking replica of that plexus of energy which they feared above all else: the hood, gown, face. The burning eyes. Lips, vestibule, root, trunk, fruit. Zuleikha was a tree, high on a mountainside. Laila was the sea, rising from the rock. Man was not a part of this world; man remained only in the mind, a phantasm, a construct. The words of a song, caught in the breeze of their conjoined breath, swept along the surface of the sea, laughing at all the pricks, cocks, wankers who thought that they were free.

Futti a volu lu merru, e lu cardiddu

Yes, thought Zuleikha, as she opened her eyes and let her gaze drift along the opened blue vulva of the sky: yes, I will dream of this in the moment before I die; I will dream while, far above, black birds and cardinals will screw on high. The ocean began to wash its might around their ankles, teasing the sand off Zuleikha's toes and turning the silver hair on Laila's scalp to writhing snake-heads. In spite of the difference in their ages, Laila's energy level was far greater than Zuleikha's, who found herself panting as though suddenly she was coming up to the wall of a marathon. And again she thought that, amidst all the love-making, she heard Laila singing. It was an alto song that had no words – or at least none that Zuleikha could recognise. Cardinals? Blackbirds? It was all a game; the whole thing was a great act of play, nothing more. Boxes, vaginas, skulls, songs, journeys, love, death. She and Laila were cuntastorie, jongleurs, trobairitz, minstrels. Yet through this play, these songs, these canti erotica, the science and art in Zuleikha seemed to be merging and growing into something quite new. And as though she were the earth, newly-mulched, or a crystal that was coalescing from the deep blue liquid at the bottom of the sea, she felt the rhythms of the song fill her and create her and the rhythms set her swimming through the turquoise, the azure, the deep blue, toward the dark embrace of the open ocean. And there, on the fiery shore, upon the joyously hard mattress of the old-fashioned sprung bed, Zuleikha closed her eyes at the point when she felt that if once she gazed into those of the other woman she would turn to stone – to limestone, tufa, granite; to the white marble of her mother's tomb with its ruba'i in broken Persian, the nastaliq which now Laila with her expert fingers, breasts, tongue, was drawing in tiny droplets of blood upon Zuleikha's skin. And the verse was singing; each of its letters was a world in itself, and the song was the sacred howl of the sireni, of the half-beasts, half-humans, of the peoples of the sea who had sailed from Egypt's reedy delta, across Al-Bahr Al-Abyad Al-Muttawasit, the Darya-eh-Meditaraneh, all the way to the stones and light of Hibernia and Scotia. The two women were fighting vines, rolling over and over in the silver sand, the grains adhering to their skins so that after a while they became like rocks being moulded on the shore over aeons by the vertiginous movement of the ocean, and by the clear milk of the moon that, just as it flooded the forest, the lake, the uncurtained windows of their bedroom with light, also poured into the sea's blackness and set it on fire. And together, in the great overflowing jaam of the ocean, they found a union of great purity. At a certain point, Zuleikha felt the warm arms of the oceanu lift her and her lover and pull the air from their lungs, slash their necks with gill slits and haul them back into its heaving body. Now they were lying prone, side by side on the bed that was like hot stone, and as the high moonlight burned on their backs, they were fin-women, sireni, skin-witches howling Ogham songs beneath the stars.

And yet Zuleikha knew that her other lover was missing, that it was a freezing night, that what she was doing was at the very least irresponsible, and at worst, downright cruel. Maybe she was taking some kind of revenge. Not on Alexander personally, but on the man who had given her a child, and on the Man-God who had taken her child away. Or perhaps this had nothing to do with men, maleness, the entire bloody edifice of patriarchy with its Doric pillars rammed deep into the soft sand, seven millennia deep, right down to the magma of the earth's liquid mantle. But this whole thing was too weird. Yes, that was it: she couldn't fucking cope with the weirdness; it was filling her head and spinning her thoughts. Did Alexander exist, or had she imagined him? Surely not; you can't make love to someone so many times and then discover that they didn't exist! That was ludicrous. But what about incubi and succubi? She could never remember which was which. And who was Laila, this ex-hippy and all-time feminist, this drug-dealer and witch? Why had she been wandering through the woods during a snowstorm? *Looking for vistas*, she'd said. For her artwork. Or had Zuleikha imagined that she'd said that? Things were beginning to collapse in on themselves. Logic, rationality, the steady flow of time and person, it was all becoming scumbled like a landscape in a snowstorm or like a mind out of joint. Or rather, on a joint. Waves of laughter erupted from deep in her belly, from a particular kind of happiness she hadn't known since her mother's death, perhaps not even since Daoud's death. She knew it was artificial, drug-induced, chemical, transient, but then, she thought, weren't all of our joys transient and to some extent determined by factors outside of our control? Economic factors, say, or factors to do with personal relationships? Wasn't our laughter doomed always to fade into silence? Weren't our bodies fated to end in chemical dissipation?

And now she was up and was dancing slowly to the tropical music. For the first time in years, dancing properly without inhibition, without the terrible corsetry of the spectacle. She'd been a not-bad dancer once, and now, on this night, the movements returned to her body as though all this time they'd been buried deep in the fibres of her muscles, in the warm liquid of her joints. And Laila was dancing too, in a different style, yet somehow their movements seemed complementary, like two strings on the same instrument.

And the music played also for those older ghosts of servants, mistresses and masters who had slunk in the candle-less night along the corridor on their way to secret assignations beneath a moon that had been not quite full. And there, a mile away, by the frozen window of the forest lake, by the body of water which in those days had been broader, deeper and darker, the mollies and morrises stomped and stretched through the reeds to the sound of gut strings and the plaintive voice of a bull-headed woman that issued from the very land itself. And Zuleikha told Laila everything, right from the morning by the Clyde when she had gone for a walk and ended up wading into the river, to their travels across Argyll and now Lindsey. She told her too about Daoud, her dead baby with the sapphire soul, and, sorrowful mother that she was, she wept a little as she related the events surrounding his death. She told this stranger things she had never told even to her best friend, nor to any member of her family. She told her things she had never told Alexander. And Laila, in turn, related the story of her father, the ship's captain; of his voyages, his many red skies, and of his family back in the old country, Sicilia. Laila still had relatives there in the province of Palermo, in the city itself and in its western hinterlands. Her cousins lived in one of the villages up on the big plateau, north-facing and surrounded by the peaks of the Madonie mountains, a desolate place called San Giuseppe ru Casteddu Nivuru. Or rather, they lived in Palermo but owned land around the ancestral village. Laila had been there a few times, mostly to gain inspiration for her paintings, but after a while had found the family life a little stifling.

'I needed peace, and it was difficult to get. You know, many centuries ago, that place was one of the last stands of the Moors. It's old name was San Giuseppe ru Calta Nivuru. "Calta" means "castle" in Arabic, I think.'

'The Black Castle of Saint Joseph...' Zuleikha murmured.

'More like "Saint Joseph of the Black Castle",' Laila corrected her.

'So what's it like? Barren, peaceful?'

Laila shrugged.

'We're talking twenty years ago. It's moved on since then. Sort of. In Palermo, forget contemplation. In San Giuseppe, everyone knows exactly what you're up to, even if you're not up to anything in particular. Everybody always assumes the worst about you. If you praise someone, they put themselves down, even though secretly they're happy you've praised them. Cui vecchiu voli campari, a bon'ura voli accuminzari.'

'Eh...?'

'"If you want to live to be old you need to start early."'

'Sounds like the west of Scotland!' Zuleikha retorted. 'Can you speak Italian?'

'To some degree, but almost no Sicilian, I'm afraid. Stock phrases only.'

'But Laila is an Arabic name.'

Laila shrugged.

'My mother always said that she'd liked it because it was different, especially in those days. Remember – she'd married this strange dark sailor, so what better than to give their child – born after his death, remember – an exotic name. It means "night". I was born during a very dark night. Anyway,' she said, pouting her lips, 'it's a Sicilian name.'

Zulie closed her eyes and pronounced the syllables of Laila's name in an exaggerated, luxuriant manner.

'Laila Sciacca Asunsi ... like a serpent.'

'No, that's scursini, or maybe scorzone – different kinds of snakes. "Sciacca" means cliff, or maybe fissure, in Arabic. Ash-sciaqqah.'

'"Night cliff" – nice. A crack in the night.'

'Thank you. So's yours! Nice. Your name, I mean.'

After Laila had left, Zuleikha eased herself down onto the mattress, let her head sink into the feather pillow, and gazed up at the single light-bulb in its yellow fan shade. Just as she felt her eyelids begin to close, she was sure she heard footsteps coming from the room above, and she wondered whether there was a room there, and found that she couldn't remember how many floors the house had, and pondering on this impossible conundrum, she fell asleep.

Chapter Nineteen

At around four in the morning, at the most silent, dark and cold moment of that long night, there was a loud knock on the outside door. The first time, as she emerged reluctantly from sleep, Zuleikha thought that she had imagined it. But the second set of knocking was more insistent, and she sprang out of bed, completely adrenalised, and peered through the window. Because whoever was knocking must have been standing right up against the wall close to the porch, they were invisible from her bedroom. But she did make out a lute-case some distance back, propped up against the trunk of the ash tree.

He looked a little dishevelled and his hair was out of order, but considering the length of time he'd been out there in the snow and ice, he seemed really not too bad at all.

'Alex! Are you all right? I couldn't sleep. We phoned the police.'

'I'm fine.' He turned away, lifted the case and entered the vestibule.

Laila had joined her at the door.

'How did you know I'd be here?' Zulie asked. She was shivering.

'I didn't. It was the first house I came to, outside the forest. I got lost, I think. I didn't expect anyone to answer at this time of night.' Yet he didn't seem at all surprised to see her. 'You went on too fast. You didn't wait for me.'

'Yes, I know. I'm sorry. I didn't realise that the snow would come down so fast.' She paused. 'There really was no excuse. I was stupid. I'm very sorry.'

There was an awkward silence. The surface of the snow looked perfect, like the iced top of a Christmas cake, and Zuleikha remembered that in less than a week it would be Christmas. She half-expected a set of plastic reindeer to come galloping toward them. She shook her head to try and rid herself of the after-effects of the marijuana.

'Come in,' Laila ventured. She stuck out her hand. 'You must be Alex. I'm Laila. Nice to meet you.' He stepped over the threshold. 'Don't forget your lute.' Laila pointed at the instrument, propped up against the wall of her house.

He returned to pick up the lute-case, and as he came back in Zulie reached up into his hair, which had turned cold as ice. She pulled him towards her.

'I'm sorry, love,' she whispered. His lips were intensely cold, like those of a dead person, like those of ... and he seemed nervous, embarrassed perhaps in front of this older woman who, she remembered, was a complete stranger to him, even if Zuleikha could no longer think of her in that way. He's probably angry with me, she thought, and she looked at the floor. He was reeking. Where the fuck had he been?

'Cup of tea?' Laila asked Alex, and then she also glanced at Zulie, who nodded. There wasn't going to be much sleep that night, anyway. 'I'll let the cops know he's come home.'

Home? That seemed an odd turn of phrase. It was her home, Laila's home of three hundred years or more. But it wasn't Alex's home, or Zulie's. She figured that Laila too had been half-asleep and now was acting on auto-pilot, especially with the bhang still swirling around in her brain. She was certain that Alex would be able to smell it.

Alex bent down to remove his boots. He figured that Zuleikha must've told this woman – what had she said her name was? – that the instrument was a lute. He wondered what else they'd discussed, but right then, with the sudden change in temperature, he found he needed to use the bathroom and he asked their host where it was. She pointed him to a door which lay on the left side of the entrance hall. As he washed his hands, he glanced up at the mirror above the wash-hand basin. For an instant, he thought he saw the face of an old man gazing back at him. The face was thin and deeply lined and, as though already the flesh had become mummified, the skin stretched tight across the bones, the lips had involuted, and the mouth lay slightly open. But the eyes stared back at him, intense, blue, undimmed. He found it impossible to look away. In the blue skies of the man's irises, Alexander saw dog-fights, ten thousand feet up. He felt the undertow of the Atlantic Ocean pull at his feet; he tasted the sweet aromas of sub-tropical cerulean palaces, and he sensed the proximity of a cyanotic death in the room of the broken mirror.

And he knew that Archie was dying and that, many years earlier, the airman had been here in this forest, and had chanced upon, or been led to, the writings of an eccentric aristocrat who once had owned all the land hereabouts. He knew that this one defining episode in Archie's life had remained secret, unspoken till now, until in his hallucinatory state he had become some kind of conduit for much older forces. The same forces, perhaps, which had taken over Alex's and Zulie's lives, which had pulled them together that spring morning by the riverbank, and which perhaps had taken Susan from him forever. The face darkened, became impossibly elongated, and tears fell from the eyes and turned to blood. He closed his own eyes, and when he opened them again the face had vanished – or rather, had been replaced by his own. He realised that his fingers had turned white from gripping the edge of the bowl, and he ran them under hot water to try and bring some life back into them. The hallucination – for Alex supposed that that was what it must have been – had lasted for only a short time, yet the memory of it seemed to linger like a note sustained into eternity.

'You didn't come looking for me,' he said later, as they lay in bed and tried to get some sleep.

'I knew you'd be okay.'

'How?'

She turned to look at him.

'I don't know. I just knew.'

'Oh well. It's good to know someone's worrying about you when you go missing.'

'I mean, we phoned the police. What else did you expect us to do?'

'Us?'

'Laila and me.'

'You just met the woman.'

'Yes, and she's been kind enough to put both of us up – strangers – in the middle of the night. So shut up now and get some rest. We have a long drive tomorrow.'

The next morning, before they left, Laila insisted on making them a sizeable breakfast, but even before that she insisted on showing them around her large garden. Zulie reckoned it must have covered approximately half an acre. Well, it had been a vicarage, she remembered. In an old album there was a photograph of the previous occupants, the last vicar and his wife. The photograph had a white border and looked as though it had been dipped in the pond before it had been developed: it had the distant poignancy of a vintage watercolour. The image had been snapped somewhere behind the house on a florid midsummer's day. The vicar was half-bald, looked around forty-five, wore plus-fours and seemed appropriately monkish. By contrast, his wife, almost a head taller than he, seemed – at least in the picture – to be a coquette. It was as though she was a loose WAC-WAAC woman, come straight out of the gin dreams of World War Two. They were not touching. Behind the couple was a row of tightly-planted rose bushes, and behind these, the dense green mass of the forest itself. There were no children.

Out in the garden, as Laila showed them around, were the remains of sweet-pea trellising and climbing roses. There were wild roses of the type that would've graced the English countryside, or at least, the English Court, in the fourteenth century. There was a giant rockery, a vegetable patch where Laila grew everything except grass, and towards the outer edges, where garden met forest, the vegetation grew wilder and in places was rank. Laila told them that no matter how assiduously she had cultivated these areas, they had always seemed to revert to the wild. In the end she'd just allowed it to happen, and now it was enough that she could stop the forest from taking over completely. The vicar had left a weeping fig tree and a trident made of ash in this part of the garden, but she'd told them that for as long as she'd lived there, at any rate, the tree had never borne fruit. The trident was to placate evil spirits. The vicar in the picture had dwelt in the house from the late 1930s until some time in the sixties. One day, apparently without warning, his not unattractive wife had eloped with the village doctor. Slowly the vicar had turned to drink, and after that there had been just the elderly, inebriated, by then more or less forcibly retired man of God, the rambling garden and the shambolic, stinking house.

'He died in your room,' she said, nodding slowly at Zuleikha. 'The body lay there for weeks.'

'Oh, thanks for telling me! I'm so glad you didn't mention it last night.' Zuleikha smiled back, though it failed to dispel the sense of unease that had begun to disturb the timbre of the morning. Laila threw her a mischievous glance.

'What, you mean he didn't come and say hello?'

Zuleikha didn't reply. The woman in the photo had seemed almost elated – though then again, that might simply have been fake. Yet the thought kept insinuating itself that, while she may not have been getting it at home, she must have been getting it good elsewhere. Perhaps, Zuleikha thought, the vicar's wife once had been a flapper whom he had lifted off the dance-floor and saved for God. But, as village wags always said, *bad blood will out!* She smiled to herself as she pictured the scene, somewhere in London, Sheffield or Manchester, the ageing scantily-clad flapper chasing the randy doctor around the bull-brown wooden examination couch. The garden seemed inordinately bare. It was midwinter, yes – but there was something more. She thought that Laila was taking the piss again. Yet she remembered her father, and a sense of desolation came over her.

'When they found him, there was a sweet smell that filled the house. There was almost no decomposition.'

'Like a saint,' Alex intoned. Laila shrugged.

'I suppose. Or it might just have been midwinter, like now, and here in the east it gets very dry, you know.'

'Maybe it was the alcohol,' Zuleikha cut in. 'It preserves things.'

Laila and Alex both laughed, but then stopped when they realised that Zuleikha had not been joking. Suddenly, she wanted away from the old house with its echoing, half-remembered miseries. She needed to be somewhere out of this cold climate and its blasted aerodrome, away from the taste of Archibald McPherson's last breath dying in her lungs. She wrapped her arms around her chest and looked at the other two, then turned away, walked slowly across the garden's border regions, and peered into the perpetual darkness of the forest.

Over the long breakfast, Laila told them that the house had lain empty for a good many years prior to her purchase of it, and that it had been in a terrible state of disrepair. Zuleikha's assessment of her the night before turned out to have been correct. Laila was not a 'New Age' woman: there was something much darker about her than that. Zuleikha had heard of people from that time, from the sixties, who had become involved with ... not really *cults* as such, but with strange letters and codes, stuff they hadn't fully understood, and whose power therefore they had underestimated. Playing with fire; bad trips. All those nuts who'd spun records backwards and had thought that they'd contained hidden messages. Leila had known a load of weirdos, activists and ex-cons; the world in those days hadn't been as hermetically-sealed as it is now – that was how she'd put it – and they'd helped her renovate the place.

Somewhat tactlessly, Alex asked her how she'd come to know such people, and Zuleikha gave him a glance that would've turned Hell into Slough – but Laila just smiled and, with a wave of her hand, declared that while she'd been a hippy in the company of artists and musicians in London she'd got to know all kinds of crooks and wheeler-dealers – especially wheeler-dealers, and that she'd even lived with some of them when they'd been in the process of becoming, as it were, that particular kind of entrepreneur, and that now they had well and truly done their time and were into deep health, and of course that included renovating houses far into the marches of the countryside, especially ones in which from time to time they could store quantities of hash. As she'd explained to a slightly dumbfounded Alexander, nowadays all that was controlled by transnational corporations – but still there was room for the small businessperson. A sort of niche market for the lamps of the world. Zuleikha wondered whether she was making fun of them, and thought the probabilities more or less even.

After breakfast, Laila took them upstairs to the second floor and to her attic studio. It had a sloping roof that was almost completely made of glass, so that as they perused the art they were serenaded with the soft thumping rhythms of melting snow hitting the ground. Laila had laid out great canvases of oils and scrolls of cartridge paper covered with watercolours and poster paints. It was a bright sunny morning, the type of morning during which one could convince oneself that it was really summer – except that the sky was just a little too pale and breezy, and the angle of the light was wrong, the sun too far to the south. The studio was filled with light, and since its walls had been white-washed, the illumination drew everything in classically correct proportions, so that at times it felt almost as though they were strolling through a public gallery.

'I paint using all the media available,' Laila said. 'Did you know that it was Antonella da Messina, a Sicilian of course, who injected oil into the Italian Renaissance?' And she showed them some pictures which she had constructed from a mélange of paint and different types of earth, stone and sand. The paintings were filled with ghostly, psychotic images, and the whole lay somewhere between Munch, Chagall and Blake, but with some other less definable element too. There were images of ropes around the necks of goats, and the ropes had been made out of sea-sand. There were images of a sinister hunched figure walking along a rocky path up a mountain slope with only his back visible. There were yet others of bright red spiders, dancing. Zuleikha was certain that all the spiders had seven, rather than eight, legs. But although the three weirdo painters may have been sources of inspiration for Laila Sciaccia Asunsi – or rather, for *Laila S* – the paintings were by no means derivative. Laila was not just a clever copyist, or even a gifted master syncretist. There was something nightmarishly original about her work. Faces and bodies predominated, and even the landscapes had been anthropomorphised, so that as Zuleikha gazed more closely she saw that, as in the old fairy tales, the trees had eyes and mouths. Such effects had been very skilfully executed, and the longer you looked, the more convinced you became that the features were actually moving. By contrast, many of the human figures seemed to be turning back into animals or plants, so that while their heads swung free, their feet were bound fast to the substance of the earth or else were in the process of being transformed into sleek carp fins in the river.

'I make my own pigments. I travel all over the country to get these materials. Sometimes I even dig them out of the ground with my own hands. It's something you can't get on the web, thank God! And even if you could, I would still prefer to sink my feet into the ground and draw up the stuff I need to create these images.'

'Do you paint while you're stoned?' Zuleikha asked, briskly. There was the slightest pause, and at her side she could feel Alexander cringe ever so slightly.

Laila smiled. Those lips of hers, Zuleikha thought. Delicious fruits.

'I have done. But I find that it works better either before or afterwards. I mean, you can't really do much when you're actually stoned. It's either the anticipation of being stoned or else the aftertaste (or both) that can trigger inspiration, can set off some kind of flow. I don't interrogate myself too deeply about it, you know, for fear that if I concretise it, it – whatever it is – might not come back.'

'But this place,' Zuleikha persisted as she found herself aroused by Laila's voice and by the light against her skin, 'this place and its history. I mean, three hundred years. That must affect what you do, no?'

'That's why I'm here and not in some city.'

Then Zuleikha noticed, propped up against the wall in the far corner, a large canvas that looked quite different from all the rest. She went over and touched the white cloth which half-covered the painting. Still holding the cloth, she looked questioningly at Laila.

'Skin,' Laila said.

'Skin?' Zuleikha exclaimed, letting go of the sheet. Her mind, rigid on caffeine and insomnia, tried to compute. Laila moved towards her, lifted up the sheet.

'Yes, parchment. It's very old. I've just begun this one.' She whisked off the cloth, which they now saw had been sitting on a metal frame above the surface of the ... skin. 'See ...'

Zuleikha looked down and saw that the centre of the canvas had been covered in thick black paint, in the shape of a solid circle – or perhaps it was a sphere, she wasn't sure. That had always been her problem, not being able to see things in three dimensions. She'd never been any use at making things, or at playing instruments. Hers was a proprioceptive problem. She hunkered down and stared at the black paint. It gleamed and stank of oil.

'It's still wet,' she said. Laila nodded.

'I began it last night.'

'Last night? But you were with me,' Zuleikha blurted out, then blushed deeply as she saw Alex catch her eye.

'After you went to bed, before Alex arrived at the door, I came up here. Don't know why.'

'You were stoned then.'

'I know. Perhaps the black sphere was all I could paint, though

313

at the time it seemed highly significant!'

'It always does,' Alex chipped in.

How the hell does he know? Zuleikha wondered. Has he ever been stoned? Not since I've known him – not that I've known him long anyway. But then, she thought, how long have I known him? He was probably just saying the right thing, trying to show off in front of a sophisticated English artist. Fucking men. Fucking artists.

'But you did it on this old parchment,' Zuleikha went on.

'I've had it for years and never figured out what to use it for.' Laila shrugged. 'Somehow I felt that I would be able to do something on it last night, but obviously I was wrong. You get that sometimes. Dead ends. But paintings can develop over time, so we'll see what happens with this one. Right now, I can't say. I don't know. I got it in a sale, from one of the old houses around here. Just a blank parchment. Nobody else wanted it. Got it for a pittance. There you go.' And carefully she draped the sheet over the painting.

Zuleikha stood up straight and, using her knuckles, she began to knead the small of her back.

'So it was you,' Zuleikha said. 'I thought I heard someone last night, pacing up and down in the room above me.'

Laila looked at her.

'Oh no, that wasn't me. This studio is above my bedroom, not yours. The space above where you were sleeping isn't used. It's through that wall.' And she pointed to the wall at the far end of the room. 'I think there used to be door there, but it had already disappeared when I bought the house. I mean, there's a roof-space in the plans, but no indication of any access.'

'You didn't open it up?' Alex asked. 'When you did up this studio, you didn't reinstate the door?'

Laila shook her head.

'Maybe some day … maybe not.'

'So whose were the footsteps I heard?' Zuleikha asked.

Laila shrugged.

'Oh, you're probably correct. It was probably just conducted sound from up here. In winter, in the middle of the night, apart from the owls and bats soaring through the trees, there isn't much noise hereabouts. You can hear a pin drop.' There was an awkward silence and then Laila threw out her arms, turned to Alexander and said, 'Well, that's my music.'

Zuleikha felt the stab of an épée of jealousy. In and out, quicker than a flash, but it left a trail of bitter coagulated blood in its wake, together with that scent again. She had never been any good at art, either in its narrow meaning of drawing and sculpting, or in the broader sense of creating, re-creating and transfiguring the world. Yeah, she'd always been the boring one, the not-quite-scientist who'd acted as the foil to all the quasi-artistic boyfriends she'd ever had. Not that she'd had many. She could almost feel the half-moon specs weigh on the bridge of her nose, even though she was too young to have needed them. A good deal too young. At least she didn't have a room full of sprouting hemp which she pretended she didn't have. But then, who had the footfalls belonged to? Zuleikha figured she must've been either dreaming or hallucinating. After all, for the first time in years, for the first time since Daoud had been conceived, she had got herself stoned. Stoned and fucked. Or at least, that was what her memory told her. And it had felt good, she admitted. She thought that perhaps she might ask to buy some weed from Laila, though she was unsure of Alex's position on the matter. And anyway, she thought that Laila had sort of half-winked at her, and this suggested to Zuleikha that the whole thing had been a piss-take. *Half-Sicilian ex-hippy grows hash in haunted house box-bedroom?* What was she, the Avon Lady of the N'drangheta? No, it was too much. Nonetheless, she would find a moment.

'And on that note,' Laila announced as breakfast ended in a mess of rattling and sunshine, 'can we hear your lute? I know it's early and you've had hardly any sleep, but...'

Alex still seemed almost hypnotised by her story and by the images in her gallery and, almost automatically, he brought out the instrument and began to tune it up. Zuleikha noticed that its structure had altered again, and wondered what might have happened out there in the night. She'd have to ask him about it later. This woman was nosey enough as it was. And if what she was saying was true, did they really want to have anything more to do with her? You'd have to be almost as sick to have made that sort of stuff up as you would for it to be real. A confabulator.

315

The world was full of them. But maybe it was appropriate that they had all met like this. After all, Laila's story, while possibly criminal, at least was rational. How could Zuleikha have explained to herself what was happening to herself and Alexander, without thinking, not unreasonably, that either one or both of them were either clinically psychotic or else permanently intoxicated? Better the latter, she thought.

Laila was now going on about how, thirty-plus years ago, she'd listened to the Third Ear Band play live with Mediaeval instruments. 'You know,' she said, 'those guys who were in Roman Polanksi's "Macbeth",' and then she and Zuleikha looked at each other and burst out laughing. Laila was on full form.

'Well, if MacBeth is now with us, sitting at the table, perhaps Banquo should take up the lute and perform!'

That joke again.

Alex relaxed into his role and began to play.

And Zuleikha could see that the lute had reverted to a simpler construction than before. Its eight courses now had reduced to six, and the neck was completely straight and was flush with the fretboard and body. Its sound was lighter, there was less bass, and Alex was using a plectrum which looked as though it was a piece of bone – though it couldn't be, she thought. Bone from a human phalange. No, that was daft. But there was no mistaking it. Alexander was playing a madrigal or something similar, and he was using some dead person's finger. What the fuck had gone on during the night? she wondered. Where had he been? She had a dream-like feeling of vague remembrance, but nothing more. She hadn't had a chance really to ask him about what had happened after they'd got separated in the snowstorm. He'd just mentioned wandering through the forest. Well, yes, but that hadn't told her very much, had it, she thought, and then she wondered whether Alex was beginning to keep secrets from her. And she became impatient for them to return to the hotel and attempt to open another box. Because, she thought, if we can, then I'll know that something went on last night and he had better bloody tell me what. But right now he was playing a slow round-dance. Yes, she thought, that was it: it wasn't a madrigal after all, it was something that bordered on the Pre-Renaissance. That was the other thing. While, as an accomplished lutenist, Alex had always seemed able to play almost any style of music, now she sensed that the very form of his instrument limited his possible repertoire. After all, she thought, he couldn't exactly play music that had been written for strings which no longer existed on his lute! And that led her to another thing: increasingly, the music for the pieces which Alexander played would never have been written down in the modern style, but if it had been inscribed at all, it would have been only as tablature or notation. He would be playing with the ear of a dead man. Or singing with the mouth of a tree.

Alone, abandoned by all joyous pleasure,
Pain is that in which I shall languish.
All affirms that I shall never experience joy;
I am and shall be for naught that I can see.
As long as I live I shall have only displeasure.

Well prepared for all bad that may come,
Without ever leaving I remain inconsolable
Wherever I find myself.
Alone, abandoned ...

In my thoughts I have no memory
Of any living thing that I may delight in.
I do not wish for a long existence,
And so I pray to God that death may take me away soon
Since never will I experience any better.
Alone, abandoned ...

Laila's eyes were closed and she was swaying gently back and forth at the table. At first Zuleikha found this amusing, but after a while it seemed vaguely threatening. Quickly, forgetting her resolution, Zuleikha brought out a cigar. What's she trying to do, the bitch, seduce him? Is this how the groupies had been in those days? The go-go girls, the pole dancers, the women in the silver cages who disrobed rhythmically to the sound of some stratospheric acid guitar solo ... fucking AC/DC cow could have it both ways.

And now I can well cry, "Alas"
And my eyes be consumed in tears
O damned, iniquitous tongue,
Which is the reason for such evil,
Hanging high by the neck,
I shall finish my life.

But then she told herself to remain calm and to maintain an Apollonian sense of proportion – which, with the chaff of the grass still blowing somewhere in her hindbrain, she admitted to herself was not going to be the easiest thing to do. The middle frequencies did seem a little larger than they ought to have been, and though there hadn't been much of a bass at the beginning, now she was sure that she could hear an undertone – or was it an overtone? She looked at the unlit cigar as it rested stupidly between her fingers. Or perhaps it was just that the natural frequency of vibration of some part of the house – the joists perhaps, those weird paintings upstairs, the empty room which hadn't been used since the vicar's time or even before (or else which now was a drug stash) or the three-hundred-year-old iron bolts that had been bashed into the oak – held within its substance an affinity for the notes that Alexander was playing. With a sense of ceremony, Zuleikha lit up.

An image from the 1940s, of a party being held across the entire half-acre of the vicarage and spilling over into the nearest parts of the forest. Summer, big hats, hot sunshine. Even in wartime, food was more plentiful out here in the country. There was rationing, yes, but farmers and those who kept chickens, cows and other livestock – well, you know, you got a bit extra, the verger's wife had been telling her. And she had nodded and smiled in a peculiarly 1940s kind of way – a respectful, respectable kind of way, since the good vicar of Saint Cuthbert's Church had laid on this delightful party for the men and women stationed at the local aerodrome. The vicar had buried some, both corn and chaff, and no doubt would come to bury more before this damned war was over. Perhaps, in the spacious grounds of his vicarage, he had also interred statues of St Joseph in the old Roman Catholic manner. After all, was that not what people did in times of strife? They reached across the centuries, folded themselves back to the time before the arrival of reason and steel, in search of any charm, any bit of rancid magic that might possibly work, that might possibly make the edges of the shadows glimmer. And over there, in the far corner of the garden, was the man she was going to marry in twelve days' time. Archibald Enoch McPherson, a Scot, a ranked Aircraftman.

His forehead and left hand were bandaged from when he'd fallen off his bicycle, and his eyes seemed hooded, so that he resembled one of those ancient photographs from the American Civil War – but she knew that it was all just the effect of an excess of night patrols. And too many warm, daft nights with the two of them rambling and rolling about in the lee of some farmer's old haystack – or else, like now, standing naked in the middle of the darkling forest, their skins mingling with the bark of old ash and elm. She would be stood up against the hard trunk, her feet splayed, the soles tickled and at times pierced by the sharp stems of the uvvers. He would be lifting her splauts and shammacks high into the air, or turning her suddenly sky-wannock as though he were a pilot and she were his aircraft. Those new rubbers sometimes hurt inside, but she didn't mind. Hurt was better than death, and pain meant that you were still alive. One way or another, pain was the lot of womankind. She knew he took other women, rafty sheeders more expert than she – in Lincoln, in the old Jews' abodes-turned-whorehouses that backed onto the cathedral. And also in Scotland – she didn't know where, but right then, in spite of herself, none of that seemed to matter. Those women were like chumpy clags and Archie was like a farmer and, once in a while, a farmer took even the filthiest of the sheep. It had always been the way, and to pretend otherwise was to bury oneself in an illusion. And in this war, in this life that was war, one could not afford to have any illusions. Perhaps those women too felt nothing but pain.

As he clammed and clanched at her body, as he knagged at the white bone of her shoulder with the rhythmic force of his goat's pyramid against the soft cone of her flesh, Margaret felt a tingling gradually spread all over her body as her gaze shifted to the tops of the trees. Poplar, beech, elm, ash, oak. They had been here since before the house had been built and they would be here after all the people at this garden-party were dead. Time seemed to stretch out beyond the green line of the forest to a place nearby where she could hear the cries of men playing cricket in a sandy clearing. Time seemed to reach up into the sky and pluck down the machines of death and blood and turn them into musical instruments, tubas, trombones, double-basses, and the trees, the metal, the still, hot air – all of it seemed to be distilling a melody which she had never heard before and which was like the imperceptible sound of oak trees, growing across the centuries. This was the crawk, the centre of everything; she would take this moment with her to her clumpsed grave and beyond. Archie! Archie! Archie! The arch of his body upon hers, the clean quivering line of his cock – a right kelcher it was, lungeous and terrifying, its taste beautifully bitter like that of gooseberries on the point of ripeness. There it was, sprung like old magic from the box of his body; there it was, its hard snake's spine encased now in red vulcanized rubber like the skin of an aircraft wheel, vulcanized, vangalized, as he readied, wacker and all, to fill the space in her belly. And now the hay was stabbing into the skin of her back, stabbing in a rhythm that was one with the cadences of the J-hangar concerts and her long brown hair, unbound for once, mingling with the sandy dirt, the spores of hay, the leaves of wacker trees, the moment when the happiness spread like hot wine across her body, when it turned to music that huzzed in her ears, his breath singing like that of a god in her face. *Whoever drinks from my mouth will become like me; I myself shall become that person, and the hidden things will be revealed to him. I am the Way, the Truth and the Life.* His breath giving her life, truth, the future, everything that in sixty years had ever passed between them...

Then his movements dackered, became slow and deep like those of the elm tree at her back. The angle of the sunshine against the side of his face, his profile sharpened in azure, his diamond-shaped eyes, newly-opened, gazing into the substance of the tree, the white and blue, softened with haar, a baby's eyes – all this made him seem almost heroic, and she wished that he might not ever move from that position, with the musculature of his being in perfect repose, from that afternoon of that day, which for all they knew might just be their last. And she would not have been sad if, at that moment, the earth had opened its sweet jaws and lapped them up into its warm darkness.

Like one of the paintings in Laila's studio, the scene faded and another took its place. Zuleikha was climbing a path that had been cut into the side of a cliff, up by a series of boulders to just under the lip of a waterfall, when she felt the surface of the stone split asunder. She became liquid and sank into the rock. Then she was in a cave, facing an image of herself as a priest with, all around her, the stink of ancient oil paint on wood. The priest's eyes stared out at Zuleikha, boring a hole in her skull and pouring his consciousness, like wine, in through the orifice. And the wine made her begin to chant and sing like a poet or a sufi in search of the power of the Doric reed, and mathnawis, qasidas and ghazals flew from the opened mouth of her skull, the cantastorii of khanqahs that sprang up in the middle of the desert and the songs of sacred goats who could change form, die and be resurrected at will, who could empty their souls from their bodies and then, through devotion, have their skins filled with the spirits of Sufi Masters seeking truth, the muwashshahat of mountain trees which were older than the gods themselves, the songs of jugglers, whores and slaves and of the memory, life, obedience and beauty which they all sought to possess, the chants of soldiers who, through sacrifice, became sages and who climbed to the tops of hills to light naphtha fires, the irregular rhythms of Kufic texts that wrote themselves in a thousand tongues in a single night and the murmurings of headless corpses who sang the neck verse and stepped along the points of the spider-dance, the Moorish dance, and who turned slowly black beneath the gaze of stone Madonnas.

Zuleikha was in the skin of a cat that raced around an earthenware pot, awaiting the word. Archie was dying; he was sinking into an unconsciousness that might well have been final, and now she was waiting for him to give her the word, the gift, the musical note. And the word was Joseph, Giuseppe, Yusuf. She had no idea what it might mean, other than being a man's name and probably a product of her chat with Laila Sciacca Asunsi, some kind of weird Sicilian-Arabic-Jewish-whatever thing – but nonetheless, the letters and the music seemed completely clear in her mind. She knew that Alex had been in the cave, that this was where he had gone that night in the snow which now, in the morning, already seemed a million years ago. And she knew that they both were ready for the next door to open. Or rather, that the door was ready for them. She had no idea though where it might lead. Behind the door there might be moonlight – or death.

Zuleikha realised that she had closed her eyes, and that through the phantasm of the night and this winter morning's frozen frost of cigar smoke her body too was swaying in tune with something-or-other. It was as though she was there in the kitchen and yet was far away, in many places at once, and after a while, though she hadn't realised that grass, bhang, benj, hashish could give one such a powerful recrudescence so many hours after it had been imbibed – she wondered whether perhaps Laila had mixed something else in with the hemp or whether hash itself was a lot stronger than it had been in the days of the anatomy hall's heads in pots – it did seem as though the entire house, including the sum total of its previous occupants (whoever they might have been) was part of the music which Alexander was playing. There were those footsteps above her; they were coming from the very top of the vicarage, and she was back in the studio leaning against the far wall, gazing at the dark parchment sphere when the footsteps grew louder and all of a sudden the wall fell open in the shape of a triangle and there, through the horsehair and freestone dust and the thick scent of a hundred roses, as the winter sunshine fissured the thick murk, she saw a long box filled with darkness. Next to the box was a burning oil-lamp, and otherwise, the only light in the closed-off attic room came through the cracks in the old thatching that had been covered over and through the woodwormed fissures in the ancient beams.

From the box that was shaped like a tower, a figure stood up and began to walk, began to measure out the same footfalls across the wood which Zuleikha had heard the night before, and the book-bosomed figure was clad in a palmer's amice and had neither face nor shadow. He was chanting words in a minstrel language that seemed familiar to her, a language of alef-laam and nûn ghunah, the Song of Giuseppe, of all the Giuseppes, the saints, the prophets, the revolutionaries, the peasants, and at her back she knew that with each stanza the parchment was filling with wildering symbols and pictures, each one drawn in red ink. The figure reached out his left hand and laid it upon her right shoulder and, at that moment, the parchment flew up and into Archie's right hand.

He lay on his back and stared at the ceiling. Only it wasn't the ceiling as he had known it, the off-white, slightly cracked artex surface that he had come to associate with constant pain and nausea and the sensation of a stone pressing on his chest. The roof was covered with symbols and letters, with pictures in the shapes of words and words in the shapes of pictures, with eremitical, imagistic, syllabic and logographic scripts. And yet he saw now that it was his own hand that was writing the symbols across the sky. And as the page of the roof rolled on – and it seemed to spin as though it was on a mechanical roller or else, he thought, perhaps it is I who am moving beneath the words – as in the times when he had dreamed that he was in the sky over England, dancing dog-fights with the dark legions of Messerschmitts, or when he had lain with Margaret in the thick golden bed of the harvest freshly-cut, or when he had touched the hazelnut skin of Zuleikha – it seemed that everything was becoming comprehensible to him, that all languages, songs, poems, howls, screams, grunts were within his ken.

Archibald Idris, Son of the Parson, reached out his left hand and touched the plastic button that regulated the flow of heroin water into his bloodstream. Seven times he pressed the button. The scroll speeded up and became a blur, yet still Archie found that he understood both the elements and the whole, even as the blur turned into the shape of a spinning head with three legs attached to it. A woman's head. He raised himself up till his face was flush with the ceiling. Oddly, it smelt of horsehair and roses, just like the barns in which he and Margaret had made love, just like the old tenement where his mother had washed herself dry and where, countless times, he had raised the silver of his seed though the glass of the winter moon. It smelt of that night he had patrolled the outer perimeter of the aerodrome, of the stench that had risen from the whore's body as in the mirror she had died beneath his rope of sand and as with this same hand he had raised her from the dead. And he pursed his lips and he kissed the face of the spinning woman and yet, though she continued her unstoppable pizzica tarantata, her great black spider-dance, his lips did not unclasp.

The uncharacteristically bright midwinter sun was rapidly melting the snow, turning it to a clean slush. Laila drove them to the aerodrome, from where Alex and Zulie returned to the hotel in Lincoln for the night. As soon as they entered their hotel room they went to the cupboard, hauled out the box, and opened its fourth lid. Inside they found a silver statuette which had been placed upside-down and which Alex proclaimed was an image of Saint Joseph, patron saint of lost causes. The silver had become tarnished in places and the face was bearded and almost black. And Zuleikha had fallen over backwards onto the bed; she'd fallen over, laughing. She was laughing so violently she couldn't get up. Partly, she was laughing at Alex, who was holding the statuette up to his face, inspecting it as though he was a jeweller checking out a diamond. She reckoned it might have been due to the hash – but really, she thought, this whole thing is laughable. I am laughable, we are laughable. He was searching for a join, a cliff-edge, a fissure, a sciacca, ash-sciaqqah, and when he found it she stopped laughing and propped herself up on her elbows and it seemed as though the whole world was tipping on its axis as Alexander twisted the statue at the waist, as he turned the head and chest round and round as though in some esoteric ritual. The two halves separated. He tipped both of them out onto the bed, right in front of the deep valley formed in the mattress by Zuleikha's prone elbows.

Two days later, they hardly talked as they took it in turns to drive north; three hundred miles through greying slush and wan daylight which, reflected in the surface of the water, became at times quite blinding.

Chapter Twenty

It is as though he is being sucked into a jet engine. Not that he had ever fixed a jet engine; by the time those had come along, he already had turned to ships instead. But that is what it feels like. Being pulled, inexorably and at high speed, through a vacuum into some distant, indefinable place. Then suddenly he is there, and it is as though his skin is being peeled from his bones; the light is all-consuming. There is neither up nor down, neither past nor future, there is nothing to which he can relate. Except, perhaps, his dream of flying. Every time he had fixed a bolt to the undercarriage of an aircraft, Archie had dreamed of going upside, of seating himself in the womb of glass and steel, opening the throttle and ...

His eyes are open, yet he is unable to see anything save for the brilliant luminosity of the air around him. Yet it is something beyond air. Every part of him is open; he is a page, a papyrus, a parchment scroll; his perceived reality is completely exposed.

Then he is entangled with the whore from sixty years earlier, but now they are on the other side of the broken mirror and he sees that beyond the room, beyond the window, there is nothing, no street, no War, no early spring 1941, no nothing. Then the whore's face changes, though not her body, and Archie is lying with Margaret and she is smiling yet does not seem to see or even feel his presence and he tries to shout at her, to tell her that it is him, but there is no sound in this place and it is not like any other hallucination he has ever had, not like the ones he had as a child when he had nearly died with the scarlet fever, not like the nocturnal wanderings he had undertaken through the Lincolnshire forests, not like the reveries of mesothelioma. No. This feels real. Then the face changes again and it is Zuleikha.

Then, before he realises it, he is falling, faster and faster, until he is a rocket, a bullet, a streak of flame.

BOX FOUR: SICILY

You'll become a lot better if you think about your death.

Sicilian proverb

Chapter Twenty-One

The bay had been formed millions of years earlier by volcanic eruptions, which even today continued to mould and define the east of the island but which here, along its northern Tyrrhenian shelf, had long since ceased. So she had read on the plane flight – or rather, on the two plane flights it had taken to get here. There had been no direct route from Glasgow to Palermo and so, as with most things, they'd had to go via London. London was the greatest city on earth, or so some Londoners liked to claim. Maybe it was true, but only if you lived within the circumference of the M25. It demanded your unquestioning allegiance and was a terribly parochial place, a centre of arms-dealers and carpet-baggers. She was always glad to see the back of London, to see it fall away in swathes of gunmetal grey, to rise above its piecemeal clouds, its casual rudeness. The higher you got, the smaller and more obviously finite London became, and usually, along with the transient sense of trepidation that accompanied any journey to another country, Zuleikha would feel like shouting out loud in a childlike excitement. She knew it was illusory, yet there was always a sense that finally she was getting away, escaping, shedding a heavy gown and a long chain. This time, instead, she sighed and let her head sink back against the stiff seat. *Make sure your tray-tables are upright; this safety demonstration may differ from others.* But it had always been the same, on every flight she'd ever been on for over twenty-odd years. The rituals never changed; the readying oneself for death.

Sitting in the aisle seat, Alex had fallen asleep even before they'd hit the Channel. She was glad for him, since such a big man would never be able to get comfortable in those crappy chairs. So there was no conversation – though to be honest, she wasn't sure she was in a conversational mood. She just wanted to get there. *It wasn't the journey, it was the destination.* She smiled, right at the moment when the air stewardess bent down and stretched over Alex to ask if she wanted to buy any drinks. Nothing nowadays came free on these airlines. It was all bare bones. Still, it was supposedly a budget airline – though with all those taxes and so on it could hardly have been described as cheap – and you couldn't have everything.

They had left a Scotland still in the grip of midwinter – or rather, in that lengthy pallid period of leaden misery which, like some epic lament, spanned from the beginning of January to the middle of April. It was a time when the cold damp wind seemed to intensify and elongate and when most suicide attempts tended to be successful. On her return from Lincolnshire she had learned that Archie had tried to commit suicide. She had avoided going to visit him, even though she had known that he would have found out from the district nurses that she was back in Glasgow. She'd felt heartless, but then she didn't want any more bizarreness, any more visions, hallucinations, tactile telepathy or whatever the fuck it had been. After all, what had she to do with this old bastard, this tankard-lunged shipbuilder, this working-class non-commissioned technician who had never really flown in the war but who had merely fantasised about flying, and who meanwhile had tried to screw every piece of skirt he had been able to lay his hands on. Or at least had been able to pay for. Okay, so he was dying. Okay, so secretly she had hoped that he would be dead by the time she returned. She couldn't continue this on-off thing with the locum. She would have to live for a while on the money from her mother's life-savings. Fuck, there was enough guilt about that, let alone having to wade in with some hoary old chancer who even on his death-bed was still so randy he'd tried it on with his own doctor!

As they came in to land the angle seemed dangerously acute, and Zuleikha found herself issuing a quick internal prayer of the sort she always made on flights, especially at take-off and landing and sometimes also during periods of air turbulence. Just the kulma, Lailaha-illala-Muhammad-ar-Rasullullah. It was an invocation which even the most casual of Muslims would learn in infancy, and it would serve to combat all manner of fears – from the interminably long dark nights of childhood, through those frosty, Presbyterian job interviews, to the rows of icy gravesides in winter. It was like an internet connection to God; you dialled the number, you got the power. Some people had broadband. Like the synchronised performance undertaken by the flight attendants, it was imbued with a power far greater than the sum both of its words and its meaning. Zuleikha could have rhymed off the semaphore in her sleep. *Before you fly, up into the sky, lend us your eye, and think about how you might die.* Flying really was a terrible thing. Not that she was a jet-setter. She'd heard that in First Class and Business Class it was incomparably better, that you could spin around the world and feel that you'd been just around the block. And you'd probably get to sit next to subtly rich guys who smelled nice and who didn't wear their riches on their (beautifully tailored) sleeves. Lord Such-and-Such, the third son of Earl So-and-So. Not that Alex smelled bad. But wealth carried with it an unmistakeable aroma, a kind of pheromone, you might say. Silver spoons, sleek yachts, offshore accounts... But they couldn't play the lute and weren't much cop at cunnilingus. Chances were.

As the plane wheeled giddyingly over the water she watched the sunset, the early March light turning the wave-crests from deep magenta to gold. The lights of the city had already been switched on and, glowering behind these, Zuleikha made out a dark circle of mountains topped by clouds. So that's why the plane feels so wobbly, she thought: it's caught in the vortex formed by the bay. She forced herself to focus on particular points on the terrain. From time to time, discrete areas would become illuminated by the dying sunlight – it was almost like a Byzantine mosaic – so that suddenly out of the twilight a gorge would become visible; but then she became confused as to whether the slopes on which she was trying to focus were actually clouds. She was becoming quite nauseated, but held down the thought of it. It was all in the mind, she told herself. Alex seemed quite relaxed, his bulk squeezing her against the plastic that surrounded the cabin window. This only accentuated the sensation she had of falling out of the aeroplane, falling into the open purplish mouths of the sea. That's what you got when you booked a cheap flight, she thought. But they hadn't wanted to use up all their money on trivial things.

The airport was at Cinisi, a town that lay a little to the west of the capital. It was properly dark by the time they arrived in Palermo, and so they took a taxi to the rather basic hotel with which they had arranged a booking, close to the old port. Even though they were up on the third floor, the sounds of police sirens and revving scooters kept her awake for much of the night – though,

331

again, Alex slept like the dead. He was lucky that way. He wasn't a worrier, as the old wives might have said if they hadn't all been dead. He'd brought his lute and the map in the hand-luggage, but had thought that he might run into problems with the airport staff. Alex was the sort of guy who adopted a shifty look at airports and so tended to get stopped. Added to which, because his hair and beard were black, by evening he would end up looking quite unshaven. So the combination of his height, fleeting eye-contact and aggressive grizzle would almost invariably alert security staff, and out of the long line of passengers, he would be the one whose hand luggage and person they would stop and meticulously search. Miraculously, this time nobody bothered. Must be me, Zuleikha thought. I'm his resolution, I bring out his essential innocence. He's got me, so he can't be a nutter, right? Right? Life was an ocean of ironies.

In the morning, they would make the phone call and would arrange to meet Peppe Ayala. A little embarrassed, they had taken the statuette and map back to Laila. She identified it definitively as a black alabaster statue of St Joseph which at some point had partly been plated with silver. Then Alex had shown her the two scraps of paper on which, in fine calligraphic style, had been drawn a map. Laila looked at them strangely, as though suspicious of some ulterior motive. After all, these two people had appeared out of nowhere in the middle of a blizzard and then Zuleikha had told her some freaked-out story about an old box, a river, a disused subway and an aerodrome. And all the while, both had seemed to be hallucinating – as though they were on a trip that had never really ended. And now they had started producing Catholic statues and weird maps of the land of her origin – or at least, one of the lands of her origin. Both sides of the paper had been covered with squiggles.

Part of her wished she hadn't shared the grass, let alone allowed them to view her studio. In the space of a few days they had set off something while she, Laila Sciacca Asunsi, had lived in this house for so many years and nothing untoward had ever happened. Well, that might be exaggerating a little, she thought. But she'd reached a kind of homeostasis with the spirits of the place, the old men who seemed reluctant to retreat into the walls, or to ascend, or descend, or whatever. The vicars of this land, going all the way back to Roman times. Britannia Inferior. Yeah, right, they were all stirring in their very old graves and were seeking the warmth of her place, her mind. The Day of the fucking Dead. That's what you get for being generous, she thought. You attract freaks. People start bringing their nightmares to you and then the nightmares start becoming real.

Sicily begins to become real. She hadn't told them the truth about why she hadn't been able to paint in San Giuseppe ru Casteddu Nivuru – partly because she wasn't sure it was the truth, and partly because – well, it was none of their bloody business! This fucking Zuleikha woman had set all that off again. The old Arab thing, the old Jewish thing. Saint Joseph. Yes, she'd been there at that time of year. Well, she'd been there all through the year actually, but had decided never to return. She could just about take the cold English spirits, could sublimate them through her art and her magic potions. But Sicily was different. Even today, with all the EU blah-blah-blah. She'd gone there and had stayed a year and it had torn something out of her, something which she'd never got back. Sanity, perhaps.

Nonetheless, it was clear that the statuette was that of St Joseph, and by its design it looked Sicilian: the shape, the look of the limbs, a particular cut of the eyes. She also put together the double-sided map which Alex had shown her, carefully sealing its edges with a glue that stank of goatskin. Then she sat down with them and tried to translate it. The map depicted a small area of land and, while on one side of the paper it was perhaps just post-War, the plan on the reverse side was indecipherable – save for the swirling lines that indicated the rising contours of the land.

'It's not in any language I know,' Laila said to them. 'It seems to have been drawn to a larger scale than the other one, as though it's a plan of a much smaller area. Bits of it look like an archaic version of Sicilian, but…' Zuleikha was unable to recognise the script. It wasn't Arabic, Cyrillic, Greek or Latin, yet it seemed to posses elements drawn from all of these. 'The big map is of the area around San Giuseppe ru Casteddu Nivuru.' Laila looked up at Alex. Pierced him with a stare. 'Is this a joke?'

He shook his head, slowly. She glanced at Zuleikha, then back down at the map that was spread out on her dining-table. Then she stared at him and, for a moment, he was reminded of the bull-headed woman in the cave. He glanced away, down at her hands. Those hands...

'You know, don't you, that Zulie has told me everything?' Alex started.

'What? When?'

'When you stayed that night.'

Zuleikha looked sheepish. She hadn't mentioned Archie to Laila. That had been the only thing she'd kept to herself.

Laila leaned back in her chair, removed a cigarette from her pocket and lit up. She puffed away, slowly.

'This,' she said, 'is fucking crazy.' She looked at Alex again. 'You know that, don't you?'

Alex nodded again. It seemed all he was capable of doing. Laila swung forward again, careful to avoid tipping ash onto the map. She'd offered one to Zuleikha, but since she smoked only cigars and hash the latter politely had refused, and so now, like some human version of the original psychedelic caterpillar, Laila Sciaccia Asunsi was generating enough fumata for the two of them. The three of them.

'Yes, well. This, my newfound friends, is a map of my hometown. Or, at least, of the area around my hometown.'

'La C...' Zuleikha began, then realised that she'd forgotten the full name.

'San Giuseppe ru Casteddu Nivuru. Saint Joseph of the Black Castle. Yes.'

More puffs. The room was filling with a slightly bitter smoke. 'Sangu del mio sangu. Blood of my blood. Mind you, my prejudices are out of date. Things have changed a lot there over the past fifteen years. For the better, I think. Gattopardismo. Depends on who you talk to.'

And after a moment's hesitation she'd given them the contact details of her cousin Peppe, and had said that she would telephone him to let him know they'd be arriving. She picked up the statue and gazed at it and her hand trembled, just a little. Then, carefully placing the figurine on the table, she went over to a tall wooden bureau that looked as though it must have been an heirloom, and rummaged around in the drawers for a while. Eventually she produced a small portrait, perhaps ten centimetres square, which she'd painted some years earlier. She told them that this was Peppe. The painting had been done in oils on wood, and had been coated in a gloss varnish in the old manner, and except for his face and hair, the entire image was in primary colours. In the December light it seemed crude and garish, not at all like her other work. It was more like folk art than art, Zuleikha thought. His face was long, though not exaggeratedly so as it would have been in a Modigliani, and his mouth curved slightly downwards at its ends. His eyes were brown and his skin was a shade of sand – but streaked though with a low-key rubaceousness. His nose was also long, but not bulbous, and in the painting his eyebrows were clearly defined – prominent without being bushy. In style it was Byzantine, yet there was no gold leaf, no halo.

'This is him. It's about ten years old, though – from when I was last there. I don't have any photos.' She straightened up and smiled. 'He doesn't look at all like me, does he?'

'You won't ... tell him anything?' Zuleikha began, looking anxiously from Laila to the portrait and back again, and wondering whether she could trust its eyes. Laila looked at her, and Zuleikha thought that she was about to smile – but then she didn't, and the effect of this was a little disconcerting, especially when she realised that Alexander too was staring at her – but in a completely different way.

'He'll think you're mad.'

'Exactly.'

Laila flashed her a mischievous glance.

'He's quite crazy, you know. Giuseppe.'

'Giuseppe?'

Now, at last, Laila did laugh.

'Half the men in Italy are called Joseph. Especially in Sicily. And the women are all Mary, just in case they should give birth to miraculous Baby Jesuses! Or else Anna, she of the Immaculate Conception, as decreed by the infallible Il Papa Pius the Ninth from 1870 onwards.'

Zuleikha laughed, then stopped.

As they had driven away from the vicarage, and as Laila's figure had receded into the distance, Alex began to question Zuleikha about why she had told Laila what was going on, and exactly how much she had told her. Zulie shrugged, and replied that this kind of thing was exactly what made women different from men: they talked to one another about everything. But even she didn't really buy it. She knew that she had confided in Laila because of the grass, yes – and the weirdly physical dream she'd had (though now, once again, she found herself unable to decide whether or not it had been a dream – mermaids, fuck!) but mainly because there, in the middle of the night, in the middle of nowhere, she'd felt the need to confess. Alex had been about to take issue with Zuleikha's partial explanation when they heard a noise that sounded like a scream: a long high-pitched scream that seemed to possess some kind of direction, a disturbed melody which coruscated with the light that was coming through the leaves – the leaves which, by rights, by nature, science and all the normative absolutes of the past three hundred-plus years, absolutely should not have been there at this time of year. They figured that it must have been birdsong, though as they drove through the woods it was never repeated.

They wouldn't have been able to see, through the studio skylight, a naked figure lying flat on the wooden floorboards, gazing at the heavens. Her pupils were tinier than the heads of pins and her mouth was opened wide, its dark rugosity mirroring the colour of the lake of paint in which she lay as though in a mess of blood. Lying on its side, close to her left hand, was an emptied goblet shaped like a skull. They would not have been able to have seen that, as the Lindu night came down and fastened its grip on the land, the woman began to roll from side to side on the enormous canvas, to roll and howl a strange obsolete song, a guttural ejaculation from the isola bellies of those who swung and heaved giant nets into the swaying sea. And they were unable to see that her face was turning slowly black, her eyes silver. They did not see the woman of the night who was in contact with the dead. But now, lying in the double bed in the Palermitan hotel, Zuleikha fell into a fitful sleep punctuated by the raucous sound of men shouting at one another in Sicilian, by the never-ending yet arrhythmic traffic noise, and by the image of Laila Sciacca Asunsi, dancing barefoot as she moved through the etiolated light of her studio that lay next to the sky, scoring her thick parchment canvases with a cutting tool that resembled a ceremonial dagger. Zuleikha was unable to make out, in the dream, exactly what it was Laila was painting – but then she realised that this was because she was trying not to look at the easel. Every time she plucked up the courage to look, some or other sound from out in the street woke her up and, as a consequence, it became increasingly difficult to recapture the essence of the dream. Finally she gave up, and Lincolnshire and Palermo both faded away.

In the morning after breakfast they went for a walk. It was just about coming into spring here, though the storm of the day before had failed to clear the dank smog which hovered over the city. Zuleikha found herself coughing, at times uncontrollably, from the fumes. She wondered whether people here ripped the filters off their exhausts – or maybe added something on – to make them noisier. Not that she would have dared to take up the wheel herself in this fucking crazy traffic. Nonetheless, coming from the dear green place to this manifest part of Magna Graecia, the temperature had jumped around twenty degrees. It had that feel of a world lived out of doors which hits you as soon as you've crossed the great marcher sea, the glistening ribbon of water known as the English Channel. Rising steeply to the south was the wall of mountains she had seen the evening before, though now in the changed light she saw that their lower slopes were covered in green. Even down here in the metropolis, through the heavily salted air, there was the aroma of almond blossom, and beneath and within that, the more delicate scent of campion.

They'd arranged to meet Laila's cousin Peppe in a café which, according to his directions and their street-map, lay between the quarters of Albergheria and La Kalsa. His English had seemed good over the phone, though Alexander had found him difficult to understand because of his thick accent – which was very different, Alex thought, from the way northern Italians enunciated the language. But he'd passed the phone over to Zuleikha, and she'd found it a little easier – because, as she'd explained afterwards, if you're used to hearing multiple languages and accents, your ear acquires flexibility – so that even if you're not technically multilingual, you still have a certain polyglottal flexibility. Besides, she'd gone on, the longer you stay in a place surrounded by a particular range of noises, the better you get at managing to decipher which was which.

Not that they were planning to stay here long. Their funds were far from limitless, and both felt a heavy sense of guilt at using their respective closest (deceased) relative's life-insurance money in this way. Alexander felt almost as though he really was committing adultery, but money tended to concentrate the mind – or perhaps it was just that it brought out the worst in people, even dead people. Zuleikha too felt as though she was betraying Nasrin Zeinab's memory in some way, though at least she wasn't spending it on booze and nasturtium bulbs, the way her father was doing. And beneath his wife's very eyes, right under her ghostly nose! Well, Zuleikha thought, he'd done it all while she was alive, so what was there to stop him now that she was ... She still found difficulty saying the word to herself, though she'd said it to other people often enough. Fuck it, she was a woman of science, of the scientific method, of method – not madness. Bodies on metal tables, heads in pots. The sum total.

Yet, for both Alexander and Zuleikha, seamed through the guilt was the realisation (brought on by the events in Lincolnshire) that what they had experienced was most likely to have been some aspect of Jungian consciousness – though she'd known even as she'd said it that really she was spouting a lot of crap and that neither she nor Alex – nor perhaps even Jung – had any explanation at all for what was happening. Bluntly, they were in it together; the box was the only reason she and Alexander had met and become totally involved, fallen in love – yes, whatever word you used, however you said it, there it was. And now somehow it had carried them all the way to this triangular island, to the place of Europe's last swinging kick. Yes, on the map it looked as though Europe in general, and Italy in particular, was aiming to boot Sicily halfway to Brazil. But did that mean then that Scotland was Europe's brain?

Secondly, whatever the box meant or didn't mean and whatever it contained or didn't contain, and whyever it existed, it was going to alter the course of their lives – indeed it had already done so – and in the whole scheme of things (if there was one) they really had little choice but to try and pursue this as far as it went. At least, that was how they rationalised it. As soon as they set foot amidst the shambolic phenomenality of Palermo, however, rationalism once again flew out of the window. Zuleikha had a smattering of Urdu and a little French, both rather impoverished now, but nothing that would be any good here. She'd been to Florence once on a long weekend with a previous boyfriend. Acquaintance. Whatever.

Palermo was an intriguing city, if in places dirty. Though, being from Glasgow, Zuleikha thought, really I shouldn't be so prissy. It was a metropolis of around one million people, and seemed to have fallen together with little regard for any guiding architectural principle, so that it was almost the polar opposite of somewhere like Siena. She was forced to the comparison through ignorance, she knew. It was like comparing, say (to be completely ridiculous) Barrhead with Cheltenham. Yet there was something energetic about the place, with its nutcase traffic, its clothed balconies, its angular date palms and swaying eucalyptus trees, and its Mediaeval monuments that lately had been requisitioned by entire extended families of squatters – some of whom, no doubt, were illegal immigrants from as far south as Niger and as far east as Pakistan. As they'd say, welcome to Sicily! A saluta nostra! Long life! Sicilia Zindabad!

But the comparisons were spurious, and in fact the centre of Palermo really seemed very prosperous indeed, not unlike that of any other twenty-first century European city. No dark-eyed men with twitching moustaches and Kalashnikov violin cases, only Alex with his lute. He'd left the instrument in their hotel-room, along with the box.

It seemed to Zuleikha that almost everyone in Palermo smoked, though since the ban they all did it outside. So whenever she sat on a bench, the person sitting next to her would immediately light up, and the breeze invariably would blow in her direction so that in the space of half an hour she would reek of tobacco. But it wasn't like in Scotland, where folk hung around doorways in the most inclement of weathers, shoulders hunched like junkies, beggars, prostitutes or paranoid schizophrenics, guiltily cadging a puff or two of Raleigh's deadly weed.

As each lid had been opened, the smell which the box gave out seemed to have become steadily stronger. It was a not-unpleasant scent of mixed woods – presumably, she thought, of the woods from which the box had been made. The pictures on its sides and on the lids had become more defined, and it was clear that they had been etched in lighter finer wood than the main body of the box. Now, as they placed it in the cupboard in their hotel room, even when the cupboard doors were closed the scent was still evident. In fact, when they closed the windows and door of the room, the odour became quite noxious. Zuleikha hoped that the hotel staff would just assume it was coming from a designer deodorant bottle.

It was raining, though there was only a light breeze; to Zuleikha and Alexander, compared with Glasgow rain, this Mediterranean squall was as nothing. They'd arrived on a Tuesday and Peppe had not been able to meet them till the Friday. They spent three days wandering around carrying paper bags and munching cannoli and calia e semenza, though with Zuleikha's dreadful sense of direction, more often than not they'd got completely lost. But she'd decided that she liked the place: she liked its disorder, even the grating sounds of its souped-up scooters and its nocturnal howling dog orchestras did not, in the end, irritate her as much as she'd thought they would.

She'd always thought that western Europeans tended to go on a little too much about how poor their less affluent areas were, as though in some twisted attempt at contrition or penance or maybe to avoid the guilt of having ripped off, and continuing to rip off, the economic south. This place had come a long way in the past forty years; you could see it in the buildings and in the people – who, as elsewhere in Italy, were able to fit into perfectly-tailored clothes, the material and cuts of which you simply couldn't get anywhere else on the planet – at least, not at semi-sane prices. Even the priests, cops and traffic wardens had super-duper outfits. Fashionable bars abounded, and even though often they were sited in old buildings, many of them seemed to have been opened quite recently. In Pakistan, for example, to be poor meant that you were likely to die before the age of five and that your life would be wholly without succour. Fifty or sixty years ago in Sicily it had been not entirely dissimilar, and the post-War boom times had arrived on the island only during the 1960s and 70s. Nonetheless,

Zuleikha had awareness enough of the relative deprivation within Glasgow to understand that such things were complex. Here, at least, she thought, I've not seen any beggars. In the UK, you fall over them – literally – they're in every single town, outside every bloody supermarket and railway station and hovering around every cash-point. Thirty years ago, she thought, you never used to see beggars in Britain. They appeared during the 1980s. However, in the newer parts of Palermo, there was a great deal of building work going on. Cranes everywhere. And, as with Glasgow, someone somewhere was making a pile, for making a pile.

Yet in the city centre, obvious neglect and stylish affluence coexisted. Enormous areas had been bombed out and then not rebuilt; like the hulls of stone Marie-Celestes, the sides of five-storey buildings gaped obscenely, revealing kitchens with pots and pans and guest-rooms adorned with pretty horticultural wallpaper from the 1940s that now mutated into real vegetation. These bomb-sites sat side by side with glittering designer shops, ancient agorae and horrible grey blocks of flats that also seemed to have been plucked from Glasgow, circa 1972. Right, so there was money here, she thought, but it was all lop-sided, so that the city had become a violent – albeit vibrant – hebephrenia of times, places and musics. The parks had been swallowed up by decidedly precarious concrete monstrosities. One gust of wind or a slight earth tremor, she thought... Or maybe this sense was conjured by the traffic, which resembled nothing more than a dodgem circuit on speed. Drivers in enormous four-wheel SUVs would tear up narrow one-way streets, going always in the wrong direction, so that you had to pull yourself into shallow doorways in order to avoid being crushed like a fly against the wall. She wasn't at all surprised that many of the cars, even those that appeared almost new, already had large dents in their bodywork.

As they moved closer to Albergheria, the neglect got steadily worse and suddenly Zuleikha realised that they were walking through a slum of narrow streets, noisy markets, corrugated iron, dirty cloths and overhanging seven-storey structures permeated by the back court smell of rotting fruit that was ubiquitous in hot countries. Would I stroll casually through Possilpark or Dalmarnock, in Glasgow on a wet Friday morning? No, I would not, she thought. So why am I being so naïve here? Because Possilpark and Dalmarnock don't have ancient pink stone palaces, she thought, nor do they resemble some bit of Arabia, with domes, cupolas and arabesque designs and churches that looked more like mosques than most mosques did. Any history in those places in Glasgow had been long erased, or else like so much of Britain had been subsumed into the nauseatingly pious and quite meaningless – and above all, powerless – concept of 'heritage'. *I am highly Baroque. It is my heritage to be a drug-dealer.* In Palermo in the twenty-first century, even the churches were falling down. But then she would come across a perfectly sculpted Arab window or a geometrically harmonious Norman arch and the city's architectonics would assume a benevolent orchestration like, say, that of a Xenakis composition – seemingly disordered, chaotic and maddeningly obfuscatory, yet with a quantum logic that leached through everything.

Even at this time of year, the sun felt hot on her skin. The café was actually a bar and was unmarked, so they had some difficulty finding it, and yet again Zuleikha was glad that Alex had a good sense of direction: without him she would have been completely lost. Peppe was there, sitting at a round table on the terrazzu near the door, sipping dark coffee from a small cup. He looked up at them, smiled, then rose slowly and greeted them with lingering handshakes. Zuleikha recognised him instantly from the portrait in Laila's studio, though he seemed a little older and less gaunt than his facsimile. When some people with very ordinary faces smiled, their skin turned to plasticine and their appearance changed dramatically, demonically – it really would be like something out of a horror film.

And it was a little like this with Peppe now, as he stuck out his hand towards Alex, whom he'd obviously realised was Scottish as soon as he'd walked in. Zuleikha knew that whenever she moved south of a certain line of latitude, say around 45 degrees North, she blended in almost perfectly, so that for the first week or so until the sun had tanned her skin to somewhere beyond the European, the locals took her as one of their own. Until, that is, she opened her mouth. The fact was that even today, in the twenty-first century in all parts of Europe, where no-one ever talked of these things any more, if you were with a white partner – or if they thought that you were white – you were accepted and dealt with in a relaxed, everyday manner by everyone from functionaries to shop assistants to hotel managers. Whereas if you were alone and tanned and/or were in the obviously intimate company of a brown or black partner, an unseen barrier instantly went up – though as with all things liminal, its existence could be perceived only by those on the wrong side of it. Zuleikha had always thought it odd that while, for a mixed-race woman, her face and arms (relatively speaking) were quite dark, her legs and other parts of her body were really rather sickly pale, so that whenever she'd gone swimming she'd thought with some degree of hilarity that she resembled a physical map of the world – the kind of map that had no borders.

After the introductions, small-talk and a light lunch of bread and pecorino cheese, they settled down to cups of coffee. The air was azure with the mixture of sky and cigarette smoke – they were sitting just outside the café, in a place where smoking was only just legal, and Peppe too lit up and began to puff away, sending symmetrical rings of blue smoke up towards the yellowed canopy. Zuleikha was no longer used to smoky dives, since in Scotland for some years smoking indoors in public places had been outlawed and again she made a mental note that her clothes would need to be washed. I gave up only a couple of months ago and already I'm thinking like a convert, she thought. Peppe was in his mid-forties, with lines etched moderately deeply into his skin and a sleek of thinning, greying hair growing backwards and outwards over his ears as though once it had been accustomed to being worn long. Yet his facial expressions and the lithe movements of his trim body belied his age. There was a subtlety about the manner in which he held and expressed himself, as though every muscle of his face was attuned to a separate note, as though each were illumined by its own peculiar scattering of light. He was clad in a dark, casual suit. Everyone here seemed to dress up all the time, she thought. Or maybe it was just that the clothes fit better. To Zuleikha, clothes in Britain had tended always to cast the wrong kind of shadow.

'Laila said that you were coming here on a kind of holiday.'

'That's right,' Zuleikha answered, with perhaps a little too much alacrity. What did he mean, "a kind of holiday"? What had Laila told him?

'So what's the connection?' he asked.

'Connection?'

'With Laila.'

Alex butted in.

'We're pals of hers. Friends, I mean.'

'Friends? How long have you known her?'

Zuleikha was beginning to sweat.

'Actually, we're undertaking some research of a musical nature. Alexander here is a musician.'

Peppe rubbed his hands together.

'Ah! Which instrument do you play?'

Alex and Zulie glanced at each other and they knew immediately that Peppe had picked up on this glance.

'The lute.'

'Right...'

The devilish smile again. 'Professional?'

Alex shook his head.

'No, it's just a hobby,' he lied. 'Anyway, there's no money in it. Guitar would be more lucrative. Lutenists all over the world are junking their tools.' He spread his hands. 'After all, who wants to play an instrument of sixteenth-century melancholic romance? Tights and bone-frills, a peculiar fetish.'

But Peppe didn't seem to get the joke.

'You must let me hear some of your music. Have you brought the liuto with you?'

'Of course,' said Alex, but Zuleikha had already cut in.

'Signor Ayala...'

'Peppe, please. Everybody calls me Peppe.'

Zuleikha smiled nervously. A light rain had begun to spatter the canopy.

'Peppe, we would very much like to see your ... I mean, the village you and Laila were – are – from.'

'Laila was not from any village in Sicily. She is English, you know – just like you two.'

'We're Scottish...' Alex broke in, but Peppe either ignored him or else hadn't heard.

'Her father may have been Sicilian, but he left the island as a young boy and became a sailor. Did you know that one million Sicilians left here? My father was the eldest, so he got to stay and work the fields. They were contadini – peasants.'

'We're Scottish, actually, not English,' Alexander repeated, his accent suddenly becoming broader. Zuleikha knew that Peppe was not likely to have noticed the change, any more than she, had she been fluent in Italian, would have been able to recognise the various accents of the mandamenti of Palermo.

'Where you're from is not necessarily where your family is from. The world has changed.' They fell silent. Zuleikha lifted her cup, but it was empty. 'More coffee?' Peppe asked.

She shook her head, ever so slightly. God, did this man miss anything? It was beginning to feel intrusive – this place, his attitude – and she was beginning to regret even coming here. Suddenly a flock of children burst in. They rushed up to Peppe, smothering him with hugs and kisses, and the youngest one leapt into his lap. Peppe's son resembled him in the structure of his features, but the boy had bright blue eyes. It was a little odd, seeing Peppe smile that way at the boy, who can't have been much more than four years old; but then she supposed that the boy would be used to it. His father's smile. Perhaps, when he grows up, he too will smile like a demon. All these guys – how odd it is that their sense of humour can transform them into another animal. Behind the boy was a girl who looked to be around seven years old and a woman in her early forties. It turned out that they were the only children in the café, but children always seemed more than they were.

'My wife, Zita. And this,' he said, patting the head of the boy sitting in his lap, 'is Giuseppinu, who was four last month.'

'And I am Nilla Dacia,' added the girl, who looked quite different from her brother: she had brown eyes and black hair which fell over her ears in a girlish version of Beatles circa *Rubber Soul*. 'And I am exactly eight years old,' the miniature female version of George Harrison added.

Everyone laughed at the girl's scholastic interjection, though Zuleikha was more marvelling at the fact that already she had such good English. Zita was bottle-blonde; Zuleikha could see that her roots were black and that though her eyes were small, they had that gleam of intelligence which was instantly engaging. She had a face which Zuleikha thought most men would find intensely attractive. In fact, as they talked, Zulie found her attractive. She tended to smile a lot, and her gaiety did not seem forced. She had laugh-lines around her eyes and that, Zulie said to herself, is always a good sign, isn't it? Her skin, albeit to some extent desiccated by smoking – and from the state of her fingernails and the pitch of her voice, Zuleikha had known instantly that she was a smoker – was fairer than that of her husband, though the contrast was not as great as that between their two children. In spite of repeated dyeing, her hair remained thick and silky, though today she'd bound it back behind her head. Before they'd come out to Sicily, Zulie had had hers done in a kind of perm streaked with light brown and Alex had said that he'd loved it. She'd thought that perhaps he'd been sincere about that. He must have been sincere because, for the first time since they'd met, he'd made love to her in Susan's bed. She'd felt slightly freaked out by it, but had said nothing to Alex. Perhaps she should have. But no, she'd thought: if he feels comfortable with it, then so do I.

He'd altered very little in the house since his wife had died. And there had been a lingering scent. She hadn't dared open any wardrobes. It had been none of her business anyway. There had been a photograph of Alexander and Susan on the mantlepiece. Susan had been blonde too – though her blondeness clearly had been natural. She was thin-boned, sort of flighty-looking, clearly neurotic, Zuleikha had thought, then had felt guilty again. Yes, neurotic, she thought. Or a Roman Catholic.

And Zita seemed to have many of the qualities that Zuleikha had attributed to Susan, except that she didn't seem at all neurotic. She had big hands with long fingers, and Zuleikha could tell that while usually she kept the nails polished and well-manicured, today the gleam had fragmented a little and so the yellow tobacco stains were showing though. While not anorexic, her body was slim, the curves just right – and after two kids, too – in that lithe, southern European way. Unlike many Scottish women, her butt didn't hang limply at her back. Lucky Peppe! she thought. Zita didn't light up on the terrazzu of the bar, though, and Zuleikha thought that perhaps this was because her kids were around, yet she made no attempt to stop her husband from doing so – repeatedly. She would have had a perfect telephone voice. The fingertips were calloused from typing and housework, and there were hints of tar and detergent around the joints. Tell-tale signs. A working mother. Zuleikha hated that phrase; it made it seem as though mothers who didn't have jobs outside the house were not really working. There was operative nowadays, she thought, a kind of reverse discrimination: a form of female machismo, where a woman who had paid employment would look down on one who stayed at home, looking after God-knows how many kids, elderly parents or whatever. We do that to one another, she thought: we weave spiders' webs around one another's throats. Then we hand the silver rope to the men and tell them to tie us up too.

Mother and children had a somewhat messy lunch of many little things dominated by the scent of provola cheese and the crunching, gulping sounds of garbanzo beans and limoncellos rapidly being consumed. During all this Zuleikha and Alex learned that while Peppe's family still owned a small area of land near the village of San Giuseppe ru Casteddu Nivuru, they rarely stayed at the old massaria nowadays, returning only for weekend breaks or when they needed to get away from the grime and dust of the city where Peppe worked as a restorer and archeologist.

'He brings things back to life,' Zita informed them.

'While I try and stop them from dying,' Zuleikha countered jovially, then she thought of Archie, lying in his bed, the sheets turning slowly to sack, the creases writhing and twisting like worms through the white cotton.

'Then perhaps he could bring me back to life,' Alex joked.

Peppe joined in the laughter, but immediately afterwards added, 'There were other things I used to do, but those are gone now.'

He did not elaborate, and Alex did not pursue it, but he had noticed the look which Zita had given her husband. Meanwhile, Zuleikha pushed the image of Archie out of her mind; sent it flying across the tricornuate island all the way to the main caldera of the volcano. Peppe's job, working on churches, palaces and a whole range of old buildings, took him all over Sicily, supervising the discovery and restoration of friezes, mosaics, stone, plasterwork and all manner of miscellaneous materials. Zita, on the other hand, worked in what seemed like a fairly lowly post in administration, here in the Ospedale Civico e Benfratelli, a prominent institution in Palermo.

Right now, Giuseppe was working on a church in La Kalsa, which was the reason he'd arranged to meet them here. Just as well, Zuleikha thought, because parts of the area looked like a slum, and though this place they were in wasn't really a dive, it wasn't particularly stylish either. Though on reflection maybe that was a good thing. The work in La Kalsa was almost finished; just another few weeks and he would be ready to move onto something else. The family lived for most of the year in a modern flat in a northern suburb, where Nilla went to school, but their roots were rural.

'I try to persuade Peppe to shift to a proper house, with a garden – for the children.'

'I like flats. They're easier to maintain,' he retorted. 'Anyway, gardening, farms...'

'Yeah, you leave all that to me,' Zita retorted, and Peppe shrugged.

'You're an artistic family,' Alex commented, 'with Laila and her paintings and you, Peppe, with your work.'

But Giuseppinu was acting up, marching around the bar inside and out, so that his father had to cajole him into sitting in one place and remaining there long enough to begin to finish his cuscusu. Zita smiled at Zuleikha.

'They make you old before your time! Do you have any?'

Zuleikha shook her head, her own smile plastered across her face. She wondered how old she would be when it came time for her to die. This scene of domesticity made her feel that she had missed out in her life, and then she thought that they would have terrible rows, wouldn't they, and right now because we're strangers they are putting on a good face and trying to control the kids without shouting at them in an overt way, but really at home or if they were on their own wandering through some shopping-mall, they would be raging maniacally and tearing one another's hair out at every turn. *Raising children engenders love.* Yeah, right. Still, it was a life. But raising dead kids engendered nothing at all. And what did she have that was so wonderful? Alexander? Okay, a good man. But what about after this box thing was over? What then? In fact, what really did they have in common, Alex and she, other than their musical box romance? You couldn't live a life based on that. That was only for songs and fantasies. Life was based on messy lunchtimes and screaming blue murder, on planting apple trees and watching them grow apples. And then eating the fuckers, forcing your teeth down through the substance of the earth. Like Daniel John, like Nasrin Zeinab, like Peppe and Zita, life was feeling a sense of connection with ... something, someone, the land, maybe. Anything.

'This weekend we've arranged to take you to San Giuseppe,' Peppe announced. 'Laila said you were interested in seeing the countryside...'

Is that what she'd told them? Well, okay.

'That's very kind,' Alex said.

Peppe waved him off.

'I need to clean out the old house, the barn...' Peppe and his wife exchanged a glance. Zuleikha noticed a rhythmic sound from above. The rain was coming down harder than before. 'The spring here begins very quickly. All of a sudden, everything starts to grow faster than you can deal with it.'

'Anyway,' Zita added, 'it's La Festa di San Giuseppe. Big processions! Zeppoli! Great fun!'

'Great fun!' both children repeated, as though they were in a family comedy routine.

'But you'll miss that,' Peppe corrected. 'It's two weeks away.'

There was a pause.

'I have a map,' Alex began, and he removed the pieces of paper which Laila had joined together and spread them on the table, careful to avoid any risk of staining, and careful too to keep it out of reach of the four-year-old. 'Laila told us that it was a plan of your...'

'How did you get this?' Peppe broke in.

'I ... I found it.'

'Found it? Where? Did Laila give it to you?' Suddenly there were no more smiles.

'No. She told me it was a plan of your farm.' Alex began to regret showing it to them. Peppe inspected the map carefully.

'No, not the farm as it is today, but the farm as it was when my great-great-grandfather acquired it during the Risorgimento.

The area then was much larger and there have been many changes since that time. But I recognised it immediately. There is only one other copy and that's in the Archivio di Stato. How could you have come by this? I don't understand.'

Alex was blushing. He looked at Zuleikha as though pleading for help.

'It's ... we've ... come a long way ...' he flustered.

Zita was looking down at the floor. Zuleikha took up the baton.

'Alex lost his wife last year. An accident.'

'That's terrible,' Zita exclaimed.

Now Alex was looking down.

'And I ... anyway, you'll think we're mad.' Zuleikha plodded on regardless. She glanced around for support, but found none. Peppe was staring at her. His expression was like granite.

'I'm very sorry about your wife,' he said quietly to Alex.

The sky was falling down; there would be floods.

'Would you like a drink?' Zita asked, leaping to her feet.

'You don't need to get up, there's a waiter,' Peppe said calmly without removing his gaze from Zuleikha's face. There had been a change in the tectonic. Zulie realised that suddenly the terrazzu had fallen silent – well, not exactly silent, she thought: it's just that everyone has one ear on what we're saying, though they're pretending otherwise.

'Umn, I'll have a glass of red wine, please,' Alex blurted out, as though he hadn't heard what Peppe had said. 'Look,' he went on, 'can we talk about this somewhere else? I mean, maybe if we go up there ...'

'No.' Peppe brought his index finger down onto the map and his eyes flashed for a moment. Then he seemed to relax. 'Listen,' he said, removing his hand from the table. 'It's fine. Laila has asked us to help you and to take you to San Giuseppe ru Casteddu Nivuru and we're very happy to do that. But we need to know why. I mean, I thought you were just tourists, you know, visiting.'

'Alex plays the lute ...' Zuleikha began.

'The flute!' Peppe exclaimed.

'No, the lute. Remember, we said – before?'

'I play the flute,' Zita interjected and she laughed, a high-pitched artificial laugh.

'Really,' Alex said, with a desperate inflection towards the end of the first vowel syllable that made it sound as though he was really interested.

The waiter had arrived. They ordered the wine and then Peppe called him back and asked for a glass of cognac.

'And while searching in an old archive in Lincoln, in the east of England, we found this map.' Zuleikha held up the piece of paper and waggled it about as though to demonstrate its inconsequential nature. 'What you see is a reproduction – obviously they wouldn't let us take the original.'

'I see,' Peppe murmured.

'We have no idea what the link is between the Lincoln archive and here, but we think that it may have something to do with the Church. I mean, that was the common factor in the Middle Ages ... right?'

Alex was watching her, almost open-mouthed.

Zulie was on a roll now. She must always have been a good liar, he thought.

'And we think it was an amazing coincidence that we met your cousin. Your uncle – her father – was a sailor, right?'

Peppe nodded, slowly.

'So we think that maybe, somehow, he brought it to England when he emigrated and that eventually it found its way into the archive there.'

Peppe spread his hands. The skin was hard and dirt had whorled its way into the tissues. He looked up and raised an eyebrow.

'So what's the importance? I mean, it's just a poor old farm.'

The kids seemed to re-animate at this and began to fight over a piece of bread. Their mother separated them and placed them both back in their respective chairs where they sat like semi-active volcanoes.

'We don't know,' Zuleikha replied. 'Really, it was just an idea of Laila's, us coming here. She was keen for us to meet you and see the place and we're very grateful...' Alex was nodding vigorously and she wished he'd stop '... very grateful indeed for your kind hospitality.'

Zita was resting her chin on both hands.

'We could have a duet,' she said, looking at Alex.

'What a good idea,' Zulie said, also looking at Alex.

Peppe was staring at her again, as though attempting to apportion her truth and meaning. She did not allow her gaze to wander in the slightest. She felt sweaty in spite of the chill, though she knew that her hair, at least, had remained immaculate.

The refreshments arrived, including a big jug of orange juice for the kids. At last, Peppe seemed properly to relax and he poured drinks all round. He raised his glass.

'A saluta nostra!' And then Peppe explained that when his family had migrated from the countryside during his grandfather's generation, they had moved initially to the part of Palermo called La Kalsa. 'Palermo has always been a bit shabby,' he said, 'but to be honest, I like it. There's no pretension.'

'Yes, but it would be good if just occasionally some of the money went to the right places,' Zita corrected him as she stood up to get the children sorted.

'I know that. But that's not all there is. People have these ideas about this place.' He wheeled his arm around the terrazzu, which was about a quarter-full. Zuleikha wasn't sure whether he was referring to the bar, La Kalsa, Palermo or Sicily in general and then she thought that perhaps it was all four.

'He gets quite worked-up,' Zita began.

'It's not that I get worked-up, it's that when there's a problem, there's a problem.'

Zita did not answer.

'Corruption, you mean?' Zuleikha ventured, somewhat tentatively.

Peppe laughed. Three cell-phone jingles went off simultaneously, two of them from the belt of a single individual – a young man with greased spiky hair. He reminded Zuleikha of some of the Asian kids she'd known in Glasgow who'd ended up rotting their brains through the excessive use of mobile telephones. At the time, she remembered, it had seemed like a pathetic kind of freedom – though, granted, she had never faced the unremitting suffocating pressures of the baratherie, the honour-and-shame-fixated extended family network which in those days had acted as the vehicle by which South Asian communities had attempted to transpose the imagined life and codes of their villages onto a postmodern cityscape in a cold country. Yet Sicily was not a poor country, and though nowadays down here there were more immigrants doing the crappy black-market jobs than there had been in the past, Sicilian youth too seemed almost to have been fitted at birth with a superheated microchip that would predispose them to portable gadgetry.

'This bar will be paying money to avoid being burned down. Most of the businesses in this great and tranquil city of ours will be paying pizzo. I tried to fight it when I was younger. It's not the only thing about this island, you need to understand that. All the films about Sicily – at least, the ones made in America – they're only about that and nothing else. They're all rubbish!'

Zita placed her hand on her husband's shoulder. While they'd been gathering up the kids Zuleikha had estimated that Peppe was around five foot-eight, his wife perhaps two inches shorter, which meant that Zita and Zuleikha were more or less the same height. She thought there was a nice symmetry in that.

Zuleikha interjected, 'There's corruption in Britain too, you know. It's just more hidden there. It doesn't tend to form part of daily life. But it flows through the darkness like the kanats of Palermo, it's never talked about, never acknowledged and it resides in the class system. The world of commerce is largely rotten.'

'Kanats?' Alex asked.

'Yeah. Underground watercourses. I read about them on the plane. Aircraft. Boeing 737.'

'Oh,' Alex said, looking disinterested.

Peppe's cheeks had turned redder as he had gone on with the subject. He was obviously trying to control himself.

'Yes, well here it does affect daily life. Even in the villages … especially in the villages. Bustarelle. Progettisti. Consulting fees.'

Alexander laughed.

'Oh, that happens in Glasgow, too, believe me. All the time.'

Zuleikha broke in.

'Yes, but unless we're talking some national military secret, if you stand up and say so, over there the worst that can happen is that you're ignored, shunned, blacklisted, made a laughing-stock. The local council or whoever is unlikely to get some hood to visit you at home and shoot you.'

'Unless you're a microbiologist,' Alex interjected.

There was a pause.

'You can't do it alone,' Peppe retorted. 'You need an army – or at least, a mass movement.'

Zita nodded and Peppe turned and looked up at her and their eyes locked.

'It's history,' said Zita softly. 'Everything is history.' Then she glanced around at the others. She took Peppe's hand in hers and said 'It's important, isn't it, never to be alone.'

Later, in the hotel as they packed, Alexander turned to Zuleikha and asked,

'Did you tell Laila the same thing?'

'No. I told her about the box.'

'How d'you know she won't tell Peppe about that, too?'

Zuleikha shrugged.

'I felt I could trust her with a secret.'

'You hardly know her.'

'Look, it'll be all right.'

Alex watched her fold her clothes neatly into the case. He wondered what kinds of feelings she really had about him, and whether they might be changing now. He didn't think he would be able to take that, if word and emotion became dissociated, or if she was playing some kind of game with him. He hadn't been lying, and up till now he had assumed that she hadn't either. But he had seen her dissemble, apparently successfully, in the bar, and now wondered whether perhaps mendacity was a habit that came easily to her. And in any case, relationships were more complex than that: they were like the bloody British weather. Here in Sicily when it rained the clouds burst, and Alex worried that the roads to San Giuseppe ru Casteddu Nivuru might be blocked with mudslides. Peppe had told them that while the village lay on fairly high ground and so itself should be immune from cascading water, in the old days, during the winter, the route there would sometimes have been interrupted by rockfalls. But that kind of thing was in the past.

Peppe and Zita's small two-bedroomed flat was in a modern

apartment building on the northern outskirts of Palermo. They had managed to buy it only five years earlier, when they'd moved from an even smaller rented place situated closer to the centre of the city. Property was expensive and most jobs didn't pay enough on their own to be able to get a viable mortgage, so both partners needed to work full-time – and that had childcare implications.

'Without our families, we would not have been able to have bought this place,' Peppe explained, gesturing around the walls, the lower parts of which were covered now in children's scrawls. Every article of potentially breakable furniture or ornament had been removed. In Britain, too, house prices had gone crazy. A million pounds for a postage stamp. But then again, when she thought back to when her own parents had been trying to buy a house, back in the 1970s, it really hadn't been that much easier. Hardly anyone then was giving mortgages and pay had been very low, and as always you'd needed inherited money. While Peppe worked long and sometimes back-breaking hours as a restorer (but at least I love what I do, he'd said) Zita had a job as a secretary, even though she knew that there would be little chance of advancement, say, to Consulente per la gestione delle risorse umane. Because it was like everything: you needed to go on courses, and to get onto the course you needed to know the right people, otherwise who would put your name forward, give you recommendations? And if you had money, you could pay for that – but then, she'd said, if you had money, you wouldn't be doing this job in the first place, and you would not be the one needing the raccomandazioni, you would be the one giving them!

And Alex was saying that in Britain, the levers of inequality were hard-wired into the system – there wasn't overt corruption or conspiracy in everyday life, because there didn't need to be. Public school, Oxbridge, the class system, the security state, all ensured that in the main, the people who got the jobs with power were on 'our' side.

'But at least there are some checks and balances,' Peppe retorted, 'whereas here, in Sicily,' he went on, 'if you're not favoured, you have absolutely no chance. Why d'you think so many Sicilians still leave for other parts of Italy – the north, mainly – or for other countries in Europe? In the past, it was absolute poverty that drove them away. Now it's unemployment and this cancerous corruption which is not a deformation of the system, it is the system. We are dealing with a medina mentality,' he said, pointing to his right temple as though he were a Renaissance philosopher.

Zuleikha winced at this, yet felt compelled to smile and then was angry at herself. Every so often, continentals would come out with some overtly racist remark and would remain totally unconscious of it. It happened less often in Britain; people in general had become more aware of sensitivities – sometimes superficially and painfully so. But that tended to put one off one's guard, and just occasionally, there too she would feel the sudden shock of disappointment at some comment indicating an underlying global view with whose parameters she did not feel in any sort of alignment. Gradually she had learned to forgive, though try as she might, she'd found it difficult to forget.

He probably thought he was being clever saying that. A medina mentality meant an Arab mentality, and the use of such a phrase suggested that being an Arab was synonymous with being corrupt, duplicitous, untrustworthy, lacking in moral fibre and incorrigibly psychologically backward. The word medina meant simply the centre of a town. Palermo's centre was a medina, since it had once been an Arab city, Bal'harm. In fact, Zuleikha had read that in those days, Palermo had been known as simply Al-madina: the City. La Kalsa, Al-Aziz, Piazzetta Garraffo, Seralcadio, Lattarini … there were so many Arabo-Muslim names for neighbourhoods, for rock and stone and glass, for rivers, mountains, fields, food. And yet here was Giuseppe – Yusuf – who spent his waking hours bringing back to life architecture from the past, including Arab and Normano-Arab architecture – sleepwalking into using such a phrase as a medina mentality. And his smiling wife, who was still smiling at Zuleikha, also was apparently unconscious of any slight that might have been given to her guest. And here was Zuleikha, inured to colluding in the casual bourgeois racism of Europe, once again complicit, indulgent, defeated, crushed, just like the contemporary Arabs, the Muslims, who couldn't even stop any old hick from the militarised economic North invading and destroying their countries – acts which were possible partly because of a conflated metaphysics of historical and political denial.

The children were playing noisily in the background. The children, with their Arab-Jewish-Muslim blood, with a past replete with possibility secreted somewhere in the cells of their brains, in the chords of their souls. Alexander was looking at her. He at least was not smiling. Slowly, she took a deep breath. The city smelled of fruit and fuel.

'Yes, but…' she began, aware that her heart was beating slightly more rapidly than before. 'Yes, but isn't oppression the reason? I mean, centuries of feudalism and all that. I mean, when the Arabs were here, it was a thriving and modern state. Modern for the time, I mean. Surely, it's not so much the medina as the latifondo.'

There was a pause. As though sensing the sudden change in atmosphere, even the children seemed to have quietened down for a moment. The hint of a smile hovered around Alexander's face. Peppe nodded, slowly, in acknowledgment.

'You're quite right,' he said.

And he started on that subject with as much alacrity as before. Although she agreed with much of what he was saying – after all, he knew every contour of this place, it had been embedded beneath his nails and had been scrubbed into the toughened skin of the palms of his hands – Zuleikha found herself wishing that just occasionally he would allow his wife to break in. Surely, she thought, Zita must have something interesting to say – about her job, her colleagues, her children, her daughter's school, the history and politics of this large island, or just about life in general. Peppe was the big revolutionary for whom the revolution had never happened. And instead of going towards either drugs and mysticism or extreme politics as others in the great generational riflusso had done, he had immersed himself in reclaiming – or at least preserving – the physical manifestations of the past. *He who controls the past…* But really, Peppe must have known that he had no chance of controlling anything, and he tended to over-compensate for this sense of societal impotence by dominating his household.

Peppe was part of the reflux from the Long-1960s, a period that had existed as much in people's minds as on a clock-face, but which roughly might be calibrated as spanning the quarter-century from 1955 to 1980. In Britain, the 1980s had been a time of intense rearguard action, while the time thereafter had spelled definitive defeat – at least on this turn of the socio-political wheel. But Italy had been different. Zuleikha had understood the dynamic within minutes. She'd seen it often enough in the west of Scotland, that deep valley of bitterness and failed revolutions – but not, perhaps, of riflusso. Mind you, she thought, trying to start a political movement here in Sicily would be suicidal, and some of Peppe's friends from his youth had paid the price of standing up to the Mafia, the cosy Cosa Nostra political establishment and the corporations. Some of them, he said, had been beaten to death on deserted roads, beaten so badly that it had been as though they had been accosted by leopards, while others had been kidnapped and thrown off volcanic escarpments into one of the many gaping orifices of Etna and still others had simply disappeared. Lupara bianca. White guns, packed with wolf shot. No traces.

His story made Alexander and Zuleikha's journey look like self-indulgence, while the incandescence of his demeanour made her feel like a pallid herbal tea-sipping northerner. But at least we're not harming anyone, she thought. Though even the fact that we are able to do this, to globe-trot in this way, is surely premised on a whole load of societal and economic pre-requisites. And then immediately she thought of Archibald McPherson and Susan Wolfe. But, she corrected herself, Archie wasn't dead yet. How could she have imagined that he was? Her sense of guilt and betrayal – would there be no end to it? And for some reason she remembered her mother's Chehilum. The forty days of remembrance and spirituality following a person's death. Seemingly ever-present family and friends, a constant flow of milky tea and Quranic ayats. Yet during that time, for once in her life, Zuleikha had not felt suffocated or restricted in any way by the hustle and bustle, the prayers and liberally offered condolences. The Scottish side of her family had been personable and warm on the day of the funeral, but the Asian branch had formed themselves into a corral around Zulie and her father for six whole weeks, bringing food and beverage, yes, and sympathy and clichés. Like the white coffins reserved for children, clichés were mental rituals which assured us that there was some order in the physical universe of random disposition. This had happened after her son's death too, though outside of the terrible carnality of her son's body, she hardly remembered the details of that time – she had been so completely out of it.

She really felt for Alex – who, she suspected, wouldn't have had that kind of support following Susan's passing. But then, he'd had her. Or rather, he'd found her. She found herself sizing up Alexander's body, as though she suddenly had become aware of his presence in the room. It was like that. Love. It was a physical thing, and not just in the sense of the congress they'd enjoyed in the thin-walled hotel room the night before and all that went with it. Zuleikha knew that even after the passion had cooled, love would still be capable of disarming her in this way. A volcanic sense of joy, possessiveness and relief at having Alexander surged through her belly and chest, so that she felt as though she wanted to sing. But she maintained her composure there, though when Peppe became momentarily distracted by one of the children, she couldn't help giving her lover a mischievous smile. He returned it, a tender, mutual moment, savoured over the rims of their porcelain coffee cups.

Every so often, the young boy would stop his rampaging (boys really were worse, thought Zuleikha, it wasn't just programming) and would gaze up at her with his sea-blue irises, would stare straight into her eyes brazenly as though, like an animal, he was trying to suss her out, determine whether she was friend or foe. She would smile at him and stroke his long flaky chocolate hair and would find herself pursing her lips and mouthing noisy kisses at him, the same kisses with which she would greet friendly cats. Very quickly she realised that in Sicily touching was allowed: one could caress children, sit them on one's knee, even kiss them and not be considered a paedophile. Whereas in Britain, where so many parents – at least in public – seemed not to render physical affection to their children in the unmeasured and immeasurable way Asian people did, you thought twice before even looking at a child, far less smiling at one. Oh, she thought, now I'm stereotyping horrendously. Her own father had always been warm with her. In those days he hadn't needed booze to be companionable. Nonetheless, she supposed that it was worse for men, especially if they were solitary. At one point in her life she'd been quite prepared to be a single parent, and then, for just nine months, she had been one. But she'd never tried again. Life wasn't like climbing Etna. It wasn't like Robert the Bruce sitting in his cave of talking spiders. That was all sport and war, things we did very well. A child was of a different order.

Nilla Dacia was in that phase of middle childhood when children, especially girls, tend to make up imaginary playmates, and where in their perception such wraiths at times can almost come to have more substance than people in the physical world. It was not overt: Nilla did not run around talking to invisible presences – there was too much clutter and noise in her home to have allowed that – but Zuleikha caught a certain soft focus in her eyes, a particular fluidity of movement which seemed instantly familiar to her and which she knew reflected some inner wordless experience that only girls can share. And which for a while, perhaps until the onset of periods or perhaps even for a little while after that, serves as a membrane between them and the world. Though Nilla's hair was black, like her mother's (or what Zuleikha thought her mother's hair would have been like beneath the streaks of grey and the tired years of bottle blondeness) it had a natural reddish tint and flowed like silk down over her shoulders.

Zuleikha had always thought that just as in the womb, over the nine months of human gestation, foetuses passed through the various evolutionary stages of life on earth, so following birth some children as they grew reflected the various historical conjunctions of DNA which had gone before. And so many southern European, Syrian and Iranian children early on looked almost like Pakistani kids, only for their features to change and their skins to stretch and grow paler as they approached adulthood. She'd never seen this written in any book and had never vocalised her hunches either, for fear that they might smack of eugenics, diffusionism, cultural essentialism or long-discredited Aryan invasion theories. Nonetheless, in physical appearance Peppe's children seemed almost like a microcosm of the historical population shifts which, like successive waves of sand rolling onto a beach, over many centuries had come to shape the island. She wondered whether Laila too had been darker as a young child and had etiolated over the decades, finally taking after her English mother rather than her Sicilian father, or whether perhaps she had received the Norman,

Frankish, Langobard or German genes which nestled within the nuclei of so many people's cells in Sicily.

Scotland was such a white place; a person of colour stuck out like a sore thumb. Zuleikha had taken most of her physical genes from her mother, and though the Afghan blood had been fair, the Mughal component had been admixed with pre-existing Indian and so had darkened her commensurately. You just had to look at old photos of the last Mughal Emperor, the sad-eyed poet Bahadur Shah Zafar, whose excellent plaintive Urdu and Persian verses people still recited to this day, to realise that. And Zuleikha had received this deep Indian inheritance of which to some extent she was proud, but which in Scotland at any rate had marked her out forever as non-European, beyond the bounds of the central Asian and trans-Mediterranean tribal diasporas who held sway from the Atlantic coast of Morocco to Khawafi's Attock Fort on the Indus crossing that lay halfway between Peshawar and Islamabad. Funny, how going abroad tended to bring these things into focus.

But now, she thought, I'm the one who's in a reverie! And she realised that Zita was talking to her, asking if she would like some coffee. Alexander too was staring at her, wondering why she was being so rude. Zuleikha nodded quickly, then blushed and smiled apologetically at them both.

Alexander was eagerly telling Peppe all about lutes: their history, the manner in which they had evolved over the millennia from obscure origins in Persia as the barbat or even from the gngnti, nth or nefer of Egypt or else the pantur of Sumeria, through the Arabic oud, which was simply the Arabic word for 'wood', to Europe (via Sicily and Spain). Nefer was the word for beauty, and had been given to the lute because the hieroglyphic of 'beauty' bore a similar shape to the instrument.

'But you know,' Alex continued,' just as the lute in Europe has changed since the Middle Ages, so too has the oud in Middle and Near Eastern countries.'

Peppe seemed interested – after all, she thought, he restores old buildings. And he was telling them that history and archaeology were well-developed in Sicily, and that unlike some disciplines they had strong credible systems.

'We're very good at the past,' he said. 'Though if the developers get hold of anything, they ruin it. Look at what they did to that Greek temple. A disgrace!'

Alex nodded. The rain was battering against the windows and she could hear a wind blowing off the grey surface of the sea. Some things were the same wherever you went.

'The scirocco is fighting with the tramontana,' Peppe explained. The season was changing and soon the weather would begin to warm-up. February was the coldest month, the storm before the calm. Eventually, the Sahara would win. 'You must give us a recital,' Peppe told Alex. 'I will not allow you to stay at my house unless you promise to give us a performance!'

He was joking, but nevertheless Alex agreed that at some point during their projected stay in the massaria he would pick up his lute and begin to play. And the inference was that Zita would accompany him, or at least that both in turn would perform. She had been classically trained, Peppe informed them. Zuleikha was on the point of asking Zita why she hadn't pursued the music, but as the words were about to roll off her tongue she looped them back in. Something told her that she would have crossed an invisible boundary.

Now the coffee was ready, but they couldn't have coffee on its own, not in Zita's home. And Zuleikha cursed herself for forgetting to offer to go and help Zita prepare it. But I did offer, she remembered, though perhaps not forcefully enough. I was supposed to ignore Zita's remonstrations that there was no need for her to help in the kitchen. Silly! she thought. It's not Britain, where to do such a thing might be to infer that a particular woman wasn't competent enough even to rustle up some grub on her own. As with South Asian households, here in Sicily you were expected to say the opposite of what you meant. She would have to re-adjust her social codes again.

As if to compensate for her gaucheness, Zuleikha got up and busied herself handing out plates to the men and babes, though she had enough presence of mind to allow the hostess her prerogative in dispensing the beverage itself as well as the torta and straws, orange juice, etcetera. Zita had brought out far too much food and again, unlike in white British households, where an excess of eagerness might have been taken as a sign of inordinate gluttony and therefore of an essential class or race primitiveness, here one really needed to accept second and third helpings of everything. The coffee was strong, just the way she liked it, and would serve to fire them all up for the raucous circus of taking young children on a journey.

Chapter Twenty-Two

The next morning the weather had changed dramatically and the sun shone unimpeded from a clear blue sky. Whenever they were in its thrall it felt as powerful on their skin as it might during a Scottish summer. A breeze came off the sea, turning the air fresh and salty, and there in the roof of her mouth Zuleikha tasted something of spring. But it was deceptive, and as soon as they moved out of the sunlight the chill hit them to the bone.

Four adults and two children were crammed into an average-size saloon. They crossed the mountains that ringed Palermo and, in spite of the overcrowding, Zuleikha could feel the temperature in her feet and in the lower parts of her legs begin fitfully to drop. She twisted back to look through the rear window at the sea, and far out, beyond the almost perfectly-shaped golden bay, halfway to infinity, she made out the tiny black speck of a boat. Ahead of them, towards the southeast, she could see the beginnings of a forested mountain-range whose summits were still covered with brilliant white snow. This, Zita informed them, was the extreme western end of the Madonie Mountains, a range that teemed with wildlife and oleasters, enormous holly trees and the occasional fir.

They weren't sure what they would do once they'd reached San Giuseppe ru Casteddu Nivuru. The map didn't seem to indicate anything specific, just an old plan of the village as it had been a hundred and forty years earlier. At first they followed the Strade Statali 188, but then they left the trunk road and, after a time, they reached the broad plateau that constituted much of central western Sicily. Here, the undulating fields stretched all the way to the horizon. Eventually they left the road altogether, and Peppe had some difficulty controlling the steering-wheel as he attempted to negotiate his way along what was really little more than a country track.

San Giuseppe ru Casteddu Nivuru was a large village – or possibly a small town, set atop a plateau in the west-central part of the island. Its heart consisted of a rough church of yellowish stone with a crumbling façade, an emerald-coloured dome and no campanile. There was a school and an oval piazza around which were clustered a few bars, cafés and basic shops. Here in the village the stone was golden-brown and porous, so that it seemed almost as though the houses simply had erupted one day from the soil. Peppe's wife informed them that this was tufa stone, and that it had been quarried from Isola Favignana in the Isole Egadi archipelago which lay off the northwestern coast of Sicily, in the Tyrrhenian Sea, but that the quarries there had long since been abandoned. The houses were clustered more or less around the piazza, though there were a few outlying farmhouses and, scattered even further out, among the fields and woods, more diminutive cottages that once must have belonged to agricultural labourers. Now they looked as if they'd been done-up to serve as country retreats for weary city folk.

It was almost deserted when they got there, though Zita explained that it was siesta and that life would begin again around four. This was a clear difference, Zuleikha thought, from Italian cities in the north, where the siesta had been fired to nothing by the industrial-strength caffeine of transnational capitalism.

Peppe's house lay some two kilometres south and west of the village. It consisted of some outhouses scattered around a two-storeyed massaria, and was built of grey stone that looked as if it had last been whitewashed a very long time ago. Beyond the garden, in which Zita and Peppe had cultivated a vegetable patch and some fruit trees, most of the land had been allowed to lie fallow – or rather, as Peppe explained, had simply been abandoned.

'It's just too much work to keep it up. Besides, I have other work here.'

He didn't elaborate. But surely, Zuleikha thought, his job was restoring old buildings in the towns and cities of Sicily, and there couldn't be much to restore in villages like this. She figured that he would spend much of his time suspended from the roofs of churches, and she pictured him abseiling, sporting a bright red helmet and tethered to the sky by a brace of synthetic ropes. Or perhaps, she thought, like Michelangelo he is lying on his back atop a pile of scaffolding, drawing a fine brush across ancient stucco and plaster while the polyphony of choirs erupts from far beneath and he thinks steadfastly of Mata Sicilia. And maybe, for him, Mata Sicilia is this place, San Giuseppe ru Casteddu Nivuru.

Saint Joseph of the Black Castle. It sounded as if the name of the village had been derived from some arcane legend concerning the step-father of the Saviour. She smiled. Perhaps that's why he still acts so young, she thought. Peppe was a redactor, a man who brought things back from not merely the dead but from oblivion. He uncovered classical Greek frescoes that had been painted over a thousand times across twice as many years; he smoothed down layers of earth, cement and straw to unveil some hoary pagan statue from the tribal epoch of the Siculi or the Elymians, and like Abu Abd Allah Abdullah Muhammed ibn Muhammed ibn Ash Sharif al Idrisi, the author of the *Book of Roger*, he mapped out the edges of reality that comprised Sicilia, and thence of the trans-Mediterranean continuum.

It was a pity there weren't more like him. Not much money in it, she guessed, but in some ways it would be a dream job, the schoolboy swot's equivalent of being a train driver – as long as you had a head for heights. He hauled dry corpses from the ground, lovingly restored every millimetre of their integuments, and set them on shelves for all the world to see. No secrets; everything – every deity and its trail of blood, spunk and Damaschino – was documented precisely, illuminated in a case of air and light, right down to its radioactive, carbon-dated lineage, its irreducible cellular DNA fragments. It was as though, crack by dusty crack, he was revealing an entire world of lost language. In Giuseppe Ayala's cosmos there was no room for mysteries, miracles, superstition. Peppe's world was the future, the new Sicily, freed at last from the mentality of feudal bondage and capitalist Mafia terror; cities and towns where black had become merely a fashion accessory; a land, a people, able at last to breathe without the stench of the omertà rising from the marrow of their bones. A land where the dead rested easy and where there was no need for the beautiful blue of jettatura.

'You can't keep secrets from a Sicilian,' he'd said to her. 'We invented secrets. Secrets, fear and the Evil Eye. Every conqueror carried with them a mirror which they left here, and now instead of getting on with life we are like rabbits staring into countless mirrors, wondering about what reflection the neighbours might see and hoping that our image is larger than theirs. We should have smashed the mirrors a long time ago, like we should have smashed the windows of all those designer shops that are really money-laundering outlets. But we didn't, and that's our own fault. Instead, we helped to crush those brave individuals who wanted to break the glass. Palermitanata. The truth is, every single person here has a different version of the truth.'

'You're too pessimistic, always. Things happen slowly, change…'

'No! You can change the world in fifteen years. It's a fact. If there was the will … look at what's happening in South America!'

Zuleikha wondered why Peppe was being so open with strangers. She broke in. 'In Pakistan, over the past twenty years, the literacy rate has fallen because nobody in power gives a shit and those that do, get shot.'

'Exactly,' Peppe concurred. 'A hundred and thirty years ago, at the completion of the Risorgimento, in this village the literacy rate was almost zero. It had been higher a thousand years before!'

But then, sometimes it was easier to be open with a stranger.

'You have to take reality as it is. You can't wait for utopia.'

'Now who's the pessimist?'

'I just want a reasonable life. For them.' Zita ran out of air. She indicated the children, who again were trying to hide the fact that they were listening to every word. Zita's face had become increasingly flushed with the effort of remaining polite, and Zuleikha could tell that behind Peppe's mask-like face there was a veritable war raging. With his lack of fear he was stuck in a Corinthian column in the Royal House for Crazy People, and year by year he was chiselling his way out, while they – the successful, the fearful ones, those who had compromised and learned to accept the way things were – had been jet-setting around the globe since the time of the late (but hardly lamented) Salvatore Lima, the Mafia Mayor of Palermo. Meanwhile, magic shows stained the airwaves with their grasping legerdemain, *Radio Maria, Listen!* and the lawyer, the cop, the professor of agriculture, all set wooden daggers by their pillows just in case. Who then was truthful, and who insane?

So this, Zuleikha thought, is how married couples argue. Everything they say to each other has a subtext that relates to basic structural problems in their relationship. The personal, the physical and the political become one. Father, Son and Holy Ghost. She wondered where Alexander and she might fit in to that dynamic. Mother, son and wife, perhaps? Nasrin Zeinab, Daoud and Susan. She shivered suddenly at the thought that their love might be defined by the strictures of the dead.

Peppe rose and began to tidy up the room with a perfectly controlled ferocity and with his back to them all. Although the Ayalas' massaria was quite different in style, shape and materials from the forest vicarage in Lincolnshire, Zuleikha did think that there were subtle similarities. It was something in the arrangement of the furniture perhaps, or the décor ... no, she thought, here it was much more basic. After all, the family didn't really live in this place; it was just a poor man's cottage which had been extended a couple of times and then left to crumble in the sun. It looked as though once, some years earlier, someone had attempted to whitewash the outside walls but had neglected to renew the wash thereafter, and so now the coating of paint resembled the skin of a lizard, with pinkish bits of stone showing through.

The original cottage had consisted of a single large room with a kitchen at one end where several generations would have slept, including Peppe's grandfather, who had been the second oldest among eleven – four boys and seven girls. And that, Peppe told them over a lunch of pasta with eggplant and cheese, white wine and Geraci Siculo mineral water, was not counting the three who'd died in infancy. The kitchen originally had been out of doors and had been covered with only a slate roof, but Peppe had had it enclosed and brought properly into the main fabric of the house. There would have been no toilet in those days; the building had been constructed during the first decade of the twentieth century and had replaced an older structure which, Peppe emphasised, would have been still more basic. In the decades following the Risorgimento, Peppe's forebears had worked their fingers to the bone to save for a small plot of land. Even by West Sicilian peasant standards, they'd lived frugally and had acquired a reputation for miserliness. But they'd been 'good coppolas', they'd sucked up to the aristocrats, and in the end that was really how they'd been granted this little piece of land.

'It still runs in the family!' Zita joked.

'But it paid off,' Peppe then retorted, almost contradicting himself. Because, he reasoned, by the turn of the century – that was, thirty years after most of Italy had been united and had thrown out both its foreign and domestic absolutist rulers – his great-grandfather had managed to acquire this piece of barren land, and with his own hands and those of his now almost-grown elder sons, had built this house. They had hoped to move up one social class, from that of peasant to that of burgisi. This epochal task had fallen to Peppe's grandfather, after his elder brother Salvatore had died in a cholera epidemic just before the outbreak of the First World War. Salvatore had died officially childless, though rumour had it that in fact he had fathered three illegitimate children from various itinerant farm labourers. However, they would have had no claim over either land or house. Peppe's brow furrowed and his countenance grew dark.

'But still, even after nearly a century, these people harbour resentments.' It turned out that the descendants of these possible bastards of his great-uncle's had joined the local gang and become low-level mafiosi. From time to time, Peppe would find that an old tree had been uprooted or that a crop of cauliflowers had been stolen during the night. They were of nuisance value only. The younger members of this tribe had shifted to Palermo and Catania and continued the family tradition of doing dodgy deals for dodgy deals' sake. However, it was a fact that even the lowest of the low of that world could suddenly become dangerous. Put a Kalashnikov into the hands of a chimpanzee and the chimpanzee will become a killer. 'If there is a straight, clean way, they will take the dirty, winding, hidden path. Actually, that's what it's like here still. It makes me feel a little like a Fascist sometimes, talking about them,' he smiled. 'But I'm not a Fascist. The Fascists were just another criminal gang. Worshippers of death. Different instrument, same song.'

There was no television in the massaria. As Peppe explained, why would he want to watch yet another beauty pageant or listen to the latest clown from the Global Parliament for Friendship, Solidarity and Safety-Pins pronounce self-righteously on the state of some malaria-infested corner of the world as though they were at all interested in doing anything about either that or the buildings

369

falling down next door. While, in central Palermo, seven-year-olds wearing designer gear flogged heroin and families lived like rats in those basements with no windows. Building plots in tourist areas was a good way of turning filth into dream. They even had the saints in the palms of their hands. Gold taps, gleaming brass, glass and trash everywhere … the preferred interior of a mafia wife was basically the décor of an African dictator: bright pink and gold for everything. Wives who ran front companies, selling varnish. A clown with a wallet, swollen to bursting point with consultancy fees and European gold. Meanwhile, beneath the heavy weight of the burned hand, the pipes leaked, the island was turning to desert, the place swarmed with incompetent doctors and all around was idle talk and boasting.

Back in the mid-1980s Zita Mossuto had been a feminist, which in Palermo in those days had not been an easy thing to be. She'd read Maraini, Ajovalasit and Cutrufelli, and had joined various radical organisations campaigning for legal abortion and occupational rights, such as the right not to have to render sex to get a job. In those times, women had begun to commit suicide rather than live under the sweltering jackboot of honour and shame, of fuitine and abusivismo edilizio, of crooked white-suited very rich doctors and grotesque mammane wielding bloody knitting needles. She had rebelled against having to watch every word, every tiny action, and had refused to be chaperoned and constantly surveilled by men, for either the promulgation or the protection of fuck-fantasies. Fathers, brothers, strangers.

And she had rebelled against the greatest obstacle of all: fear. Fear that over the centuries had grown to be as large as Mongibello; fear that smouldered and burned and led women to swallow poison, to hide away their bodies in convents or to throw themselves in front of trains. Fear that was ingested with each swirl of bread in olive oil, in the slow opening of each sugared martorana eye, fear in the slash of every pupi's blade. The feminist movement had grown strong in other parts of Italy, especially in those northern cities like Bologna – which some people in rural Sicily in the 1970s had still thought were towns in America – but in Trinacria everything was more difficult, everyone was isolated. It was an island whose body was burning like that of a martyred saint in a mass of fire and light. At least in Palermo there had been outside influences. The situation in provincial towns and villages had been ten times worse, Zita told Zuleikha when they were alone together, preparing lunch. Yet often, it was women who had stood up to the Cosa Nostra. Things had improved since the 1970s, mainly through the struggle of women like Zita, the women of *Mezzocielo*, those committees who had hung white sheets from their balconies, the women who had fasted in solidarity with pentiti and those sisters, mothers, daughters and wives who had dared to stand up to the Mafia, often in the face of opposition not only from their own families and other women, but sometimes even from so-called left-wing males.

But what could you do? Capitalism drove people to exist in only certain modes, and so now Zita Ayala was a wife and mother as well as a secretary. She'd got far more freedom in terms of her personal life than her own mother had ever dreamed of, yet still she was expected really to do everything, to be all these things and then to be more than the sum of her parts as well. She kept her mouth shut and smiled and her smile was a perfect arc, a Cupid's clasp that held fast the broken dreams of this triangular island. Well, she preferred that to talking all the time about nothing. Pay differentials still existed, as did rampant sex discrimination. But even here in Sicily things had moved on: women were no longer willing to accept the garbage that had been forced down their throats for so many centuries. Millennia. So now Giuseppe could say that he didn't want his daughter to become merely a flight attendant. And Zita had given her daughter a middle name, after the Christian name of the feminist writer.

And Zuleikha thought of her own mother; of how, through the bluster, the domineering attitude, Zuleikha had known – or at any rate, had sensed – that above all else Nasrin Zeinab had felt fear. Perhaps it had been the deep scars of having been brought up in a country which had an ambivalent attitude towards immigration from what, in those days and for some time afterwards, had been termed the New Commonwealth – but which really had been the old empire. Or perhaps it had been simply the existential dislocation of a woman living in a post-industrial society who had never worked outside the home. Whatever had been the dynamic,

Zuleikha thought, her mother's fate – the fate of being born in a certain place at a particular historical moment – had framed her mother's life and to some extent her own life as well. For most of her nearly forty-three years, Zuleikha had had the feeling that one way or another she was always attempting to escape. Though the problem was, she had never quite been able to pin down with any precision exactly from what it was that she was trying to run away. Yet for both her mother and herself, death had come to define their interaction with the world, so that even in the midst of their struggles, from the cold darkness, there had leached a certain consent, a surrender, a submission. They existed.

After lunch, Alexander played with the kids in the garden, while Zuleikha went for a long walk. It seemed strange that there should be a harvest – a word which in her mind she had always associated with the onset of autumn and of things brown and gold – in the middle of May. They'd sampled some of Peppe's home-made wine, a pungent red that had been much stronger than most commercially available vintages and which had gone straight to her head. The land had been barren for centuries, Peppe had explained, and only now, after a hundred years of cajolery, was it beginning to yield a little sustenance.

'But like his family, it's mean,' Zita had added. 'The Ayalas. Suco della pietra. Blood from the stone.'

Peppe hadn't smiled at this, but simply continued to fill their glasses with the strong-smelling liquor.

'Good for winter,' he'd said. 'It warms you up.'

And as she'd sipped at the liquid, Zuleikha had thought that it did resemble properly-prepared mulled wine, something which in Scotland she'd always associated with the more pleasant aspects of that otherwise awkward and irritating festival of Christmas and New Year. To Peppe and his family, she thought, this is still winter and there is a chill up here in the hills. But to me it seems much more like May, High Spring. And so the wine was yet another discordance, but as she drank the pungency of its aftertaste seemed to lessen these feelings and she found herself enjoying, and indeed being delighted by, the sense of incongruity of being here in Sicily with this family and with her lover and his lute and with, ballooning all around them, the silence of the box.

And now as she proceeded along the bridle path it became obvious that spring had erupted, perhaps a little early. But then, she thought, the whole world is meant to be heating up like the inside of a volcano, so that soon all the seasons will begin to merge, winter into spring, summer into winter, and in the confusion no doubt strange exotic beings with irresistible aromas and large membranous wings will sprout from the earth and cover the seas. And sure enough, as she descended along the path, she seemed to enter a small sheltered valley where, along with rosemary, almond blossom, sorrel, acanthus and lavender, the first bougainvillea already had begun to bleed a richer shade of purple, the blood gathering in the tiny cupolas and spidery branches that arched over the stone walls. At one point she was sure that she could smell orange blossom – but surely not, she thought; even here in this heart-shaped island at the centre of the world there are limits – but there were definitely hints of mulberry blossom and wisteria. How the fuck do I know all this stuff? she wondered. Suddenly I've turned into an empathic botanist. From being simply a physician, a sympathetic cartographer of human form and function, a good listener, a careful restorer of homeostasis, now she had become an expert on time and place and on the passages of the one over the body of the other. A gardener of the soul, you might say. At this point a large bee buzzed past her nose in a kind of Spitfire Doppler effect, though when she attempted to trail its flight-path it deliquesced in the sunlight that spread its measure evenly as though it were a finely-sewn net thrown taut across the still afternoon air.

She inhaled deeply and closed her eyes, allowed her pace to slacken, and then she stopped altogether. She became aware of every little sound, of the scratching of hedgehogs and squirrels in the incongruously mixed undergrowth of winter and spring vegetation. And this was what Peppe had called barren land. Maybe in June, July and August, she thought, these same hillsides would smoke under the heat of the sun and the grass would turn the colour of dead skin. She could feel her skin pull tightly around her bones and she could smell the silvery dust that flew into people's lungs, into their blood and their minds, and which turned them into walking corpses.

She opened her eyes and realised that in fact she had walked further than she had thought, and that due to the folding pattern of the land the cottage was no longer visible. She was no longer on Peppe's land. But she wasn't worried. There would be plenty of time later to study the map. She needed to be alone for a while. The busyness and discordant noise of Palermo had been of too short a duration for inurement, and besides, she was no longer in her twenties, or even thirties. She'd been to a techno-style club once only and hadn't felt compelled to go back. She'd been and experienced whatever it was you were meant to go and experience, and it had been no great shakes really. And anyway, she liked to talk, to be heard and to be able to listen. Yes, she was a good listener, they said. Her patients. As a locum, she thought, the entire city of Glasgow potentially is under my care. She laughed out loud at this, but her laughter also made her shiver as she moved parallel to a stone wall some twelve feet high and the colour of freshly-mined gold, which had blocked out the sunlight.

She felt a sudden affection for Peppe's family, for Laila, Zita and for the two children. They're good people, she thought, and then she wondered what that meant. By all conventional criteria Archie had been a good man. During the War he'd served his country in the Royal Air Force, he'd risked his life on the plains of Lincolnshire, and for several decades thereafter he'd helped to construct the massive silver ships which had given Glasgow, Scotland, Britain, their renown and their overarching power. And after the shipbuilding had shifted to Japan, the port work to Singapore, Karachi, Marseille, Rotterdam, he'd done his bit in respectable skilled blue-collar jobs. Okay, like the rest of the country he'd stopped actually making things and had taken to simply repairing them – before that function too had been rendered obsolete, since under the iron laws of Late Capitalism nothing ever got repaired any more, but was simply tossed away so that low-cost production could continue and consumer spending could be maintained at an artificially high level.

And he'd been a husband to his wife, to Margaret. So he'd been unfaithful a few times, mostly during a very difficult period of their lives: during the all-consuming war, when the individual, if not the collective fibre of the national morals had seemed to waver. But really, in the final analysis, what had he done that was so terrible? Yes, he'd engaged in a little horseplay with a prostitute or two, but for goodness sake, did that justify him dying slowly, painfully like that, losing oxygen by the molecule so that each cell in his brain would feel every millisecond of his demise? There was no justification, she knew that. She had known it always, ever since the days of heads-in-pots. Even then, in her serious lack of intelligence, Zuleikha had known that there had never been any kind of god – here, there or anywhere. The death of her infant son, her pure cherubic love, had not been a test of faith. It hadn't been a test of any sort. It had been merely a concatenation of biochemical reactions. The rest – the funeral rituals, the endless weeping that had wracked her body and destroyed her mind for months on end and from which she knew she had never fully recovered – all that had been merely displacement therapy, somatisation. An ape-dance.

Bits of the tufa wall had crumbled and come loose, and broken stone littered the pathway, some of which was overgrown with moss and fava bloom. She bent down and took a flower between her thumb and forefinger, gazed at the velure of its petals and at the strange black markings that looked almost like the theta of Greek script. In the old days – not so very long before – in order to get into university to study Medicine you'd needed both Greek and Latin. But that had died away long before Zuleikha had 'gone up' to Glasgow – though no-one had ever said it like that; students went 'up' only to Cambridge and Oxford. But even those echelons of privilege had relinquished the requirement for Cicero and Scipio, Catullus and Archimedes. Eureka! No more chariot races and rhetoric, no more wild Cyclopean epics etiolated through the dreaming spires of Cam and Isis. Yet when she'd been young the grumbling ghosts of dead masters still had seemed to roam in their long black scapulars through the halls of her school, and she had always walked that bit faster past the War Memorial that commemorated the dead of both world wars, lest the insipid shades, drawn like the wavering spines of asphodel flowers to their tarnished bronze names, be attracted also to her vital fluids.

The wall was impossible to see over and it seemed to go on and on – but then, quite unexpectedly, she came to a deeply-set gate. Her palms turned orange with rust as she gripped the railings.

On the other side was a garden overgrown with trees, bushes and weeds, at the centre of which was a dried-up ornamental fountain. Behind the veil of branches and freshly-sprouted leaves, only just visible from where she stood, was a large house. In Britain she might have called it a manor house, but here in Sicily she had no name for it. It rose to three floors and had been constructed of pink tufa in the same Baroque style as the palazzi she'd seen in Palermo – except that here the roof remained intact. Birds had made nests high up in the cedar and chestnut trees, though there was no sign of a bird anywhere nearby. She wondered whether, like so many of the houses, the nests too had been left year upon year to desiccate in the burning heat of the summers.

Tall weeds grew everywhere and the iron gate had been completely smothered in a corona of leaves and flowers bearing blue and yellow petals. She pulled on it, but the gate had been locked with the largest padlock she'd ever seen. A cartoon padlock, as though whoever had set it there had possessed a sense either of farce or else ridiculous grandiosity. Serious burglars would hardly have been disturbed by such a thing – one clip of the cutters would have been enough – though this set Zuleikha to worrying about whether there might be guard dogs. But no, she reasoned, the effects of the wine seeming to intensify now, an hour or more since she'd imbibed the last sip. If there were any dogs here worth their salt they surely would have begun to bark at her approach by now. Dogs worth their salt? She laughed again at the clumsiness of her metaphor. Her serious lack of intellectual capacity, her constitutional inability to define truth, was a deficit common to most of humankind – even to the people, good, bad or indifferent, who had built this palazzu here in the hinterlands of the Province of Palermo on the Island of Siqilliya. And in the late winter, in Glasgow, Archie was alone and was dying. While here she was, conning herself that the future would be any different.

To the left of the gate was a whitewashed enclave filled with the disordered remains of old leaves, green, blue and white candle-stubs and, right at the back, a statue of Saint Joseph. Who else, she thought. After all, he is the patron saint of the village and, de facto, of the whole island. It was a typical rendition, quite unlike the black figure she had secreted in her coat pocket. This votive Joseph wore a long brown robe and had a cream-coloured complexion, blue eyes, wavy hair the colour of hazelnuts and a somewhat Iberian beard to match. He was smiling cosmically. San Giuseppuzzu, a technicolour beatification.

She glanced to the right and then to the left. It is as though I am commencing a Muslim prayer, she thought, and in front of this very Roman Catholic statue even the thought seemed blasphemous. She tried to conjure up the face of her son, but all she saw was the whiteness of his coffin. She was a scientist, not a penitent. Not allowing herself to ruminate any further, Doctor Zuleikha Chashm Framareza MacBeth climbed over the gate and jumped some five feet down onto the ground on the other side.

The fountain was small and cod-Baroque, a product of some arriviste member of the Palermitan bourgeoisie rather than that of the old Norman-Swabian-Anjevin-Aragonese-Bourbon latifondo aristocracy. Too many urinating angels, she thought; they make the funtana look like a pisciatura. Long fronds of ivy had looped themselves around the stone structure, rendering to it a bizarrely Southern Gothic feel. She ran her palm over the pink stone head of one of the cherubs. The silence was almost complete. This was about as far south as you could get and still be Gothic and get away with it, she thought. Well, no; that would maybe be Andalucia or Palestine. But go much further and it begins to look quite ridiculous. Like women's Kirk of Scotland hats among the desert fathers, or like those English church spires in India, she thought. Or the red-brick colleges of Pakistan. Owzat! The varicose world of cricket. Thwack, thwack, fuck.

The grounds were strewn with last autumn's leaves, not yet decomposed but matted by the recent rain into a springy brown carpet, and she could see that she was walking on what once had been the driveway of the manor. There I go again, she thought, turning this pink Sicilian palace into an English biscuit-tin lid! On the side of the building opposite the fountain there was a large zinc tub which was about a quarter filled with brackish water. It didn't look like a bath-tub – it had no taps, no handles and none of the decorative features she might have expected a bath from a house like this one to have had – and it gave off the sweet odour of putrefaction. Who knows, she thought, perhaps it had been placed here simply in order to collect rainwater. But earth and all kinds of other gunk had got into it. She peered into the muddy liquid, but couldn't see whether there might also be a dead bird or animal floating in it.

Round the back of the building, in a small garden separated by a hedge from the main body of the iardino, half-hidden in deep undergrowth, was a small abandoned graveyard. Most of the tombstones had been cut from marble that once had been white, though closer to the outer wall there were a couple made from tufa. Some had half-fallen over, or had been pushed out of position by a combination of the vegetation, the elements and age. Zuleikha bent down and tried to make out some of the writing, but it was impossible. The graves must be very old, she thought. As old as this palazzu, or possibly even older. At the far end of the cemetery was a wizened hawthorn tree that looked more ancient than both graveyard and palazzu. Nonetheless it was in full flower, exuded a rich scent and sprinkled a pinkish-white snowfall over the gravestones. On one of the stones she saw what might just have been a portrait, an old monochrome photograph which had been touched-up with colour. As with the writing, the portrait's features too had been scuffed away, so that all she could make out around the blank face were the ends of shoulder-length black hair. It freaked her out a little, crouching there before the grave of someone who once must have been a resident – perhaps even the owner – of this house; but then she thought no, the owners would have had far grander tombs. These tombs must be the final resting-places of the servants. But why aren't they buried in a churchyard or a proper cemetery? Then she saw that there were black and red insects crawling over the flowers of the hawthorn. With its ebony hair, the figure reminded her of Alexander. She sprang up, turned away from the tiny necropolis, and made her way back round to the front of the villa.

Zuleikha went straight up the stone staircase that led to the doors. Suddenly she was assailed by the not entirely rational fear that the house might not be empty. What if the gate over which she had just clambered was simply old and disused? What if the family now lived in one wing of the house, leaving the rest to the ghosts of their ancestors? Worse still, what if the place was a secret rendezvous for members of the local cosca? After all, as Peppe had told them during one of his rants, this whole area – western Sicilia – was meant to be crawling with them, and everything, from the deepest roots of the old vines to the stars that hung like tiny lemons from the vault of the sky, was supposed to exist only on their say-so. Indeed, one might say that across the land there was a veritable plague of tightly-bound artichokes. Had they not usurped God, science and the state? Had they not altered the landscape itself, the landscape that was the repository of memory? One day, the whole of Sicily would slide into the sea or else into the molten lake of Etna and everything would be forgotten. Past, future, truth – all gone. They. The ones who vomited up those shit-houses among the temples, those ecomonsters slammed down on every bay of the beautiful coastline, the buildings of sand and clay constructed over public sewers. Il bel paese. Italy was the land of concrete and cars. Abusivismo.

Palermo had been raped long ago, her parks levelled with cement, her palazzi demolished during the night. At least the Borgias and Medicis had built beautiful buildings and patronised the arts. Whereas this lot wouldn't know art if it hit them on the head at a thousand metres a second. And once those breeze-block Godzillas were up, even though they were illegal, they could never be demolished. The bulldozers had fallen silent a long time ago. It was a simple logic: what didn't exist couldn't be removed. And once it did exist, on the ground if not on paper, then it couldn't be removed either. The entire construction industry, tendering process and housing market was run by the Eco-Mafia, while on magical boats, planes and trucks, drugs from all corners of the pharmacopoeia flowed across the land like sacred tributaries of the River Alpheus or the Papineto that ran beneath Palermo and that followed the tides of the Nile. But none of this was real. Oh yes, and then there was the control of the water supply too, by means of which the Cosa Nostra could quite literally dehydrate and hold the country to ransom. Perhaps, she thought, it is this thirst which drives everybody here mad. Everybody, that was, except the rich, the Beat-Head politicians and those who licked the raw cocaine of power off of these jackals' arses. But that wasn't real either. Reality was all beautiful hotels and golden beaches. A perfect sea, filled with teeming life in its savage state. A paradise on earth where all sins always were pardoned, condoned, condono.

The sun was warm on her neck; she was sweating again. She removed her coat, slipped her jumper over her head, then replaced the coat. Carrying the jumper over her left arm, she approached the doors. So that they can see I'm not a burglar, she thought. Anyway, do I look like a burglar, for God's sake? The windows all had been boarded up, though here and there a plank had either fallen or been ripped off, revealing a cuboid area of dark glass that had been smashed at its centre but whose shards still clung to the frame. The heavy wooden double doors were ajar; one of them had become stuck, jammed onto the floor, and a pile of leaves had accumulated close to the aperture. The opening was not quite large enough to allow her access and she peered into the murk, trying to adjust her vision away from the sunlit garden. There seemed to be no furniture in the hall – not that she'd have expected any, and plaster was peeling off the walls while twisted cords hung down from the ceiling like sleeping serpents. At the far end was a broad staircase, leading presumably to the upper floors.

The floor was made of a different type of stone from that of the walls. Somehow, ludicrously, Zuleikha had expected marble. How stupid, she told herself. Even here, where marble is so plentiful, by now it would have been gouged out and stolen, carried on the backs of flatbed trucks all the way to some dark warehouse in Pantano d'Arci, where it would have been crushed into a fine powder that would have been mixed with opiates and sent out to junkies all over Europe and North America – to induce them to part with their dosh and to help them destroy their brains just that little bit faster. Most of the heroin that came to the West came through Sicily – though in recent years, as with most other sources of capital, diamorphine also had been outsourced. She wondered then about Laila's 'spare' room, and about whether this apparently deserted palace was really a transit point of some sort. But then they wouldn't have left it unmanned and the door ajar like that! It would have been guarded like Fort fucking Knox! And she told herself not to be so stupid. She managed to contort herself so that she became thinner than before and, thus aligned, she succeeded in squeezing her body through the opening.

She was in a large hall with a fifteen-foot-high ceiling. The walls once had been adorned with light pink paper which originally might have been silken, but which long since had faded and peeled away from the paint and plaster underneath. She tried the light switches, but they were all dead. There were large holes where ornaments or paintings once had been affixed and, over to her right, framing a chimney, was the shadow of a mantelpiece. At its central point, the ceiling was gashed as though gravity had torn down the chandelier – which, she imagined, once must have illuminated the chamber with scintillating glass. She heard a scuffling sound from above. This place had to be infested with vermin, with rats, bats and the other creatures that crept in once human life had withdrawn. Thick webs hung like hammocks in every corner. Eight legs? – it was unnatural, otherworldly. It meant that, like a demon or a jinn, you could move at high speed in any direction. She shuddered and moved on.

The leaves had made it to just the first six feet or so back from the doorway. The remainder of the floor was coated in a mixture of dust and glass, the very sight of which made her cough. She put her jumper back on. The hall smelled musty. She wondered about asbestos, then decided that it was unlikely, since this building clearly was far older than the invention of either white or blue asbestos. But what if they'd renovated it at some point, put in all the most snazzy mod cons, including a fire-proofing layer? The white was bad enough; broken or frayed, it could trigger various pulmonary diseases, particularly if someone were exposed repeatedly over a period of time. It was what they had used to use in ironing boards: the square platform for the hot iron.

But blue asbestos was the real killer. A single microscopic filament of it would fly into your lungs and sit there for thirty, forty, fifty years before all of a sudden one night you would wake up to find that you had three months to live and that your mode of death – for death, like music, consisted of countless modes – would be one of slow suffocation. Just one filament would be enough. The workers – shipyard workers, builders and all manner of tradesmen – and their families had had to fight a prolonged war to secure compensation from transnational corporations, even though the firms which had employed them had known full well about the dangers of asbestos for some years prior to its use being banned. Asbestosis, mesothelioma. Sometimes they would fail to get any dosh at all, and even when eventually they did win in court, often the money would arrive after the worker in question had died. The firms deliberately had allowed people to be exposed to this stuff, knowing that it was likely to kill both them and their families. That, Zuleikha thought, was mass murder. And that was how corruption and murder happened in Britain. It was sanctioned by the highest court, by the Law Lords, who also functioned as the lawmakers and the protectors of big property. And they talked about Sicily! They should take a look at their own front yard! Archie the airman was dying – perhaps, she thought, he is already dead. There was no-one to fight the bosses, and really he was being murdered by multinational corporations with fingers in every pie, including pornography, arms trading, drugs – the lot – and offshore accounts of such magnitude they could, and often did, purchase entire states. Sicily was just a tiny part of it all. The real villains were not the guys with violin-cases and big mamas: no, she thought, that stereotype had been shot down a long time ago. The real culprits today – the composers and conductors – were the guys and gals in suits who all had gone to the same private schools, and thought the same way, and who functioned as perfect cogs in this worldwide edifice, this machine oiled with the blood of millions. War, starvation, pestilence.

An image flashed into her mind of Archie's face, his battered body lying white and listless beneath bleached sheets, his eyes child-like with the life-force that was flaring one last time before it went out. But he is not a child, she reminded herself. Nor was he a saint. Or perhaps he was the only kind of saint we can have in this world: a saint with blood on his hands; a mortal being whose suffering was some kind of penance ordered by a relentlessly vengeful deity. Bloody Joseph. She fingered the statuette in her jacket pocket, felt its pointed head, its arms that were abducted at an angle from the sides of its body. It had been sculpted in severe lines from black alabaster and the sculptor had had no illusions.

The other rooms on the ground floor were similarly filled only with dust. From time to time she thought she made out shapes on the walls: the remnants, delicately embossed onto paper, of the subtle forms of angels and hunting-scenes.

She climbed the staircase. The noble floor was similar in design to the ground level and was equally empty, though more of the windows remained intact. Up here, the scent which she had noticed as soon as she had entered the house was far stronger. It was a sweet smell and it seemed familiar, yet irritatingly she found that she was unable to pin it down to a particular memory. Against the far wall of one of the rooms there lay an old-style white porcelain bath. The pipes still seemed to be connected to the convoluted silver-coloured taps, and their other ends disappeared into the wall. But it was clear to Zuleikha that the bath could not have been used for many years. It was dry and dusty and bore only a permanent plimsoll line. Beyond the bath, in the upper left-hand corner of the fireplace, she saw something fluttering. She drew closer and saw that it was piece of paper which had become caught in the frame. She half-knelt and curled her wrist and hand upwards so that her fingers were in a position of leverage. She pulled, but it was held tight. She lay supine on the cold marble and pulled harder, this time utilising her shoulder and more of her body-weight.

At the third attempt she sensed a movement, then the entire thing came down on her in a blinding fug of soot, feathers and stoor. Coughing, spluttering and cursing loudly, Zuleikha slithered her body off the marble, sat up and tried to clean out her eyes. Her jumper, coat and dress were filthy, her hands and face blackened. After she'd brushed herself down as best she was able, she noticed that the object which she had pulled from the chimney was a rolled-up old newspaper. Some workman no doubt had shoved it up there after eating his sandwiches. She picked it up and saw that, save for the edges which had become torn on the way down, it was almost complete. The writing was in Italian, not Sicilian – even she could tell the difference. She glanced at the date: 10 Maggio 1978. On the front page there was a large photograph of the back of a car with a boot that had been sprung open. Somebody had been assassinated. It was several decades old, which suggested firstly that the palazzu – or at least, this chamber – had remained empty since the late 1970s, and secondly, that in spite of the apparent shapes of rising damp which she'd seen downstairs, the air up here carried very little moisture.

Zuleikha was aware suddenly of how dry her tongue was against her palate. She wished she'd brought some water. Her mouth tasted of soot and there seemed to be tiny grains between her teeth. Her gums gave off the flavour of piss, as though like a dog or a lunatic she'd slaked her thirst by kneeling before an overflowing chamber-pot. A wave of nausea flooded over her and she spat heavily, several times, onto the floor of the palazzu. The force of this made her slightly giddy, so that from the left-hand corner of her visual field she caught a movement that was almost like the swirl of a dress or the billow of a curtain – though when she looked up, there was nothing but broken light seeping through the glass plates of the big grimy windows.

Partly because, quite literally, she was following her nose, partly because she was fed up at her own stupidity, and partly because she was beginning to get freaked, Zuleikha did not explore all of the rooms on that floor. Instead, she continued on to the floor above. As she approached the final flight the light grew dimmer, the opposite of what she had expected. She began to move more slowly and by the time she reached the head of the staircase, she found that she had to pause and grip the balustrade, and she remained that way until her eyes had begun to accommodate to the murkier conditions. The smell here was far stronger.

Half-feeling her way, Zuleikha moved like a spider along the corridor, which was a good deal narrower than those on the floors below. Indeed, the proportions up here seemed altogether more diminutive, and she reasoned that originally this floor must have formed the servants' quarters. Every so often, her hands would run over irregularities in the fabric of the wall, rough areas that were not quite circular in form, though these did not seem to occur as part of any particular pattern or sequence. She found that she was becoming intensely aware of touch, and aware too of the exact weight and dimensions of the stone saint in the right-hand pocket of her jacket. The air had grown much colder, and the temperature continued to drop the further along the corridor she went. At a certain point she had the urge to turn and run, to retrace her steps along this dark corridor and to race down the stairs, taking two at a time, to sprint across the hall and squeeze herself back out through the doorway, to get back into daylight, sunshine, birdsong, spring. But the anticipation of something from this dark place following her down the staircase as she ran outweighed any fear she had of proceeding.

She almost fell to her left as her hand missed the wall. Panicking, she groped for something solid; she managed to find what she assumed was the jamb of a doorway. The colder air seemed to be emanating from here. Tentatively, she wheeled her body around and entered the room.

The chamber was square and all of its windows had been covered with black cloth, each one outlined with a thin border of light. The room was empty – except for a circular wall of bricks, some four feet in height and perhaps ten across, at its centre. Raised over the opening thus formed was a thick wooden beam from which was suspended a ladder. She moved closer. A breeze blew back her hair and clothes. The air smelled of spring, primavera, bahar. She leaned over what must have been either a well or else a tower of some sort. But a well, up here on the second floor? Wells were set in the ground, weren't they? She remembered an old hospital in Glasgow whose entrance was on the sixth floor but whose exit lay at ground level. This house too had been built on an incline, but the hill was not steep enough, nor the house sufficiently large, to have produced such an effect. Then she remembered that the hospital was rumoured to have been built on a cholera-pit and that through the rising blue smoke of their wavering cigarettes, the night-nurses had been like storytellers. The stone saint felt warm in her pocket. Roman Catholic attitudes were like potent bacteria: they conjured up a feverish diorama of blood and ossuary. And there was something else, too. In the cold air that issued from the opening, Zuleikha made out what she thought at first to be the sound of water lapping against the sides of the well – but no; it seemed too rhythmic for that.

While playing hide-and-seek with Nilla and Giuseppinu in the area behind the garden of the farmhouse, Alex had found himself crossing a field of wheat on the far side of which was an old barn. As he entered, he heard the children's voices coming from far away. He realised that he must have gone in completely the wrong direction and that, in the midst of the children's keen concentration on their game, mercifully he had been totally forgotten. The barn was an outhouse which functioned now as the repository for a defunct olive-press. Alexander ran his hands over the metal and stone of the machine, the bowls, wheels and rollers, which seemed not to have been used for a while. He imagined that the contraption may just have lain idle over the winter, given that the olive oil harvest would have taken place during the autumn. Or perhaps there was a newer machine somewhere on the farm. This was a traditional one, of the type that would have been pulled by long-legged mules.

A voice from behind startled him. He spun round.

'Olvari di tò nannu, cèusi di tò patri, vigna tò. It was my grandfather's. When my family first got the land, he tried to grow both vines and olive trees, but the soil was not good enough. The wine you had at lunch was my doing – we manage to cultivate a little patch but it's not enough to sell. And it's quite strong!'

Alex nodded and smiled. Peppe had folded his arms across his chest and in the subdued light of the barn he seemed far more proprietorial than before. His face seemed to elongate, but it was just the shadows and those tiny, well-practised muscles.

'I liked it,' Alex said. 'Strong's good.'

Peppe moved closer.

'You drink, when you play?'

'Pardon?'

'Your lute – do you drink before a performance?'

Alex shook his head.

'Not usually. It makes your fingers clumsy; you hit bum notes.'

Peppe smiled broadly.

'So, no more wine then, tonight.'

'I don't know if I ... I mean I ...'

'You brought it with you.'

'I know, but ...'

'And you did promise.'

'I know.'

Peppe turned away and ran his hand along the wooden shaft of the press.

'You're here for other reasons, aren't you?'

'Well, sort of.'

'You brought the map?'

Alex nodded.

'Tonight, then, after the children are in bed, we'll take a look at it. We have another two days. There's plenty of time.'

Plenty of time for what? Alex wondered.

There was a pause while Peppe circled around the press, as though he were inspecting it. Every so often he would kneel down and scrape off something with his nail. Then he looked up at Alex.

'I am working on something, too, you know. Out here.' He inhaled and thrust his arms backwards and to the sides, but failed to elaborate. 'You know, once, a left-winger hid here, in this barn.'

'Oh really?' Alex said. 'That's interesting.'

'Yes. There are lots of hiding-places here.' Peppe smiled at him. 'It's peaceful; there's space to think. No phones ringing, no e-mail to check, no cells, hand-helds, laptops – none of that stuff. I try to keep it that way. When I get back to Palermo I will find that people will have left messages on every machine possible – friends, family, work colleagues and men-in-grey, and all of them say the same thing: How dare you be away, even for a single day? How dare you ignore us? How dare you do anything outside of the box?'

Alex laughed.

'Yes, I know what you mean.'

Peppe was staring at him.

'What is that thing you have brought with you?'

Alex felt a shiver run up his spine.

'What thing? The lute, you mean?'

Peppe shook his head, slowly.

'You had it in the car trunk. I saw you lift it out. It wasn't like a case, exactly…'

Alex wondered whether Peppe had been into their room. He must have been: it was his house, for God's sake. Alex felt a gulf open up between them. Beneath the warm hospitality – and Peppe had gone out of his way to be hospitable; after all, Zuleikha and he were more or less complete strangers, not only to Peppe Ayala and his family but also to his cousin, back in England – Alex sensed that he and Peppe had come from very different places. These differences, he thought, they catch you unawares. They pull you up when you least expect it – and yet you should expect it, you with your northern European prissiness around the concept of personal privacy and private ownership. When he thought about it Zuleikha too lacked insight into her deficiency in respecting his things. She'd gone fingering Susan's photos, for a start. He swallowed hard. Susan would remain an inviolable part of his life always. No-one could ever touch that, and no-one should try. He realised that he was blushing, though he was unsure whether his anger was directed at Peppe or Zulie. It would not have been good form for Alexander to have gone poking about among someone else's belongings, not even if they had been those of his own brother (if he'd had one). It was an affront. Yes, he thought: we have our silly codes too. We are not, and never were, the elevated objective beings we like to project ourselves as: we're just glorified homesteaders (though we can no longer see the dirt on our own skins). He knew that if Peppe had been rummaging among their things, he would have opened up the various lids of the boxes before reaching the one which wouldn't open. Perhaps he would have wondered what the box had contained, what it still might contain. Alex thought for a moment of confronting Peppe, but that would've been stupid, inappropriate, an overreaction. And so instead he smiled and said,

'Yes, it's a box.'

At first, the temperature in the stone well was freezing and she had to button up her coat and evert the collar to prevent herself from shivering as she measured out each step on the metal rungs of the ladder that had been bolted to its side-wall. But after she had climbed down about fifteen feet or so the atmosphere began to moderate somewhat, though she was unsure whether this was from the shelter provided by the enclosed space or from the heat generated by her own exertions. I need the exercise, she thought, as she found the muscle tone in her left calf suddenly insufficient to prevent her from wobbling just a little, so that the fingers of both hands went into a rictus around the iron of the ladder. It was more difficult climbing down than it would have been to have ascended, because while the circle of dim light at the top of the tower – was it after all a tower, she wondered – cast a little illumination from above, yet at her level she could not make out even her own hand, held up before her.

The sound of her boots on the iron echoed more loudly the further she descended, and she attributed this to some effect of physics – Newton's nth Law, no doubt, which stated that, 'In an enclosed, cylindrical vacuum, the amplitude of a sound-wave will be equal to the square of its distance from the sun'. But this was not a vacuum, otherwise she wouldn't have been able to smell that scent which lay somewhere between jasmine, cedar and sulphur. Nor would she have been able to hear the unmistakeable twanging of a Jew's Harp, a marranzanu, which also had grown louder. What if I get stuck down here, she thought, in this dried-up well in a deserted villa in the middle of these barren lands? When I do not return to the massaria people will become worried, but no-one will know where to look. After a few days without water, I will grow weak and will be unable even to stand, and then slowly I will become delirious and lose consciousness. My breathing will become stertorous, just as my mother's did in the hours before she died, and like Archie McPherson's breathing has been for months on end. No, she thought: that is inaccurate, unscientific. Nasrin Zeinab had died of heart failure, part of the multiple organ collapse brought on by disseminated cancer. Her lungs had become flooded with her own serum, the blood minus the cells. But all of Zuleikha's science could neither create nor destroy even the tiniest atom. Archie was dying from a type of neoplasm which had been triggered by the skins of the big ships, a meso-tumour which grew like a giant red spider. It was filling up the darkness of his lung tree with its deformity, its fast-growing cells whose nuclei had been programmed from their inception to do nothing but destroy, even to the extent of causing their own demise. There was logic, but no sentience.

She kept on going, a few more steps, a few more feet down into the earth. Every so often, her hand would brush against something soft and she would recoil, imagining that it was the head of some fungal growth or else that of a lizard or worse. The tactility became more prominent as she descended and seemed to comprise two distinct qualities of sensation. One was like touching a vein, a dead person's vein, the denervated blood vessel of a corpse halfway through dissection. Cold, cylindrical, solidified. The other was more like a thick sugar paper redolent of primary school. But after a while, there was only the irregular surface of the stone and the smooth iron of the ladder. That, and her own heartbeat. She was proceeding by touch and smell. And by the sound of the Jew's harp.

Again, she wondered what would happen if she got trapped down here. Down in the well, she thought, perhaps I would be forced to begin drinking my own urine. But the mineral balance of urine was wrong and anyway, with less and less input, its production would slow and then stop and the total lack of water would cause the cells of her organs to cease functioning. Chemicals would build up and would poison even more cells, including those of the muscle of her heart. Zuleikha became obsessed by this thought and, as sweat broke out under her armpits and along the whip-line formed by the join between her neck and skull, she found herself impelled to follow its trajectory. Wrapped in its clothes, my cadaver slowly would desiccate; the cheeks would implode; the belly, bloated with anaerobic microbial activity, first would burst open and then later, partially eviscerated, would fall in; the globes of the eyes would grow opaque and then shrivel to plastic skins. If I am not eaten by rats and spiders, in death I will be propped-up against the wall, a queen of the dead, my shoulders swathed in white flowers, my gaze piercing the future, my mouth set in an inanimate grin, and from my tissues will erupt the aroma of sainthood and the aroma will fill the well, the palazzu, the countryside. And the land and my body will become one and will gather within itself, as though it were a miniature paradise, the heady reek of mint, carnations, roses and myrtle, the great and multifarious sex of spring.

Then she found herself dwelling on those women who, during the Indian Partition in the 1940s, had leapt into wells rather than be captured and gang-raped, tortured and then slaughtered. Eventually, so many bodies had piled up that they had formed a cushion of flesh, and so some women had survived the initial fall. However, because no-one had been left alive at the top – all the men having either run away or been killed (if, that is, they hadn't gone and joined some reciprocal killing gang of their own) – these women had been unable to escape. They'd sat there on top of the pile formed by their sisters, mothers, aunts, grandmas, daughters … some already dead, others dying from their wounds, moaning, screaming, pleading, scalped, mastectomised, incontinent, broken. And eventually, in the heat of that particular August in India, in the water the bodies would have begun rapidly to putrefy, one by one to burst open at the belly and to let out the intestines and then slowly to boil, like lobsters in a pot. And amidst all this, the women closest to the top of the well would have died slowly from dehydration. The Black Hole of Calcutta. Yeah, right. People dug their own black holes and then they jumped into them. And she thought of her own visit to the big bridge. Of Alexander and the box. Had she really been suicidal? She was no longer sure.

Suddenly the rungs stopped, her foot flailed wildly, and she panicked. The noise had become loud and its wavering, bent-back notes filled up the tower so that it became hard to think straight.

She let her foot probe just a little further and then peered deep into the darkness. She realised then that in fact the darkness had become diluted ever so slightly and that the ground lay about six, or possibly seven, feet beyond the end of her boot. She climbed right down to the bottom rung and hung onto it with both hands. But the gap had been deceptive, rather like the depth distortion produced by the water in a pool. Kicking her toes against the wall, she caused her body to swing outwards and then she let go. Simultaneously she realised that if the bottom rung of the ladder was higher up than she was able, at maximal jump, to reach, then she would not be able to get back up again. These thoughts were cut short by her landing, which was rough and awkward. The depth had indeed been deceptive, and when she looked up again towards the tiny ring of light, Zuleikha realised that she must have just leapt about fifteen feet down from the last rung. Since she was five foot-six, this meant that, at the point of release, the ground had lain some nine and a half feet beneath the soles of her feet. No wonder she'd jarred both knees. Luckily, her boots had probably saved her ankles from being badly sprained, though she knew that sometimes the full extent of any such damage became evident only a few hours after initial injury.

She gathered herself together. She was at the foot of either a tall tower or a deep well that surely, she thought, must reach far down into the ground. The light which she had perceived earlier seemed to be coming from one side of the brick wall. The bricks felt

391

slightly warm to the touch, but as she followed the light and knelt down, at the lower part of the wall she saw that the stonework gave way to wood. Zuleikha realised that she was pushing against a small door. There did not seem to be a handle or lever and it did not respond to her attempts to force it open and so, stepping back a few paces, she took a run and kicked hard with the steel toe of her boot. She felt the wood splinter but still the door did not yield and so she repeated the action twice, and at the third blow it gave way and light flooded into the tower.

At first, Zuleikha could see nothing for the clouds of dust and ash that her commotion had raised. The stench caught her in the centre of her chest and caused her to cough repeatedly until she felt that her head would explode. She desperately needed a drink of water. When at last the dust had subsided, she wiped the tears from her face and licked the salty liquid off the back of her hand. Now that light had filled the tower, Zuleikha saw that from about a third of the way up the surface of the brick was veined with tendrils and small white flowers whose petals were shaped like clubs. Each flower had five – or maybe six – lobes, and exuded a scent so powerful it felt almost like a drug – a scent which seemed now to be drawn and concentrated as though through a vacuum down to where Zuleikha was standing, at the foot of the tower and on the threshold of a chamber. The music had stopped as soon as she'd blasted open the hatch. She crouched down and crawled through the aperture. She closed her eyes to avoid the dust and, as the aroma of flowers filled her brain, it was as though Zuleikha was a lavureddu: a receptacle in which these flowers of the night had been germinating, perhaps for years, perhaps for centuries. She remembered now. Jasmine, chambeyli. The Queen of the Night.

As soon as she emerged into the room, she realised that the structure down which she had been descending was neither well nor tower, but an enormous chimney whose upper portion had been removed and in whose hearth she had been standing.

'I'm Santa Claus!' she said aloud.

Her clothes were filthy and she brushed them down as well as she could. She was in a small low-ceilinged room whose walls seemed to have been whitewashed fairly recently.

At the opposite end of the room to the fire-place was a doorway from which there protruded a single brass hinge. Beyond, the space opened out into a much larger chamber – again, totally bare and with whitewashed brick walls, but at whose centre, reaching almost to the flat ceiling, there stood a pink cubic structure some twenty feet square.

The surface of the structure seemed to be peeling, so that as she walked slowly around it Zuleikha was able to make out several layers of stone at once: white, pink, bluish-grey, black. Right around the top there was a narrow band of stone into which had been carved the angular letters of a script which looked like a mixture of Greek and Kufic. She wished she could read either of them. Immediately beneath this was a broader area occupied by images coloured in pale pigments: yellow, green and purple. There were two such scenes on each side of the cube. Beneath a heavily pregnant vine she made out the figure of what she thought was Dionysus, while on another panel was Pan. Both deities were surrounded by creatures which looked like archaic horned goats, or else goat-antelopes, or perhaps muscular sheep.

But the dominant theme around the cube was that of the incarnations of Persephone, from fertility goddess to Queen of the Dead. In places, these pictures had been overlaid with other images: drawings of musicians, some in Arab clothing, others dressed like Mediaeval northern Europeans, and one even resembling a Norman knight from the Bayeaux Tapestry's depiction of the Battle of Hastings. The musicians included women and they played all manner of instruments: gitterns, oddly-shaped fiddles, bagpipes, a Jew's harp, various types of drums and tambourines, a small recorder and a single hurdy-gurdy, but most prominent and varied of all, several ouds. And, watching over the entire scene, eating couscous speckled with raisins, badams and pine nuts and no doubt listening to the music – which in ten centuries or more, never seemed to have ceased – were the great sultans: Manfredi, chess-master and Lord of the Saracens; al-mu'tazz bi-llah Roger II; and Emperor Fredericus Secundus, the Stupor Mundi. Zuleikha wasn't sure how she knew all this stuff, but then her attention wavered and she could have sworn that at one point she saw a woman dancing between the panels, dancing through time and space as though from one agora to the next, from the time of bone and horn, through the bronze gleam of Hamilcar Barca and the gold leaf of Byzantium to the era of the three emperors and beyond. The figure shifted between the human and the non-human and from male to female. It seemed to possess no fixed structure – or rather, the fluidity of its transformation was infinite.

Further down the cube were numerous pictures of chimaerae – figures painted in ochre, sepia and pale blue – children whose fingers became waterfalls, and lute-shaped women whose hair turned into gardens of fig trees. She felt as though she was standing at the summit of one of the hills she had crossed earlier on her way to the villa. The air smelled of almond and sorb apple blossom, of asphodel and narcissus, the scents of early spring that normally were placid and understated like an English cup of tea, but which, thrown together in this enclosed space, now in the aromatic decadence of their music, quite overpowered her senses. And she was certain that she could hear music, somewhere deep in her head. Not sound, not the noise of instruments, but something that held the quality of music, the transfiguring of form, the intersection of the physical, mathematical and spiritual that threw up windows, portals; what in another place she might have called insights, intuitive realities, illuminations. It was obvious now that this building was being painstakingly restored, its layers uncovered one by one, right down to the bare limestone. She could see the marks of tools drawn across its surface, and she knew that the work must be taking years, decades – at least, if it was being undertaken by one person, and she was certain that one person was responsible and that he had fallen in love with the building, with its walls, its arkan, its pillars and all it represented. Giuseppe Ayala, whose grandmother's name had been Asunsi and whose father's mother's name had been Scime'.

On the walls of the room, Zuleikha began to make out the imprints – almost like silhouettes – of the symbols, aleph, beth, gimla, daleth, and then she wondered whether this might have been a burial chamber of the Marranos, the Jewish converts who sometimes had continued to practise their old religion in secret and who had been rooted out and burned here in Sicily at the hellish hands of the Spanish Inquisition. Perhaps, when persecuted, a spirit would secrete itself in airless grutti, in sea-bed jars and inside the hearts of human beings. And at times the music seemed to attain the coherence of words, so that it was as though Zuleikha was picking up an ancient radio broadcast:

...petra disprizzata, cantunera di muro...

And then it sank back again into a morass of noise. And it was as though the force of the music had thrown this great stone block from out of the mouth of the Mountain of Mountains and carried it to this place where, long before the palazzu had been constructed, the cube had burned down to the very bedrock of the island.

Sweat ran into her eyes. She blinked several times, threw back her head and drew out a hankie. But instead of the hankie, there in her hand was a man. San Giuseppe ru Casteddu Nivuru, cut a thousand years ago from the very lip of Etna, from a seam of black rock, long ago cooled, that now lay deep beneath the surface, and that with God's grace had held up the wall of a sulphur mine. The saint's right hand protruded slightly from his gown as though inviting, enticing the believer to follow him, to follow him down into the deepest shafts of the mine, the shafts into which no-one ventured any more, the mine that had been sucked into emptiness by the ghosts of those who had died beneath its yellow fumes, by the contadini who had been burned to the bone by its white-hot magma. The music was much louder now; the smell was almost palpable and it was as though, through the music, Zuleikha could see deep into the interior of the cube. And she could see that it was filled with nothing but light, light from which she was shielded by layers of stone, paint, mosaic, stucco, by every accretion that had formed the skin of the complex polytonal organism called Sicily. The images began to move between panels so that it became impossible to attribute a particular one to a specific scene, and then the cube itself seemed to begin to move, to spin, to become almost liquid.

And then, from the substance of the cube, at a level around seven feet from the floor, eyes began to form – eyes that were black at their centres – while the smell emanating from the structure grew stronger, the music louder, until, with the density of sensation, Zuleikha felt as though she might lose consciousness altogether.

And it was the music of the wheat as it burst, full and green and speckled with carmine, through the heavy moistness of the soil, and the notes caught sharply in her throat with the pungency of zàgara. It was the music of all the earth that rose up beneath the widening sun, an octagonal music that bit her in the neck and infused her body with a delicious poison that turned the balls of her eyes upwards to gaze again at the gold and white stucco, at the vaults and shadows of statues which lay buried in the walls of this secreted oratory deep in a disused sulphur mine. Flitting along the walls, she saw the weeping shades of child-miners, the long bloody history of yellow death on this island. And at the heart of the music there was the face of basalt black that had been cut, burning and molten, from the mouth of Mongibeddu, the fire mountain, Gibel Utlamat, and it was the face of Wali Yusuf of Sicilia, Yusuf of the great palaces, Joseph the Just, the Miraculous, the Bethrothed, Nutritor Domini, Joseph of box-makers and carpenters, of travellers and the dying, of the inner soul, the Old Man of the Lily. And behind everything was Beautiful Joseph of the Nile, the Moon of Canaan.

And the face was weeping tears of liquid sulphur, tears of rage at the priests, the bishops, the kings and at all those who burned forever in a lake of sulphur, who burned for their sins, for the life of each child they had murdered down in the tunnels of the lemon-stone tomb. The face was singing an old lament, a Scottish lament for the African's body that had been washed-up dead, white and bloated on the southern beaches of Sciacca, Licata, Pantelleria and Lampedusa; for the African who a thousand years earlier had brought irrigation, palaces, mathematics and most of the fruits of the island, but who now disembarked as, seventy years ago, Sicilians of the family classes had arrived on other shores as slaves, beggars, hookers: people with swarthy mysterious lives. Terrune. Dirt people. People of Aadam. Now it was the Africans who sold trinkets, sitting on mats in the centres of Palermo, Agrigento, Gela, Marsala, or who sold their bodies for pyramids of cocaine in the brothels of Catania, Siracusa, Ragusa, Salemi. As-salaam alaikum. Al Banurmu, Mars'Allah, Sirako, Rogos, Qalat al Nisena, Katane, Gergent. Peace and granaries. The markets of Al Madina. The people of the scirocco, peace be upon them, who bathed in the holy spring water of sacred gebbias and who brought forth revelation to the land and the sea. The Congolese, Ethiopians and Malians who nowadays were captured like bluefin tuna from the depths of the ocean; the people who swirled upwards through the chambers of death, and who now lived amongst the shit and spunk of the Vuccinia and who eeked out a living on the edges of death row vara and who were stuck in sweat-cellars, spending their lives being played shamelessly upon the fingertips of the Honourable Men, the Men of Respect who, when asked what they do, reply that they are *in security*, or else that they direct cars to resting places in the excessively well-protected mandamenti of Palermo.

The lament was for the intelligent goats who find ancient buried cities beneath the thrones of archbishops, for the shades of ragged children and tightly swaddled babies who drink milk from goats' udders and who sing to the flickering dance of nache lights, and it was the song of the Lady of the Chain, of the carusi, those bones of the earth who emerge from the zulfare during only the deepest, blackest of nights to howl madrigals at the empty moon, of the penitents with bleeding heads, of the curatuli who commune with the stars and with the face of the beautiful Joseph. And all of these joined now with the grizzled emirs of Kasr Yanni and the dancing animals cut into golden sandstone and the sugar dolls of the devil as together they sang laments across the stillness of the mountains. The forgotten songs, the songs of those rushing towards death. *Ad Mortem Festinamus.* And the saint was also weeping for Archibald Enoch McPherson, peace be upon him, who at that moment was sinking into a final unconsciousness, and for all the shipbuilders, roofers, plasterers and their wives and children who had been poisoned by those same lords of silver and gold who had filled the Temple with their heinous breath, with the substance of their foul sulphurous lungs, and who continued to receive great medals and honours and peaceful spiritual deaths at advanced ages with several generations garnered around them like petals, like devotees, disciples, acolytes. There were no devotees or disciples, no family at all around Archie's deathbed. Only the faded images, their lower parts half-hidden behind coloured winding-sheets, of dead lovers who danced on brass balconies, lovers who spun in the arms of the juggling spider, lovers who screamed in the music of arks and the songs of aeroplanes, the lovers who, with their bare fists, punched holes in heaven. Peace be upon heaven.

And Zuleikha reached out her hand, the bones of her fingers wrapped tightly around the black body of the saint, and she placed the saint's form upside-down in the niche which had opened up in the cube. She felt that somehow the statue had led them here, that she and Alex had been drawn to this hilly place in the heart of Sicily, to this village of San Giuseppe ru Casteddu Nivuru, to this palazzu in the middle of a sea of wheat, to this node of penance, by the power of a face, by all the faces of Yusuf the Prophet, the Technicolour and the Black, San Giuseppe of the Night, the man who in his dark nakedness had risen from the face of the zolfara. She had been drawn here by the music of the Hebrew, the Catholic, the Muslim Yusuf. Joseph, the architectural restorer, the patron of causes lost and dying, of dead airmen, of whores, jugglers, soldiers, sufis, poets, of n'er-do-wells, of those who were lost in wells. Yusuf the Greek with his face of light.

And now at last she was returning the saint to his rightful place. To the tomb that lay beneath all the layers, to the house cut in red porphyry, the crimson residence of the soul of Sultan Rujari whose blood flowed to the place where all the knowledge of the ages was stored, knowledge that awaited a new revelation, a different justice, a law that would be administered by dishonourable women. A vision of beauty: an image of sea pigs riding untrammelled through the open ocean, of the stone skulls of ancient children, of the courses taken during the night by holy feral cats from al-'Attabiya, of the dance of tornados as they tore open the skin of the ocean. And there, in the middle of the great stone cube, was the face, the body, of Daoud – of her son, Daoud. He was asleep and was nine and a half months old and his skin glowed with a perfect lustre, while his hair was cast across his forehead just as it had been in life, each strand purest gold beyond measure. It was as though he had been captured at the very moment before death, caught deep in the night in the midst of a perfect sleep in his cot, in the act of taking his last ever breath. In death he would remain immortal. His eyes perfect sapphires. Yaqut, jachitu. Yes, naturally, that's right, she thought; he was here, cut into the dry stone of Black Joseph, and not six feet under the sodden soil of the

Cathcart Cemetery. His spirit resided in the arms of the saint, he played happily among the ghosts of lost carusi, he was protected and sung to as he never had been in life. No, that wasn't so: she had sung to him; she had sung sestinas till her voice had grown hoarse, till her breath had died within him. And even after he had been taken from her, she had sung to the empty walls which once had been kissed by his shadow, had tried, through the music of her mothers, to bring him back, just for a second or two, just for the span of a single warm breath.

Zuleikha felt the music grip her body as though it were a muscle and thrust her down onto her knees and then press her flat onto her chest, so that she was prostrated like a nun or a slave. The tears burned the skin of her face, branding her with the soot and bone dust of this place, turning her face black like that of the Old Madonna. And she wept and worshipped at the same time. She wept for her mother, Nasrin Zeinab, the beautiful woman to whom she had never said goodbye and with whom it had not seemed possible to have made her peace. And she wept for her father, Daniel John, as he sank into his pool of lilies and dark whisky; for Susan who, in a long second of despair, had taken her own life; for Alexander, whose tangent would never have coincided with Zuleikha's had it not been for Susan's act of self-immolation; and for Archibald of the Blue Asbestos, her patient, the man who had started all this, the man for whom at last the box had come. And she wept for the disarticulated skeleton of her own long-dead child, of Holy Daoud, buried seven years in the children's section of the Cathcart Cemetery among the plastic windmills and the faded streamers, the dog-eared teddies that had been propped up by strangers against the headstones of tiny graves.

And there, sprawled on the floor of the zolfara, her lips kissing the stone that had been yellowed with dust and age and the heavy tread of calloused skin, she swore obedience to Saint Joseph. She swore always to be his slave, to do his bidding, to follow the path which he had laid out – across continents, across time, faith, spirit. The ground tasted bitter, like human seed; but then she and the cube were moving together as though enveloped in a single integument and, as though through the spirit beatitude of the spider, truly they had become one.

Chapter Twenty-Three

That night, after she had washed away the grime up in the attic room which had been assigned to them, Zuleikha and Alexander came across an almost full bottle of limoncello. They found it in a capacious cupboard stuffed with old counterpanes, blankets, cuttunini, cupierte and other assorted material bric-a-brac, some of which, from their appearance and smell, seemed to date from the era of Peppe's grandmother, and among the moth-balls, dusty portraits and alabaster statuettes of various obsolescent saints whom even the Roman Catholic Church had de-beatified, un-frocked, defenestrated, stripped naked, pronounced heretical or schismatic, or simply had declared had never existed in the first place. They took it to bed with them and passed it from one to the other, swigging crazily like adolescents and trying to suppress giggles as the liqueur – God knew how old it was, but with liqueurs that didn't really matter, did it – warmed their stomachs, while in a comfortable symmetry, the smouldering dome, the brass and willow of the cuba kept their feet from freezing.

On her return from the palazzu everyone had been in stitches at her appearance. It had seemed as though she'd rolled around for several hours in the fields and ditches of Giuseppe's inheritance, as though she'd been attempting, like some typical British religious pervert – an acolyte perhaps of that upper-class loony the other Sikander, who'd christened himself 'The Great Beast' and who eventually had been thrown off the island – to bury herself alive in the fecund Palermitan earth, so that like Persephone she might rise with the spring that broiled just over the lip of the south-eastern escarpment. The more she'd tried to explain, the greater the hilarity had become. In the end, what with the hunger, dehydration and surreality of it all, Zuleikha had begun to feel that she was going mad – though in a peculiarly comforting sort of way.

At some point, Alex awoke quite suddenly with the sound of a lupara and found his head filled with stars. A few seconds later he realised that it was an effect of perspective, and that one of the shutters covering the outside of the skylight had blown open. It was most probably the banging of this heavy wooden contraption against the roof tiles that had caused him to awaken. He was gazing up at the night heavens. Argo Navis, l'ursa maggiuri, the Dog Stars... And it was as though each pattern of lights had its equivalent down here on the Sicilian earth, down here among the ghosts of the contadini and the living people, on the land whose very flesh had changed so much since those ancient times. The stars had a smell, even from millions of light-years away: he could smell their sulphur and phosphorus, their hydrogen and helium, their monumental and continuous explosiveness, their instability as they – or rather, as their ghosts – flickered against the basalt black of infinity. Canopo, Orioni, Algorab...

The smell brought back the deep yearning for his mother and father which he thought he'd overcome, matured through, or at least compartmentalised, years ago. Perhaps the loss of Susan, or meeting Zuleikha, or this strange journey, or just this sudden glimpse of the very deep past was bringing back all those old emotions. He sighed, then chuckled. Or maybe it was just the yellow drink. He glanced over at Zulie but she was fast asleep, and occasionally lightly snoring. In the starlight, the exposed angle of her shoulder gleamed with the lustre of ripe wheat. Her face was relaxed, the skin barely creased. When they slept people seemed young, vulnerable, innocent. He reached out, but held back from touching her face or her shoulder and instead slowly, carefully manoeuvred himself again onto his back so that he could gaze some more at the heavens. He had forgotten how dark and clear the sky became in the deep countryside and it reminded him of his childhood on the southern borderlands of Glasgow. His house had been right on the edge of what later he had learned had been denoted as the green belt, but which at that time, to Alex, had seemed like the start of the great green wilderness. There had been a disused railway-line near to where he'd lived that had been closed probably during the Beeching so-called reforms of the early 1960s. As a child he'd spent countless days playing in the deep cutting, and he had come to know every inch of the old track-bed with its rotting sleepers and white rubble. During the summer months especially his playmaking, the stuff of future memory, had taken place amongst the unruly weeds, barbed thistles and indestructible gorse bushes which had begun to sprout even as the whistling wind of the last train's passage had faded forever into stillness.

As an only child Alex often had played alone, and though at times in the absence of siblings he had sought out company with other children, mostly he had found contentment in his own world – a world which, weather permitting, had been discovered and re-created largely out of doors. His mother's voice, high-pitched, would carry on the breeze and would find him wherever he was. Now, so many years later, he thought that it was odd that her voice calling *Alexander*, with its rise and extreme sustain of the last two syllables, should have been audible to him some two hundred yards or so away from the house as he'd played down in the gully of the old railway. Or in the opposite direction, at the very bottom of the dense deciduous wood of beech and sycamore, the trunks of whose trees were infested with a parasitic fungus that had grown over the surface of the bark to resemble giant, white brains. And now, as he lay on his back and gazed at the Sicilian stars, he wondered whether truly it had been her voice or whether his name, enunciated as in a song, had been transmuted somehow from her throat to his head with no physical intermediary.

His mother, with her straw-blonde hair perpetually bound up behind her head, her blue pinafore tied tightly around her waist, her arms drowned often up to the elbows in soap and grease and cooking pots – hers had been a respectable life. It had been understood in those days that a woman would be like this, that those women who went out to work did so out of necessity, so that they came to be looked down upon as dubious characters, very possibly with loose morals – especially if they also smoked, painted their toenails and lay on low-slung deckchairs, displaying themselves scantily clad beneath the sun. Alex's family had had a record player designed in the 1960s manner of sharp angles and clean spaces with a subdued red lid, grey casing and a silver grille, and which had settings for vinyl at speeds of 33, 45 and 78 rpm. His mother had used to pile on several records at once beneath the angular black arm – that was the way it was supposed to be played: you kept on adding singles. Yet it wasn't the raucous beat songs that teenagers of the time listened to, but big band music, swing, hot jazz and white heathery Scottish singers. This was the stuff of the War generation, those people whose lives forever had been marked and blighted by the great conflagration of the 1940s, so that everyone had known someone who had died, or whose mind had been turned on the fields of blood or by the wars in heaven. He could almost feel the hard heavy black of the vinyl: vinyl that could weather the boom of heavy artillery and that would never bend but only crack.

It seemed such a long time ago now; a different world, really. Like something out of a museum or a Pathé film – and yet for so long, as he had grown up, it had been mundane, overly familiar. But that was what happened, he thought: that is what happens to people like us. People who die. We become extraordinary, larger than life, identified always with sunsets or sunrises or hulking mountains, reedy rivers, seas swaying with fish.

His father had been an electrician, a skilled worker, and had had to negotiate his way through most of his colleagues, who had been active members of the Orange Lodge. Electrons, asbestos and the sash. Rugged men with short backs and sides – what hair they had had been matted down flat with Brylcreem – and trotting along beside them were their flea-bitten wives. In those days, in the time before showers, casual continental or American clothes and centrally-heated tap water, many domestic toilets had been sited down at the end of a path at the foot of the back garden. People had had baths only twice a week and had wrapped up warm. Yet with all their faults they had been real people; they had helped one another out in small but significant ways. Mentally they had never lived in the suburbs. They had moved with a sureness born of the knowledge of humanity's advancement. They were like Scottish versions of Yuri Gagarin, John Glen, Paul Robeson. Each of their faces would have made it onto a Soviet coin or an American banknote. With their muscular affection, their social class certainties, their ingrained industriousness, they had been the salt of the earth. He could taste the salt, as though it had been freshly-cut from the earth or as though just now, at this late hour, it had been hauled in on silver nets from the dark heaving sea. It was a taste of the stars. Alexander found himself smiling and he realised that the constellations had shifted ever so slightly. He'd drunk too much of that stuff and his mouth felt parched; his head was light and airy. It must have been at least several hours before dawn. Alex decided to go down to the kitchen to get a glass of water or heat up some milk and maybe to read a little.

It was no longer raining and the darkness had eased, so that Archie was unsure whether dawn was imminent or whether it was just an electric effect of the city. Shadows flitted across the windows, the walls, the photographs, the map of his life, compacted here in this last room. This tomb. His breath seemed a little easier now, even though the moment he had awoken he had pulled off the oxygen mask and opened his mouth as though to taste the flavour of the night. And this night tasted of trees, blossoms, flowers. He thought that perhaps, like witches, the district nurses had sprayed some kind of toxic air-freshener all around the house, but this was neither stale nor synthetic: it was like fresh air. And then he noticed that there was a breeze blowing across his face, lifting the lank strands of hair off his scalp. He glanced over at the oxygen cylinder, though he knew that he'd already turned it off. Mulberry, hawthorn, alder, his mother's perfume, which she'd used on the rare occasions when she'd been able to raise her arms from the dirty water of the sink. And there must have been some damned car out there on the gleaming wet street playing its stereo at top volume – and at this time of night, for God's sake – because now he could hear music, drums, horns and pullulating flute, and maybe beneath these the sound of a plucked guitar. But no, it wasn't that: the timbre was too soft, sad, elegant. The music was growing louder and the breeze stronger, and it was a cool breeze, a tramontana, and it had blown off the ice and stone of the peaks that lay far to the north. He thought that perhaps someone had left the window ajar – yet the curtains lay still. And then, high on the shelf which he no longer used, but which once had held a full Everyman's Library, Archie saw a single volume bound in brown leather. He knew that he couldn't possibly have got up and removed the book, yet somehow he did raise himself up, carefully avoiding disconnecting the infusion pump, *and where were those bloody nurses, anyway. There was supposed to be one here every night. He was sure he remembered her arriving, but perhaps that had been the night before this one, or the night after this one, or the night sixty-odd years ago...*

For the first time in weeks he stood up – properly stood up, straight-backed like he used to, as would have been expected of him in the Royal Air Force and in the shipyards too, where there was no time for slouching, where slouching could get you – or someone else – killed. He inhaled and found that his lungs filled with air. It felt strange, the feeling that oxygen would reach even his skin, the marrow of his bones, the outer edges of the sky. He reached upwards, but the window seemed to have turned on its axis so that he was standing directly beneath it. And he took an even deeper breath, and then another, and with every breath he took the yawning chasm of the night seemed to grow more vibrant. The brilliance of the stars was almost painful, so that after a while he could hardly bear to look. He stretched out his hand and circled his fingers like the legs of a spider around the spine of the book, then he pulled it towards him and clutched it to his chest. He looked at its cover and he saw that the cover was blank, just plain brown leather, it smoothness broken only by the whorls and fissures of whichever beast's skin had been taken and tanned into buckram.

He felt a slight pain in his right forearm and realised that the pump had become disconnected from his body and that his blood was flowing through the tiny orifice thus exposed; that it was pulsating with the rhythm of the music which now had grown to fill the entire street *and what was happening, for fuck's sake, was there a Carnival going on out there? Someone should phone the Polis or the Noise Control Department of the Local Cooncil!* But now he could hear the stamping of bare feet on stone and dust and his blood really was flowing like a river over his skin that was as pale as marble, and the sky was coming down and was flooding his room and he opened the book and saw there the exact same pages he had seen all those years earlier in the deserted black lakeside house in the Lincolnshire forest – except that now it was as though he could read at high speed, could read faster than a spinning bicycle, faster than a coursing Spitfire, faster than a bomb spiralling down towards the runway shelter. He was reading at the speed of light, at the speed of the stars whose movement through the black velvet of the sky gave off the stink of sulphur, the stench of oxyacetylene that came from the hulls of big ocean liners.

And then he looked down and saw that his body was naked and that his blood had turned to water and that he was standing up to his thighs in a cool clear lake and that reflected in the face of the lake was the full moon and that from behind him a woman's hands had met, the fingers intertwined right at the centrepoint of his chest and he wasn't sure whose arms they were but he felt her warm breath on the back of his neck and the music was coming from her breath – she was singing a song that flowed in tides and dastgah-ha across thousands of years and then he breathed in one last time and all other scents in the room had been replaced by the strong smell of salt, of sea-water, of seed, of the black sirens, of the Mother of the Sea.

In Zuleikha's dream she was sitting cross-legged under the shade of a large olive tree which she knew was hundreds of years old. The tree was on top of a hill, so that she could see for miles around, and yet the areas immediately by the foot of the hill remained hidden. The land was undulating and verdant, though in places already it had begun to look wilted, yellow and parched in the manner of early summer. Rising behind her was a much higher mountain, a proper mountain whose summit, shaped like a dark skull bared to the sky, was still circled with snow. In the other direction, beyond the hills and the plain, lay the limpid vermillion sea. The water was so clear that she could see, swimming far below the surface, the sleek beautiful bodies of i sireni – giant squid that were as long as ships – and i pisci, the beings with enormous teeth who came up to feed on stray gulls and scorpion fish.

She looked around, trying to find Peppe's house, but it seemed that she was in another part of the country altogether. Or maybe in fact she was close by and simply was unaccustomed to the local geography. Yet it did not alarm her, this loss of memory, this sense of knowing unfamiliarity. The air smelled of gunpowder. Then she saw, littered over the ground, the burned-out casings of rockets and Catherine Wheels, fireworks which sometime before dawn had been launched from the valley, from the town, and which had arced across the sky and had ended up here, scattered over the summit of this hill, with its dusty winding track and its ancient Saracen olive tree. The day was hot; she had on a sleeveless cotton dress decorated with a print of small flowers that was of a cut of the sort which women had used to prefer in the 1960s. Her feet were bare, the skin hazelnut brown, the ends of the toenails broken and splintered, and the hardened soles scuffed with a yellow dust that was finer than sand. Her hair grew long, thick, untrammelled. There was no breeze.

From the foot of the hill she heard the sound of drumming. Then she remembered that she had been there, in the piazza of the town, and that she too had risen early with the crack of a single gunshot and had moved with the crowd, greeting people she knew, watching the fireworks take flight, and ending on the broad stone staircase of the church where the scent of incense mingled with the sulphur of the comets, rockets and Roman candles. And when she ran her tongue around the roof of her mouth the aftertaste of Communion Wine lingered on the soft skin – not so very unlike the taste of a man. The snare drumming grew louder and was accompanied by the brash sound of horns and then the procession emerged over the ridge and beneath the drumming there was a hubbub of voices from people of all ages: old men with sticks, swaddled babies, widows dressed in black, young women and working men. Some were in white hoods, others in capes, some carried trays laden with sculpted breads that had been baked in the shapes of castles, ships and churches, while others ported baskets piled high with fava beans, marzipan and all manner of trinkets. Some of the contadini wore chains around their necks, ankles, wrists, while the clothes of others had been made entirely of thorns and brambles. Many were bleeding from their foreheads, arms or feet, and some even from their palms as they clutched rosaries cut from thorn bushes, so that as they walked, as they carried aloft their angel ships, they left tiny trails of red along the track. After a while it was as though a line of miraculous snails had just passed by the olive tree.

Right at the centre of the procession, in a garishly decorated litter carried by four men, Zuleikha made out an ebony Madonna, six feet tall and partially clothed in a long blue gown decorated with gold traceries. Behind this litter was another, also carrying a Madonna, but this statue had a cream-coloured complexion and a sorrowful expression. Though of similar size to the first, this

Queen of Heaven wore a black robe adorned with crystal teardrops and white carnations. Behind these Mothers of God came pilgrims dressed in bizarre apparel: red demons wearing fur cloaks, armour-clad angels, and a lone figure draped in yellow who was carrying a crossbow. As they passed by no-one seemed to notice Zuleikha sitting under the tree.

The music was a dirge, a slow heavy sound that was painful on the ears. Zuleikha saw that many of the mourners – for she realised now that, save for the Mediaeval-like figures she'd noted earlier, the villaini were all dressed in black – were carrying large unlit candles. It was an otherworldy sound, as though the Solemnity of San Giuseppe had merged with the Addolorata of Good Friday and the Easter Dance of the Devils. But beneath the slap of bare feet, which every so often would stop as the penitents knelt and offered prayers, once again through the rising cloud of yellow dust, the haze produced by the heat which had levelled the land and turned the flowers of spring – the fuschia, bougainvillea, scéusa and sulla – to fire and ash, there was the sound of an oud. An oud playing the maqam Saba, the maqam of sadness, pain, dolorousness, and yet it was a misery which swung like a nache through the burning air, a misery which illuminated and transfigured, a misery which transcended mortality.

And then Zuleikha saw, rising all around her, the grey buildings of a town – a town quite different from those others she had seen; even the stones had a different quality. None of the buildings were whitewashed, but all had been bleached by the sun and eroded by the centuries. The land was like a giant labyrinth: the villages, the hills, the track and the plane trees. She saw that the hill on which she and the olive tree were perched was far higher than at first it had seemed. At the heart of the town was a church built of black and white lava. There was the thick dizzying reek of lemon, and as the penitenti rose from their dust station and moved slowly forwards, the twin Madonnas turned their faces, moved their eyes and they were smiling at her, at Zuleikha, daughter of Daniyal and Nasrin Zenobia. The sad statue was smiling at her through crystalline tears and the joyous Queen of Heaven was grinning ecstatically in her direction and from both of these painted women of wood and stone, these women who had held God within their wombs, there came the delicious aroma of black Persian mulberry. With the full extent of the muscles of her neck and chest, she inhaled as though she were taking in the entire island and all of its history that was layered in stone beneath the bared soles of the penitents, beneath the great white beard of Saint Joseph up there on the coronal mountain. Bringing up the rear of the procession was a large goat which did not seem to belong to anyone and which, Zuleikha noticed, had been castrated. Blood dripped from between its hind legs as it sang, in the rasping voice of a raìs,

Aimola! Aimola! I have to leave,
To follow the light of the Dog Star
To sail on the sea where the sirens roam
To hear their song, to be taken down
To merge with their green flesh
To sing through their willowy throats
To sing the Song of the Sirens
And to free myself from the mattanza
That awaits all mortal men
Aimola! Aimola! O Madonnie di Mare!

All of a sudden, from that hillock with its olive tree, Zuleikha could see across the land, right through the big windows of the deserted palazzu. Except that it was no longer deserted. Now the enormous rooms were filled with the forms of waltzing couples, long lines of dancers, a string quartet, people feasting, chattering, smoking, drinking. In an enclave somewhat shaded from the bright wax light of the candelabras and chandeliers were the bandolier shades of a general or two, drawing up war plans. The pictures embossed in the wallpaper ballooned into the warm smoky air so that the hunts, the deities, the cherubic infants all became as real as the forms of the men and women spinning around on the polished wooden floors. It was night-time and it must have been cold, for there was a fire burning in the great hearth, the same fireplace in which she had lain and up whose chimney she had stretched her arm. But when she looked more closely she saw that the logs in the hearth were actually words that had dripped from the newsprint, and then she saw that the dancers too had been formed from letters, and as soon as this realisation hit her they seemed to begin to come apart, the young lovers, the old soldiers, the spinsters, the crooks, the self-important dreamers – all of them lost their human forms and became simply the words of the goat's song.

And then the windows of the palazzu became shuttered once again and Zuleikha was back on the hill amidst the marching column of pilgrims. When the procession had moved on up the mountainside towards the ring of snow, and after the sounds of the drums and horns had faded in swirls of dust and light, Zuleikha knew that it had been the procession of the dead and that the grey buildings which surrounded the olive tree were really tombs. Through the dead of the centuries were the living linked to one another. The trees, plains and hills, the dark mountain, the sky and the sea that flowed around all of these, were turning into pure colour as though the entire scene was becoming a painting. And then she looked down at her own body and she realised that she was not breathing.

She woke up suddenly and saw that the skylight was uncovered and that the stars were rushing like comets across the heavens, the Seven Sisters, Serpens, Draco – they were all dancing around, chains of stars just like in a rope dance, and her chest felt as though it had fallen as still as a stone. Too much limoncello, she supposed, and she raised herself up on locked elbows and got her breath back, and with it a deep sense of relief, and then she turned to her right and there in bed beside her she saw Archie.

He was staring up at her, his eyes clear as the blue of a noon sky, and he was smiling. His face was pale as ... But it wasn't Archie as she had known him. This was a younger Archie, Archibald Idris McPherson, Aircraftman Royal Air Force. He was breathing without difficulty, without any hint of a rasp in the throat. The skin of his face was fleshy yet taut, and his hair was full, thick, brown and was bunched up over the tops of his ears. His breath smelled of jasmine. He looked like a perfectly fashioned marionette, and when he moved his legs she could see that beneath the sheet he was nude.

He did not speak a single word and she did not expect him to. He removed her night-dress and then methodically, sinuously, as though he were untying knots, he brought her entire body to a fever pitch. Then he turned her onto all fours and, working between her legs and over her back and breasts, he made her whisper his name repeatedly, as though it was the hidden name of the god in a rosariu, in a tasbih. And then, when she could bear it no longer, she pulled him into her body, pulled him in where for so long only death had lain, pulled in the harvest of his seed, for the most fertile soil is the soil whose mouths are filled with dead leaves and rotting bones. His body was pure muscle, his movements instinctual yet perfectly timed, like those of a pupa or like the maqamat of night birdsong among the papyrus reeds of Sicilia. She was gasping for air; there was a tightness around her throat. It was as though she was in a room without windows, high in some dark mountain – and then the bassi itself was a window, or a mirror, and through the black glass the stars moved above her, tickling her skin with their passage, every tiny fire a needle in her body, a drop of freezing rain on a magma river.

The rhythm of their dance quickened so that it was as though they had become stationery: he a pointed arch over her spine and she a stained saint, her skin refracting the light from the stars. She felt the bones of her neck nearly dislocate upon one another as her head was bent back almost double and as he filled her mouth with his substance, his flesh, the whole of his tongue and the air of his lungs. And she realised that throughout he had not breathed, not even once, yet now he was emptying everything, the sum of his life, into her body, into her soul. And though he did not speak, a song seemed to issue from the pores of his skin. Six words, repeating again and again like the notes of a maqam or the words of an old hymn that were no longer understood:

> *I will give you my blood*
> *I will give you my blood*
> *The ciuri will be stained with my blood*

And still his eyes were open, staring into hers, flooding her moistness with the cold blue ice of the deep night, with the sulphur rock ice of the high mountains, with the sangu from the still-beating hearts of revolutionaries murdered by the honoured society, the blood which someday, insh'Allah, would give birth to new rivers; with

411

the asbestos of the iron ships, with the metal of the bullets that hit the aerodrome tarmac, with the WAAF woman's body that had fallen from the tail of a Hurricane Mark IIA Series 1 fighter, with the sound of her long scream. And now Zuleikha's legs were numb, unmoving; it was as though they belonged to a creature in a fresco or to the pendant body of a catacomb figure. From far above, from 10,000 feet or more, she heard the scurrying noise of insects, the distant howl of a goat, the dark music of a bomb being loosed in the night from the belly of a Heinkel He-111, the growl of the hoary Dog Star. Then she lost consciousness and sank into a deep well.

Chapter Twenty-Four

The next morning she barely spoke to Alexander. Her whole body ached and she felt slightly feverish, and she put this down to the booze. Except that around her neck there was a thin red line, as if a large insect had bitten her. Yet it was far too early for mosquitoes. Following breakfast she went out into the fields, and after a short while she realised that Alexander was following her. She tried to get away, but his pace was too fast. When he stopped her, turned her around and asked her what the matter was, she gazed into his eyes. And then she broke down and buried herself in his chest. The only words she was able to say at that moment were,

'He's gone! He's gone! Archie!'

On one level, Alex wondered how the hell she would know whether or not someone two thousand miles away was living or dead – someone with whom surely her relationship had been merely professional. Yet he knew that, in Archie, Zuleikha had seen and felt the sinews of history, just as through his lute he had played out its soul. In the cave behind the waterfall in Lincolnshire and again in Laila's house he too had had visions of the airman, who through that peculiar distortion had felt almost like a dead brother. Sometimes in the middle of the night Zuleikha would call out his name – Archie's name – with an unmistakeable desperation. When she did so it would be in the strange, archaic accents of rural Lincolnshire, yet Alex had not been surprised at this. After all, he thought, every conjunction of lovers is a conjunction of history, from the vast circle of the sky right down to the smallest atom, the oldest sin, the decorative wooden box which Pandora had opened, the lid she had flung open and then quickly had slammed shut again, allowing for only the merest glimpse of the eternal, the tiniest flicker of hope.

There was no breeze, yet the scent from the few trees there were seemed to intensify and gather around them, and Alexander pulled her closer and held her trembling body that had been racked for so long by grief, by a grief that burned slowly, that burned like the decomposing sulphurous gases in the bellies of dead creatures, a grief that had festered for years like a dying river, like the Papyrus

413

Wadi of Palermo, like the Papineto – a grief that flowed unseen through the darkness like blood through a muscle. It was a shared grief, which one day – one chilly morning in the shadow of a grey northern bridge – would explode in that terrible music that had conjured up the box, the lute, Alexander, Iskander, Sikander, and Susan, yes, even Susan, her death foretold on some scroll from the dark cave. Yes, he had read it there in Lindsey as he had played his music behind the waterfall, he had read of her moment of self-destruction, he had touched the unspoken depths of her despair. Her fear of oblivion, of purposelessness, of having no issue, no god, no music. Susan had merged herself with the Clyde River, with the secret rivers of Siqilliya, with the fast-flowing torrents of the Sindh Darya. From Susan's dead white hand, as from the hand of Bibi Fatima, Pandora, Persephone, had come the sacred drops of river water, the seeds of the underworld, the songs of the box. The Hidden Maqam of lutenists down the ages, the song of Rujari d'Alì, of Alessia Aldobrandini, Barbara Strozzi, Lady Arabella Stewart, Tarquinia Molza, Dilhayat Kalfa, Jane Pickering, Mary Harvey, Lady Mary Killigrew, of Ya'qub ibn Is'haq al-Kindi, Abu Nasr Muhammad ibn al-Farakh al-Farabi, of Milinda and Iskander, and it was the dastgah of the lost dream of Yusuf.

The smell became overpowering. It made him dizzy. Or perhaps it was just that Zuleikha was wearing a new perfume – but he hadn't seen her buy one, and she'd never smelled this way before, and it wasn't coming from the back of her scalp, from the sparse hairs whose roots already had turned to grey. They were too far away from the sea, surely. Yet Alex could've sworn that in the air that morning, in that place where, through the copse of cedar and chestnut, past the tiny votive chapel buried in the wall, where if you looked carefully enough, if you narrowed your eyes and then closed them, burned into the back of the retinas you could just about make out the pink walls of the deserted palazzu – there was a strong and unmistakable smell of salt.

Peppe was washing his car and he seemed a little coy when Zuleikha asked him about the mine, the palazzu, the cube. He hid behind a cigarillo, which he seemed to take ages to manage successfully to ignite.

414

'I'm working on it, restoring the stone, bringing it back to life. It's what I do. It's my job.'

'But here, in the middle of ...'

'Yes! In the middle of nowhere.'

She looked down.

Peppe told her that the big house belonged to a rich family, the Garufis, who once had ruled this area and who had acquired wealth over many centuries through agriculture but also through sulphur mines. Over a short period of time they had lost a fortune in a series of bad business ventures. It would have cost more to demolish the palazzo than simply to have left it to rot. Peppe had ventured in and had found the tower – originally the start of a mine shaft or possibly an air vent, turned later into a chimney – and then he had discovered the building down below.

'It is as though the house had been built around the shaft. It is still not finished, the restoration. It will take years. It is one of the reasons I come back here.'

'But it's not yours.'

Peppe shrugged.

'No-one cares about the place. Anyway, I am not doing it for myself.'

'For whom, then?'

'I don't know. Perhaps for all those who worked in the zulfare, the sulphur mines, over the thousands of years they were in operation. The picconieri, the naked men who cut the rock, and the carusi, the women and children who hauled the heavy sacks of sulphur to the surface and who often were raped along the way by the zolfatari. It was a hierarchy of Hades and, like the galleries themselves, some of the people who worked there seemed to slip down ever deeper into evil. But it simply reflected the system that existed above ground. You know, people used to sell their children to the mine-owners in order to survive. Some of the carusi managed to run away, but most never got out. Their whole lives, from the age of nine till the age of ninety, passed in the zolfara. We're talking here about the 1950s or even later. Eventually, the zolfatari and the women who worked as carusi banded together and went on strike, fought for their rights, for safety regulations. This mine, the one on which we are standing right now, was one of the smaller ones – and they were the worst. Sometimes I wonder just what the point is of me doing all this work. My senseless mission to resurrect the angry dead. This world up here in the fresh air has not changed its mode of working, and so the anger down there is unabated. They may try to cover it up by turning it into a folk museum: *Here, children: behind this clean transparent glass is a facsimile of how the miners used to live! Isn't it exotic? Isn't it exciting?* But they won't succeed. We are not children and Hell is a place of rage. Centimetre by centimetre, we will take back this land.'

He shrugged, looked into the distance, and blew on his cigarillo as though attempting to re-ignite its embers.

'That's the dream, anyway.' He paused, and his eyes almost seemed to moisten with tears. He spoke quietly. 'Late at night, occasionally I think I can hear the sound of singing. Perhaps, once, we too were carusi.' He resumed polishing the body and both of them were silent for a while. A light, cool breeze teased the ends of Zuleikha's hair. The chemical smell of the polish was reassuring. Almost as good as a cigar would have been, right then. 'Sulphur mines began to close down during the 1980s, and now simply have been replaced by sand quarries and other forms of exploitation, often of migrants from Africa. Any old Beat Head can come and buy up an ancient ruin and build a useless shopping-mall, brothel or drug processing unit on the site of temples to Dionysus, Aphrodite and Saint Oneiria. Who gives a shit?'

'Beat Head?'

Although they were in the middle of the countryside and had seen no-one since they had arrived, Peppe glanced around. He leaned closer and unintentionally blew cigarillo smoke into Zuleikha's face.

'Capo Bastone. Beat Head, Underboss and all the rest of the Beautiful People. The incandescent faces of the Holy Saints of the Mafia. Blood and fire. In the name of Palermo, Trapani and San Giuseppe ru Casteddu Nivuru, for the sake of the future I'm trying to preserve history, while they rule the present!'

'What does your wife think about it, you coming down here every weekend? Going down … into that place.'

He laughed, and then talked with the cigarette still between his lips.

'You're lucky you found the easy way out! You would have had difficulty trying to leap three metres up onto that ladder in the chimney.' He continued to polish the metalwork. Far above, a flock of swallows cut a V-shape through the sky, heading inland. 'Anyway, I'm not here every weekend. That's why it's taken so long. She knows my madnesses and I know hers. It's how we stay sane. You're not married, are you?'

'And what is her madness, Peppe?'

Now it was his turn to avoid eye-contact.

'Music. The flute. U friscalettu.' Peppe threw back his head and swallowed several deep draughts from his plastic mineral water bottle. It must have been a little too much because then he started coughing. Clearing his throat, with a flushed face, he resumed his account of the Sicilian Mafia.

He's not the stereotypical Sicilian man of few words and many expressions, Zuleikha thought. I was wrong before. He is of the Left, his interiority is all about discourse, dialectic and so, in both respects, he is legion.

'Water is always the best.' He smiled and Zuleikha smiled back. 'We are not just vegetables: give us water and some fertiliser and we'll grow. No, people are more than that. My grandfather worked his fingers to the bone just so that we could have a small piece of land that we could call our own. For centuries, who knows, probably since the Normans or else the Angevins came, we had been villain. We had been servants of the landlords, those owners of palazzi and Houses of the God of Eternal Punishment and now, at last, after a thousand years we came, through the blood of our teeth, to own land that had been cursed like some black-cloaked widow, land like this –' he motioned his arm outwards and the movement sent soap, dirt and spray all around '– land damned to sterility, barrenness. Love is like a cucumber, it starts off sweet and ends up bitter.'

Peppe paused for a moment while he resumed wiping the handle of the rear passenger-side door, but Zuleikha knew that he hadn't finished. He stood up and did not look at her, but indicated a place, some hundred-and-fifty or so metres away from where they stood, where there grew the crooked form of a fig-tree.

'My grandfather died there, on that very spot as he was harvesting a few shrivelled figs. We buried him there. We uprooted the tree, placed his coffin two metres down and then replanted it. It survived – in fact, it thrived like nothing else – and now every August it renders a rich harvest.'

Zuleikha wheeled around towards the house.

'Ah! That smells nice!'

Peppe smiled.

'Dinner will be ready soon. And then we shall have music, yes? Tomorrow, I'll clear up the mess you made in the villa.'

'Oh, I'm sorry. I'll help you,' she ventured.

But he shook his head.

'No. Thank you. I'll do it.'

The sun had grown hot, and it was as though during the course of that single day it had gone from winter to spring. She wheeled around, taking in the green fields of wheat, the rash of colour that almost overnight had appeared across the land. She filched in her pockets, but her pockets were empty. She gazed straight into the sun and again her face broke into a smile.

That evening the children were in bed by eight-thirty. It had taken a lot of persuasion, plus Zuleikha's involvement, to get them there, and possibly only the presence of the two guests had prevented a four-way tantrum from breaking out. All the while Zuleikha could see that normally, in spite of himself, Peppe would have been likely to have taken out the frustrations of the day on his kids, and that he and his wife would argue incessantly about this too. But tonight he was on his best behaviour, and she marvelled at the lengths to which people would go in order to fulfil the exigencies of being a host.

Giuseppe brought in some black wine with glasses and a plate of cassata which he set down on a centre table. Alexander removed his lute from its case and, looking only slightly less weary than Zuleikha might have imagined, Zita went upstairs and returned with a small flute case. Zuleikha smoothed down the white cotton dress she had donned for the evening meal, the hem of which reached to just below her knees. She had on sandals and wished now that perhaps she'd worn something a little warmer. The cold here was deceptive. In the sun, she thought, one could be forgiven for imagining that it was already spring – which in some ways it was. But as night fell, the underlying chill which now one realised had been present all through the day sleeked like a killer through the copses and wheat fields, through the tufa walls of the farmhouses and the hard pink structures of the deserted palazzi and held the land, the blackening sky, the distant sea, unbreathing in its grasp. Thank god for braziers and brassiers! she thought. Thank God for the fire of the cuba and for San Giuseppe ru Casteddu Nivuru!

Peppe rubbed his hands together, swung back against the settee and announced,

'L'omu a cinquant'anni o è papa o varvajanni. At fifty, a man is either the pope or a fool. Five years to go! Music! Let's have music!'

Then, in a manner reminiscent of some grizzled patriarch, he gestured to Alex and Zita as though to say, "Be my guest" or "Commence the entertainment!" Zuleikha and Peppe smiled at each other, amused, and also pleased by the irony of his performance. Peppe lit the coals in the open hearth, at first conjuring the flames and then, as though he were a magician, causing them to subside. And Zuleikha knew that Peppe again would make sure that later there would be old-fashioned braziers in their rooms upstairs. But this was his time to relax, Zuleikha thought. He spent his days effecting a seamless conjunction of art and craft, of inherited wisdom and hard graft. But he never earned quite enough to make ends meet, to be able properly to relax, and instead he and his family lived cramped in a mess of noise and fumes while he was forced to watch others distort the world.

As the musicians tuned up she pictured Peppe, his revolutionary dreams forever crushed beneath the weight of corporatism and the exigencies of feeding a family while pursuing the love of his life in the darkness of the old sulphur mine. Far beneath the Baroque hem of the palazzu that belonged to some dog-eared aristocrats perhaps descended from Norman soldiers with proboscis helmets and almond-shaped shields who had fought and shed blood here, on this fertile island and there as well, in England's green but not yet pleasant forests and on Scotland's sleeping, purple-heathered mountains – there, surely, deep in the earth, lay the centre of Giuseppe Ayala's being. La Cuba was his message to the future.

He was like one of those humble Dark Age masons who began work on the foundations of a church building, knowing that the structure would be unlikely to be completed during their lifetime – indeed, perhaps hoping that it would not, since it was to be their epitaph, their perfect note, played out in stone, light and silence, into eternity – for only the dead live forever.

And now Alexander cracked his knuckles as though he was an òpira fina, a tragliu pulitu, a master of the axe, a carpenter about to build an elegant cabinet, table or box. He was ready, his hands all set and, like Peppe, Zuleikha also sat back and allowed herself to relax just this once. For she too was a healer of the sick – though of people rather than buildings – and from the arc of her presence, with her hand held across their flesh, from the most ordinary of materials in manner indeterminate, like those wild women of old who had painted themselves blue and danced in strange formations upon the stony shores of lochs, Zuleikha was a lens through which the generations might glimpse their own infinity. Every little thing you do counts, she thought. In some mysterious way, it all adds up.

God! This wine was good! She inspected her glass, swirled the dark liquid around slowly so that there seemed to be a rhythm in her movement. The first strains of music began to emanate from Alexander's lute, which now she saw was really much more like an oud, a Mediaeval oud with its four courses and at the centre of its body the ornate dark rose. He was playing with a white bird-feather which in his hands looked almost like a quill, and the strings of the instrument, silk and gut and metal, now seemed more loosely wound than before. The graduated frets narrowed as they proceeded up the neck, each intersection of fret and string like partners, like Zulie and Alex or Peppe and Zita, being scored by a different letter of the Arabic alphabet, aleph, bey, Tey, tey, gim, hey … as though their lives similarly were marked in some way, as though during their time on this earth there was only a certain span of meaning they would be able to traverse.

As was the way, he started off slowly and at the lowest possible pitch. Or even at a pitch just beneath the possible, a Phoenician pitch coming across the water, something barely audible, a disturbance of the winter air merely, a risha in the wind. It was a maqam bayati, a maqam of joy, femininity and life, a maqam to bring in the spring, but played in a manner unique to Alexander Wolfe and singular to this evening in early March. Or was it now mid-March? – she'd lost count of time since the wine really was very strong. Peppe – dear, revolutionary Peppe – had said that it was home-grown, that it was the fruit of that difficult deadened land which his great-grandfather had cajoled back into a kind of life – perhaps through a song and a dance, a tarantella, a tarantata, a taran-whatsit – and she didn't want to be one of those nutty northerners who came here and essentialised everything Sicilian into just that: being Sicilian. Ah! The swashbuckling, dark-eyed piratical men who sported bandannas and moustaches of the old-fashioned style and who resembled those supporting actors from Errol Flynn movies – the ones who had talked in funny accents; who probably had been able to talk perfectly well in Standard – or at least, Hollywood – English, but who had been commanded, paid to exaggerate the way they spoke in order to come across as vaguely Oriental – or at least what they had used to call 'Near Eastern'.

Nobody ever used that term now, because originally it had referred to the territories in the Ottoman Empire, many of which lay within the ecclesiastical borders of the bull-fucking Mata Europa. And also because, from Cape Fligley to Ayia Napia, from the carnation of Iceland to some God-forsaken piece of tundra up beyond the furthest reaches of the realm of Ivan the Terrible, we were now all good Europeans, she reflected, and we black, brown and somewhat off-white ones were especially good Europeans, so long as we had Euros busting holes in our pockets, dear Liza, dear Liza. It would have punctured the grand psychosis of Europe to have claimed that Bulgaria, say, or dear white-pillared Greece was in any way 'Eastern'. My God! The anathema!

And here was her man, her Glaswegian man, white as the white of a playing-card and trunk and arms as big as the steel crans that once on a day had overhung the magical green river of Thaney and of her holy son, the Chief Lord, Kyentyern otherwise known as Munghu, otherwise known as the dearest Friend, the buon'anima, and Alexander was playing the bayati maqam with considerable expertise, with expertise that could only have been gained through a lifetime's apprenticeship – or even through several generations of apprenticeships – to some wizened-faced, whiskered phantom of a master. You didn't just learn to play the oud; it wasn't like a computer game or a ready-to-assemble set of furniture. The interplay between the notes may have remained the same, but the rhythm was unique to Alexander. And indeed, to this particular time and place and to the company he was in: to Zuleikha and Giuseppe and Zita. Especially to Zita, who was holding her friscalettu as though it was an arrow ready to be loosed. The instrument was barely the length of a woman's double hand-span. She was waiting for some cue to enter the music, which was quite different from the style to which she had been accustomed. Her blue eyes were fixed on the oud and on the swirl of Alex's hands across its body, and her brow was furrowed with concentration, and Zuleikha thought that perhaps she was trying to identify the dominant note, the jins, or else the tonic, the spinning nucleus of the maqam. Bayati Shuri, Nahfat, Husseini, even the names of the different maqamat evoked love, happiness, poetry cut in words of nastaliq silver, mother tongues, moist, pungent, vigorous, southern dialects that undercut, that slipped beneath the anthemia language of the fathers. Ah, the mysteries of musicians!

Zuleikha let her head fall back, closed her eyes, then opened them again. She found Peppe smiling at her as though the same thought had just occurred to him. Music always brought into being a certain telepathy between listeners and musicians. It was not so much an entertainment as a communing, though most definitely it could be both. And every time this happened a new language would be forged, a language that was hot as Mongibello's many caldere, a tongue through which might be brought into being new thoughts, new ways of constructing reality.

It was the music of ghost players, of notes wrought in the night by the skeletal fingers of the Pure Brethren, of the perfect compositions penned for the Shah-en-Shah of instruments, for al Ajfa and Jamila and Ziryab and the al-Mawsili father-and-son team, Abraham and Isaac, of notes sung from the airless throats of qainas, of notes sung in sulphur and salt, of windmill songs of love and desertion, of the chants of the forests of holm-oak, mulberry, pine and aloes wood, of the hundred songs of al-Isfahani that once had covered this island of Siqilliya, that had blown into

422

blossom the spring of this place and from which the ouds of the world once had been fashioned. The music was of this land; each note resonated with a specific type of stone, every interval with the quality of the light at a particular time of day in Kalat-abi-Thur, Rahal-mut, Qalat al Nissa. The stronghold of the vulture, the farmhouse of the dead, the fort of the women. Zuleikha bit off a piece of qashatah and let it dissolve in her mouth. She would return to healthy eating … later, tomorrow, eventually. It was hard work, dealing with young children. It was a dance for schizos. The mothers of the world were welcome to their collective rapacious motherhood. All I need, she thought, is a bottle of good vinu russu and this large slab of cassata.

As the oud shifted up in register, as Alex began to play the second melodic sequence in the sayr, Zita bent her head over her instrument, which she held straight out from her body almost as though she was recognising and acknowledging the dominant note, the ghammaz, of the music, as though she was greeting the music in the old way, with a long sweeping adaab, as though she was saying, *In submission, I acknowledge that I am the servant of the music.* She pursed her lips around the orifice of the flute and began to blow into the cane, into the reed that was encased in the cane. The friscalettu had a sound that was pitched at the higher end of the scala, yet the instrument seemed to be played in an overwhelmingly minor scale. It reminded Zuleikha of the swoop and dive of a bird, and though there was a certain melancholy about its sound, it evoked a sense of loneliness which, say, a classical piccolo flute would have lacked entirely. Zita's knuckles normally were red with household chores, yet now, as she played, her fingers turned slowly white until it was as though Zuleikha was gazing at a skeleton playing a hollow stick. A reed cut from the banks of the rivers that had vanished along with the forests, the vast ciumi that had been burned down into narrow seasonal streams or which had been driven underground but which now sprang, fresh yet plangent, from the flanks of the great black mountain. The Mountain of Mountains. Mongibello, Mongibeddu, Muncibbeddu, Etna, Aetna, Gibel Utlamat, Jabal al-Nar. The Mountain of Fire. The Land of the Pure. Sicilia, Alba, Paak. It was the music of the people who, one way or another, had been lied to, and whose wealth had been stolen from their calloused hands by pretenders bearing sulphur, salt, asbestos, oil and religion. It was the song of the people who had been turned into servants, serfs, slaves, saints. Etna. Kaf. When the music of the people exploded, the earth would shift its orbit.

And gradually, over the course of the night, with the drinking and the eating and the interjections in several languages, Scots, Sicilian, English, Italian and Urdu, the music became faster, the pitch higher, and it was a miracle that the children were not wakened by it. But then, as Peppe had explained, this house was very old and had two-metre-thick walls constructed of tufa collected from the ruins of an ancient calta, a castle that was far older than the abandoned Baroque palazzu through which Zuleikha had wandered the day before. Zuleikha was surprised that she could remember some of the poetic phrases her mother had used so many years earlier, the poetry that was intrinsic to, that formed the very bone structure of, languages like Urdu and Persian – yet some modulation in the music brought this memory to life so that as she spoke, whispered, almost sang the words, it felt as though she was becoming another person, or perhaps that she was becoming, God forbid, her mother. Or else, God knows, the person she had always been.

Then, at midnight, Peppe took out the map which they had brought from Lincolnshire and he spread it out and flattened it down against the wood of the table and there, right at its centre like a dominant note around which everything else revolved, was an image of the cube. It seemed obvious now, but over the months, as they had gazed at it, neither of them had been able to make out the lines. They had seemed to be merely disjointed scribbles, clashing notations, half-Byzantine, half-Ifriqiyan, and though – while Zuleikha had been away exploring the chambers of the deserted palazzu – in the old barn of the olive oil press Alex had managed to score a series of musical sequences from Lord Jack's lunatic diorama, the plan had seemed simply to have been the syphilitic wanderings through oxygen-deficient hinterlands of an insane aristocrat.

It seemed to Zuleikha that once again the music was radiating from the cube. She felt its vibration in her haunches, in her spine, in the soles of her feet which now were bare since she'd kicked off her shoes awhile back. The fire purred away like a sleeping tabby, every so often flickering into incandescence before settling down again into the low heavy brass of the grate. The flute poured out its liquid music – yes, she thought as she watched Zita's tightly closed eyes, this is her lunacy, and though Zita had never been trained in Arabic music she could obviously play Sicilian folk, and it seemed as though Alex's measuring out of maqamat had reached out and caught the sequences of notes common to both forms, and that the maqamat had led Zita to a high mountain place where only goats and dead men climbed, where priests got drunk on Communion Wine, where the ground hissed like a giant snake and where the saints walked on lava.

Alex and Zita played without needing to look at the positions which their fingers assumed upon their respective instruments, and the density of sound and the manner in which notes seemed to be being played over and over again, as though each musician were seeking to perfect that one sound, that particular sequence, before moving on to the next, reminded Zuleikha of artisans weaving an elaborate carpet, or d'òpira fini sculpting a perfectly symmetrical article of furniture, a table perhaps, or a writing-stand, or a box. Zuleikha's head spun with the wine and the music and she saw that Peppe was slumped back against the settee, his eyes closed, the globes roaming as though he was dreaming.

She leaned forward, grabbed the unmarked bottle and poured the remainder of the wine into her glass. The room now was shifting slightly from side to side, yet it was not as though she was drunk: there wasn't that sense of heaviness or nausea that she associated with inebriation. She felt as though her limbs were feathers, the bones hollow like those of a bird. She felt as though it was her body which Alex, her lover of almost a year, was moving across the fretless soundboard. Fretless! She fingered her neck and felt a rough bit of skin which had begun to ache just a little. She tried to remember where it might have been acquired and then she became aware of her heartbeat accelerating as she realised that, though the discomfort was minor, it seemed to be worsening by the minute.

Peppe held his glass up to the light. The wine, which at first had seemed quite black, now appeared as a dark shade of red. He threw his head back and drank the glass right down to emptiness. He lowered the glass slowly and for a moment did nothing, just stared at it or else at something through it. Then, turning to Zuleikha, he smiled: a difficult, bitter smile.

'History, Zuleikha, history is not blind.'

Zuleikha had been watching Alex's oud, and even through the smoke and booze she was sure that earlier she had made out distinct bands of frets, precisely measured, their spacings calculated to al-Kindi accuracy, positioned right up and down the instrument's neck. She was moving from side to side and then she was up on her feet, but she couldn't remember having risen. Giuseppe, great bridge between heaven and earth, protector of innocence, he who breathed life into the forms of the dead. In the old days they had ventured deep into the forests and had hewn from magical trees the figures of chivalrous knights, orafa, and had set them reciting poetry in muwashshah stanzas, a poetry of almonds that dissolved slowly beneath the tongue, of bird-sellers and small valleys, of the dead screaming through the buried ruins of palazzi and night air-raid shelters. Peppe's grandfather had died with a hail of bullets to his chest; he had died with an iron holy heart, defending his land from those who would deny ordinary people everything, from those who would turn men and women into schiavi and butane, from those who shot children in the face and strangled pregnant mothers on their kitchen tables. Latifondi, Mafiosi, the scum of the earth. Revenge would come like blood, in thimblefuls, and it would be bitter, acidic, like the taste of wine fermented from lava.

The music was turning and changing. Yes, she thought, the music must shape the instrument as much as the instrument generates the sound. She was rising through the seven chambers of the tonnara: the levante, the camera grande, the bordonaio, the bastardo, the camera, the bastardella with its gate shrouded in jasmine. Yes, she thought, the melancholy runs deep and blue, it weeps and explodes with each breath, like the flesh of la camera della morte, it howls in despair, for we humans are like the fish, we are caught, and are struggling in a net, we are being pulled, wave-upon-wave, into the crashing rock and smashed bone of the shore, into the silent darkness of the earth. The lute is changing.

And since Alexander is really a part of his instrument...

She allowed her body to relax into the dance. Because that is what Zuleikha MacBeth was doing there, in that stone massaria in the middle of the bosco: she was swaying, shifting, bending, contorting. She had moved out from behind the table and was dancing in front of the fire, the musicians playing behind her. In the lucid glass cube of the music Zuleikha ceased to have any awareness of time, or perhaps it was time that ceased to hold Zuleikha. She had escaped the black boats and the leering hungry faces of the tonnarotti and was swimming in the open ocean.

She feels as though her whole body is breathing, every pore is open before the sound. To the music of the oud and the friscalettu, to the lignu of sycamore, lime, walnut, reed and cane, she is dancing the pizzica tarantata, the dance of the spider bite. She lifts her arms above her head and it is as though she is pulling down the ethereal cacophony of the Capella Palatina. And then she too begins to spin, clockwise at first, her arms lifted as though by an unseen partner. But it is not a smooth dance; her body and limbs are shaking violently. It is as though she is having a seizure, yet her eyes remain open, staring and black like those of a spider. There is a beat and it comes from the ground, from the movement of her feet, driving down into the stone. She convulses and her throat sings, she is singing in fat tongues from the opened vein of her neck. The spider stands behind her, a shadow of her movement, a geometry of stillness at the core of her chorea. Then it lifts each of its three black mouths, one that of a young maiden with flowers growing from her skull, the second that of a bearded old man, and the third that of a pallid child. Its long niuri snake hair sways behind its back and the spider takes a bite. Zuleikha's voice, suddenly raised, is tremulous, uneven, and like the muscles of her body it quivers – not with fear or weakness, but with Lydian fire.

The music accelerates; she is moving faster across the hot floor which is a tamburello for her feet, for she is the figliola, the black mountain, the white rose, the castle of gelsomino, the bottomless lavureddi of the well, the fruit garden at the bottom of the surgiva. For three days and three nights she dances all over the land, through the aisles of the churches, along the beds of dried-up crocodile rivers, the emptied gorges, the trees petrified in the sun, the blustery cliff-edge towns, the nameless country lanes down which the devil dances at noon. She dances by the rock from which are hewn charms against the M'al occhio, she pirouettes among the cocks from whose bulging bodies are pulled red eggs, she spins through the casa that grow straight from seed on the side of the mountain, she drifts between the dark and ancient wombs, cut in bronze, where people first learned to dance and paint and through the cemeteries filled with the shapes of the Bal'harm dead who rise again every night at the sound of the Virgin's song. She dances beneath the deserted miraculous shrines of forgotten saints, through the echoing manzils of barons and emirs and amongst the forests of ungo baskets that hang from thousand-year-old hazelnut trees and which are boudoirs for witch's heads. She slips between the sainted souls of children found spinning on the Holy Wheel in the mignotta night and the herds of Mafiosi shepherds who flay their wives alive, melt the fat over seven-wick torches and turn their skins into zampogne which howl all night long. She enters, and then takes leave of, the country shacks where the magical piovra lives; she bends down and kisses the black stone where the paesana goes to crack her chain while calling out the name of Hazrat Maryam to the sound of the pig-iron bell cracked with gold, silver and pumpkin juice...

Zuleikha went upstairs into the cupboard and she reached up to the shelf, cradled her arms around the box as though it were the body of a saint, and carried it downstairs. And there, as Alexander and Zita continued to play, and as Peppe slept through his own fugue state, she lifted the next lid and thrust her hand down into the darkness.

Chapter Twenty-Five

Archibald Enoch McPherson is in bright light. For the first time in seventy years Archie sees his father's face. In the days after he had left the house there had been no photographs, not even wedding snapshots. Only the tenuous memory, solidifying into bas-relief, of the big man who had scooped him up in his arms. A smile, a jowl, a gust of breath – and that was it. Now he sees his face, but it doesn't seem to have any awareness of Archie. And anyway, how would his father know him? He has changed so much. His father vanishes and in his place is Archie's mother and Archie feels a well of sorrow flood over him. And the sorrow wipes away his mother's face.

And now he is falling again and the light has become less intense so that it no longer hurts and from somewhere, possibly from below – though here there is neither above nor below – he makes out a thin coil of white smoke. His old workmates from the shipyards and the aerodrome appear before him but he has no time for them, he never had time for them, only for the machines and for Margaret who has been lost to him for so long and who did not seem to see him before. He sinks again and the darkness grows deeper, the smoke thicker. And now here are the machines: the Spitfires, Hurricanes, Wellingtons, Lancasters, the battleships, ocean liners, cruisers, aircraft carriers, the metal, paint, wood, oil, the sulphur and TNT, the river water, the deep black blood of the Clyde waters swirling in the Govan Prince's Dock, the shouts of the dockers, the platers, the flame throwers, the asbestos men. The men and machines become monstrous, their faces fall apart as flesh turns to pus and as worms slither at high speed across their bodies. The boats sink and are swallowed by giant sharks and the aircraft fall from the sky and like torn sheaves their pilots burn to nothing.

Archie feels all of this, every lick of flame, every invertebrate twitch, every last sound of pain and decay. Finally, it is happening. Cremation. Ah! The joy! At last the tumour is dead, its cells denatured, its flesh turned, in the yellow alchemy of fire, to black dust. And it is a terrifying music; it is complete, all-consuming; it fills up his world. No-one sees him and he is thrown down into a place where there is no light at all but simply the fear which has become a single unimaginably large mirror and he gazes into the mirror and sees nothing. Then he is cast back into the world.

Chapter Twenty-Six

'It's in Sicilian,' said Peppe, but it's like none I've ever seen before. It's very old, I think. So old that perhaps it was never written down.'

'Except that obviously it was,' said Alex. 'If this is what you say it is.'

Peppe looked at him with the type of expression he was good at, and which instantly made Alex regret he had said anything at all. After all, the man was an expert – not in languages exactly, but in the fields of the past, the tongues, scripts, imagery and structures of history. It was his life's work.

Peppe studied the scroll.

'It's in Latin script, but is heavily inflected with words from Arabic and some other language which I don't recognise,' he said.

'Can you translate it?' asked Zuleikha.

The luminosity from the bedroom skylight was bright enough to illuminate the manuscript, and Zuleikha worried that it might damage the ink before they'd had a chance to decipher it. Then she cursed herself for being so selfish. This isn't about you, she reminded herself. This is possibly a historical document. It belongs here in Sicily, and Peppe will figure it out – or else he will ask some expert in ancient linguistics to help him. It has nothing to do with me or Alex, she thought. We're like the Bedouin peasants who found the Dead Sea Scrolls, or the Palermitan squatters who came across the ancient Carthaginian codices under the tiles of the deserted palazzu, or the goats who discovered the ruined Greek city near the town of Gibil-Gabib. It just so happened that we were around, that the box came into our possession. All the rest is fond imagining, fantasism, and an excess of limoncello and black wine.

The writing had been undertaken by hand and it seemed as though it had been effected by means of a stylus or possibly a quill. The manuscript had not come in the form of a single scroll but as a bundle of papers which had been fastened together with a thin leather strap that was somewhat dog-eared and worn in the area nearest its knot, suggesting to Zuleikha that over the years it had been opened and closed repeatedly. When she had lifted the fifth lid there had been an explosion of perfume that had nearly knocked her off her feet, and which had swirled around the musicians, around Peppe and the wine bottles, the glasses, the furniture, everything. And around Zuleikha, whose dance had become even wilder, until she'd felt as though her limbs might be torn out of their sockets and the crown of her skull fly in golden light from the brainpan that was modulating the rhythm of her feet. Alex had told her later that she'd ended up writhing on the floor, twitching, her eyes firmly closed yet still roving in their orbits, her white dress pulled up to the level of her thighs, her long black hair fanned out around her, mingling with the hot ash from the brazier which she had upset on her way around the room. Peppe had had to douse her with cold water to bring her back and even then, for close on an hour she had seemed glaze-eyed, not completely with it, not the full Euro, as it were. But then, she thought, I've not been the full Euro for quite a while. Perhaps it's not a magician I need, but a shrink. It was embarrassing. What had Zita thought of her? But then, she thought, Zita had been in a trance of her own, some bizarre flautist's dance of sublimated feminism. Yet it was something which they had constructed together, and if the manuscript belonged to anyone, it belonged to the four of them. And to Peppe's grandfather, Laila Sciacca Asunsi, and Archibald Enoch McPherson.

Magic. That was what the manuscript looked like: a series of instructions on the modes of performing various spells. There were drawings of decanters, alembics, aludels, bustuqahs, ghadhar cups, luted pots and all the other tools of alchemy. Yes, but alchemy had been just a metaphor, thought Zuleikha, for the perfection of the human spirit. It hadn't really been about turning lead into gold: that had been just a cover, a simple explanation for simple times. Ironic then, she thought, that it was the lie which had led to modern science. It was the filthy literalist fools who had continued to potter away in their dark Satanic workshops, trying to turn base lead into shiny gold, who had invented chemistry and so had given us the transmuted modern world.

Archie's touch had started all this off, and he'd got it sixty years earlier from Lord Jack in Lincolnshire, and he'd got it from a Sicilian lutenist and composer, who'd got it from some old monk or wizard and he'd got it from … who knows? The trees, the birds and the bees. When someone dies they acquire the quality of a spirit. They are no longer the beloved mother, son, friend: they are now simply a spirit and will behave accordingly. We love them when they are alive, but we fear them after they die. Her mother had told her that, when Zuleikha was a child. It was after the death of her own mother, whose spirit she'd claimed she'd seen one day in what Zuleikha reasoned later must have been a hypnagogic vision. With all our resources and technology, still we knew very little about the mind. We had discovered many things, yet still we were unable to define consciousness. What does it mean to be alive? We don't know. *I think, but I haven't got a clue.*

Peppe agreed to get the manuscript translated. Zuleikha and Alex couldn't afford to stay in Sicily indefinitely, and so they returned to Scotland at the beginning of March, and tried to regain some normality in their lives. Zuleikha undertook locums – though not in the practice in which Archie had been a patient, and not booking ahead more than a few weeks. Alexander finally got round to giving away or selling off Susan's things, including some of the ornaments which he'd associated with their life together. At the risk of seeming cruel or cold-hearted, he wanted to keep only a few tokens: it was too painful to have constantly to walk into a living-room filled with the heavy scent of bereavement. Now, at last, he would be ready to invite Zulie to come and stay properly in his house by the river, the river where it had all begun. They would both keep their pads – it was far too soon for anything else – but he felt that, gradually, their lives might attain solidity and commitment.

Zuleikha found out where Archie had been buried, but first she paid a visit to the graves of her mother and son in the Muslim section of the Cathcart Cemetery. It had always dismayed her that the Muslim section of this graveyard was the least well-tended of all the sections. There were no paved pathways between the lines of the headstones, so that for most of the year you had to wade through mud – you either had to wear Wellingtons or else to slip polythene bags from the supermarket over your shoes if you were to avoid completely ruining them and simultaneously sinking into the soft wet clay soil and walking about on damp feet for the rest of the day and very possibly catching flu as a result. Yes, she thought, visiting the graveyard of your loved ones was never going to be a pleasant experience, but surely there was no need for you to catch your death of a cold as a consequence! It was really the fault of the Muslim community, she thought. Just down the hill was the Jewish graveyard, and that was so well-tended that it resembled a theme-park: wooden walkways, the lot. There would be a committee for everything. And even the older parts of the Christian section, containing the graves which nobody visited any more, the last resting places of souls who had ceased to exist in living memory – even these relatively overgrown plots seemed less disordered than the new ones in the Muslim area. Or rather theirs was a genteel, natural abandonment rather than one which rankled and saddened, splayed as it was across a blisteringly cold hillside. It wasn't that the graves of Muslim people were unvisited – quite the opposite – it was rather that nobody seemed to give a shit about the ground they walked on, or whether there might be a bench for the elderly or infirm, or just for someone to sit on and ponder, dream, cry. It was a graveyard for people who, in spite of everything, still regarded themselves basically as peasant immigrants, people whose dead had only a tenuous claim on the land, and whose living continued to be pursued by the nightmare that they might just have to pack up and leave at any moment.

Her mother's grave sat right at the top of the hill, and unlike the majority, which had been hewn from the harder-wearing black granite, her headstone had been cut from Carraran marble. Zuleikha had insisted on white marble, and also had had a line of Persian poetry from the Letter Nûn section of the Diwan of the classical Persian poet Hafiz Shirazi inscribed in Nastaliq script halfway down.

> *The heart's grief how can one suffer, when time remaineth not,*
> *Say – Be neither heart nor time – what will be?*

Unfortunately, there had been no sculptors in Glasgow who'd been familiar with Arabic script, and so the regular stonemason had done it himself. He'd made a pretty good job of it, she'd had to admit, except that once the stone was up they'd noticed that a single dot was missing from one of the letters. This might not have seemed like such a big thing, but it wasn't like, for example, a dot over the letter 'i' being left out – after all, whether or not it's got a dot, 'i' can only ever really be 'i'. In Persian, Arabic and Urdu, on the other hand, a dot over, under or inside a letter makes all the difference between a sublime poem with fifty levels of meaning and a piece of hogwash. And so she'd asked the stonemason if he could rectify the omission. She'd expected that perhaps he would have removed the stone, taken it back to his workshop and, using the appropriate tool, made the correction. But instead, the bastard had come to the graveyard with his chisel and had gored a hole in the white marble. He'd created an irregular orifice so that it looked as though someone had taken a pot-shot at her mother's headstone. So there was this elegant script with a horrible gash above the last of the letters, which every time she visited drew her attention so that everything focused down onto this grotesque flaw.

She'd hoped that finally this country would have been able to have done her mother right, that she would have been able to have done her mother proud. Yes, she thought, as the breeze gathered strength, pace and frigidness: Hafiz of Shiraz, considered in the East to have been possibly the most accomplished Persian poet of all time, combining with genius, as he did, the different qualities of Omar Khayyam, Sa'di, Ferdowsi and Rumi, was said to be untranslatable. She drew the big floppy collar of her coat – an elephant's collar, she'd always thought – up against her cheek, and held it there using the tips of her fingers. But that was just a cop-out, the result of which was that in the English-speaking world Hafiz's words did not exist. If even the topmost class of professors couldn't get it right, no wonder the stonemason had got it wrong.

Her son's grave, situated close to the foot of the hill, was much smaller, and had attached to it the remains of a plastic windmill and a clutch of primroses. His was a small grey headstone on which had been inscribed simply his name and dates of birth and death. She still couldn't bear to think of his small body down there. It seemed Mediaeval, people burying their children, though she was aware that even here in Britain, right up until the middle of the twentieth century, both childhood and maternal death had

435

been commonplace – expected, even. You just had to listen to the words of the folk songs and nursery rhymes; you didn't have to read the barely credible columns of rows and numbers secreted deep within the worm-eaten archives of the reference libraries. This lost memory had become a hidden death, a denial perpetuated by most films, where history had been cleaned up in favour of ridiculous character arcs and high tragedy. Then and now, in the real world people seldom died in high tragedy. No, Zuleikha thought: people just died.

In the distance, beyond a dense area of woodland, there was a moderate-sized river, but not once when she had visited the graves of her family had she heard the river flowing.

Archie's grave was not difficult to find. This cemetery too was perched up on a hill, but this hill, situated some ten miles or so to the west of Glasgow, overlooked the majesty of the Clyde. It was nowhere near where he lived, but it had been where Margaret had been buried. Already, newer fresher graves had been dug on the far side of Archie's headstone. Zuleikha was quite surprised that he had acquired a headstone so soon. It normally took at least a few weeks, since they usually waited till the earth had settled before planting the slab. But then, she thought, his nearest relatives had been the nephews, and perhaps they had ordered it to be respectable but basic. There was a single bunch of flowers whose stems had been stuck through the wire mesh at the foot of the headstone. Already the flowers looked faded, bedraggled. The writing was simple and clear and had been chiselled neatly in gold into the glossed black granite:

ARCHIBALD ENOCH MCPHERSON
BELOVED HUSBAND OF MARGARET
AND SON OF WILLIAM AND EUPHEMIA
RIP

A few dates, a stylised flower – taken, she thought, from the internet – and that was it. A life, in stone. Even though, with her hat, scarf and woollen coat wrapped tightly around her she was over-dressed for the weather – returning from Sicily to a full-blown Scottish winter had been a shock to her system – she still found her heart sink like a cold stone as she thought of her own situation. Who will there be for me? she wondered. The odd district nurse, perhaps. She thought of Alex, but that was ridiculous. They'd met a year ago. Less! Still, there was something which she'd really never felt before. Not the grand guignol passion which they wrote about, or around which entire films were shot. She'd always wondered whether such a thing had ever really existed. Hadn't it just been the fevered imaginings of sex-starved guys and gals in gardens and garrets? Shirin and Farhad, Heer and Ranjha, Romeo and Juliet, Yusuf and Zuleikha... these were just ideals, airy-fairy fantasies. Music, the food of love, and all that. Reality was stone, bread and worms. There was a particularly enormous monster crawling towards her foot. It looked a foot long, but she knew that it couldn't have been. Earthworms didn't grow that long here in the west of Scotland. Maybe in some dank, dark corner of the Amazonian jungle...

She walked around the grave. The earth was beginning to solidify and sink down upon itself. The sun shone brightly, though the air up here was still piercingly cold. She pulled her hat down over her ears. It was April, and some years in Scotland that was still winter. Right now it slipped like ice into her chest. No, she thought, I am not over-dressed. This is a cold country. God knows what it must've been like in the old days, before electricity, hot water, inside lavatories, social security, hospitals. Archie's life had spanned massive changes. People forgot too easily. Historians scribbled away, documenting this or that Act of Parliament, the details of some or other foreign war, while film-makers made documentaries, trapped the voices of those about to depart in flickering tin machines – and yet no-one really seemed able to capture ... reality, pain, loss. The despair that lies beyond both art and artifice. Archie had meant something to her, that was why she was here. He'd been an evil bastard at times. She found herself smiling. In the last few months, his honesty had been total. She slipped her hands out of her gloves and examined the palms. The skin was dry and was scuffed around the edges and the pads were lightly calloused. Life-lines, heart lines. They were the hands of a working woman over forty. She put the gloves back on.

To her left, beyond the cemetery wall, the ground sloped

away rapidly down towards the river. The grass had been almost flattened by the wind that rose constantly from the surface of the water as it rushed away westwards on its way to becoming the Irish Sea. This was the bend beyond which the river widened out into estuary, which stretched for tens of miles so that sometimes it seemed that the sea was simply an extension of the river. She knew that the rivers of Pakistan and India were many times the size of the Clyde, yet on this day the sky seemed enormous. Everyone committed acts of evil, she thought. You bore them, you lived with them, and you hoped that they died with you. Did the dead ever forget or forgive, as the living surely couldn't forgive themselves? She fished in her handbag, conscious now that some people had entered the cemetery from her right. She had run out of hankies, so she wiped the cuff of her coat across her face. The wool felt coarse, cold and damp on her eyelids, and she realised that though the sun was still shining it had begun to spit with rain. Now all the worms will emerge, she thought; they'll poke their little pink heads out from under clods of earth and will stretch their dirty bodies, stretch and contract, each segment cracking with ecstasy at the diamonds falling from the sky.

The people were coming closer. There seemed to be several generations of them; there was even a child in a buggy. You shouldn't bring children to graveyards, she thought. The spirits will envy them, will make them fall ill, will take away their souls. Another nugget from her mother. And anyway, she hadn't taken Daoud to any graveyards, and the spirits had taken his soul away regardless. She inhaled sharply, controlled herself and focused on the concrete, the material, as she had had to do countless times since the days of the Anatomy Hall. She hoped they weren't coming here, to this grave. The visitors. She felt like an interloper, but then she relaxed just a little as she noted that the group were moving slowly down the hill, towards the wall, to the area where the oldest graves lay. They were facing away from her now and seemed to be gazing out towards the opposite bank of the river where Dumbarton Castle lay in a heap of black ruin. The cemetery was perhaps fifty or sixty years old, and many of its inhabitants were part of the original overspill from the generation who, after the Second World War, had been moved en masse from the slums of Glasgow to the various suburbs, estates and new towns built in a ring around the great city.

She knelt down, pulled off her gloves, and with her fingertips gingerly touched the wet earth. Then with some force she laid her palms down flat. Then she dug her fingers in – one inch, two inches, three inches – right down to the knuckles. First her right hand, then her left. The soil felt warmer the deeper she went. She was disgusted by what she was doing and yet there was also an attraction, a pull that was stronger than her prohibitive sense either of embarrassment or hygiene, stronger even than her fear and disgust at the creatures of the earth. Yes, she thought, but Archie's body is not down there. He's just a heap of ashes in a box buried beneath the soil. There are no bones, no hair and nails growing like the roots of yew trees. The clay soil had closed in around her without her realising; it had sucked her down further, to the wrists, the elbows. She rocked on her heels and almost fell backwards as she tried to pull her hands out of the mud. This wet Scottish earth was claiming her as it had claimed her mother, her son. As a Muslim she would not be cremated; she would be buried, warm. One day…

There were no fresh leaves on the trees. It had been a long, dark winter. It took all of her strength to get free. She raised her hands to her face and smelled the earth. Tasted it. Almost vomited.

The people were staring at her. The baby was crying. They had not wrapped it up adequately. They should have brought a blanket. Stupid bastards. They shouldn't have brought a child to this place. She wouldn't have… Then she was crying. The words on the slab blurred and began to dance. Margaret's grave was behind her, several rows back. Perhaps Archibald and Margaret are dancing together, she thought, dancing in the giant aircraft hangar in the sky, stepping lightly to the sound of trumpets and trombones, to the open rhythms of swing jazz, those silly songs of betrothal and annunciation: happy songs; songs of a better world to come. It was a lie, yes it was: music and love are dancing lies, but we need them to get through, she thought. Without them we are just ashes, just earth. Perhaps there is a beauty in that, but it is a hard and unforgiving beauty; it is a beauty that does not permit mistakes or imperfection; it is a beauty that brooks no guilt. The breeze was

439

blowing around her ears, shutting out the sound of her own sobs, shutting out the light of the day, the swing of the music. And the letters and dates embedded into the stone were jumbling, juggling; each stroke and dot was flying back to its earliest form. Perhaps, like the lute, that was where they were heading, she and Alexander: back to where they'd started, whatever that meant. Argyll, Lindsey, San Giuseppe ru Casteddu Nivuru ... connections of light, letters, codes, notes. Of wood, stone and river. And who, in the beginning, had sent the box? Perhaps it was simply a message from the dead.

She took one last look at the headstone, but the noise had become deafening. The noise of the wind was blowing harder now; it was an afternoon wind, fresh, clean but deadly cold, and it carried with it salt, dirt and urgency.

Chapter Twenty-Seven

In mid-May, when they got Peppe's e-mail to say that the work had been completed, they booked flights back to Palermo. He had refused to send them a transcript over either the internet or through the post. Both Zuleikha and Alexander had wondered why he was being so coy; after all, hotel accommodation and flights were expensive, especially as they were now in the high season. While as a matter of courtesy Peppe had offered to put them up in their flat, everyone had known that it was far too small: what with the kids and his books, papers and God knows what else, it would have been impractical. And they couldn't have expected Zita to cook for them, and Zuleikha wasn't going to, that was for sure. Also, it meant time not working, which meant more expenses with no money coming in – or rather, that she was continuing to spend her mother's money when really she should have been doing something useful with the cash. Like buying a new car, or visiting one of those crooked Asian estate agents, getting a dodgy mortgage and investing in property. Something sensible like that, instead of taking up with someone who obviously was equally crazy and chasing around the world together after a weird box.

But she'd had no choice. It wasn't something she had chosen to do. Not that she had been chosen, either – to think that would been the height of vanity – but … well, there was something. Ever since that awful day at the cemetery, she had been unable to get the taste of soil and grit out of her mouth, her nose. Every time she thought she'd got rid of it, it had surged back, its bitter, emetic flavour seeming to dwell even within her breath. At night she would wake up covered in sweat, panting as though she'd just run a hundred miles. This began to happen with such regularity that she began to wonder whether she might be hitting the menopause. She was only forty-three, but it could happen; it did happen, she thought: every day it happened. Not that she was planning to have … not that she would ever want to go through that again. There was Alexander, but still …

No, it wasn't the change of life, though there was no question but that her life was changing. She and Alex were spending most

441

of their spare time in each other's homes, and only seldom now did she sense the discomfort in his house which had assailed her on her first few visits there. Routine tended to flatten all that down, to make it history, water under the bridge, you might say (though she would never have dared) so that the unspoken hope, the assumption, the underlying necessity of life was that eventually mundanity would save folk from the ghosts of their pasts. She was becoming inured to his presence, so that even though at times privacy still remained attractive to her, increasingly she felt a gaping sense of absence when he wasn't there. And they were having rows now – like those, she supposed, a married couple would have. Deeply referential rows, often about silly things. It was the first time in twenty-odd years that Zuleikha had forged anything like a permanent or long-term relationship with any man. Now that she thought about it, perhaps really it was the first time in her life, and she found that she was unsure of the parameters. These things were so bloody complicated, so full of ins and outs and in-betweens, and it wasn't as though they were just some couple who'd met and got together. 'Shacked up', as they'd used to say in the seventies. Theirs had never been a teenage romance, dizzy with overdoses, slit wrists and carnal liaisons in public places. For fuck's sake, they'd been far too old for all that! Yet there was an intensity about their relationship, rather in the manner of a tensile string wound as tightly as it could go. A metal string on a lute, say. And Zulie liked the music which they made together; there was an incipient, yet secreted, ecstasy about it which at times made her want to sing. But she couldn't sing – at least, not in tune, and so instead she often found herself laughing. Yet now, as their plane flew into Palermo, following that same wheeling trajectory as before, the sunlight blasted through the cabin windows as though it was coming from an interrogator's lamp, and a nauseating sense of uneasiness hovered like motes in the clear light.

Peppe was as welcoming as ever. It had been really magnificent of him, Alexander thought, to take the trouble to arrange for the text of the manuscript to be deciphered so quickly. Alex asked him whether he'd had to pay anything, simultaneously offering to reimburse him for any expenses incurred, but Peppe waved away his concerns.

'The Professore is a friend, a linguist. We've worked together in the past and will do so again in the future. We just help one another out from time to time.'

But beneath the genuine bonhomie, there were lines of worry etched across his face. And it was a lot hotter now. Zuleikha had read the web forecast, but the temperatures they gave in those things always seemed to be the very lowest possible, as if the thermometer had been set at the summit of a mountain, in the hollow of a swamp or at the breezy perimeter of an airfield. Maggiu in Palermo was heavily scented by the African Sea. Zuleikha understood some of Peppe's concern. She was certain that Laila would have been pestering him to reveal what had happened in San Giuseppe ru Casteddu Nivuru. Unveiling the past little by little and making a serious lifetime study of it so that you might better restore its structures to something resembling their former appropriateness was one thing. But for some foreigner to go and find your life's work down a secreted cistern in the centre of a villa in the middle of nowhere, and for her man then to be such a virtuoso musician that he could induce your wife of how many years to play like an angel (or a devil) was quite another. And now, Zuleikha thought, poor old Peppe has got himself involved in having to translate some ancient manuscript which very likely might turn out to be simply a Mediaeval shopping-list of the type of which Italy was full. But then, she thought, surely if it was just another shopping-list, he wouldn't have called so urgently at one in the bloody morning (two a.m. in Italy) so that they'd been thinking, my God, perhaps someone else had died, or that a burglar alarm was going off above the headboard of Alexander's marital bed.

Peppe removed the manuscript and smoothed it down on the large table in his office. Its consistency was like that of bullskin parchment. The A/C was broken and the intense heat of the day took ages to dissipate, so they had to make do with fans and copious amounts of mineral water. The three of them had gone there at night, an hour or so after the place had closed for the day, in order to avoid both the children and Peppe's colleagues, who would have been unbearably nosy. Peppe's office was in the Albergheria, a run-down part of town filled with holes in the wall where people lost themselves in drink. Worse, it was a locus that had a bad reputation: some of it well-deserved, but some simply exaggerated. Peppe knew what Palermo had looked like eight hundred, a thousand years ago. He didn't need computer simulations, he had it all in his head. Europe's jewel, she had matched Cordoba and Baghdad in size and splendour. But now, in spite of the adiopizzo businesses, in spite of the fight-back and the refusal to pay protection, all the buzzers on all the doors to power had been smeared in glue, had well and truly been fixed so that the doors could never be opened. Across the globe, the false economy of consumerism was everywhere triumphant.

Alexander, Zuleikha and Giuseppe sat around a rectangular table and pored over the two sets of documents: one, the manuscript which Zuleikha had pulled from the fifth chamber of the box that night in San Giuseppe ru Casteddu Nivuru, and the other a fresh new set of sheets: its translation, or transliteration. The words had been written first into Italian and then into English.

'There's this map,' Peppe began, 'and then, through it, is this text:'

Just as all rivers are connected and speak – or should I say, sing – to one another, the Nile, the Tigris, the Acesines, the Fiume di laci, the Achates, the Cantara, the Sindh, the Styx, the Sarasvati, so it is with mountains. The Apennines connect with the Nebrodi, the Madonie, with the Atlas, the Alps with the Carpathians, the Taurus, with the Caucasus, the Scottish Highlands with the Appalachians, the Hindu Kush, Karakoram, Kunlun, and Tian Shan with the Pamirs. And then there are the Himalayas... Very few people understand the words and almost none can pick out the notes, which can be played only on certain instruments that have been fashioned from particular trees or cut from certain mines. The monks who were thrown to work in porphyry far beneath the deserts of Nubia discovered a seam of ancient metal, samples from which they managed to smuggle out to three monasteries that had been built on the tops of desolate mountains.

One night, beneath Mongibello, I came upon the great

444

Lord Maughis, King of the Sleeping Knights, the pure of heart. He was seven feet tall and was clad in green armour and he had a red beard that was so long that it had grown right through the slab on which he had been lying.

Peppe told them that the Professore had found himself unable to translate beyond this point, or even to find anyone who was able to translate it. It had been written in a script which had never been seen before. The Professore had wondered whether in fact it was an intelligible script at all, whether it might just have been the equivalent of doodles on the part of the scribe. A joke, perhaps. But he had made one last comment, and that was that if it followed any pattern at all, it appeared closer to that of some antediluvian musical or architectural notation than to the rubric of human language – though it is true, the Professore had told Peppe, that there is a theory that language itself grew out of music, dance and stone. But he was an academic, and therefore would not admit to anything on the basis of one book, and especially not one that had emerged from a single, somewhat dubious, source.

Zuleikha gazed at the original manuscript and saw that only a tiny proportion of it had been translated. The remainder seemed at first to peter out into blank spaces, but then, as she flipped the sheafs, the writing re-appeared and grew more dense again so that the letters seemed to tumble and dance into one another and effloresce into wild designs, calligraphic zoomorphism, curlicues, arabesques and shapes that more closely resembled characters than letters.

'Oh God,' she sighed, 'this is so bizarre. I need a drink.'

Peppe looked at Zuleikha.

'You know,' he said, 'everyone makes fun of Sicilian universities and sure, there is corruption, and sure, it's all grey-beards, but you should not underestimate the quality of the best individuals or of the student body as a whole. Let Roma, Bologna or Torina take this –' he held up the manuscript '– and run with it! Look ...' He pulled out a large piece of paper and began to superimpose various sheafs of the wafer-thin manuscript over it. At first, Zuleikha could make out nothing. But then, quite suddenly, as though she was recognising an image for the very first time, a legend did indeed emerge. A legend, a map. 'Laore,' Peppe said, folding his arms and smiling mischievously.

'Pardon?'

Alex looked baffled.

Peppe opened his mouth, but Zuleikha broke in.

'He means Lahore. As in Lahore, Pakistan.'

Peppe nodded sagely. There was a moment's silence as Zuleikha slowly ran her hand over the surface of the manuscript.

Alex glanced at his watch.

'Let's grab that drink.'

Zuleikha exhaled and leaned back against the chair. She was covered in sweat. The streetlights were going on and darkness was falling fast, as it always did at this latitude. She allowed her gaze to come to rest on a fixture set almost at the mid-point of the ceiling.

Alexander turned to Peppe.

'Do you know when it was written?'

Peppe shook his head slowly.

'According to my colleague, the ink and paper, papyrus and vellum seem to have come from many different eras. He's never seen anything like it. He thinks that perhaps some collector...' Peppe paused, fingered at the edges of the papers. '... that it may be a clever forgery.'

Zuleikha snatched the sheet away from him and pored over it as though she was a jewel expert inspecting a diamond for impurities. The sheet smelt of musty paper, as she might have expected, of something that had been stored in a box for ... how long? But underneath that there was another, older smell. She didn't pick it up at first; it was more like an aftertaste, or a *before-taste*, she thought. It was the scent of blossom. She wondered whether it might be coming from the street outside rather than from the manuscript. But even at this hour the street was filled with belching, barely-moving traffic. The traffic system in Palermo was crazy, even by Italian standards. No seat-belts. And besides, here in Trianacria it was no longer spring and the land was withering, the blossoms fading fast. For the next three months, everything would be heat.

The manuscript's edge was rough and worn and fibres the colour of ripe cotton had begun to fracture away from the main body of the paper. She wondered whether, like the vampires in the stories, it might simply vanish in the sun. Zuleikha thought of Archie, of his body, cold and still, of his organs, wrapped in spiders' threads. And she wondered whether she might be a lunatic, locked in an asylum somewhere. Lie back and think of the evidence-base, she told herself. Archibald had been cremated. He was dust.

She turned to Alexander.

'Why did we meet, that morning by the river?'

Alexander glanced nervously in Peppe's direction. The restorer was gazing studiously at the manuscript as though he was still trying to decipher the hidden part of it.

'I see your point,' Alex replied quickly.

Men were so fearful of losing face, she thought. It was one of the things that hadn't yet been bred out of them.

Zuleikha had visited Pakistan only a handful of times and possessed only a very basic understanding of one of its many languages. She reckoned that she had been bequeathed a rather distorted view of the place by her mother, who had disparaged it with the passion of a true lover. Or perhaps with the dispassion of an ex-aristocrat: one whose fortune had been squandered by the stupid men in her family (men who had possessed neither the desire nor the ability to remove the silver spoons from their scowling mouths). Yes, she thought as they made their way through the bust Jewish streets of the Albergheria: Bahadur Shah Zafar, the last Moghul Emperor and a distant relative of sorts, may have died, or been poisoned, in a jail in Rangoon, his sons put up against a wall and shot without ceremony, his daughters sold into Calicut brothels … and, in a more genteel parallel, in the metropolis of Lahore, the supra-clan of Sadozais, the one-time kings and queens of Afghanistan, may have sunk into the dusty narratives of resolute imperial or post-imperial Scottish travel-writers.

However, particularly as she had grown older, in Nasrin Zeinab's mind they had lived on – at least as long as she had lived on – as dancers who had never quite resolved the patterns of their chorea, musicians who had continued to perform well beyond their allotted time in a world in which no-one any more had been able to listen to the strains of their music – save, perhaps, through the media of dream or madness. Death was everything. Her mother had dissolved into a mass of pain, a bundle of fired-up nerve-endings, whereas her son had slipped away silently, with no warning, no signs or symbols, no history, except for the nine and a half months she had nursed him on her breast, and the nine months before that through which she had carried him, fed him, grown him, created him. Yes, she thought, as they dodged the early evening river of scooters, cars, trucks and people which flowed down the pavements towards the cafés, bars and tratturi, and as Alex looped his arm around her upper back – he was so tall that his arm reached almost to her shoulder – yes, now she understood all about boxes-within-boxes, chambers that led only to other chambers, and about homunculi, marionettes, pupae, the spirits that could possess ordinary life and turn it upside-down, make it never be the same again. She understood all about the spirits who destroyed innocence and necessitated the development of love. In similar fashion she reciprocated Alexander's affection, and together they joined the elegant jouissance of the passegiata. No, she corrected herself: it's not all dead. Not yet.

Chapter Twenty-Eight

Although the box had continued to change ever since Zuleikha and Alexander had hauled it, dripping and dark, from the Clyde over a year earlier; although its wood had lightened and become variegated and the pictures etched into its surface had proliferated – yet inside, with its multiple chambers, it had remained bare as the gut of a well, its wood smooth enough for each lid to close without difficulty over the next. She was unable to tell from the patterning of the wood how many more lids there might be – or indeed, whether there might be an infinite number of them.

Once the interior of a compartment had revealed itself, the join became obvious; yet before a lid had opened, one really couldn't tell whether or not it ever would. None of the lids had had either handle or loops to indicate that they were lids at all, and when you rapped them with your knuckles the wood sounded solid, not hollow. The box was an acoustic and structural puzzle, one which she was certain no joiner would have been able to unravel – though she had never dared to take it to one. A mathematician or physicist might have understood something of the box's architectonics, but unlike the various manuscripts, objects and cartograms which had comprised its slow revelation, neither Zuleikha nor Alexander was willing to share the box itself with anyone.

When it had been X-rayed as it had moved through airport security, she had seen that its interior had appeared as a single chamber – though it had had an awkward shape. This understandably had irritated the cabin crew, who had insisted on secreting it in a special compartment. They'd said to Zuleikha that really she ought to have sent such a thing through baggage. She'd told them that it was an artefact. The authorities periodically got twitchy about hand luggage and seemed ready to declare World War Three every time some under-sexed Salafist nutcase with bad dentition, an existential crisis and a silicon super-chip on his shoulder decided to try and bring down the government with a tube of toothpaste (allegedly). Then she too had become paranoid, and had begun to fantasise that the box might be confiscated, or that some stewardess might simply steal it and have it cut into pieces and donated as miraculous gifts to the stiletto lovers she had stowed away in her many different ports of disembarkation.

The box had changed and developed; its imagery had shifted almost as though it was a story, written in wood and time. The box was a garden: its pictures resembled those of pagan frescoes, with barely-clad couples cavorting through the clearings of deciduous forests. Yet there were other panels, carved from different woods, which displayed animals and letters in a veritable Babel of tongues – in Latin, Greek, Ogham, Arabic, Hebrew, Ethiopic, Pali, Tamil and in various Chinese scripts. As time had gone on these designs had became increasingly complex, until there was hardly any blank space left. Sometimes, in the hypnagogic semi-darkness, the shapes would begin to move and change. The human forms would become those of animals or buildings, while the abstract designs would cluster together, spin and become animated. But then she would fall asleep, or else lose concentration, and the vision would be gone.

But since that second visit to Sicily, Zuleikha had begun also to hear music emanating from the box. At first she'd thought that perhaps she had left a radio switched on, or that one of her neighbours had turned up their music centre. It seemed as though it was coming from all directions at once. And the walls of old tenements were hard and thick, cut from great blocks of Giffnock sandstone. The thought of all those sleeping ghosts freaked her out enough, without having to know their names. Names were important; that was something which people in Britain had never really seemed to understand.

First, they found it difficult to comprehend the truism that every name has a meaning, and sometimes more than one. For example, her father's name, Daniel John, modestly meant 'God is my judge, I am God's gift'. And he did tend his garden rather nicely. Appropriately enough, her mother's first name meant 'White Rose of India, ornament of the father'. 'Zeinab' meant 'life of Zeus', and had been made famous by the Syrian queen Zenobia, who was descended from Cleopatra and Mark Anthony and who, having been deposed by the Roman machine but living in wealth and comfort in Italy, had become a philosopher – and even, in her own day, a kind of pop star. Yes, well, Zuleikha thought: with that

450

kind of a legacy for a name, as well as the (relatively speaking) more recently accumulated blue blood of Genghis Khan, Akbar the Great and Ahmed Shah Abdali, it would have been difficult to have been anything other than slightly imperious. 'Alexander' signalled 'a defender of men'. How useful, these days, she thought. Her own 'Zuleikha Chashm' meant something like 'the eye where a man slips', or 'most beauteous eye' – and she'd always been happy that her eyes, at least, had been well-fashioned. And as far as men were concerned, in her time…

And what about 'Archibald'? Anglo-Saxon for 'Bold prince', according to her book of names. Archie, Arkady, Arky, Arch. Yeah, okay, that would be about right. The flying prince who had emerged like a thinking golem from the sand and blood of the tenements, and had ridden on the wheel all the way to the memoirs of some demented nineteenth-century aristocrat in eastern England who in turn had stumbled upon … what? A shrine, perhaps, high up on a mountain slope, somewhere in the region they called 'The Roof of the World' – as though the world had a roof, or limit of any sort. There were an infinite number of things, a list of possible throws of the ball that would stretch all the way from Glasgow to the furthest stars – the ones that were so old, dark and distant that they could only be hallucinated. The resonance reached back to the beginning of time, to the moment when, from over the cold waters of the absolute, God said 'Be!' *And the box was.* And 'Enoch' was 'Idris', the mystical flying prophet.

But anyway, she thought, in the East people often would shift through a series of names during their lifetime: from a pet name as a child, maybe to a given name as a young person, then to 'Mother of' or 'Father of', or else simply 'Mother' or 'Father'. And then perhaps, via an occupational denotation, ascending at last to a respectful honorific in their old age. Furthermore, men often had the name of the Prophet Muhammad as a prefix to their given name. Hospital staff, for example, never seemed able to grasp this simple concept: that the reason why every second Pakistani man was called Muhammad and every other woman was called Bibi was not because of a lack of imagination on the part of their parents, but because those names had been given in the hope that the power of the letters – or even of the single

451

letter, 'M' – would in themselves offer protection, love – and, yes, hope to the bearer of the name. The British bureaucrats with their massive iron computers didn't seem able to understand that these individuals should rightly be called by their middle names, because those were actually their personal names. But then they weren't viewed as individuals, were they?

Furthermore, while every name had an original meaning, each one had through countless millennia been through so many personages that surely they should have acquired at least an accretion of dust from each of the people to whom they had been bound. 'Giuseppe', for example, which often was shortened to 'Peppe' or 'Peppino', had been the name of the Prophet Joseph, one of the twelve sons of Jacob, and meant 'the bountiful'. But it also meant 'to sigh, to groan'. And it also had been the name of the step-father of Gesù, hence its ubiquity in Italy in general and Sicily in particular. So 'Yusuf' was a paradox of a name. It was a name with many faces, many voices; interpreter of dreams, carpenter, and a thousand other things. And Laila meant, 'black', 'night', 'sweetheart', 'night jessamine fragrance of wine' (an intoxicating mouthful, thought Zuleikha, yet no doubt pleasing to the palate) and it was also the name of a Quranic surah. So there you go, thought Zuleikha: even the woman's name is like a psychedelic song from, say, the summer of 1968.

Okay, so knowing the names of the deceased – or soon-to-be-deceased – people who had lived in her house would serve no purpose other than to set off a whole bunch of trains of thought which she really didn't need right now (or indeed, ever). Perhaps the walls do have ears, and perhaps, as some claim, they can retain sound for aeons. And if only we knew how to extract that sound from the broken stone of, say, Rome, Mecca or Maryhill, then we would be able to listen to the sound of archangelic revelation or to the conversation of Caesar, or even to the fevered worries of a Glaswegian family on the eve of World War Two. But since that was just idle supposition, all she had to go on with this music was that if it wasn't coming from or through the walls, then it had to be issuing from the box. And it was lute and oud music, and some other older sound around which she could barely get her brain. The volume was so low that she really wasn't sure whether what she was hearing was some transmission through pots, pans and pillars – as used to happen occasionally in the old days, when radio transmissions were of a certain wavelength and frequency, and accordingly used to flow not merely through transistors but also through normally dumb metal. 'The News from Britain and around the World at One O'Clock' through a pot of rice; 'The Afternoon Play' in a knife-rack; 'Brain of Britain' served up on a holey spoon. When you said that kind of thing to young people, they looked at you as though you were mad. People always assumed that their own normality was the same as everyone else's.

The music tended to hover around the lower limit of the audible, so that at times, as with the ticking sound of a clock, she would become unsure whether or not it was still there. She began to wonder whether in fact the music had been playing the whole time, ever since the box had come to her flat, and whether it was this music which had generated everything that had happened: the manuscripts, skulls, statuettes; her strange interaction with Laila and with the tarantismo, and Alex's trance performances. And that, she thought, was where common sense went wrong. There was never absolute silence, even in the farthest deserts, in the deepest mines and up on the highest peaks. There was always some kind of sound, even if it was just the sound of one's own breathing or the tinkling of the oxygen all around. In this world, the rockers were correct: music never died. Like the pots and pans, like Alexander's lute – or like the lute in his brain – one simply had to be attuned to it in order to be able to pick it up.

Not that there was anything simple about it.

She laughed at herself and at her pomposity. As long as you could laugh at yourself, she thought, you weren't completely insane. The genuinely mad not only possessed absolutely no capacity for small-talk, they also had no sense of humour. Quite the opposite; they tended, at least in the early florid stages of an illness, to feel an excess of profundity: to believe that they were Einstein, or Napoleon, or Jesus Christ the Nazarene. Of course all three of these individuals had had a great sense of humour. But with psychotics the depth was always fake, the persona superficial, the concept puerile. In any case, this kind of lunacy had been romanticised out of all proportion by people like R. D. Laing and other 'cool docs', since really, Zuleikha had always felt, even on their own terms, such psychoses represented an abject failure of the imagination. They were usually banal, obsessional, repetitive, a one-step dance in ever-decreasing circles. In a nutshell, she thought, mental illness was neither romantic nor dramatic; it was simply monotonous, boring and destructive.

And quite why the Little Corporal would have chosen to reincarnate himself in – or been assigned the corporeal vessel of – a Glasgow lunatic, never seemed to occur to these people. Nobody ever seemed to suffer from the far more plausible delusion that in another life they'd been, say, a fisherman's wife (as opposed to a fishwife) from Madonna della Scala who had had twelve children, who had never learned to read or write, and who had died of puerperal fever, diphtheria, cholera or typhoid at the age of thirty-two and a half. Furthermore, she thought, such people hadn't pondered on the fact that, while Jesu Pantocrater Basileus had been tempted by and ultimately had vanquished the great winged farishta Iblis upon the edge of the wilderness cliff, the great Prophet of Love had never once threatened to cast himself off that cliff. Jesus had never been parasuicidal. His Hospital Anxiety and Depression Scale was probably minus five hundred. That was why he was a prophet (or, if one preferred, the son of God) and not a fucking general practitioner in this green and muddy land which some Greek with an over-developed sense of humour (and therefore an intrinsic sanity) had christened 'Alba'. Except for the indigenous population, there was nothing white about it. You had to have lived through forty-three Scottish winters to know that. During the frigid months, the place was like a tomb.

But this was the time heralding the June solstice, when the light faded for only three or so hours before the sun, having simply slipped a few degrees beneath the hem of the horizon, began to illuminate the eastern sky. In a couple of weeks, Zuleikha and Alexander would be catching a flight to Lahore. Laupor, Lokhot, Lohawar, Lohar, Rahwar... Yes, she thought, I will be returning to the land of my mothers, to the city of Lav, son of Rama. She knew that it would be unbearably hot at this time of year – hot, dusty and bad-tempered – but she had had no choice. Thanks to

Peppe's ingenuity and Alex's computer skills, they had discovered that the strange half-pictorial scripts which had so baffled the good professore universitario were contiguous with a map of the Gardens of the Mughals. Or, to be more precise, not of the gardens themselves but of the district known as Heera Mundi or the Shahi Mohalla: the district of music and red lamps that sat in the lee of the great Fort. Lahore, city of a hundred gardens and a thousand saints, city of poetry and light; built by the old emperors, descendants of Changez, Timur, Babur ... and at the centre of this map there was a particular address, marked with the symbol of infinity.

BOX FIVE: LAHORE

Separated from my love the nights have grown longer
The flesh is worn out and the bones have started rattling
Love cannot be hidden howsoever I may try
The affliction has taken root

Shah Hussain (1539-1593)

Chapter Twenty-Nine

Pakistan was an interesting country. That was the diplomatic way of describing it. In some ways it was like Brazil without carnival, and gifted with both the thought police and one third of its literacy level. Infant and maternal mortality, education, life expectancy ... the dismal catalogue of which Zuleikha was all too well aware. The statistics burned away at the back of her mind; they were like viruses trapped in the nerve-bundles of her spine. Most of the time it seemed as though they were dormant, but at some level everything she said or thought was mediated by these facts and figures. There was more than one way to insert codes into reality and more than one type of dissonance that rang out from the deep past, through three hundred years of Western supremacy and the consequent assumptions which remained unspoken and nowadays unsayable, but which for all that nonetheless were extant and powerful. Even the bellowing tee-shirted drunks of Alexandra Parade carried with them a whiff of malt imperial swagger.

Anyway, Pakistan does have plenty of festivals, she thought, and Lahore in particular. The Festival of Lamps, the Festival of Kites, mushairas galore ... there was even a street named after food. And in that city the nightlife, the clubbing, the eating, the ogling, the art, the culture – it all goes on till the early hours. (Whereas, she thought, in Karachi, famously, it never stops.) But some folk there would rather it had none; would rather the people, many of them deliberately denied the most basic of life's necessities, were not able even once in a blue moon to step out and enjoy themselves, to lose their head for a night and a day.

Those pusillanimous groups, originally and over many decades funded, trained and armed largely by the USA and the UK – partly via the latter's client-state, Saudi Arabia – would rather that there were no kite-flying events, no musical instruments, no dancing of any sort; no sufi shrines (in fact, no sufism at all) and no singing. Except perhaps of naaths, talaawats and the azaan (the last of these, repeated not-quite-simultaneously, across four thousand tinny loudspeakers turned up beyond maximal volume, part of a plot, Zuleikha was convinced, to turn the intrinsically sublime into the expressively diabolic). In short, if the Great Western Empire was a brothel owned by distant American landlords, and if the UK was the old Madam, then Saudi Arabia was its pimp and Pakistan its factory-floor hooker.

Not that lots of people weren't breaking both sweat and mind to try and change things. Women were, mainly. You get two men in the same room and you get tribalism; two women, and you get progress. Well, that was the theory. It was probably complete bullshit. Yet slowly, Zuleikha thought, things were happening; things were changing in some areas. In cities, mainly. But the state itself was an addict. Okay, it wasn't monolithic. There were people, even inside the state, who wanted to improve things. But they had to tread very carefully if they were not to end up hopelessly exposed. Like that Government minister: a woman who had spoken out for women whose security detail suddenly had evaporated, leaving her to be assassinated by some supposedly misogynistic 'lone nut'.

Yes, Zuleikha thought, there seem to be an awful lot of lone nuts in the world – Lee Harvey Oswald, Mark Chapman, Prince Faisal Bin Musad Bin Abdel Aziz – but the likelihood was that they'd all been manufactured in the same plant and had borne the brandings of their creators in the walls of their hearts. Regardless of which government was in power in Pakistan, how much of the GDP went on education? Answer: two percent. And on health? One per cent. Less. And how much was swallowed up by debt servicing and 'defence'? Twenty per cent each. Redirect even a third of this, even a quarter, and within fifteen years for ordinary Pakistanis the world would irreversibly have changed. Correction: the state was not an addict. In general, deep down, addicts are sad about being addicts. No, like its alter-ego, its id, its over-sized doppelganger India, Pakistan was an acolyte. For the state, God was not invisible, ineffable, shapeless. No: God had a very definite structure and could be quantified right down to the very last piece of lead shot. For the state, God was war.

Alexander was a Glaswegian – yes, he too wore tight tee-shirts – but he didn't swagger or bellow drunkenly at the moon. He seemed to be of a generation that finally had transcended all those old imperial tropes and archetypes, all that nonsense. She watched Alex as he dressed, watched as the dappled light that filtered through the mosquito-proofing swung across the large windows played about his skin. His skin, which here suddenly seemed untenably pale. In Sicily, everyone had assumed that she was southern Italian. But then again, she thought, throughout centuries there had been extensive trade all the way from China to Britain, trade which had been effected by a whole host of middlemen, from the Greek and Roman merchants based in Cochin to the Persians who had accompanied Asad ibn al-Furat to Mazara del Vallo, to the Arab geographers who had crossed the English Channel to explore and delineate the intimate curvatures of the farthest isles.

And then there had been the people of the south coast of England who, as recently as the seventeenth century, regularly had been kidnapped from their beds and taken to the Barbary Coast to be sold as slaves. Some later converted to Islam – perhaps in order to gain their freedom, and perhaps also because their lives in Ifriqiya were actually far better than they had ever been in Sussex, Kent, Cornwall, Hampshire or up the mouth of the Thames. Perhaps the Barbarossas had come as far north as the Clyde and the Forth and, a hundred years or so before the birth of Robert Burns, had abducted peasants, scribes, magicians and hookers and taken them to mingle with the ghosts of Carthage, with exiles from Andalusia and with the ex-pat cavalieri of Lucera and Caltanisetta. Slaves, artisans, merchants, a whole host of long-forgotten individual lives, had thrown their genes around like scented flowers and sometimes, even in the most unlikely of places, Zuleikha had spotted what she had felt was a kind of throw-back, an indigenous but very Indian-looking person with a name like McDonald in some provincial Scottish town who was not known to be of mixed heritage and whose relatives were all porcelain-white.

Along the coast of Sindh the Makranis were as dark as Congolese, and it was widely assumed that they were the descendants of Africans who had sailed, or been brought, across the Indian Ocean – probably from the region of Mozambique. By contrast, in the north of Pakistan there were people with blond hair and blue eyes, people whose skin was as fair as a middle European. She'd even known a few Punjabis like that. These were facts that remained generally unknown in Britain where, for example in children's picture-books that she'd seen, every race had its own distinct appearance and costume. People seemed to have forgotten that the land empires had worried a lot less about racial purity than the nineteenth-century maritime British had. But then, she thought, whenever I have been in love I seem to imagine that the man is outside history, that love lies beyond the long throw of politics. Yet the concept of love itself is defined by politics and history.

So many of the pioneers and imperial residents across the British Empire had been Scottish. Men with names like Elphinstone, Robertson, Jamieson, Ochterlony and Burnes: upright learned men from the Presbyteries of the Lowlands and Southern Uplands who, through public school and Oxbridge, Edinburgh or St Andrews, had been systematically anglicised and had thrown in their lot with the City of London. Such men had maintained a psychic distance from the locals and, unlike their dissolute Georgian predecessors, had never taken Indian wives or mistresses. (Though mysteriously, in spite of this, some of them had managed to catch the clap, a public health prevalence which suggested that like many an occupying army, they had preferred instead, to visit whores.) They had tended to write about the subject nations in an anthropological manner, with an inquisitiveness and prolixity conceived, Zuleikha had always imagined, from a repressed and suppressed sexuality that was the hidden side of the British Imperial coin. Manfully, they had laid out infrastructure across the womb-and-tubes of Hindustan and had given them names like Lawrence Road, Queens Road, North Western Railways and Charing Cross Police Station.

Well, she thought, I too am a product of those routes, of that history and of its demise. I am living proof of a changing breeze, of Sterling silver stamped with Urdu letters. *MacBeth Avenue.* Yes, that sounded about right. Zuleikha's generation was at the vanguard of a quite different demographic, an epic of mingling and mixing that had become the story of Britain in the late twentieth and early twenty-first centuries. Within a few decades, or perhaps a century, she thought, in many of the large metropolitan conurbations of the United Kingdom – or at least those of England – people who now were described as 'of mixed heritage' would become the majority.

Scotland had always been different. The Asian population there had been far smaller than those in, say, London, Birmingham or Manchester. And there were hardly any blacks at all. Furthermore, Scottish people – white Scottish people, that was – really did seem to prefer their own. There were far fewer 'mixed marriages', as they'd used to call them, than in England, and in those that did exist, it often turned out that one of the partners was English, not Scottish at all. She wondered whether it had been this same prudish sense of separateness that had been carried to India, Africa or wherever by the Scottish imperial adventurers and administrators, the clerical and military men – and especially by the Caledonian wives who had followed in their wake, a provincial selectivity that somehow, subconsciously, had persisted down to the present. She was an exception – half-Scottish, half-Pakistani – and in general those white Scots who had coupled with Asian partners tended to come from a lower social class and to be of Catholic Irish-Scots extraction. It was as though this group, traditionally the underdogs of Scottish society, had already sensed their own depressed status and potential hybridity, and so had been less prissy about with whom they had kissed, slept, and made children. Her father's name was an anomaly. MacBeth was about as Scottish as you could get. It wasn't really Irish at all – or at least, not recent Irish. Nonetheless, Zuleikha's surname had given her a kind of credibility in the eyes of white people, an acknowledgement of rootedness which deep down was seldom granted to full Asians. Better a white villain than a brown hero.

Because her father was white, she had no feeling of awkwardness with white men. There was no sense that, in going out with Alexander or any of her previous male friends, she was doing something unusual. This was what people from London never understood: the extent to which, outside of that heavenly (rich) polyglot metropolis, the old silent codes still mattered. Sometimes, in moments of idleness, she would gaze at herself in a mirror with the tips of her fingers pressed pink against the glass, and would try to extract the whiteness from her body, try to draw it out like ghostly ectoplasm, try to hold it, dance with it as though it were a succubus. But to look into a mirror was to look into all

463

the mirrors that had gone before. Being three-quarters Scottish, Daoud had been almost entirely white. Everyone had marvelled at the clarity of his complexion, the sandy waves of his hair, the azure pigmentation of his eyes. He was her Alban seed, her eternal fossil, planted forever in the clay and mulch of Scotland.

Zuleikha silently chastised herself for thinking these thoughts. It was all nonsense, surely. Yet there was a peculiar transparency to classic Irish and Scottish whiteness, almost like the notes played from a clarsach. Alex's skin is like cartridge paper. When we're together, it's as though I'm making love to a ghost. She smiled. And she wondered what kind of lines her body might draw upon that surface and upon the life that lay within, and where the points, angles and tangents of their map together might lead. Nobody talked about these things now, she thought, because it isn't fashionable to talk about them. It's a subject that is deemed offensive; it's a blast from the past against which people would rather wrap up. But that didn't mean it wasn't still operative. And whenever she came to Pakistan, in the midst of the heat and (supposedly) the scent of jasmine and (allegedly) the taste of mangoes, from time to time she felt reminded of this icy mountain wind which seemed to her to carry within it a disturbing music like that of a phantom dastgah – a mode that changed every time, yet which in essence, at root, in its inner bone truth, remained the same.

They were staying at a guest-house of the type in which Pakistan excelled, and which all seemed to have been built in the open-plan, Lloyd-Wright American style popularised across South Asia during the cocktail age, which had extended from the 1950s to the 1970s. Flat-roofed, white on the outside and with wood-panelled interiors, some of these abodes had shadowy reputations. The call-girl economy had really taken off in the past decade, yet like booze and lesbianism and unlike the glittering electrical cornucopia of internet cafés and high-tech billboards, in some senses sex was definitely undercover. In another sense it was utterly indiscreet, and paraded with ferocious vulgarity through the kotees and kotas of the ancient city. Alexander and Zuleikha had brought the box with them to Pakistan, though this time in the plane there had been even more trouble than before and they'd had to put it in the hold – there simply had been no choice.

With its enormous peepal trees the broad Mall Road, site of annual Hogmanay battles between celebrants and Islamists, formed the spine of central Lahore. Arrayed around it were the Zamzamah cannon, the Minar-e-Pakistan, the shrine of Data Gunj Baksh, the elephant walk of the fort, the covered market of Anarkali and the numerous sweet-smelling gardens ... from the seventh century on, Lahore had been a city of poetic ambience. Yet as they were driven along behind steadfastly sealed windows – it was too hot and dusty to open them, even a crack – towards the centre of the city, Zuleikha did not detect even the ghost of a fragrance of jasmine, bougainvillaea or gulmohur. At length they came to a certain point beyond which the car could not go; they would have sat in a traffic jam for hours. So, leaving the dutiful driver to find his own route back, they decided to walk the rest of the way.

The address indicated by the manuscript lay deep within the walled city, close to the old Fort, which was built in the mid-sixteenth century by the Emperor Akbar. Originally, the River Ravi had looped around qila, mosque and Old City alike, but over time the river's course had meandered into irrelevance so that now it lay virtually at the metropolitan boundary. The Andrun Shehr consisted of a series of not-quite-concentric circles, and originally each circle would have held traders of various sorts. For example, the outer loop would have been filled with the tiny shops of, say, carpenters and then, as one moved a little further in, there would have been the shoemakers, then the textile shops, the bazaar of healers, and finally, in the innermost circles, the sellers of incense, aromas and books. And to some extent this pattern still applied; the Old City of Lahore was a working casbah, a methodical medina. But more importantly, it was the bejewelled casket in which lay the spirit of the city. And the spirit of the city was the Word. Well, Zuleikha thought, perhaps 'bejewelled' was going a little too far.

With a shock, Zuleikha had realised that the address was in a particular section of the Andrun Shehr called the Shahi Mohalla, the Alley of the Kings, or Heera Mundi, the diamond market, which as far as she knew, had never sold a single jewel, an area

465

which since Mughal times had been the city's premier red light district. During her previous visits she had never ventured into this sector and, though she had expressed interest in seeing it, no-one among her extended family had been agreeable to taking her there. While everyone was quite happy to joke about it, or to express regret about its decline, its descent into artlessness and vulgarity – which, roughly and probably not by accident, seemed to have been paralleled by that of Pakistani commercial cinema – no-one among her courageous and liberated cousins had been willing to show her around its narrow galis.

It would have been pretty much unthinkable for her to have ventured there alone, mainly because it was an unsavoury place but also because she knew that, without a local guide, she would certainly have become lost. And it wasn't the sort of place where you would want to ask for directions, especially not in broken Urdu, spoken with a British accent. In any case, she would have to wrap herself tightly in a sharif dupatta to cover her hair and breasts and to be accompanied at all times by her tall male chaperone, Sikander, so that no-one could possibly mistake her for a pro – or at least, not a cheap pro. It was yet another reason for not alerting her family to her presence in Lahore. But then, she thought, maybe I'm just making stupid excuses. After all, they're not village people, for God's sake. They're aristocrats – old money, not new, though it was true that along with the national ethos they'd rather gone to seed over the past three or four decades.

Her Urdu was not really up to much, but she'd always found that her fluency improved the longer she stayed in Pakistan, so that after a few weeks she could make do. The accent of Lahore was a particularly attractive sing-song version of Punjabi. She suggested to Alex that he wear a shalvar-kamise purchased off the peg in one of the hundreds of clothes stores in the fashionable Liberty Market. That way, he would be likely to attract less attention. If it had been winter she would have bought him one of those Pathan caps, the woollen ones with the rolled-up hems, but to have worn such a thing at the height of summer – though some men did – would have been madness. The cap, particularly if accompanied by a four-day beard, would have allowed the tall Alexander – Sikander – to pass as Pushtun or Pakhtun, a mountain-man from the aptly named

North-West Frontier Province. And nobody messed with those guys. Pushtuns had a culture of vendetta similar to that which existed in Corsica and Sardinia and in the mountains of Albania, Puglia, Calabria or Sicily. If you insulted them, you could set off a feud that might last for generations. Well, not all Pushtuns, she thought. Over the centuries so many had settled in the Indus valley and had become indigenised, had been caught up in the feudal capitalism that was the operative system in Pakistan, and gradually had become denuded of the tribal qualities which ruled the hills and peaks to the north and west. It was a bit of silliness really, but instead of the Pashtun cap Zuleikha bought Iskander a Swati cap, made of grey felt embroidered with dark red threads around the crown and rim. It performed the dual function of keeping the psychotic sun off his head and making him blend in. Or at least, making him stick out in the right way.

Zuleikha felt the sweat pour down the undersurface of her kamise. Five minutes of this and you were covered in perspiration. Ideally, you had to have four showers a day, and even then ... And it felt as though they had to be the maddest people in the entirety of Pakistan, India, Sri Lanka, the Maldives, Nepal, Bhutan and Bangladesh (including the territories of Kashmir and Jammu that were disputed, for enhanced excitement and close encounters of the nuclear kind, between not just two but *three* countries) as now they were tramping the streets at noon, for goodness sake. Some of the shops closed for several hours (or at least retreated to the darkest depths in an attempt to find a source of cool air) during the daily qellulah, in a futile attempt to avoid the most intense of the heat. Only the poorest people, who had no choice, still hauled themselves up and down the avenues of singed trees, coughing in the dust and fumes thrown up by taxis, four-wheel drives, motorised rickshaws, motorbikes and other unclassifiable vehicles that had probably been knocked-up – or rather, raised from the dead – by mechanics whose names must have included that of Hazrat Issa, the carpenter's behta, since their skills were little short of miraculous. These were machines that had been re-enervated amidst a haze of blue and gold sparks in some tin shack by a chowk named after the moon or a sixteenth-century saint or the second-brightest star in the sky.

The dust in Lahore, especially at this time of year when everyone was praying for the reluctant monsoon rains, was like castor sugar: hot, silvery and almost weightless, it would inspissate into your lungs, triggering malevolent coughing fits that no medicine, whether allopathic, homeopathic, Yunani or Ayurvedic, would be capable of sorting. In the time of folk cures, she thought, they hadn't had fucking diesel. But they had had tuberculosis, and Zuleikha was certain that most of the poor people in Pakistan suffered, to a greater or lesser extent, from this disease. In the same way that the underclass in Victorian – or even Interwar – Britain had been decimated and literally consumed by the acid-fast bacillus. Streptomycin might not have done any good for George Orwell, but across the globe it had saved millions of lives. And adequate nourishment, sewerage, vaccination … okay, she thought, I've got to stop this now. In Pakistan you just have to accept it, otherwise you would go insane at every second street-corner. Most left-wingers who hadn't been killed, corrupted or exiled had gone insane and now wandered like bloodied shadows through the ghostly mohallas of ruined cities, drunkenly coughing and spluttering and cursing the skies.

At the very heart of the city was the King's Mosque, the great red sandstone masjid of Aurangzeb, which dominated the skyline of the Andrun Shehr and which luxuriated in the space once occupied by the famed palace said to have been built by the emperor's usurped elder brother, the wondrous aesthete Dara Shikoh. And in the background the occasional colonial silhouettes of nineteenth-century buildings that had been constructed in the style that was somehow jarring to her eye – a style known as 'Mughal-Gothic' that, like much fusion music, seemed to be out of place everywhere, and which reminded her of so many redbrick town halls in Britain. The King Edward Medical College, the Aitchison College, the House of Wonder … These buildings seldom seemed in harmony with their surroundings. They weren't like the Normano-Arabic palazzi of Sicily; no, the architecture of Victorian Britain had always been triumphalist, colonial, an imposition from master to slave, and as such even the stone seemed to secrete an indigestible melody of trumpets, flag-drenched cathedrals, esoteric English public schools and the pointless and vulgar flatus of Highland bagpipes. The corollary of this consisted of Asian women in Britain wearing gaudy satin shalvar-chamises, Western shoes polished black as fresh tar, and dun-coloured woollen overcoats. Serious mismatch all round.

Here and there were elements of earlier periods – Sikh, Afghan (yes, she thought, my family once ruled these streets!) and Mughal. Anything beyond that one had to seek out, and she didn't have the time. She and Alex seemed to be engendering the only purposeful movement along the street, at least as far as pedestrians were concerned. God knows, Zuleikha thought, what people had done before air-conditioning had come along. Coolers, most likely; and before that, just big electrical fans; and before that, for the well-off, high ceilings and thick walls, shutters, damask screens and blocks of ice – oh, and punkah-wallahs: poor bastards whose sole function in life had been to act as human bellows, giant bags of air. For the poor, then as now, there had been fuck-all.

Some of the guys driving motorbikes wore chirurgical masks, so that for a bizarre moment they looked like brain surgeons going about the business of repairing the cerebral cortex of this most ancient and venerable of cities which once had been known as 'The Paris of the East'. Once, just a few decades ago, Lahore had had boulevards, beautiful parks and wondrous marble buildings. Now it was all being eroded by unmitigated industrial pollution and by a temperature that seemed to rise by half a degree every year. Why were cities always related to Paris? she wondered. As though love had come to stand for utopia. Why not 'Faisalabad is the Slough of the East'? Or perhaps that should be 'Slough is the Faisalabad of the West'. She smiled with her mouth open and then found herself coughing. It was killing, to tread even a handful of metres along these streets in this heat. She had walked along these same roads in November and still had felt the sun oppressive. Now it was 120 degrees in the shade, and they weren't in the shade because there was none.

Many of the vehicles were overloaded with people and produce, and Zuleikha always felt that you really did take your life in your hands when you embarked on the roads of any city in Pakistan – except perhaps those of the capital, Islamabad. If Palermo had been manic and irregular, its history weighing heavily upon its

469

broken crooked shoulder, Lahore was positively hallucinatory. It was as though time had become quantum, so that the highest technology – a Pakistani had invented the world's first computer virus, for which Zuleikha thought he ought to have received an anti-matter Nobel Prize – coexisted with the severest levels of serfdom and under-development imaginable. Okay, she thought, I am just being a typical BBCD – British-born Confused Desi (as opposed to an ABCD – American-born Confused Desi). Pakistani people complained about the same things, yet when you mentioned these faults to them they instantly became defensive and began to treat you as an outsider. Which you were, but that didn't mean that you weren't correct.

Alexander was becoming breathless. She could hear him wheezing beside her. He wasn't asthmatic, but perhaps, she thought, his airways are slightly more sensitive than mine and with this level of dust and pollution… He didn't talk as they walked. She pulled him back, slowed him down. He was walking too fast, too purposefully; you couldn't do that in this heat. This country was not for sprinting; its people were all marathon-runners. You had to pace yourself, or you would hit the wall. As though she was some kind of expert! Alexander seemed suddenly to have lost the ability to negotiate; it was as though he was at sea, and she understood that it had been a culture shock for him to arrive here. It had been, even for her. Whereas in Sicily he had taken the lead, here in Pakistan he seemed to have become a lamb, allowing Zuleikha to do all the talking, find the places, read their way through traffic and across streets that had no name-signs but seemed possibly to be marked somewhere on their map, depending on which way up you held it. Their modern street-map, that was, not the old Siqilliyan manuscript – so that most of the time, while trying to figure out just which corner of the off-kilter square that was the shape of the city was meant to be pointing due north, they got hopelessly lost, hot and dehydrated. It became impossible to think, much less find their way.

One couldn't even go into a shop, she thought, and buy just any old bottle of mineral water. Some of the mineral water bottles were adulterated and dirty, and the liquid would lay one up for days. Might even thin out and kill you. At one point Zuleikha had wandered into a shop, thinking that it was a chemist, only to discover that it was a store selling veterinary supplies. The shopkeeper and his (human) customers had had a good laugh at that, a laugh in which she'd joined while simultaneously feeling irremediably stupid and gauche. It was the need to think about this kind of thing that exhausted her every time she came here. Her family had visited on occasion, mainly for weddings and suchlike, but it really was rather expensive and jet-lagging to fly such a long way – especially as her mother hadn't even been born or brought up here. There was her mother's family, what the physician in her might have called second-degree relatives, but that was another reason why she'd made a point of not telling anyone that she was coming to Pakistan. If even one relative, or even a friend of a colleague of a relative, found out that she was in Lahore, she would be obliged to visit one by one every single family member simply in order to avoid giving offence. To have come four and a half thousand miles and not to see anyone was offensive, but she had neither the time nor the inclination. Their very hospitality was suffocating: the endless meals, the cups of hot sugared milky tea, the secondary and tertiary visits that went on till three in the morning … really, she couldn't be bothered with all that. Especially not now that she and Alex needed to find this bloody address in the middle of the sex mohalla. That was another thing she couldn't allow to get back to any relatives, the fact that she had visited Heera Mundi – a place where no respectable woman ever went. Plenty of respectable men went, of course; though generally, unless they were so rich as to have no worries about reputation, they kept it pretty quiet.

She felt that she was thinking like a mem-sahb, a liberal imperialist – like one of those etiolated women brought over by educated Pakistani men as trophies of their time in Amrika or Inglistan. For the first few years they'd go all out to integrate, but sooner or later they became either sick or sickened. Zuleikha had always thought that they managed to find the plainest, most colourless women, whose one defining characteristic seemed to be a total lack of eyebrows. These wives lasted a maximum of five years before running back, with or without children, to Baltimore, Uxbridge, Stirling. To properly exist in this country necessitated the activation of a different level of consciousness, and not everyone had it in them. She wasn't sure if she did.

And now here she was, hauling along her trophy – or boyfriend, she supposed one might call him – as well as her own Britishness, European-ness – a quality which, like a shadow, seemed to accentuate, to darken her mind as well as her visage the longer she remained in the studied chaos of Pakistan. Then she stopped herself from going there. It was a dead-end road, a road blocked off by a paramilitary barricade and a row of guys with sten-gun moustaches, guys who chewed pure tambaku and who would shoot up their own dead in the kabaristan so long as they were paid for it.

Now she could see the cupolas of the qilla up on the hill to her right. A long time ago Lahore had been protected by a wall with (presumably for luck, kismet or karma) thirteen gates. Now, however, while the original archways of some of the portals still existed, much of the old walls had been destroyed. First of all in the British conquest of Punjab in 1849, and again a century later, during the Partition from which the modern states of Pakistan and India had resulted. Though subsequently (to some degree) both gates and walls had been restored to something approximating their pre-colonial magnificence, in practical terms these orifices were really just names for certain places on streets: psychic nodes, like the points of the star-shape which bound together the tightly-packed gallis of the Andrun Shehr. Although many of the houses in the Old City had been constructed during the period of Sikh rule which had occupied the first half of the nineteenth century, nowadays there were no obvious signs of the Hindus and Sikhs who, for hundreds of years, had dwelt within the Old City and who had been forcibly expelled – and worse – in 1947.

They entered the Shahi Mohalla by passing through the Taxali Gate, an enormous structure on one side of which was a public garden. As they walked the street became visibly narrower, and in places was shaded by buildings that teetered beyond the perpendicular some fifty or sixty feet above their heads. It wasn't that there was any discernible difference between this mohalla and any other in the Old City: there were the same door-shutters, closed just now against the heat; the same ruts in the road; the

472

same scooters tied to lamp-posts; the same bicycles rattling past; the rickshaws whose filterless engines emitted a sound similar to that of an angry hornet; the exhausted donkeys hauling tangas and heavily loaded carts that seemed constantly to only just avoid getting stuck between two buildings; the same decaying shambolic four-storey habitations linked by hammocks of brightly-coloured clothes, and the ubiquitous garish posters written in a ferocious mélange of Punjabi, Urdu and English, of Lahori filmi acts in which the male leads always seemed to sport the heavily-oiled cock-mullets of the 1980s. Indeed, Zuleikha had always thought that much of what was considered normal in Pakistan – and for that matter in Pakistani diasporic society – held to the line cut in the flesh of their country by the Great Leader of Handguns and Heroin, General Zia ul-Haq, as though in some essential mythopoeic sense the cultural ethos had not really moved on since then. As though, whether in Lahore, Bradford or Glasgow, every stone of every chowk had been branded with the petty-bourgeois normative absolute of small-mindedness, vulgarity and prohibition that somehow had been embodied to oilaceous perfection in that man whom she'd always thought of as 'The Fucking Bastard'.

But she thought that this was in spite of, not because of, the essential spirit of Pakistanis themselves. It was as though the creativity of an entire nation – creativity which you could see here, on the streets even of this most frowned-upon of areas – was at bursting-point, was yearning to blow apart the restrictive skin imposed on it. Here in Heera Mundi, with the dancers and musicians and the roving bands of film producers who always had an eye out for the pretty thigh or the suave loin, the creativity was molten. And yet – and so – the state repressed it into a mere two-hour period. And this, Zuleikha thought, was like a small but existential paradigm of the entire country.

There were the same food, clothing and other small shops, mostly closed just now, and the occasional specialist store selling kites. The same goat testicles being grilled in the open air, in skillets. Well, not testicles from the same bakra, otherwise it would have been a mutant goat, with hundreds of the soft sweet blighters. But seriously, Zuleikha thought, this was a typical street in what they called a developing country, and as such, with some regional

473

modifications, it could have been situated almost anywhere south of a certain latitude. This was what white people found exotic, fascinating, attractive, scary, she thought. It reminded them of a past which had ceased to be linked with the reality of their present, and it also served to confirm them in the holy position of intellectual and moral superiority which they preferred, usually silently, to adopt. The rest of the world was just their cinematic whorehouse. So many white middle-class women she'd known had been so full of themselves and hadn't even realised it.

During the Raj, the British had begun the degradation of this area. Whereas the Mughals and their cohorts had wanted culture-as-well-as-a-fuck, and the tawaifs, who had been among the most highly educated people in the Empire, had tutored shahzadas and other aristocrats on the metrical aspects of Persian poetry and lots more besides, the Tommies, Taffies and Hamishes had wanted merely a fast, furious – and above all, cheap – screw. Nonetheless, until the 1950s the gaikas had continued to recite the poetry of Iqbal, Zauq and Ghalib, and had learned and practised classical dance to an extremely high level. Whereas now they were expected only to provide some coarse words, jigged-up into a catchy tune redolent of contemporary Punjabi films and executed through supposedly voluptuous body movements and throats tied remorselessly to a beat-deck. Indeed, she had heard of tourists from Britain and North America who had visited this area and enjoyed themselves – not necessarily having sex with the hookers, though the prices were dirt-cheap, and a simple fuck with a rundi could be purchased for as little as one pound sterling (a more elegant ritual would cost anything up to fifty pounds, though that was exceptional).

Nonetheless, the whores here were far cheaper than the she-camels monopolised by pirs and mullahs, and were certainly less expensive than the upmarket mem-whores of Gulberg, say, or of the Cantoonment. Strictly speaking, one might call those latter types call-girls, since many of them 'called' in during the hours of darkness, earning fat fees for purveying a wondrous universe of perversions and returning like phantoms, like bhoothes, to their hovels in Heera Mundi on the puttering monochrome rickshaws of dawn. But it came to the same thing. Other – dubeez – women were more discreet, and hid behind the yellow furze of laburnum in plush hotels or respectable guest-houses like the one in which she and Alex were staying. And even richer, hyper-sharif ladies and gentlemen owned the whole racket and made very fat bucks indeed out of the glistening vulva trade.

Zuleikha was somewhat suspicious of the receptionist and the odd-job man in the guest-house: they looked as if they knew something you didn't, and the way they eyed her up, as though in their minds they were slowly disrobing her, caused her some considerable irritation (as an Edinburgh lawyer might have said). Alexander had noticed this and hadn't understood, and had got really angry – or perhaps just jealous – but she had steadied him by informing him that it was common and to be expected. That uncultured under-sexed men here stared unashamedly at women as though they were gazing at magical treasure or at some mythical heroine which they hadn't a hope in Hell (or Heera Mundi) of ever getting for themselves. It was the look of men who watched more pornography than they let on, who hid themselves in the airless rooms of some dead-beat kota where blue flicks would be screened and no questions asked, or who became pilgrims at sufi shrines where among the qawwals, prayer-flags and ayats, the cheapest hookers of all, fallen women from the villages of Punjab, Sindh and wherever, sang, prayed and opened their legs to anyone and everyone for the price of a (non-alcoholic) beer. Many of these shrines were like great open-air brothels, and also represented good custom for the drug-dealers, who operated food stalls and the like.

In Heera Mundi, on the other hand, at night the prostitutes paraded themselves brazenly in doorways, through the opened shutters of big windows or up on wooden balconies. The very pukka Islamic government had however restricted their active, official, legal office hours to between eleven p.m. and one a.m. – which surely, she thought, was a recipe for a whole of host of sexual dysfunctions and quack abortions. Not to mention God-knows-what diseases! Yep, this was the area of dirt and cunts, of hash, heroin and hydroxzyine (though nowadays in Pakistan drugs were everywhere, scattered like the seeds of pomegranates from the Siachen Glacier to the pearly Arabian Sea) of glittering celluloid culture – most of the Lahore film industry's actresses still came from the families of kunjarees – and of the delicious aroma of risk, antithesis, counterpoint.

Yet perhaps because of its proximity to the fort, the area's name, Shahi Mohalla, meant 'The Royal Neighbourhood'. On its other side it was bordered by the minaret of a most holy Sufi shrine, while the old Grand Trunk Road formed a crescent around it, so that in fact – as well as in essence – it lay right at the heart of the city. There were covered balconies on the upper floors of some of the buildings, but these remained unoccupied, and apart from the stalls of kebabs and the hole-in-the-wall cobblers, there was a stillness too about the houses themselves. Daylight did not seem to penetrate at all into some of the narrower alleys, yet because the battleship-grey buildings were so high and close-knit, the heat in these mohallas was even more intense (if that were possible) than in the relatively broader streets. Mountains of flies were everywhere, and if they provided a kind of underlying melody, then the coursing legions of rats were the harmony. Pimps who might once have been weavers sat in the shade of fast-food outlets, eating gallons of nihari and haleem, sporting big bellies and low-slung bulges that were either genitals or handguns. Far in the background, from the top-floor shacks of ruined havelis on the point of collapse, Zuleikha was sure she heard the rattling of chains, the shackles of women who had been bolted to iron pillars and left like Andromedas at the mercy of the chorails and bhoothes of the top floors. But then she realised that it was merely the sound of ghung Roos as someone somewhere began to rise and get dressed and maybe to rehearse. Heera Mundi was a place of cartoons and caricatures, of juxtapositions and strange coordinates. It was a place where some men dressed up as women and painted their faces with florid make-up that ran down their cheeks, the heat turning them into parodies of parodies, overgrown boys clad as precocious girls who whirled their eyes suggestively at passers-by as though they were imparting atomic secrets. And here and there, through broken shutters, the falsetto ankle-bangle laughter of khuserah houses.

Then Zuleikha noticed that the ground floor entrances were set at a higher level than in other areas of the Old City. Several feet higher in fact, so that getting to the doors required steps, and often the steps led, not simply to a door, but to a verandah which ran along the fronts of several doors. Old women, their skins all henna, wandered down the street loudly munching paan, their gaits in spite of themselves still redolent of youthful licentiousness. Like squirrels, they kept the paan leaf tucked away in a corner of their cheek or behind their lower gum, where it seeped and festered and eventually resulted in carcinomas which gnawed away slowly at their faces until they were a mass of blood and gore, until they were like ghouls out of some Pashto horror flick. One or two seemed to be eyeing Zuleikha up. Quickly she turned away from the frightening naikas with their betel-nut mouths. There were only one or two younger women about at this hour and they hurried past, their honour wrapped tightly in dupattas, though mixed groups of better-off youngsters from the more modern parts of Lahore on their way to some café or other rollicked, rippled and jived along the gullees that were so hot their fingers seemed to quiver like thick transparent liquid. A junkie roasted in the bright sunlight, his form crumpled, swept like rubbish to one side close to an open drain, his body emaciated, his mind stoned to the deep unconsciousness of outer space and his long matted lice-ridden hair seeming to have sprouted not from his scalp but from the dust itself. Sherbet-sellers and ice-cream wallahs were everywhere, doing a roaring trade, and although by now both Alexander and Zuleikha were parched, they didn't dare drink or eat the stuff. The chipped ice was fatal.

'I think it's this one,' she said, not daring to take out the copy which they'd made of the manuscript. But it wasn't.

A passer-by seemed to have overheard her, or perhaps he had noticed that they were outsiders, and instantly he leapt to be beside them and to become their guide, although he was followed by a huddle of gawping men and boys. In broken Urdu, which she knew carried a terrible British accent (which the man would think English since he would never have heard of Scotland) Zuleikha explained to him that they were looking for a particular house on a certain street. For an instant she thought that she had caught a knowing gleam in his eye, but then he was off ahead of them, occasionally turning back to make sure he'd not lost them in the throng which now pressed them on. The crowd apparently had come to the conclusion that they were two white English people. It didn't matter that Zuleikha had light-brown skin; here, in general, it was your words which defined you. In any case, she was with a white man, so she must also be an Angraise. She knew that exaggerated deference would be conflated with a desire to rip them off. But then, she thought, this is what they do. To eat, they must get as much money as they can from anyone who ventures into their orbit. In this respect they were no different from a bank, insurance company or building society. The man led them into a warren of streets so narrow that they were able to shed the crowd, who had seemed anyway to lose interest once they had discovered from Zuleikha that Alex was Pathan. The man stopped suddenly and went up a set of stairs no different from any other in the mohalla; he knocked firmly on the blue wooden door three times in a particular rhythm. At first there was no reply.

'There's no-one in,' Alex said, and his voice betrayed his desperation. Zuleikha had become so used to Alexander's deep voice that nowadays she found that she hardly noticed it. She still found it attractive; it was simply that, as with the man himself, Alex's voice had become almost a part of the music of her life, so that unless there was something amiss, she would no longer feel that frisson which had possessed her at the start of their relationship. Maybe this is how infatuation shifts into love, she thought. A necessary indifference.

Alex was seriously baking, and he felt that if he didn't sit down in the next five minutes he would simply collapse. The sky was as heavy, jaundiced and dusty as the road. The paint on the door was badly peeled, and it looked as though where once there had been a handle now there was merely a glue-filled hole. But their guide, who obviously understood more English than he let on, or who perhaps was simply a very skilled reader of body language and voice tone, took great pains to reassure them. Just then there was a sliding back of bolts and the door opened just a fraction, just enough for Alex to see a single eye in a face and a lemon-slice of mouth. Their guide and the man behind the door exchanged rapid-fire Punjabi in a rhythm which seemed to Zuleikha like that of a fluid metal song. But then, she thought, all foreign languages sound as if they're being spoken really fast, and anyway Lahori

Punjabi is a beautiful, poetic tongue, no question. These folk of the old city, of the andrun shehr, descended, they said, from the families of rajas whom the Mughals had vanquished over the years, were the purveyors of the most pukka West Punjabi of all. Those who were chauvinistic about Urdu said that this was because in the Royal Courts of Lahore – and for hundreds of centuries, this city had been the capital of the Mughal Empire – the language had been influenced by both Urdu (the lingo of the soldiers and ruling classes) and Persian (the language of the court and of all official documents). But then, Zuleikha thought, language is a hot potato. And the ground was an oven that burned through the leather soles of their sandals, so that as they stood waiting before the door, they had to shift stupidly from one foot to another. Everything around them seemed to be running in disordered yet nightmarishly slow fashion, as though a frenetic reality had been filtered through hot glue. She became aware that they were being watched by another group of men. She pulled her dupatta tightly around her head and shoulders and gave the men a brief dismissive look.

Alex heaved a sigh of relief as the door swung open, and they were beckoned in by both their erstwhile guide and the man who had emerged from the darkness. They gave the former a wad of low-denomination notes as the man closed the door behind them. He was wearing black patent shoes and a shalvar kamise the colour of earth, and had a regulation Punjabi moustache. Presumably he was a servant.

It was an old-fashioned type of house known as a haveli, and she knew that it would consist of a square shape with several floors set around a central courtyard called a dalaan. Many of the houses in Lahore's Old City were of this design and had been constructed before British Rule, during the eighteenth or nineteenth centuries or even earlier. The rooms had high ceilings and each would have a giant electric fan set at its centre, and generally these would be used instead of air conditioning during the short spring or autumn seasons. Zuleikha and Alexander found that they had to step up to go through the doorways, as each was set about eight inches above floor level. The first room measured around thirty feet square. Its walls once must have been bright blue, though now the paint was chipped and faded. It had several firmly shuttered wooden arches for windows, a number of diwans and ornate tables covered with white throws, and three electric glass chandeliers-cum-pendant fans. It looked like the sort of evening khana in which people might entertain guests.

The servant led them through one chamber after another and Zuleikha realised that once again she had been wrong: this was not simply an ordinary haveli, otherwise by now they surely would have reached the courtyard. All the rooms were identical in size, though not in décor; but they became less ornate the further in they went. Each had at least one small heavily grilled window set high up, and by the time they'd passed through the third internal door the illumination had become so dim they could barely see each other, let alone anything else. The servant switched on the light, but the single bulb hanging from the twelve-foot high ceiling was insufficient to illuminate the space, and the air bore the stagnant odour of naphtha. Against one wall there was a settee that was upholstered in a silver-coloured satin-like material, and running parallel to this was a long heavily stained coffee table garrisoned by several wooden chairs. Over in the far corner was a battered chirpae that looked as though it had been lain on every afternoon for a thousand years. The absence of other furniture rendered to the room a certain asymmetry which irked Alexander. Why were the chairs and table not in the middle of the room where they ought to have been? He shook his head, as though trying to clear a spider's web from his thoughts. God, I need a glass of water, he thought, but I daren't – not here. The people living in the Old City might be immune to the local bugs, but he certainly wouldn't be.

The muntazim asked them to take a seat, and said that he would bring tea. Somewhat reluctant to occupy the low-set sofa, they perched on the chairs instead. More tea, Alex thought. Everywhere you go, people offer you tea. It was very nice and all, and he quite enjoyed the taste of cardamom, but after a while even a good thing, if repeated too often, can begin to pall. I need either a bottle of iced water or a cup of espresso. I need to wake up. He almost voiced this to Zuleikha, but then noticed that she seemed a little distracted, and indeed looked more interested in inspecting the contours of the room than in engaging with him.

She understands the language, he thought; I don't. That's

what makes it different from Sicily. Here, I am like a man struck suddenly dumb and deaf. A shadow man. He crossed one leg over the other. He hoped that this house would have a proper toilet. Some of the older buildings had those squat affairs which he'd never been able to use for anything more than peeing. And with this shalvar, how the hell did people avoid getting crap, piss and water all over them? There was an art to it, he supposed, and since he didn't have this art and was never likely to acquire it, he was also a man paralysed. Codes, he thought. Everything is fucking codes. He wondered whether he had decoded Zuleikha adequately. No, he thought; women can rip us apart at a glance, yet we spend decades trying to seek them out and still miss by miles. He had never found Susan. Not really, otherwise ... but it was too late for that.

Now he was in the Land of the Pure, and he was with his new woman who was part-Pakistani, and he was in a stuffy room in the brothel area of Lahore, waiting for ... what? He'd come a long way since that early morning walk along the banks of the Clyde. What if he'd never ventured out of doors that day? None of this would have happened. His lute would still be a lute, all sixteen courses of it, and his head would still be in one place. But he would have been alone and still grieving. Then he felt guilty; he felt that he ought still to be grieving. Just after they'd returned from their first visit to Sicily, one of Susan's relatives had spotted him and Zuleikha, out for dinner one evening. And now the whole family knew about it. His family and Susan's. Tongues had begun to waggle and dark suspicions to burrow their way into the collective mind.

He'd left his lute – or oud, as it was now – in the cupboard of the room in the guest-house, and he hoped that some thief in cahoots with the shifty-eyed receptionist wouldn't make away with the instrument. In general in this country, musicians tended not to be well-respected unless they were either classical ustaads or very rich and famous pop stars. Otherwise, the word 'musician' conjured up this place, Heera Mundi, and the mirasis who played for the dancing girls. Kebabs and cobblers. He knew that much.

The servant left, quietly closing the door behind him. His shoes made a faint crunching sound on the marble floor as the rhythm of his footsteps receded. They were alone. There were no noises from the street, and though high up on the wall behind the settee there was an air-conditioning unit, and though it must have been switched on – since otherwise the room would have been stiflingly hot – try as she might, Zuleikha was unable to make out the sound of the mechanism.

This room differed from the rest in that it was at least basically furnished and it had only one door. On the wall opposite the door was a large oil painting whose frame reached down almost to the floor. While they waited Zuleikha went up and, without touching it, closely examined the painting. The frame was made of heavy gilt convoluted in the form of a vine. Well, she thought, this is Heera Mundi; but still, not every house is a brothel. The painting was of a mountain whose lower slopes were filled with terraced fields, cattle, chickens, goats, forests and low houses, and whose single pyramidal peak was covered with snow. Curling through the land like a long silvery worm was a river filled with clear water and large boulders along the course of which had been inscribed, as in a painting-within-a-painting, the words of a script, the nature of which she was not able to discern. Zuleikha glanced around and then, seeing that no-one was coming, she ran her finger along the line of the river. The surface was thick and bumpy, as she'd expected, yet when she drew her finger away from the painting and sniffed at the skin, it smelled not of oil-based paint as she'd expected, but of pine cones. She rubbed the smell off on her shalvar. It seemed incongruous, hanging there in the semi-darkness of the haveli. Though there was nothing inherently disturbing about the image itself, somehow its presence disconcerted her and made her shiver in spite of the intense heat.

'No air-conditioning,' she said quietly to Alex. 'Not even a cooler. Fans are no use when the temperature's this high – they just circulate the hot air.'

He nodded, and grimaced. She and Alex looked at each other and she tried a smile, but he looked pissed off. He was obviously dehydrated and exhausted and was badly fazed by a combination of cultural dislocation and jet-lag. She had experienced the same feelings during the first few times she had come to Pakistan, and it still took a couple of days for her to sink into its difficult and slow, yet frenetic, routine. But now, after several more visits over the years, she had become less disturbed by its apparent chaos.

Nonetheless, she had not been used to dropping in during the height of summer, when everything seemed sharper. She wasn't used to heat of this magnitude and it would take a month properly to acclimatise. But, she thought with a mischievous frisson, Alexander was experiencing an echo of the White Man's Burden. Nowadays, this derived not so much from diseases and parasites as from a lack of boundaries – or, to be more accurate, from boundaries that were hidden. Paradoxically, there was a forest of red tape in Pakistan, a legacy of the anally retentive paranoia of the British Empire which in post-independence Pakistan had been maintained and nurtured as a necessity, since if systems became easy, smooth-running, efficient, there would no longer be any need for palms to be smoothed, for favours to be granted by big important men who sat on big important committees and who knew big important generals, landowners, factory bosses.

And as a consequence of the clientelismo that was the secret pact between the forces of capital and those of landed feudal patrimony, and with which over the past three and a half decades or so it had become wholly necessary to engage if one were to enjoy even a vaguely normal daily life, the palms in Pakistan were so smooth that you could slide a tank, an opium factory, a housing construction project, a flyover, a training camp for nutters, or even an atomic bomb, off them with no-one noticing. Except, perhaps, the occasional solitary academic, the civil societal conscience of the nation, imprisoned like a levitating Anarkali in a marble tower. Just as Zuleikha was thinking these subversive and possibly revolutionary thoughts, the door opened and a man who was clearly not a servant walked in.

They both rose as he shook their hands, beginning with Alex.

'Salaam alaikum. Petrus Dihdo Labokla. I have been expecting you.'

Alex shuddered, since even as he sputtered out his own name in reply he recognised, in the timbre of the words, those of the man who had given him the lute all those years earlier. *I have been expecting you.* Corny, yet somehow, even on this burning summer's day, also chilling. How could he possibly have been expecting them?

'Please, sit. Has Abdullah gone to fetch tea?'

In unison they nodded, and sat down. Petrus Labokla followed suit, positioning himself lightly upon the settee – which, they were somewhat surprised to note, was in fact at the same level as their chairs. Deceptive again, Alex thought. Appearances.

'Abdullah is not very efficient; he may take some time, I'm afraid. But tea will arrive eventually. We call him Zulfikar, because he's so slow.' He glanced towards Alexander. 'Lightning,' he explained.

Zuleikha wondered who 'we' were. Did that mean that Petrus Labokla did not live alone, that he had a family, or that other families lived in various of the wings of the haveli? Or had he used the term simply in the archaic, plural version of the nominative case? No doubt they would find out sooner or later.

Petrus Dihdo Labokla was tall. Not quite as tall as Alexander, but certainly at least six foot. But he was also very thin. He was wearing Peshawari chuppals, and his shalvar kamise hung off him as though he'd bought the wrong size off the peg. Zuleikha, though, could see that his clothes had not been bought off the peg. As was usually the way here they had been tailored, and though there were good, bad and indifferent tailors in Lahore, surely no tailor could have been so very incompetent as to have fashioned such ill-fitting garments as these. Nonetheless the cotton was spotless, with signs of vigorous starching having taken place close to the sharpened seams. Possibly, she imagined, by the man who'd been ironically named 'Lightning'.

She wondered whether Petrus too was a nickname. Peter. His complexion was that of a fair-skinned Punjabi and he had blue eyes. In Britain, she thought, if he wore Western clothes he would not be taken for a South Asian at all. Perhaps for a northern Arab or southern European. Or maybe a Central Asian, since his eyes were almost 'Chini'. His head was long and his age indeterminate. He might have been anything between forty and sixty, and though in places, such as around his eyes, his face was deeply furrowed, the skin over his chin and cheeks remained taut. This, together with the litheness of his movements and his languid mode of speech, suggested the younger end of the age-range. Petrus's fingers were long and thin and bore no signs of manual work, and apart from his slim moustache his jowl was clean-shaven, his browny-black hair bundled up into a pony-tail. With the exception of a few red-headed or blond Afghans and other extreme northerners, most Pakistanis' hair was either brown-black or blue-black, although some peasants' hair had been bleached to a dusty pallor by the constant exposure to the sun.

And then there were the radioisotope heads, the ones with hair that glowed in the dark with the cartoon luminescence of mehndi. Outside of the NWFP and the Northern Areas people in general did not tend to wear headgear, except for poor elderly guys in wrap-around turbans or the devout in prayer-caps. The further away from Peshawar and Gilgit you got, the further east and south you went, the more sparse the head-wear became. It was not like South America or southern Europe: here in Pakistan, people's heads were exposed to the full force of the sun. It was different for women, who wore dupattas around their shoulders or on the backs of their heads, or who pulled them right over the whole head. Then there were the few (the few compared to Britain, anyway) who insisted on wearing hijaabs, chadurs, niqaabs, burkas, the increasingly chic couture of the unbeatably, and unbearably, holy.

'You have come a long way to see me today.'

'Yes,' she began, 'we're staying in Garden Town.'

But he waved her aside.

'No, I mean from England.'

'Scotland,' Alex broke in, but Petrus just looked at him as though he'd said something in Martian. His eyes narrowed and Zuleikha thought that this was how he would look when he was being cruel.

Then he smiled, and as the smile caught the ends of his pencil moustache, his face seemed to change completely. There it was again. Daniel John MacBeth, Peppe Ayala. Or maybe with her father it was just the whisky. And then she caught a whiff of liquor. Yes, when he smiled he did seem older. She began to wonder whether his angularity might be due to illness. Alcohol was plentiful in Pakistan, even though it remained illegal – except for personal and ecclesiastical use by Christians. But that had always been a joke, and even during the tightest darkest years of Islamist military rule during the Hell that was the 1980s, people in the know had held drinking parties disguised as tea-parties, the dissimulation extending right down to the teapot and fine bone-china cups. But as he had breezed in, there had been something else as well. Petrus Dihdo Labokla was a weird enough name, she thought.

Alex scrambled through his bag.

'We've got this map ...'

'I know,' Petrus broke in.

'You know?' Zuleikha shouted in astonishment. She and Alex exchanged a glance. 'How do you know?' she asked again.

Just then, the tea was brought in. Zulfikar took his time over the ritual of pouring and distributing cups and mitai. God, Zuleikha thought, every time I come here, I put on an inch! Yet it would be rude to refuse to eat anything at all. So she nibbled as slowly as she possibly could, in an attempt to spin out the crumbly green pistachio sweet. Petrus stared her straight in the eye so that she lost coordination and let the plate slip to one side, only just managing to stop the mitai from sliding right off the sleek porcelain. Finally Abdullah left them alone, though since she didn't hear any receding footsteps this time around she fancied that he might still be listening at the keyhole. But then, she thought, perhaps this too has become internalised in my brain. I no longer hear the footsteps of ghosts or servants. She sipped at the tea, but it was still too hot.

'So, how do you know?' she repeated, more quietly.

Petrus did not seem perturbed either by her question or by the scaldingly hot chai. Alex shifted in his seat. Labokla took his time to answer.

'Laila is a good friend of mine. We have known each other for ... how long? Over thirty years, probably. She was here, you know, back then.'

Zuleikha felt the compass begin to slide along with the mitai. Leaning forward, Alex broke in.

'You mean, Laila was here in Pakistan?' His voice was level, low-pitched, as though it had been seasoned by the chai. 'She was here, in Lahore?' he persisted.

Petrus smiled again, less broadly this time, and nodded slowly. 'Have you ever heard of the hippy trail?'

Naturally they had heard of the hippy trail, which had run from London, through Europe, Iran, Afghanistan, Pakistan and Kashmir, reaching all the way to Kathmandu. They also knew that some of the travellers had not made the full journey, but had stopped off for varying periods of time, anywhere from Istanbul to Srinagar. Yet they had never supposed that any of them had remained in Pakistan. But then, Zuleikha thought, that is because we no longer have any real memory of Pakistan as it was before General Zia and the Salafists took power. We have only the whispered testimonies of those who had lived before and who, against all the odds, had retained a sense of the possible. She was also annoyed that Laila twice had breached her confidentiality. Still, it was her own fault for confiding in the woman. After the first time, in Sicily, she really ought to have known better. Laila seemed to have become a key figure in this whole thing and Zuleikha wondered whether in fact their original meeting in the forest of Lindsey had been an accident after all.

'Laila was on the hippy trail and that is how we met. I too was a hippy.'

'You were a hippy?' Alex asked, a smile almost dancing upon his lips. 'I didn't know there were any hippies in Pakistan.'

'But then,' Petrus replied quietly, 'you don't know Pakistan.'

'She … she stayed here, in this house?' Zuleikha asked.

'Here, there and everywhere,' Petrus replied, dreamily. 'The Café Orient, Zelin's, Falettis, Griffiths, the Indus, the Park, the Braganza, the National, the Intercontinental, the Gymkhana Club, the Pak Tea House, the Garden of Open Hearts. You know, in the 1960s the Mall was known as "Cool Street".' He laughed wistfully. 'Many people stayed here, in this house, and they – we – used to drink, smoke … and listen to poetry, music. In those days, we were free.' He let his head fall back against the wall and closed his eyes.

Ah, thought Zuleikha, so that was it. You are a drug-dealer and this is your den. Again, she wondered who the 'we' might be, the 'we' who had named Abdullah 'Zulfikar'. There had to be people who did the cooking and the cleaning – servants, who would live on the top storey or perhaps on the one just below, since sometimes top storey rooms had no roofs and tended to be occupied only by the occasional wandering djinn. And was there a wife, she wondered, or was this Petrus Dihdo Labokla also a pimp? Did he have his pick of women from the kunjarees of the mohalla? Was that why he was so thin? Did he, in fact, have AIDS? She realised that she had her tongue halfway across the rim of her cup and so she swiftly removed it and set the cup down. Swallowed uneasily but too quickly. Felt the liquid burn her oesophagus, millimetre by millimetre, as it went down.

'They were good days, good days…' Petrus murmured, his eyes still closed. Alex looked at Zuleikha as if to say, what the fuck is this you've got me into? She inhaled briskly.

'If you know about Laila and about the map, then you'll know what this is all about. You'll know about the box.'

Alex was burning a hole in the side of her head. She could feel the cheese of her brain begin to frazzle and turn to liquid which began to leak just like milky tea across her body.

Petrus came awake suddenly.

'Box? What box?'

Idiot. Shit. Fuck. Zuleikha could've kicked herself. So Laila released only the information she thought people needed to know. She was like a fucking secret service. She avoided his gaze. He was becoming expansive, he had cast out his arms as though he were a cod-Jesus, a twenty-first-century Issa with a charcoal moustache and dressed, not like a first-generation hippy in sandals and kaftan, but in an ill-fitting shalvar kamise and Peshawari chuppals.

'This house is the house of my ancestors. It goes back a long time, and before it was here there was another even older house, and before that one another, and so on, even unto the time of Sikander. Eighty years ago, some Red Russians lived here. Did you know that?' he asked rhetorically. 'A famous juggler and his family. The Samarins. They sat right there, where you are sitting. On those very chairs. Afanasii Aleksandrovitch Samarin, Rada Mirovna Samarina and their two children. The son, Arefiy Afanasiyevich Samarin, and the daughter, Darya Afanasiyevna Samarina. In those days Lahore was the capital of the giant State of Punjab that stretched from Attock to Patiala, and this was all India.'

Petrus spoke as though he had been there in the 1920s as, a few hundred miles to the north, the Reds and the Whites had battled it out on the snowy plains and burning deserts that had formed the southern frontier of Revolutionary Russia. But that was ridiculous, she thought. He'd have to be ninety, a hundred years old. Don't be so silly, she told herself. Yet still she felt unease creeping up from the base of her spine.

'They were escaping from the civil war. When after many years the Partition of India came, they had become disheartened. Although Christians had been almost the only religious group left relatively unscathed by the whole disaster, one never knew which way the wind might blow next. And so they had left for Europe, or maybe Amrika, I'm not sure which. This is the story which came down to me and which I have been repeating, in my mind, for ... how many decades? They left trunks stuffed full of equipment – who knows, perhaps they'd intended to return one day – and some years later, as a child, I would play with the glass, twine and rubber balls, the wooden spheres, the sticks with white ends, the rings, the plates. In a sense, I was the jamura to their madari. I was the boy raconteur to their master juggler. This was the 1950s. Yes, that's right, around the time of the Rawalpindi Conspiracy Case. I spent hours, days, nights, practising my juggling skills. Everyone used to laugh at me, but when I got really good they stopped laughing and opened their mouths in marvel. The Russians also left books. They say that Madame Rada used to dance here in this room. She would not have been able to have danced anywhere else in this area, because then she would've been mistaken for a kunjaree. And because she was fair-skinned, she would've fetched a very high price – for those days. But she wasn't a kunjaree; she played the piano and the kobza and they say that she was able to call down the spirits.' He whispered. 'Those spirits are still here. On some nights I can almost feel them, spinning up there on the roof, in the dalaan and in the inner rooms of the haveli. I can almost hear the whispers of lovers filtering down through the walls of the barsati.' He leaned forward, so that he appeared to be balancing on the edge of the settee. He was no longer whispering. 'You know, if you juggle fast – I mean, really fast – sometimes it is no longer skill, but jadoo.'

'What?' Alex asked. 'What did you say?'

'Jadoo,' Zuleikha repeated. 'Magic. White, black or in between.'

Petrus nodded.

'In olden times, jugglers were not trusted. Even now – I mean, while the Russian family lived in this house, Stalin's secret service

agents came here to try and poison them. The house acquired …
a certain reputation. People used to come for cures, or to apply
curses on those they didn't like.'

'But how did you come to live here?' Zuleikha asked.

'We used to live in the house across the street. When the Russe
were leaving, they sold the haveli to my mother at a knock-down
price. After all, who would want to live in a house of jadoo in the
Shahi Mohalla? There were rumours … there always are.'

'Rumours?' asked Alex.

Petrus sighed and then sipped his beverage meticulously as
though he had been educated not in magic and juggling, but in
the art of the Japanese Tea Ceremony. Zuleikha suddenly realised
that his skills and training explained the litheness of his body, his
stature, his bearing. It wasn't faked; you really couldn't fake that
sort of thing, any more than you could've faked having been to
Eton. It was in his muscles, in the fibres of his bones and ligaments.
It was in his very breath. It was magic.

'Ignorant people – envious people – said that my mother had
an affair with Afanasii. That I was a harami, a bastard. You know,
illegitimate.'

'Half-Russian,' Zuleikha mouthed and then realised that she
had actually said it, albeit quietly.

Petrus nodded.

'Eventually it drove my father to suicide. He was found hanging
from a roof-beam in the room next door.' He indicated the door
through which Alex and Zuleikha had passed earlier.

'The third door,' Alex whispered.

'Pardon?' Petrus said.

Alex shook his head and leaned back against the wooden
chair. He could feel the carvings indent the skin and muscle of his
back, just as, he thought, they must have indented the body of the
Russian juggler, Petrus's real father.

'And … and your mother?' Zuleikha asked nervously.

'While I was on the road, I heard that she had eloped with
an army officer – one of her long-standing clients – and had
gone to East Pakistan. I never heard anything more of either of
them, except that they may have been massacred in Dhaka by the
Bengalis during the riots of 1971.'

Zuleikha was taken aback, both by his candour and by his dispassionate rendering of this terrible story. Again she found herself doubting its veracity, but then she chastised herself with the thought that so many awful things had happened to people in South Asia over the past seventy years that sometimes people had become ... not exactly inured to tragedy, but resigned perhaps to its inherence in their lives and in the lives of their families. It had developed into an outlook that was a kind of psychic defence mechanism: always expect the worst. So, because he had been illegitimate – or, to be more precise, since illegitimacy on its own was fairly common in the Mohalla and indeed was an occupational hazard-cum-benefit – because his existence had been unacknowledged, Petrus had been abandoned in different ways by first his father and then his mother. Yet he seemed to look back on his time as a child in the haveli with nostalgia.

'Once on a day, the dalaan was filled with the laughter of children, and every room of every floor was occupied by families of the baratherie. In our family the women were always performers, artists; they earned a living while the men stayed at home and did the cooking and looked after the children. Then, gradually, the world changed. Nobody wanted art any more.'

'So,' Zuleikha began tentatively. 'Your family are ...'

'Yes, we are kunjars.' Alexander looked perplexed. Petrus turned to him. 'Prostitutes, but also artists.' Alexander inhaled sharply, and then blushed, crimson. 'But I did not want to remain at home, especially after my father died, and so I ran away. I dodged and darted between the desi tangas, the old Victoria buggies, the black bicycles, the palanquins which we called dolis, and the gleaming new cars. I learned from the travelling mirasis and the magicians, najumis and amulet-sellers of Mochi Gate, how to be a proper juggler. With this troupe I travelled all over Pakistan, and India too. In those days it was still possible to slip across the border and return with no-one knowing. You could cross the frontier over the peaks of Kashmir, or else through the hot marshes east of Karachi that led to the Rann of Kutch. Both paths were dangerous, but possible, and still there are smuggling routes which have continued to be operative, ever since Partition.' He rubbed his thumb and index finger together. 'Rishvat.'

Zuleikha nodded.

'We would perform at villages and in towns – occasionally in cities too, but there was less custom there. City loag had become addicted to the cinema. No, it was the people of the earth who remained fascinated by our act, by our magic. I spent years on the road. Really, I grew up as a travelling magician. I learned from an ustaad; magicians are never called that but they should be. The really top-class magicians are virtuosos. The girl-jugglers of Orissa, Augustin Daly's *Zanina* jugglers who so electrified the Stateside mother of modern dance, Mister and Misses Ramaswamy, the first professional jugglers in Britain, who fired the great Hazlitt with energy and inspiration, Sena Samo, the first sword-swallower in Amrika, Enrico Rastelli, Pauls Conchas, Cinquevalli and Spadoni… Yet I also designed my own tricks. When I performed magic, it was as though I was alive! While the troupe were in Abbottabad, my ustaad died and then I became the lead magician. But when, in '65, the war broke out between Pakistan and India, I had to return home and I found that everything had changed. The families had all left and the house was almost deserted. The house belonged to me, but I needed to pay the bills, to maintain its upkeep, and also I needed to eat. So when the hippies began to come through, I would rent it to them and provide them with … entertainment.'

He smiled as he related the past, and despite the room's dimness his eyes began to shine with a clear blue light.

'And that is when I met Laila. Long hair, tall, she was the most beautiful woman I had ever seen. In those days, it was not so easy to get up-to-date records. The Ajays, The Bugs, Dad's Gratitude … party bands. *Ko ko korina!* Here, in Pakistan – and I think in India, too – we were always somewhat behind Amrika and England in pop music: about five years behind, so that in 1972 we would be listening to stuff released in 1967. In those days there were dance halls, all kinds of places you can't imagine now. It lasted until that elephant-fucker came along.'

'Zia,' Zuleikha said.

Petrus nodded.

'Did you know that he banned all the films that had been made in this country in the preceding thirty years? Every single one. Even the comedies. He ruined the industry, he destroyed the arts. I curse his memory, I hope he rots in Hell. Many of the stars came from this place, from the Shahi Mohalla, and after Zia it was all screwed. Everything went downhill. Try juggling with a Kalashnikov at your back. The whole country was playing Russian Roulette. I left my magic tricks, went into the hills and became a revolutionary.'

'My God!' exclaimed Alex. 'How dreadful.'

Typical British understatement, Zuleikha thought.

'What? Becoming a revolutionary?'

'No, I meant the Kalashnikov, the Russian Roulette.'

Petrus formed his hands into the shape of an arch as though he was a Protestant Pilgrim Father beginning a prayer.

'The Samarins left behind books – revolutionary books. Mainly in French and Russian, neither of which I was able to read, but some were in English. One of my mother's clients, a teacher, agreed to give me lessons in return for ... favours.'

'Your mother did that?' Zuleikha was aghast, but also found herself filled with a kind of sad admiration for this long-dead woman.

'She wanted me to become educated, to get out of here. It's ironic, isn't it, that out of them all I was the only one who stayed. Or should I say returned. And then I began to read the books and then I got my hands on other books. I have had no formal education, only what I have read with these hands, these eyes. I became involved in the Left, I helped set up groups in the city and beyond. I became a target.'

'Yet you have servants.'

'Only one – Abdullah. I cannot afford any others.'

'But why will no-one rent this building?' she asked. 'It must be massive. We just came through – how many rooms, Alex?'

'Four, including this one.'

'Four rooms...' She pointed upwards. '...and there are obviously more.'

Petrus looked directly at her.

'No-one will stay here because they say it is haunted with jadoo, djinns, piries and the ghosts of those dead Russians. No kunjeree will dance in the kotha, no tamashbeen will smoke a hookah, no notes will fly like the verses of ghazals, across the air, lightened with the scent of rosewater. It is beyond the pale, as they say. In

493

the hills and mountains of the NWFP...'

('Northwest Frontier Province,' Zuleikha translated for Alex's benefit.)

'...in the Tribal Areas, one can hide out for years – decades, even. The people there will protect you with their guns and their lives. You are their guest, their cousin. They will kill anyone who tries to get you. The police are not permitted to go there. And until recently, even the army was afraid of venturing east of Jamrud Fort. There are people who have been hiding out in those deep gorges for centuries. They don't know the war is over. Well, the war isn't over. One way or another, this country is in a state of perpetual war. With India, with itself. When I returned, the Left had died. So I have no comrades any more. Once you could walk across this city. Now you require an oxygen cylinder.' His glance fell and he looked down at his hands, which seemed to have become restless. He sighed. 'I am alone.' He looked up at them. His hands moved to his kamise pocket, situated high up on the left side of his chest. 'Do you mind if I smoke?'

They shook their heads.

'So you went to the Tribal Areas,' Alex began, once Petrus had lit up properly and inhaled a few times.

'I knew some people there: families who in those days, just after the coup of '77, were willing to take in left-wingers on the run from the military authorities. It was Tribal Law, local, village jirgas. Even the Army dared not interfere with the affairs of the tribes, or they would risk an all-out war on their western flank. Which, with India only twenty-three miles to the east of this spot, they could ill-afford.'

Zuleikha wasn't sure how much of what they were being told was true, but she was willing to suspend disbelief for a little while, at least until she knew what the connection might be between all this and their map.

'But ... Mr Labokla...'

'Petrus, please.'

She nodded.

'Petrus. Why are you telling us all this? We're very privileged.'

'Because your map has led you to my door. My house, into which no-one has ventured for so long. My haveli, that has become

494

like a tomb. Laila has led you here, to the place where, for a few short years, we had happiness.'

'You and Laila …?'

Petrus nodded.

'We were lovers.'

Alex glanced down, a little embarrassed.

'I'm sorry. You are uncomfortable with this. I will change the subject.'

'No,' said Zuleikha, raising her hand. 'No, please, it's fine. It's just … a bit of a surprise, you understand, us coming here in the first place out of the hot summer's day, and he's not used to it – Pakistan, I mean – and the summer, well, it's quite different from Scotland. And then there's your story.'

'It's not a story.'

'No, I mean the story of your life, Mr … Petrus. It's pretty unusual, I think you would agree?'

'Here in Heera Mundi, where the mirasis have played music for centuries, first for the landowners and now for the tamashbeen and where every kunjeree – if she's lucky – sleeps with several different men every night and dreams of being a film star, it is not so unusual. It is ordinary life – the life which you people outside, in Garden Town or Model Town or Muslim Town or Scotland or Amrika consider to be normal – that is unusual for us. General Zia ul Haq, General Yahya Khan, General Ayub Khan, General Pervez Musharraf and all the corrupt civilian presidents with their palaces here, there and everywhere and the jagirdaar cronies without whom the combined economies of Switzerland and Grand Britagna would collapse overnight – these things are truly unusual. Abnormal. Wrong.'

'So,' Alex continued slowly, 'you were saying that Laila and you lived here for … a while.'

'It was a kind of commune. You know, Afanasii Sahb had left behind these Leftist kitaabain and they'd also left books on juggling and magic. Laila and her friends lived here, cooked, cleaned – when it took their fancy to do so – and over there, I juggled…' He pointed in the direction of the outer door whence Zulfikar had brought them into the haveli. 'There, in the front-room of the kotha. We had a great act. I would juggle and then the hippies would come and play music. And we had the dancers, too. Our kotha was unique in the whole of Pakistan. People would come from far and wide, just to see our performance. In those days, the kunjerees could still dance properly. I mean classical dances, to real poetry – Mir Taki Mir, Zauq, Ghalib, Bahadur Shah Zafar – and not just to some cheap Punjabi punch-and-fuck-song. It was as though we carried the whole history of this country on our backs – not in a bad way, not as a burden, but in the sense that somehow the magic which had freed me as a child had returned with me and attracted these hippies to come and stay here and not to go on to Kashmir or Nepal. Somehow that magic also fired us up, turned us all into genuine performers, real artists. It was as though the music had infected us and made us glow with light.'

'The music...?' Alex asked, suddenly intensely interested.

'When you are juggling, there is a certain music that emerges from silence. No-one else can hear it, or at least, they don't know they're hearing it. But the really good Jadugars, they know. When you are juggling, there is nothing else.'

He smiled, that demonic infectious smile of his, so like the smile of her father. Though this man was maybe older, maybe younger, his age indeterminate just like his inheritance, and now she believed his story. It was simply too bizarre to have been made up. Anyone who had wanted for some reason to fool them would have concocted a much more believable tale, and it would have been a tale of unremitting woe, designed, like the kunjareon ke mujre, solely for the purpose of extracting as much money from 'visitors' as was possible. No, she thought, Petrus was not after money. There was an odd smell now in the room. There was tobacco, yes, but not just that. Petrus's eyes had begun to droop and the cigarette – a home-made one – was teetering dangerously between the ends of his index and middle fingers. She woke him up.

'Petrus!'

'Umn?' He looked up and smiled again. He filched in his pocket, pulled out a makeshift cardboard packet and offered her one, his expression suggesting quizzical amusement.

Is he playing with us? she wondered, and then the heat, the airlessness and the general incipience of the long-dead and departed got the better of her and she reached out and accepted.

496

'Zulie…?' Alex began, but she smiled and shrugged as Petrus offered Alex the end of the pack. Petrus leaned back against the sofa, nestled himself into the silver-coloured satin as though he were burrowing into a well-dug hole, and began to exhale smoke-rings towards the ceiling.

'We had the best records in Pakistan, Laila and me. I knew a guy who worked on the boats, down in Karachi, same guy who supplied us with drugs. Yes … Brian Auger and the Trinity, the Kaleidoscope, The Stooges, The In Crowd, The Talismen, The Keynotes, The Action, The Red Crayola, The Rotary Connection, the MC5, Erkin Koray, Wilma Reading, Pink Floyd, Chad and Jeremy, Mohammed Yousuf and the Mods, East, Moğollar, Mighty Baby, The Grateful Dead, Bariş Manço, we were the absolute best! Especially in bed. Screwing on lysergic is incomparable.'

By this time, neither Alex nor Zuleikha were shockable. There was definitely some top-class Royal Afghan Black in Mr Petrus Labokla's cigarillos. But it's strong, Zulie thought. My God, it is strong! And inadvertently (or maybe not), she inhaled. Yes… Strong and spicy.

And she realised that, at some point, Petrus – or perhaps Abdullah – had put on some music, though she couldn't tell from where it might be coming. She let herself sink further back into the wooden chair so that her body became part of the architecture of the chamber, of the haveli, of the Andrun Shehr of Lahore. Labokla's five-storey haveli had been built during the reign of the diminutive Ranjit Singh, on the site of earlier Afghan and Mughal habitations. But perhaps really it had been conjured out of dust by the magical tenth-century governor Malik Ayaz, who, it was said, had rebuilt Lahore during a single night. Zuleikha could almost smell the history.

That's an oud, Alex thought; a very early 'ud. So early I've never heard the sound before and didn't know it had even been preserved, let alone recorded. It was playing a dastgah, and as he inhaled more of the marijuana it became clear to Sikander that the instrument being played was in fact a barbat, an early Persian lute, or perhaps a mizhar – a word which he couldn't quite remember the meaning of. Perhaps it had been an early Arabic lute or a lyre or something. In spite of his exhaustion he had the urge to join in, to follow – or perhaps lead – the notes as they were being played. But that's silly, he thought. This music was probably from some distant time and place. Or perhaps it was from here, from the next room, the fifth chamber, from 1938. Say June 1938, when Afanasii Sahb had taken out his props and begun to practice for the evening's performance. But who had played the lute? His wife, perhaps, who had learned in some conservatoire in Moscow or St Petersburg or Odessa or Kiev or in some far northern city where the ice cut the music clean and sharp.

Here, in the Andrun Shehr during the long days, Rada Samarina had learned to play the kobza. In those days of celluloid silence serenaded by Master Nissar and Miss Nadia, of Iqbal, Sajjad Zaheer and Akhter Husain Raipuri, of the Braganza Hotel, Diamond Talkies and live snake-eating professors, of Austin Sevens, Master Buicks, Armenian muscle dancers and Anglo-Indian flappers. In this fusty haveli she had tapped into something, or perhaps the djinns up on the roof had swept invisibly into her instrument, changing it string-by-string, wooden strip by wooden strip, so that as she had played, it had returned to some original form. These early versions of the lute were not like the ouds of today, he thought. As with the lute in Europe, so too the instruments of the Middle East and Asia had moved on over the centuries. Yes, thought Alex, it is a barbat. I see it, even as I hear it.

And there she was, up on the flat roof of the haveli at the height of summer; there among the wakeful sleepers, the paindu sahibs fresh from the villages, the gulli-danda boys who never rested, the mast malangs whose abode lay in the ruins and kabaristans of the scrublands and who saw visions of the Hindu cremated as they turned to smoke and rose into the sky, the hookers of all grades, the washerwomen, the sardarjis and the charsobees pattebaz, the crawling shrieking devotees whose heads were shaped like those of rats. There, in that time and place, with her lustrous wheaten face, was the Russian lady, holding the instrument at right angles to her body, its ancient mulberry wood caressing her belly, its face invisible to her as she played with an eagle feather on a hot summer's night, as she played to the moon and the stars, as from her watered wooden platform she serenaded the sleepers, living and dead, on the roofs of the houses all around with her prayer, her dastgah.

Far away across the Old City, up towards Bhatti Gate, two kites were doing battle, pecha larana, high up in the sky and with their paper bodies turned translucent by the stars. They seemed almost to be darting and dancing in tune with the music. It was as though she was cradling a giant pear with a tiny stalk and a bent-back peg-box. Alexander could smell the mulberry as he pressed the nail of his fourth finger down onto the string, the old way. Its tone was like the song of a small bird, flying from the top floor, flying over Lahore and all its gardens and palaces, sweeping through each of its thirteen gates, including the invisible ones no longer in existence. And as her husband juggled downstairs, she picked up the angles and notes which he produced and played them to the darkness. Bo-kata!

Not a very revolutionary instrument, thought Alexander, but then those early Bolsheviks, Mensheviks and Socialist Revolutionaries had been cultured people who had watched impotently as friends and colleagues had been arrested, incarcerated in some God-forsaken prison camp and then shot without ceremony and their bodies burned, the memories of their existence erased forever. Manuscripts, symphonies, feature films, ideas, dreams, mercy, humanity, hope, truth, bureaucratically, scientifically, were annulled. Afanasii Sahb, Rada Bibi and their family had been the lucky ones. They had managed to escape, riding on the backs of mules, avoiding bands of Basmachis, through the white sun of the desert and across the blank frozen surfaces of the high glaciers. They had travelled from the lands of Turkestan across the Pamir Mountains, the Jayhoun River, the long Wakkan corridor of Afghanistan and thence into the Chapursan Valley and British India. Alexander had imagined all this from what Petrus had told them, but also from the quality of both the music and the reefer which Labokla was smoking very slowly, very luxuriously as they were enveloped by the middle tones of the dastgah Segah. It was a dastgah of other dimensions, it was the music that had been torn from the belly of Mother Russia. It was the rhythm of Rus connecting with its eastern soul, with Byzantium, Pars, Armenia, Samarkand and Felix Arabia. And with Sasha the Great Plunderer and the prophets, Pagan, Buddhist, Jewish, Christian and Muslim, who had come in his train.

'I hear a lute,' Alex said, though his voice sounded as though it was issuing from far away, as though it were one of the kites – a piri or a teerah – or maybe one of the khilaris, the expert flyers from 1938, from upstairs, from the roof, that was speaking.

Petrus nodded.

'It is you, Sikander, who is playing.'

Alex glanced down at his hands and saw that indeed the fingers were moving as though he was holding and playing the four-stringed barbat and he wondered whether perhaps he might have been possessed by the spirit of Rada Mirovna Samarin. For surely, all the Russians of that generation were dead now. If they were alive, they and their Victoria buggies would have to be a hundred and ten years old. Well, perhaps if they ate the yoghurt of the Caucasus and drank the arak of Pakistan like the old Quranic Patriarchs, they would live to unimaginable ages. Perhaps this house was a giant Ouija board or a magical mirror; perhaps its walls, made of God-knows-what, retained not only smells, sounds, atmospheres, but also personalities, histories, truths. After all, what is juggling but a dance of the spheres? And what is a barbat but a model of the universe? And thus spake God, or Zoroaster, or Ziryab, or Milinda or Rada: And barbat begat oud and oud begat lute. And Alexander and Susan begat death and Zuleikha and Iskander begat ... what? It wasn't as simple as that, though. Nothing was. He was smiling broadly at Petrus.

'I am a hundred and ten years old,' he said, and his words, hummed possibly in Cyrillic, seemed to float across the room.

Petrus smiled back at him, that transfiguring smile of his, and Alex realised that he resembled nothing as much as an icon, a golden Byzantine or perhaps Nestorian icon.

'You must bring your barbat tomorrow evening and we will have a mujra! Or perhaps a qawwali, since the best dancers here are really dancing and spinning for a higher master. If you paint their steps through space you could write a symphony, or a dastgah, or perhaps an even older form. I will juggle silver spheres and you will play your instrument and perhaps the ghosts of the tawaifs will begin to dance.' He sighed. 'I haven't seen Laila for ... how many years? A quarter of a century. Yet with your presence here today, I feel her presence too. Isn't that strange?'

Zuleikha nodded.

'She is a good woman. She helped me out of the forest.'

'In which you were quite happy to leave me to freeze to death!' Alex interjected, glaring at Zuleikha.

'You found your way all right,' she said. 'Through the music you found your way, Alex.'

'Who knows who or what has drawn us together. Perhaps it was always going to happen,' said Petrus. 'Perhaps the Samarins knew that, back then.'

But Zuleikha thought that was rubbish. Did that mean that Daoud was always going to die, that her conception of him, her giving birth to him, had been futile from the start? These things just happened. Their coming here, their going to Sicily, Lincolnshire, Argyll and into the bowels of Glasgow had been mediated by the conjunction of their own wills and by someone's sense of humour. Laila's, perhaps. Nothing was written in the stars, except trillions of light-years of empty space. Dark matter.

Alex wondered how Petrus had known that he played the lute, but he figured Laila must have told him. It seemed she was in contact with people on all continents. Perhaps for her the Hippy Trail had never ended.

'I can't juggle as well as I used to,' Petrus was saying 'I'm a juggler who can no longer juggle, a revolutionary who has no revolution to join, the son of a kunjeree with no kunjerees in the house … All in all …' He raised his bidi as though it were a glass of pepper vodka. 'I think you would agree that I am a great success!'

'We agree!' sang Zulie and Alex in unison.

And it seemed as though not only the ghosts of old Reds and creaking beds were inspissating the air of the haveli, but also those of the Heads, of Laila, the Hippy Queen of the Night, whose weird trek through the mountains and valleys had foreshadowed their own journey. But it was all too confusing and beautiful to make sense of right at this moment. And in this way, amid thoughts of flying spheres and dancing kites, darkness and a modicum of silence at length began to descend on the old city of Lahore like the black coverlet of a magician upon a box.

Archie moved stealthily through the elms, dodging from one tree to the next. There was no-one about, yet he felt that he was able to sense the movement of every single worm in the ground, every leaf as it desiccated in the sunshine. For though here in Lincolnshire it was deep night, it was as though he was moving through all times simultaneously. At first he had been consumed by an inchoate terror, and he'd wondered if he was in Hell. But then, as he had noticed that he was no longer naked, that his internal organs were no longer exposed to the blinding light or the freezing darkness and that the terrifying mirror had faded to nothing, he had begun to attain something approaching equanimity. And now, wearing, for the first time in over sixty years, his World War Two Royal Air Force uniform, Archie found himself beginning to revert to the old forms of discipline. And it was so good to be able to breathe properly again. He took a deep breath in and held it there at the apex for a few seconds, to savour it, to hold and caress the oxygen as though it were a vintage wine or a finely distilled single malt whisky, to let it fill his being and set him alight, so that he would feel like an angel, or like God. Granted, his throat was barely a fist's diameter and he was hungry yet unable to eat. Nonetheless, this fugue had rendered him a certain lightness of touch and existence which was far from being uniformly unpleasant.

He wasn't sure how long it had taken, but by what seemed like several weeks later he had figured out how to travel great distances without having to … travel. He could go in all directions at once, through time and space. But although he moved unseen through the affairs of the living, who now seemed like shades, he had not yet spotted any other spirits. Only once had he become disturbed, when a woman wearing narrow-rimmed spectacles of the sort his mother had had in her younger days had been able not only to see him, but also to pull him down into herself – into her mouth, for Chrissake – a most unpleasant experience, especially as she had halitosis! He'd told her in no uncertain terms to fuck off, but he wasn't sure the words had come out quite as he'd intended, since her tongue and palate had simply howled as though she had been a wolf. She'd scared him half to death – or would have, if he hadn't already been dead. After that, at the slightest hint of psychic activity he'd streamed himself away, flown up beyond the furthest plane – or at least, the furthest he'd been able to go; there had seemed a point, or rather, a great translucent ceiling, beyond which he was unable to rise. The fact that he no longer needed to eat, drink, piss, shit or bath had come as a pleasant surprise. Once or twice he'd tried to talk to people, but had ended up producing only music. So Archibald Enoch McPherson had come to the conclusion that he was completely alone, and though he was startled by this realisation, he felt that in some respects solitude wasn't so bad: indeed, that it could be liberating. Especially when you knew things.

He was at the lake shore, in the middle of the forest. In sixty years the ground had sunk, the trees seemed taller and the house was a ruin, but the air and the night were the same. He half-expected the ghost of his twisted bicycle to come spinning out of the woods towards him, but even thinking about this gave him a headache. How can a head ache, when it's not there? he thought. He reached up to his temple and when he brought his right hand down again, he noticed that there was blood on the fingers and palm. I have just fallen off my bicycle and have walked through the forest. It is June 1942 and Hitler is at the height of his fucked-up power. But I am in freshly laundered uniform. Furthermore, the house was definitely in a far worse state now than when he had taken refuge in its interior. Indeed, there no longer seemed to be an interior. Perhaps only some things reproduce, he thought. Strange that I haven't seen Margaret yet. Then a harrowing sorrow welled up from the pit of his belly.

By the edge of the jetty, at the place where the small island sank into deep water, he saw a figure diving and splashing. He thought at first that it was a dog, or an otter. Cautiously he moved closer (he had become much more cautious following the encounter with the medium) and saw an arm raised as though someone was swimming. His watch had been screwed from the beginning, its hands spinning at random. Looking at it made him dizzy and he thought of flinging it into the long grass, but then the swimmer was moving towards him at a rapid pace, switching styles noisily. Instinctively, he hid behind the great brain of a fungus that had attached itself to the trunk of a large beech tree.

The swimmer hauled herself onto the bank – yes, through the

substance of the tree Archie made out the figure of a woman. She was completely naked and her thin body gleamed in the moonlight. Her skin, pale as milk, had gathered and atrophied in places and her hair was lank and silver. Yet she moved across the grass, moss and sandy earth like someone rejuvenated. She sat down on the bank and Archie saw that this was where she had left her clothes and bag. Removing something from the latter, she held it close to her mouth. A sudden flash, a momentary illumination, startled him. And it was odd, but for a moment he fancied by something in the manner in which she paused that perhaps she had sensed his presence. But then, as she began to smoke, she eased herself down onto the grass so that she was lying down, staring at the circle of sky formed by the ring of the highest leaves of the clearing.

Her breathing was deep and relaxed and reminded Archie of the sound of flowers growing from moss, or the sibilance of a breeze teasing the edge of a counterpane. He crept around the trunk and positioned himself so that he was directly above her. She was in her late fifties, maybe older. Her pubic hair largely had turned white and her small breasts sagged. An unfamiliar smell, a certain lightheadedness. He could see that once she would have been attractive, alluring. He could see back through her life, to the time when she was in her twenties. And the old feelings began to return. The old physical compulsions that had used to drive his being into the hunt, into the fire, into war, into Margaret. And again he wondered why it was not the young Margaret he was seeing lying there, her back taut against the cool moss laid atop stones old as creation. He wondered why it was not Margaret, whom he missed so terribly it tore his insides out, whose absence wound an unseen thread around his body. But then the web was formed by the physicality of the forest, by the night, by the Queen of the Night, by this stranger who was bathing in the lake of his soul.

And Archie began to seep like liquid through her skin and into her flesh, so that the lake inside him began to heave and roar as it had done when he had gone to war or else to the whore, the woman whom he had almost killed with his own hands. Or perhaps he had killed her, it was all so mixed up now in this state of distorted clarity. He was caught in the sweeping electric discordance that was rising from this crone's flesh. He struggled wildly, but was unable to reverse the movement, and at the point where the guitar hit crescendo, Archibald Enoch McPherson found himself inside the body of Laila Sciacca Asunsi, inside her childless womb. And from there, inside every cell, every coiled protein of her being, the being of the woman whom he had never known and who simply had taken a short grass-break from her regular midnight swim in the place, upon those very blades of grass and those broken twigs, those dead leaves pressed layer upon layer into the bosom of the warm earth where, over six decades before, he had entered the narrative and the song that was of a quite different loka.

A sudden jolt hit Laila as she was contemplating a particularly bright star and sent her springing to her feet. Everything was different. Like the Hamun Loch of Khurasan, the lake seemed suddenly to have become much larger, and the rubble on the island had vanished. In its place was a fully-restored house with a long front door and dark windows. Even the air seemed sharper, its quality more clearly defined, and the smells of the forest were intense, giddying. But the weirdest thing of all – and this was weird with a capital 'W' – was that she found that she could see through things. She glanced down at her hand – the one holding the joint – and she could see the bones, the blood flowing through her arteries; she could see everything right through to the moss on the ground.

'This is bizarre,' she said, aloud. 'Biz-fucking-r.'

And she looked again at her joint, rolled it between her fingers. Some bastard had adulterated the hash. Momentary anger at her stupidity was succeeded by a feeling of spreading warmth and a lightening of mood. She looked up again at the sky and saw that the stars were brighter than before, not glaring but rather as though an entire layer of atmosphere had been removed and she was viewing the heavens from the vacuum of outer space. She could make out every crater on the moon, which was not quite full. And the stars were dancing; she could see them pullulate and spin and she knew the names of the planets and the nebulae. And the constellations appeared to Laila as they had appeared to Archie that night in 1942 when he had spent the dead hours in an empty house. Where he'd come across the book that had started all this. The stars danced a little further back and she remembered that once before she had been filled with a vision of this nature. Of all the substances which she had ingested over the past forty years, from gig speed during London concerts to these grassy nocturnal naturist summer swims, the only time she'd had a similar experience to the one she was having now was during the early 1970s in Lahore, when she'd been with Petrus among the cigarette-toting, mini-skirted, freely sexed dolly-birds of love's city. Petrus Labokla, the weird revolutionary, the Red Head, the freak, the juggler of balls, words, images.

She had stayed behind in the Old City when her companions had trundled on towards Kashmir and to their ultimate destination of Kathmandu, capital of Nepal. She'd stayed and had become a part of the household, and when Petrus had juggled and they'd smoked (always in that order, since after smoking he would be unable to juggle a child's soft toy) she would find that she was able to see right through the integument of the house – all five floors of it. Not only that, but she would also be able to gaze into the past, from the time of the Afghan conquerors, through the Sikhs, the British, the Partition, and on through the military coups and the civilian crooks and the magnificent courage of the people and the shades of those Russians who had taught Petrus to juggle. Some nights he had juggled so fast that she hadn't been able to discern the props at all. The world had begun to distort and she'd had the sensation of being able to travel through time and space, to change her shape, to become an animal, a bird or a goat, and to wander for years through the Old City and then up north towards the mountains, and to return after a lifetime to find that in fact no time at all had passed. A mir'aj, in the true sense of the word.

Sometimes she would become Sassi, the girl in the box who had perished in the desert while searching fruitlessly for her drunkard lover. Or Sahiba, the woman whose beauty had caused nine angels to die and who ultimately had fallen on her sweetheart's sword. At other times she would be Heer Salehi, the free lover from the Punjabi myth, and Petrus would be her Ranjha. They would get high together and would fly over the peaks of the mountains, carried on the sturdy shoulders of jinns. And they would soar upwards and would enter the sky through an invisible door and on the other side they would be able to read the old Aramaic – or was it Syriac? – of texts, gospels, epistles. The gospels of Matthew, Mark, Yahya, Thomas, Judith and Maryam. The songs of the hod-carrier, Almalaak Jibraeel, the angelic saviour of Joseph in the well, and the songs of the Karubiyyun and Seraphiel, of Hazrats Daoud, Sulaiman and their massed jinn orchestras. She'd had that hallucination, or dream, or whatever it was, so many times while she'd been with Petrus that it had seemed to have become almost a part of his body. It was as though, when she had made love to him, she had been making love also to all of these texts, tales, songs, demons, piries.

She'd left hastily after Martial Law had been declared in 1977 and Petrus had had to flee for his life, far into the Tribal Areas where, in the past, any military that had ventured had sooner or later ended up being massacred. They'd been separated one stormy night in Lahore by an army patrol. Petrus had run for cover and had ensconced himself deep in the whorls of dead havelis and hidden cellars of whose existence no living person knew. He had known the Old City better than the muscles of his hands – and that was saying something. Indeed, she remembered, Petrus had drawn his strength from the Old City of Lahore just as Samson had drawn his from his hair. Even before the onset of the third – and most brutal – Martial Law, that of General Zia-ul-Haq, the Andrun Shehr's magic had seemed commensurately to dissipate once the developers had begun to encroach upon its sleazy grandeur. And Petrus too had begun to withdraw from the world and to console himself with studying the unfinished writings, the five hundred volumes in Persian of Hama Ibn 'Ali, a mystic who had lived during the fourth century after the Hejira and who had been known as 'The Juggler'. Or else to sally forth with the farang magician, Baba Ilyas Paperoissole, who had used weapons of sorcery against the Crusaders. Or else to commune for forty days in snow chillas along the north-eastern Marches with Fatima Khatun, the shape-changing horse-witch of the Taklamakan.

And she'd lost touch with him; she hadn't known if he was alive or dead. It was a period of her life about which she didn't like to talk; even after all these years the separation, the wrenching sense of unrequited loss remained too painful, the guilt too bitter. Yet still, on wild nights, even here in Inglistan, his ghost had appeared and had danced upon her skin, had struck up leaping dark epiphanies and, in more ways than one, had taken her to places no-one ever went any more. Places where there were no words but only numbers. PETRUS: 99. Petrus Labokla, Doctor Maximus, holy offspring of a blue-eyed Bolshevik and a courtesan, a Jadugar who was descended from a scuffed-shoe conjunction of imperishable catacomb saints and Arif of the Road, great lover, miracle-worker, and dancing ruffian grandson of Jalaluddin Rumi.

In the years before her departure the juggling had kept him supple, and they had spent many long nights making love on creaky chirpaes, or on the marble floors which during the summer had been the only cool places in the city. Or on the spiral stairwell that had led to the upper storeys, and especially in the room of the djinn which had lain between the house and the moon. And even as they had come together, Petrus – mad, beautiful Petrus – had continued to juggle, with one hand or sometimes even with two, so that Laila had felt as though whatever song or music was in his hands, shoulders, back, belly, the insides of his knees – that all of this was being played into her body. That each step, every move, was branding itself onto her spirit so that wherever she might go in the future, Afanasii's dance and Bibi Rada's music would go with her, would follow her or perhaps would lead her, as once she had been led by the shade of Saint Joseph, the Restorer, the Protector, the Divine Carpenter. But she had never been into the fifth room of the kota. Petrus had told her that it had been locked since the old Russian had left and that there was a curse on it. Anyone who opened its door would never be able to stop dancing, would never be able to escape from the world of visions, deos, jinns, piries.

But once, while he was out, she had got high on some ancient psilocybin, had picked the lock and had slipped in. That night was a gap in her memory. She could barely remember how she'd got into the room or even where in the haveli it had been. Perhaps it had never happened, that night in the Shahi Mohalla, in Lahore in the 1960s. It had been a different world. A world when there had still been hope. But no, she corrected herself, she had been different from her fellow-hippies, many – though by no means all

– of whom eventually had returned to believing in the boundary conditions of their social class origins. She had been unlike those who had become big business tycoons, dealing maybe drugs, maybe underwear, maybe stocks, shares and offshore booty. Unlike the ones who had taken the easy way out – though she knew that it had never been easy, that way – and unlike the ones who had grafted themselves onto the grass, halfway up some ancient Nepalese mountain. And, unlike all of these people who once had been her friends, her comrades, her fellow Heads, Laila Sciacca Asunsi had never lost hope. Because, like Pandora, she had known that to lose hope in the world is the final defeat.

And now, here in the forest of Lindsey, once again Laila felt her body stretch; from her toes to the frayed hem of her hair she felt herself elongate as she remembered climaxing in the Andrun Shehr to the sibilance of kite glass. Finest cotton, Paisley thread, spun all the way from the red-brick factories of J. & P. Coats to this joyous dancing painch of the kites, of bamboo, paper, glass, tamarind, egg-yolk and emptiness. The whispered music of maanjha. But each string had a weakness, an invisible point of fracture. After so many years, it was happening again. She could almost feel the powdered kanch fall like stardust from the tails of the night birds of freedom. She remembered those freaky books the Russians had left behind, the hermeneutical texts, tomes consisting of aphrodisiac spells, some in ancient Cyrillic, of transcendental shape-changing jadoo. Spells for summoning friendly fatas, beneficent djinns or perfect spheres that had been cut from the bleached skulls of the Old Men of the Even Older Mountains. And she laughed out loud as she remembered that this was why, during their sojourn in the Old City, their kota had been the most successful and popular of all the kotas in the Shahi Mohalla. Men had rendered up entire fortunes to the kunjerees just to watch them dance, just to touch the fleeting wavelets of their lengas, just to inhale their candamom and rosewater breath. Decadence, perhaps – but decadence of the highest order. Notes, cut clean and pure, steps of light and fire-music from the mountain.

On this night, once again she could taste the arak which she and Petrus had distilled from Baltistani mulberries, and she could hear, in the room of mirrors, the swaying madness of a thousand keys. This same music – psychedelic, yes, but also very, very old. Older than anything she had ever come across before or since, in Lincolnshire, in London, even in Sicily. And now here it was again, here in her forest sanctuary. Her body was supple and languid. She'd almost forgotten how that had felt. And yet, the realisation came to her all of a sudden, as she gazed down at her legs and pelvis, as she cupped her breasts, as she threw back a full head of hair that after so many years had turned again to reddish-brown. The old desires, the ancient needs.

The warmth which at first had been pleasant now streamed painfully up through the soles of her feet, and the moss no longer felt cold and soothing, but molten as though the forest bedrock was beginning to turn to lava. Laila was Heer, the great lover of Punjab, the woman who had taken up a hamza and beaten mullahs black and blue, the woman through whose veins flowed the five rivers, the strength of Raja Rasalu and the wisdom of paanch pirs. But where was Ranjha? Where was her consort? She felt her throat break into song in Punjabi, as though she was calling to him across the void of the night, across the broad expanse of the Father of Daryas; as though once again she had heard the plaintive sound of his lute, the wood that had caused her to begin a dance which had never really ended.

> The month of July has descended in flood
> And the barrier sands have been carried away
> Deep, deep and as fierce in my heart and my blood
> Rolls the river of love – can you turn it with threats, or with
>   menaces stay?

It was perhaps the beginning of a ghazal. But no, she thought: the rhyme scheme was all wrong and, like the Ravi, the darya had changed its course. The river water had broiled and the river had burst its banks and flowed down through the poem, the song, the dance, sweeping away all breath. The heat began to burn the skin of her legs and belly and the air in her chest felt like fire and she felt the urgent need for another plunge. In any case, her cigarette had gone out – not that she needed any further draws right now; whatever was in that thing was good enough as it was, and even if she was hallucinating – man, it felt fucking good. And so Laila carefully tucked the joint into her bag and then, looking once more up at the sky, began at first to walk and then to run in the direction of the lake. She was Sohni, preparing to swim across the river to reach her lover, Mahiwal. Sohni, who was betrayed by a surahi. She was a burning woman-soul. The stars and moon seemed to form a great arch as she dived in at the point where the darkness was deepest. At the last moment before she hit the surface of the water, Laila thought she heard the sound of a voice. The face that had gazed up at her had not been her own.

Night-time in Heera Mundi was something else. Before they had even passed through the Taxali Gate, they were already hearing the sound of music and had been engulfed by the heavy sticky scents of hanging grapes and motia purveyed by the legion of flower-sellers. For two hours, between eleven at night and one in the morning, very young women and girls – Zuleikha was sure that some of them couldn't have been older than twelve or thirteen, their faces bleached, their eyes kohled and their skin heavily made-up – spun like marionettes on every balcony and verandah and in every archway, porch and vestibule. The women leaned over wooden and marble balustrades and danced suggestively, enticed the men, either through tiny well-practised movements of their bodies, through a lithe fluidity which Zuleikha knew had been passed down in matrilineal fashion since the time of Akbar the Great, or else with coarse gestures, garnered, it seemed, from the juddering and increasingly vulgar Nordic physicality that spewed from the screens of commercial Indian cinema. To Zuleikha, it seemed that the line between soft porn and these mainstream family movies had become so thin as to be indeterminate. But then there was nothing remotely soft or vicarious about this place. This was the market. This mohalla was where the business got done. This was the reality that lay behind the films and behind the pantomime curtain of dupattas, chadurs, hijaabs, niqaabs, burkas. And yet, still, she thought, even a kiss on the lips was strictly forbidden on screen. The whores may be puppets, but even they resist giving their customers pupees.

And there, on the glittering streets of the Diamond Market,

among the pot-holes and discarded mango-stones, they seemed to be witnessing a battle for the soul, not only of this red light area and all the exploitation that went with it, but also for the spirit of artifice itself. While the remaining few top whores here studied song-books filled with classical lyrics, the industrial pornographers with enormous bootleg budgets plied their trade with walnut-oiled streamlined efficiency in the upmarket salons, hotels and Cantoonment guest-houses of Karachi, Islamabad and the City of Lights. Successive military regimes had atomised the talent-base, dispersing red light areas throughout the city, so that now, if someone said that they were from Allama Iqbal Town, people would raise an eyebrow. Invitation-only, topless shag concerts for the top brass and the feel-me-up burqa hookers of M. M. Alam Road. Most whores now came from the near-shanty-towns of the periphery, bra-less, changeling girls ever-ready for camera crew and casting couch. The overriding feel of places like Heera Mundi, on the other hand, was of melancholy, a sense of loss. Once the Shahi Mohalla had been the residence of artists, singers and ustaads. Of courtiers and kings.

The women wore their make-up so thick that Zuleikha could almost taste it. She wondered what lay underneath all that pale foundation, the glitzy stars, the fresh red lipstick which, even as they opened their legs to total strangers, would remain untouched, pure, virginal as the sound of their breath moving steadily through the lips of the night. Each woman was a song, but as in the folk tales of Heer, Ranjha, Mirza, Sahiba, Sassi, Sohni, every song would end in some essential sense tragically. Poisoned, burned, drowned, eviscerated. And in reality the djinns of the Old City of Lahore, as with those of Delhi, Agra and all the others, many years ago had fled into nothingness – or else into the imaginings of women and men. And when the time of reckoning came, when all the books were opened and the maps deciphered, there would be no strong arms to carry into the air the pure of heart.

While most of the people looked either Punjabi or Upeean (these latter would have in their mouths the sweet knives of charm for which their people were renowned) some of the women here in Heera Mundi seemed to Zuleikha to be tribals from either the upland parts of northern Punjab or else from the real highlands beyond, from the Northern Areas or the NWFP. They had those tell-tale parallel scars that resembled sergeants' flashes on their cheeks. The appetising smells issuing from fast-food joints and the general upbeat hubbub barely subverted the sense of *last kathak in Lahore*, the feeling that in some essential way the area had gone to the dogs. With its desperate rushed glitz and its thick-lipped coarse hookers, Heera Mundi seemed more like a theme-park for crystal meth heads than a whorehouse paradise for your classic sharif aadmi. Beyond the faux innocence of the pahjah ke pi restaurant and the Lady Wellington Hospital, there was an all-pervading scent of rot, of fruit and munnashiyaath – bhang, heroin and many other, unidentifiable compounds. From time to time, skulking in the shadows in the narrowest of alleyways, she would spot gashtiyan, prostitutes who wore the cheapest clothes and who from big-bruiser pimps rented mattress-and-room on which they provided unvarnished sex for a hundred rupees or less. These kharaab women were the dross of the Shahi Mohalla and would undoubtedly die of AIDS or hepatitis B, C, D or whatever else men decided to piss off the ends of their pricks.

Alex had allowed his salt-and-pepper beard to grow so that now, she thought, really he could pass properly for Pathan. And he towered head and shoulders above everybody else in the street, so that it was unlikely anyone would dare to mess with him. In or out of the Old City, in Lahore or anywhere else in Pakistan, you didn't mess with those people; you didn't fuck with the women or pick fights with the men – unless, that is, like a randy goat at the Big Eid, you wanted a quick fix to heaven's gate. The predominant smell of bhang and lemons was just another dislocating factor about this whole area which lay between the Mughal fort with its Dream House and its Palace of Mirrors and the reddish, curiously modernist, sixteenth-century Badshahi Masjid. As a consequence, the Shahi Mohalla seemed thronged, less with the bodies of those present on that night – the tamashbeen and kunjerees, the mirasis and cooks – and more with the ghosts of those soldiers, poets, sufis, slaves, jugglers and whores who had gone before. Alex seemed much more at ease now than the last time they had come through here. Perhaps he had acclimatised; perhaps his jet-lag had lifted so that now, with his clothes and beard, he was able to move around, at least in his own mind more incognito. Nonetheless, he was carrying his lute in its case and this would have made him stick out anywhere. There was no way he'd have been mistaken for a mirasi! And anyway, everybody here would know one another like they knew the callouses on their palms.

They'd left the box in the guest-house and this was something she felt uneasy about, especially with those creepy-looking guys that came around during a certain shift. Then again, the fact that she could speak basic Urdu and appeared to be from here – at least, originally – seemed to make some difference. They knew that with her, they wouldn't get away with the stuff they sometimes got away with, with Farangi. On the other hand, the fact that she was with a white man seemed to irk some Asian men, as though she'd sold herself like a stock or a share on the floor of the City of London. She never told them that she was half-white. These were discomfitures and negotiations of which Alexander would have had no idea. Yes, she thought, he seems much more at home now. It's been only a week and already he's settling in – since that day at Petrus's house and the stuff they'd smoked together, that peculiar melding with the middle tones that you get with good hemp.

On their way here, travelling by taxi along the broad Mall Road, they had witnessed an accident. An elderly woman dressed in a faded brown shalvar-kamise had attempted to cross in the midst of busy traffic, and had been knocked down by a scooter which had not been travelling particularly fast, but which had simply been unable to dodge past her slim but inexorably moving figure. They had been immediately behind the scooter, and with incredible adroitness the taxi-driver had taken evasive action. The bareheaded driver of the scooter – only a few riders in Pakistan wore a crash helmet – had been thrown over the handlebars, but had risen at once and clearly wasn't badly injured. The woman, on the other hand, had been spun backwards and to the side and had struck her head on the tarmac. She had lain still and Zuleikha had seen blood coming from her scalp. The taxi-driver hadn't stopped and they hadn't asked him to. Yes, it would probably have been suicidal for anyone to get out of the car at that point. She had no mobile phone, nor any idea how one might call an ambulance, and yes, she had been in a rush to get to her appointment on time, but if such a thing had happened in Britain she would have stopped. It was part of the Hippocratic Oath and she had just broken it. Again.

Petrus's haveli was the only one where there was no dancing or performance of any kind going on. Once again they knocked loudly on the door. But the street noise must have prevented the lightning-footed Abdullah from hearing, and so after they'd waited for what seemed like minutes (and by that time once again people were beginning to get curious and to mill around them, smiling for no apparent reason) Alex banged with the ball of his fist on the wood, causing the door to shudder and bringing forth an emanation of dust that made Zuleikha step back for fear of coughing.

Finally, with a grating of bolts and the turning of what seemed like several enormous keys, the door wheeled open. Behind it was not Abdullah but Petrus himself, and he looked completely different from before. He was wearing an elaborate Mughal-style outfit, a chugha with a belt affixed around the waist, and on his head was a tall black hat of the sort worn by Mirza Ghalib, the mid-nineteenth century poet famous for his Persianate philosophical and mystical ghazals. Attached to his belt was a small leather pouch. Petrus looked as though he'd just stepped out of one of those black and white etchings in the books reproduced in Pakistan from the hundred-and-thirty year-old travel writings of British residents and other colonial servants. Books with titles like *Costumes and Scenery of Afghaunistaun,* or *A Memoir of Journeys Through Upper Punjab and the Land of the Kaafirs,* whose authors always seemed to have anachronistic names like Major H. S. Jarrett, Mr. Jebbs, Mr. James Darmesteter and, best of all, Lt. Col. H. Wilberforce Clarke, Royal (late Bengal) Engineers, author of *Notes on Elephants*; and of *The Transverse Strength of a Railway-Rail.* Good God! Zuleikha thought: with a mouthful like that, no wonder the guy had been unable to translate into English even one iota of the poetry of Hafiz of Shiraz. In 1891 he had completed the militarily methodical yet utterly soulless translations of the words of the Diwan-i-Hafiz as though he were measuring a thousand-mile length of railway-rail. Once again she was struck by the fact that many of those who had been in the van of empire had been Scots, so that a nation which itself had been colonised in some respects had transmuted its spirit into a very dynamic and entirely self-righteous aspect of the mind of the coloniser. Men from the middle and upper classes of all sorts of Scottish provincial towns had gainfully gone off as preachers, soldiers, merchants and administrators, while the working classes had taken the Queen's Shilling and become Redcoats, Tommies, and killers.

Not that some of these people hadn't been conflicted, especially early on. There were some amazing journals in which the writers had expressed regret at the new British paranoia around miscegenation, for example, which nowadays the British (at least within the enormous valley of their capital city) seemed to be going like the clappers to abrogate. And good luck to them, Zuleikha thought. She and a million others were proof surely that human life and conflict arose from countless factors other than things like race and religion, about which so many people for so much of the time seemed in a state of utter vexation. It was as if they'd forgotten that money was – well, it was the coinage of empire and nation state alike. And here, in the middle of the Shahi Mohalla, in the heart of the heart of the ancient city, was Petrus Dihdo Labokla, possibly half-Russian, half-Punjabi; a conception from the rollickingly nutcase middle part of the twentieth century; a result, like Zuleikha, of troubled macro-history; a cutting from that tall foliate oak known as the Great Game, which seemed still to be growing and casting its seed in all directions of the compass. His eyes were flaming Archangel-blue, as though not only the pupils but the globes themselves had expanded, and perhaps through an excess of oxygenation the shades of their tissues had become heightened and intensified.

Even as Petrus greeted them with the politeness characteristic of that vague concept known as 'the East', it was evident to Alexander and Zuleikha that he was somewhere else altogether. He had shed the heavy weariness that had seemed to afflict him the last time they'd visited, and his movements now seemed even smoother, more practised and flowing than before, as though in the intervening day his body had turned all to muscle and elastic. There was a sense of unconscious elegance about Petrus that was intensely attractive to Zuleikha and Alexander alike, though in different ways. He led them through the line of rooms, through the strong scent of jasmine and sandalwood, and all the while the gentle melancholic music they'd heard before was playing again – though, since Zuleikha's spatial sense was all scrambled, she was unsure from which direction it was coming.

They paused in the fourth room, the same chamber they had visited the day before, but this time Petrus didn't ask them to sit down. Instead, he went over to the painting and touched the frame with hand movements so fine that Zuleikha could barely make them out at all. He seemed to be manipulating the painting somehow, though she could have sworn that through all of this it did not move even one millimetre from its place on the wall. It was their host's body that moved, that pivoted and half-turned upon its axis even as his feet remained planted firmly on the marble floor. Indeed, she wondered whether his juggling act had already begun, or whether perhaps this might be some kind of limbering-up routine. She swung back round and saw that Alex too was transfixed. He smiled at her, just the slightest acknowledgement, but quite suddenly she found herself becoming aroused, and the smile that formed in response was framed by a blush.

God, she thought, it's this place. The erotic ambience is beginning to get to me. Perhaps Petrus was right. The spirits of the natchnaywalis have never quite left these dark closeted rooms of purdah and revelation. Perhaps, just like in the story, some poor beautiful nautch, her hair flowing with pomegranate juice, had been walled up here, or maybe the jasmine scent and barely audible footfalls of an undead raat-ki-raani still permeate through the beam and plaster of the high ceiling, or through a deep fissure in the old walls. Yes, there it was, she could see it now: the light of a thousand flickering oil-lamps shining through a gap in time, blinding her as the past always had. But then she realised that it was not the past but the painting that had blinded her. With a single well-practised movement and amidst a considerable quantity of fine white dust, the picture disappeared as Petrus swung it on its hinges round and forwards so that it ended with its face to the wall. Behind the picture was not a hook and a blank surface, but a large set of wooden double doors. The dust made Zuleikha cough, and now it was Alexander's turn to step back a few paces. She wondered for a moment whether the dust might contain asbestos, but then reminded herself that these houses were at least a hundred

517

and fifty years too old for that. Anyway, asbestos, cancer, drink, a road traffic accident, sudden infant death syndrome … there were a million and one ways to die in this world. Death was singular, yet ubiquitous.

The doors had been made from what looked like thick oak, and were adorned with carved images which seemed to depict a folk tale or epic of some sort. There were larger-than-life heroes and animals – wolves, leopards, snakes, what looked like a type of hairy bull, and a smiling bipedal goat. Among the human figures were musicians playing instruments that looked like elongated trumpets, others who ported reed flutes of the type that are held perpendicular to the lips, some who sat cross-legged cradling dholaks and others reclining on cushions and playing what looked like some sort of very basic lute. In physiognomy and couture, the people seemed more Central than South Asian. The pictures were set in twelve panels, and behind the whole was the outline of a large pyramidal mountain. The doors smelled strongly, not of any of the woods of the plains but of the oak of the high places, the tall oak that for thousands of years had weathered even the strongest storms. For a moment the figures seemed to move ever so slightly, but Zuleikha blinked and realised that it had just been the effect of the flickering light. Behind the picture, she thought, lies another picture, and behind that …

Petrus paused before this fifth door of the house and from the bag tied to his belt took out an extraordinarily large and ancient-looking skeleton key – even larger than the one he'd used for the external doors. It was old and rusty, and both bow and bit were ornate to the point of uselessness and seemed to have been fired to resemble a rose in full bloom. The key turned in the lock for what seemed like a whole minute as Petrus half-reversed the rotation several times before finally something in the mechanism clunked and the double doors responded to his firm pressure and swung slowly open, away from Zuleikha and Alexander. They entered the room. As Petrus closed the door behind them Zuleikha saw that the other sides of the doors also were covered in images: the same figures, but in a slightly different configuration, as though these inner pictures depicted other versions of the tales.

The room was windowless and was larger than the others,

measuring some fifty feet square and perhaps twenty high. The walls were white and seemed to have been re-painted recently, and the cornicing was unbroken. A large silver chandelier hung down from the central rose. It was of the old style, filled not with electric light-bulbs but glass candle-holders and fresh white candles which had just been lit. All four of the walls and all of the ceiling, save the decorated areas, were covered with large gilt-framed mirrors, but each mirror consisted of a mosaic made from hundreds of tiny octagonal pieces of glass, so that as Alexander, Petrus and Zuleikha entered, it was as though the room suddenly had become filled with a crowd.

They removed their sandals and Petrus motioned them to sit on some large green cushions that had been propped up against the far wall. The floor was made of a pearly marble which gave the impression of translucence, and which felt refreshingly cool beneath their feet. There was no furniture as such, save for several tasselled hookahs and, on a small table over in the corner, an old wooden gramophone, the source of the music they'd been hearing. They sat down, and the machine produced a rasping sound as the record ended and the stylus spun on clear vinyl. Petrus went over to the gramophone, lifted the arm and switched it off. Close to the table was a battered trunk big enough to contain a small man. The trunk was closed and padlocked, and consisted of panels covered in Air Force-blue buckram held together and reinforced by a series of plain wooden strips.

Abdullah brought them some papaRs and a large earthenware jug filled almost to the brim with a sabz liquid that smelled strongly of aniseed. They ate the papaRs and drank the green liquid until only a sediment remained.

Petrus knelt and, removing yet another set of keys from his bag, he unlocked the lid of the trunk. One by one he began to draw out props. He removed balls of various colours and sizes, made of glass, rubber and twine, sticks with white ends, clubs, spools, torches, steel plates, star-shaped objects, sets of daggers, cigar boxes, barrels, Trilbies, hoops, and finally a whole host of carved wooden animals. He closed the trunk and arranged the objects on its lid. Meanwhile, Alexander had taken out his lute and tuned up. It now looked like a very simple instrument, consisting of only four strings, a bent-back peg-board and a pear-shaped body. A barbat, as Alex had told her. And as he tuned it, the sound which it produced was of a higher pitch even than that of an 'ud.

Once again Zuleikha was struck by the irrationality of the whole thing. A solid body does not simply change form; that surely was one of the basic physical laws of the universe to which we belonged. But then there had been an age when people had thought that the world was a big round disc surrounded by emerald mountains, and that all the stars and planets spun around this disc, as though the universe was the stage-set of some omniscient juggler. For millennia, that had been the overwhelming orthodoxy. There had been occasional dissenters well before Copernicus, most prominently in the Arab world, but they had failed to shift the mainstream of thought on the issue. For most of history, God had placed Man at the centre of His universe, and now each religion fretted and engaged in incredible contortions in an attempt to prove that actually there remained some kind of essential truth in this vision. And this uncertainty had generated the completely ridiculous belief that the words of religious texts, which in every single case had been formed by many different hands, mouths and minds over periods of hundreds and sometimes thousands of years, were the actual sonic words of God that had been laid down in one take, bass, drums, lead and rhythm guitars, like a Beatles song from 1963.

It occurred to Zuleikha that Alex might have a stock of such period instruments at home and that he might simply be substituting one for the next as they progressed. He certainly possessed several lutes, though all were of modern provenance and none of the others had ever altered their form through the playing. It was the kind of magical idea that you'd have thought fishing out brains from glass pots and slicing through their soft substance would banish forever. Not to mention twenty years of watching people die at different speeds, of holding (or rather, of being too scared to hold) her own dying mother in her arms, of feeling her own dead child stiffen beneath her fingers. You'd have thought that the concept of the soul – eternal or not – of God, transmutation and so on and so on would have been sliced and sectioned like the anatomist's brain into wafers, and then blown like so many dried flowers into textbooks of psychology, anthropology, sociology, paleon-bloody-tology. You'd have thought.

But beyond all that, for God's sake, she had been in his home. She had slept with this man, she had held him as he had wept again for Susan – they had progressed thus far – and it would have been inconceivable as well as physically impossible for him to have pulled that sort of trick with the lute even if he'd wanted, or been able to. And anyway, with her own eyes she'd witnessed the change in Scotland, Lincolnshire and Sicily, places far removed from Alex's home and to which she knew he had brought only this miraculous instrument. And anyway, unlike Petrus Labokla, Alexander was no magician. She'd lifted each lid of the box and the fact was that while they'd remained fixed and immobile, there was no way anyone could have opened those lids without in the process destroying both the box and its contents. But when Alex had re-composed and played the appropriate piece of music, the lids had opened as though they had been affixed with brand new hinges and liberal quantities of olive oil. Was it possible for a piece of music to have such physical consequences? To be capable of altering the structure of matter in this way?

No, she thought: it was impossible. Every millilitre of rationality in her being told her that such a thing was beyond the pale. And yet here she was in the Old City of Lahore, about to watch a performance of juggling and barbat-playing which both she and Alexander hoped would lead to yet another lid, another door opening. And it was only then that she noticed that this room too had two doors: the one through which they'd entered earlier and another, positioned exactly opposite. So then, there are rooms beyond this one, she thought. How deep is this haveli and where does it lead? Such a strange design. The Mughal (or Afghan, or Sikh) who built it must have led an interesting life. Or perhaps had had lots of wives.

Zuleikha realised that her image of eighteenth-century Lahore was essentially a nineteenth-century Orientalist one, handed down through numerous oil paintings executed usually by itinerant Scots fresh from the monarchical world of the glen. And little wonder, she thought, since from the onset of dear old Queen Victoria onwards, in the midst of their severe sexual deprivation, those guys had clung desperately to their three-piece suits even at the pinnacle of the Indian summer, and so must have been hallucinating most of the time. The whole of the British Raj had been a fevered dream which had lasted at most two hundred years, a product of the metrical chants of Presbyterianism enveloped in the bishop's vestments of Mother England and cast into the spider dance of Hindustan. But underneath all the persiflage, the engaging rubbish about railways, roads, nabobs and cricket, every hog-grease bullet had been melted down from the pig-iron bells of the Eildon Hills, of the Lindsey Wolds, of some far western isle. *Onward Christian soldiers!* Yet in a thousand years perhaps the Brits too will simply have a bit-part in some unreal warring myth set to song in the dust-bowls of Middle Bharat. Who said music couldn't change anything?

Petrus removed his flowing robes to reveal a pared-down white outfit, an old-fashioned juggler's costume with leggings wound around the calves and shins and low-cut flexible-looking shoes. It was not that dissimilar, she thought, from a set of archaic cricket-whites. She wondered why he hadn't bought more modern gear. Yet his clothes seemed to fit perfectly, so that unless Masterji Afanasii Aleksandrovitch and Petrus had been of exactly the same build, it meant that Petrus would have had them made-to-measure. Not so difficult in Pakistan, where the tailors were nothing if not malleable and innovatory, if sometimes wired to the moon and lacking in finishing skills. Zuleikha found him attractive, though not in a sexual way. She admired Petrus as one might admire an athlete or an eagle. Alex was sitting cross-legged on a large green cushion, playing the barbat with a simple shell plectrum which was about the length of a finger. He had removed his Swati cap and had loosened his hair so that his dark locks swung around his shoulders, and now he was beginning to sway from side to side. While Petrus limbered up, shaping his muscles into perfect tones, Alex was setting up a rhythm, an ambience. Zuleikha, meanwhile, lit the huge joint which Petrus had handed to her, saying,

'It is very old bhang: it is very special. I bring it out only on certain occasions. It was used by my ustaad, Afanasii Sahb and his wife, Bibi Rada. He got it as a gift from the Sheikh of an Afghan khanqah where he had performed. He kept it in a secret compartment in this trunk.'

Black Peter. And the spliff did taste rather bitter, as though it had been kept in a very dry place for a very long time. As she inhaled the fumes the end of the spliff turned pitch black and seemed almost to liquefy, and she was afraid that it would drip off the end and burn a hole in her clothes. But sixty years or more? As old as the trunk in which it had been hidden away? Would bhang keep for so long? She had no idea. She smiled as the smoke flooded into her brain. Surely not. It would decay, rot, or else transform into something else altogether. Perhaps, she thought, in the end that is all we will find in our box. A stash of best quality Royal Afghan Black. She chuckled, but then pulled herself up. Our box? It was the first time she had referred to the box in this way, as though she and Alexander had joint ownership. At first, Zuleikha had felt very possessive of the object. But the marijuana was softening her brain, melting her resolve, dissipating her Presbyterianism, or her West Scottish Catholicism or her Capitalist sense of private ownership, or whatever it was. And who were these long-dead sufi pot-heads from Afghanistan? The boundary between British India and the kingdom of Afghanistan had been as porous as the blood-brain barrier, as holey as the limestone of Lincolnshire or the tufa of Sicilia.

Over the years ideas, people, music and transformative substances had flowed easily in both directions. Indeed, the current border was yet another nineteenth-century British imposition: the famous Durand Line that had been drawn willy-nilly through the tribal heartland. So, like some itinerant jester, the old Russian had toured around the place, throwing up his props in numerous permutations, playing at mathematics, geometry, calculus, creating new, albeit invisible, formulations. And perhaps his wife had gone with him into the tribal regions, disguised as a man, and there, amidst the dust mountains perhaps she had played lute to his dancing figure. And so Petrus and Alexander, in this fifth room of the haveli – were they now going to replicate those old performances? Or would there be new elements which each might add? Would the whole thing be like the performance of a dastgah? Such thoughts rushed through Zuleikha's mind as Petrus completed his warm-up and began to juggle – though she'd found it difficult to determine exactly where preparation had ended and performance had begun.

The smoke from her cigarette formed words in her mind. Yes, she thought, there is definitely much more than simple hashish in this stuff; there are grains of something positively, if gradually, psychedelic. Yes, I can feel the grit roll beneath my tongue, even though it is somewhere up there, halfway to my skull, and then she was moved to laughter and through the laughter words were forming in nastaliq script, that most elegant and mathematically-proportioned of Arabic scripts. Now, in the haveli of Petrus Dihdo Labokla, she could read it perfectly well, even though she had thought that she had forgotten long ago. Ever since the evenings when her mother had tried to teach her the Urdu and Persian alphabets, making her draw out the cursive forms of the letters, aleph, bey, pey, te, seem, sheen … on old geometry exercise-books, because each figure had twelve different possible meanings and so to write in those languages was to be an artist, a geomancer, a composer. It is something, she thought, that the modern Anglophone world simply was incapable of grasping. The requisite neuronal connections had never been formed, or if they had then they had been smashed out decades earlier in the cultural jihad that dominated all discourse and the delivery of every concept of aesthetic value.

Barbarians, she thought. Yes, that was about right. Yet, with the right catalyst, even the al-'ajamiyya tongues could be turned into poetry. Kharjat, aljamiado. And all in a rush, in a rich heavy haze, came the aroma of her mother's perfume, an old scent that could no longer be manufactured and which somehow reminded her of the dark inner doors of tenement flats. She'd thought that she had forgotten; for so long the Urdu-Persian continuum had seemed to her almost like Ancient Etruscan or like the old language of the Nile, its doors to meaning had remained firmly closed in her face. But now it seemed the darvazay had opened just a chink. The music was pitched low, as low as it could be. And the word which she was seeing, or perhaps which her mind was writing, was *pishdaramand*. Prelude.

At first, Petrus juggled rubber balls in cascades, columns, fountains and showers, switching with ease between styles until

Zuleikha felt herself becoming almost hypnotised by the effect of his constant modulated movement. Within one minute of beginning his dance Petrus's clothes had become adherent to his skin, and from then on every movement seemed perfect, raw, unmediated. Alex played the slow beginning of a dastgah, although Zuleikha still had no idea how he might have learned to play this type of music. It was as though his brain had become porous and could absorb any style without having to pass through years of training and osmosis. Perhaps he did have a form of epilepsy, she thought, with seizures that were provoked by only certain types of music. Maybe he ought to be on medication of some sort. But then perhaps such medication would block out his abilities.

And the notes were coming out slow through the three sound holes, as though the barbat was being woken from a long sleep and was just beginning to breathe again. One of the holes was bigger than the other two and they all had been carved in a rose-shaped latticework and were set in a triangle on the upper part of the instrument's body. Although she was sitting some four or five feet away from Alex, through her spliff Zuleikha could smell the walnut wood and indeed, though she was even further away from Petrus, the stink of old vulcanised rubber began to mingle with the other scents of the chamber. The wood of the doors, the freshness of the marble floor and the soft cotton and wool of the rugs and cushions meant that, despite the lack of windows and the consequent blocking-out of all street noise, the underlying atmosphere of the Old City yet seemed to have permeated every inch of the haveli. As though, rather than having been erected like some modern prefabricated concrete block of flats, this haveli and all the others in the Shahi Mohalla had simply grown from the air and sound of the place.

The cigarette was as long and thin as a stylish cigar, and as she pursed her lips around its proximal end, Zuleikha wondered whether perhaps Bibi Rada had smoked these in her zenan khana while her husband had practised his routine. And whether, as she'd smoked, like some heroine from a long-lost silent movie she also had listened to an ancient dastgah on the wind-up gramophone. She felt the substance tickle along the flowers of her lungs and flow through her muscles, felt it emanate from the glands of her skin, so that she could almost see it, the drug, the music, there, dancing in smoke-rings, in curlicues, the substance of the old film-stock pungent in her nostrils, the daramand rising in tetrachords from her body which had become as porous as limestone, as Alex's mind, as the spaces between the balls which Petrus was casting up into the emptiness of the Lahore air. It was as though her body was the aqaz, the note on which the dastgah began; it was as though the dance of the city was beginning from this very room. She saw reality through superimposed layers, as in a film, turning to white light. And there had been fewer cars in those days and more trees, birds and parks. The Victorians thought they had invented parks, but in fact they had got the idea from the Mughals, just as, earlier, courtesy of Granada, Cordoba and Palermo, the landscapers of love court and Enlightenment had drawn on the symmetries, cupolas, gates and funtani ianchi of the Muslim Paradise. She closed her eyes, and all these images dappled her brain like the droplets of water from a fountain. But the movement made her giddy and so she opened them again. Petrus was pacing around the room, slowly but with a deliberation that seemed to be leading up to something, some great trick or sleight of hand perhaps.

But Zuleikha didn't want any evil phantoms floating around her mind, not now, just as Alexander was getting into his stride, as he was riding the breeze of the shahed-bazi, the rising air produced by the king note of the dastgah and as, almost imperceptibly, the music was beginning to hasten, the pitch to lift, to shift from the daramand with which every dastgah began, to the forud, the musical thread that bound each gusheh, each melody, to the next so that gradually the whole would build up into a richly decorated carpet of sound. She was drawn back into the intense architecture of the music, each gusheh being formed through the angulation of a narrow set of notes by Petrus's movement, which had altered, since now he was juggling not balls, but sticks whose ends had been painted white. The wheeling patterns produced by his dance seemed to mirror the structure of the music. His feet moved within a small invisible circle while his hands fibrillated, so they had become merely splashes of colour.

Yes, she saw it now; she saw it just as it had been written by Abu Nasr Farabi, the incomparable Khurasani philosopher, in the

Book of Music. The very first gusheh's melodic form had been played by the man named Barbad, the Great Manichaean maestro after whom the instrument had been named. Almost mirroring each other, Alexander and Petrus were playing an awaz, yet the tone wavered and shifted ever so slightly so that it was as though in this piece, with its thousand separate reflections, nothing was fixed. Perhaps the limited range of two and a half octaves was forcing the music into distorted patterns. The music was walled just like the Old City, and its beauty lay partly in its restraint as they, the queens, kings, kunjerees, mirasis, Jadugars and saints of the city, spun on white marble and as their arms, hands, fingers, ankles, feet, toes, every inch of their bodies moved to the music that was like a heartbeat, a syncopation from the shehr ka dil, its rhythm coiled, constrained, fired deep in the memory of every cell.

In the Shahi Mohalla the people of the night, the people of light, the people of hope had only two hours in which to perform, in which to soar, in which to earn a living. No wonder they needed mirrors! There were so many mirrors in this room that it seemed as though Petrus was juggling not six or eight, but hundreds of sticks, their white-tipped points causing manifold geometries to arise, coincide and then part again in baffling tangents and configurations. It was an older music, a mausiki that had lived before the twelve dastgah-ha had been organised, a music in which the modes, the mayeha, had run free like herds of wild horses. It had been the music of the Safavids, the Sassanids, the Saffarids, the Samanids, of the Ilkhans and the Abbasids. Alex was holding the instrument before him as though it was an extension of his chest, and Zuleikha knew that she would be unable to see the plectrum as it kissed the strings, and that up on the short neck he would be using the fingernails of all four fingers of his left hand to stop them. Except for his hands his body seemed incongruously relaxed, the muscles almost flaccid, as though while he was setting the tone for Petrus's juggling moves, the latter, in turn, was affecting the manner in which Alex played his barbat. The sound reflected off the marble and rose towards the plain walls and the high ceiling so that it was as though the entire chamber was acting as a supplementary sound-box, spinning the music outwards across the Shahi Mohalla, the Old City, the great rumbling spewing metropolis of many towns, the place of borders that Lahore had become.

And the music seemed to tell of the complexity of cities and she saw now that Petrus was juggling with knives whose blades never clashed and that he seemed always on the point of slicing off a piece of his own anatomy and that his steps had elongated as though he was one of the old gods of this place, as though he was the son of Rama after whom in the time following the Greek kingdoms Lahore had been named. He was making the daggers dance along his body, using not merely his hands but also his back, the flexor aspects of his knees, the soles of his feet, every part of him, and she wondered just how a man in his sixties could possibly be so athletic. He would have to have practised for twelve hours a day every day for decades. He would have to have practised even in his dreams. But as she puffed away on the fag which seemed never to get any shorter, Zuleikha knew that to Petrus juggling was like breath: it contained all of the past, both his and that of the Old City which had conceived him and which bound him in a kind of creative purdah within which, as within the frame of a maye, he had been able to explore and perfect every movement, every feat of legerdemain. And through this process of constant honing, shaping, sculpting, loving, over the years his dance had become a dastgah, a symphony through which the tales of the past were sung.

This symphony had carried with it the heavy scent of revolution which had been drawn through blood and air, just as, before departing again and forever for some far-off city by the Kara Deniz, Afanasii Aleksandrovitch had cradled his newborn son in his arms and in a moment of sentimentality had named him in the style common among Christian minorities in Muslim countries, after Saint Peter, the Rock upon which had been built many things, including Leningrad, née Petrograd, née Saint Petersburg. And because she had known of the fecund infidelities of her husband, Rada Bibi had taken to the roof on moonlit nights where, beneath the awning of the roof terrace, by the light of flickering mustard lamps, her music at times had been sparing and melancholy, at times raging and ferocious as it had poured like monsoon rain down upon the secret pathways of the lovers' trysts.

Alexander was plucking out a cheharmezrab, a fast section,

and was swaying like a ship at storm. Or like a clandestine aashiq, trapped in the ecstasy of the barsati. His eyes were closed and Zuleikha knew that he had passed from her into that state of consciousness in which the human mind's true form can be transmuted only through the memory and pedagogy of music. Or juggling.

Petrus was leaping through the air and was catching plates, spheres and clubs; he was spinning sticks on devil spools and skilfully was sweeping scimitars held simultaneously in both hands – or in many hands, since it seemed to Zuleikha that really, he must possess more than two – and at any one time he seemed able to cause ten sticks and eight torches to pirouette, each lit while in motion with a taper from the wick of an oil-lamp. He juggled gigantic inflated balls the size of pumpkins and a dagger or two, or three, or four, and as Zuleikha glanced again towards the closed wooden doors, again she thought she saw the figures move. She thought she saw the musicians' hands shift across their instruments, the animals turn to courtesans and tamashbeen and the courtesans' feet stamp on the floor and then their forms fly through the air. She thought she saw the mountain rise and swell as though the old wood suddenly had become filled with sap. And then she was no longer certain whether the music she was hearing was issuing from Alexander's barbat or from the fifth door, and as a mountain stream strikes a stone it struck her quite suddenly that the wood of the door was the same as that of the box. And she had a sense that the box, of which at the beginning she had been so possessive, had never really belonged to anyone; that like this door, this house, this city, it was not an object to be bought and sold as though it were a television or a whore, but a living being, made of countless different woods, born from the saplings of one, two, three thousand years ago, the blood of their channels reaching back perhaps to the very first tree, the tree of mountain, lake and moon. But then Petrus was moving as though he was made not of solid substance but of shadow, or fire.

The man is a jinn, thought Zuleikha. He's not human; he can't be. He's almost flying through the air, the air which is filled with the smoke from my fag. Or perhaps Afanasii Aleksandrovitch was a jinn and his son, Master Petrus, half-Punjabi, half-spirit, has flame running through his veins. Chyorniy Pyotr. Maybe the jinns have taken over the bordello. Yet there was a continuity of rhythm in his movement. It was as though with every pace, every bodily contortion, Petrus Labokla was mapping out the cartogram of the manifold paths of the dead. As he danced, everything seemed to orbit around him so that he began to resemble a white sun, in the scheme of things a dying sun, perhaps, but one which gave off an immensity of light.

Alex's playing had grown frenetic and, as Zuleikha watched the soundboard, it seemed as though he had snapped a string, because now there appeared to be only three. She looked quickly away and puffed some more. She found that her own body was swaying in time with the music and the dance, the underlying rhythm of the Old City that played backwards to the eighteenth century, to the walls, towers and gates of ghost mohallas and back further into a place obscured by fog. And as she looked into the face of Petrus Labokla, she saw that the face was preternatural – or rather that it was a face which she had known from somewhere before, perhaps from her childhood of ta'liq drawings and visits to the circus where the trapeze artists flew like letters through space.

She could not help but look behind the juggler into the thousand mirrors of the room and see Alexander's visage as he played the old barbat, and the face she saw there also was known to her as though it had belonged to some old female friend or distant aunt. His black hair was long and was combed in perfect tresses and his skin glowed as though it had been coated in paint or as though it had become a mask. His body was covered with a white silk shalvar kamise and his nails were painted glass-red. Thick lipstick played around his lips as he murmured the song of the kota. The song that told of the Russi Jadugar who once had lived here in this haveli, and who had mingled and fused with the dancing women, the kunjareon who had painted themselves with mehndi in patterns so intricate that their bodies had been like the gates of paradise, and who had lined their eyes with kohl so black it had turned them into love-poems.

And the song told of how their conjoined spirits had run free through the mohallas and across the chowks, and of how, between the flickering lights of dusk and dawn, they had danced with the bhooths of dead naikas, the wraiths of elegant tawaifs, the living dead huddi addicts of the Badshahi Masjid, the crooked cops with their tight blue jumpers and their five foot-long laathis, the beat-head drug-dealers who held sinister cabals in the quiet hours, the wandering long-haired dervishes who saw God on every doorstep, the mullahs who came down for a quick one with the rat-eyed choRails in the stink and shit of the Tibbi Galli, and the martyrs whose forms hovered, soft and fragrant, over the Shahi Mohalla, the Andrun Shehr, the broad swathes of Garden Town, Model Town, Muslim Town, Allama Iqbal Town, over the white fountains and cascades of the Shalimar Bagh, the posh chrome and glass and high-class hookeries of Gulberg, the cotton, silk and blue neon of the Liberty Market, and the cocked rifles and cooked books, the puttees, sentry boxes and manicured watered cottees of the Cantoonment.

With their luminous knowledge, the Russian pirs had lifted like kites from the tops of golden domes, from the shroud flags and silver panjey of Heera Mundi; they had coursed through the stanzas of Shah Abdul Latif and Bulleh Shah and had danced among the Words of Waris that shone with light and that had blown from the very mouth of God. At the tops of their voices they had belted out the songs of freedom, the ghazals of revolution that had been penned by Miraji, Faiz Ahmed Faiz, Noon Meem Rashed and Kaifi Azmi – for in those times Lahore had been not merely the capital of Punjab Province, Pakistan, or even of Punjab State in a unified Hindustan, but had been the premier cultural node of an entire civilisation.

For though they had been persuaded to return to the Land of Joseph Vissarionovitch Dzhugashvili and had been sucked into the lingering aftershocks of the Great Paranoid Purges which had swept away all hope of freedom, and although along with the leaders of the Revolution in some basement in the suburbs of Kiev they had been shot in the backs of their heads – in the occiput bone where, it is said, the soul resides – Afanasii Aleksandrovitch and Rada Bibi had learned the jadoo of the Old Women of Lahore, those ancient concubines, each one of whom spoke thirteen languages and who played an entire ensemble of musical instruments. They had learned thus how to transmute their forms from matter into energy and so had transcended the firing-squad, and over the years they had been spotted playing the circuit from the White Sea to Siberia, from Donegal to Jakarta, from Glasgow to Palermo.

One rumour maintained that Afanasii Sahb had been seen dining with a gentleman of Scottish appearance in Dinoli's restaurant in Soho, London. And, like the ghost of Shamshad Bai, the teenage singer who had been first murdered and then ravaged by a stinking-rich sayt, or Tamancha Jan who had been the sepoys' sweetheart during World War Two, like the great praestigiator, Eurybates of Oechalia, like the Malika-e-Taranum, the Queen of Popular Song, Nur Jehan and the Malika-e-Mausiqi, the Queen of Classical Song, Roshan Ara Begum, the bird of magic alighted inside them. Tausendkünstler. The jadoo of the Jadugars. By this time, they had added anagrammatical feats to their prodigious act. At the end of their performance they would drink large amounts of wine and then set it alight inside their mouths, whereupon the incandescent couple would turn into cats and would slink off, taking no bows, giving no encores. On other evenings there would be a decapitation, followed by a recapitation. One night in Upper Hungary, in the town of Okos Bokes, the particularly wayward genius whom they had released decided to decapitate the entire front row of the audience – which, since the seats in question were occupied solely by dignitaries of the town, could have led to a very sticky situation for the Aleksandrovitchs. However, amidst screams of horror (and a few of delight) the duo kept their own heads and managed to reign in the phantom, and thus they succeeded in the correct apposition of caputs with trunks. At other times they would invite an audience member to approach the stage, whereupon the unfortunate volunteers would find themselves being swallowed by Rada Bibi. In the manner of Zedekiah the Jew, the Mystagogue of Lyon, the regurgitation which followed would result in an unharmed but very wet and completely transfigured individual.

Afanasii Sahb had returned to the old haveli that lay in the wondrous depths of the Shahi Mohalla and had appeared to Petrus's mother, the virtuoso kunjari, in a shower of silver spheres ... and had given his chaharmezrab, his most virtuoso performance yet, a play through four plectra, turned to liquid, to the Red Church, to the four rivers of Paradise. Quiet, into the palms of the great dai of the earth, flow the Don, the Clyde, the Ravi, the Sarasvati, the Papineto, but above all, the rivers that are no more or that have vanished, far underground and through which the notes of the dastgah sing – yes, Zuleikha was sure she could hear it now, the sound of chanting as though from a mosque or a khanqah, yet no-one in the room seemed to have opened their mouth.

She realised that the awaz was coming from her own body, that her body was singing tawaifon ke gaane, the songs of the concubines, and that she too was dancing – not for any tamashbeen, but for a higher master, and that her dance was the circle-dance of the women of Punjab, the luddi, and that she was Heer, the queen of free lovers, and that she was Laila, the night dancer, and that through her movements she and all her sisters were spinning out a possible new architecture, a possible new Pakistan. And through the broken mirrors she saw in a million images a land purified of the rule of the landowner and the gun, a verdant soil where the deserts were turned back to fields and forests, and where the hidden rivers were pulled drop by drop through the grains of golden earth, and where Islam meant submission to no mullahs, generals, jagirdaars, to no-one but only to Almighty God, and where women and men were equal as the colours red and blue … and then she was passing through a stone arch formed by the music, by the shape of the music danced that night by Master Petrus Labokla.

She realised that the darvazay had swung open: the doors into the fifth chamber of the house, the doors that perhaps had not been opened since Afanasii Aleksandrovitch and Rada Bibi had packed their cases, gathered up their family and left. The night they had bequeathed their books of necromancy, alchemy and composition, for in the Shahi Mohalla the jadoo of the Russian jadugar had entailed levels of skill and inventiveness never again broached, levels which not even men at the peak of human skill, men like Cinquevalli, Kara, Brunn and McBann, had reached, feats about which the great Rastelli or the cosmic Ivanov perhaps had dreamed, but which even they, with their preternatural skills, had never been able to master. No kraftjongleure had developed the strength and control now demonstrated by Petrus Dihdo Labokla. No modern juggler had crossed over from simple dexterity and oscillation to prestidigitation, to reaching down into the deep memory of the body – the memory which, like that of Heer and Ranjha, went back all the way to the time of Sikander and Menander and which, like the two Yunani generals-turned-sages, untied knots and opened doors by means of music and dance and through the working of miracles upon the air. Masterji had no dwell ratio; the props no longer touched his fingers at all, or if they did then it was for impossibly miniscule spans of time and with velocities greater than any neurological impulse could possibly have attained, and these infinitesimal fractions formed the core of the music which Alex the hijira was playing.

Zuleikha gazed up at the highest point of the room and for an instant she saw everything. All the objects which Petrus was spinning in the air appeared to her in their arcs, fountains, showers and cascades, and it was as though he was conjuring not merely inanimate objects but an entire living garden with arches, fawwaray, bêr berries and massive sheesham and chachra trees. It was as though there was a great unseen firdaus here, right in the very heart of Lahore, and that the energy from this garden was spreading out along lines of multiple symmetry, right out across the city in the forms of arches, cupolas, minarets, mihrabs. And the energy was helping to nourish all the other gardens and places of shade, all the other dances, songs and stories that bound the city together and gave it breath.

At times the juggler moved so fast that it seemed as though he was all velocity and light. Petrus Afanasiiyevitch was dancing so fast that his head became almost invisible, so that he was like Zaki, the decapitated martyr saint whose body had fought, headless, against the Mughals for the span of an entire day. Petrus the Guru of Dancers was dancing a kathak, and each step and every movement of his fingers carried within it a story without words. It was the story of Lahore, of Punjab, of Arachosia, Gedrosia, Gandhara, Saraostus, Sigerdis, Patalene, Puspapura, Palibothra, Minnagara and Méthora; it was the tale of the Greeks, the Yunanis, the Yavanas who had entered into the epics of Hinduism, Buddhism and Islam alike; of the White Huns, the Black Huns, the Mongols, Persians, Turks, Afghans, Sikhs and British; of the travellers, merchants, mystics – and of all those who had left their footprints on the spiralled stone staircases of the kotas and their spirits in the rooms of the dancing soul. Just as his own home had been formed from a template of the andronitis, the deluxe dwelling-place of the Yunani, with its central courtyard and its rooms that were closed-off to the street, so Petrus Labokla the Juggler himself carried within his body all of these stories and in the magical box of his throat he held the songs of thousands of years, of entire lands, continents, seas.

And like Ranjha, the prince of free lovers, Alex was playing a reng, a dance, and he was playing the barbat faster than he'd ever played on the strings of the lute – the lute that one night, on the strong back of the green river, had taken away Susan and brought Zuleikha into being. Yet he could no longer separate out the physical from the spiritual, for the fingers that played that night in Heera Mundi were those of Mirshikari the Storyteller, who had been given a bîn, a barbat, by Khwaja Khizr, King of the Greenwood, the same spirit who had shown the Deo of Yarkand five dreams and who had blown onto the deo's eyes so that she had become a shape-changer and who now, through the Suite of the Juggler, here in this house of refuge and revolution in the world of jewels, in the Diamond Market, the Shahi Mohalla, the alley of the kings, prepared at last to open the doors to the sixth chamber. Khwaja Khidr, Khizr Elias, the patron saint of streams and brooks, of daryas, burns and dykes, the immortal man who had danced like a lion through the most beautiful gate in the old city walls. Like a dance master wandering through the mohallas of Heera Mundi, through his music, through the Gate of the Lion, through the portal of light, Alexander had become an ascetic, a devotee, a khuserah, a hijera, a dervish, and his essence had become manifold.

Zuleikha turned towards the rear of the room and she saw the doors swing open and she stepped forward and took hold of their edges, steadied herself against the scented breeze whose force was so strong that it almost blew her body backwards, and whose scent was so thick that she felt her mind begin to spin along the course of yet another music. It were as though the room had become filled with charas smoke so that she could see only by means of the greenish light that came from the fifth chamber and which seemed now to pull her forward as though it had assumed substance in the form of a hand, a panja, each of its fingers grasping her by the belly and enfolding her into its embrace.

Ranjha was on his hands and knees down on the translucent white marble, his instrument was somewhere behind him and was playing on by itself. Or perhaps, he thought, the gramophone had been switched on again and was broadcasting this distant basic music that circled around a single note. A music of the broken people, a music of truth and lies. The mulberry arak flowed through his body like the oiled hands of a malish and he arched his neck backwards and up, then swung his head from left to right and around in a circle, first anti-clockwise and then in reverse so that his bones, muscles, brain and the room itself felt fluid, weightless, empty. In the unbroken heat of midsummer the air felt like hot lead and his clothes had adhered to his skin so that he felt as though he could no longer breathe. He felt a pair of hands with soft palms and long tapered fingers draw away the cotton: first the kamise, then the shalwar. He felt them rub the sweat all over him so that now his infinitely malleable body was oil beneath the hands of a malish. The music circled around him as a spider circles its prey, its dance upon finely balanced fingers spinning an intricate jharoka, a lute window through the air, and the ends of its feet painted long black mohallas, those brilliant glittering gut-strings of the city which the sun never reached.

The mere expectation of its strong liquor already was massaging, softening, ripening, and with insistent force its voice sang high-pitched notes against the cool marble in a ghazal that opened the mouths of his soul as at the time of musical climax a barbat opens the notes of an auj. Then all of a sudden it flowed through him in a great rush as though he too was the spider with splayed legs and opened jaws. And as the spider music entered him, as it entered slowly, millimetre by millimetre through the soft welcoming rugosity of his anus, at first moving slowly, even tentatively, entering and departing, entering and departing, but then faster, faster, harder, like iron, like fire, his body began to tauten with the loha of its timbre and the dance quickened, the eight-legged dancer hastened her pace across the cold marble skin as the flesh of Petrus Dihdo Labokla became one with that of

Sikander Ranjha Wolfe in a rhythm of bodies turned to quicksilver beneath the immobile electric fan. And before he faded into a delicious unconsciousness that smelled of motiya and rosewater, Alexander opened his eyes so wide that in the midst of the dance, turned now to frenzy, he felt that the globes would fly out of his skull, and as the blindness of ecstasy covered him with its damask veil and as the prints of his fingers burned into the stone, the marble itself seemed to melt and he gazed deep into its white liquidity and saw a face filled with light.

The door – my God, she thought, veritably, this is a city of doors – was open and Zuleikha passed through. Inside, everything was green and smelled of buffaloes and musk. There was a bright light that seemed to illuminate evenly, though she was unable to make out its source. Set against the walls were cameras, tripods, reflector screens, boom mikes, circular metal cans, square-shaped heavy-looking grey boxes, folded-up cloth chairs, redhead lights, blondes, brunettes … the general messy panoply of film-making. Scattered about in piles were monochrome prints of heroines, all heavily made-up and smiling or pouting lasciviously, some clothed, others in states of partial or complete undress. Some were posing solo, others plainly coupling with men who had the bodies of pehlvaans. The room was a porn studio which doubled as a cinema – or at least seemed to have been done up to resemble or evoke one.

At its centre was a raised stone tomb, around twelve feet long and almost entirely covered with a green cloth which had been embroidered in golden nastaliq letters with couplets from Maulana Rum's *Mathnavi*. Zuleikha felt her head swell with the music and the light burned into her skull so that she found it difficult to think or feel. The ground here was not of marble but of dry earth, and her feet were bare. She was finding it difficult to breathe, and it was as though she was swimming underwater, with the trees set in a ring around the deep black lake of the tomb. She lifted her right hand and pulled off the green cloth. The water slicked against her body as though it was another skin. She was a tonno, she could see through the darkness without blinking, and as she rose through the red dust of the chamber's floor, though she had no need of breath, yet she could smell its powerful scent. The tomb was topped with a dome of fresh white flowers, each one of which bore several miniature petals. On the inside the cist was lined with silver, and into the silver had been cut a complex abstract design, a series of concentric circles of diminishing size. In the fifth chamber, she could see right through stone and metal.

And there, staring up at her from the belly of the tomb as though through the thinnest film of alabaster, his face perfectly preserved, was Master Peter. Petrus Dihdo Labokla. His blue eyes were open and the faintest of smiles played around his lips. He was like a Byzantine icon, a Russian saint; his face was long and thin, his features set in a state of holiness. But his body was the corpse of an addict who had not yet joined the empty-eyed ghouls and zombies who crawled through the gutters and smoked, injected and died by the pomegranate walls of Akbar's mosque. It belonged to a juggler who was only just managing to hold it together: the muscles, the finger-dancing, the songs. It was the body of a man about to sink forever into a dark mohalla whence there was no return. His hands were crossed over his chest, his feet nestled close together, and instead of a kaftan he was wearing juggler's whites. And as Alexander played and Petrus juggled, and as the tuberculous strains of a church organ billowed around her, Zuleikha found that she could read the poetry and also, at the side of the tomb, the name cut into the stone:

HERE LIES PETRUS DIHDO LABOKLA
BELOVED JADUGAR OF THE NIGHT

In and around this city of Lav, scattered tombs turned into shrines and luminous mazaars became takias, manzils, rahls, caravanserais, pillows of the body and soul, where all in a single night, the traveller might seek and find beautiful poetry, super-tight vulvae and Almighty God – triangulatory proof, if any were required, that in essence these three have always been one. Out in the scrubby fields that surrounded the city, as though in defiance of death, people served street-food from stalls set up around marble sarcophagi. The graves of the emperors, with their processions of mourning, became sites of joyous carnival and of carnality, of filled bellies, opened spirits and sexual gratification. Loud emetic nodes of energy, like Saturn's rings these mazaars encircled the city in unashamedly raucous perpetual celebrations of the now. Zuleikha felt suddenly elated, as though she had become filled with light. But as she looked again into the face in the open tomb it seemed to have altered, the hair to have lightened, the jowl to have broadened, the structure of the skull to have changed to that of Afanasii Aleksandrovitch Samarin. And just as the music was shifting, its tone wavering between states, so too the body before her continued to change.

Zuleikha fell to her knees as she realised that she was gazing into the face of the young Archibald Enoch McPherson, flying juggler extraordinaire. And he was still smiling, even as she threw herself upon the alabaster and wept. The music had eased and had become slower and more distant, and as she emerged from the water she knew that she would be purified, as surely as if she had bathed after sex – that she would be clean, white and ready for prayer. For the music now had assumed the form of a naath, a hymn to the divine, and it was as though the very wood of the barbat itself was singing.

Chapter Thirty

Zuleikha couldn't believe what she was hearing. The woman who had given them shelter and who had sent them off on their journey through first Sicily and then Pakistan, was dead. Laila was dead. Her body had been found floating face-up in the forest lake. It had been there for perhaps three or four days, and in the absence of any known relatives had had to be identified by DNA and dental records. Alex turned white when she told him. He began to drop things. He said it was because of tiredness, but Zuleikha knew that it was because he was scared. Things were turning very bad. His hands trembled every day and he could not have played his lute even if he had wanted to. Not that he had wanted to. Not after the experience in the Shahi Mohalla.

Zuleikha felt suddenly old. Although as the years had gone on she'd been aware of the onset of a subtle but inexorable emotional lability – especially in the direction of lachrymation – nevertheless, paradoxically, the extremes of her emotions – like bookends – seemed to be drawing imperceptibly closer. It was as though she was on a kind of mental valium that would disinhibit even as it ameliorated. And now she thought that the relationship of the living with the dead was like the touch of a poisoned goblet, that every memory was laced with a dull pain – the happy ones most of all.

When they had woken up Alexander and Zuleikha had been alone in the house save for the old servant, Abdullah, who had offered them yet more tea. When they had refused this, he had begun to close and lock all the doors. Zuleikha had challenged him, and he had replied that, as he thought they would be staying in the house, he was intending to shut the place up for the day. Zuleikha had informed him that neither she nor Alexander had any intention of remaining for one second longer in a madhouse and that they were leaving right away. Obligingly, and with no sense of having been offended, he had opened the doors for them. They had thought that it was merely the morning of the next day, but when they returned to the guest-house they discovered that in fact three days and nights had passed.

Zuleikha remembered that when she had come round, both she and Alexander had been in the drawing-room, the outermost of the chambers, and that therefore either they had smoked so much bhang or whatever it was Petrus had given them that they had lost their memories, or else Petrus and Abdullah had dragged their bodies through five – no, in her case, six – rooms and had left them splayed across the various diwans in what had used to be the kunjerees' dance-hall. But then, she thought, if Petrus was not what he seemed, then perhaps the entire thing had been simply an hallucination. She'd panicked and phoned her father, and also Peppe in Palermo. And that was when Peppe had told her about Laila. There were no suspicious circumstances, he'd said through tears. Now Laila was a buon'anima, a good soul; she was now the late Laila Sciacca Asunsi. Zuleikha had gone straight to the box, and even as she'd dreaded it, had thrust both hands into the darkness and eased open the next lid. Because it was in a walk-in cupboard whose light-bulb had fused, she couldn't see inside the box, but she could tell that her fingers had closed around a hard irregular object about the size of a human hand. With some dread she removed the object and carried it to Alexander, who was lying on the bed looking pale and ill. He turned to look at her.

Zuleikha was cradling a large green-coloured rock. It caught the light which was filtering through the window's mosquito-mesh, but seemed also to be emitting an autonomous luminescence. Involuntarily he glanced over at the lute-case, which he had propped up against the wall in the far corner of the room. Slowly he sat up and took the stone which Zuleikha proffered to him. It felt warm, and within it were a series of points of concentrated colour. But as he gazed into its substance Alex saw that the rock was multi-layered; it was as though, over the years, different sediments had been laid down like the rings of a tree, so that when he looked at it from one angle, the many areas of brightness assumed a particular form, while if he turned the stone a little in his hand, an entirely different pattern emerged from the green substrate.

'It's like a crystal,' he whispered. 'It's grown over many centuries. Grown like an animate thing, rocked to and fro by the cadential motion of fresh mountain water.' He brought it close to his face. 'Smell it,' he said to Zuleikha.

And it did smell of mountain flowers, of saxifrages, stonecrops, rock jasmine, red willow herb, columbines, asters, anemones, delphiniums, louseworts, and even though very few of these grew in Alba, their ambience transported Zuleikha back to high places, to Argyll and the old seat of the Kings of Dalriada. The chapel by the loch seemed like a lifetime ago, though it was barely a year. It would be pleasant there now, she thought; summer in the west of Scotland was humid, breezy, unpredictable. Scotland was defined by the shifting seasons of the Atlantic Rim, the Celtic Fringe, the Gulf Stream's dying breath.

The sound of the Lahore traffic invaded her reverie. July in the Subcontinent. Before they knew it the monsoon would be upon them, and with it down here in the plains would come a measure of relief. Further north the monsoon brought havoc: mud slides, rockfalls, foreboding skies. North – where this rock had come from, she was certain. She'd never been beyond Murree, the old hill-station some forty miles north-east of the capital, yet from that point above the town – where, they said, Bibi Maryam had been interred – she had felt the chill of the high mountains. Mai-Mari-de-Asthan. The resting place of Mother Mary. And now, when she gazed into the emerald – fool's emerald, perhaps, she thought, if there was such a thing – she imagined for a moment that the points of brightness, joined together, would form the shape of a script – though she knew that she would be unable to decipher the letters. But then it was gone again and the pattern formed within the rock was a chart, a facsimile of some mountainous valley. Yet it assumed this aspect only when held at a particular angle in a certain light.

Zuleikha sat on the edge of the bed while Alex moved the stone to one side. She turned to look at him. He didn't look at all well. In spite of having been in Pakistan for several weeks his face was pale, as though he'd remained in purdah all that time. His eyes were shot through with red streaks, the quality of his hair seemed to have deteriorated, and his skin was coated with fine beads of sweat. He had a fever. She hoped he'd been taking the anti-malaria tablets properly. She tried to think of any instances when he might have had even a sip of water. In Pakistan, you had to watch out for so many things, especially if you were a foreigner. You had to watch your back, front and sides. If you were a woman on your own, you would never take a taxi anywhere. And no matter your gender, you would never get a taxi at night, even if you were not alone.

For a woman there were various degrees of covering-up, from the dupatta flipped like a talisman over the backs of your shoulders to the full tribal burqa, worn only by mountain women and city nutters. In a place like Lahore it was relatively relaxed, and even more so in Karachi, where the night-clubs went on till four in the morning and where booze and drugs flowed as fast as the tides of the Arabian Sea. And the contemporary art scene in Pakistan was so much more exciting and real than in Britain, where everyone seemed bound hand, foot and brain by the dry and constricting notions of postmodernism and, in truth, by an unresolved sense of the superiority of the Western canons. The tedious British love for the Land of Bharat and the essentialist Hinduphilic prism through which they saw the land was startling in its complacency, whereas they would see Pakistan, and Pakistanis, much as they viewed Islam: always through the spectacles of a cold critic. What Pakistan needed was really quite simple: land reform, proper sewerage, universal education, mass vaccination and wealth redistribution. Together with India, dump the missiles. Let the Kashmiris vote and decide their own fate. In other words, a revolution. After a while it became tiring, all this vigilance, the constant need to negotiate even within one's own brain, and like the arrival of the monsoon, returning to Europe would come as a relief. Never mind the rockfalls.

She smiled and looped her arm around Alex's back. He laid his head down on her shoulder. She could feel the heat pour from his body. Fuck, she thought. Pakistan isn't a good place to fall ill, especially if you're not staying with family. Her family and their history were here, in this city, but … here in this guest-house, she felt like an alien. Yes, she thought, and as in this guest-house, the men in Lahore had an infuriating habit of staring at women. Any women. It wasn't like when she went to continental Europe: the emotional dynamic was entirely different. She was bound to this place by blood and history. It had reached out across five thousand miles and by stages had pulled her in as though she were a bluefin swimming up the hill of death.

In spite of the warmth coming off Alex's body she shuddered, and she hoped then that whatever he had was not catching. She would have to go and buy some paracetamol. Again, that was not simple; in the residential areas you had to know where the chemists were, or else you had to be driven there. Unlike the old city centres, the suburbs had been built in the Amrikan style and were not pedestrian-friendly places. People were obsessed with the Amrikan style, with its casual grandiosity, its gigantism, its evangelical car culture and its clean-cut Modernist lines. It suited a sunny country where big was always deemed to be best. Big landowners, big army, big missiles, big four-wheel drives, big bellies, big noise, big money, big mullahs. The King of Coins. The dominant forces in this place had junked the sensibility of the miniature. In any case, for Zuleikha and Alexander a driver-plus-car removed many headaches. With the exception of motorised rickshaws in the Old City or tangas in the countryside, she couldn't imagine travelling on public transport here. The painted buses were interesting but uncomfortable, especially if you were a couple, what with the gender segregation of the seating. But it was their driver's day off – it would be, she thought – and so she'd have to venture out on her own and search for this simplest of things. She wished her Urdu was better, or else that she'd learned Punjabi. As it was, she knew only the expletive end of the latter's lexicon.

She laid Alex down on the bed, pulled a sheet over him and drew the curtains. He seemed to have shrunk, but then people did contract into themselves when they were ill. When she was certain that he'd fallen asleep, she picked up the rock and turned it around in her palm. It had many smooth facets. She held it up to the chinks of natural light that shone around the edges of the blinds and felt its green luminescence pour over her face. She needed to sleep. It had caught up with her, all this running around, this crazy music, these crazy people. Archie, Alex, Laila, Peppe, Petrus … and Zuleikha, the maddest of them all. Now Archie and Laila were gone and Alex had fallen ill and in the daramand of the music of their transition there seemed an increasingly disturbing sense of malevolence. Above all, she was fed up with herself. And yet it was irresistible. Cradling the stone, she drew up her legs and reclined sideways onto the bed so that she was resting next to Alex but on top of the sheet which covered his body, so that together they formed the symbol of infinity. She let her head sink into a nook formed by his looped arm, and within seconds she fell into a deep sleep and, somewhat incongruously at that time of the afternoon and in this Amrikan-style open plan suburb, it was a morphoea whose parameters were formed, it seemed, by a recrudescence of the old music of the Shahi Mohalla.

Archie was flying at last. After years of telling people that he had been a pilot during the big war, now at last he really was looping the loop. It was enough to turn a man into a believer. The blueness of the earth was stunning – those space walkers had been damned right! He'd been soaring for a while when he saw below him a great sea – he didn't know which one. And there were no anti-aircraft guns firing up at him and so there would be no bailing-out over the side of the cockpit, none of the heroic idiocy which necessitated a posh accent. The upper-crust English and their pals the Scots who'd been to English Public School. Guys with names like Farquahar or Laughlan. The suffocation of a nation in the bed of empire. Perhaps this was the only way for a working-class man really to be free. He liked it, this limbo state, though he didn't know how long it might go on. He wondered whether perhaps he was simply dreaming, whether he would wake up and find himself still attached to that wretched oxygen cylinder, that damned infusion pump. Perhaps, when he opened his eyes, he would be staring into the face of Doctor Zuleikha MacBeth. Now that would not be so very bad, he thought. Especially now he knew what it was like to be inside a woman's body – to really be inside, to feel her tissues contract against his mind, her fluids seep through the channels of his spirit. To exist in the span of her arc, the curvatures of her neck, her spine, her thighs…

Archie could make out the individual waves as they flowed over the top of the sea. He thought there was a breeze, and found it odd that he was getting hotter. Then he realised that he was falling.

The sea rushed up towards him at an alarming rate. It was as though ninety per cent of his vision had been occluded so that now he was hurtling through a blue tunnel and he could make out only a single wave, becoming enormous directly beneath him. He could already taste the salt and, beneath the water's surface, he saw the shadowy forms of large fish. Then he saw the even darker outline of a net. Just before he spiralled into the sea he felt himself swept suddenly upwards and to the side, and for a while he was completely without the possibility of orientation.

When he regained his bearings the blue was gone, and in its place a black and gold carpet spread out beneath him, the dark earth and shining roofs of the villages and towns of La Provincia di Catania and, here and there, a scattering of green where the land had been shaded from the burning eye of the summer. He could see rivers flowing, but the rivers were red, and as they flowed they carried with them rocks the size of fishing-boats. He was buoyed up by a current of air that was rising from the largest of these sciumi and he was travelling upstream. And now he saw the side of the great hulking mountain, its strange hybrid vegetation, the trees that in the ascent moved through several climates, the summer snow curled like a necklace around its base, and then there was nothing except bare black rock and smoke and the stench of sulphur. He had been drawn somehow to an opening in the surface of this burned earth, to the apex of the mountain of fire. Because he was not yet an expert at this kind of thing, the thermals sucked him downwards, so that he was growing hotter and hotter the closer he came to land. Perhaps I am going to Hell, he thought; yet the concept seemed dispassionate, as though he were discussing someone else's fate – that of a tuna fish, say, or of a dead beat-head. And then everything was red and black and he was in the fire and all thought burned away in an instant.

He was a ragnu, he had eight legs and his body was the earth, moving. He was flowing underground, all the way from Mongibello, beneath the provinces of Catania, Siracusa, Ragusa and Messina to the high plateau of Palermo's hinterland, and towards the village that lay at the very centre of that plateau, the village of Joseph and the Cube. And just as Joseph had been raised from the dark well, so now with his black spider's body and his octagonal music, Archibald Enoch McPherson took hold of La Cuba and raised it up through the plasterwork and stucco of the Garufi villa, so that the lava of his body cast rocks and houses into the air and made them dance as though they were pupae in the hands of a puppet-master or balls in the hands of a juggler.

Standing outside the door of his peasant's shack with his wife and children behind him on that night, the seventeenth of the month, Peppe the Restorer felt the earth begin to flow and dip as though it were water and he looked up at the sky and saw it redden and he felt the droplets land on his face and he stretched out his hands and let the liquid concrete come down thick until it had entirely covered his body. In the timpesta the land itself was being re-formed, turned over, maqlùb, maccalube. And just before the hot mud covered his head he saw all the way to the sea where the black boats were burning and then he saw the villa fall and the cube rise and he saw that the lava had cleared away all the detritus, the lies of seven centuries and he heard the sound of a crowing rooster and he saw that the cube had grown into a castle and that like a fontane ardenti, a blazing well, it was shining with the white light of Giuseppe the Carpenter and the black light of the Madonna. And behind both, behind even the bursting of the dawn, there was another, even brighter light, but then the white concrete covered his eyes and took him and his family down into the belly of the mountain, to the place of renewal, the abode of the fearless ones, whence to the sound of a lute one day the future would arise and as in the beginning, it would be sung in Sicilianu.

Alexander was a mess of music. He knew that he was dreaming, but that didn't lessen his frustration at not being able to sort out the scores. So many pieces of music: a sea of sound, from the Dundee laments of Master Beck to the Flowres of the Forrest of Skene, from the Puirts of Straloch to the secret loves of the Border hills to the last good night of Lady Margaret of Wemyss … the vanished music of Scotland was returning in a lutar flood of spruce, rosewood, plum, pine, cherry and ash, a green monsoon that hovered right at the very edge of the horizon. And there it was, the great emerald mountain range that surrounded the disc of the world. Alex could sense its immensity and, like a single hair off a skull, he was blown backwards by the wind which was its antecedent, its herald, its archangelic Israfil. For behind the Scottish music was the Italian, and behind that the Sicilian, the

Arabic, the Persian, and behind that... He stared into the stone and could make out only kufic, naskh and nastaliq and underneath these letters, the long tomb of Petrus Labokla, the Fata of Lahore, the jadugar sister of the knights of Mongibello and there she was, doing her jadoo, cooking up her black spells, her incantatory necromantics sung to the words of the spider and beat to the hollow rhythm, the dastgah, of the skull.

Somewhere there was Susan, but he couldn't reach her, couldn't touch her. And behind Susan there was the apprehension that in some way his music had caused her death. Perhaps it was better not to know, better never to play any music at all, but simply to live and die, dumbed by the masquerade of TV fantasy, by mendacity hammed up as truth, and by hook-lines that pretended to be music and that caught hold of and sank into your mind as surely as if they were the strings of an eight-legged net and your brain a tonno with eyes in all the wrong places. Then Zuleikha was the Fata, the piri, the jinn's offspring. After all, wasn't she too from this place, this old city with its marbled emperors' cists. Had she not risen from a whole host of tombs, from the Durranis, the people of light, the Abdalis, the angel people, from the Mughal poet-kings, from the Sons of Beth, the sons of life. And hadn't he been caught in the swell of her tide, even that morning by the fast-flowing Clyde? Had he not been caught like a ballad on a string, his naked body held in the water and kissed by the lips of Joseph? And had he not lifted up the box as though it were an offering to the grey sky, and, sinking, had it not driven him like a tidal marker down into the river-mud, the box-within-the-box, the river-within-the-river, the music-within-the-music, on its walls, the images of all those who had come to define Zuleikha and Alexander? Had it not bent back his fingers until the bones had cracked, until the architecture of his mind had turned to water, to lava, to blood?

For several days and nights Alex slipped in and out of a kind of delirium that now did not seem to be associated with any fever as such, and which, like the shifting demographics of Pakistan, was difficult to distinguish from a series of simple dreams. Except that during these episodes people were speaking to him. A soldier, a poet, a sufi, a slave, a juggler and a whore – six people of either sex and varying appearance were speaking, singing and telling tales in many languages and dialects. And as they sang, so too did he, even though he had never had a voice – yet now, unaccompanied, with staring eyes Alexander sang, and Zuleikha scribbled down his words, though at times even his English was barely comprehensible. And after every session, which might begin at any time and last through the night, both would sink into a sleep so profound that when they rose in the mornings it seemed as though they were waking from death. Zuleikha was worried that the staff or perhaps the other guests in the guest-house might have noticed that something was amiss. Yet there did not seem to be any other guests and the caretaker and receptionist seemed as taciturn, disinterested and suggestively curious as ever. They seemed obsessed with sex, and Zuleikha was thankful this time around that their obsession seemed to blind them to everything else.

It took six days for Alex to recuperate sufficiently for them even to consider taking the train journey from Lahore to Rawalpindi, far less jumping into a jeep and heading up north. When Pakistanis talked about a jeep, they were generally referring not to some open-topped khaki military box, but to a four-wheel drive, the grossly inappropriately named Sport Utility Vehicle. This was the minimum requirement for anyone contemplating a journey beyond Abbottabad, especially following the earthquake which several years earlier had killed many thousands and wrecked the entire region. They could have flown to Skardu, the capital of Baltistan, but there was the problem of the box and of the lute, and in the end they decided that it would have been too much hassle. They would go by road. Either method could end up being screwed: the former by the sudden mists that came down around Skardu airport and which required aeroplanes simply to turn tail and return to Islamabad, and the latter by completely unpredictable, and often multiple, rock-falls.

But then, at the last minute, an ashen-faced Alexander informed Zuleikha that he would go no further. She stood in the vestibule of the guest-house, so exasperated by his attitude she could barely move, let alone speak.

'I'm not going, Zulie. I'm sorry. I know we've come a long way. You go. I'll stay here, or maybe fly back to Scotland.'

'What?' she yelled, arousing the immediate interest of the receptionist, who twitched his moustache and began to pretend that he was not listening. Even though it was a ball-point, his pen made scratching noises as it tore across the paper, as though he'd watched too many period movies in which people with frilly cuffs always seemed to write feverishly using quills, styli or fountain-pens.

'I know…' Alex began.

'No, you don't. I've just nursed you back to health, we go through all this fucking…'

'Don't swear.' Alex glanced at the receptionist, who met his gaze momentarily and then resumed his incredibly important business.

'Why not? Why shouldn't I swear?'

She inhaled slowly, then stared upwards and let her breath out. The ceiling of the vestibule looked as though once it had had some cornicing. It was not an old building – 1960s at most. It was the sort of place where those relatively liberated films made during the time between Independence and the rise of the Salafis had been made, the ones starring people like Mohammad Ali – not the American boxer, but the tall left-wing Pakistani thespian, or Saaed Khan Rangeela, the satirical comic actor-director-singer, and Waheed Murat, the heart-throb known, on account of his dark complexion, as 'The Chocolate Hero'. Good actors, all.

'I just have a feeling…'

'A feeling,' Zuleikha repeated, looking Alex straight in the eye. Now she felt as though she was in one of these movies, except that Alex was neither a chocolate hero nor a revolutionary. Perhaps he was a comedian.

'Yes, a bad feeling, just like…'

'What…?' she snapped. 'Just like what?'

His voice dropped.

'Like before Susan died. The night she died. The ninth of May, two thousand and…'

Zuleikha moved out of the vestibule and cut in a little too quickly.

'You never told me that before.'

His countenance reminded her of a Renaissance portrait: the black full set, the blue eyes, the sadness. And she wanted to embrace him, wanted to fold him inside of herself.

He was gazing into the marble floor.

'I'm sorry,' he said. 'I had a sense, before she died, that something was going to happen, but I didn't know what. You know, you get that kind of feeling lots of times, only mostly, nothing happens and you forget you ever had it. But that time...'

'So what have you seen?'

He shook his head.

'I haven't seen anything, exactly.'

'Then what?' She threw her arms out to the sides, trying to dissipate her exasperation. Most of what he had said during his delirious ravings had been nonsense.

'I don't know. It's a shadow, a darkness and it's very close.'

'You're freaking me out.'

'I know. I'm freaking myself out.'

'It's just the stuff that happened back there, in...' she looked at the receptionist '...in Labokla's house.'

'Yes, but there's something else.'

Zuleikha was silent. She felt things begin to skew.

'It's Archie,' he said.

'Archie? But you never even knew him. He was my patient, that's all.'

Alex looked around him, behind him.

'He's here.'

'What, in the guest-house?'

'He's free, you see? It's not good. Zulie, please don't go. Just leave it. We'll chuck away the box, throw it back where it came from.'

'But we haven't...'

'I know. But perhaps it doesn't matter now. We've got each other, right?'

He moved towards her, reached out, touched her shoulder, drew her to him. She was like a zombie. He kissed her. The receptionist's hair almost stood on end.

'Alex, you don't understand. I have to follow this, and I need you with me.' She felt his body tremble. She stretched up onto her toes and kissed him on the lips. Whispered. Drew her index finger down over the right side of his face. 'Don't be scared. We'll be together.'

He looked at the floor. The moment had passed. Then he smiled at her, a wan smile, the smile of a convalescent just emerging from a shimmering realm of dark visions. They embraced there, in front of the honourable staff of the guest-house; they hugged and kissed. He'd lost weight; through his clothes she felt that.

'Let's go, then,' he said, quietly.

The front of her chest felt warm. Her body still pressed close against Alex's, she glanced down and realised that her blouse was wet. Right on time, like a clockwork gland, she was lactating.

BOX SIX: BALTISTAN

To erect a pillar to hold the sky
To separate milk and water

Balti proverb

Chapter Thirty-One

As they sat in their air-conditioned First-Class compartment and sped through the baking fields of Punjab, past the railway junction of Gujranwala, Zuleikha downed her third cup of doodh puthee. She drew herself away from the brick-kiln villages encircled by pools of green slime and gazed instead into the substance of the rock which they had removed from the sixth box. The stone contained scripts drawn from various languages of the Northern Areas – Burushaski, Balti, Domaaki, Gujari, Shina, Wakhi and more – and, when spun anti-clockwise to a different position, appeared to be a kind of three-dimensional map – but of an area they hadn't yet been able to identify. So the tall woman from Punjab University had told them as she'd marvelled at the rock and asked them where they'd obtained it from: whether real or fake, there was a profitable black market to be had in ancient artefacts.

Shortly after their arrival in Islamabad Zuleikha had paid a visit to the Lok Virsa, the folk museum. She was put in touch with a Professor Hawwa Issa Daoud Stakpa-pi, who was herself from Skardu and who was an authority on the Northern Areas – and in particular on Baltistan, which was where they were heading now. She gave them a number of contacts as well as helping them to hire a Balti driver, Zulfikar (they're multiplying, Zuleikha thought. What is it about that name?) who knew the area well. Zuleikha told the Professor that she'd inherited the green stone from a great-uncle, a Pathan who once had been a commissioned officer in the Pakistan Army and before that the British Indian Army, and who, once upon a day, must have been stationed somewhere up there in the far northern wastes. She had concocted the whole story so beautifully that she'd even found herself beginning to believe it, and was half-expecting that she would see this fictitious great-uncle standing impossibly to attention on the peaks of Rakaposhi, Nanga Parbat and K2 – even though, in his time, Pakistanis and Indians hadn't yet risen to the lunacy of war on a glacier.

But that was wrong, Zuleikha corrected herself. It hadn't been Indians and Pakistanis, but the Governments of India and Pakistan which had done this. Crucial distinction. The people didn't build the atom bomb: the state did. Yet it was individual fathers, husbands, sons, brothers who raped, bayoneted and slit the throats of their counterparts' mothers, wives, sisters, daughters. They'd done it in every war since time began, and here in South Asia they'd done it in '47, '65, '71, '84, '85, '87, '94, '99, '01. Except in poor bloody Kashmir, where it had been happening continuously, day-in, day-out, since at least 1989. Good sharif mamma's boys with coiffured hair and Rishi Kapoor smiles did this stuff. So what was that about? Woman as territory. Which then was the greater lie? Zuleikha's, or the state's? Perhaps on her father's side she'd had an ancestor who had lived here in British India, and had stood in tightly tailored suit and knee-high leather boots on the granite cliff-edge overlooking the gorge of the Father of All Rivers. As she gazed into the stone, she could almost see through the thick glass of his monocle.

At this time of year, early July, Islamabad was almost as hot as Lahore – though here at least there was less pollution, the boulevards were broader and leafier, and the occasional breeze would float off the tops of the Margalla Hills that rose in a verdant crescent to the immediate north of the city. But throughout Pakistan there was the perennial problem of load-shedding. The country was self-sufficient in gas, most of it coming from Sui in the south-western province of Baluchistan. And yet frequently – especially during the summer, as a result of the necessity for air-conditioning – the demand for electricity would become so enormous in that land with its steadily urbanising population of a hundred and seventy million and rising (and anyway, nearly all the villages too now had electricity) that the system would simply be unable to cope. It would have to be switched off for several hours at a time, usually at the height of the afternoon when the day was at its hottest. If this happened in the evening, it would mean no artificial light for as long as it lasted. Many well-off folk had domestic generators and voltage stabilisers, but the power from them was usually insufficient to run much more than light-bulbs, fridges and freezers. It definitely wasn't enough for fans, let alone for air-conditioning, and so everyone would simply swelter in temperatures of up to fifty degrees Celsius. It would be a relief to get to a cooler place.

On the morning of their departure northwards, Alex still seemed rather wan. He was definitely thinner than before, which Zuleikha thought was no bad thing in itself – though the way it had happened had been quite bizarre. They started really early, aiming to cover as much ground as possible on that first day. They had no idea how long it would take, nor what they would find when they got there – wherever 'there' was. They weren't tourists and had no interest in sight-seeing, or in comparing themselves and the freedom of their manifest destinies with those of the locals. They weren't interested in getting a high from someone else's poverty. Zuleikha thought this seemed to be the reason most Western people – excepting, of course, Alexander – came here, though many good souls had helped during the aftermath of the earthquake, there was no disputing that.

Their driver was a slim man of around twenty-five, about five foot six inches tall (the same height as me, she thought) with hair spiked fashionably at the crown. Like the Balti professor, he had Chini angkon, though his face was thinner and his features sharper. He dressed in a tee-shirt and blue jeans, spoke excellent English, and was a fan of the Asian Dub Foundation and other hip-hop and metal bands. As they drove – or rather, as he drove the Toyota Land Cruiser and they held onto their seats – he began by playing CDs of that sort, but Zuleikha insisted that he kill the music system as soon as they left the outskirts of Rawalpindi.

Zulfikar by name and Zulfikar by nature, he drove like a maniac. He drove as though he wanted to turn their white jeep into a magical stallion, a Pegasus, a Bucephalus, a Buraq. It was no way to drive any vehicle, but certainly not a four-by-four, and definitely not one that was heading up the Karakoram Highway. Zuleikha had no wish to embark on a Mi'raj, nor to slice off the head of a Gorgon, invade the Northern Areas, or journey in the span of a pico-second through the planets of Heaven, Hell or Purgatory. But, as Zulfikar Ali explained to them while Alexander tried tactfully to get him to decelerate, he'd driven up this road hundreds of times in all seasons. He'd been trapped between rockfalls, had slid down mudslides, had almost fallen into the Indus River twice, and once had even been held up by Kohistani – Yaghistani, he called them – daakoos who had threatened to take him hostage but had been persuaded to back off when he'd offered them an entire set of Def Leppard CDs and a fully-loaded Kalashnikov pointed at the capo's skull.

And today too Zulfikar Ali had a gun stashed by the driver's seat: a proper army-style rifle loaded with deadly bullets. He knew how to use it, he said, and you could never be too careful. Then he glanced at Alexander, who once again was done up in Pathan style, as if to say: They won't be fooled; the Dakoos will know a foreigner when they see one. In fact, over the generations, the bandits of Kohistan had evolved their sense of smell to the point where now they were capable of detecting the presence of an alien from miles away. They assumed that all foreigners were unimaginably rich and almost certainly American, and so they adopted the poses of Maula Jats, Robin Hoods, Salvatore Giulianos. But actually, Zulfikar Ali told his passengers as he sped along at nearly seventy kilometres per hour, they were all simply murderers, goondas, tugees, charsobeeses, chorails, bastards.

This was the Wild North, where anything could – and frequently did – happen. Part of the area had been hit hard by the earthquake of '05, but these people had built an impossible road across the peaks of the highest mountains on the planet, and just as they hadn't been beaten down by two nuclear powers facing each other off along every inch of an artificial border cut halfway through their land, so neither were they going to be defeated by mere continental drift.

Zuleikha and Alexander hadn't heard about the enormous landslide that had occurred in west-central Sicily, the eruption of an entire river of hot sulphurous mud; it hadn't been covered in Pakistan, and indeed even in Italy, where it had filled the newspapers and TV stations for exactly half a day, it had been reported as no more than an act of God, a random occurrence of nature. The open-faced deck-chair attendants of the southern beaches concurred with the Vatican's view of Satanic involvement, while the political parties of the Alps had blamed it all on North African immigrants and Sicilians, Calabrians, Apulians, Basilicatans – and especially the people of Lampedusa and Pantelleria, whose blood had been adulterated over time by wog concubines. And indeed the next morning a motion had been raised in the Rome Parliament to expel the Pelagie Islands and the other outcrops of the African continental shelf, soil-and-rock fifth columns that they were, from within the marble-white body of the Repubblica Italiana. Believe! Obey! Combat!

A village and its people had disappeared overnight, had been swallowed up by the land, and then had been covered with a seven-lane super-highway leading from a hill to ... another hill. Yet simultaneously, in a kind of yin-yang harmony, to the sound of castrati choirs intoning *appalti! appalti! Potere è meglio di fottere* in a polyphonic Gregorian counterpoint with the word *menefreghisti* bathed in the mollifying light of the full moon, five twenty-story hotels had been erected along the line of the coast near Agrigento (that haven of Enlightenment). A veritable quintet of tall white cuboids cast up taut and shiny, Egyptian pyramid-style, on a web of pulled strings, all of which had been granted retrospective planning permission by officials of the local government, whose smiles were like treble clefs, or like folding deck-chairs. Those wondrous, sunny European exemplars of democracy in its final, its purest meaning. Demos Kratos: Rule by the (Beautiful) People.

Alex, with his now-full set of facial hair, sat in the front with the driver. That was always the way in this country: the women sat in the back. Unless it was a woman who was driving, in which case the gender placings would have been reversed. All this fucked-up etiquette had begun to tire her. She longed for the thoughtless ease of Europe or America, where it didn't matter where you sat, how you dressed or spoke, or with whom you slept. Yet her lover made a pretty convincing Pathan, and there was a sexiness about that. Now I am thinking like a typical Farangi, she thought: a mem-sahb, an Anglo-Indian. A few weeks out of my tight white bodice and I'm throwing the walls up, locking fast the iron gates. No, she thought: this is my land, the land of my people, the Afghans, the Mughals, the tribes who had coursed down from the north, from Central Asia, all the way from the cold haunch of Siberia. This was where her ancestors were buried, their bones laid out in a cartogram pointing toward the Holy City.

Up here, every valley had its own language. Effectively isolated for so many centuries, with their goats, their stones, their circle dances and their strange nasal songs, the peoples of this land had dreamed entire worlds in different tongues. And as she reminded herself, she had never ventured beyond the elegant decrepitude of hill-station Murree. She was a passer-by; she could hold neither the brilliance of its light nor the giddying sweep of its geology; she could not find its span, her past, in metaphor and yet...

Eventually Zuleikha gave Zulfikar Ali an ultimatum: slow down, take proper breaks, or take us back. Fifty miles an hour on this road is sui-fucking-cidal. You're not driving a bloody painted truck now. This seemed to work, and the Lightning Boy eased off on the accelerator pedal just enough to make them imagine that they might make it to wherever they were going without joining the ranks of the KKH martyrs. Recently, Zuleikha had noticed the tendency to post flowers, plastic toys and teddy bears at points on busy thoroughfares where children presumably had been knocked down and killed. They were terribly sad, those places. Whereas in the middle of deserted mountain vistas there was a certain haunting quality which attended the cairns, on busy urban dual carriageways the toys just became mud-spattered and grew faded in the rain. After a while someone had to remove these animist outpourings. Whose job was that, she wondered, and what did they do with the stuff? In the postmodern machine that was the city, death couldn't be pinned down, couldn't be made to stop and lay its claim on reality. People died, were hygienically disposed of, and life had to go on. That was the phrase: *Life has to go on.* Except for those for whom it no longer goes on.

Laila's drowning hardly seemed real. According to Peppe, she had been found to have an inordinate amount of LSD in her bloodstream. Not enough to kill, but certainly enough to cause rabid hallucinations. Her body had been dragged naked from the lake in a state of partial decomposition, so the assumption had been that she had got high, stripped off, gone for a midnight swim and thought perhaps that she was a fish. Misadventure. But Zuleikha remembered that Laila had mentioned quite casually to her, as they'd smoked joints on that long winter's night in the forest, that she often went for nocturnal skinny-dips in the lake, since during the summer, in spite of the droughts of recent years, it would fill up again almost to its original depth. There was supposed to be an underground stream of some sort which fed the lake and whose sources would tend to freeze in winter, thus depriving it of water. Funny how you didn't remember the things people said until it was too late. Not that she could have done anything about it. But after all those nights in Lahore when Laila must surely have got high with Petrus – the weirdo juggler who'd had his own tomb built in his back room – it seemed awful that she had died alone in that way, at that time. Perhaps she'd been having a bad trip; who knows?

On the other side of the Margalla Hills they passed through Haripur, with its ruined Sikh forts and gurdwaras. After Havelian the road traversed a rising landscape of maples, oaks and cinnamon ferns to Abbottabad, where they stopped for a snack at a tea-house, and where the ghosts of the British hung heavy around the cantoonment in cricket whites, pig-iron bells and more of those hideous Indian Gothic mansions and the even more bizarre English suburban homes, courtesy of Major Sir James Abbott. Already the smell of pine, woodsmoke and maybe ash poured into the Land Cruiser, so that when she closed her eyes Zuleikha felt almost as though she was in rural northern Scotland. Yes, she thought, India had been the Scotsman's burden. Up on a maple tree she spotted the particoloured plumage of what might have been a hoopoe bird, a hud-hud, as it was known hereabouts. But then it was gone.

Through Mansehra, up the Black Mountains and into fields of golden wheat stubble and terraced rice paddies, then more pine and old ruins, and on into the Land of the Mountains, Kohistan, where the highway seemed to teeter precariously above the gushing Indus and Zuleikha was glad she had a head for heights. She tried making conversation with Alexander but his replies were clipped, and she realised that he had a phobia about sheer drops, and that right now the only thing between them and the rocky floor of the gorge was Zulfikar Ali's lucky charm against the Evil Eye, which pendulated from the stalk of the rear-view mirror.

The land around them seemed to have shattered, as though it had been wracked by an ancient giant or, more likely, by a series of earthquakes which had thrown up mountains and isolated ridges seemingly at random. Though perhaps, she thought, they did conform to some weird diorama laid out in the lava ocean that heaved and rolled far beneath the fields and forests, or perhaps

561

this Spaghetti Western land of Kohistan was a working-out of pre-existing forms, of the Tethys Sea that once had separated the Eurasian from the Indian continental plate and which, as the giant landmasses had moved closer together, gradually over aeons had been forced up into rock sculpture. She thought of their belongings, stowed in the boot – which Zulfikar Ali, Amrikan-style, referred to as the 'trunk' – along with Alex's lute and the box. There seemed to be no substance left in the box, as though they had opened out all there was. And yet deep down in its belly there was another lid, another door. Each successive box had been slightly smaller than the previous one, and so the rock which they had found in Lahore had occupied almost the entirety of its compartment and its rough corners had scored the wooden walls on the inside. The drawings and inscriptions on the outside of the box had become clearer and more extensive with each stage of their journey, and now seemed to display scripts from every possible era – from Latin, through Greek, back to a proto-Sanskrit, and from Hebrew and Arabic to strange archaic writings. Phoenician, perhaps. One day she would get them all deciphered, but just now there wasn't time. She had to follow the box's lead; her whole existence seemed to have become dependent upon it. And now Laila had died.

She had no reason to think that the woman's death had been in any way related to the box, or to either of them – yet it made her uneasy, the manner and timing of her demise. As though there was ever an easy manner and time – yes, yes, she knew the platitudes: knew them like the undersurface of her own skin. She wondered what would happen to Laila's house, to all the paintings, to the hidden room... Recently she'd been dreaming of Archie, of the young Archie, and in her dreams he was flying through the sky and was burning like a comet. At times she felt that he would be waiting for them, up there in Baltistan, in Little Tibet, in the towns of Skardu or Khaplu, or in the place beyond which the pattern in the stone seemed to end. She felt that he would be waiting to begin some demonic dance, this strange man who had emerged from the Glasgow tenements; who had longed to soar but who had been riveted by his social class to the shanks of aeroplanes and the hulls of ships. Zuleikha worried about her father and about Alexander, and all this worry crowded in on her like the peaks of angry mountains converging in the sky. Soon the monsoon would come down, and in Kohistan it would whip up electrical storms and tidal waves in the sky.

Down at the foot of the gorge Zuleikha made out the smashed rusting hulks of buses, lorries and jeeps. This was where Zulfikar Ali had to be slowed down again. It was also where they had to stop to allow Alex to throw up against the roadside, as Technicolour Bedford trucks painted with badaams, roses and the enormous visages of film stars and holy saints wheezed and roared by, and as Zulfikar Ali maintained an unobtrusive but continuous vigilance born of great experience. Although at the time Alexander had looked dreadful, the act of emesis seemed to give him some release, and after a few sips of water his colour began to return. Afterwards he seemed less afraid of the mountains, the maniacal rivers and the spiralling road.

Zulfikar Ali, it turned out, was an art student in his third year at the Beaconhouse National University in Lahore. He did this driving job during the summer vacation, mainly for the money, but also because he enjoyed showing people around Baltistan – and because it was an excuse to go home to Khaplu for a little while. He was into oils and also sculpture, and sometimes drew on his hometown and the area around it for inspiration. He admired the work of the Pakistani artists Abdul Rehman Chughtai, Sadeqain and Jamil Naqsh, as well as that of Chagall and Modigliani. Zulfikar Ali wasn't sure what he would do after graduation. He would have liked to have become an artist, but that was a laugh. He knew that he would be likely to end up working in a bank, or as a graphic designer for a pharmaceutical company, or else being part of the army of NGOs which had the country sewn up from top to bottom.

Zulfikar Ali's tirade was cut off abruptly as they rounded a bend and there, to their right, soaring in a massive wall of sheer grey granite, was Nanga Parbat, the naked mountain. The ravine also was completely bare, save for a torrent of white water that foamed and writhed like a tortured snake against the rock.

A few miles beyond the eastward turn-off from the KKH, they stopped for lunch at the village of Sassi. The fields and terraces of the hills were covered in masses of yellow flowers and it was much cooler here, though the light remained strong. With the thinning of the ozone layer, Zuleikha had found that she needed sun-block even during Scottish summers, something that had never been the case when she had been a child. And up here the atmospheric barrier was far thinner and the ultraviolet light would burn straight through to bone. The people were already beginning to look Tibetan, with high cheekbones and broad fleshy faces. The smells were earthy. On all sides – to the north, south, east and west – lay enormous snow-covered mountains and glaciers which, even through dense sunglasses, gave off a blinding light. Poor people in Pakistan never wore sunglasses and this, together with the unending dust, made their eyes narrow to slits surrounded by wrinkles so that the conjunctivae would gleam like rivers rushing through deep gorges.

The sun was low in the sky behind them as they pulled into the hill-town desolation of Chilas, just outside of which they spent the night in a rest-house. It had taken longer than usual to get here because of a traffic jam further south – the result, as so often on this highway, of the mountain discharging a torrent of rocks across the road, each one the size of a Bedford truck. Half the people in and around the town seemed to be trekkers and climbers, nearly all Europeans with large-boned frames and state-of-the-art costumes and equipment, Alpine people to whom the Alps had become pedestrian. They were the World's Burden.

They took great care unloading their luggage from the jeep, as though somehow the fragility of the lute and the box might be intensified by the greater elevation. As they failed to find sleep in the hotel room, both Zuleikha and Alexander noticed that the light coming from the rock seemed to be getting brighter as they travelled further north and east, so that now it gave off a palette of yellowish terracotta and deep maroon. They attributed this to the purity of the darkness here in the deep country.

Zuleikha was troubled by the thought of how little divided her from those trekkers, those conquerors. She, too had the white glacier blood in her veins, not so much genes as attitude, mindset, the relentless pursuit of personal gratification, the quest for El Dorado. The box was an excuse.

Even when sleep came it was in the form of a mountain torrent, and she did not feel refreshed the next morning as they headed through the brown mountains and high dust desert on the road to Skardu. She'd dreamed of her father, of Daniel John. Even when she'd phoned, she hadn't told him she was in Pakistan. Stupid, yes, but as she'd kept telling herself, she'd wanted to avoid any hint of her visit reaching her relatives. And though it hardly seemed so as they bumped their way across the planetary surface of Little Tibet, in terms of human networks it really was a small world, a world of mirrors, shadows, reflections. It had been a strangely coherent dream; it had possessed certain sensate qualities as well as a linear narrative. Even as she'd had the dream, she'd been sure that she would forget its content the moment she woke up. But she remembered.

During the middle of the morning they were delayed for several hours behind a line of grumbling, smoking traffic backed up from another small rockfall. Zuleikha got out and walked right to the edge of the road, to the site of a memorial cairn. From this vantage-point she spotted a flock of egrets – or maybe mountain vultures, their white plumage barely visible against the snowy peaks and the massive sky. As the birds turned eastwards through a gap between giant mountains, Zuleikha made out, far to the south, a thin black line running along the horizon. The south-west summer monsoon had risen from its watery source in the Bay of Bengal and now would be raining hard across the plains of Punjab, and while it rendered joyous life to the country, it also would wash away the takhts of the dead. But even the monsoon would be broken finally by these great mountains. Later on, as the drivers cleared away the fallen rocks by hand, she thought she saw some snow pigeons.

As they had travelled up the spine of the Northwest Frontier Province, Zulfikar Ali's conversation had been about art or music or the scenery around them. But as soon as they'd crossed the Ayub Pul bridge which represented the border between Gilgit and Baltistan, he assumed an altogether more thoughtful expression and began to relate stories of his homeland, of Baltiyul.

'Did you know that the literacy rate in Pakistan is one of the lowest in the world? And that here, in Baltiyul, it is the lowest in the whole of Pakistan? In some of the valleys, there is cent per cent illiteracy, especially among women. Why is that? Their agents are everywhere, crawling like lice.' He turned to Alex and smiled, grimly. 'I paint them as tarantulas, insects, rats with seven tails. Perhaps this is why I am doing Art.'

'To get back?' Alexander asked.

Zulfikar Ali went back to concentrating on the road and half-whistling, half-humming a space-rock song through his teeth. After what seemed like several minutes, he spoke again.

'The only things that work efficiently in Pakistan are, one: the Army, and two: death. We are very good at funerals. Within twenty-four hours we have our dearly beloveds safely tucked up in the earth, their bodies perfectly clean, their eyes fixed only on heaven. Okay, it's the religion. But think about it. What are we trying to hide? No-one asks how they might have died. No-one cares. "Natural causes" covers a multitude of sins. Meanwhile, the sinners sit in their palaces, their souls slooped somewhere in offshore accounts on some Caribbean island or else up some white-topped mountain in Switzerland. Tinkering at the edges is useless. What we need here is a revolution. Nothing less will make any difference. But it's not going to happen.'

And as she looked around, Zuleikha began to spot handmade signs outside shops. Inscribed on them were letters shaped almost like pieces of pasta, which didn't seem to denote any language of Pakistan or India. There were also some swastikas, symbols which, even though she was fully aware of their provenance, and even though they were not in the reversed form of the Nazi emblem, still made her shudder. Zulfikar Ali must have noticed this, because then he explained that shopkeepers, in protest at the suppression of their mother tongue, had begun to do this: to erect signage in Tibetan.

Zuleikha spotted some women wearing brightly-coloured clothes walking along a dirt track and carrying huge baskets of apricots on their backs. Their hair had been tied in small plaits; they looked totally Chini, and they were smiling as one of them pointed at the jeep – though then they hurried off, as though conscious that they had ventured too close to the main road and to the male gaze. But it was a relief to be able to see women's faces at all after the sartorial morbidity of the NWFP.

The Indus at this point was broad and flat, and it flowed with more composure than had been the case further south. Its waters were opalescent from the silt and mud of the glaciers that formed the river's source. Yet Zuleikha knew that the source of the Indus River, the Choughou Rgyamtso, the Darya-e-Sindh, the Sinthos, lay some four hundred miles to the north-east, in Central Tibet. Here the slopes of Mount Kailas met Manasarovar, a lake that had been born in the mind of Lord Brahma, whose energy flowed down the river's two thousand-mile course all the way to its seven mouths which opened in song to the Arabian Sea. This one river provided for agriculture, industry and drinking water. As we were seventy per cent water, she thought, it meant that essentially Pakistan was the river. But like the Clyde the Indus too was tidal, and now Zuleikha peered through the glass in an attempt to spot the eager that she was convinced any minute would go roaring upriver in direct opposition to the current, the tidal bore that would roll back the water as though it were a curtain and expose the creatures, the swords and the bodies that lay beneath.

But I'm stupid, she thought: we're much too far upstream for that. Just as the Clyde ceases to be tidal around Glasgow Green, so the Indian Ocean's force must subside somewhere in the burning deserts of Sindh. The thin air and the lack of sleep must be confusing me. I'm not twenty-two any more, she thought. Every five years, I tumble down some cataract. And for a moment, in the light refracted from felspar, she thought she saw the triremes of Iskander lying on their sides, completely wrecked, their hollowed-out hulls beached along the sandbanks of the Sinthos, their frames destroyed by the sudden force of the rising tide. When she looked again, she saw that it was only the outline of a ruined Buddhist lamasery through the gate of which, incongruously, a herd of long-horned goats was emerging.

As they passed through the small villages and slightly larger towns that dotted the roadside, they saw that the houses up in the foothills were flat-roofed and mainly two-storeyed, with floors linked by rickety-looking ladders. The half-submerged ground floors seemed reserved for animals, while the roofs were stocked with vegetables. The houses were built of closely packed brown-coloured stone that had been cemented together, and which reminded her a little of Orcadian dwellings – except that here in Little Tibet, often the walls had been whitewashed, each roof was contiguous with that of its neighbour, and at the centre of each dwelling was a small opening to the sky. The trees grew in copses around the villages and along water-courses. The mountains in this region didn't seem to be snow-covered, at least not at this time of year, but in concert with the walls that looped around every drong, they too were predominantly brown. The women wore traditional tribal clothes, and on their heads were tall black woollen hats with reams of black cloth hanging behind, while some of the younger women braided their hair in complex patterns and attached silver jewellery to the hat – which, Zulfikar informed them, was known as an urdwa. The men however wore the Punjabi shalwar kamise which, back in the 1970s, Bhutto (the Elder) had promulgated as the 'national dress' of Pakistan, and which – among men, at any rate – largely had replaced Western jacket and trousers and regional costumes alike. Some of the older women looked all crumpled up, as though the sun, wind, ice and sand had sucked away their flesh and left them only dry bone and cracked skin.

The sky seemed to darken as it rose, and towards its apex it was the deepest blue she had ever seen. Though technically they were not now as high as they had been earlier in northern Kohistan or southern Gilgit, here in this high desert the horizon seemed perpetually to recede, and it felt as though they were on the edge of outer space. Zuleikha stretched out her legs along the back seat of the jeep and propped up a cushion beneath her head, though the sweeping irregularities of the road and the fitful nature of her own consciousness made sleep impossible.

There were special places along the way where, day and night and in between, little men (or at least, men who seemed to spend most of their lives crouching) would brew tea in voluminous black pans and pour it skilfully into metal teapots so that it was perpetually ready for consumption, together with spine-tingling cigarettes and cakes laced with a pinch of hashish. Right from the depot in Rawalpindi, all the way to outer Baltistan, the chai-wallahs all had been cut from the same cloth. Tea from tin pots tasted better than tea from china cups, especially out of doors, the steam rising in the starlight and the landscape closing in around them like a goat's wool blanket as they were serenaded from some far-off forested gorge by the howling of moon bears. The drivers of those psychedelic trucks were all high as kites. They had to be, to be able to cover the vast distances they covered, the terrains they traversed. Riding on the smoke of lung-dun-she they journeyed through war-zones, bandit country, police and army checkpoints. Real police, fake police. They coincided with bands of bearded Jihadis ploughing the Hippy Trail, in reverse.

These unassuming yet somehow heroic truckers scaled the highest mountains in the world, and the hottest deserts where great-headed snakes ruled and sang anthems of the many lost Edens of the Indus Valley. They coursed along the flat beds of desiccated mythical rivers and all the while they were working, watching the road, delivering goods and consuming great bowls of hash. If the Indus and its tributaries supplied the plasma, then the truckers were the corpuscles of this country. Without these caravaneers, and without the navvies who bent their sun-toughened spines, pulled the rocks up out of the hard land, matched them with the bones of their skulls and then laid them down as roads, Pakistan quite literally would grind to a halt. They were proletarian Michelangelos who laid on their backs and daubed wondrous paintings of film-stars, sufi saints, Quranic words and symbols and images of Paradise all over the elephantine wooden structures they'd built on the metal frames of their flatbed Bedfords.

Alexander laughed, and his laughter seemed terribly small inside the almost pressurised cabin of their jeep. This was about as far from Bedfordshire as you could possibly get without going into orbit. And these guys – the truckers, with their cabs painted inside as well as out, with their taavizes and their talismanic eyes – these guys were really sailors, with a woman – or at least a whore – in every province. They were skysailors who were flying upside-down, their feet attached to the stars; they were coursing through an ocean of bhang, tea and dust. And mountains. Perhaps that was why Zulfikar Ali drove so fast: he wanted to turn the anger into lightning.

Smoke rose from some of the houses, and because there was no breeze the smoke lifted into the sky in straight lines like bluish-white string. It was a comforting scent which took Zuleikha back to childhood bonfires in the days when you didn't need a permit to light one in your back garden, to Bonfire Nights on cold clear

November evenings when the crackle of logs would be syncopated by the explosion of fireworks and the miraculous illumination of children's faces. That acrid smell of sulphur, a scent which in her mind always seemed to herald the opening of winter, but which here in the primal topography of Baltistan would be more likely to suggest the proximity of hot springs. At times, she felt that she wanted to just curl up in one of those shelters which the women of these villages had built right on top of the roofs of their houses: a place set aside, a place of privacy, safety, solitude; a place where they might bathe in the ecstasy of the silvery darkness.

Up in some of the crannies she thought she even spotted a few tiny cannabis plants. Yeah, she thought, no wonder both Herodotus and the hippies had passed this way. But along with the wood, hanging around every settlement through which they passed there was the stink of dung. Yak dung and sheep's dung, she imagined, though the sheep here looked more like goats. And then there were several hybrids too, some of them with horns shaped like curved swords and others with hides that were coloured greyish-blue. Goats that would be capable of scaling even the steepest slopes, ibexes that were wiser than men in their healthy lack of respect for borders.

Again that night in the hotel in Skardu, Zuleikha's dream erupted vividly inside her head. It took place in a cold high valley filled with black grass. Her mother was wearing a necklace of white, red and blue stones, and was dressed in the manner of the old Byltae, the Baltistanis of ancient times – not simply as a woman but as a warrior woman, a Mother of War. They lived in a house cut from tree-trunks, thrown up as four high walls with slits for windows and a skylight, and from whose door there wound a long crooked path that seemed to spiral all the way up the mountainside. The smell of pine and willow had seemed so physical that Zuleikha felt that she'd be able to quantify it. Close by, two broad rivers – one blue, the other brown – met in a swirling confluence of rocks and foam that churned for hundreds of yards downstream. Between the house and the river there grew an enormous tree, so tall that she was unable to make out its top. Or rather, the tree narrowed as it grew, so that its end was like a needle pointing towards the dark blue apex of the sky. Her father was dressed like a Dardistani peasant from a hundred years ago with a short reddish beard, a belt worn over the top of the shirt in an almost Russian manner, and black leather boots reaching to just below his knees, He was dancing a slow stomping circle dance. He moved with intense deliberation as he marked out the line of the circle on the ground with his boots. He did this seven times, moving gradually inwards, so that the seventh circle was drawn simply by him turning in a single movement, a full 360 degrees on the axis of his soles. Every time he did this, every time he struck the ground or spun, a cloud of fine dust flew into the air. But since there was no breeze and since it was the height of summer, the dust did not disperse but simply grew more concentrated, so that by the end of the dance of seven circles, Daniel John was surrounded by a cloud which billowed and gleamed like a silver chugha in the sunlight. Her mother was staring up at the sun and her mouth had half-opened, just as it had behind the high-concentration oxygen mask the night she had died; when, because of the tightness of the tumour as it had wrapped itself like a dark glove around her heart, she had been unable to breathe properly.

But now, in this thin air, in this light that burned off the shining surfaces of ten thousand feet of rock, Nasrin Zeinab was not breathless or blue. She was pink and healthy and was singing as she had not sung for decades. Her song was unaccompanied, her voice pitched low: alto, perhaps, though it wasn't on a level that could have been described by any Western scale of which Zuleikha was aware. Except perhaps a kind of Phrygian… yes, that was it, Zuleikha-in-the-dream thought and Zuleikha-outside-of-the-dream recalled – it was Phrygian. It was Yunani, Yona, Yonaka, Yavana, Greek, Ionian, Macedonian, Hellenic, and her singing was bringing a herd of goats down off the side of the grey-brown mountain. And around the song, wrapped like stems around its notes, were thyme and mulberry, briar bushes and scrub grass. But nothing lived up on the white summits except eagles, vultures and snow leopards. Even the lower peaks were still three times the height of Ben Nevis, the Evil Mountain of Scotland. The land of bya nuks and bya kurs. And the words of Nasrin Zeinab's song were in a language whose enunciation seemed to Zuleikha to require a different set of mouth and throat muscles altogether.

Tibet-e-Khurd. An old, old language, a tongue of the dust and the light, a hymn of the empty places, the long time.

Into all the heights of the sky, none flies
Besides the king of birds, none flies
During the three summer months
Whatever can bloom, blooms
Except in the summer months
There are no flowers

Besides this one lifetime
I shall not belong to my mother
In this one lifetime

Whatever can be happy, is happy
Enjoy this one lifetime
As ever you can enjoy it

The song progressed as Daniel John danced his agonisingly slow dance, and at its climax Nasrin Zeinab was almost howling at the sky. Her voice no longer seemed human. It was one of those moments when Zuleikha had felt a rush of sheer terror, the feeling she'd had occasionally at home, at night, when she'd been woken by what she'd thought – had been convinced – was the sound of a baby crying. Her baby, crying again, breathing again, back from the worms and the mud and the darkness. She'd leapt out of bed and had rushed into the spare room, only to find ... emptiness, cold. The voices had come always from outside the walls, from beyond the glass, their timbre sustained beyond what was humanly possible. No wonder people had thought cats were devils. And now her mother was singing in a voice not so dissimilar from that song of the cats. Lower-pitched perhaps, yet just as other-worldly.

And then she thought that no, she'd been wrong the first time when she'd gazed up at the tree. Zuleikha saw now that the tree grew downwards from heaven and that it had twelve branches and that it was watered by the paradisiacal rivers of milk, wine, honey and water and that one of the branches lay open. *Your mother is a spirit now; she will possess the qualities of a spirit and will behave accordingly. She is no longer your mother.* Zuleikha turned away from the fortified house, the dream house, the House of Sadness, of Weeping, of Loneliness, the wilderness house of canes, and she tried to look at her father, but the white dust had risen so high that the cloud now whirled around him as though the earth itself was dancing, and in its dance he had moved beyond the farthest point of visibility.

She had woken up covered in sweat and with the taste of blood in her mouth. Panicking, she had run to the bathroom, flicked on the electric light and stared at the mirror. She had a nose-bleed and the redness cascaded down the smooth sides of the porcelain sink. The taste of iron made her want to vomit. She could still hear the music and she realised that there were indeed cats outside. In the distance she could make out the dark shapes of tall trees – pine, spruce, birch, plane – as they swayed to the song of the dead children, the children who had been taken by the piries to the valley fields and the high meadows, the children who among the rolling boulders, elegant pear trees and tangled, ancient vines, among the blue goats and wise yaks, had put on magical caps and become invisible.

Chapter Thirty-two

Skardu was a scrubby, brown place, set in an enormous valley formed by greyish mountains. By the time they got there the sun was setting, and the shadows seemed to Zuleikha to resemble strange alien beings with etiolated limbs who would be able to defy gravity and cover great distances in the stride of a single day. Unlike us, she thought. In spite of Zulfikar Ali's driving skills, which now she recognised were indeed considerable, it had taken them the best part of three very long days to reach here from Rawalpindi. A mere fifty minutes as the crow – or rather, the propeller plane – flew, but over five hundred miles by road. And after sitting for all that time in the jeep, her back and limbs were aching as yet again they carried the box out and secreted it in the cupboard of the hotel room. With trekkers, climbers and miscellaneous travellers, it was end-of-the-pier season in Skardu, and the rooms had not been cheap. The town, the Old Bazaar, the New Bazaar and all the other bazaars seemed to be swarming not only with buses but also with jeeps, similar to their own but scruffier, and filled with local guys, Pathans, Punjabis and others, all hanging out of the windows or else perched precariously on the rear running-board.

Balti sounded quite different from the other languages she'd encountered over the past two days. In its assonance, in the gaps between words, in its short monosyllables, it was clearly much more like Chinese or Thai, say, than Urdu, Persian or Pashto. She realised that somewhere back there, around the time Zulfikar Ali had begun to open up and talk about Baltistan instead of hip-hop, Hollywood and heavy metal, they had crossed an invisible frontier. A frontier not merely between language groups – though that was profound enough – but also between continents, music and the conception of the sacred. Zulfikar Ali had told them that his real name, his full name, was Zulfikar Ali Lobsang. He had reclaimed the latter of those names in the manner of many of the younger educated people of Baltistan, as a statement of his cultural ties with Tibetan and Ladakhi culture. Ali, of course, was the name of the Holy Prophet's son-in-law, himself a pre-eminent prophet of Islam and, for Shias, the first of the Imams. Zulfikar meant 'lightning' and Lobsang meant 'brightness' – and so, he explained, his name spelled illumination.

In the old days, this whole area had been part of a single kingdom. The kings had made their winter capital in Skardu and their summer capital in Leh, and Mahayana Buddhism and Islam had co-existed largely peacefully. In fact, most people had not become Muslim until the sixteenth century or later. Even now, most Muslims belonged to either the Shia (of the Twelver or Sevener persuasions) or Nurbakshi Sufi sects, both of which effectively had become targets for the Wahhabi and Salafi nutcases who seemed hell-bent on turning Islam into a religion bereft of love, tolerance, humanity, philosophy, theology, common decency or even common sense. But over the preceding thirty years they seemed very successfully to have infiltrated the army and security services, to the extent that every single one of these organisations played a double or even a triple game between the Americans, the Chinese, the Indians and God knows who else.

Or rather, Zuleikha had thought to herself, probably He doesn't. Actually, she thought, the fact that all these shit-heads behaved in the way they did probably served as proof that He didn't exist at all. Either that, or God had smoked a large dose of crack cocaine on his famous day of rest. Heresy! Blasphemy! Shirk! Yes! So fuck it. The people around here, in their dark valleys scarred with both poverty and the discarded rings of Coke cans – what kind of God did they have? A God who tore the children, dead and blue, from their bellies? Kids cretinized by the simple lack of iodised salt or else destined, one in ten of them, to perish before the age of five? If God had been living in Glasgow he'd be on the fucking paedophile register, she thought. He'd be locked up for eternity in a State Hospital. This was a land of dead children. The earth seethed with their tiny bodies, the rocks echoed with the resonance of their cries, their cat-yawls. It wasn't more God that they needed, these folk: it was sewerage, education, health provision, the opportunity to sustain their fields as they had managed to do for centuries, and the chance to prosper without having to abandon everything for the hubristic, cannibalistic, suicidal economics of capitalism.

But Zuleikha had come to distrust narratives, potted explanations framed with neat borders. You shouldn't believe everything you read or hear, she thought. There's always an agenda. This thing about Baltistan – or Baltiyul – and its heavy Tibetan-ness had probably been dreamed up by some nineteenth-century roaming aristocrat. And now the young hotheads of the Baltistan Students' Federation and the Baltistan Cultural Foundation knew that the West would swallow anything from a tin with the label *Tibetan* plastered on it as though it was the new manna. Whatever had happened to 'Bod yul', the 'Land of the Buddhists'? Well, she thought, Baltistan is no longer a 'land of Buddhists' and hasn't been for five hundred years, since the time of England's Henry VII, the Huguenots of France or Scotland's James IV. 'Tibet', or 'Nub Ti-bat' – 'Western Tibet' – was as much a construct as the Ghàidhealtachd, or 'Scotland', 'England', 'Pakistan', 'Italy', 'Sicily'. It was not the new manna, it was just another tall tale. Nothing was as it seemed, a blade of grass was no longer simply a blade of grass (as the Red Lamas might have said).

Even though the sun had set it was still burning hot, and then the electricity too had gone down so that the entire valley was in virtual darkness, and then the hot darkness wrapped itself like a bearskin around the town. Sparse dots of tungsten were spat across the invisible landscape by the occasional generator, and though the hotel had one, as usual it was sufficient only for light, not air conditioning. And so, in spite of cold-showering repeatedly and sleeping nude without sheets, Alex and Zuleikha felt as though they were trapped inside the corpse of a giant animal. They began once again to swelter, to toss and turn, and their bodies began to come inadvertently into contact with each other in that apparently casual manner which can lead rapidly to disinhibition. The lack of moving air, the intensity of the night heat and the strange wildness of the setting made her feel as though, like the junior wife of the Emperor Akbar who had fallen into an adulterous relationship with her stepson, she was alive and was being walled-in somewhere far way. This feeling of slow suffocation was simultaneously maddening and erotic (*Ah, could I behold the face of my beloved once more…*) and, after all, it had been perhaps two weeks since they had screwed at all and that was the longest they had gone since … since that first night in Zuleikha's flat. Oddly, this comforted her, thinking that now they were becoming a little like a couple, not so rabid, more relaxed about it all.

And Zuleikha needed comforting, because she was scared. Scared she might be losing her mind. She needed to feel the closeness that can come only though sex; she needed to feel its immediacy, its reality, its suspension of disbelief, logic, rationality; she needed its ferocious theatre for those few minutes of an entire night; she needed to obliterate her mind. Maybe Alex needed to do the same. And so, even though they were exhausted by the journey, the low oxygen level and the unfamiliarity of the place, they did have sex that night, panting noisily because of the deoxygenation and the difficulty they had in perspiring, so that Zuleikha thought that they were like a pair of wild dogs fucking in the dust and trying to lose heat through the surfaces of their tongues and soles. She also thought that Alex had pretty much fully recovered on this journey which had been so tiring for her. He seemed to have gained in energy the thinner the air had become, and as he hit an orgasm that was hard as iron and which seemed to penetrate her body right up to the base of her neck, she reached out and touched his spine and his back seemed like the curved body of a lute and in that moment, although she had already climaxed, Zuleikha came again, and this time her breasts, which she had thought had subsided into repose after their annual liquefaction, now began again to leak as though it was she, and not Alexander, who was ejaculating. It was all she could do stop herself from screaming like a cat, or like a woman sealed in brick and stone and in pretty, poetic, pomegranate verses.

Yet still, respite and sleep did not arrive until around three or four a.m. when the A/C finally went back on. In the distance there was the sound of a short-wave radio, some sad song in Persian from Tajikistan or Kirghizistan. She became preoccupied by the thought that maybe she'd wanted to scream like that to block out her thoughts about Archie and the unremitting respiratory struggle to which his body had been subjected by the close embrace of the tumour. And then, as though to serenade her imaginings of the dead airman, from somewhere up in the mountains the real dogs began to howl – presumably heralding the false dawn or the setting of the moon, or whatever it was dogs howled for. Or maybe it was cats. Or maybe it was babies. No, she didn't want babies, not now, not ever again, and anyway she was too old.

She woke him and they made love a second time and she held onto him, held tightly onto his shoulders so that the ends of her nails threatened to pierce his flesh and, with her legs wound around his loins as though in a python's grip, she pulled him closer, closer to her skin so that every pore was joined with his, so that they fused like rock, like sand, like snow, so that the waters of their flesh flowed into each other like the rivers in her dream. Zuleikha was in every note of his music, she was flying across land and sea, across centuries and quarter-seconds, and once again his voice sent delicious sa-re-ga-ma shivers up her spine, right from *I Love My Love in Secret* to *The Lament of Heer and Ranjha*, so that as yet again they arched into a tortured almost Tantric climax which seemed to centre around a place in the base marrow of her spine, she felt as though their roles had been reversed, that now she was the musician and he the instrument. Deep inside her body the pain was intense, yet sweet. And then they were out over the emptiness, they were mountain climbers perched on the hundred-foot-high edge of a glacier, dangling together from a rope that was beginning to fray ... she felt a warmth between her legs and realised that as they were fucking, she was starting to have a period. Fucking Christ.

Perhaps, she thought afterwards as Alex's breathing eased finally into the regular undulations of sleep, perhaps in Glasgow she had been cursed by some wandering khuserah. Babies invited misfortune. With its long fingers, death stalked babies like a shadow, like the shadows cast by a mountain sun or a flickering tungsten bulb somewhere out in the wilderness. That night, in Skardu, in the Valley of the Stars, the first time she'd come, for just a second as she'd opened her eyes she had thought that it was Archie's face above hers, staring at her. She had blinked hard. The man was six feet under, the worms were eating the asbestos out of his eyes, they were purifying the bastard's toxic soul. But they were also gnawing away inside her brain – or maybe it was woodworm from the box. But then, Archie was ashes. He didn't have any eyes. Fucking freak, she told herself. You're a fucking freak.

Tonight it was raining hard; the water hit the windows as though the darkness itself was trying to punch through. Summer, right. July, okay. Scotland! A time for drink, liquor, fire-bloody-water, that was all there was for it now. Sun's gone, drink up! He raised his glass, saluted the electric light-bulb, put the rim to his lips and swung back his head so hard he thought the whisky had fractured his spine. He slammed the glass down, almost snapping it at the base. Exhaled. Looked up at the photos.

He'd seen Nasrin Zeinab on many occasions since her death, mostly when he was on the marches of sleep. Though once he'd imagined that he'd spotted her form moving swiftly across the corridor, passing from their kamra into the living-room. He'd called out but had received no reply, and when he'd ventured into the living-room, it had been empty and nothing had been disturbed. The room had been no colder than the rest of the house and anyway, when you died, you died. So he'd paid no attention to his dreams and gradually, along with the smell of her clothes, they had faded. Some people drank to get high or mad, but Daniel John drank simply to get numb. Well, no; that was an untruth of the first order. He leaned his elbows on the dining-table and looked at the chairs ranged around its rectangle. Six chairs, one person. He laughed and looked down at the whorls of wood. One person. The rest, all ghosts.

He'd always enjoyed a tipple, as the euphemists said. And since his wife's death there had been no-one to moderate him, no-one to screw the lid back on and put away the bottle in the wooden secretaire along with the finest teacups and crystal glasses. It had begun as an alternative to watching the dumb TV – especially in the winter evenings. There had been nothing else to do; it had helped him clear his mind of a lifetime's detritus. And yes, he thought, at seventy-five my life is nearing its close. But the thing was, he thought, sipping some more from the small glass, you never knew just when your moment would come, nor how it would come. He didn't want to be like Nasrin Zeinab, drowning slowly in tumour. No, when it came he wanted it to be quick. Did all people his age dwell on death like this? Perhaps. Yet maybe others had distractions – grandchildren, for example. He laughed and then drank some more. The whisky burnt the roof of his mouth, producing a slightly rancid taste, a sensation which he quite savoured, and he drank some more and then poured another glassful of the single malt. Daoud, the grandson he had had, and then lost. A summer's night, just like this – only not stormy like this one. No, on that night death had crept up on them unseen, unsuspected, a slick blade upon the throat. Bastard!

It is a wild night, this, thought Daniel John, his arms moving round in a parody of a white heathery welcome. Aye, new year, old year, last year, this was summer in Scotland. And yet, because of the season and the high latitude, the evenings remained light until around ten-thirty, and instead of pitch black, a mauve ribbon would stretch along the southern horizon, moving eastwards in the time before the dawn burst through. But because of the thick cloud-cover, on this night there would be no such dawn. The deep grey clouds hung low and heavy over the earth and the atmosphere was leaden. As Daniel John sank forward in his chair, he was aware that the side of his head had made soft contact with the polished wood of the dining-table, and he felt himself slip into a rough sleep.

He must have got into his car and driven, which he shouldn't have done. He knew, like so much in life, that it was stupid, illegal, dangerous, unforgiveable. He'd looked after her for the nine months it had taken for the cancer to kill her. At the end, he'd cradled her head in his hands as though she were a newborn baby, her eyes gleaming with their last light and his glistening with tears that he would not allow to fall until she had gone. All around them, beyond the crumpled form of their daughter, the night ran with the idiot rhythm of lighted machines, the theatre of false hope, inexorable the rise of the morning in that period when the night-birds had fallen silent and the day-birds had not yet awoken. Inexorable, the sound of psalms, of one particular psalm, that of Asaph, Psalm 77, the chant of the bereaved, the lost, the living who know that in the long trumpet-note of time they too were merely a rank among the legions of the dead. Its low hum was barely discernible, but it was there: in the stones of the city, in the raindrops that hit the pavement as they had done for sixty years or more, in cantillations of his own heart which had stopped just at the moment of ... then, nothing. All around them, nothing. Silence, emptiness. No God, no psalms, hymns, naaths, talaavats, nothing at all. And silently his tears had fallen onto the face of his beloved, but like all human tears they were impure and had failed to lift her from the darkness.

He must have got into his car, for now he was at the cemetery. And he must have climbed over the fence – or perhaps had forced his way through the bushes and thorns, the densely packed trees, for his skin was torn and bleeding and the air was black. The rain poured down and struck the ground with such force that the drops bounced a whole foot into the air. He was in shirt-sleeves and the graveyard was deserted. The wind blew the shadows of the trees hundreds of feet across the slabs of the long-dead and the mounds of the freshly-deceased alike, and Daniel John's silver hair whipped across his face, his eyes. He had lost his glasses somewhere on the way here, and with the rain and wind that drove into his eyes, he could barely see.

Then he saw her.

She was standing, smiling, some thirty feet or so to his left. She was young and slim again and was wearing a trouser-suit of the kind that had been fashionable in the early 1970s. Although everything around her had been battered by the water and the darkness into a pullulating monochrome, Nasrin Zeinab's face, her hands that were outstretched towards him, her cotton clothes, all were brightly-coloured, her skin burnished olive, her vestments red and yellow and green. Yet he saw that she wore no shoes and that as she walked across the sodden earth, as she came through the rain in his direction, not a single hair on her head seemed ruffled by the storm. He saw that his feet too were bare. He shook his head and closed his eyes, tried to dispel the vision. It was just the whisky, the extreme weather conditions. He was just an old codger who was losing his marbles, whose marbles were rolling downhill to their final resting-place, to the dark box that would lie beneath white marble, into which his name would be cut in Persian, Gaelic, English. His name, a poem, a song, an exhalation. This was just a dream, a nightmare, the cohorts of grief catching up with him. But when he opened his eyes he was still there, kneeling in mud, his hands gripping the sides of her tombstone, his hands and feet bleeding into the earth. That sound again, the sound he'd heard in the few seconds before she had passed – there it was. But this time it was clear like glass, like the surface of a lake. A single string, plucked at regular intervals; the song of a life, the music of a soul that was eternal. She was standing before him and she felt closer to him than his own skin. She turned over her hands, opened the palms. Smiled again. And in her smile, the Urdu ghazal turned to a Highland lament. A psalm of David.

I lifted my hand in the night without tiring,
My spirit would not be comforted...
You have pulled my eyes open,
I will think of music in the night

The sea has seen you and it suffered
And the deep places were disturbed
you are walking in the sea
you are moving in the multitude of the water,
you have left not a footprint...

In her face the bones of Zuleikha, their only child – their sainted future whose song would be carried God-knows-where and with God-knows-whom, and the tiny broken bones of their grandson, poor Daoud, who had never learned to sing and yet whose short life had seemed to them like a joyous ode that later had turned into an incurable wound. It was a song of wafers and wine, of flesh which through death had become trans-substantiated into words. Nasrin Zeinab was the logos of his soul. Without her, he held no meaning. But perhaps there was some place where everything added up, made sense; some distant universe where you could stand and take hold of the stars and grasp in your fingers every burning melody, every last note as though each one were a drop of blood from your own heart.

Along the horizon there was no light, no sign of dawn. The rain did not cease that day or the next, and so much water came down from the skies that Glasgow Fair weekend in July that at high tide the Clyde River rose and burst its banks, flooding the drains and the subterranean streams and all the old abandoned railway stations, right the way back to the flat place where, fourteen centuries earlier, amidst the oak and hazel trees, the saints had first bathed the bodies of the faithful in the warm salvation of the green marshes.

It was dawn and the surface of the loch was completely still. The shoulders of the mountains were still in shadow, as though the short tenuous night had not quite loosened its grip and even now only reluctantly slipped away westward, chased by the rising light coming over the cliffs from the inland direction. A pair of white birds – possibly seagulls – chopped and swirled the water and then rose smoothly, spraying droplets like tiny flying lamps from the ends of their wings. Around a hundred yards from the shore the old chapel was dark, closed-up, its hulking wooden door sealed firmly against all comers. Parts of the roof had fallen in, while in places the sandstone of the walls had crumbled, leaving small mounds dotted around the base. Some of the mounds had become covered with moss, lichen, grass and rangy plants with pale pink flowers which hung loosely as though they were either still sleeping or else exhausted from the night.

Down in the vault the Whore was fixed now, her figure cut perfectly into the middle layer of the glass, her long blue robe sweeping elegantly around golden slippers, her hair long and wavy, a fox-brown dupatta upon her shoulders and her face a shade somewhere between olive, pink and cream. Her hips were full and were shaped like the slopes of old hills or like the billow of ocean waves. Her eyes were almond-cut, the irises the colour of hazel. A smile played around her modest lips, which lay slightly open, the gap between them remaining unstained, so that when either the sun or the moon caught that particular part of the window, the Whore's mouth would send a polychromatic light through the dust and darkness of the vault, onto the stone of the opposite wall and onto the sculpture of the door that lay embedded in granite. The Whore's left hand was outstretched, the palm facing upwards, as though she was offering solace – or else prophecy – to the sheep that passed by.

At midnight, at the apex of the full moon, the Whore's lips would bring the chapel to life. The door would swing open and the drowsy sheep would raise their heads as they heard the sound of giggling and singing, and beneath these the notes of the first, the original lute, the instrument that had been fashioned from the wood birthed from the tree, high up on the mountainside, among the clouds and pennants and disembodied tinkling bells, far to the east. Shadows would flit across the wall as the whores of the night danced like luccioli up from the vault and into the belly of the church itself. All the figures from the stained glass would melt into being and would begin to dance, to spin on the flags that had been worn smooth as marble by the feet of the living and the dead and there, beneath the open sky, beneath the stars that shone so clear, to the sound of a single string, they would dance the round-dances of the old days and would raise their voices into a beauteous alto, mezzo, contralto that made the angels envious and which, if the wind was blowing in a propitious direction, could be heard right across the bay. Sailors and fishermen would hear the song and would fall into a trance and, like the whores, they also would begin to dance, round and round on the decks of their ships and then, unable to contain their desire, would leap over the rail and into the cold dark loch whose depth was unknown and whose currents flowed from countless rivers and whose tides ran with those of the sea until the ships, bereft of steady hands on the tillers, would run aground. Most of the sailors would drown to the sound of the beautiful voices, but one might manage to clamber ashore and stagger over boulders and rock pools to the ruined kirk from where a flickering yellow light shone. And this one would stand in the opened doorway of the caravanserai and would feel himself sway in the burning air until his hands both were taken hold of and his body pulled whole into the church, into the dance.

And there she was, the whore that Archie had strangled, the woman whose soul had slipped through his tightening fingers, whose spirit had flown out from between the taut blue knuckles of the airman, the holy kunjeree who had blown ennisa dust into his chest and who had followed him down into the air-raid shelters, the forest, the shipyards, and who had been his bridesmaid up the aisle beneath the war flags. And there, in the midst of the churchen labyrinth, she had smoothed the skin of her body down against the names, cut deep into stone, of the dead of countless wars upon which England, Scotland, Britain had been built. Baraka, baraka, baraka. There she was, there in the chapel, all those years after she had nearly died at the hands of the airman, as though her form had been leached off the glass plates of colour photographs captured during the time of Swing and miscegenation. Dazed and impervious to the mass destruction all around, the chemical fires, the screams of the dying, the smell of burning flesh and oil, she had wandered off to the docks of the holy city and had gazed into the swirling waters for hours, had watched as the ocean current had caught the river's skin. She had watched the water turn from grey to black and had watched the full moon filter through the clouds and from time to time there she had contemplated suicide, had wondered what it might be like to stand on the edge of the wharf, to caress the metal cheek of the mooring bollard and to feel the breeze sweep away her hair and blood, which during her life had mingled in rigor with those of ten thousand men.

Amidst the firestorm, she had wondered what it would be like to gaze one last time at the stars and the clouds and the moon and then, like some lemon-cheeked heroine from al-Tabari's *Chronicle of Apostles and Kings*, to leap over the wooden edge and into the cold darkness. She had slept there for days, sheltering beneath a steel piece of roof that had been blown off the top of some factory. She knew that it was more than likely that her own tenement would have been destroyed, along with everything in it: the cracked mirror, the broken bed, the Pope. No-one had bothered with her; so many people had been displaced during those two days of the Clydebank blitz. She had gone to the edge of the broken wharf and had walked down the steps and had bathed in the freezing river. But as she had risen to her feet, a large ship flying the merchant ensign had moored alongside. Suddenly, she had remembered how hungry she was. Where there were ships, there were sailors, and where there were sailors … Ignoring the stars, she had straightened out her hair and her skirt and had begun to walk with a practised louche ease towards the gangplank that had just been lowered.

The *mv Junaghar* was headed for India and the Whore – who had decided to name herself Lily, since in the old days all whores had been called Lily – took up with a sailor. With his help she managed to stow herself away in the deepest of the holds, the place where only bilge, sluice and crap went. And in the foetid darkness, against the coarse wooden planks and rough industrial steel of the hull, a bride of the sessions, she provided carnal services for the entire crew, from the Captain and the Mates down. And as the latitudes grew warmer, the Captain brought her out of purdah and into his own cabin and when they reached the cosmopolitan shores of Karachi, great seaside metropolis of Our Respected Lady Fisherwoman of Kolachi, the city of the Indus delta which recently had been pulled away from the Bombay Presidency and designated capital of Sindh Province, she became the captain's own little woman-in-a-box.

He set her up with some money and a house which quickly she turned into a kotha, with blue and red illuminations, velvet and muslin furnishings and all. Lily's Palace. *Lily ka Mahal*. And she invited the loose whores of the port to come and dance in her bordello, to learn properly from a dance master, and within a few years the Glasgow Whore had become renowned as the most auspicious naiqa in the Old Port area of the city of Barbarikon. She became so popular that her kotha drew tamashbeen from the far sides of the Vomiting Bridge of Makran and the Nahr-as-Sabt, the Sabbatical River of Baluchistan. But then, after some years of profitable enterprise, she heard that the Captain had discovered her business venture and was after her. And so one night, by the charsobees light of the crescent moon, she decamped along with her fortune and fled upstream on the tidal bore, a thousand miles or more, all the way to Lahore.

It was there, in the Shahi Mohalla, the Street of Kings where once had dwelt the emperor's court – the bards, the officials, the musicians, the dancers, the artists, the poets, the jugglers – there, beneath the perfect spiritual shadow of the Badshahi Masjid and in the wondrous swirling orbit of the great qila, that one night of the new moon, to a background chant of dadras and thumris and full-throated ejaculations of *Wa-wa! Bohoth khub!* and *Marhaba!*, with the moist kissing lips that lay between her thighs, she rolled back the freshly-sheared petals of the foreskin of none other than the young, the handsome, the fair, the conjuring, the nose-ringed, the virginal Petrus Dihdo Labokla, son of the naiqa down the street.

And though he had still been learning he had juggled for her, and she had given him a first-edition copy of the sex-instruction books the *Hidayatnamas*. Every day after that, while the rest of the Mundi slept, they would meet in a secret passageway beneath the old city, a conduit that had been hollowed-out by white eunuchs (as opposed to black bhoothes, red deos and silver jinns) during the time of that dreaming romantic, the Great Mughal, Jahangir, so that tawaifs might hold night trysts with their poet lovers. And over the years the salt wind of the sea, the keening breezes of the river and the relentless sunlight of Bharat had walnut-stained her skin to a shade similar to that of, say, a Sicilian or a Greek. It was in this form that to an entire generation of Sikha Lalas whose bundis had been softened and turned almost to nectar by Amritsarian money and the ever-giving calf-leather of Packards, Pontiacs and Master Buicks, that Lily the Glasgow whore had become the doyen of renowned catering and hospitality establishments such as Stiffles, the Standard and Elphinstone, and, most particularly, of the Metro on the Mall.

But then she had caught TB and had returned to Scotland to spend nine months in a sanatorium, her body wasting away to the breadth of an oak stick, her bright blue eyes fading to yellow, and her skin drying and becoming coarse as hoghide. And when she'd got out, cured at last of the rectangular bacillus, she'd found that her partners in joy had run off with both her money and her clients. So she'd gone solo again, and as she grew older each man she had aged her by one week, and then like debt it seemed to catch up with her all at once, and with interest too. All in all then, calculus-upon-tangent, by the time of her latter-day encounter with Archie and his Mai Margaret wife the Whore was ten centuries old, both wizened and wise, a brown madonna with a cunt the size of the Clyde. As her body had swelled and had begun to decompose, she'd had to resort to gathering a coin here, a coin there, from junkies, methsmen and the frankly insane, and maybe if she was lucky and if the man felt sorry for her, a meal for the night. She was no longer called Lily; indeed, once again, she no longer possessed a name. This is what happens to old whores: they don't die; like the maghi of Siracusa they vanish into thin air.

That day by the south bank of the Clyde she had hovered around the tree from whose branches they had used to hang witches, and she had walked up the street in full view of Archibald McPherson and his pristine saintly WAAF wife. He had looked at her as though in his mind that morning she had risen like a grey rock from the dank earth and granite plinths of the Glasgow Necropolis. And in spite of the countless travails of her life and in spite of having had a thousand men a year for forty years, as she'd passed the couple she had smiled at the thought of this man who unwittingly had sent her off to make her fortune way across the ocean. And now on this night there she was again, the fata of the loch, the jinn of the sea, the queen of the dance, her hands outstretched like those of the first Madonna, the Madonna of the Volcano, the nameless molten woman, the woman of spring and of winter who had drawn the Scots tribe across the long reaches from the hermit caves of the desert fathers, all the way to these cold islands where the stone set slowly into silver and the soul faded into window glass. There, in the kirk by the Black Loch, she was young again; and once again as in Lahore so many years before, she was Heer to all the Ranjhas.

The Whore was dressed in a crimson shawl adorned with silver brocade and she was dancing the old dances of Scotland, the circle dances of the fisherfolk, the crofters, the women, the dances that were stories of land, sky and sea, of the northern raiders with goats' horns and of the southern fathers with magical books. Her angular stepping movements mimicked the shift of the seasons, while the sounds blown from the tissues of her throat replicated the tales of her people in a language no longer spoken, in thoughts long since washed away. With every step, the ghungRoos tiered around her ankles jangled to rhythms cut from the rock. Yet whenever he had turned a street-corner at twilight, Petrus had caught her shadow in the corner of his eye. She had hovered always close to his skin, her feet slapping down onto steeked earth in the old way, the way of the temple whores, the devadasis, the tawaifs, the women who danced the sadir, who dressed always in white and who, like the old Greeks, spoke only in oracles.

Petrus, Chief Jadugar of Lahore's old city, guru extraordinaire of the Andrun Shehr, son of the Rusi Jadugar, Afanasii Aleksandrovitch, and Rabia Bilqis Labokla, dancer, kunjari and whore, Petrus Dihdo Labokla, the spirit of the city, was there too in the Auld Kirk, with his body distilled to bootleg whisky. He was putting on his make-up, adjusting his tresses, rubbing his integument with almond oil, climbing into his khuserah skin, his juggler's outfit, shalwar kamise and green chugha, and he was bending back his double-joints, cracking his knuckles, toning his

limbs and limbering up for a special performance. He had with
him his box full of props and his body filled with stories, and all
around a juggling cascade of acolytes, their silhouettes penned
like notes against the whitened stone, their mouths red with blood
and paan. And hovering within his breath was the spirit of the old
Russian who had juggled his way across steppe and mountain pass,
all the way to the city of Rama's son. Perhaps one of the chelas
was Rada Mirovna Samarina, sitting as an acolyte would, cross-
legged, her lute splayed across her lap, her back arched over its
frame, her long fingers caressing the strings as though they were
the sinews of a lover.

The Whore stopped dancing as they assumed their positions.
They were waiting only for McPherson, great son of Glasgow,
builder of planes and ships, mason of modern times, whose children
had been machines, whose every action had held significance, and
whose story would be re-lived now as though he were the grand
laird of tamashbeens. In the granite breath of the Auld Kirk, amidst
the hermit graves of ancient cavalieri, he would be transmuted to
dance, song, music. Everything he had ever done would come at
him through stone and blown glass, through the air that tasted
of salt even though, here by the shore of the loch, they were far
from the sea.

And as Archie swam across the water, his body whitened by the
moon, at last he remembered the lake house and the vision he had
had there of the woman with white hair, the woman who had bent
over his sleeping form and taken him into her. After all these years
he remembered the song she had sung, the words that had vanished
as soon as he had awoken, and the book he had found lying on
the floor. Amidst the burning hulks of war, the book had seemed
like a dream. Yet now, as he swam through the sea-loch and felt no
chill, no fear, it was the life he had led in the wasteland tenements
of the Depression, the oil and grease of the Lancasters, it was the
burning trombones of the lunchtime orchestras that seemed light
with unreality. His mother leaning over the sink, her skin burned
red by the hard soap and cold water, his father roaming through
the oases of Morocco, his sisters one by one marrying, procreating
and dying, the big ships he had hammered and swung into being,
the vessels that had carried their nets into his life, a life tied up,

doomed, fated, caught in the fibres of blue asbestos. Nothing seemed real any more, nothing except the touch of water against his skin, the undertow of the ocean, the call of the backwards-flowing rivers, hauling him to their sources and, through it all, this song: the song of the Whore, the spinning notes of wood, rock, water, moon. The swirling motion of aircraft oil in a puddle. The smell of apple blossom. The touch of stone, the kiss of the wind. The tiniest of thoughts and images, the inconsequential detritus of a life, a distant song filtering from the mesh of a valve radio, a song that was like the skin, the touch, the breath of Margaret, or of his mother, a song in which every note held its own beauty.

When he arrived at the oak door of the chapel the nachne walli had assumed their positions on the stone flags. Each of the dancers, jugglers, magicians, musicians was ready, set as though in the still frame of a film, their hands poised, drawn out in the shape of a majuscule. As soon as he stepped over the threshold the dance began. Other hands took hold of his and pulled him into the mujra. Round and round the whores were spinning, their movements now slow and perfectly measured. They were in pairs facing each other, and it was almost as though they were fighting or casting spells. They were falling to the floor and then being brought back to life again; they were kissing one another on the mouth. This was an old, old dance, a mill-dust dance of the Cailleach, a parade of the twilight dead. Bîn, tabla, dholak and the singing sarangi and shehnai all began to play slowly, slowly as the dancers wheeled upon the stone like planets, their hands, feet, faces and bodies united as though each one were a musical instrument, an eagle quill, a stylus, the pen of a sha'ir. And Archibald Idris McPherson knew that all through this long night, which bore no relation to the chronological night of summer, he would be a ghazal, a plaintive song of terrible longing that would be sung over and over again until sunrise.

Chapter Thirty-Three

The next morning they drove eastwards, following the big river through a dusty rock-strewn landscape, a creepy plateau broken irregularly by mountains which resembled enormous women wearing black chadurs. The road had been blasted straight through the rock and followed the meandering course of first the Sindh and later the Shyok Rivers, and at a point approximately midway between Skardu and Khaplu, in a torrential dance of blue, grey and white, the two rivers came together. From the visceral power of their conjunction in the wide gorge far below the road they emitted an evenly pitched sound, a note which seemed to draw even the hard stone of the mountains into their flow. Clumsily, as she was sorting stuff out, Zuleikha managed to bash the side of her arm against the dashboard and the glove compartment fell open. She realised then that it had been Zulfikar who had been listening to the small battery-powered short-wave radio the night before.

Hamlets clung to the terraces, each drong an island of fertility in an ocean of wilderness. At first Zuleikha thought that all the roofs had been painted bright orange, but then she realised that it was the early harvest of apricots which had been laid out to dry in the sun.

It took them the best part of a day to get from Skardu to Khaplu, yet when Zuleikha looked at the map she saw that they had travelled only around one hundred kilometres by road. But distances here were deceptive and up on the high peaks five miles, one mile, a quarter-of-a-mile, an inch could mean the difference between life and death. This whole district of Ghanche was frequently cut off during the winter, so that the only way in or out would be by helicopter. And yet, paradoxically, as they drew close to the whitewash and carved wood of Khaplu, the land seemed to open up into a concentrated fecundity, as though the centuries themselves had been irrigated and had drawn all the seeds and spores of every plant in Baltistan to this curvaceous valley.

In the town of Khaplu, in the lee of its hilltop castle, they booked into the only hotel which still had rooms. Zulfikar would have introduced them to his family, but the whole family had decamped en masse to a wedding in Islamabad. At night, people slept on the hard-packed mud roofs of their houses – something which was not uncommon in Pakistan, though over the past decade a series of gang robberies and murders in the cities had discouraged the practice. The sky was dark blue, almost purple at its apex, and in spite of the diesel exhaled by the legions of trucks once again the air was filled with the ubiquitous scents of woodsmoke, livestock and apricots. While the older buildings were made of wood and in design and structure – like the people – seemed more Tibetan than South Asian, their eaves inclining upwards in a clasp that resembled praying hands, the town was teeming with brightly attired big-booted hikers, unshaven trekkers and Neanderthal mountaineers whose faces seemed to have come to resemble their conquests. Intense guys with number-half haircuts and '666' tattooed across the tops of their heads. Varangians, Normans, Franks. Farangi. It was as though several teams of rugby players from some lower grade English public school had arrived to play in and conquer this valley. Imperialism as high-risk sport. In spite of all this frenetic activity the weather was noticeably cooler than it had been in the burning tandoor of Punjab, and the fresh air felt like heaven after the choking dust and diesel of the road. The sound of the Shyok River was everywhere, so that at times she almost wished the waters would rise and sweep away the Westerners. Until she remembered that she too was a Westerner.

The light which the green stone seemed to emit had grown so sharp that it had become painful to inspect the rock for too long, and Alexander and Zuleikha had to don sunglasses in order to trace the trail which its features seemed to delineate. Alex took out a detailed map of the area which he had bought in Skardu, and laid it out alongside the stone on their hotel room's coffee-table. Zuleikha quickly gathered up their plates. The taste of salt, mixed with the sweetness of honey, still lay heavy upon her palate. Zulfikar was out round the back of the hotel, washing the jeep.

'This is Khaplu,' Alex announced, pointing with a biro at a particular place in the small rock.

'How do you know?' Zuleikha asked.

He shrugged.

'Well, look – there's Skardu, and there's the course of the

Indus…'

'But how do you know this is right? We can't just go trekking about like those idiots with their crampons and tent-pegs. They may get a high shitting into a glacier, but I certainly don't.'

Even as she said this, Zuleikha remembered all the things they'd done. Defaecating into a crevasse would be the least of it.

'I can't make out the end of the trail,' he mused, as though he had not heard what she had said. 'The luminescence seems to fade.' His finger, poised just above the waxed surface of the map, had stopped at a point on a wavering brown contour some ten miles or so beyond Khaplu, somewhere high up on a mountain. 'The rest is unmarked. In the stone, I mean.'

Zuleikha sighed with exasperation.

'We'll have to take Zulfikar. He's from here.'

'I wouldn't go alone in any case. It's another world. Even the buildings…'

And Zuleikha remembered those arched eaves, the carved wood around the doors.

'The air's clean,' she whispered. 'It's as though all life is here, held in the leaves, the berries, the flowers.'

Alex turned her around and they kissed. He tasted of sweat and mulberries, and of kurba, unleavened bread, and as their kisses deepened she felt the rhythm of his heart play through her body, but she thought that perhaps it was just the distant sound of singing, a summer song, a happy song of abundance, of fertility. Baltistan lay beyond the Himalaya and so was in another climate zone altogether. Far above and inaudible from where they were, a swarm of military helicopters gathered like bees and the sunlight coming through the windows burned. Yet they hardly noticed, or if they did then it was only because the heat lent an insistence to their embrace. Zuleikha felt as though he was lifting her high in the air and then bringing her back down to meet his lips, his tongue, the hard muscularity of his body that she needed to envelop, as though he were a tree and she the wind.

In the depths of a long period of darkness she had driven out one morning, thinking of death, perhaps casually thinking of suicide, and instead had found Alex … and the box. And the box had brought them across five thousand miles to this high place of rock and sky, to this place where the embrace of continents racked the land. Perhaps it would be a casket of destruction.

She had a sudden image of her father sitting alone in his mahal, gazing out over his garden and sipping whisky, slowly becoming more intoxicated – though in a genteel, almost mystical manner as he watched the fruit on the trees ripen in the afternoon sun, the Scottish summer sun that, like the Scottish landscape, was moderated by latitude, age and ocean. The sun and this breeze that was soft but insistent like the music of a Rowallan lute. *I Never Knew I Loved Thee...* And as the light danced across Alexander's skin, as the shadows played about his eyes and his hair, Zuleikha felt that in the midst of his unending grief and perhaps as a consequence of it, her father yet had within him a complete knowledge of his life with Nasrin Zeinab, that year by year his memory had been sharpened by his unspoken faith which manifested through every song that had passed between his lips, and from which finally he might make sense of that song of songs around whose radif, whose root everything, including love, revolved.

The next morning, carrying the necessary supplies together with a large-scale map of the locality, a small portable easel and, hidden away deep in Alex's rucksack, the green stone, Zulfikar, Alexander and Zuleikha left Khaplu on foot and began to follow a sandy track which ran parallel to an irrigation channel. The perfect golden stalks of the barley swayed in the sunshine in a tableau for which an advertising executive would have given his right arm. Birdsong was everywhere, though Alex couldn't make out any individual species. And he glanced at Zuleikha and he saw that her face had acquired an almost alizarin hue. It was as though, like Zulfikar, she too was returning to some original form which her body had hauled up from a distant genetic pool, framed presumably by a circle of pencil cedars. Another perfect image. Or perhaps it was just that her heart was having to work harder because she wasn't yet acclimatised. Alex had got much fitter in the time he'd been with Zuleikha, what with all this running around and also with him having ceased to comfort-eat, but up here even he was struggling, and after a while both talk and thought became subsumed into the simple act of walking. She wondered whether the tarantulas in Baltistan were related to the ones in Sicily. Octagonal migration … Zulfikar had to stop every so often to allow them to catch their breaths. Zuleikha was glad she'd finally chucked the cigars. Otherwise I'd have been dead by now, she thought.

Occasionally they would pass a male villager – a jungli, her mother might've said: a wild person of the jungle – with whom Zulfikar would exchange a brief greeting before moving on. Unlike in the NWFP or Punjab, the women hereabouts wore long dresses but no dupattas, and though they seemed keen to avoid contact with even female foreigners there was no staring at Zuleikha, for which Alexander was both grateful and relieved. One man in Yaghistan had even come up boldly to Alex and asked if they were foreigners – to which, in suddenly flowing Urdu, Zuleikha had replied that he ought to mind his own business: they were from the capital. That had scared him off, the instant knowledge that she was from a far higher social class than he, that she had certainly been educated abroad. And also, hidden behind his leering countenance, the fear that they might just be spies of some sort. Tooled up with cameras in their prayer-wheels, Nepalese pilgrims had been hired as spies by the Farang. In some parts it seemed that everybody suspected everybody. But Pakistan was like Pandora. No-one considered that someone had stuffed evil into the box in the first place.

Somewhere to their east and south lay the Line of Control that split Ladakh into two parts: one administered by India, the other, Baltistan, by Pakistan. Wherever else war had erupted – Punjab in 1947, East Pakistan in 1970, Afghanistan from the late 1970s onwards – it had always seemed to come to roost on these mountains. This, Alex thought, is what six-plus decades of incipient war and rule by the machines that generate, and profit from, the constant state of unresolved conflict does to people, to the norms of an entire region.

But then, he thought, if Britain is the second or third-biggest arms-dealer in the world, what does that say about Britain and its people? When your hands moulded missiles and bombs, something of those missiles and bombs must surely insinuate itself into your being and eventually, entirely without you knowing it, begin to dictate your impulses, come to define you. How many people whom he had known had worked in the local ordnance factory for decades, until finally, some years earlier, to much community dismay, it had closed down? Lots. And they'd seemed like normal pleasant people, both men and women, most of whom had had children they'd dandled on their knees and who they'd cuddled up close to – no doubt in the certain knowledge that none of the explosive-stuffed metal projectiles which day and night they had constructed with those same fingers that had leafed gently through the hair on their children's heads, would ever be landing on their roofs. They'd rather be cascading from the soft white hands of some deadly juggler in the sky, down onto foreign lands where, most likely, the inhabitants would have black or brown faces and would talk funny languages. What did you do in the War, Daddy? *What did you do to the peace, Daddy?* But no-one would ever ask those questions any more, because really, when it came down to it, people didn't give a shit about some wogs being burned to a crisp. We would never know of those people, since missiles, semiconductors, high-tech circuitry – those things weren't individually traceable. Or, to be more precise (smart, you might say) the people who made the things never knew exactly where they ended up.

Perhaps they should, thought Alex. Perhaps there should be exchanges, so that factory workers from the UK could tour around the villages, towns and cities which their labour had helped to 'degrade', and through the cemeteries and orphanages – indeed, through the entire history in soil and blood of this world which they had helped create. Conversely, the survivors of 'pinpoint' bombing and 'collateral' artillery strikes could wander around the crèches and arms factories of Scotland, London, Chester, Chorley and marvel at the sense of peace, productivity, happiness and job satisfaction which exuded like a hymnal of positive feedback from the faces of the workers and their families. Human resources. High on a crag, he saw a raven preen itself. He sighed. Yes, he thought, wandering among birch and fir trees up here in the high places of the world is far easier than facing the truth.

Khaplu sat in the base of a valley and itself was at two and a half thousand metres. All around the town rose massive mountains whose slopes changed from green and yellow at their lower reaches to dust-brown further up and ultimately, in the morning sunshine, to a brilliant white that seared heavenwards in a series of pyramidal shapes – almost as though the peaks recently had been sharpened by some giant sculptor's chisel and then sprinkled with icing sugar. And now they were climbing slowly above the town, through the terraced fields of barley, potatoes, onions and cauliflower, the tall walnut and apricot trees, the plum and peach, the pencil cedars and the perfectly-shaped poplars that reminded Zuleikha of Lincolnshire.

And now she gazed into the clear water that rushed down the irrigation channel. She stopped, bent down and let the water from the irrigation channel run over her hand. It was colder than blue ice, and yet it seemed to induce in her body a paradoxical sensation of warmth. The soil here was somewhere between greyish-brown and khaki, depending on the angle of the light, and was soft, crumbly and easy to brush off the fingers. She looked up and saw that already Alexander and Zulfikar had moved far ahead along the track. She straightened up and hurried after them, but then felt a little dizzy and so slowed her pace again, and wished that she had kept herself fitter, and promised herself that she would do in the future. She was enjoying the bitter taste of apricot seeds, which was far better than the saccharine heave of chewing-gum. The seeds contained cyanide. One way or another, she thought, up here on the lip of the sky I will go blue.

After a while the track left the water channel and began to climb through scrublands where the vegetation grew sparse and wild and where the boulders, larger than those in the valley, looked as though they had only recently became separated from the overhanging crags. And then they were walking on bare rock, inching through narrow defiles and carrying themselves across terrifying gorges supported only by the loose netting of swing bridges known as zambas that were made, for God's sake, of yak hair, or else by glorified buckets that had been set up and strung from double ropes like very basic cable cars. As periodically he gazed into the green stone and checked their position against his map, Alexander seemed preoccupied, distant somehow – though Zuleikha thought that this might be just the effect of the terrain, which seemed epic, as though suddenly they had entered a world that was not quite real, a larger-than-life place where the narratives recounted in the old tales seemed almost to rise into plausibility. Though they knew that it was fanciful, they had wondered whether the rock might have come from an asteroid, and now Zuleikha thought that Alexander's mind was way up there, somewhere among the glowing peaks of outer space. She hadn't realised that she would have such a good head for heights, yet now it was as though she'd lived for years up here among the spikes and schists, the white-water swells and the sheared rock. It was nonsense: she was a city girl, a fast-lane woman who somehow had wandered off on this bridle-path of madmen and flying horses. Yet there was a headiness to being in such extreme terrain, and she began to understand the motives of those climbers who came back to repeatedly risk their lives in the snow and ice.

This was where it had all started, surely; this was where the people had come from, these valleys and slopes, this life of subsistence and worship. Occasionally, cut into the sides of the boulders, some of which were the equivalent of nine-storey blocks of flats, she would make out letters carved in unheard-of scripts. On occasion the words were accompanied by images, some of which were set so high that she had no idea how anyone could have got up there. At other times she thought she spotted square holes, very like windows, though there didn't seem to be any means of entry and so she supposed that these latter must simply have been generated by either erosion or else tricks of the light. Yet the light here was perfect.

Spies, armies, allegiances – so much seemed fluid here. The greater and lesser powers played their games and meanwhile, one way or another, ordinary people suffered. And ultimately, she thought, 'ordinary people' usually meant women and children. But had it ever been different? When the Mughals had fought the Afghans, or the Sikhs had clashed with the Tibetans, or the Greeks and Scythians had engaged in battle, had it really been any different? Or was war more pervasive now? In the old days it might have resulted in a change of king and ruling class, whereas now war seemed limitless and constantly invaded the peace, so that the mohallas, the galis, the village prayer-walls – all had been breached by the bloody requirements of the modern state. And so, instead of being sites of communing with God or with the emptiness, the walls had become lines of control. Bengal: split by Curzon; Pashtuns and Afghans: split by Sir (for drawing bendy lines these guys always got knighthoods) Mortimer Durand. Pakistan and India: split by Sir (there, see) Cyril Radcliffe; Kashmir: split by ... everybody.

The people were still living with the consequences of these men's pencils and dividers. Dividers and rulers. Perhaps, whether or not they knew or intended it, on some level de facto they were all spies. All those researchers who went always to the most inhospitable regions, who pretended to go native or to be recorders of some arcane anthropological ritual, really were feeding back information to military intelligences who sat in impregnable and mysterious buildings overlooking the Thames, Potomac, or just the local swimming-pool.

She thought of her father, of his meekness, his descent into whisky, his unconditional love for her mother. He was not a spy; he was not an imperialist. His people, the Highlanders, had also been crushed underfoot. The vicious Clearances of the late eighteenth century had torn both the spirit and the flesh out of Scotland, had emptied her mountains of human habitation and filled them instead with sheep, so that nineteenth-century travellers had felt able to comment without even a pang of guilt or a hint of irony on *the great romantic wilderness*. Haggis, whisky, tartan (no underpants please, we're Scottish) and white heather ... and so now larger-than-life Amrikan tourists came 'back' to search for their roots as though they were exotic plants rather than a completely different species. *We love your country. It's so cute.* Oh, good. Does that mean that you won't bomb it, then? But that too was a stereotype, and people tended to fold themselves into such patterns when they found themselves in threatening or unusual situations.

Back in Khaplu she'd heard the legend of a miraculous 'Angrezi', a healer who moved among the people doing great deeds. Or maybe she'd dreamt it; she couldn't remember now. And anyway, in general one only saw a very small sample of Americans in Europe. The older, richer, invariably white ones; the equivalents of the equally repulsive ex-pat Brits who had migrated to Sicily,

Portugal, Spain, Cyprus. Yes, with the slabbering complicity of her ruling classes Scotland too had been sliced up, divided between Highland and Lowland, industrial hub and wasteland, Gaelic and English, Protestant and Catholic, bourgeoisie and proletariat. The Clan Campbell of Campbellpure. Och-fucking-aye. Yet she had always felt comfortable within herself; all that stuff about mixed-race people being somehow conflicted had never really rung true with her. Prayer wheels, rosary beads – it all came round eventually. At times like these, it was as though you were standing before the edge of an invisible mirror in which dissonance and counterpoint would grow loud, brash and edgy. With its rock and sky and vibrant colours, with its whiff of frontier in every direction, this place was all edges.

As they gazed up at the grey surfaces Alex took out the stone, and saw that the light coming from its depths had grown so bright that it shone almost like a torch, even though the sun was directly above them. And she saw it now: the stone really was the same shape as the mountain up whose haunches they were climbing. It had been a map leading them here to Baltistan, and now it was a mountaineer's chart on which every pass, every rushing stream seemed to have been marked. She wondered who had cut this green stone, and from where, but that led her up the dead-end street to the question of who had built the box and filled it with lids, spaces, objects, music. It would have been far too large for them to have hauled all the way up here. It would have been nuts. Yet somehow she felt that it would have been right and proper for them to have done so, that since that very first morning and possibly even before, the box had lain at the centre of everything that had happened to them.

From the many different types of wood from which it seemed to have been carved, Zuleikha had come to the conclusion that it had not been built in one place, at one time, by a single hand; but that rather, like a holy book, it had been put together gradually. In between it must have moved about, possibly following one or other of the old roads, the trails across Eurasia, the trans-Siberian highway or perhaps the Silk Route, along one branch of which they had travelled to get to Skardu. Nonetheless, Alex had insisted on carrying his lute, strapped like an extra tent across his back. How bizarre he looked! He must be the only person in the entire geological complex of the Hindu Kush, Pamirs, Karakoram and Greater and Lesser Himalayas who was porting a musical instrument up a mountain. Not that they were intending to climb a mountain – at least, she hoped not. Between them, Alexander with his lute and Zulfikar with his easel seemed to know where they were going – or at least, the general direction seemed to be becoming clearer as they progressed. Alex had shown her the stone, had held it up to the sunlight so that its green luminescence had streamed all over her face, almost blinding her.

'The path only becomes clear once you've reached the end of the section that comes before,' he'd said, as though suddenly he had become a cross between a Buddhist arhat and a chartered surveyor.

Which meant that, in fact, they didn't have the faintest idea where they were going.

Now the terrain had changed yet again, and suddenly, from bare rock and dust, they had entered a broad vista of swaying meadows adorned with dark purple flowers and jasmine whose scent intoxicated them and slowed them down; forced them to walk with loping strides through the sea of yellow, green and indigo. From above there came the sound of whistling as snow-cocks swept across the surface of the floral sea. Occasionally they would come across a herd of goats or a solitary grazing zomo, for whom these lush meadows were summer pasture.

Every so often in the midst of this bucolic scene they would stop and consult the map on which Alex had drawn a thin red line. Alexander had a multicoloured biro which he would draw out like a magic wand and, as they progressed, after consulting the stone he would use the pen to mark the course ahead. Every time he removed the stone from his rucksack he seemed wary, as though perhaps he feared that Zulfikar would become inquisitive, or else think that they were typical Western nutcases like the ones who had used to come through in the hippy time. The ones perhaps who had ingested a little too much *Raven's Beard* and who had lost the trail to Kathmandu and become bearded hermits, held perpetually in a state of deep bovine meditation in the darkness of some distant mountain cave; or else who had turned by degrees into latter-day geomancers attempting to pursue a course, guided by only the eye inside their head and the scent of jasmine. Or like the crazy Russian mystics who, fleeing revolution, civil war and blood purges, had crossed mountains and rivers to secrete themselves in hidden high valleys to which in those days no-one had ever come, save for the occasional salt merchant or gem seller. The descendants of some of these people still lived in Yarkand and Kashgar, cities that lay a little further to the north, in Chinese Turkestan.

The further north they had journeyed, the more Zulfikar's posture and features had begun to assume their normal configurations, as though at last he was beginning to dream again in his mother tongue: in Balti, which he had never learned to write down – at least not in its proper Aiggy Tibetan script – but which, when spoken, was a staccato song that ran through the land like a mountain brook. Now he moved like a mountain goat; this had been the terrain of his childhood. He had been lucky to have been able to pursue his studies, though since there was no institute of higher education in Baltistan and only one in Hunza, in order to do that he'd had to leave the Northern Areas altogether. Back in Khaplu, through the mist, amongst the fleeting morning ghosts of dead musicians, Alexander had seen the soldiers out from their barracks, part of a mule caravan heading no doubt for some God-forsaken redoubt, and he'd sensed that unmistakeably casual swagger common to armed men the world over.

Masherbrum, Gasherbrum … the mountains hereabouts seemed to have Alpine names, so that you might believe that you were in Switzerland or Austria and that round the next bluff you would bump into a fairy castle, all spindly turrets and waving triangular pennants. And, hiding somewhere in the dungeon, an unimaginably aged witch, and up at the top of a windowless tower, a golden-haired sleeping princess. Or, in his case, a raven-haired, very wide-awake doctor. But though sometimes strange and unexpected, life most definitely was not a fairy tale. Whatever these episodes might have been, when he went back home there would still be Susan's presence hovering around the house, the river, the hills that were like mere bumps in the road compared with the magnificent and terrifying mountains up here in Baltistan. From time to time her smell and the memory of the way she had died would return to haunt him, and even if he emigrated to some

602

anonymous English metropolis, Susan's dark epic would go with him. You can't just efface the dead. Perhaps 'haunt' was the wrong word. It was more that Susan's being, and the end by which it had been defined, had become a part of him. He knew that even on his deathbed the wound would remain; it was not something that his physician-lover, his alchemical lady of the river, could ever heal. He could feel it now as he walked alongside Zuleikha, the woman with whom he seemed to have become almost symbiotic, as though she was the bone and he the sinew. And yet, even as her breath caught in the thin air which he had just exhaled, Alexander knew that in his very essence he would never stop loving Susan, would never stop feeling guilty that gradually over the years with his selfish indifference he had destroyed that love. And it occurred to him that what he was going through now with Zuleikha, with enough effort on his part, he and Susan might have... But then the hypothetical too was a cop-out, an evasion as subtle as the way in which the sunlight played upon the flowers of the meadow.

Then they left the valley and once again entered a desolate place where the trees were lightning-struck and where dust eddied and swirled around their ankles and coated their clothes with a granular patina. There were more of the engraved dun-coloured boulders here, and from time to time they made out isolated conical shapes projecting upwards approximately ten or twenty feet from the tops of what at first glance had seemed to be just more rocks. Cut into the surfaces of some of the boulders were images of deer, ibexes, birds, horses and strange chimaerae possessing the heads of humans and the bodies of goats. Suddenly, Zuleikha thought she saw something move behind one of the chortens. She'd heard of bears and of snow-leopards and yeti, all of whom were supposed to be very elusive, and she hoped that this was true. But then the movement ceased and she attributed it to optics.

They were passing along the summit of a narrow gorge. Hundreds of feet below the path a silver river wound its way through solid gneiss, while above, the shape of a bird sailed across the sun's face. There was no breeze and the path was so narrow that they had to walk in single file – Zulfikar in the van, then Alexander, and finally Zuleikha, bringing up the rear. It wasn't a position she relished. It was always the person at the back that got picked off. But then this was not Afghanistan and she was not a British soldier circa 1839, 1878, 1919 or 2001. There were no hostile tribesmen hereabouts. Just adventurers with furrowed brows and purposeful eyes. Not that she'd seen any of these on this journey. They seemed to have wandered far from any beaten tracks, far from the routes that led up to the big glaciers with Germanic-sounding names. She thought she made out a sound. While the others went on, she paused in order to be able to listen more carefully. But there was nothing. The bird, or whatever it had been, had disappeared. The sun was warm on her face and she closed her eyes.

There it was again. It had sounded like a single blast from a trumpet, but surely, she thought, it must be some sort of bird. An eagle, perhaps, or one of those black-winged crows which live at high altitude and which she'd seen once in the Alps, circling around a white peak some ten thousand feet up. But they were higher than that now. They were maybe closer to twelve, fifteen thousand feet above sea-level. Beyond eighteen thousand you would need oxygen. Some of these mountains went up to above twenty-five thousand feet. No-one lived and nothing grew above this height. From there to heaven was desert. The enormity of the terrain disconcerted her. Over the last few days she'd thought that she'd grown used to these hulking perceptual distortions. But the sudden clarity was giddying. Perhaps she was beginning to hallucinate. Altitude sickness, cerebral oedema, waterlogging of the brain. She glanced around and began to make out people's faces in the rock, their features punching out like American presidents from the greyish-brown stone. A quick intake of breath.

'Archie?' she said, quietly.

She blinked, hard, and the image was gone. Fuck sake. It wasn't cold, yet within her brightly-coloured synthetic gear she shuddered. Her companions had vanished around a bend. She could no longer hear their footfalls. With an incipient sense of panic, she hurried on.

They now seemed to be in a high valley of chortens, boulders, mani walls set at knee-height and red and yellow prayer flags. Some of the chortens had had eyes painted on their walls, while the flags seemed either very old or else badly weathered. There was more of the stone script which, it was now obvious, was sometimes

Greek, sometimes Chinese or Tibetan, and in other places more like an archaic version of Sanskrit. There were no trees, no bushes, no vegetation of any sort. Zuleikha spun round.

'What is this place?' she asked Zulfikar.

He seemed as puzzled as they.

'I've never been up here before. In this direction, I've never been past the big grazing meadows. It's not on the usual trails. Even hyags and hyaqmos – I mean yaks – don't come to these places. I don't know...'

Alexander and Zuleikha exchanged a glance. They had assumed that Zulfikar knew this territory like the back of his hand, but obviously the land was larger and more complex than they had realised. They rested on a trio of small boulders.

Alex spread out the map on a rock, then he took out the stone and held it up. He circled anticlockwise slowly, twice. She almost laughed out loud. *Sir Alexander Wolfe, the Explorer and British Resident of the Lands of the Bulti and Eastern Dards.* He's nuts, she thought. My Alex. He's finally lost it. The seizures have done his brain in and now he is hallucinating – or, at least, is delusional. Then she heard the trumpet sound again.

'Did you hear that?' she asked, urgently.

But before they could answer, a figure appeared from behind the largest of the shrines. He was emaciated and was covered from neck to ankles in what looked like a green cloak fastened at the waist. From what she could see, he had a long beard that had acquired the same colour as the rocks. He was hurrying towards them – not running as such, but scurrying, and for a moment Zuleikha thought that he was using all four limbs and that he had a tail which curled upwards; but as he came closer she realised that the 'tail' was in fact a short metal trumpet, slung loosely over his lower back. Alex quickly put away both map and stone.

When the man came to a halt, Zuleikha realised that he was completely naked. The muscles sleeked close to the lines of his bones and there was not a single millimetre of fat on his body. He stood about five feet tall, but his posture was flexed, and so she reckoned that his true height must be nearer five-five. The green that she had mistaken for a cloak was moss, and it grew on every part of his skin except for his palms, soles and lips, and became more dense over his genitalia. His integument was thick and wrinkled like zo leather, yet there were neither the paps nor hanging folds which she might have expected in a man of his age. His beard reached down to the deep pit of his navel; it had been this large bulbous umbilicus which, earlier and from a distance, she had mistaken for a belt. His penis hung long and loose, the foreskin intact, and behind it his scrotal sac bulged like that of a goat. It was as though his physical being had been reduced to the most minimal shape compatible with continued life. Though it was clear that he could not have had a bath for years, he smelled not of excreta as she might have expected, but rather of grass, trees, berries and fruit. His eyes were bright blue marbles which darted from side to side as he inspected each of them in turn. From behind him there protruded the battered silver horn of a rkang-dung, an instrument which he carried strapped over his left shoulder. The strap was made of twine. Beneath the moss, the dirt, the physique, it was clear to Zuleikha that this was a white man.

When he opened his mouth, his teeth, all of which remained intact, were long and feral. He said something, but none of the party understood. His voice was grating, low-pitched, as though he'd not used it to communicate with other human beings, for decades. It was as though she was listening to a record being played backwards very slowly, so that the phonemes sounded like speech, yet were consistently nonsensical. He said some more, but when their lack of comprehension became clear to him, he beckoned to them and began to move back in the direction he had come from. She thought that he might be one of those psychotics who lived alone in these high places, or perhaps that he was a xi'anren who had wandered over the border from the plain of Tibet. In which case, she thought, he was immortal.

The old man was moving too quickly even for Zulfikar. He led them over boulders, through canyons and along dried-up riverbeds, and all the while the tattered flags and symmetrical chortens punctuated the landscape as though, instead of words, the old man was using these stone shrines with their forgotten scripts as a means of communication. As she followed him, Zuleikha saw that his anus was large and red like that of a monkey, and indeed that this was another place where no moss had grown. Zulfikar looked as though he was having a bad dream. In an instant he had gone from being their cool confidant artist and local guide to being completely at sea. Perhaps he too was wondering whether they were all having some kind of weird collective hallucination, but on the other hand, perhaps he was deeply suspicious of this green gora, lest he too be a spy. Perhaps, she thought, this is what happens to climbers, trekkers, hippies who get lost along the way. They meet this monkey-man and are led forever off the beaten track.

The scent of flowers had grown far stronger the longer they spent in the old man's presence, and now Zuleikha realised that it was the same scent she had experienced in the mine-shaft in Sicily, the church vault in Argyll, the pergola and studio in Lincolnshire and in Petrus Labokla's cist. Those delicate white flowers. Gelsomino, chambeyli, jasmine. The only sound was that of their own breathing and the fitful, yet rhythmic, fluttering of the prayer-flags. From time to time, as they walked, this almost eerie peace would be broken abruptly by the noise of a rushing stream. The old guy seemed to feel neither the coldness of the water nor the hardness of the rock. He moved as though he were a part of the earth, moving over itself, and she wondered whether in fact he had been following them ever since they'd left the fields around Khaplu village. The soles of his feet resembled thick goat's hide, and as he clambered over rocks and bluffs his rkang-dung bounced against his buttocks and spine. While at first Alex had thought it to be metal, now it looked more like bone, buffed so that it gleamed like silver. Perhaps he had used his moss-covered skin for the purpose.

Alex had heard of saadhus living in the plains of India who would retreat to caves where they would sit for years, growing wisdom in their minds and grass on their bodies; but up here in the villages of these northern mountains, where during the winter the temperature dipped to minus twenty-five degrees Celsius and where even the redakhmo, hyaqmo and zomo were brought indoors, here, surely, it was impossible. And where was he taking them? Alex had not had a chance to consult either stone or map since the saadhu had appeared. They moved through several valleys and then began to climb an enormous scree at the top of which sat a row of oddly shaped grey and black boulders which resembled great perching birds. Doves and crows. Climbing up the scree was made much more difficult by the pebbles which kept slipping underneath their boots so that it was almost like walking up a stone waterfall. The old man, who had had no such difficulty, disappeared over the top.

When finally they reached the ridge they realised that the boulders were actually standing stones, set in an elliptical arrangement as though to catch the rays of the sun as it rose and set. The three of them paused for breath. What they saw from the summit of the scree took their remaining breath away, for on the other side was a broad green valley filled with orchards and meadows and dotted with shrines of various sorts. Some were stone pyramids coloured red, black and white, while others were more like the chortens and stupas which they had seen earlier. A narrow river emerged from the mountain at the far side of the valley, wound its way through the grass and around the shrines, and then vanished beneath the flank of the opposite ri. Both mountains gleamed brilliant white – not from snow, but simply from the reflection of the light, and Zuleikha was glad that she had worn sunglasses. In the middle of the valley was a dark blue lake whose surface was so still that it resembled very fine porcelain. On the island at the centre of the lake stood a large complex of whitewashed buildings. Far in the distance they made out the man's form as he crossed an arched bridge and made his way towards this central structure. There was just a hint of juniper in the air.

As they drew closer, the broken rock and shale gave way to soil which at first was hard, but which grew softer as they progressed. They passed through a meadow, more fertile than any they had yet encountered, and this was followed by an orchard of tamarisks and mother-willows, of walnut, peach and apricot trees, and then a garden of wild rose bushes whose flowers were black and whose thorns were as long as Greek swords. Zuleikha thought it strange that roses should be able to grow at this altitude, though the valley did seem very sheltered compared to the others through which they had passed. Lying hidden among the big glaciers, she thought, this is the land of roses. Yes, it's perfectly logical, just as history, the army, the earthquakes are all perfectly logical. The sun was beginning to dip and she began to worry that they might need to spend the night out here – wherever 'here' was. They had brought along only minimal camping equipment, and although it was mid-summer she knew that at night in the mountains the temperature would drop precipitously. Each of the gardens was bounded by a low stone wall to which had been attached pennants and what looked like votive offerings. The surrounding meadows were unoccupied, save for a white goat which oddly had climbed halfway up a willow tree, and a large hyag which had long sharp horns and which swung its head towards them as they approached – but then grew bored with watching their slow progress and resumed chewing the cud.

They too crossed the bridge, and as they did so Zuleikha gazed down into the waters of the lake. She had thought that the view from the top of the scree had been deceptive, that really the surface of the lake would not be quite as still as it had appeared. Yet here, in the middle of this high valley in the Karakorum, the waters really were unmoving – so much so that at times as she gazed, she wondered whether in fact she was looking not at mountain water, but at ice or silk. It was not transparent, but translucent, so that she was able to ascertain neither its depth nor what life, if any, might dwell within its substance.

The saadhu disappeared through a gate set in a stone arch. At the centre of the arch had been affixed the dried head of a horned goat. As they passed through, Zuleikha saw that the frame of the gate was made of a white stone quite different from any she had seen elsewhere in Baltistan, and that at its apex the stone curved upwards in the Tibetan style. Around both lintel and jamb had been carved pictures of various kinds, calligraphies in Arabic, Persian, Urdu and Greek and, once again, also in the cursive characters of Aiggy. Zulfikar whispered to them that at the very top was the number 786, the figure that preceded all Muslim holy verses and incantations, and they saw that above this number was a stone dome topped by a tapering spike. The gate swung loosely on its hinges and pieces of coloured material had been tied to its grilles and some of these had had messages written on them.

'It's a shrine,' said Zulfikar. 'I didn't know about this. I've never heard of it.'

Alex was poring over the chart.

'After a while, all the contours begin to look the same. We're here ... somewhere,' he said, and he circled his finger over a large swathe of territory. He took out the stone but its light seemed to have faded. Exasperated, he announced, 'We've lost the trail.'

'Oh fucking great,' Zuleikha exclaimed. 'So now we're following this nutcase into a ruin and we don't know where we are, nor how to get back. Perhaps we should ask him, though the chances are he won't understand us and we won't understand him. The blind leading the blind.'

'He's not blind,' Zulfikar said, quietly.

'It's just a saying,' she snapped back.

'I know it's a saying,' Zulfikar replied. 'What I'm saying is, I think he knows where he's going. I think he's lived here a while.'

'Who is he?' asked Alex, putting away the map and stone.

'He looks like a white man,' said Zuleikha.

'It's hard to know,' Zulfikar explained. 'The people up here are a mixture, you know: Dards, Mons, Tibetans, Persians, Greeks, everyone who ruled, fought, traded or passed by left their seed. He could even be Russian.'

'Russian?' Zuleikha exclaimed.

'Yes, why?'

She exchanged glances with Alex and then shrugged.

'Nothing. I was just surprised. It's not what you expect, is it?'

'Maybe he's a soldier from the Afghan War of the 1980s,' Alex ventured.

'He's too old,' she replied. 'How does he live? I mean, he's stark naked, for fuck sake.'

Zulfikar blushed and Alexander made to enter the courtyard.

Again they had lost sight of the old man, but the moment they entered the complex a loud note, something like the sound made by an Alpine horn, echoed across the valley. The note was so deep that the whole valley floor seemed to tremble, and for a moment Alex wondered whether it was one of those earth tremors that had plagued the entire region of Jammu, Kashmir, Hunza and Ladakh ever since the devastating earthquake of some years earlier. The courtyard was open to the sky, which now had turned a livid blue, the sun having dipped behind the sloping roof of the surrounding buildings. The ends of each of the roofs turned upwards and formed a point, again very much in the Tibetan manner, and yet this was clearly a Muslim shrine, with arabesques carved into the walls and into the white fountain that stood at the centre of the courtyard. No water emerged from the stone spouts, and the edifice was coated in a fine moss of the same sort that had covered the skin of the hermit.

Again the horn blew, and then a third time, and each time its vibration seemed to grow more powerful so that even after the actual sound had died away, they felt as though the energy emanating from the instrument continued to flow outwards from the main building, out over the high stone walls and the carved iron gate and on across the wild garden, the orchard, the meadow and up over the scree, the boulder-strewn wastelands, the Greek and Tibetan inscriptions, the summer pastures of the goats and zos and down into the marcher lands and the irrigated terraced fields and low mud houses of Khaplu itself.

There were a number of outhouses built right up against the walls, and two cupolas that were set equidistant from each other and from the entrance to the main building. The entire surface of white stone and dark brown wood was covered in what looked to Alexander like a continuous story, perhaps an epic of some sort, or else religious scenes from the lives of the twenty-seven prophets. There seemed to be knights on horseback, and dragons, lions and strange chimaerae, as well as the more familiar flora and fauna he had come to expect in mosques and palaces. Yet this place did not seem like a typical mosque or palace. Apart from the figurative imagery there was the Tibetan ambience, though with the flags here less tattered than in the open valleys, yet he had spotted some other buildings scattered around this part of Baltistan that had seemed syncretic: with Persianate, Mughal and Turkish styles merging, through the local materials, with Mahayana Buddhist architecture. As they entered, they passed a fifteen foot-high wooden door – also covered in carvings – which they assumed must have been eased open by the saadhu.

They entered an enormous hall which at first looked to be more or less square, but which, as their eyes became accustomed to the dim light spread by a number of silver butter lamps, they saw was actually polygonal. An over-arching scent of burning juniper issued from the incense burners dotted around the chamber. The only other light came from small windows in the ceiling. Although the basic fabric had been carved from the same white stone as the rest of the sanctuary, much of the interior structure consisted of wooden beams painted with yet more of the scenes from whatever epic had dominated the courtyard. Here, however, the pictures were like miniatures and the art was cursive rather than figurative, though as she peered into the murkier corners of the chamber, Zuleikha thought that the letters seemed to form a knot which, when gazed at for long enough, might come eventually to resemble a face. There was one in particular which seemed to recur throughout the complex: that of a man whose visage was long, pale and almost Byzantine, though the features were arranged in a different style. The man was wearing a white gown that reached to his ankles, and on his head there was a plumed cap from which extended several flaps. The face seemed to recur a thousand times, sometimes overtly as a portrait and sometimes half-hidden in letters, symbols and orange-coloured flowers, so that when she stared at him it was difficult to be sure he was really there. He seemed familiar, somehow. But then, she thought, you can do that with a simple crack in a wall, or a fly on a windowpane, or a cloud against the moon. Like Petrus Labokla, you could conjure up anything out of anything. With enough knowledge and practice, you might even be able to raise the dead.

She realised that the others had moved away and that the three of them seemed to be exploring the chamber separately. She wondered where the old guy had disappeared to, yet still, beneath the strong tug of juniper smoke, she found that she was able to detect a hint of the more delicate, almost subliminal scent of jasmine.

There was a small rectangular area set at the far end of the hall. The walls were covered with paintings that had been executed on cloth and each of the paintings took the form of a series of interlocking circles, or ellipses – blue, red, green and white, one for each wall. Each of the circles was occupied by a single figure dressed in ancient Sassanian clothes, and each was engaged in a different activity: one was dancing, another singing, a third making chiromantic gestures. Some of the figures were male, others female and one looked indeterminate. The woman's face in particular attracted Alexander – not really in a sexual sense, though she was captivating, her eyes glinted at him and her hair fell in curls across her forehead and temples. She had on one of those hunting caps beloved of the Ilkhans and her hands were pale, the fingers slim, clearly defined in space. He glanced at Zuleikha and then realised that the woman on the wall resembled his lover. How strange, he thought. But then he figured that to men, all new lovers looked like Botticelli's Venus. Now here he was in central Asia amidst a mélange of cultures and peoples, and so it wouldn't be surprising if some of the images of their deities or angels or demons might resemble Zuleikha Chashm Framareza MacBeth. The outer loops were also different from one another and consisted of multiple circular niches, each one occupied by a smaller figure bearing vague similarities to that of the large central portrait. The orbits further out on the wheel were decorated with incense, lamps, flowers and mounds of what looked like powder or spice. In between these giant hangings, which reminded Alexander of Mediaeval European tapestries, were inscribed words in again that mixture of scripts, some resembling Persian or Arabic, others closer to a kind of cursive Chinese or what he imagined Mongolian might be like.

Much of the central portion of the floor was covered in a large red and yellow woollen carpet with variegated images of the doubled gardens and rivers of Paradise. This carpet incorporated elements of Chinese, Persian and Turkish art in a tightly-woven and structurally unified image which seemed almost to have grown from the stone flags themselves. And now they saw that the carpet had been woven in accordance with the architecture. The roof consisted of several sections, each successively higher than the last, so that the whole had a stepped progression, each section overlapping and mounting the next, right up towards the highest, most diminutive of the roofs which sat at the centre, directly above the carpet. As their eyes accommodated to the murk, they began to notice more and more of the ornamentation, yet the sputtering light cast by the lamps caused the shadows to lengthen fitfully. It felt as though they were being assessed by the spirits of the place.

Then the hermit reappeared, and now he was clothed in a

saffron gown – not like that of a Buddhist monk, but more akin to the apparel Zuleikha had seen worn by the man in the images. It was more like an outer garment, a gown, a chugha or a serge-lined chu-pa. Zulfikar shouted to them to gather close to the building's sacred eye, its mihrab, a facsimile of the modulating angkh of the mother of Hazrat Jesus, through which the faithful directed their prayers towards Mecca. And surrounding it was the Quranic verse relating to Bibi Maryam and her guardian, Hazrat Zakariya, the verse that induced one to sing the song of Gabriel's wing from which all songs derive, to close one's eyes and fly.

The hermit was standing behind a low table on which were several wooden beakers that resembled beer pots. When they went up closer they saw that the beakers were filled with a liquid whose colour, in the subdued light, seemed indeterminate. The hermit said something completely unintelligible.

'I don't know what he's saying,' whispered Zulfikar. 'It's not Balti, Ladakhi, Burushaski or Central Tibetan. I don't recognise it at all. I think maybe he's mad.'

But then the old man indicated to them that they should drink from the beakers.

'What should we do?' asked Alex.

'One doesn't want to be rude, if it's expected,' Zuleikha enjoined. She looked to Zulfikar for guidance. 'Besides,' she went on, 'I don't think it's water.'

Zulfikar nodded slowly, though he really didn't seem any more certain than they of what he was doing. He was out of his depth. They all were. Perhaps they had been ever since that first morning by the Clyde. Or perhaps even earlier, since the day in the Barras when Alex had been given the lute, or else the first time Zuleikha had met Archie. He was part of this, she was sure, though she didn't know how.

'But he's not drinking,' whispered Alex, nodding towards the hermit.

'He looks like he's drunk enough already,' she joked.

Tentatively, she sipped at the liquid and found it to be not unpleasant – a little bitter, perhaps, in the aftertaste, but essentially its provenance seemed largely that of aniseed and alcohol. And she saw now that it was colourless. Yes, she thought, it was definitely bitter and reminded her a little of leeks which were either unripe or else which hadn't been properly cooked.

It took them several minutes to completely empty the beakers, and then the hermit led them behind the mihrab, through a doorway and down a narrow corridor. This can't be a working mosque, Zuleikha thought: not with the alcohol. Then she deduced that each of them was following the hermit down a separate corridor, so that either he had managed somehow to fracture himself into three, or else all along there had been more than one old man in the complex. Oh fuck, this is too weird, she thought, and she realised that she had begun to giggle like a schoolgirl. Yet the old guy didn't seem to notice. Perhaps he's deaf, she thought, and this made her giggle more uncontrollably than ever. The only light came from porcelain oil-lamps placed in niches that had been carved at regular intervals into the rock face. Not every niche was filled with a lamp, and every so often Zuleikha would make out the shape of a bird, a partridge, and these bird-sculptures had been so skilfully carved that they seemed real.

They entered a small room with a low silver roof whose walls were draped in green, and at the centre of which was a long stone casket raised on a dais. The atmospheres in all of these subterranean places possessed similar qualities: the mixtures of smells, the echo, the disconcerting sense they conjured of time merging into itself and losing its linearity, and somehow of the incipience of music – and yet here, in this innermost chamber of the khanqah, the dominant scent was that of apricot oil.

The twelve round stones that formed the base of the cist bore an old gold hue, while the casket itself was a dull silver, inlaid with sandalwood and divided into sections by pillars of a lighter gold. Beneath each of the stones was a sculpted aureate vulture with opened wings and the bodies of these birds were hollow and had been filled with spikenard and ambergris. The cist was hung with scarlet cloth studded with seed pearls and had been pulled open by means of gold and silver chains.

The hermit motioned to her to lie in the casket. She stepped onto the dais and peered over the edge. It was just bare stone, the same white rock from which everything here seemed to have been hewn. It was some twelve feet long by eight feet wide, and

615

its interior had been fashioned from sandalwood. The khanqah seemed to have been carved out of a seam of the mountain rather than constructed independently as a free-standing structure, and indeed, it seemed now that they were no longer in a mosque or temple at all, but at the heart of the mountain itself. She glanced up at the hermit, who was standing right over her. Still he smelled of juniper smoke and jasmine, and now she realised that even though his mouth remained closed, a low hypnotic hum seemed to be emanating from him. She didn't fear him; his cold blue eyes now didn't dart about as they had when she had first encountered them, but remained perfectly focused on hers. They were the same colour as the mountain lake which surrounded this place, the colour of the apex of the sky. She climbed into the stone casket and lay down. She had expected it to be rough and cold, yet as she eased down her back and head she discovered that the stone was soft like silk, and that it was slightly warm as though from the effect of some subterranean hot spring. She saw that directly above her was suspended a large drum. She closed her eyes, but though her head felt light with the chhaang, she was not in the slightest bit sleepy. She was aware of the hermit around her and of the air in the room and of the circular hole in the ceiling just above her head through which no daylight issued but merely a deep darkness and the heavy scent of sandalwood. And through the stone and wood, through the still air of the chamber, she heard the sound of her own name, echoing, over and over again: Zaliqa, Zaliqa, Zaliqa...

Zulfikar Ali Lobsang followed the hermit out to the edge of the lake where, in a place he hadn't noticed before, a small white boat was moored. They embarked and, with no visible means of propulsion, the boat began to move. When Zulfikar gazed into the waters of the lake he made out the silver form of an enormous sang sang nia which seemed to follow the craft for a time, but then the fish disappeared as it dived into deeper waters. Soon the boat had left the lake altogether and entered the river which they had crossed earlier. Dusk now was upon the valley and Zulfikar watched the emergence of first the stars and then a sliver of silver moon. Lzaguay lzaut.

He scooped some water into his palm and brought it to his lips. It was cool and fragrant. He wondered whether this might be the Dgihun Darya, the Oxus, the Jayhoun, which was said to have as its source an ice cave, and which had been named as one of the four rivers of paradise. But that lay further to the west, did it not? Who knows, he thought; so many rivers have their sources here amongst the glaciers. Throughout the voyage the hermit said not one word, though the same low hum seemed to come from his throat that Zulfikar had noticed the moment he had set eyes upon him, way back in the Valley of Chortens. He wished he had told the others about this, but now it was too late and the ship was moving more quickly downriver – or was it upriver? He had noticed that the waves seemed to be travelling in reverse. It was as though as they journeyed without a sail up the mountainside; they were riding atop a wall of water, though there could not possibly have been one this far upstream. And then the boat entered a narrow defile formed by cleft rocks and they were in complete darkness. They had entered the mountain.

Zulfikar was blinded painfully as they emerged from the far side of the ri into a world of snow, ice and a night sky that was like black glass. Gradually the pain subsided and, as he peeked through his fingers at the enormity of the glacier-flow, he saw that the boat had slowed and then ground to a halt. This was where the river began; this was the point at which the ice burst forth from the mouth of the glacier and began its long journey to the sea. Perhaps it was the Indus, the Sengge Chu, which turned green as it entered Baltiyul; or perhaps it was the Sarasvati, the great vanished river of myth and fable. And yet once this entire area had been flat and had lain deep under the ocean and over millions of years its creatures had turned to stone. This was the place from where both gods and demons had emerged. This was the source. All his life, growing up in his village that was named after the moon, on winter nights, through the long tongues of women, Zulfikar had learned of this place.

Winter was the season when the characters in the stories emerged from the rock and ice and trod the earth like ghosts, draey, djinns. Lha Kesar, Rgyelpo Gesar, Emperor of Gling, the great invisible shape-changer whose mother was the Queen of

Heaven and whose wayward, beautiful, broken grain of a wife was a song of the earth, whose palace was made of sulphurous wax, whose life, steeped in saffron juice, ran to ten thousand pages and whose story from beginning to end could not have been recited even once during the span of a single human being's life. The Dark Tara of Nepal and the White Tara of Chiin. Shakti. The tongues of the women reached down deep into the earth's belly and drew out strange and magical words, songs from the rock, the tales of the Old Religion, and this was the music which underpinned all other musics and which had assumed the form of a bird and then one bird had become thousands, so that over the centuries there had emerged countless different versions of truth.

Alexander followed the hermit up a windowless spiral staircase which seemed to go on forever, so that he had to stop on several occasions (though once again, the old man didn't seem to have this need) and finally, by the time he reached the top, not only was he light-headed and completely whacked, but he saw that the hermit had already gone over to the edge of the platform which sat atop the tower. As Alex moved towards him, he glanced over the edge of the giddyingly low wall. And what he saw made his light-headedness even worse. They were not at the top of a tower at all, but were standing on the white stone platform of what appeared to be a shrine hewn from the sheer side of a mountain, so that when he looked out over the wall's edge Alexander saw the mountainside fall away vertically beneath him. The sky was no longer a uniform blue but had become interspersed with clouds, while closer to hand mist curled like a silk cloak over the mountainside. Tied to posts around the shrine were more of the ubiquitous red and yellow flags, and growing up through the centre in a manner which made it seem as though it had actually split apart the rock, was the trunk of an enormous tree which was so tall that its top seemed lost in the mist. When he peered again over the edge, Alex saw, stretched out below him the white walls of the gompa, one tier upon the next, with tiny rectangular windows cut into the sides. Again he had the feeling that the entire complex – temple, mosque, gompa – had been raised from the rock of the mountain. So this was what it was like on the other side of the mountain, he thought: nothing but a great gulf of fog and cloud. And yet here in this white shrine, cleanly cut from the mountain's flank, and in the tiered vista of the temple of the pure and real, there was a peacefulness, a lack of ornamentation, a simplicity that appealed to him, that appealed to the Scot in him.

The hermit was sitting with his back to the trunk and a low hum seemed to be coming from either the tree or the man – Alex was unable to tell which. The hermit was staring at the sky, and his eyes were glazed over. He seemed to be breathing inordinately deeply, yet he wasn't out of breath. Quite the opposite: his chest rose and fell so slowly that every inhalation seemed to be a terminal one. By the side of the hermit lay a human thigh-bone that had been fashioned into a horn. Alexander went over to the tree and removed his rucksack and lute-case. He sat on the stone floor in the same manner as the hermit, his legs splayed out before him and his back rubbing against the tree's rough bark. It was not cold, even though, with the sun vanished behind clouds and mist and with the onrushing of night, it ought to have been. Metrical psalms. That was what he was hearing. The Outer Hebridean psalms of Hazrat Daoud, the Great Songs, led in the old Hebraic manner by precentors, Masters of the Sang Schule who held within their ear a crystalline expertise in line ornamentation and grace, and whose bodies were reincarnations of the tiompain, the old Gaelic lute, their throats of the carnyx horn. And through these songs of the stone, A' Ghàidhealtachd connected with the Ethiopic, the Coptic, the beginning.

Through the wavering tonal figure of the basal hum there came trochees, dactyls and rhyme. And he was hearing a voice, and words which he did not understand but whose significance, for him, reached beyond their meaning to something deeper, or perhaps higher. The Zabur, the lost chironomical Book of David, was playing in lamentation, joy and triumph through his body. Then he realised that the music was coming from his fingers and that he had taken out his lute, which now had assumed the appearance of a simple ektara, an instrument with only a single string, and that he had had no need to tune up, polish anything or position himself, since the gut-string, the wood and his flesh had become as one and now drew their measure from the air, the sky, the stone

619

and the holm oak tree.

Alex played as he had never played before. On that single string he found resonances, overtones, undertones, sounds that lay beyond the human range, notes that were like dwarf-women, notes which lay hidden within other notes. And his bones danced in the shape of the dragon and the amban and the letters Z, R, R, A, so that he became the bard, Zarra, daughter of Natshab Ali of Sheh because although as a young girl, as a middle daughter, she had wandered far and wide and had sung for the adventurous imperialists who had seemed to glut the fag-end of the nineteenth century, yet over a century later, here in the khanqah, in the clay and dust of a chorten, she lived on in form, lithe, young and beauteous. Her visage was yet protected from the fire of the sun of the high places by a tasteful modicum of goat's horn powder, her voice was as clear as those of the Crystal Monastery, and her song was an gling-glu epic.

Chapter Thirty-Four

In the disused chapel by the shore of the loch, Archibald Idris McPherson was dancing the dance of the natchnaywalis. The coordinates of his being were replicating those of devadasis and round dancers, of the Cailleach Bheur, the old veiled woman of winter, and of Brigid, the whore of spring. He was clothed in full Mughal-style costume; in his hair was a piece of metal shaped like an old half-crown, and through his nose was a ring, while his face was covered in make-up so thick that it was like a mask. His body hair had all been plucked, his toenails painted bright red, and around him spun his sahelia, his female bosom friends, his colleagues in the way of the night with, at their centre, an invisible unmarked radif, a hole, a punctum, the entrance to a well, which repeated through the music, minute on minute, hour upon hour.

For, during the night, like beasts they had emerged from the loch, each one an Etive, and had encircled and then entered the auld ruined kirk, the kharabat, intoning in ethereal song the beautiful words of *Lepo Kesar*, the Epic of Kesar, the Tale of the King. His partner in dance was the Whore, the blue-faced woman who many years earlier he had almost strangled and who had gravitated to this shore of hurmuzd, this loch ruled by the planet Jupiter, Zeus, kesar of the forces of lust, of the animal soul. Now he learned from her the steps of the mujra, the paces of the blue women, the cailleachan, those mothers, sisters, daughters of the little sun, those fallen angels who had been bought and sold like cattle or swine, the lovers who had been killed without ceremony and bricked up beneath palaces, the lovers who had been burned in acid or buried by murmuring priests in unconsecrated ground or else thrown into rivers, to swell and rot and provide nourishment for bhoothes, ghouls and wild boar. The music of the blue women was the music of the mountains, of the Minch, of the Sciacca. It was the psalm of the empty mohalla, the anthem of the great fissure between the worlds, its notes drawn from a hidden fascicle of the Rowallan Manuscript, a lost madrigal of Rujari d'Alì and his disciples, its soul leached from the songs they sang in the morphia of male post-coital bliss, its rhythm traced from the rocks of Baltistan, from the flight of a thousand green-tipped arrows loosed one summer's morning from a cliffside gompa.

Like newly fired rocks from Mongibello, the music erupted in silver and gold from the heart of the khanqah, from a place hidden deep in the mountain, from the cave where perhaps, long before, Milinda the King-turned-Seeker had found shelter, become naked and gained insight into his journey, and around which had been constructed a stathmos, a fortified post-house, a simple cuboid with tiny windows set high in the walls. And this place was the very furthest koinan, a watch station in a web of such stations which had spread eastwards on the way to the Yonu conquest of Chinese Turkestan. And because many of the Yona cities in India took the names of their mothers, so that Tyre, Elymaide, Daedala, Calliope and so on replicated themselves across the swathe of Eurasia and Africa, right down to the borders of Ethiopia, the koinan up here in the mountains of Baltiyul took the name of Panormus.

And then later, as the settlement had grown, gymnasia and theatres had been constructed on the mountainside in a white stone that had been made by crushing the bones of the dead into a fine powder and then mixing this powder with ash and clay. The dead were buried thus in the walls of the houses of the living, and their spirits continued to inhabit the low walls, the deserted lanes, the hilltop shrines. And Milinda's portrait was everywhere, painted in egg-shell and ochre on the walls of caves, carved in gneiss on the outcrops of mountains, and scattered among the chortens of the dancing dead. There he was, with his knowing smile, in an image that was quite unlike any other painting of a Yavana king anywhere from Siracusa in Sikelia to Barigazi on the Gujerati coast to the Menander Mons on the frontier of Burma. An expression that derived perhaps from his discovery of the griffin gold route from Siberia and the trail of the aureate ants of Rajasthan, and then perhaps his good fortune came from the power he held over ants and griffins alike, even though the ants had the skins of leopards and the griffins were made of solid metal that had been washed in the swirling headwaters of the Yenisei River.

In this way, through the music of the ektara, the Cailleach Bheur, Archibald Idris McPherson spiralled through the world of the witnessed and the world of the absent and like the Persian ancestor of the great shaykh, Wang Tai-yu; he surveyed high into the nine heavens and deep into the nine seas.

And now, in the kirk, in anticipation, appreciation and wah-wah, the tamashbeen poured notes upon the silver-white hair of Archie's bewigged scalp and upon his newly blackened body. Yet like a freshly carved statue Archie was young again; his skin felt pliable, his muscles lithe, and both his lungs and his mind were like mouths that had been freed and opened. And he was dancing as he'd never danced before, not in the hangar jive parties with assorted local WAAF, not in the drunken shipyard public houses where the Glasgow whores had congregated in search of welders, panel-beaters and men of the hammer who would shower them with sperm and blue asbestos. He danced as he had never danced in the genteel church charity drives when he had matched palms with Margaret, their entwined silhouettes against the chintz wallpaper as chaste as a prayer and as sleek as the form of a Hurricane swooping along the horizon. A barefoot khuserah dancer with red betel-nut teeth, Archibald Enoch McPherson moved elegantly through unseen ellipses, his skin sweating beneath the arched roof, his body an arc of brass forged from a juggler's hands. It was as though he had become the goddess of the hundred arms, the thousand rivers, the deva who resurrected ruined cities from the deserts of Saca-land, who pulled luminous green snakes from the insides of tree-trunks in the Naga jungles, and who caused to wash up ancient fired-earth surahis from the Arabian Sea, jars in which had been secreted the lost manuscripts and tablets of Asterusia, and with them a horde of hungry ghosts.

Like the red-faced devils of Baltistan, he and the Whore danced all through the night, moving faster and faster upon the stone flags until one by one his companions began to spin as though from the tips of his fingers. And the tamashbeen too no longer were spectators but had been caught up in a web of movement and glitter, a round dance of Baltistan, of Alba, a spider dance of Siqilliya, a dance of swaying hair and unashamed fecundity, a dance of women everywhere, with Archie and the Whore at its centre as though the church were a door and they the capstone. And then they seemed to merge into one. Just as music issued from the hands of the mirasi, the musicians who paid attendance upon the fey-folk, so Archibald's being was re-created through the breath of the dead. And now the zangstung sounded from somewhere so deep it was as though the mountains themselves were singing and the damans pounded and the single string of the tree pulsed its silent music across the world. And so Archie became the Dead and The Dead took the form of a woman.

When the rim of the sun touched the still, far edge of the loch, The Dead donned a veil and spun through the stone walls out of the church, and began to dance across the land, the glens and braes of mid-Argyll, the place where the Scots had planted their first kingdom, there the holly tree, the gorse bushes, the marsh reeds, and there the mountain of darkness whose summit reached into other worlds. And there the hollow where kings had swum and were consecrated through freshly slaughtered horse's blood, and there the broch of the piries, and everywhere she danced her feet created miracles, her fingers spawned animals, buildings, ships, technologies, people.

The Dead journeyed far and wide, dancing through call centres, superconductors and sado-masochistic television programmes and into the heads of the call centre workers which were filled to bursting with the opiate darkness of the TV programmes. She danced deep beneath the earth into the tunnels of disused railway lines, the ghost stations where the time remained fixed at the moment of departure of the last train: Glasgow Botanic Gardens, 5th October 1964. The gaze of the last passenger in the last carriage … the wayward father who ran off to Spain and never came back again, the mother who washed herself away in the swirling soapy waters of the wash-house, the WAAF wife with the laughing eyes who had never known the depths of her lover's darkness, the mother who had held pride and love together in her heart, scion of Afghan and Mughal alike, descendant of the old Jews and Greeks of Khurasan, of Bactria, of the Sindh Darya, of Peshawar, Multan, Kabul, Jalalabad, Taxila, Sialkot, Mathura, Patna, Rajgir.

And as she danced through the hinterlands of Scotland, as she spun music along frequencies which no-one knew how to capture any more, in a rapid succession of shadows which skipped along the surface of the grey stones, she was accompanied by the people on the trains and in the cars, the farmers in their fields, the psychedelic rock musicians whose power chords echoed across the lakes, forests and aerodromes of Lindsey, the WAAF women machine-gunned on the tarmac, the crews who had lifted off into the darkening skies and never returned, the shadows of all the generations of humanity, each one as it passed causing its name to be etched into the stone: Nasrin Zeinab MacBeth, Daniel John MacBeth, Margaret McPherson, Lord William Michael Jacobus de Ruthyn, Laila Sciacca Asunsi, Giuseppe Ayala, Zita Rosalia Zafarano, Petrus Dihdo Labokla, Zulfikar Ali Lobsang, Archibald Enoch McPherson, Susan Wolfe, Alexander Wolfe, Daoud MacBeth, Zuleikha Chashm Framareza MacBeth. For she sowed the gravestones too of those not yet dead; with her painted fingernails she etched their names deep into the white marble, she mixed bone with dust and thrust the stones up through the hard clay skin of the Scottish earth to form a line of chortens along the horizon. Wherever she went she was accompanied by hordes of black and white hogs, sacred pigs and devil swine, herds of beasts gathered up from forgotten cemeteries and hidden rivers, and wherever she went a cool breeze followed, not dank and cold like that of a Scottish winter but fresh, light, invigorating, as though people were drinking whisky through the pores of their skins, as though they were gathering in the liquor from the air. The sacred Dead brought illumination, friendship, hope – above all else, hope – to the living.

From the khanqah of Baltiyul, Zarra, daughter of Natshab Ali of Sheh, her face smeared liberally with red ochre, sang the Epic of the Dead in a perfect voice not of this world. It was the voice of the daughter of the bone, the old woman of the high snows and the grey rocks, the Cailleach Bheur, the veiled one, and as she sang, *Do you want to hear more?* and as the Dead themselves replied, *Yes, yes, tell us more!* and as, sitting against the tree, Alexander played and as, climbing onto the surface of the white glacier, Zulfikar journeyed towards the river's source, lying in the stone cist, the breath of the arhat flowing through her, Zuleikha dreamed that she was on the summit of the mountain. She was sitting on a slightly moist, flat-topped rock amidst a world of snow and ice, looking down on the broad shoulders of the glaciers, of Baltoro, Siachen, Kaberi, and on the sources of all the rivers, of Sindh, Ganga, Brahmaputra, Papineto, Sarasvati, Clyde and she was conversing with the arhat of the khanqah, and though this figure's countenance was veiled from her, Zuleikha could tell from her frame and her bearing that she had the body of a woman. Between them was a small wooden table, octagonal in shape and inlaid with white copper set in a roseate pattern, and on the table was an inkwell, a pen and a blank scroll of paper. There was no breeze and the air was still and cool, and though it was the height of summer, the sun shone with an etiolated springlike quality. Zuleikha gazed up at the sky and saw that there were no clouds. Far below, to her right, she could make out the khanqah, its white crumbling walls built in tiers into the mountainside like the walls of a wedding cake. Perched there on the mountain, it reminded her a little of an old Highland castle: a black fort, a white monastery.

On her left side, at a level some three hundred feet or so below where she sat (though she found that distances here were quite deceptive) there ran the immense sweep of a glacier which seemed to begin from the sky and slowly to roll down to an edge of stone where the ice crumbled finally into a scree the colour of lavender. Nothing grew on the surface of the glacier, there were no trees or houses, no fields or bushes, yet somehow, around two-thirds of the way down, it looked as though the snow had begun to move and for a moment she was alarmed that it might be an avalanche. But then she saw that the snow was simply turning to a thousand burns and that the burns flowed through the ice sands of the glacier until finally they re-emerged further down the mountainside, transformed into waterfalls and rivers. Walking towards the moving glacier was a tiny black figure who paused every so often as though to get its bearings before moving on again at what seemed like an inexorably slow pace. She shuddered. The glacier was a white shroud, wrapped tightly around the mountain.

Zuleikha wheeled around and there, a thousand feet below, was a small promontory circled by a low wall and at the centre of which was a tree. A multicoloured haze of prayer-flags surrounded the shrine and beyond this a ring of black birds glided soundlessly. Even in the context of the sky and the land, the tree seemed enormous, and she felt its roots burrow down deep into the earth, down through the hardest rock and the hottest fire, right down to the white-hot serpentine rivers that swarmed at the earth's centre. And, thinning upwards into invisibility, like the spokes of a giant wheel its branches seemed to reach into the sky, so that in the light breeze it seemed as though not just the tree but the khanqah with its shimmering face of crystal, the valley with its streams and rivers, and indeed the entire landscape itself was slowly spinning. But then she thought that perhaps she was gazing at the tree the wrong way around and that in truth it had grown down from heaven. She made out two figures leaning against its trunk, but she was unable to discern any details. In fact, Zuleikha thought it highly odd that she was able to see anything at all from this height. She turned back to face the figure, who had remained quite still throughout.

'Who are you?' she asked.

The woman took in a deep breath, and it was as though the entire scene, the mountains, rivers, glaciers, shrine, gompa, sun and sky were about to be sucked in and dissolved as though they had been merely a thanka, a painting on cloth.

'I am not one individual, and neither are you,' The Dead replied, and, like the single string on the wood that was being played from somewhere in the distant background, her voice spanned all the audible laryngeal octaves and was simultaneously rumbling as a Russian night song, as haunting as a Scottish lament and as trilling as a Chinese opera.

'Who are those people down there?'

'Don't you know them, Zuleikha?'

'You know my name?'

'I know the names of all the heroes, the sages, the kesars, the fools. I know every blade of grass and every tiny stream that forms from the mouth of a pebble.' The woman looked up towards the sky. 'I know every face of the moon.'

But Zuleikha could see no moon, though indeed she had thought that by now night ought really to have fallen and the stars to have become visible. It was so strange that it was day again – unless she had been wandering for longer than she had thought, unless, as with space, her perception of time also had lost its bearings and no longer held validity.

'In Death, there is no time.'

Zuleikha started. It was as though the woman had read her

thoughts.

'Lamaji, am I…?'

'In the face of nothingness, everything that lives is dead. Every coil of your being knows exactly the moment at which you will die.'

'Do you know when I will die?'

'Only the greatest sufis, saadhus, arhants and prophets know the time and place of their own deaths. And that is the way it should be.'

Zuleikha glanced down at the inkwell, which seemed to be empty.

The woman lifted a sheep's hair calligraphy brush, dipped it into the mouth of the inkwell, carefully laid the tip of the brush on the paper, and began to write.

'There are numerous possible versions of every tale. It is only at the source that tales can be altered.'

'Is this the source?' Zuleikha asked.

But the woman did not reply and simply continued to write. Zuleikha didn't understand the script.

'The words change with every footstep. The dance of life is a knot with no beginning and no end. Yet truly to know the dance, the sequence of the words, is to sing it. Can you hear?'

And once again, Zuleikha listened to the words. They did not seem to be coming from a specific direction; rather, it seemed as though they were emanating from the mountain itself. It was a girl's voice from a long time ago. And as she listened, and as she followed the long cursive lines of the letters and characters which were being drawn by the woman, Zuleikha felt that she was beginning to understand. And these were the tales related to her, in poetry, epic and song, by the Beda girl, Zarra, daughter of Natshab Ali of Sheh as they sat facing each other on the mountaintop.

Zulfikar's Tale

Zulfikar the Noble-Minded found himself wandering among towers of ice. It was broad daylight and there was absolutely no sound. But that was not quite correct. After a time of there being no sound, he realised that all day there had been a single sound, low-pitched and continuous. He was certain that it was not his heartbeat, though at first he had imagined that it might be the music of the glacier, the sounds of the tiny crystals of ice and stone which were in a state of constant slow movement upon the base rock of the earth.

Whereas on the sides of mountains, even up above the snow-line, the whiteout would be punctuated occasionally by rocks covered with green lichen, here on the glacier the lack of life was absolute. Other tour guides would lead intrepid Westerners all over the gung singay, the enormous glaciers of black gravel and white ice, but Zulfikar had been content to stick with historical monuments, old rock inscriptions and semi-manufactured tableaux of peasant life. He had tried to keep the capitalists away from willow trees that grew near springs, from newly threshed wheat replete with talismans and from the fitful sound of whistling peasants. He tried to keep these new invaders away from the heart of the house, from the pillars laced with ripe stalks of corn and the ibex statues that drew moisture and verdure up from the land. For Zulfikar and his people, there was no dividing-line between rock and wheat, between the high pasture and the low, between the human and the non-human. Yet the hunters of Baltistan, who had been plying their subsistence ritual with the ibex for two millennia, now were no longer permitted to hunt, but had to make do with being coolies.

Some summers ago, Zulfikar had gone portering among the junglis, for money but also in the hopes of maybe meeting some cool white trekkers. Even up on the glaciers during the three months of the trekking season the sun had been burning hot, and this strange paradox had seemed to heighten his desire for the luxuriant, smiling bodies of the gorees. But he quickly had discovered that the tourists, travellers and trekkers – for ethical reasons, they liked to differentiate between themselves – once they had arrived in these primitive marginal zones, tended to revert to a single Imperial type. In the redoubt of their gated multiculturalism, these gods of the door expected the porters to exist on roti and chai, to wear plastic shoes and no waterproofs, to sleep on naked ice with one blanket and a crap tarpaulin – pilched from the UNHCR – and to carry, on wooden contraptions strapped to their backs, barrels weighing twenty-five or even thirty-five kilos over ice, rock and bottomless crevasse. And to be paid shit wages! In the villages, he'd seen hideously deformed ex-porters. The Army had properly-designed glacial shelters, so why not the porters? After all, without coolies, there would be no tourism, no mountaineering, no profit and loss, no nothing. Even beasts didn't sleep on bare ice. Welcome to Baltistan, in the twenty-first century! Peace, love and profits!

And what was so different about these two? Nothing, perhaps. They held their fantastical spiritual ideas close to their chests and they treated him well because he had appeared to them as an apparition of the bourgeoisie, an artist. They too were imprisoned in their box of history. He wasn't going to tell them this, but he had heard the hidden tales, the stories, songs and jokes that had been hacked into the granite, of coolies rising up and rebelling against their 'sahibs'. Tales that had never been written down, stories the words of which had never been birthed beneath the iron hammers of the imperial print machine. Deep in the rock, beneath all the detritus of colonialism, there lay the truth. This was the inner land, which Outsiders never saw, heard or smelt. The truth about Outsiders was that whether or not they knew it, they were colonial, racist and violent. Yes, he thought, Baltistanis are no longer the coolies of empire. At least, not in their own minds. On his third day as a porter, when the sirdar had attempted to overload him, Zulfikar had tossed away the wooden contraption and had walked out of the expedition.

There was a purity about these high places that defied the crass individualism of Western civilisation. Assuredly, that was what they came for, the ones who liked to climb as far as they could go: they sought the clarity of elevated spaces, but they didn't seem to realise that they had jettisoned any possibility of such things years ago. They were like water demons: everything they touched turned to slush. Turned to drugs, bullets, money, death. Within a crew-cut radius, five or six armies stood daggers drawn behind the rocks that were carved in the shape of music.

Now here he was, going God-knows-where up this glacier which he didn't recognise. Yet he was not cold, and that surprised him. Beneath the warmth of the midday summer sun, the glacier's bones were ten thousand years old and frozen solid. Gloom leached from the brilliant white, and through his sunglasses the perceptual distortion was becoming so pronounced that he seemed to be confusing one sense with another. He told himself to get himself together; after all, he was from this place, the soil and ice lay deep within his genes and the mountain blood ran fast through his veins. But the beloved was forever elusive. Up here, death and beauty walked hand-in-hand, singing their silent songs and mouthing their eternal music. And if ever you heard those songs, you would know that you were dead. Zulfikar's father's generation had taken up their own fathers' musical instruments and had smashed them and their fearful beauty against the rocks. If you ventured too close to a well where one of these creatures dwelt and if you leaned over the wall, smelled the nectar and milk and gazed into the darkness, the Naginis would bewitch you with their beauty and you would be sucked down into the rock and ice and would be doomed to live for eternity in their world of black fire and snakes. But he had left that behind a long time ago. Scientific rationalism was the way forward; it was the only way to lift these people – his people – out of their subsistence poverty. He thought he saw something move and wondered whether it might be a snow leopard or an ice lion, but then it turned out to be just a large icicle, melting in the noonday sun.

He had been following a melt, which had led him around a corner formed by a rise in the glacier when, quite suddenly, he came up against a wall. It was entirely white and it resembled a waterfall frozen in the middle of its cascade. It was fifty feet high and stretched around as far as he could see and he knew that there was no way he would be able to climb up its slender fibrils of ice. He would have to turn back – but turn back, where? When he looked behind him at the stream, he saw a blue snake glide through its clear waters.

He remembered that they had drunk that strange-tasting liquid and then had begun to follow the hermit down – or had it been up? – a long, dark corridor. He had become separated from the others and had been taken on a voyage through the mountain. And when he had emerged he had been suddenly blinded by this white world, and by the time he had regained his vision, the hermit and his boat had been nowhere to be seen and there had been no sign of an entrance. Everything had been mountain, glacier and sky. Zulfikar had begun to walk, because there had seemed to be nothing else for it. He realised that all this time he had been climbing rather than descending and that had worried him, but he imagined that perhaps the khanqah might have multiple entrances on different levels and that somehow he might be able to locate one of these. So this way was a dead-end. Right. Suddenly, he realised how tired he had become. In spite of his fitness level and his semi-acclimatised blood, there were limits. Because they recognised and respected these limits, unlike the lunatic Westerners who seemed to view every foetid jungle as their own personal delta of Venus, his people had seldom ventured up into the high glaciers. He was about to turn away, to attempt to retrace his steps, when he spotted a blue-coloured goat.

Now there were goats, both sikins and dalmos, males and females, that ventured up beyond the high summer pastures and clambered about the loose shale and scree of the mountainsides which led to the edges of glaciers. But never had he heard of a goat who had traversed the actual surface of one. There was no food up here – at least, no natural food. He and the goat stared at each other for such a long time that Zulfikar began to feel that the only difference between them was that, unlike the goat, he did not possess horns. Then the animal turned around and was gone. It was as though it had simply vanished into the side of the ice. Zulfikar hurried after it, but when he reached the place there was nothing to be seen. Just another wall of white. He thought that perhaps he had begun to hallucinate, that this was the first sign of hypothermia or ice-blindness or brain death. He took out his little silver radio and tried to tune it to ... anywhere. But there was just white noise.

A little further on and to his right, Zulfikar noticed an irregularity in the surface. Nothing more, just a shadow, an area that was slightly less than brilliant white. He ventured towards it and as he drew closer, he saw that it was formed by an ice overhang which made that part of the glacier look like a sculpture. As he passed beneath the overhang, he saw the entrance to a passageway.

Some way down the passageway, suddenly he thought that he heard laughter, and he turned and saw a young woman with turquoise tresses smiling at him. She opened her mouth and began to sing, and then he realised that this was the sound he had been hearing all along, and that the girl was the spirit, the lha-maung of the glacier. She was wearing a white goonmo and tsaynoo, the Balti equivalent of a shalvar kamise, and he saw that her hair was actually red but that through her tresses were scattered turquoise stones shaped like ringlets. In her right hand was a small drum and in her left a spray of white flowers. On her feet were kratpa, soft goatskin shoes. She began a languorous dance, yet her feet seemed to possess no weight so that it appeared as though she was flying, or perhaps gliding. As she danced she sang, and she sang nine songs, and at the end of the ninth, amidst its resounding echo that was as clear as ice, she bent her head as though in acknowledgement of his presence, and he saw that through her thick tresses two small horns protruded from her scalp. Perhaps she was a sky-goat, a khaanami-bia, and perhaps she would take him away, as no doubt she had taken other travellers with her into the mountains of ice. The last three lines of her song continued to fold, echo upon echo, rather like the layering of the land.

> When I, a boy, was still in my fatherland,
> I always had a pair of teapots, like the sun and moon
> Then I, as a boy, went to sleep under a cedar tree

And then he knew that she was indeed a lha-maung, one of those mountain spirits possessed of great beauty who had many names but whose mark was always the same. Suddenly, she lay down on the ice and splayed her legs and he saw that she had not been wearing a shalvar-kamise after all, but rather a zjhindu chun nating, an ancient Balti dress, except that it was white instead of black, and then she exposed herself to the open air and parted the tissues of her vulva, but her vulva was an ice cave which suddenly swelled and grew and seemed to engulf him. Reflexively, he threw his arms over his head and blinked hard several times – and she was gone. It had all happened so quickly that he hadn't had time to be shocked, and now he doubted the veracity of the entire vision.

Further along the passageway, out of the corner of his eye, Zulfikar saw an apricot tree, heavily laden with ripe yellow fruit, growing straight out of the ice. He reached out, plucked one and put it to his lips. It tasted like no pharing he had ever tasted before.

Its flesh was yielding but not yet rotten, sweet yet not sickly, its texture and aroma were exquisite and, as it entered his body, it seemed to warm his flesh. The taste of the fruit made him realise how hungry he was, and he paused for a while and ate half a dozen of the fruits before continuing on his way, newly buoyed by this unexpected and somewhat impossible meal. Yes, he thought, I must be hallucinating, and the fruit which I have just not eaten do not really exist. Yet I feel light as air. Further on still an ice lion roared at him, sending tingling sensations up his spine and causing his hair to stand on end.

After about half an hour (though time here seemed relative) Zulfikar reached an iron door with a loop handle. He turned the handle and the heavy door swung open. He entered a chamber of ice and rock that was as large as the prayer-hall of an enormous mosque. He counted seven walls and each wall was covered with a single giant carving that stretched from the ground to the ceiling, and which must have been made by some very sharp implement that had been inserted deep into the permafrost. There were scenes of horses, musicians, dancers and merchants, and of people carrying long horns and playing barbuds and pibains, and even though the images had been cut from ice and rock, each one seemed almost real and indeed, multicoloured. It was as though Zulfikar was gazing through stained glass windows into the past. This was the history of his own people, of the many peoples who made up the Baltis. He was drawn to one of the scenes – one filled with armies, soldiers, horses, chariots, swords – and tentatively reached out and touched the ice wall. The sensation was unusual, tingling rather than cold, but before he had time to assess it further, the central section of the carving swung away from him so that he almost fell forwards as it opened like a giant door onto another room. In this room there was a man dressed in the robes of the Shagari, the Greeks who had migrated from Bactria to Ladakh during the reign of Dimitra I and who had become Maqpon kings and had ruled right through until the Hindu Dogras had unseated them in the mid-nineteenth century.

The man did not notice him and seemed preoccupied with slowly stirring an enormous wooden milk-churn that was filled almost to overflowing. Zulfikar tried to put his hand through the doorway into the chamber, but found that he could not; that even though there seemed to be nothing between his fingers and the room, the air held some invisible force which barred entry. Yet as he watched, the milk began to curdle and froth and some of it spilled down the sides of the churn and onto the floor. The scene faded and once again Zulfikar beheld the unbroken picture of horses and soldiers – of Lha Kesar and Milinda; of Ali Sher Khan Anchan and Dimitra; of Kalzang the Musalmaan Balti princess who had become the Lady of the White Parasol, an incarnation of the goddess Tara, and to whom a thousand tiny temples had been dedicated; of Iskander and Asoka; of Akbar, Sandracottos, Kanishka and Strabo the Saviour-King, and of Kesar, son of an ibex and saviour of humankind – and all of them were talking through the dance of the hands that was mutually intelligible from Hibernia to Ethiopia, from Sikelia to Palestine, from Hindustan to Chinese Turkestan, the chorea in which the first music had been composed and the first texts written.

Then there was a thanka picture of old men wearing conical hats and elongated silver beards, seated on the summits of mountains, their right hands extended towards the sky and their left inclined towards the earth. In the long cloth Zulfikar thought he recognised the faces of the sufis Syed Ali Hamadani and Shah Syed Muhammad Nurbaksh, as well as that of Dara Shikoh (*Oh, may Lahore always be full of bliss!*) and, along with the mystic prince-who-should-have-been-king, Zulfikar saw the books which he had written: *The Greatest Mystery* and *The Mingling of the Two Oceans*, with their gleaming singing Upanishad pages. In the chamber behind was a rolled-up carpet which looked fat and asymmetrical, and there seemed something not quite right about it, and what that was became suddenly obvious when the carpet quivered and then rose up on four legs and Zulfikar fell back as he realised that this was a live, completely white snow leopard, something he had never seen before. He inhaled sharply as the animal leapt towards him, but thankfully it was unable to penetrate the unseen barrier that lay between them and the big cat fell back to pacing about the chamber, purring softly and continuing to fix him with its green-eyed gaze.

The next door bore a picture of sha'irs and sha'iris sitting on diwans which had been placed against three sides of a room whose walls were covered in soot. Jami was there: Jami, who for the fifth of his *Seven Thrones* had written a version of the *Romance of Yusuf and Zuleikha*; as was Rumi with his massive *Masnavi-I Ma'navi*, and Sheikh Saadi with, fanning out behind him, the vast bustans and gulistans of Khaplu, Ferghana, Kabul and Shiraz. And there too, wearing naatings, the caps of Baltiyul, were Ba Mohib and Hussain Ali Khan; and Zulfikar recognised Farid-ud-din Attar with, circling around his head, thirty birds of various species; and, along with him, Sana'i, Nizami and Yonaka, the last of whom was carrying, in numerous loose sheafs under his arm and in a bag on his back, the unedited transcripts of the conversations held between the Ionian King Milinda of Uttar Pradesh and Nagasena, the Buddhist sage of Pataliputta and disciple of the Yonaka monk Dhammarakkhita. Behind the poets was a thanka scene from the Greek Gujerati city of Yonagadh. And right at the centre of the room, sitting on a small circular stool, was the poet Al-bDe, and beside him was a mountain goat whose skin was blue and the poet's mouth was open as though he was singing to the goat and his song was a skin-jug, a mournful bridal lament. Zulfikar reached out, and the scene opened into a long room filled with people. Half the people were at one end of the room and were weeping loudly, while the other half were at its opposite end and were laughing without restraint, so that the whole was a cacophony that echoed off the ice walls and caused the overhang to vibrate painfully and Zulfikar clapped his hands over his ears, but it seemed to make little difference. Quickly, he turned away.

Then he came to a picture of men and women dressed in long robes and wearing tall conical hats of the type worn in the Kargil region of Ladakh, Indian-administered Ladakh, which lay a few miles away on the other side of the Line of Control. They were busy cleaning a two-storeyed house, washing the apricot roof and the insides of the ground floor, which during the winter became a stable; scrubbing the living-quarters, beating rugs against the outside walls, sinking clothes into a clear stream and cooking in vast pots filled with marzan, thsodma, chuli-chhu, hyag-meat, buckwheat and barley. As they worked the people sang yurmi-khlu, the seed songs of the women who knew no borders.

The LoC was so very convenient for the masters of war on all sides, but for more than six decades had divided families and destroyed lives. No wonder the areas around this artificial red line, the palaces, forts and mountains which lay between Skardu and Kargil, were fissuring from bedrock to sky. No wonder the glaciers were cracking apart under the weight not of continental drift, but of pollution and fratricidal war. And just where were those bodhissatvas, arhants and black goddesses anyway, that such things were permitted to happen? Perhaps, thought Zulfikar, they were all dressed up and were spending their days posing for tourist snapshots on the main street in Leh, while in their prolonged absence the Sufi houses, Buddhist temples and Balti forts had become haunted – though quite how the ghosts got any peace in between the periodic sniping and mortar attacks and the overweening pointless grandiosity of Asia's Punch and Judy was anyone's guess. Beyond this image was a room in which a man was seated on a stool and the man was polishing a long silver sword.

The fifth carving was of two goats butting horns, and behind this one was a chamber filled entirely with brass spheres. The sixth was a vision of thin dark figures with red eyes and white hair who slunk along a high wall, and behind this was a room which at first Zulfikar thought was empty but which, as he peered into it, became filled with numinous phantasms who seemed to be moving aimlessly and silently around the room while from all around, perhaps from the mountain itself, again there came the sound of Rtse-glu, the songs of the dance.

Over in the far corner of the chamber Zulfikar saw some much more mundane objects: cooking utensils, a discarded black woollen dakhun chadur, a broken box – the desultory accoutrements of human habitation. As he examined the objects he realised that they had been there some years at least, and that perhaps some refugees had found this place – God knows how – as they ran from the Indian missiles that rained down upon their villages during the war of 1999. So they had got out, he thought, but that didn't mean that they had survived. Suddenly, a news broadcast in Uygur, a language which Zulfikar could not understand, came from the cooking pot. Why not, he thought: since everything else is possible, why not this? But then he realised that the broadcast, punctuated by adverts, was actually coming from the radio in his back-pack.

The space for the last carving was empty: just a flat white square. As Zulfikar touched its surface for the first time, the wall felt cold – so cold that even though the contact had been with merely the tip of his finger, it sent a powerful shiver through his body and he had some difficulty disengaging his hand from the ice. At first he thought that it would not open, but just as he turned away the panel swung round, and there before him was a dark room whence there came the sound of sawing. As Zulfikar watched, he saw emerge out of the darkness a carpenter who was fashioning a long wooden box. But the carpenter was a woman and her face was veiled. Then Zulfikar saw that each of the chambers was connected to all of the others by means of narrow passages, and as the realisation came, he saw that it was on the axes of these conduits that all six pictures began to turn and spin as though they were parts of a wheel, and they spun until they had become merely shapes, mandalas, each of a different colour; white, blue, yellow, red, green and black.

He sensed a movement behind him. The lha-maung had reappeared and this time, except for the turquoises in her hair, she was completely naked. With all the images swirling around her, she walked slowly towards Zulfikar. She was smiling and her Chini eyes sparkled with ice from the sacred mountains. And yet to Zulfikar she was like the fire that burns within the ice. Her hair was long, wild and reddish-brown, her face white as snow. Her breasts were small and were shaped like pears, but were sharply pointed, and the nipples were the colour of fresh blood. There seemed to be a kind of music coming from her, the music of a one-stringed instrument played by the ghost of a dead cho-ruh high up on a mountainside, or that of a single horn blown with the last breath of an arhat. It was the music of the instruments that had been smashed along with the songs of the people, it was the rapture of the grandfathers.

She unclothed him as though she was relaxing with him in the handhok, the exposed yet intimate grain-storage space formed by thatch that projected from the roof of every Balti house. The handhok was a place of illicit congress, a space of filtered light where widows took their consorts, their husbands-for-a-day-

or-two-or-three and where, as the sky poured in through their sanctified skins, they breathed in the ecstasy and fluid of their lovers' bodies. She unclothed him as though she was peeling a plum, and then she laid him on the ground and began to move over him with her mossy tongue, her anemone lips, her long fingers, her stone nipples, her small, deliciously sharp horns, all lifting his skin into tiny mounds of pleasure that glowed as though they were fuelled with electricity or lighted phosphorus. The lha-maung's mouth was a sea-horn and his skin was an ocean. Then she enfolded her soft lips around his phallus and began to sweep up and down, her hair rising and sinking in slow waves as though a gentle breeze was blowing backwards against her breasts. He saw that tattooed on the upper part of her back was the picture of a sea creature, a great prehistoric water-dragon with flaming eyes and fiery jaws, and that the dragon's skin was covered with pearly shells which changed colour as the lha-maung's long thick turquoise hair began to move more rapidly over his belly. The music had become faster and louder so that their bodies made no sound as they writhed together on the rock ice.

Zulfikar laid his head back down and closed his eyes. It was impossible to think when his whole body felt like a pulsating glans, its lips trembling, the muscles tensing around the opening, pulling open the doors, letting in the warm breath of the lha-maung, the breath that was pure gold and which flowed over him and through him and which filled his heart and his brain with its substance until he felt that he would burst from his skin like one of the ancient rivers which cut through the rock of the black mountains as though the rock was soft as pumice. They were moving as a water-dragon moves as it rises from the darkness, as once enormous creatures had sleeked like liquid rock through the ocean. They moved in a single spinal arc, seamless in its formation and perfect in its curvature. He felt his heart would give out, he thought that he was about to die, and then all at once in a single spasm his body let go and in the movement it felt as though his entire substance was flowing out through every pore, it felt as though flesh, liquid and spirit were sweeping and gushing into the lha-maung, whose body had become completely contiguous with his own so that not a single millimetre remained between them. Now she smelled of musk and her horns were like those of a mountain deer. She had wrapped her arms, legs, shoulders, her entire integument right around his corpus, and he felt the mingling in every detail, he sensed his bones dissolving and re-forming, the axons of his neurological system splicing with hers, the wet bags of his organs, the memories which he saw now were intimations not of a dead past but of a present that was perpetually unfolding – all of these became transformed and replicated into infinity, into the images that were spinning around the lha-maung's head as she arched over him and as she brought her lips, filled with his semen that smelt of flowers, to his in an apposition so perfect that there on the hard ice floor of the glacier they were like a single dancer, a mound of white stone rising molten and slow from the bowels of the earth. The stone screamed without breath, sang without instrumentation, rose without energy. And Zulfikar Ali Lobsang was in a locus that ran to a different scale of time, a loksor, a place where the years spun in a cycle of twelves and it was a place where at last he was able to separate milk from water, lies from truth.

Then quite suddenly she was gone and he was upright and was dressed in his clothes again, as though nothing had happened. Yet his body felt as though it possessed no mass but only cold fire, and every movement seemed to hold a fragile significance, so that as he walked around the walls of the chamber he felt almost divine. The pictures also had vanished and in their place were words. Some of the words were in Aiggy, the most ancient script of Baltiyul which had been carried into Skardu from Jullundur, from the auspicious conference of 1st century AD Buddhists, while others were in Tibetan, Persian and Urdu. The scripts ran from right to left, left to right and top to bottom. And beneath each word were many other layers of words, yet far from undermining meaning, this multiplicity rendered temporal substance. It were as though the memories of all the preceptors, the arefat and jawanmardin who over the years had lived here in the khanqah, had been preserved on these ice-white walls in a shifting textual dance so that the glacier was like an enormous library, a giant crystal that stored voices, thoughts, feelings, truth. As Zulfikar spun around and tried to read what he was seeing, he began to feel dizzy with all the letters, which now seemed to be singing at him, singing as though each one was a bard intoning a redakh-si-khlu, an ode to a mountain goat.

> *I am not a goat, I am lightning!*
> *I am not a poet, I am frightening!*
> *I am not a rock, I am brightening!*

– he thought to himself, but then he wasn't sure whether perhaps he too had sung the words back at the wall, had sung them in all the forgotten scripts of the high places, the words which lay beneath the skin, the words that flayed. Perhaps it was at that moment that he became filled with proverbs and aphorisms, so that his fragile skull felt as though it would explode from the cumulative weight of their wisdom. Zulfikar undid his rucksack, removed his foldable chair and easel and his painting materials and there, in the middle of the glacier, he began to paint. And everything he drew was like a lost memory. At last, Zulfikar was coming home.

Zuleikha turned to the Green Woman and asked,

'What does all this mean? Did he really mate with the ice-woman? What was she? Why am I seeing this? How is it I knew even the thoughts which he was thinking, as though I were reading a story?'

And the woman replied,

'The music of stories has gone on since the beginning of time, but one will only hear the sounds, thoughts, actions which bind us if one is willing to become a reader, a listener, a watcher.'

'Have I reached that stage?' Zuleikha asked.

But the woman did not reply to this question and instead went on to reveal the meaning of what Zuleikha had just witnessed. Her voice was quiet, yet easily audible and it sounded as though it issued not from her throat but from her belly.

'The first room was the room of soldiers, but of soldiers who became other things – wanderers, sages, mystics, sufis. Just as milk curdles and turns to cheese, they remain the same and yet are irreversibly different. And so, Milinda the Greek General was reborn as a sufi.'

Zuleikha thought of the underground railway station, of the looped track which had been disused for so many years and of Alexander and herself, losing each other down there in the darkness. That had been the start of their journey together, and the songs of the dead trains had become their songs. The toxic sweltering mass of human history was a long trail of blood sacrifice. The conduits of empire had occupied and colonised people's minds, bodies and souls and the empire of steam had turned the world into a great engine, the engine for which Archie had worked all his days. Perhaps, she thought, in some distant future when the lords of London are made to melt their guns and bombs and missiles into ploughshares, then at last this foundation would be transformed. Instead of war and peace, she thought, let there be war into peace.

Yet it was only one possible path. Through the confluence of their existence, the three of them – Alexander, Archibald and herself – had raised the trains and again had set them rolling through the darkness. Yet many such transformations would be required before anything changed. The first step, perhaps, was to sing these songs and tell these stories: local songs, little people's stories; odes to partridges and lullabies sung to young children in the dead of night, cooking dances, border ballads, psychedelic riffs, subtle subversions, performed over and over again until through repetition they accumulated power and made possible a million different histories. That was the mistake which both the wandering Westerners and the modern states of India and Pakistan had made. It was not the mountains that mattered, she thought, it was the passes, the rivers, the high pastures, the people. The only line of control was death and even that was not absolute, but rather was simply a representation of fate's power over the imagination.

'The second chamber was that of the sufis. Like a snow leopard, deep gnosis cannot be known until it is upon you. It has no substance but hides itself in nothingness. Yet it is the only reality.'

And Zuleikha saw the enormous body of the loch and the tidal sweep of the Clyde River, some of whose black waters she had swallowed and from whose substance all of this had flowed. All those black goddesses that had shaped the land with their broad calloused palms and their bone feet, all those soul-bodies which were arranged in tall circles, the wells, the sacred trees: rowan, holly, yew, mulberry, apple and oak; the gods of the red rocks, the birds that whispered oracles into the ears of those who could hear. The birds who sang with the sound of scratching-sticks. Scotland, her land, the land of her bones and her blood, the rivers and lochs, the beasts, the stones and the people, all were connected on every level through past, present and future to all of the world.

'The third room is the diwan of the poets. Half the people are weeping because they have been through dark times and have not yet heard the words of the songs; the other half have lives filled with the same difficulties and loss, yet because they have heard they are laughing and singing! The poet transmutes sorrow into joy. The tales she tells, the epics, the rgya-khlu, redakh-si-khlu, gar-khlu and mGul-khlu, the elegies and goat-songs, the romantic poems, the canzuni, sunnari, muwashshah, zejels, ballate – all of these flow in a new language which arises out of the many that went before, like the waves of a river, like the rising sap in the tree. From the inside of a skull, they sound out across the universe and thus do they hold life together and they teach us history.'

There she was, in the church vault in mid-winter, a place of gloom, death, decomposition and darkness, and yet, through the playing of Alexander's lute, she had been lifted giddyingly from the tomb into the clarity of air and light. The kirk had been extremely aged and had witnessed the passage of countless generations, returning knights, heavenly musics. Each note was pristine, was cut and stained from glass, its power like the face of a saint extending outside of space and time. By the still waters of the loch, in the shadow of the cold granite arches of the House of God, Zuleikha and Alexander had fallen in love.

'And the man polishing the sword?'

'The fourth is the room of the slave. That man is in Hell.'

'But why?' Zuleikha asked.

'Because the sword which he polished was the axe of the moon which other men used to kill a thousand children.'

'But how could he have known that it would be used in that way?'

'Stones make ripples, rocks make mountains,' the Green Woman replied. 'If not for one's own life, then for the lives of others. This must be learned through experience.'

Zuleikha wondered about Archie, who had repaired and polished battle aircraft and later had built warships. The aerodrome and the shipyards had manufactured death. But then the aircraft he'd serviced had shot down the Nazis, no? And he'd built passenger and cargo ships as well. Was he too in Hell, along with Adolf Hitler? Or was it like Dante's vision? Maybe Hell had as many cells as the human brain. The cancer had turned both his skin and his mind porous. Perhaps we are both destined for Jahannum, she thought. Perhaps we are slaves, learning obedience and submission the hard way, the only way.

The Green Woman's song (for even as she talked with Zuleikha, she was still singing) was now a yurmi-khlu, a women's work song. And as though the Green Woman had heard Zuleikha's thoughts, she answered:

'In this one life, we are many people.'

'And the room full of brass spheres?'

'Did you notice that even though only one door at a time opened, yet throughout you were able to hear sounds from all of the chambers?'

Zuleikha nodded. She had imagined that it had been music she'd been hearing, the music of a single-stringed instrument, the music of ice and rock and snow and emptiness. The song of nûn, of time, of a concept of time that was less like a foot ruler and more like an ocean or a symphony or like the letter that spanned both worlds; yet now she realised that what she had imagined to be emptiness had in fact been filled with a legion of voices.

'We are jugglers,' the woman explained. 'Through time, upon the fulcra of our lives, many doors, chambers and spheres are balanced. The soul is not like a bottle; it is more akin to a musical instrument through which countless tunes can play.'

'A lute,' Zuleikha ventured.

'Lute, oud, kobza, pipa, pandoura, bîn, barbat, nefer, ektar, tree.'

Or like a building, Zuleikha thought – though in truth, she was no longer sure whether it was she who was thinking, or the woman who was talking – a house with many floors. History is knowledge and the search for the ordonnance of this knowledge must never end. La Calta, Mongibello, the Beat-Heads and their opponents, the anti-Mafia knights who lie sleeping beneath the smoking mountain, their forms and thoughts suspended yet made animate by the Fata Morgana, their bodies healed, re-composed, severed limbs re-attached, exploded fragments reconstituted, acid-dissolved skulls made whole, each sleeping revolutionary waiting for the day when they will be called upon to rise again and, with the wisdom of sacred fools, to save the island and the world around it from the clutches of evil. In this way do slaves become magicians.

The Green Woman swept her arm around the vista of peaks, plateaux and valleys.

'Beneath each of these mountains too there lie a thousand freedom fighters. Can you not hear their breathing, in the snow wind?'

Zuleikha felt the cool breeze on her cheeks and it carried the pungency of leopards and the sweetness of apricots.

'What about the goats?' she asked.

'The goats butt horns because this world exists in the space between hammer and nail. Reality must be forged. Reality renders consciousness. Whores exist because of a lack of love, and of the consciousness that can be mediated only through love. A dance is not an end in itself. On its own, it leads only to the room of dark figures who are perpetually lost in the belly of the cold mountain.'

Zuleikha imagined the luthier from whom Alexander had obtained – or rather, had been gifted – his lute and of the various objects, charts and other materials which they had found in the box that now she thought perhaps had been generated by some kind of compressed memory that lay outside of the parameters of the physical. And she thought of Petrus, dancer, conjuror, Shaykh of the Magians and of the qallash whores from whom he had emerged and of the darkness into which he had spiralled. And of Laila, Lilith, the Dark Queen, the woman of the night who once had been his lover, yet whose love had failed to draw from either of them a higher consciousness and which, in the end, faced with the armies of death, had left them swirling in the torpor of drugs, virtuosity and paint, the oil-and-water delusions of dead forest lakes and deserted mohallas. Perhaps together they had come upon some old parchment or ancient dream, some potter's oracle that had granted them access to a modicum of power and truth, and yet still both Petrus and Laila had drowned in the florid magic of psychedelia, in the convolutions of its artifice. But behind the wondrous chords and impossible tricks, the Phrygian modal, raga-rock licks, they had failed to recognise that these had been merely the beginning and not the goal. Or perhaps after all they had realised it, and this realisation had been the cause of their shared melancholic solitude. Midnight swims. She wondered what the last box might hold. And then she wondered how she had known that it would be the last.

'And the chamber of the carpenter? He was making a coffin, wasn't he?'

The Green Woman again began to sing words in an old tongue and again her voice was the voice of the Beda, Zarra, daughter of Natshab Ali of Sheh. She had sung for the old clap-ridden imperial adventurers and missionaries of Ladakh back when Good Queen Vicky and her fecund womb had sat astride the takhts of Albion, India and one quarter of the earth's surface besides. And Zuleikha realised that Zarra too must have sipped from the same well whose waters had been brought to the lips of Iskander's daughter, since now Zarra must surely be at the very least over a hundred and twenty years old. And yet her voice was not the voice of a crone, a Cailleach; no, her words were sung as clearly as though they had emerged from ice, or glass, or properly seasoned wood. And at times they sounded as though they were being sung from beneath the eaves of a black house on some Outer Hebridean isle; there was that sense of ebb and flow, of epic power that derived from the tidal breath of history, from the grand sweep of the Dead.

Zuleikha looked down again at the tree and she saw that it had opened and that its form now was like that of a beautiful man with a face like the moon, eyebrows like the backs of lutes, eyes of kohl drawn like musical notes, and hair that was long and which had been sculpted into dark Pharaonic ringlets. And the man opened his mouth and began to sing.

The Story of Alexander

The hermit seemed to have vanished; or perhaps, Alex thought, he has simply escaped into yet another tunnel, chorten, habitable tomb or khanqah. Alex looked up at the branches of the tree on which the leaves had begun to appear and as he played his one-stringed instrument, he saw that each one was a story, or rather, that each branch was a different version of the same story. The Syriac, Ethiopic and Latin versions, each carried on the backs of missionaries, traders, mystics and soldiers and on the winter tongues of mountain women, repeatedly had been translated, footnoted, endnoted, narrated in multiple parallels, chanted with fanciful hope and had been embroidered with the ghosts and shades of even older tales, stories that had been drawn like dust from the papyrus of hidden epistles and wonder-letters, epics that were laden with the manifold declarations of false pharaohs and true magicians and embroidered with eulogies, elegies and encomia to long-dead qalamat.

Together, in song, they told the story of the Wanderer, of Iskander the Sage, of his birth at Pella, Macedonia, of his numerous and bloody campaigns, his amassing of wealth, his scattering of cornmeal around the boundaries of polyglottal, putative, eponymous metropoli – all of which frenetic activities had led him to realise nothing more than the extent of his own ignorance and the fact of his own mortality. And the tree told of his shape-change into a magical traveller, of his learning at the feet of the Naked Philosophers, the Brahmans of Oxydorkai and Prasiake, of his flight into the heavens on the back of a man-eating ox-headed horse, of his power of prophecy and his sway over fin-folk and storms, of his crossing of the river of black stones and of his visit to Mongibello, to the land where the trees ran with sap that was like Persian myrrh, where they grew every morning until noon and then shrank back again in the night and where they produced fruit only with the swelling of the moon. The holm oak tree told of his arguments with headless soldiers, his voyage to the sea-bed, his journey to the spring of eternal life from which his perfidious daughter drank and of the arch he built at the world's end. And Alexander Wolfe saw that the green lightning-stone which he carried in his sack once had resided, like the Prophet Yunus, in the belly of a great ketos, whence it had given off a light which had allowed Iskander to spear the fish as it had leapt from the honeyed waters of the loch. Then he saw that around this tree was a circle of cypresses, and that around these was a circle of other trees of indeterminate species, and that around this second ring were flags, pennants, bits of cloth and scribbled notes, the last of which had been stuffed into the gaps between the stones of a low wall.

Then the holm oak itself seemed to change; each branch began to move as though of its own accord, as though each were a separate being with a long head and body and with eyes which morphed constantly from blue to brown to green to grey. The sky and the tree together seemed to form a giant carpet above his head, and the end of each branch soared into invisibility as though each were a track into heaven.

And in the language of the Crystal Country, the trees spoke – or rather, sang – to one another, a redakh-si-khlu, a paean to the mountain-goat. Then the song changed and they were singing a rgya-khlu, the story of Zuleikha and Alexander, a romance of sorts, spanned across the wooden body of a shape-changing musical instrument whose substance had been hewn from the very holm oak which now formed the takht for his music, for the headwaters of a song which had begun one misty summer's morning by the Clyde River at the point where it begins to turn to sea. The notes were a little like the architecture of this place that was halfway between a gompa and a khanqah, situated as it was midway between Tibet and Persia, this high place that once had been a post-station of the Greeks, a monastery whose notes inclined upwards at their ends, the ends of the lines of the stanzas that swept towards the sky and repeated themselves with only slight variations, so that like the dense foliate mass that grew above him, the song was being sung in parallels. And perhaps that had been the sole reason for his taking up the lute, to know this fact, that all things ran in parallel: death, life, states of being. And perhaps it was the massed ranks of the deceased who had fashioned the lute and rendered it unto him on that hot summer's morning in the Glasgow Barras. The box had been made from so many types of wood, with so many different designs, that now he thought that perhaps this too had been conjured into being by the fingers of the Dead and set floating down the green river, to be caught by Alexander and Zuleikha, through this act the dead being drawn at last into love.

How else could the wood have risen from Yaqub's Well into the fingers of at least the archangels, if not those of the seraphiel? How else could it have been hewn in three arcs from the oldest tree in the world and sent down in spirit form into the arms of wandering arefat, the great Ziryab at the Court of Cordoba, Manfredi the Sultan of Siqilliya, Yahya Dowland of Elizabeth's court, Rujari d'Alì, assorted Bolognese Germans and the Great Hoolet Lord Ruthyn. Or else, perhaps this metaphysical lute had gone overland from Khurasan to Astrakhan to Kiev and thence, through anonymous, mysterious and mercantile eighteenth-century Farangi, to the Land of Alba where, in the manner of poets, it had fallen into the cellars of Alexander Hume, who, having heard only the floating aural tablatures of the possible, in his will had assigned the lute, alone of all his instruments, to a certain Mister Beck, lute teacher of Edinburgh. And from there to the Glasgow Barras was merely a leap of silence, a double century's rest, the lute sealed perhaps in a case shaped like a child's casket and secreted in some dark dry place, in the vault of some chapel of recuperation as the searing winds of the machine factories burned off the demon-skin of the Cailleach of Alba. This was the music which had survived the axes and hammers of Lewis and Baltistan, alike. Love was all of this, love was everything.

The tree at his back opened up to reveal a great hall that led down into the Underworld, and in the hall were 99,000 disciples and each of these was spinning anti-clockwise, and the whole produced by their movement was a mathnavi of the Wheel, a Charkha-nama. He took out the stone and saw that it glowed with a fierce green light and that from its substance a song seemed to be issuing, and it was the Song of the Hermit. But then, Alex thought, our way has already been lighted by the box and by this wood. He half-turned and with all his strength he threw the rock as far into the hall as he could, and the moment it landed, the tree closed up again. Alex then looked down at his instrument and saw that it had assumed the shape of a figure, a long thin-faced man who resembled an old saint or prophet, perhaps from the church of Chaldea or Ethiopia.

And he saw that it was playing music without being played and he felt that this was only appropriate *since all along it is I who have been the instrument*. Surnai, dung-chen, kettledrums, a sound-box, a double-headed frame-drum, pairs of reeds, a cymbal or two, it was a music of skeletons, of bird jigs, of chiriyon that resembled letters, nga-ro, nûn, aleph ... and each utterance, every sound, was completely clear as though the oboes and elongated trumpets had been made of glass, rkang-king and rkang-dung, and as though the song had been sung by a thousand dead monks from inside the walls of a crystal stupa. It was the song of the north country, the hrtsik-khlu, the marcia, the song of death, and like the Dead the figure also wore a mask. Alexander had always worn a mask, though with Susan's death, the mask had begun to erode and then, after he'd met Zuleikha ... and now there was no skin at all, he was just flesh and bone and perhaps a song.

Alex cradled the statue as though it was a newly born baby, and perhaps it was, since its breathing seemed to be giving rise to this music and indeed, to all the various forms of music which over the years Alex had thought he was playing. And everything was connected, he thought: the rivers, the lochs, the mountain passes, the streams of history and so yes, his music had killed Susan, but no more so than had the light of distant stars or the breath of a fish in the Arabian Sea. It had been just an accident caused by tiredness, it had been the result of driver error brought on by overwork – yes, the procurator fiscal had been right about that. Though something she hadn't said was that, whether it had been accident or suicide, it had been constructed by an economic system that had driven people like Susan to work night and day just to draw even with ... what? At last he could begin his life again, in the knowledge that Susan's continuing presence, if there should be such a thing, if after death there was any thing, would be a benign one. They had loved each other and their love had existed outside of time. And now his love for Zuleikha too lay beyond anything anyone could ever kill. Alexander looked down again and saw that the statue had turned into a long stick, a sapling. But he knew now that all of these were simply objects; that, like people, no thing held singularity.

The Story of Zuleikha

Her first memory was of her mother's essence as her conceptualisation of perfect beauty. Perhaps Zuleikha was lying in a cot, or perhaps in a pram; she was no longer certain which image had come first. Suffice it to say that it was before words, or at least before words had become tools, so that in her mind they remained as pure sound, as music. She was aware too of the presence of other people, but somehow this awareness served simply to augment the manifestation of her mother. Now that her mother was no more, memory seemed to consist of a finite catalogue of images. And this seemed somehow obscene, that the woman who every day had bathed her body and who had fed her with prophecy from her own being, the being whose spirit had leached so deeply into her own spirit that she had been unable to tease them apart – that this woman had turned into an adhesive snapshot album, a series of stills and fragmentary clips which bore no relation to Zuleikha's sense of the physical person that her mother had been.

There was something her mother had said once, quite casually; it had been just an interjection as she'd glanced up from a magazine, but Zuleikha hadn't been listening properly at the time and had never really registered what her mother had said on that bright cloudy afternoon (or had it been sunny, she could no longer recall) a few months before she had died. For years she'd tried to reconstruct this scene in her mind, had tried to re-form her mother's words. After Nasrin Zeinab's death, this lacuna had come to assume enormous importance in Zuleikha's mind. She knew that it had probably been nothing significant, just a comment on whatever her mother had been reading at the time; yet her failure to listen, her failure to remember, her failure properly to conjure up her mother, felt like a betrayal of both memory and love. Because surely, Zuleikha thought, if her love for her mother had been as real and as powerful as it ought to have been, as for so many years she had imagined it to have been, then would not Nasrin Zeinab continue to possess her soul right now? Would not Zuleikha, right here in this place, be able to draw on her presence that had been as strong as the whiff of sandalwood or frankincense, as though she were sipping rose wine from a jaam? What had been the point of all that connection, that intimacy? What purpose was served by the mute shadow of her mother hovering across the bones of her face, or dancing in the bow of her lips, or gazing out from the fibres of her irises? Beauty, love, life, was it an entirely forgettable music?

'Beauty and love are not the same,' she heard the woman say. 'You are a mirror, that is all. Without the fire and smoke of separation, there can be no perception of love; without the hellish River Sambatyon that runs between people, there can be no vision of beauty.'

But the sound was issuing from the chiromantic ballet of her hands. The veiled figure held up her right hand and through her fingers Zuleikha saw, coming towards her across the empty sky, a legion of exoteric scholars, literalists, men and women whose bodies were shaped like machine-guns and whose single eye, positioned on the tops of their heads, could see in only one direction. They were accompanied by those wedded to gold and silver and the unreality of the image. These were the massed hypocrites of the world, and they bellowed like cattle and howled like wolves. Although such people claimed to worship the word, they had no stories to tell; they held within their fingers neither ta'liq nor nasta'liq, and they suffocated those around them like platinum mist.

The woman lowered her hand and the vision faded and disappeared in the sunlight. Then she raised her left hand, and there Zuleikha saw Archibald Idris McPherson. After his time as an old kunjeree, a Cailleach Bheur dancing in the nave of the kharabat, the kirk, he had found himself alone again as dawn had fallen across the weft and weave of Argyll's green carpet. He had begun to wander across the land banging on a tin lid and singing strange raucous songs that either had no words, or else held within them the words of so many tongues that they had lost all meaning. Archie had become a qalandar, an itinerant beggar, living in his own private madhouse, his footsteps tracing out a new Qalandarnama, a pilgrim epic across Scotland, a vast chronogram extending in many directions, from Out Stack to the Mull of Galloway, from the bhoothes of the Janefield Necropolis to the cloven hooves of the Eildon Hills. And his journey was being played on the strings of a lute which had been hewn from the wood of the holm oak tree and scalloped from the belly of a mountain goat and which, like the music of humanity, had passed through many different forms: dastgah-ha, maqamat, mandalas, ragas, tarantelle, redakh-si-khlu, hot jazz numbers, ghazals, laments. And perhaps this was his means of discovering every feature on the face of the Beloved. Or perhaps it was his punishment, his karma, his third bardic song, played out yet again among the flying demons and ferocious symphonies of human history.

And now he was here, just as he had been in the aerodrome forest and the Sicilian mountain, and just as his moisture had seeped through the brick and wattle-and-daub of the haveli of Petrus Labokla, so now Archie was here on this roof of the world. He was dancing, spinning, his blood-red tongue lashing in and out of a foaming mouth, his face blackened by the ice, his hair silvery-white like the mountain peaks. He was calling to Zuleikha, Alexander, Zulfikar, all three; calling to them to leap over the edge of the cliffs, to render up their skins and join the ranks of the shades, to link arms with him and continue the dance on and on unto the very Marches of eternity.

His breath was powerful; it was like the haunch of a snow leopard. It pulled at her chest so that she couldn't breathe. She remembered Alex's fear. Now we're all going to die, she thought. This is what it's all been about. Fuck. Fuck. She felt her feet skid on the stone; she saw the veiled figure bend down, lift the pen from the inkwell and begin to write, and she saw that the figure was writing their names in a thousand different scripts. And she knew that by the time the woman had stopped writing, they would all be dead. Just then, Zulfikar felt his skull explode with the intense cold, Alex sensed the keening of the giant tree trunk as it began to teeter against his back, and Zuleikha found herself standing right at the edge of an abyss so deep that its very profundity seemed to draw her in.

Far away, the light swirled into mist over the valley floor. It was the fog of Rannoch Moor in winter, the bone-cold sea haar that drifted like a claw across the pellucid North Sea and darkened the Riding of Lindsey; it was the tramontino that whipped around Catanian street corners and froze the smoke rising from

Mongibello; it was the dank cist of the inner room of a Lahori jadugar kota; and here, in Baltistan, it was the glacial blood of the deep past. And now it rumbled upwards and looped itself around both her arms and again she felt his hands on her body, Archie's hands, those calloused fingers, the hard palms thickened by so much metalwork, the muscles crushed by time's heavy wheel, the tissues smothered by endless grief. Inch by inch, he was pulling her over the edge of the cliff. She felt the warm body of her baby son curled against her breast after a night feed, for he too was here, and even though she couldn't see him she could feel the soft breath evacuate from his tiny mouth, could feel it ripple deliciously against her cheek, and then there were her own mother's arms, wrapping themselves around her shoulders, pulling her head to one side as though to allow her at last to rest. No more guilt, no more sorrow. And in the midst of the cold fog, a warmth enveloped her. This is the seventh chamber, she thought. This is the place beyond the burning river. This is it. I'm here.

The box was rising from the earth like a statue, a cube, a cuba, a kaaba, and from it there came the pressure of voices massed against its walls, voices that were straining to break through its skeletal frame, to spread their hot psalm breath throughout the world. It was the song of her mother, her son, her father – her father?! But surely, she thought, he isn't dead. But then he too came and was pulling Zuleikha down, down, into the swirling comforting fog. No, Papa! When did you, but you're not...

'Your father is dead now, he is no longer your father, he has the qualities of a spirit. Muka'ab, muka'ab, muka'ab. Everything has symmetry.'

She felt her lungs imploding, collapsing. It was a physical force and it pushed her down onto her knees. No! He couldn't be! She couldn't take any more. She couldn't. She was empty. Where is fucking God? Where are you, you fucking bastard? The anger drove her onto her feet again. Archibald McPherson, you drew me into all this, you with your long whore's cock and your blue asbestos lungs. Your skin that was so porous that we could read each other's thoughts. Your skin, my skin. Why couldn't you just die, you motherfucker? Die, you motherfucker! Die a thousand times! Die!

I love you.

Suddenly, a pair of fists seemed to throw her back from the edge of the cliff, back into the stone chair in which she had been sitting just a moment earlier. Multi-coloured flecks ran before her. She was still winded and her skin felt cold. As her vision cleared, it seemed that the fog had lifted and the baleful song had faded. The woman was still sitting before her, yet the paper was blank and the brush was back in its inkwell. Alexander found that the tree had stabilised and that he was no longer wedged painfully between its rough trunk and the ground and when he raised himself up and looked around there was no sign of the hermit. At the same moment, Zulfikar noticed a small mound to his right, which turned out to be a deep-frozen pie of human dung. Close to this crystalline turd he discovered some detritus from a camp: fag-ends, polythene and ring-pulls. Normally this would have incensed him, but now, elated, he felt the blood begin to course through his veins as though he had just awoken from a dream. He followed the rubbish trail out of the glacier, and after perhaps three hours the sporadic shit gave way to a green track that led downwards and which smelt of apricot blossoms.

Night, cars, the bridge over the River Clyde. Archie is there, standing in the middle of the northbound carriageway, beyond the point where the road dips into invisibility, on the slope down which the vehicles accelerate into darkness. And there he is, his white face glowing in the moonlight, his arms extended above his head, his hands waving like the semaphore paddles of an Aircraftman. There he is, Archibald Enoch McPherson; there, in his blue uniform, as her car comes over the hill fast, too bloody fast on this road at this time, but the road ahead of her is clear, she knows it like the sleek back of her lover-husband-musician-bastard Alexander, who loves his lute more than he loves her. But then the music swells in her head and it fills her and it takes her. And even as his neck tightens around his windpipe, Archie's face grows huge like the moon.

Archibald Enoch McPherson sank back. His hunger would not be sated, and he felt around his neck and realised that it was as thin and atrophied as ever – yet surely, eventually, there would be a way out of this song. One day, or maybe one night, he would come across a green path that would take him up instead of down, and then he would climb through successive stages and at some point perhaps he would even meet Margaret, dear blessed Margaret, the WAAF Princess of the Northern Isles, and perhaps they would dance elegant waltzes and jitterbug jives, and perhaps once again, with his slick, greased hair, he would be permitted slowly to seduce her and wrap around them forever, the dark shroud of the leine-bhàis, the shirt of death, the cloak of that warm night in the air-raid shelter so long ago. That night, when they had covered each other's bodies with the glistening balm of the marham-i-Isa, the ointment which had brought them from the death of the war into the world of light and life.

But now, instead, like all the old Cailleachs of winter, Archie followed the Clyde River up into the hills, he traced its path until at length he came to its source which, like the source of all rivers, was merely a spring that bubbled up from between clods of earth. And there, deep in the moist verdure of Little Clyde's Burn, the Cailleach had a cock hard as granite and balls filled with liquid barley and she steeked down the land with her great stone nafs, and on the last point of winter she gave out a shriek so loud that it petrified the air and scattered the birds from the trees. Archie found that again he was wearing the daytime garments of his last illness: the crumpled shirt, the baggy white underpants, the cheap greyish-brown trousers. It was as though on this journey he had come full circle, back to Scotland, to reality, to the incontrovertible fact that he was dead. The box was almost ready; its chambers had become filled with the songs and tales of the wanderers, its sides had been sculpted by the histories that in the wake of their passage had parted like the walls of the Red Sea, like the rocks and fire of the Sambatyon River. Having thus drawn his section of the ark from the earth's wet belly and having set it against the others in scenes from various of his lives, and having let the tabot thus formed fall onto the surface of the spring, he held it fast with a rock and, disrobing until he was completely naked, he wrapped his clothes around the box, tied the shirt in seven knots, one for each door, let it go on the waters and then lay down and slept. When the rains came, he turned to grey stone.

Now, up on the mountaintop, Zuleikha had the sense again of her mother's presence. Not exactly in concrete, sensate terms; it wasn't as though she could smell jasmine or asphodel, or whatever aroma spirits were supposed to carry, and nor was it held within the music that seemed to be playing from the stone, ice and wood below. It was something tenuous yet omnipresent, like the perception one has of stars dancing behind the noonday sky. And the scent of her mother was like the taste of her first ever breath, like the breath of God that had turned her from clay into being. She wondered whether it might be coming from the veiled woman, but it was something she couldn't position in space or time and anyway, the woman was singing a lament, a melancholia for lute and reed, something Scottish perhaps, or Balti – Zuleikha wasn't sure. After a while, all those folk songs began to sound so similar to one another: if not in linguistic terms, then at least in musical and emotional cadence. Through this journey it was as though her sight had been restored. It was as though, having seen words merely as squiggles on a page, now finally she had learned to read. It was as though she had passed through a house of seven doors, as though her body had been flayed to the bare letters of a text, as though she, Zuleikha Chashm Framareza MacBeth, had been burned into stone.

Her feelings towards the phantasm of her mother, who was no longer her mother but who now possessed the qualities of a spirit, were qualified by her feelings towards Daoud and by the fact that, unlike her mother, she had not been granted the privilege of watching her own child grow; that, unlike her mother, he had been snatched away from her quite suddenly, without warning or preparation. She would have given – would still give – anything to have Daoud back again, to have him back at any age. How old would he be now? Eleven years. He would be running with the boys, immersed in his own world, attempting in his own way to separate from her; yet that would have been a gradual, a natural and incomplete separation, and not a permanent one as though some killer had come wielding a silver sword and had cut the knot of his umbilical cord clean through. There would never be a family of Ibn Daoud.

For a long time she had blamed God or Fate or herself, but then she had become preoccupied with the fear that there might be no-one to blame and that such things simply happened – statistically, they just happened – and for no particular reason. She would have given her own life for this not to have been true. Was that why she had been at the big bridge, that morning which now seemed so long ago? Had she really been contemplating suicide? Had she really desired to leap off the edge and fly into the deep green waters of Kentigorn's river in a kind of Toledan baptism through flaying, evisceration and death? Had she really desired to stand in the wind that blew off the Atlantic Ocean and then to lose her balance, to sway and fall into the breeze, to let the ocean's breath take her down along the cursive line of the Alif that ran beneath the river's skin all the way to eternity? Did she imagine that she might leap into the Clyde and re-emerge in the Indus, or the Oxus? Had she been thinking this when the box had arrived?

She could no longer remember clearly what she'd been thinking. Perhaps that was simply a protective reflex, the mind guarding itself against the reality of death. Perhaps, if really she were able to remember her mother in every detail, if now her mother were to appear before her as though in the flesh, the grief would be unbearable. It was easier somehow to cope with vague concepts, snapshots, a scent here, a song there; in order to live it was possible to deal only in partial truths. And yet it had been her remembrance of Daoud and Nasrin Zeinab which ultimately had pulled her out of the well, since if she had not had her love for them – if, say, Daoud had never been born – she had never wished for this, not even once – then what in the world would she have had? What would she have known? What would her life have meant? If she had never heard their voices echoing through the chambers of her mind, how would she have been able to dance? How would her love have drawn Alexander into the river of music? How would her love have drawn the spirit of Archibald Idris McPherson out of the box of his corpse, how would beauty have pulled him through the polished brass mirrors of his bones and hauled him into the possibility of redemption and salvation?

And then there was Alexander, who had saved her from being swept into the river, or who had whirled her into a kind of romance of which previously she had deemed herself incapable and whose music had led her on this journey. But perhaps, like Hazrat Yunus who had been swallowed by the whale, or Hazrat Yusuf who had been thrown down the cistern of sadness, that morning she had simply dived with Alexander into a different river: a river that was like the Sarasvati or like the long-vanished broad flat marsh in which Thenew's son had bathed the bodies of his flock. Alex too had lost a loved one suddenly in the night – yes, and from that very bridge from which inadvertently he had saved Zuleikha. Perhaps in saving her, in helping her rescue the box, he had felt that he was doing what he had been unable to do with Susan. Perhaps that night as he'd played his sixteen-course double-headed lute he had had a numinous premonition but had been unable to act on it, had been unable to stop his sandy-haired wife from turning the key in the door and smiling as she had half-turned to say goodbye. Perhaps he had been too engrossed in his lute and had given her a cursory nod in return for her full smile, and that last smile would be branded on his brain as surely as the date and time of her death.

This time he had waded into the water, this time with her he had pulled out the box of destiny and had turned the key himself, had caused each lid to open through the playing out of his music, through the gathering of the dances of those around him, through his love for Zuleikha – a love which was complementary to that which he had for Susan. It was a love in which Zuleikha was neither an object nor a vague concatenation of memories, but a song: a piece of music that had no beginning and no end and which contained within it reflections, radifs, of the deeper love, the mighty and terrifying love that lay behind all things and which was called beauty. Yusuf, the soul, the one who needed no key and whose love had had a unique effect on each of them – on Archie, Laila, Peppe, Petrus, Daniel John, Nasrin Zeinab, Zulfikar, Alexander and lastly, on Zuleikha herself. Yusuf, the shining figure in the white robe whom she saw now coming down from the mountain whose summit lay in the substance of the sky, the mountain called Kaf, which once had coiled like a green serpent around the furthest edge of the world, but which through the ages had become light as silk and had been swept up into the air and which now lay on the other side of the sky-door. Ka'b al-Ahbar of Akiba, the great haber of the Hebrews who had crossed the river of stones and had

659

dreamed with the children of the east. The shining figure with the beauteous face that no mortal could ever gaze upon without losing their reason. The face that had turned Zuleikha's mind. Zuleikha, Potiphar's wife, acolyte of dust. The face that had caused the seven doors to open. Daoud's key that had opened up the seals of the book and had laid the stories bare, Hazrat Daoud, who had passed the letters on down through time, through the angular mathematics of music.

The woman lifted the edge of her veil and slowly rolled it up as though it were a carpet or a garden, as perhaps paradise had been rolled up before the faces of Hawwa and Aadam. And beneath the veil was another veil and she removed that one too, and beneath this was another and yet another and so on, so that with its many facets the Green Woman's face was a face of crystal. Zuleikha lost count of the number of veils; she thought perhaps that there had been four, or seven, or nine.

And from beneath the last niqaab there came a light that was so bright it blinded Zuleikha, yet she found that she was unable to close her eyes, and through her blindness that was yet brighter than the noon of a midsummer's day she saw a kabaristan encircling the gompa, and on each of the white marble tombstones she made out a script – possibly Aramaic or Ethiopic. There were written the names of the Matriarchs and Patriarchs, of Hawwa, Maryam, Rabia, Bilqis, of Nuh, Yusuf, Issa, Ilyas, Idris and all the rest of those imbued with word and dance and from whom, into the ears of the approaching Saul, streams of music had poured. And, rising from the tomb of Yusuf, the beauteous one, Zuleikha saw the faces of those who were no more. Faces she did not recognise: animal faces, the faces of goats and eagles, of spiders, snakes and sacred pigs. Then there were the faces of people from the deep past of Hibernia, Alba, Bactria, India, Kin'an. Saul, Yonatan Afghan, the eminent Sado, the dreamers of the Oxus. Milinda, the sons of Beth, the men of the old religion, each one passing through a thousand Cailleach nights in the zamin-i farang. The faces formed through multiple couplings, the joining of a Muslim female jinn with a Hebrew man, the scion of the Twelve Tribes who with his yaels and his books had crossed the river of rocks and fire and whose story, known as the *Epistle to Kabul*, had been enclosed in

660

the body of a shepherd's staff and buried deep in the bed of the River Indus, along with the libraries of the Brahmans of Kashmir.

Zuleikha knew that she was seeing the faces of the dead, of those who had died and of those who had yet to die, and even of those who had not yet been born, or who would never be born, even unto the very ends of time. It were as though she, Zuleikha Chashm Framareza MacBeth, had never been just a single isolated entity, but had been composed of a myriad of spirits, the spirits of the blades of grass, the branches of trees, the apricots, the olives, the rowan berries, the leopards up on the high glaciers, the spirits of numerous strangers in a thousand cities. The dead were the living and the living were the dead.

And then she began to see faces which she did recognise. She saw the faces of the grandparents whom she had barely known, those of her mother and son, of Nasrin Zeinab and dear sweet Daoud, of Archibald McPherson as a young man, of Alexander Wolfe, Susan Wolfe, Petrus Dihdo Labokla and Laila Sciacca Asunsi, of Zulfikar Lobsang and Peppe Ayala and of her father, Daniel John, Danyal Yahya … and as she saw his face she saw him there in the cemetery, moaning and weeping and praying over her mother's grave, thrusting his hands deep into the earth's black belly and pulling out Nasrin Zeinab's spirit, thrusting his hands, soiled with beauty, into his face, the fingertips slipping in, right to the backs of his eyes, then pulling, pulling on the red muscles, the jelly and neurons, the brain-pan substance, pulling out the globes through which sight had become unbearable. She saw him fall forwards, his face kissing the clods of earth which her mother had become, kissing the worms, the creatures with a thousand legs, the sharp-toothed red spiders, kissing them as though each were a gleaming icon. And then the woman's face became dark, black, so that no light escaped from its visage and she could make out nothing, no features, no breath sounds, no song, nothing.

In the black light Zalikha noticed that once again all around her, as though in a brass mirror, the khanqah, the mountain, the air itself had begun to spin in an anti-clockwise direction around an unseen radif and she saw that everything – all the musics, the chains of words written in gold on the skins of scapegoats, the faces of the dead and the hands of the 404 nameless saints, the snouts, tongues and cloven hooves of the beasts – all were turning towards the face of Hazrat Yusuf, towards the well, the fruitful bough. And she saw that Joseph was rising from the whiteness as though from a blank page in the Book of Heroes, and that in one hand was a rod of gold and that he was cloaked in a ketonet which possessed the quality of silk and that the ketonet was of many colours and that each of the colours revealed a secret.

On her head she felt the weight of a ring of gold and silver set with onyx stones, and yet her body felt light and then she too was up and was turning, dancing, and at times her movements were fast, violent, turns and hemi-turns, leaps and falls, her feet slapping down on the hard ground until the soles began to bleed, and at times so slow and contorted that she could barely retain her balance. Zalikha was a leopard, a wave, a bird, and her dance went on for hours, days. As she gazed into the nur-i-siyah of the woman's face, before her she saw her own face as it would be at the moment of her death. A singular moment of concentrated energy held within her body, both male and female: Mahakala-Mahadevi. And then she heard a loud moan issuing perhaps from the belly of the mountain or perhaps from her own body, she wasn't sure, but it was a prolonged dissonance and her bones shuddered with its desolate ferocity.

She had been at the bottom of a deep dark well; for years she had been trapped in a reliquary of darkness. She had been left sitting on a stone and chained to the wall and then, one foetid night, she had met Archibald McPherson. And Archie, through his dying, had helped to set her free. He was not a pleasant man, even making allowances for the fact that he had been suffering from a dreadful condition. She could tell that he had never been an easy person; he held his sins coiled tightly within – those animal furies which all his life had driven him and which later seemed to have throttled the life out of him, depriving him of air and light and love. But she also recognised that he had slowly been murdered by the same forces of history that had caused her very conception, that unintentionally had given her life and breath, the breath imparted to her by her mother and her father and by all those who had gone before. The Mughals, the Afghans, the Greeks, the Indians, the Sicilians, the Jews, the Scots, the Irish – all of them and their

662

stories, the songs that poured from their throats and the music that flowed from their fingers. There on the mountain, history and spirit were intertwined like the whorls of the red string on an oud. And there on the mountain it was as though, through some winnowing karama, Zuleikha at last was able to hear and understand all the tongues of her forebears and to comprehend the love that bound people together and the pain which they felt when they were cast apart by time, place or circumstance – and above all, by death. And in all this epic song of the earth and the stars, Zuleikha felt that maybe she was a single complex note, that the form and meaning of her life was a lament, a madrigal, a maqam, a slowly executed round-dance. And that contained within it was the music of an infinitude of songs, all accompanied by the plucking of a stringed instrument.

She knew that the lid had opened into the last box, but that neither she nor Alex would ever be able to see what lay inside, because that was not something it was possible to see this side of death. All our life we wait for the last breath, the end exhalation, that we might catch a glimpse of the soul as it leaves the body, as it passes between the lips which so often have touched our own lips. The lips of the Divine Consort, of Yusuf, whose mouth has sipped from the spring that is the source of all rivers. And all rivers and lakes are gates to the underworld. Perhaps there was nothing in the last box. Perhaps there was an endless cycle of being, or a tiered metaphysic of paradise, hell, purgatory, limbo. A parallel and multiple re-configuration of the persona in other times and places and in successively less conscious forms, a billowing of the soul that began the moment one was born. Then again, maybe there was only this music, or else a garden surrounded by adobe walls. Or perhaps there was only the silence, the dust and light of the human form. But in the final note, the note that is formed by the noise of those that went before and the silence of those that are yet to come, the seventh box is nothing more than this life. The life that is everything we cannot know. And somehow this knowledge of her ultimate ignorance was not something she could ever have put into words, yet she sensed that it ran through all the songs of all the people and through the wood, stone, metal and fire into which daily they transmuted themselves, and somehow

663

this made Zuleikha not happy, not joyous or ecstatic, but at least able to measure her pain, the imperfection of her being and the depth of her love. Because perhaps when the final tablet is written, that is the most that any human being can ever do.

Chapter Thirty-Five

The jewel, turned to sand,
slipped from my hand
and blew away...
  Melanie Desmoulins, 2002

July, not August, was nearly always the hottest month in Scotland, and in recent years the onset of summer steadily had moved to later in the year, and the warm weather had gone on longer – sometimes even into October. Yet at times the isobars would carry the wind and rain across the velvet hills in great waves, as though the Atlantic Ocean had risen from its basin and was cascading fitfully over the land.

But at some point during the night the rain had stopped, and so now the path by the river along which Zuleikha and Alexander were treading was merely damp. It was early morning, perhaps six o'clock, and so it was still a little chilly – though from the clarity of the sky, Zuleikha could tell that once again the day would be scorching. It was nothing to summer in either Palermo or Lahore, it was paltry even compared with the intense four-month season of Khaplu, yet because here in the Clyde Basin the humidity tended to be high, it always felt hotter in the summer and colder in the winter than the straight temperature readings would have indicated.

Zuleikha had not woken in the night with the rain; she had been too exhausted after the funeral, and had lain beside a beardless Alex, her hair a mess, splayed across his pillow. It had been a functional sleep helped by sedation, and she'd had only a single short dream. The bridge now was quiet, with just the occasional lorry breaking the silence, and even when they were standing directly beneath the giant south pillar, the traffic noise seemed to come from some other place. The morning was filled almost entirely with the underlying rhythm of the water as it flowed westwards. On the far bank, the hills gave way to the mountains of the Scottish Highlands, the lush lands of Argyll, and beyond those, the invisible and extreme territories of Inverness, Ross,

Cromarty and Sutherland. Yet the mountains of Scotland were senile inclines compared with those of northern Pakistan, the Pamirs, the Hindu Kush, the Greater and Lesser Himalaya, and, set against Mongibello, they seemed quiescent or even dead. And yet the beanntan were less high only because they were far older and had been beaten down over millions of years, beaten down by the fall of the slow rain. Yet these ancient mountains did not lack drama, and even now as they unfurled slowly into full daylight, even after the violent emotions of the preceding day, their rough scatter of colours and textures and the sense they imparted of inspissated age seemed to Zuleikha and Alexander to render to the morning both a profundity and a sense of heightened expectation.

The air coming off the water smelled almost sweet, as though she could have reached down, cupped the river in her palm and brought it to her lips. Perhaps such a ritual would have been appropriate: an old Celtic consecration of the host, for it was her father's blood which flowed past her face on this summer's morning. As she watched the river, every rising wave seemed to be shaped like the body of a lute. And Alexander had his lutes, instruments which would hold fast to the courses of their strings, to the sound into which they had been created.

When Alex had come round, up on the high cliff, his hands had been empty. There had been only the holm oak, rising far above him, fresh and green again, and a long-horned goat that stared at him quizzically, as goats tend to do. But perhaps some essence of the lute was in every tree, in every land, perhaps its song was carried across the air from the leaves of all the woods of the world. And although now his other instruments were all stacked in her flat and, like their owner, had moved completely and permanently into her life, fancifully Zuleikha imagined that a tune was playing, that a song was coming over the humpbacks of the hills, perhaps from the Highlands, perhaps from the Borders or from Galloway: a Scottish tune, a ballad of *King Orfeo*, a song of the wood in which Orpheus does not die or split apart but is made whole, woman, man, nature and music. But she knew that the music came not from somewhere on a map or chart, nor from within the stone or alabaster of a statue, nor even from the various woods of an instrument, but from deep inside of herself, from the

666

breath of the dead.

They carried the box between them; it weighed far less now than it had when they had hauled it from the Clyde some fifteen months earlier. Although during dank wet years the leaves would begin to turn even in the last week of July, this year, Zuleikha thought, the way things are going, they would be unlikely to shift to gold till early October. By that time, the earth over Daniel John's grave would have settled. With the last of her mother's inheritance, she had ordered a fresh slab, white marble from the quarries of Chitral, on which the engraving of both their names – her mother's and her father's – would have been completed before it reached British shores. This time there would be no errors in transcription from the Persian, no gaps in poetic comprehension. It was fitting that her parents be buried together as they had always wished, and furthermore, the peculiar manner of Daniel John's death there in the kabaristan had seemed almost to compel a twin inhumation. After all, there was room enough. For the weight of their broken love, there was the whole earth. She'd heard that in England, seventy-five years after a burial, the local authority could re-use the graves. She wondered what they did with the old bones; whether they removed them and buried them in some mass pit like those that had been dug for the plague victims of old, or whether perhaps they simply placed one body on top of another in a kind of multi-storey catacomb. After all, what did it matter? In seventy-five years time, who would be left to mourn, to give love to the soil? The odd fond grandchild, perhaps. But then she smiled. There would be no grandchildren. Her line would end with her. Thousands of years of history, spiralling into darkness, silence, freedom.

The box felt smooth now; its wood glowed in the fresh morning sunlight. The scenes engraved into its substance seemed almost alive, so that at times she could feel the tiny figures shift beneath her fingers, she could almost feel them breathe so that, rather than being many different stories, now in the manner of an epic they had come to form a whole, a continuum – from Daniel John and Nasrin Zeinab (yes, she saw them there too, and they were dancing across the wood, dancing and laughing as though caught for a moment in an old, romantic Bombay film) all the way back to the Matriarchs and Patriarchs whose resting-places had never seemed to be final. Originally constructed from many different woods, the box now had become just one: incorruptible acacia. The seventh chamber had remained unopened, and now, as they waded slowly, barefoot into the water, and as they felt its coldness rise like metal stockings up their legs, Alexander and Zuleikha did not speak. There had been enough words already, through the funeral and afterwards. Their feet gripped the mud as they felt the river-bed incline downwards into the cold darkness. Once again they felt the first of the reeds curl around their bodies, impelling them to go further, claiming them already. Death would come and sweep them away in an hour, a day, a year, fifty years, but even as Alexander gazed up at the bridge and as the light seemed momentarily to catch the metal railing, he knew that their time was not now. Death like a lover had caressed their bodies up on the mountain in Baltistan, it had forged their measure, yet it had thrust them back into this difficult messy world in which the most one might hope for were occasional flashes of joy.

A single dream. The old park where her father had used to take her as a girl, the old park with its shallow oval pond punctuated by minnows, tadpoles, triangular nets and jam jars. The pond on whose surface she had used to sail small wooden yachts, each one painted a different colour and with the imprimatur 'Birkhenhead' on its hull. They had been there, her father and herself, in the short dream, on that summer's day long ago, and he had been looking down at her and smiling as she had launched a simple blue boat from the pool's edge. She'd seen his face reflected in the water and it had been the face of a young man, a handsome perfect face. And Zuleikha had been simultaneously child and forty-three-year-old adult, and she had smiled back at him and, in the sinad metre, had said, *I love you*. And Daniel John, the youthful Daniel John, the man who was forever besotted with the face of beauty, in the hazaj style had mouthed, *I love you, too* as the boat moved off across the water, serenaded by the inchoate shouts of children that, regardless of time and language, are the same everywhere.

And in that moment of conjunction, corny as an afternoon movie, clichéd and repetitive as human life itself, somewhere in the sunshine that gleamed upon the water there was a particular kind of music. It was as though she, Zuleikha, was the boat, moving out upon the lake of Yusuf's face, and carrying in her sail the breeze of love. The Dead had cheated her up there on the mountain; they had pushed her back, they had allowed Zulfikar, Alexander and herself to go free, yet in the same moment they had taken her father down into the crawling earth. Or perhaps it had been her father's hands that had pushed her back from the edge of the cliff, the same hands that had rested upon her shoulders in the sunshine park as Zulie, the little girl, had launched her yacht onto the clear still waters of the pool. And perhaps it had been Susan's hand, held up like that of Bibi Fatima against the rising of the silver sun, that had impelled Alexander to go for that walk by the river in the late spring, in May. Pasca, Passover, Ashura, Shem el Nessim. The calendars were all becoming mixed up in her head. Maybe that morning had been the dawn of a special saint's day, who knows? There was a saint for every state of human misery. Perhaps that was all we were, a great field for the afterworld, a constantly shifting point of sorrow that only has meaning through its relation to the past and future, to its own state of extinction.

In the midst of her grief her body once again was racked with loss, this new and terrible loss which had occurred while she had been thousands of miles away, this death that she felt she might just have been able to prevent had she stayed by his side, had she plunged his fist into the opening of the whisky surahi. And now, as she waded into the river that was the opening into the cold darkness of memory, this river which carried in its dark waters all the other deaths that had surrounded her, so that now it was as though each one was fresh and had occurred only yesterday, Zuleikha thought that perhaps the dream was all we had, and that in the end these memories, these tenuous flickering songs of love and beauty, are like dust.

The Clyde River smelled like ripe apricots, and Zuleikha imagined that this was what it must have smelled like in the old times, when upriver, by the Glasgow Green, Thenew and her miraculous son had bathed people's bodies, had pushed down the corpses of the living into its soft green waters. Perhaps now if she drank of the river it would not be foul and brackish, but would taste of honey, milk and figs. And in the river, in the midst of darkness and loss, Alexander and Zuleikha had found each other, had found the box, and through its stories had found life. They had merged with its stories and with all those vanished souls through whose lives it had passed, the spirits it had transmuted into words, so that in this sense Zuleikha and Alexander had themselves become words upon the river's flow.

Alex, because he was that bit taller, was standing a little further in than Zulie. They wedged themselves in the mud but they found that suddenly the current became strong so that it was all they could do to stop themselves from being swept away. When the waves had reached the level of their hearts, when they could no longer hold back the flow and when their bodies began to feel numb, almost like wood, together they turned to the west and let go of the box. At first it just bobbed up and down on the wavelets, not moving anywhere much and seeming at times almost to encircle them, as though perhaps the sea was running somewhere beneath the surface, roiling the water, swirling it up into notes; but then, as it rocked a little further into the open darya, it was swept suddenly downriver, was carried on a fast stream beneath the huge concrete arch of the bridge, and then out into the estuary. And they stood there, almost fully clothed, their feet sinking into the sand bed of the Clyde, and together they watched as the box grew steadily smaller until it was just a fleck on the moving surface of the river.

If you would like to find out more about the world of *Joseph's Box* please visit:

www.josephsbox.co.uk

The following tales are provided in full on the website:

Primal Dream: A Man, a Woman, a Goat and a Mountain

The Tale of the Soldier: An Ant, a Rock and a Greek

The Tale of the Sufi: A Death, a Wife and a Journey

The Tale of the Poet: A Potter, a Jinni and the Queen of Sheba

The Tale of the Servant: The Prince, the Saint and the Dancer

The Tale of the Juggler: The Haveli, the Dancer and Joseph Stalin

The Tale of the Whore: The Lovers, the Saints, the Imps and the Faw

The Tale of Lord Jack: A Ghost, a Monk and a Skull

The Hermit's Song: Acid, Habibiyya, God

Joseph's Box is also available as an e-book. Please see the website for details.

New Fiction for 2009

Grace by Alex Pheby

The story of Peterman, an inmate at Greenwood Walls secure hospital, whose dramatic escape leaves him seriously injured, lost in the snow. Half-delirious, he encounters an old woman and a young girl who live deep in the nearby forest. Peterman stays with them as he convalesces, and an extraordinary relationship develops between the three tragically damaged people, until circumstances propel Peterman and the Girl back to the harsh world of the city. For Peterman, the Girl represents all the love, trust and beauty that has been missing from his life – she represents his second, and last, chance. How could he possibly survive her loss and to what lengths will he go to prevent it? In luminous, lyrical prose, Alex Pheby has created a powerful tale of love, danger and madness, in a world on the fringes of reality. With the urgency of hyper-realism and the rich strangeness of a fairy tale, *Grace* is an unforgettable work of literary fiction.

'*A world evocative of Grimm and Kafka, and furnished by Freud... Risky first novels are gutsy and Pheby's style conjures Penelope Fitzgerald, Angela Carter and A.S. Byatt... This is an accomplished fable of how we are all constantly struggling to escape our histories and reach a state of grace.*' **Scottish Review of Books**

ISBN: 978-1906120-39-9; RRP £9.99

Printer's Devil by Stona Fitch

Two warring printers' guilds struggle to survive in a world where natural disaster has become commonplace. Caught up in a risky raid on rival printer Sevenheads' bank, the Printer's Devil and the Patchwork Girl struggle to escape the city as the black wind starts to blow... Picking up where *Clockwork Orange* and *On The Beach* left off, *Printer's Devil* deals with the fate of the remnants of humanity in an extreme post-apocalyptic landscape. A fable in the spirit of Coetzee's *Waiting for the Barbarians*, *Printer's Devil* is a meditation on power and its abuses – one that echoes with disturbing parallels to the present.

'*A wonderfully dark, dystopian tale set in a world where excessive consumerism has led to an environmental apocalypse.*'
Independent on Sunday

ISBN 978-1-906120-32-0; RRP £8.99

The Winding Stick by Elise Valmorbida

A solitary cashier in an all-night garage is haunted by visions of real life and death, but is unable to intervene ... until dramatic

events force him to venture beyond his limits. He stumbles into hope, love, true insight – and Tamil London, where the hidden stories of others come to light. There's Kandy (a sex worker and psychology student), The Whistling Woman and, most important of all, the mysterious garage manager Siva. Written with compassion, suspense and verve, *The Winding Stick* is a story of London's immigrants: a novel that explores dislocation and delusion, but becomes bright with possibility and love.

'She writes like an angel'
John Madden, Director of Shakespeare in Love

ISBN 978-1-906120-35-1; RRP £9.99

The Floating Order by Erin Pringle

The Floating Order is a unique and innovative collection of stories. Erin Pringle's world is filled with the dreamlike, nightmarish narratives of children: children in danger, children at the mercy of their parents, children in all kinds of trouble. Children who continually rise, return, and haunt the pages.

'The stories in Erin Pringle's first collection possess the charm of fairy tales, the wisdom of poems, the hope of prayers, the weight of eulogies, and the intimacy of letters home. There's an old soul at the center of this book, an old soul with a passionate, lyrical, exhilarating new voice.' **Tom Noyes**

ISBN 978-1-906120-42-9; RRP £9.99

Fighting It by Regi Claire

With an Introduction by Louise Welsh

A woman revolutionary, a woman in prison, a husband seeking revenge, a child driven to sin – they are all 'fighting it', battling to retain their belief in themselves. No mere slices of life, the stories in this second collection by award-winning Scottish-Swiss author Regi Claire have the range and depth of whole novels. They give voice to men and women who seem otherwise condemned to suffer in silence and whose struggles we recognise as our own. Sometimes with humour, sometimes in despair they cry out, clamouring for our attention. Claire's prose is edgy and vibrant and, whether set in the ice-cool beauty of the Swiss mountains, the heat of Tenerife, the urban frenzy of Paris, Zurich or Edinburgh, her tales are at once deeply disturbing and almost unbearably compassionate.

'Regi Claire is a writer of compassion and determination. Her stories are filled with the details of pain and physical bewilderment and leavened with tenderness.' **A. L. Kennedy**

ISBN 978-1-906120-41-2; RRP £9.99

Two Ravens Press is the most northerly literary publisher in the UK, operating from a six-acre working croft on a sea-loch in the north-west Highlands of Scotland. We publish cutting-edge and innovative contemporary fiction, non-fiction and poetry.

Visit our website for comprehensive information on all of our books and authors – and for much more:

- browse all Two Ravens Press books by category or by author, and purchase them online at an average discount of 20% off the RRP, post & packing-free (in the UK, and for a small fee overseas)

- there is a separate page for each book, including summaries, extracts and reviews, and author interviews, biographies and photographs

- read our daily blog about life as a small literary publisher in the middle of nowhere – or the centre of the universe, depending on your perspective – with a few anecdotes about life down on the croft thrown in. Includes regular and irregular columns by guest writers – Two Ravens Press authors and others.

www.tworavenspress.com